# CIRCLE OF PEARLS

# ROSALIND LAKER

Circle of Pearls

DOUBLEDAY

NEW YORK  LONDON  TORONTO  SYDNEY  AUCKLAND

PUBLISHED BY DOUBLEDAY
a division of Bantam Doubleday Dell Publishing Group, Inc.
666 Fifth Avenue, New York, New York 10103

DOUBLEDAY and the portrayal of an anchor
with a dolphin are trademarks of Doubleday,
a division of Bantam Doubleday Dell Publishing Group, Inc.

Library of Congress Cataloging-in-Publication Data

Laker, Rosalind.
Circle of pearls/Rosalind Laker.—1st ed.
p.   cm.
1. Great Britain—History—Commonwealth and Protectorate,
1649–1660—Fiction. 2. Great Britain—History—Charles II,
1660–1685—Fiction. I. Title.
PR6065.E9C5   1990
823'.914—dc20      89-29458
CIP

ISBN 0-385-26305-8

To Hazel for her enthusiasm

CIRCLE OF PEARLS

# ONE

WHEN JULIA PALLISTER was born one October day in 1641 a rare and beautiful Elizabethan drop-pearl was placed in her tiny palm. She clutched it strongly for a matter of seconds while her grandmother leaned over her be-ribboned crib. Then it was taken from her and returned to a safe place. Neither parent knew of the incident. Robert Pallister was celebrating his daughter's arrival with his nine-year-old son and some friends downstairs. His wife, Anne, was unaware of her mother-in-law's presence in the bedchamber as she lay sleeping in the massive four-poster in which she had given birth just an hour before.

Almost as if some consciousness of the pearl remained with Julia through its cool contact, she occasionally dreamed as time went by of something hauntingly glowing and lovely, so indefinable that it could not be recalled when she woke. As it was natural to her and an accepted part of her existence, she was not troubled by it and never mentioned it to anyone.

Yet she always took particular notice of anything that struck her as being unusually beautiful, as if she might gain some clue to the mystery that intrigued her. She had watched the moon sailing amid the stars, held her breath when a swan arched its feathers on the lake as it glided against its own reflected image, and been dazzled by the display of a rare white peacock shivering its huge fan. Then one day she saw a pearl-white pony that widened her eyes with wonder.

It happened in the Roman-walled city of Chichester, which lay no more than a few miles from the gates of her home at Sotherleigh Manor. There was a ribbon shop in West Street and her mother, who embroidered many yards of silk ribbon in a year, was replenishing her diminished stock. Julia, bored with the proceedings as any lively seven-year-old would be, gained permission to wait outside by the shop door where there was plenty to see.

She was a slender, vigorous child with an ivory skin and an impish smile, her eyes large and blue. Bunches of chestnut curls bobbed over her ears as she rocked on her heels as if bound by invisible chains to the spot where she had been instructed to stand. She had an open view of the whole market-place, in the middle of which was the medieval market cross set like a huge stone crown, and within its arches she could see the butter women selling their wares. From one of the many stalls there drifted the appetising aroma of gingerbread and caramel, making her mouth water. Less pleasant and more pungent were the penned-up cattle and sheep; in another section more interesting to her, horses were being bought and sold. Amid the throng of people milling about, gentry, city dwellers and farm folk, pedlars, gypsies and beggars, there were plenty of soldiers of the Parliamentary Army, for Chichester and the county of Sussex had fallen to them early in the recent Civil War and a barracks was still maintained.

Dominating the whole scene was the ancient Cathedral, which with its separate bell tower stood on the opposite side of the street from where Julia waited. Plain glass had replaced the jewel-like medieval glass that had once sparkled from its many windows, for on the day of the city's capture, the forces of Oliver Cromwell, their Puritan minds outraged by anything they suspected of being Papist, which included the whole of the Church of England, had smashed the beautiful windows and destroyed the pictures painted on boards from earlier centuries that had long been admired and preserved. The altar had been desecrated and stone effigies of past bishops prised from their tombs and smashed. Everything had been tidied up since that day and Puritan services, devoid of organ music, with sermons sometimes lasting three hours or more, were now held within the Cathedral portals.

Julia by her dress was unmistakably the child of a Royalist family. Although she wore a plain cape she felt restricted by it and had tossed it back, revealing her elaborate gown such as no Puritan parent would have allowed a daughter to wear. Julia would have preferred her garments to be without the embroidered ribbons that adorned everything she wore on top and underneath. They were the bugbear of her days, for invariably she ruined or lost the dainty trimmings when she climbed trees or wriggled through hedges or caught them on twigs when out riding. Those on the yellow silk gown she wore today had chains of Dutch tulips on them, the stems and slender leaves linking the blooms, and the stitches so small as to be almost invisible. Other people were delighted when fortunate enough to receive a gift of them, because although woven brocade and patterned ribbons were commonplace, embroidered ones were not, the work too painstaking for most ladies, which made them extremely rare and there-fore to be treasured. Julia would gladly have given away all the bows and love knots and streamers from her own garments.

"When you were a baby," her grandmother had told her once, "you and your crib were so smothered in ribbons it was almost impossible to find you among them."

It had been a well-meant little joke and her mother had smiled, taking it all in good part, although Julia did not doubt there was a firm basis of truth as well as humour. It was as she heaved a sigh on the thought of her mother buying still more material on which to carry out the delicate work that she saw the pearl-white pony. With silvery mane and tail flowing, it came leisurely up West Street, its rider a boy seemingly about four years older than herself, black-haired and dark-eyed in a high-crowned hat with a buckle to its band and oak brown velvet jacket and breeches. He sat well, straight-backed and easy in the saddle as if he had ridden since birth. Accompanying him on a grey horse was a Parliamen-tary officer, probably his father, but she gave no thought to that. On and on the riders came. She watched with a rapt expression, her hands clasped high under her chin in sheer delight at the pony's beauty, unaware that she was on tip-toe with admiration.

The boy spotted her. His serious young face took on a look of pride that his pony should be so admired. He spoke to his father, indicating they should ride to the north side of the market cross. It was agreed. Julia beamed with pleasure. They were going to pass within a couple of feet of her and she could gaze her fill at the pony.

Then, as they drew level, she was astonished and delighted when the boy reined in, looking down at her. "Would you like to pat Pegasus?" he asked, stern and lordly with ownership.

"Yes, please!" Even as she reached out her hand both her parent and his intervened. Anne Pallister had emerged from the shop at that moment. With a gasp of dismay she pulled Julia back by the shoulders while the boy's father turned in the saddle to seize the pony's bridle and jerk it forward.

"Adam!" his father growled harshly. "Have you lost your wits? We have no truck with Royalists!"

The boy's eyes hardened on her in bitter hostility and he turned his face stiffly away, increasing his pony's pace to draw level with his parent. She heard her mother's distress.

"That was Colonel Warrender and his son, Julia! Our neighbours in name only! How could you let yourself show friendliness to the enemy? It is barely four years since the war went against us and now our King has been martyred by execution!"

Julia felt her cheeks burning from both the slight inflicted by the Warrenders and her own shame at being reprimanded by her mother more severely than she could remember. Although she would never have exchanged her own pony, which she loved dearly, for any other, she could not resist another glance at the pearly haunches and the tail of silver silk disappearing into North Street.

Now and again on the drive home Julia stole a glance at her mother, able to see that she was still upset, although not angry, for that would have been alien to her gentle nature. Anne Pallister was a sweet-faced woman, her profile classical against the leather blind that was keeping out the draught through the open window space. Her clear grey eyes were long-lashed, her dark hair worn in the current mode of bunches of shoulder-length curls over each ear, the rest drawn back smoothly to a top-knot, presently hidden by her hat. It was a coiffure that left the neck prettily bare. Hers was swanlike.

Julia supposed that when they were back at Sotherleigh her grand-mother, a staunch Royalist, would have to be told what had taken place. Katherine Pallister was a formidable old lady, likely to be fierce over a lapse on her granddaughter's part, for she was quick to utter a rebuke for any misdemeanour and to give Julia's knuckles a sharp rap on occasion—something her mother had never done. Nevertheless a strong bond of love united them, and companionship bridged the dividing years between them, all the closer since Julia could not remember her grandparents on the distaff side. Their tempers also matched, equable until fired and then a spectacular explosion of wrath.

The coach passed through the village. In the winding lane, beyond the mill and the woods, the gatehouse of Sotherleigh came into sight. Julia felt her qualms melt before the simple pleasure of coming home again. She loved her birthplace. The drive up to the house was half a mile long, flanked by elms sharply green in their new spring foliage, and beyond them, on each side, stretched the gentle parkland. As the coach lumbered on she caught a glimpse of the lake where she fed the ducks and swans. Just visible before a curve in the drive was the maze, a hundred yards in diameter, which was said to be one of the most intricate ever planned. Then suddenly the drive gave a view of the house that could not fail to please even the most jaundiced eye.

Sotherleigh Manor was south-facing and smaller than most of the great country mansions that distantly neighboured it. As a compliment to Queen Elizabeth, in whose reign it had been built, it was in the shape of an *E* with the east and west wings projecting at each end of the main block and a central porch rising from a flight of wide steps through the two upper floors. It had a warm and welcoming aspect, its russet bricks free of any encroaching creeper and its patterning of local flints winking like inset diamonds. Behind it, rising gently against the sky, were the undulating Sussex Downs, their slopes green velvet that occasionally in winter were powdered with snow.

To Julia every part of Sotherleigh smelt as sweet as if the scented Queen Elizabeth herself had just passed through. There was a fragrant blend of herbs and beeswax and sunshine, clean linen and lavender and tangy oranges piled in two rare Chinese bowls decorated in blue, green and iron red.

The bowls had been brought back by her grandfather, Ned Pallister, from one of his many voyages to the Far East. Ned Pallister had been drowned at sea before his only son, Robert, was born.

Julia had seen little of her father, a straight-backed, broad-chested, muscular man, during the first five years of her life, for he had fought for the King throughout the conflict and had not come home to stay until after the Battle of Naseby, a great defeat for the Royalists that had settled the conflict. Since then Robert Pallister, valuing family life, had tried to make up to her and her older brother, Michael, for his years of absence.

Julia knew that he savagely resented the law imposed on him and other Cavalier officers that restricted all their movements to within a five-mile radius of their homes, quite apart from the heavy dues that had to be paid. Fortunately the estate of Sotherleigh came within the bounds and Robert rode his land frequently, keeping an eye on everything and always willing to listen to a tenant with a legitimate grievance. Michael either went with him or undertook some independent duty on the estate, father and son equally dedicated to the husbandry of the land. At every opportunity Julia liked to ride with them.

"You here again," Michael would tease whenever she came trotting up on her pony as he and their father rode out of the stableyard. He was a merry youth, bony at the jaw and with a straight nose. Under his dark brows, less peaked than Robert's but adding to the resemblance, his eyes were the same grey as Anne's and never without a twinkle in them.

Julia would always laugh, retaliating to his quips. It was his joke to say that her curls were the red of his chestnut horse, but she took that as a compliment, thinking it a handsome colour and hoping her hair was really that shade. Much as she enjoyed her brother's company, she felt more grown-up when she rode beside her father on her own. She would have skipped her lessons at any time to be with him, but he was as strict as her grandmother in that respect. Her tutor came two mornings a week and in between she had set-work that had to be done. She never went with Robert or Michael to hunt, hawk or course hares with greyhounds on the Downs. Neither she nor her mother had the stomach for such sports, and no bull from a Sotherleigh farm ever went to be baited by dogs or a bear before it met the butcher's knife.

The coach was drawing up at the steps of Sotherleigh. Usually Julia sprang into the house to run and tell her grandmother all she had seen and done, but today the incident in Chichester was hanging over her. She followed her mother indoors at such a slow pace that Anne was already upstairs when she entered. She met Michael with a net of bowls on his way to play a game on the green to the east of the house with his friend from his Westminster schooldays, Christopher Wren, who was waiting for him there. Christopher had come to stay for a short while before the two young men went up to Oxford where they were to enter Wadham College.

"Coming to watch, Julia?" Michael asked her.

She heaved a sigh. "I don't think I'd better do anything for a little while. I've upset Mama."

"What did you do?"

"I spoke to a Warrender."

He looked taken aback and gave a low whistle at such folly on her part. "Nobody's going to be pleased about that."

It was rare for Michael to look severe and it should have chastened her, but she could not feel much remorse. It had been a beautiful pony and the Warrender boy had been as full of goodwill as she until they had both been reminded of political differences that were not of their making.

"I'm going to make a clean breast of it to Grandmother." Steeling herself, she went into the library where Katherine sat reading. The book was lowered at her approach and Julia related all that had happened.

Katherine heard the child out, making no interruption. She was in her early eighties, dignified and of gracious appearance with a thin, aristocratic nose, bead-bright hazel eyes and a sharp chin. Her hair was snow-white, frizzed over a high roll in the style she had not changed since her young days when she was lady-in-waiting to Queen Elizabeth.

"You were not to know either Colonel Warrender or his son, my child," she said fairly. "We have had no contact with Warrender Hall since the outbreak of the war when we took different sides, although once the Colonel's late father, Sir Harry Warrender, and I were good friends. You may forget what happened, Julia. Naturally your mother was distressed, but she will have forgiven you by now and neither will your father reprimand you for what you did."

With such generous absolution Julia felt she should have been able to forget what had taken place in Chichester, but an image of the pony's beauty became imprinted on her memory and she could not recall it without seeing Adam Warrender's stern young face at the same time. Whenever her dream came to her he was not in it any more than anyone else had been, and yet it was as though the pearly beauty that she could never quite see was now nearer than it had ever been before. Had he and his pony come galloping out of those silvery mists she would not have been in the least surprised. For the first time she felt a need to discuss the dream with someone.

Her natural choice of a confidant was Christopher, whom she considered as much her friend as her brother's. She sought him out down by the lake the day before he and Michael were to go up to Oxford. He did not hear her approach, having thrown a book down on the grass in some anger to lean a shoulder against a tree as he watched unseeingly the swans and ducks on the water.

Wondering what had upset him, for he had the most amiable nature, Julia picked up the book and opened it at random. It was in the students' language of Latin, which she recognised through having begun lessons in it, as well as French, with her tutor. As yet this instruction was a heavy burden on her, but children in her station in life often began such study earlier. According to her grandmother, Queen Elizabeth had been set to learn Latin from the age of three and at least she had been spared that!

"Why does this book displease you, Christopher?" she asked curiously.

He turned with a start and his wide mouth curled in a smile at the sight of her, his ill humour dispersing. A thin, bony youth of medium height, he had a mane of brown, wavy hair that fell fashionably to his shoulders and framed his kindly face. His nose was largish and well shaped, and he had a mannerism of setting his head on one side at times that was quick and almost birdlike. He came forward and crouched down on his haunches to bring his face on a level with hers.

"It doesn't displease me in content. I happen to be the one who translated it into Latin for the author. It's a mathematical treatise by a most eminent man in that field."

"Then why did you throw it down?"

He hesitated. How to tell her that he had been acutely embarrassed by the preface, about which he had had no warning? To him there was nothing unusual about the amount of knowledge he had acquired in the new sciences or in the mathematical instruments he had invented, for his sickly health and wheezing chest in his earlier years had kept him to study while Michael and the rest of his contemporaries had used their freedom from their schoolbooks in vigorous sports. He saw it as no cause for praise, but the author had showered it on him in the preface for all the world to see, saying that the translator of the treatise had been only fifteen years old at the time and great things could be expected of the young inventor, Christopher Wren, in days to come.

"I took offence at the preface where none was intended," he admitted, taking the book from her, "but that is forgotten now. The author was kind enough to send me a signed copy and I'll treat it with respect in future. Have you come down here to feed the swans?"

"No. I want to ask you something. Let's walk by the lake." Her idea of walking was to hop and skip, her exuberant good health giving her boundless energy, and she bounced along as she followed his leisurely stride, telling him of her dream.

"So what is it that I can't quite see?" she concluded.

He considered carefully before he answered her. "If I could work out your dream mathematically it would present no problem at all, but it's in a sphere that can't be deciphered on paper and I'm not a visionary. Yet I would say that destiny has decreed something splendid for you. You will know when it comes."

She was puzzled. "Would it be a fortune, do you think?"

He smiled at the literal turn of a child's mind. "I wasn't supposing it to be monetary. It could be a rewarding experience as you go about in life."

"Why should I ever want to leave Sotherleigh?" Thoughts of womanhood and marriage were far from her. "I love my home and all who are part of it, which means you as well, Christopher."

"I'm pleased to be included."

"I know my father might leave to fight in a revival of the Royalist cause one day, but he will come back when the war is over as he did before. Michael is going up to Oxford with you, but he will return and you will still visit. And Mama and Grandmother will always be here and so shall I."

He refrained from saying anything more on the subject. Let her suppose that nothing involving a break with her family would ever take place. The past Civil War had caused enough disruption at Sotherleigh, affecting her young years, just as it had done in his.

"When and where your dream is fulfilled is not important." He sought to reassure her. "I tell you truly that I wish such a dream were mine."

To his surprise she stopped her hopping and clapped her hands excitedly. "I'll wish hard to share my lovely dream with you."

He looked very seriously at her. "I'll never receive a more generous gift than that."

For a while afterwards she began to think she had achieved her aim, for the dream came less often, as if its power were being divided.

As JULIA HAD REVEALED to Christopher, she knew, young as she was, that her father would never rest until the monarchy was restored. He had hardened to a renewed resolve when the King was executed. Anne was less perceptive, supposing he had determined to make the best of what could not be changed and adjust to life under the Commonwealth. Katherine suspected that he felt otherwise, and this was confirmed when Robert commissioned a plaque to be moulded in plaster of the profile of the young man whom all the Royalists now regarded as King Charles II in all but his actual crowning. Within a laurel wreath the likeness was set in the north wall of the Long Gallery at Sotherleigh amid other decorative and ornate plasterwork that had been masterly created when the house was built.

"Look well on that face," Robert said to Julia, his hand firm on her shoulder, "because it is that of our King. He is across the sea at the present time, but, God willing, before long he will receive the Crown of England at Westminster Abbey."

She glanced up at him with a puzzled expression. "I don't think Oliver Cromwell knows that, does he?"

Robert threw back his head on a roar of laughter. "Not yet, my sweeting. But he will!"

He said almost the same to Anne when she viewed the addition to the Long Gallery, but she listened to him compassionately, as if he were voicing a vain hope, and patted his arm almost consolingly. She was happy and content that they had picked up their lives together again after the war's end and she refused to look ahead to troublesome times that might never come.

He was everything to her. She loved the signs of his presence in the house—the aroma of tobacco smoke from his long-stemmed pipe, the riding gloves left carelessly on the hall table and the lingering scent of the soap with which his personal manservant barbered him. There were the masculine voices and roars of laughter after he and some of his friends came home to dine after hunting. The five-mile ban applied only to those who had been Royalist officers, and a good many gentlemen who lived in the area had not served due to age, disability or responsibilities that had made it impossible for them to join the cause, even though they were staunch supporters of the King. There were always those who had been officers who chose to take a chance and ignore the ban to meet again, for Parliamentarian eyes could not be everywhere. Often there were gaming sessions while Anne entertained the wives to less exacting games of cards. Yet once these gatherings had been far greater in number. Many people were absent due to the toll of war; others had had their estates sequestrated by Parliament, which had compelled them to move elsewhere, invariably out of the county of Sussex altogether.

Sometimes on a mild evening she and Robert would go strolling on their own after Julia was abed and Katherine was being settled by her lady's maid for the night. They would take one of the paths lined by high box hedges to a rose bower or the lake. Often he would caress her lovingly and she would preen under his touch like a cat brought to purring by a gentle hand. She supposed if they had never known separation in their married life they would have long since taken each other's love for granted, worn it like a comfortable cloak, the thunderous waves of passion reduced to mere ripples. But his long absences had made them like young lovers.

When they were married twenty years ago she was fifteen, innocent as a flower and just three years over the age of consent, and he was thirty and worldly-wise. He still liked to tease her playfully about their wedding night when she had been overwhelmed by shyness that he should wish to see her naked and kiss her everywhere. He had let her stay enveloped in her voluminous nightgown until eventually he had won it from her with caresses that had almost made her swoon with sensual pleasure.

Since the birth of Julia she had suffered one stillbirth and two miscarriages, which she blamed on anxiety due to the war.

It was her hope that eventually she would conceive again.

"Don't ever leave me again!" she implored one night in bed as if some slight misgiving had caught up with her from viewing the plaque of the young King in the Long Gallery a few weeks before.

Her plea had come at the very moment he was possessing her. He chuckled low in his throat, cupped her head in his hands and looked down into her face, making a lover's jest. She smiled and he kissed her hard, leaving her plea unanswered in his rising passion.

THERE WERE TIMES when Robert tried to discuss with Anne, when they were strolling or on their own in the house, the possibility of another Royalist uprising, but she always steered him away from the subject or changed it skilfully. He and Katherine never tired of discussing such a possibility, for she had a political awareness that was lacking in his gentle wife. In the year following the regicide the two of them sat often together, both seeing Scotland as a source of hope.

"Cromwell has found the Scots troublesome from the start," Robert said with satisfaction. "What with their clan loyalties and their stubbornness and their Highland hideaways! Now they've shown their contempt of him by proclaiming Charles II as their king even louder than they did after the regicide!"

Katherine inclined her head wisely. "I agree that it's a light at the end of what has been a long dark time."

"I see it as evidence that they have been making contact abroad with the King." Robert leaned forward eagerly in his chair. They were in the library where he had located a book for her before they had settled to talk. The sunlight through the diamond panes caught the bloom on his velvet jacket and full-cut breeches pouched at the knee. Across his chest was a dress sword-band, encrusted with gold and silver thread embroidery by Anne, whose needle had also executed the flowers on the bunches of silk ribbons that flowed with the lace over his bucket-topped boots. Cavaliers took delight in extravagant wear and in having their hair long and curling—wigs if their own did not suffice—to contrast with the severity of garb worn by the Puritan Roundheads, whose nickname had been gained through a skirmish just prior to the outbreak of the Civil War between the King's men and a band of crop-headed apprentices supporting Parliament. Hardly any in the Parliamentary forces wore their hair shorter than shoulder length, but the term "Roundhead" had stuck. Similarly a derisory taunt from the Roundheads had resulted in "Cavalier" for Royalists, meaning they were as foppish and Papist as the Spanish caballeros. But the King's men had taken it up as a badge of honour and displayed their hat plumes and their finery even in the thick of battle. Anne, with her love of needlework, contributed much to Robert's constantly grand appearance.

"How old is that royal young man now?" Katherine asked. Sometimes she was inclined now to be forgetful.

"Twenty, and he is full of fire and spirit. I can't believe it will be long before he makes a move to claim his rights. Every Royalist sword-arm will rally to him again!"

Katherine gazed at his strong, well-shaped face that held such a look of her beloved husband. That he was a man of intelligence, great discipline, and courage was to be seen in the cut of his features, with Ned's blue eyes, the same longish nose and firm mouth. His hair had lost its bright gold now, so brindled with grey that only a trace of its former colour showed here and there, but it was still thick and he was destined to be one of the few men who escape baldness in one form or another. The likeness was accentuated not by the thin moustache, but by the crisply trimmed arrow-head beard, a fashion such as Tudor men had flaunted. Although there were lines about his eyes, a thickening of the neck, and the threat of stoutness to the body, he was as striking-looking a man as he had ever been, active and energetic. She wished for his sake that he had had more than one son, although Michael, presently following in his footsteps at Oxford, was as hard-working at his studies as he was when home on the estate, a credit to the name of Pallister, and that counted for much. As for Julia, no man could have had a brighter and more interesting daughter.

It had not been easy bringing Robert up on her own, not that she had ever let him know. As a boy he had been wild, which was partly due to the fearlessness of his character and to her own resolve not to smother him with maternal love. He had sobered down with regard to his studies by the time he left Westminster School and went up to Oxford. Yet there had remained in him a restlessness that she recognised all too well and that at times had filled her with dread.

"I'm going to sea, Mother," he had announced the very day he came down from Oxford, barely before he had flung aside his hat and pulled off his riding gloves.

So the moment had come. Everything in her baulked against it, but she retained an outward calm. "Indeed? And what is to happen to Sotherleigh? Did I not raise you to be master here? Is there anything you were not taught about the husbanding of land and all that entails? Have I not promised to make Sotherleigh over to you when you come of age?"

His blue eyes under the peaked brows were serious and direct; his attitude serious, determined but reasonable. "Agreed. But I'm not sailing away for ever. There'll be an end to my voyages when the right time comes. I'll marry some day and I promise you grandchildren for your old age, but in the meantime I have to see something of what lies beyond this realm."

Satisfied that he was aware of his responsibilities, she had shown nothing of her inner fears of shipwrecks and cannibals and other hazards of far-off places, but had let him go with encouragement and her goodwill. He was not to know the extent with which he had tipped her back into those agonised times of waiting and hoping and praying that all was well with a ship no bigger than a tiny cork on the mighty oceans of the world.

She had filled her time with overseeing the estate and ensuring that everything was kept in order for his eventual home-coming. At every social gathering she mentally selected one young woman, and then another, as a possible bride for Robert, but gradually they all married and she gave up her hopeless task.

He came home again after thirteen years away. During all that time he had visited Sotherleigh only twice and she was not at all sure that he had even now turned his back on the sea. Then, by sheer chance, he met Anne and any thoughts he might have had of going away again came to naught. They were married within a matter of weeks and by then he had taken up the reins of Sotherleigh as if he had never been elsewhere.

His voice broke in on her reverie. "The war was a drain on every man's purse, no matter whether support was for the King or Parliament, and I was more fortunate than many in that the estate remained productive in my absence. As you know, the bailiff could not have been more reliable and Anne kept the accounts as meticulously as she embroiders. Yet it has to be accepted that a Royalist uprising will impose a further financial strain on Sotherleigh's resources until victory is won."

"Yes, it will, but we managed here before, as you have said, and we shall do the same again. Never let concern for us womenfolk hold you back in any way."

"That was bravely said."

"When the time comes to serve the Crown again, remember that some of the best plate is safely in hand should you need funds in a dire situation."

He knew what it meant for her to contemplate his going off to fight again, but there was no show of the anxiety that she felt either in her voice or on her somewhat stern features. Neither would there be a fuss when the day of his leaving dawned, as he believed it must. "I trust it won't be necessary for me to draw on it. It belongs to Sotherleigh and those generations of Pallisters who will live here after us."

As a Royalist officer he had received no pay during his service and neither would he next time. When at war an English gentleman of wealth and position was expected to provide for himself and also to arm and clothe and supply horses to those men in his employ who went to war with him. Some of the lesser plate, still valuable enough in itself, had been looted in two Roundhead raids during his absence. Fortunately the most precious pieces, mostly Elizabethan and studded with jewels, had been buried in the kitchen garden in the nick of time and thus escaped confiscation. It was Anne herself who had dug some of it up to send to him when his purse needed replenishing and the King's cause was desperate for funds. He felt it bitterly that he had come home from the war with only the battle-stained garments on his back, his arms and horses taken from him, and his retainers who had served with him had been in similar straits. That in itself had to be revenged.

"You're a true warrior, Mother," he said admiringly.

The compliment pleased her. "I thank heaven that the late King, who was not often as wise as he should have been, had the good sense to send his son Charles and his younger brother, James, to The Hague for safe keeping when the war began to turn against us. Poor little Harry should have gone too, but at least he will be reunited with his brothers on the day when the monarchy comes into its own again."

FOR SOME MONTHS nothing happened to bring that day any nearer. At Sotherleigh the daily routine went on undisturbed, through 1650. Christmas went by and the year of 1651 rolled on through spring towards summer. The most talked-of happening between Anne and Julia was that Michael would not be coming home for the summer vacation. Julia was bitterly disappointed. The previous year's June he had come home full of a first-year undergraduate's cockiness, highly pleased with himself over his examination results and such fun with his quips and laughter. Christopher had visited for three weeks and although he and Michael had spent much of their time dallying with two pretty sisters that lived beyond the village, Julia had had many talks with him. She was fascinated by the weather clock he had made as a gift for her mother, the workings of which he had explained to her so clearly that she found it easy to understand. But this year she would not be seeing him. It caused an aching in her heart that she kept to herself and did not mention to anyone.

The reason for Michael's absence was that he had been invited to the home of Christopher's sister, Susan, and her husband, Dr. William Holder, at Bletchingdon. The purpose was that Michael might benefit with Christopher from special mathematical studies with William, who was a Cambridge don and a renowned mathematician. William had met Susan when she had lived at Windsor in the days when Christopher had played with the present King and the other royal children before clouds of war had begun to gather on the horizon.

Robert, much as he would have liked his son to come home for this summer more than any other, having had wind that events were stirring, raised no objection. This was a time of enormous interest in all the new sciences, knowledge in previously unexplored fields bursting forth, and he would not deny Michael a share of extra-intelligent tuition in the sphere of mathematics.

June had melted into July when the dramatic news reached Sotherleigh that Charles II had landed in Scotland and been crowned at Scone. In spite of its being good tidings and a cause for rejoicing for others, to Anne it was a warning knell that could not be shut out. All the sparkle went from her like a candle snuffed as anxiety mounted in her with every passing hour. Then the clatter of galloping hooves up the drive heralded the message that the new King had raised the Royal Standard again and loyal Cavaliers were joining him and the Scottish army he had rallied. Robert made immediate preparations to leave.

# TWO

THE EVE of Robert's departure came. He made love to Anne, knowing that it was likely to be a long time before they could be together again. In the morning, just before they were about to go downstairs for a family breakfast, she stopped him by the bedchamber door.

"Promise me that you will consider your safety at all times!" she implored with a desperation she had never shown before.

He held her in a close embrace and smiled reassuringly into her upturned, anxious face. "Once when I was in a far-away foreign land, an old soothsayer told me that I should never die at sea, or on a battlefield, but on my own land. I believe him. As you know, my first ship sank in a storm and I escaped capture by pirates on another. As for battles, I have been seasoned since Edgehill onwards. Have no fear, my love. We shall spend our old age together at Sotherleigh. I promise you that I shall come back to your arms. Never doubt it."

She nodded, accepting what he said in an urgent need of comfort. Then it seemed to her that within seconds breakfast was over, farewells were said, and her final kiss with him exchanged. Somehow she managed to follow Katherine's example and shed no tears when he rode off with his little band of faithful followers, who only the day before had been serving him at table or tending his land, all rearmed, newly breast-plated, well clad with fresh horses to ride. Her tears came later that night when she was all alone in her wide and lonely bed.

ROBERT HAD BEEN GONE only three weeks when his daughter had a rare recurrence of her dream. But it was dashed from her by a loud shout of warning from somewhere downstairs in the house. Julia sat bolt upright from her pillows, her tousled hair hanging in disarray about her startled face. Shaking her curls back, she clutched her rag doll closer. From far away the shout came again, reverberating up through the panelled walls and oaken floors. This time she could distinguish the words.

"Roundheads at the gatehouse!"

Flinging back the bedclothes, she sprang from her narrow four-poster and dashed to the half-open mullioned window, its diamond-shaped panes gilded by the early sunlight. Although she knew there was little chance as yet of seeing the unwelcome visitors, she stood on tip-toe to peer out in the direction of the drive.

The warm air met her, heralding another hot and brilliant day, and the elm trees were dusty with summer and faded with heat. The groom, who had given the alarm, had left the house and was running off across the courtyard, not returning to the stables as she would have expected. She saw that he was making for the seclusion of the box-hedges that lay in the opposite direction. He was a good groom, who had lost an arm in battle while serving with her father, and she was puzzled as to why he had not gone back to the horses in case they should be troubled by the presence of strangers marching by.

She felt more wary than frightened. Yet the very manner in which the warning had been given showed that some danger was imminent. Were they coming in the hope of seizing her father on a charge of treason? If that was the case they would be piqued to learn that he was not here. By now he should be with the King, who might have crossed the border into England already.

It was as she drew away from the window that a disturbing thought struck her. Suppose the Roundheads refused to believe that her father was elsewhere? She had heard what great damage was done when they searched for hideaways. She would go wild if she saw havoc being wreaked on her home! There was also the dreadful possibility that in their rage at not finding their quarry they might set fire to it.

Thoroughly afraid now, although not for herself, she began to wash hurriedly, making do with the cold water in her jug since a maid was not due with a steaming container for a long while yet. It was a source of pride to her that she was able to look after herself in many ways. Her mother had always cared personally for her instead of relegating her welfare to underlings, as would have been expected of a lady of Anne Pallister's social status. As a result Julia had been allowed to develop more

independence than any nurse would have permitted. She was also proud
of being allowed to sleep in a room of her own, admitting only to herself
that it was a comfort, when the wind howled eerily or the house creaked,
to know that her grandmother's bedchamber was next to hers in the west
wing.

Julia snatched a pink cotton gown out of one of the drawers in her
clothes-press, not quite at random, for if it had had hooks down the back
she would have needed assistance with the fastenings. As she pulled the
garment over her head and settled it down onto her petticoats, its decorative knots of rose-patterned ribbons fluttered and danced. Then she
whipped up a hairbrush and wielded it on her tangles. Normally her
mother dressed her hair, but for the time being it must hang free down
her back. When the brushing was done she returned to the window and
looked across to the east wing where her mother's bedchamber was located, but saw no sign of her. Then she stiffened. Was that a glint of steel
through the elm trees?

She dallied no longer but shot across to her door. Outside in the
corridor the silence of the house seemed to hit her. Abruptly she stood
quite still and strained her ears, but there was no distant clatter of dishes to
be heard, no clack of heels from scurrying maids, no swish of a broom
over carpets. Her pulse quickened and she swallowed hard. Turning on
her heel, she ran to her grandmother's apartment, which consisted of a
parlour, a bedchamber and an adjoining garderobe. She did not halt until
she stopped with a gasp on the bedchamber threshold, for the door was
open to reveal that the room was deserted and the bed made.

Katherine never rose early and always took a leisurely breakfast alone
in her room before emerging for the day; the only exception that Julia
could remember was when her father left recently to join the King. She
was seized by the conviction that everyone in the household, except
herself, had been up for hours, which meant they must have been forewarned of the Roundheads' coming after she had gone to bed. They
should have told her too! Now her blue eyes flashed under a deep frown
of annoyance and her stubborn little jaw tightened.

Whirling about once more, she dashed in the direction of the Grand
Staircase, passing on the way the open carved wooden screen that was one
of the treasures of Sotherleigh. It took the place of a wall, reaching from
floor to ceiling and overlooking the entrance hall below. It gave an
illusion of transparency in its fretwork effect, all the wild flowers and
ferns and grasses that had been growing on the land where the house now

stood had been depicted on the screen with a sense of spontaneity and a feeling for natural form. Through the entwining stems and leaves it was possible to view the hall below. It had long been a game of Julia's to identify by name everything portrayed there, but today she had no time for that. She paused briefly to peer through a cluster of carved hedge-roses at the hall with its black and white chequered marble floor below. It was deserted. The heavy wooden bolt, which slid out of the wall to bar the entrance door at night, was still in position.

It was then that she heard the sound of someone at work in the Long Gallery, the double doors of which were exactly behind her. Swiftly she turned the handle and entered. A handyman, far from young, who did general repairs in the house, turned with a start from plastering a section of the wall a few yards from where she stood.

" 'Ave them bastards got 'ere yet?" he asked.

No need to ask whom he meant! "No, but I think I saw them. They'll soon be in the courtyard."

He cursed picturesquely, using words she had never heard before, and she pondered them with interest as she went to him. The Long Gallery was hung with portraits under a curved ceiling painted as though arched by the branches of thickly foliaged trees, and it stretched the full length of the main block of the house, with four fireplaces to heat it in winter. It was here that ninepins and other bowling games were played and where the ladies of the household sometimes strolled for exercise when the weather was bad. She was astonished to see at close quarters the work that the man had in hand. He was slapping wet plaster over the profile of the new King.

"Why are you doing that, Mr. Ridley?" she demanded indignantly.

The handyman did not pause in his work. "Your father was a brave man to 'ave set this 'ere in the first place, but it'll do this 'ouse no good for them that lives 'ere if those Roundheads should spot it."

Julia's anxiety for Sotherleigh, already high in her, made her clasp her hands together. "Why are they coming?"

"You best ask your mama that, I don't know nothing."

It was obvious that he did, but did not feel it was his place to tell her. "But wet plaster can't be hidden!" she cried out.

"That's why I'm covering a good spread of the wall and not just the King's face. It'll make it look a bigger job than what it is. Them cracks 'igher up the wall will be a reason for my work." He gave her a wink, twisting his weathered face that was as wrinkled as a walnut. "They'll suspect nothing."

She was not so sure. Sadly she watched the carefully executed plaque being obliterated by the plaster; it was a handsome profile with hooded eyes, a large well-shaped nose and chin, the lips sensual under a thin moustache. As the last slap of plaster covered it, she shivered and rubbed her arms.

"Where's my mama?" she asked on a rising note. "Do you know?"

"Mrs. Pallister will be with Mistress Katherine downstairs somewhere." He used the old form of address that her grandmother preferred. "It'd 'ave made no difference if I 'ad started on the work last night, 'cos the plaster would still 'ave been damp this morning. Better for me to be seen at what I'm doing."

She bit her lip as she turned to go, hurt showing in her eyes. "Everybody seems to know about Oliver Cromwell's Roundheads coming except me. If I hadn't heard the warning I'd have been asleep still."

He gave her a consoling glance. "It's my bet that's what the Pallister ladies wanted. With the Roundheads coming so early it was 'oped to spare you the upset." Then he jerked his head as a knocking for admittance to the house resounded from the hall. "That'll be them! Nip down quick to your mother, child. You'll be safe with 'er and Mistress Katherine."

She ran from the Long Gallery, full of trepidation, and rushed to look down through the screen at the hall below. An entirely different scene now met her gaze. The whole household had gathered there. Her mother and her grandmother stood side by side. Behind them, lined up in a row, were the two lady's maids, eight of the nine maidservants, the cook and her scullion boy. It was a domestic staff much depleted by the need for economy and the absence of the footmen, who had gone with their master to the King. By the entrance door the ninth maidservant waited for the moment when her mistress would tell her to open it. The all-over effect was that of brightly hued pieces on a chessboard. They were facing the barred door where the hammering had increased in volume and the demand for admittance was louder.

"Open in the name of Parliament!"

Anne, very pale and visibly trembling, was wearing the most vivid gown she possessed, a rich ruby red, almost as if she hoped it might help her to assert her authority in the face of the enemy. She stood slightly to the fore of her mother-in-law as benefitted the mistress of the house, neat in her person as always, even at this early hour. Not a strand of her dark hair was out of place and her top-knot, high at the back of her head, was encased in a little cap of plaited metallic threads. It was a fashion favoured by Royalist women and she had a variety of this accessory, some with rosebuds, others of narrow ribbon, and even one with tiny butterflies. This morning she had chosen the one that sparkled most, perhaps out of defiance. In her lobes, almost invisible under her bunches of curls, were her pearl ear-bobs.

She was looking fixedly at the barred door where the butt of a musket was adding to the din. In her right hand, dropped by her side, she rotated a wispy lace-trimmed handkerchief in an agitated manner; she looked fragile and vulnerable and likely to collapse at any moment. Julia's heart went out to her, fiercely angry that anyone should frighten her mother in this manner.

In contrast, Katherine, wearing bronze taffeta with a wide lace collar, was a commanding figure in spite of her age and her need of a cane. Her whole demeanour was completely composed. She spoke to her daughter-in-law in her slightly husky voice.

"Take courage for the sake of Robert and the King!"

Anne nodded. On both the previous Roundhead rampages she had been in bed recovering from the miscarriages that had caused her such grief. On each occasion her maid had pulled the curtains around her and she had been spared the sight of her jewel-box being rifled and her clothes and personal belongings being tumbled from her chests. It was at that time that her be-jewelled and be-pearled accessories for her top-knot had been plundered.

This was the first time she had had to meet a raiding party face to face and her knees felt ready to give way. Yet mention of Robert had stirred some small fount of courage she had not known she possessed. For some inexplicable reason she had a sudden image of his love-face at their most intimate moments in the wide warmth of their marriage bed. In her heightened state of nerves there came such a surge of longing for his presence that she almost cried out. Yet if he were here now he would be drawn into fighting to escape capture and she must be thankful that he was far away. Straightening her shoulders, she gave her instructions to the maid by the door. For a few moments her voice was clear of the nervous tremor that had been plaguing it ever since the midnight warning that the Roundheads were coming for a special purpose.

"Open the door now, Joan."

Julia, who might have run to her mother at this point, had been stayed from the start by the hurtful knowledge that she was neither expected nor wanted as a member of this waiting tableau, in adult eyes still the baby to be kept out of the way. She watched the door keenly, her hand tightening on the carved leaf that she gripped as she waited. The maidservant grasped the bolt and slid it back into its aperture. Then she turned the big ring handle. When she had drawn the door wide open she scampered back to her place in the line.

A broad shadow fell across the chequered floor and a heftily built Parliamentary officer strode in, his boots bucket-topped, his spurs jangling. The meeting of thick brows and the grim set of his mouth showed his immense displeasure at not having been admitted at his first demand for entry. He came to a halt with his hand resting on the hilt of the sword at his hip, facing the group in the hall. In his wake came a sergeant, who took up a stand nearby. The door, left open, showed a dozen troopers lined up outside.

The Roundhead officer addressed Anne curtly. "You are Mrs. Pallister?"

"I am."

"My name is Captain Harding." His frown was threatening. "Why was your door not opened to me at my first command?"

Anne looked bleakly at him. How could she say that she had delayed everything by fainting on her way to the hall? Katherine had slapped her wrists and brought her round and hauled her to her feet. To her relief her mother-in-law promptly spoke up, answering the officer on her behalf.

"There was good reason, Captain." Katherine regarded him haughtily, her back as straight as she could manage. "We have a system whereby the gatehouse keeper signals to the stables and the groom then warns us here. These are dangerous times and, being a house of women, we have to be cautious. My daughter-in-law was careful to check first from an upper window that the troopers had an officer with them."

"Hmm." He thought it more likely that arrogance on this old woman's part had delayed his entrance, but he was prepared to let that go as he made an observation. "I must say I find it surprising that everyone here should be up and about at such an early hour." His gaze rested cynically on Katherine. "Even you, madam."

"I was up early for my prayers," Katherine stated imperiously.

"Is that your habit?"

"It is." She spoke the truth, for she prayed each morning in her room on her knees before returning to bed for a while. This morning she had dressed instead of resting again and had breakfasted downstairs. In her opinion if her daughter-in-law had had something to eat it was unlikely she would have fainted. Anne had not slept either, although she should have snatched some rest after all the preparations for the Roundheads' visit had been carried out in the darkness of the night. If it had not been for a friend whose contacts reported Roundhead movements to local Royalist families, this officer and his troopers would have caught Sotherleigh completely by surprise.

Captain Harding returned his attention to Anne. "So where is your husband since everyone else is about?"

She attempted a casual note, somewhat unsuccessfully. "The Master of Sotherleigh is not here at the moment."

Katherine followed up in an imperious tone. "My son has gone hawking in the vicinity." She knew her daughter-in-law would never get her tongue round a lie, but she herself had no such qualms in these desperate circumstances.

The Captain's eyes showed contemptuous disbelief. "Is that so? I suggest to you he has already broken the five-mile boundary to which he is restricted."

Katherine's chin went a little higher. "Why should you say that? My son is not in the habit of breaking the law and has never failed to meet the heavy payments demanded of him and others like him by the Committee of Compounding for failing to condone the execution of King Charles!"

The Captain snorted furiously. "That royal tyrant was poison to the country. We have freedom now."

"You give freedom only to those whose religious beliefs run parallel with your Puritan rules!"

His retort came with the speed of a musket ball. "I'll remind you, mistress, that there would never have been a Civil War if your royal despot had not tried to force his rules, religious and secular, on Parliament and the people of these isles!"

Anne knew it was the truth that he had spoken, but the trouble was that the tyranny of the late King was being matched by the extremists into whose hands the country had fallen. So many good, fair-minded Puritan Parliamentary leaders had been killed early in the war or had died from other reasons, and now Cromwell could send his men to invade the homes of those listed as his enemies. But this was no time to let a political debate develop.

"Captain Harding," she intervened hastily, "why not say where you believe my husband to be? All will go easier if we are as direct as possible with each other in these unhappy circumstances."

His gaze switched to her. "Very well," he said on a less brusque note. "Your husband has gone to join young Charles Stuart, who would have done better to have stayed where he was sent, because his fate is destined to be the same as his father's."

Anne tried to shut her ears to such a terrible prophecy. She refused to believe that this time all would not go well. No matter what this Round-head said, nothing could shake her belief that Robert had done right to ride to the new King, who was known to be a very different man to his father. Yet she dared not voice these loyal sentiments. It was a time to be diplomatic at all costs.

"Since you have guessed the whereabouts of my husband, I will name the other members of the family not here by my side. Michael, my son, is an undergraduate at Oxford. Julia, my little daughter, is still asleep in bed and I beg that she should not be disturbed. Nobody else is missing."

He did not doubt anything she said. The lie had been the old woman's and not hers. She was transparently honest. There was also an intriguing air about her of innocence-never-lost that was belied by the flowing sensuous grace of her body, which in itself was guaranteed to stir the lusty instincts of any man. As for the nervousness that emanated from her, it came like a bouquet and would have made her a natural victim for rape if she had fallen into rougher company than his.

"I'm not here to frighten children, but for another reason altogether."

"Then what exactly is your purpose here, Captain?" she asked him.

He spoke bluntly. "I am here to commandeer your horses. We have need of them for the final defeat of the Royalist usurper."

Up by the screen Julia froze with horror. Her pony was her dearest and most precious possession. These hateful men wanted to take him away. Never! Neither should they have the four old coach horses to drag their heavy wagons! As for the sleek saddle horse that her mother rode, it was ready to be exchanged for her father's tired mount in time to come if he should be able to make secret visits as he had done previously during the war years. Surely her mother would forbid this officer and his men to go anywhere near the stables.

Anne's answer came in a rush. "There are no horses at Sotherleigh, sir. Our stables are empty."

The Captain was watching her closely. "I'm well aware that the stalls are deserted," he countered with sarcastic emphasis. "I sent two of my men ahead to mount guard there and they reported back to me. Everything as clean as a new pin, I understand, and no trace of feed anywhere. What's more, whatever outdoor staff you have apparently scattered at our coming, because my men could find no one to question. However, I happen to have been reliably informed only a couple of days ago that you are in possession of four strong coach horses, a good saddle horse and a Welsh pony."

Julia's blue eyes, already wide and sapphire dark with anguish, became shot through with glittering tears. Her pony had gone already! She recalled all the talk she had heard in recent weeks about unscrupulous thieves with Parliamentary sympathies creeping into Royalist stables and stealing horses for the Commonwealth forces. Now it had happened at Sotherleigh in spite of her mother's orders that a guard be kept on them day and night. Her pony wouldn't understand what was happening to him. She thought her heart must break. A huge sob broke noisily from her throat.

It was heard in the hall below and everybody looked up. Both men reacted automatically in swift military fashion, the Captain drawing his sword with a flash of reflected sunlight and the sergeant dropping to one knee and aiming his musket, already primed before entry into the house, at the screen. Anne screamed and darted forward in panic and with arms outstretched.

"It can only be my little daughter!" She turned and called frantically, "It is you, isn't it, Julia. Answer me, please."

The tearful answer came. "It's me, Mama."

Captain Harding snapped an order to his sergeant. "Check the situation!"

As the sergeant went bounding up the flight, his musket still at the ready, Anne tried desperately to reassure Julia.

"There's no need to be afraid, my lamb. Nobody is going to hurt you." She spun round imploringly to the Captain. "Don't let your sergeant drag her down, I beg you."

"He won't."

At that point the sergeant spoke through the screen. "The little girl is on her own, sir."

"Leave her."

Anne seized the chance to call out again to her daughter. "I had no idea you were about! Are you dressed?" She knew Julia would never willingly appear before strangers in her nightshift.

"Yes, but I've only brushed my hair."

"That's not important. Come down to me, dearest." Then seeing that Julia made no move she tried again. "Do the soldiers outside frighten you? I will ask Captain Harding if we may have the door shut."

Katherine could scarcely refrain from banging her cane on the floor. She had been fuming inwardly from the moment that Julia had made her presence known. There was no denying Anne was hopeless in a crisis. She should have flown upstairs at once to her daughter and whispered to her to say nothing, for the child was intelligent enough to grasp the urgency of the situation. As it was, Julia was likely to give the whole game away by saying innocently that the horses were in the stables yesterday evening when she had gone to give her pony a special tit-bit of sugar. That did not seem to have occurred to Anne in her concern for the child's state of mind. As the sergeant came down the stairs again, Katherine moved forward.

"I'll fetch Julia."

Captain Harding levelled his sword at arm's length and made a flicking movement with it to halt her hobbling pace and make her draw back again. "There's no need for that. Let the child come down by herself in her own good time." He sheathed his sword again as Katherine obeyed him with a glare. He had good reason for his insistence. Children were guileless sources of information and nothing was to be gained by frightening them. Still less would be garnered if interfering old grandmothers were able to get to them first.

After telling the sergeant to shut the entrance door, he stepped back a few paces in order to be in a more advantageous position to look up at the screen. The child could be seen like a small shadow against it. He smiled and spoke jovially to her. "Did you hear what I said, Julia? Come down here and join us as soon as you like. I'm sure you would prefer to be at your mother's side than up there alone."

Anne added her persuasion. "Do as the Captain says, dearest." After a few moments she saw her daughter's hand give a little wave through the screen and knew that her words had had effect. Only then did she remember that Julia was liable to plunge them all into terrible danger. She was helpless to do anything about it. Captain Harding had planted himself at the foot of the stairs in a manner that showed no one should go up the flight until he had spoken to her child.

Leaving the screen, Julia dried her eyes hastily on the back of her hands. Michael had told her it was babyish to shed tears and he wouldn't have liked her to cry in front of enemy soldiers. Yet nothing could stop her weeping inside for the loss of her beloved pony. Everyone who loved horses knew they could get as homesick as people and she could not bear the thought of his being in strangers' hands, perhaps ridden with a whip or used as a pack-pony until he dropped.

She came slowly down the stairs, which were built around a well with short, easy flights with wide treads and many landings. A portrait of Queen Elizabeth hung on the wall of the lowest landing and now it glistened in a reflected shaft of sunlight from one of the hall windows which obliterated the gaze of the olive-dark eyes that appeared to look directly at anyone coming into the range of them. It was as if the Queen had shut her lids at this scene of greed and treachery against a fair house and would not open them again until these rough intruders were gone.

Captain Harding smiled when Julia came into sight. He had children of his own and although they were older, two of them wed, he knew that Julia was at an age when the truth was far more natural than deceit. It should not be difficult to find out from her all that he wanted to know. When she was just five stairs from the bottom he held up his hand for her to stay where she was.

"That's far enough for the moment." Setting his foot on a lower tread, he leaned an arm across his knee and smiled again at her. "I want you to answer a few questions for me. Will you do that, Julia?"

She did not like him. His mouth was a row of big teeth, but his smile did not reach his hard and penetrating eyes. "Yes," she said reluctantly.

"Good girl. Tell me, what is your favourite pastime?"

"Being at Sotherleigh."

"That's not quite what I meant. We all like to be at home. I'm a long way from mine and miss it very much. Do you like to play with dolls?"

"Yes." Normally she was outgoing and would have spoken eloquently of her favourites, but she begrudged every word to this would-be stealer of horses.

"Perhaps you like to draw?" He received the same monosyllabic answer. "Can you sign your own name yet to your drawings?"

She looked scornful. "I can read and write and cypher."

He feigned admiration for such talent by raising his eyebrows. "You're very grown-up. I suppose you ride too?"

She gave him a nod, gulping on this sensitive subject. Anne and Kath-

erine were on tenterhooks, able to see where the interrogation was leading. The child nodded. Then the next probing question came.

"Have you a pony of your own?"

Julia's pent-up anguish rose perilously close to the surface. Her pony
was still her property, no matter where he was now. "I have. He's a
chestnut with a white blaze." Her throat was choking. "That's why I call
him Starlight."

"Where is he now?"

"With the other horses."

"And where are they?"

"Taken by Roundhead thieves!" She burst out in an explosion of fury
and misery, thinking the culprits could only be associates of this man since
he had come for the same purpose. "They take everything and spoil
everything! Why can't you kneel to the King and then my father and
Starlight could come home again!" She dived under his arm and rushed
past him on her final words to hurl herself against her mother, wrapping
her arms about her. Anne, almost thrown off balance, clutched at the
newel-post to steady herself.

Captain Harding felt his colour deepen in anger. He removed his foot
from the stair and straightened up. The child's spontaneous outburst had
come from the heart and had been completely sincere, however roughly
expressed. So his comrades had been here before him. It was unfortunate,
for he was desperately short of horses, but at least they had gone to the
right side. It was the second disappointment since late yesterday afternoon
when one of his troopers had come running from an advance sortie to tell
him there was a stableful of thoroughbreds at Sotherleigh's neighbouring
estate, Warrender Hall. He had thought mistakenly to find himself in
luck. After setting a guard on the horses, he had discovered to his consternation that the late owner of the estate, Sir Harry Warrender, had been
one of the strongest advocates in favour of increasing the powers of
Parliament. To add to the embarrassment of the situation, the present
Master of the Hall was Colonel John Warrender of the Parliamentary
forces, who happened to have arrived home the day before. Any hope of
an invitation to supper, over which two officers might have buried the
matter, had come to nothing. What was worse, Colonel Warrender, iras-
cible over the disturbing of his highly strung horses, had virtually
snubbed a profuse apology.

Angered by the rebuff, Harding had needed to give vent himself and
had felt his vices rise up against his Puritan principles. Returning to the

nearby city of Chichester, he had begun a tour of the taverns, looking for a landlord prepared to sell him more than a tankard of mild ale, there being a government ban on the sale of what was called "strong waters." It was known that the trade in bottles of spirit was still active in spite of ruthless measures to stamp it out, and it did not take him long to find an inn-keeper well used to being bribed by men like himself, who were committed to abstinence and yet found themselves overcome at times by a deep thirst and other urgent needs. With an armful of bottles he had taken a whore with him upstairs to one of the tavern rooms. There he had drunk too much, talked too much, and bedded the drab with all the pent-up lust of months of denial. He had also been swindled, for he thought he had paid her for the night, but she had left him long before midnight, slipping away when he had turned his back to piss into a chamberpot.

He cleared his throat to deal further with this Royalist household. "You must teach your daughter more respect for the Commonwealth," he said brusquely to Anne, "particularly as Charles Stuart will soon be in chains."

"That is not a foregone conclusion," Katherine interjected icily.

He curled his lip contemptuously, riled by this old woman who was able to get under his skin, then sternly addressed Anne again. "How long since the horses went?"

She stared at him as if struck dumb. Until now she had avoided a direct lie and she knew a false answer would show all over her face. But she was saved by Katherine in the nick of time.

"The pick of the stables was taken about eight years ago after your forces captured Arundel Castle and took the city of Chichester."

He nodded. That was plausible. He had been at both the siege of the city and the storming of the castle. Afterwards the orders had been to take only the best horses in the newly over-run district. "What of the rest?"

"Those left to us were commandeered in full a few days ago."

Anne felt Julia's head jerk in surprise against her at the lie and pressed her closer to smother any involuntary remark. To her overwhelming relief the Captain accepted her mother-in-law's reply with a nod. He was not to know that Robert had replenished the stables during the time he was at home, and had taken the saddle-horses with him on his recent departure.

"Very well." Captain Harding still saw no reason to doubt what he had been told, but he had to make sure no wool was being pulled over his eyes. Experience had taught him to follow on with the servants. He strolled over to the row of women and the kitchen lad. If one of them should be disgruntled, or not wholly with the Royalists, that was where he might learn something. He walked along the line, fixing each one in turn with a penetrating eye. Then he came to a halt.

"Have any of you heard anything said since my arrival that goes against your conscience and for which every one of you will have to answer on the Day of Judgement?"

They stared at him and shook their heads, all of them Royalists having strong personal reasons to be on their guard against him, either on religious grounds or because they were the daughters or sisters of the men who had followed the Master of Sotherleigh back to war. Joe Berry, the thirteen-year-old scullion, was an orphan with no political views stronger than his allegiance to the Pallister family, who had given him a home. To him it would have been the same if they had been Parliamentarians instead of Royalists, for he prided himself on knowing which side his bread was buttered. Square-bodied and short-legged, he had a plain face, impish and freckled, with an artfulness in the brown eyes, a vulgar breadth of nose and his hair a copper-red thatch. Having a keen sense of humour, he was hard put not to show his merriment at the game being played by the Pallister ladies. He would never have believed Mrs. Pallister capable of standing up to this burly officer, who was studying him with gimlet eyes again. Quickly Joe shook his head as if to reaffirm that he had nothing to tell.

The lack of response from the servants was no surprise to the Captain, but the feeling weighed in his guts that somehow this household had got the better of him. Well, he'd get the proverbial pound of flesh out of them anyway. To equalise matters he intended to be recompensed in kind for failing to achieve his purpose here. He turned on Anne again, his whole attitude as belligerent as when he had first entered the house.

"I don't intend to leave empty-handed. Since you are unable to supply me with horses, I shall take valuables in lieu as compensation."

Anne was aghast. She unfolded herself from Julia's arms and stepped towards him, flinging her hands wide. "But we have nothing left! Sotherleigh was ransacked on two occasions!"

He knew this household would be of the Church of England or the Roman Catholic faith, neither of which was recognised by Parliament, having been officially abolished with the monarchy, the House of Lords and all the old pagan customs from maypole dancing to the celebration of Yuletide. There was every likelihood that some altar plate, previously concealed, would be in daily use since the old woman had spoken of rising early for her prayers.

"Where is the chapel to this place?" he demanded. "Indoors or located separately outside?"

"Neither. This household has always worshipped at the local village church. You may search the house and the park if you don't believe me." Too late Anne remembered with a sinking heart that Ridley might still be at the vital part of his task and if this officer thought that one thing was being concealed, he was likely to start poking about in every corner of the house. She sensed her mother-in-law's exasperation at her foolishness and her clutched handkerchief rotated with the speed of a child's windmill-on-a-stick in a high wind.

"I take you to be a woman of honour, Mrs. Pallister, and so I'll not waste time looking for nonexistent altar plate. But what of your jewellery?"

Already pale, she became ashen to the lips. She brought her left hand up to her chest and covered it protectively with her right. "Surely you would not take our wedding rings from us?"

He sighed heavily. It might well be a case of scraping the barrel in a search of this house, but he had never yet stooped to taking wedding bands from women's fingers and neither would he now. "No, set your mind at rest there. I cannot promise the house will be left tidy after the search, but it will be conducted in an orderly fashion for whatever items of value have been previously overlooked."

The soldiers were called in and split into two sections, one under the Captain's orders and the rest with the sergeant, a precaution against any personal pocketing. They began with the ground floor and then went upstairs. Anne followed the Captain and his men to the Long Gallery, wanting to be on hand if Ridley should be landed in any sort of trouble through his plastering, for the responsibility was hers as head of the house in Robert's absence and she would shoulder it.

As she reached the open doors of the gallery, she thought how in one aspect the Civil War in both its earlier stages, and again in this third, was particularly hard on her, for all along she had been able to view the conflict from both sides. Her parents were members of the Separatist movements, a religious group that had broken away from the established Church and followed Puritan principles. In the reign of James, one of her uncles, a keen Separatist, had sailed for the New World in a ship called the *Mayflower*. Her mother had always been believed to be barren and the birth of a daughter late in life had brought enormous joy to both her gentle parents. With never a cross word heard in their exceptionally peaceful home, Anne knew she had grown up over-protected in many ways from everyday buffetings.

It had left her with a need for a peaceful existence that was as necessary to her as food and water and was matched by her ability to love those dear to her with a depth and warmth that overflowed to anyone in distress. Robert had come into her life by way of a chance meeting on a market day when he had saved her from a fall as she tripped on a cobble-stone. Upon marriage she had passed from the shelter of loving parental care to another created by a devoted husband.

Although her loyalties were entirely with the Royalists and had been from the start, even as she had become a member of the Church of England through love of Robert and her wish to be with him in every-thing, she had grieved as deeply for the Roundhead blood that was shed as for the Cavalier, her compassion going out to all the bereaved families; it was something that Robert understood but which she had never dared mention to his mother, who would have taken up a sword herself to fight for the King if it had been possible.

But where was the sense in a struggle that from the first clash of arms had had monarchists on both sides? Not all Parliamentarians were against having a king, just as not all held with the more fanatical Puritan attitude in religious matters, there being men of all faiths under both the Com-monwealth and Royalist banners. The greatest tragedy of all was that men who loved England dearly, wanting only the best for their motherland, had killed one another in large numbers over the ways of achieving it and had now gathered again to continue that dreadful purpose.

She entered the Long Gallery to discover what was happening and stayed just within the doorway. Nobody paid her any attention. The soldiers had begun to examine anything there that might be of value, opening drawers in side-tables and the doors of two large cupboards that stood at each end of the Gallery, rifling the contents within; one was tossing out a set of ninepins, which spun about the floor around him.

In less dangerous circumstances she would have smiled to see that Ridley had adopted the old trick of the country-born, which was to hide their own quick wits to get the better of a townsman. It was obvious to her that he thought he had found the perfect target. He had paused in his plastering to gape open-mouthed at the soldiers and then blinked as if the Captain had appeared out of the blue at his side.

"What are you doing?" Captain Harding demanded.

"Plastering, sir," Ridley replied, letting his surprised eyes wander again to the soldiers spread out in their search.

"I can see that. What are you covering up?"

"Cracks, sir. See 'em along the part of the wall I ain't done yet? It's a big job and I does a bit whenever I 'ave the time from other work." Ridley cocked his head and lowered his voice confidentially. "Everything is going to rack and ruin with women in charge. It'll be a good thing when you gentlemen have routed the King once and for all and things can get back to normal."

Captain Harding regarded him with lordly indulgence. "So you are with us, are you?"

"From the start, sir." Ridley then shrugged his shoulders and spoke in a whining tone. "But I 'ave to earn a living and I'm too old and lame from a ladder-fall to fight."

"You should not be under a Royalist roof. Why not seek work on the Warrender estate?"

"I 'ave, sir, but the bailiff there 'as a rough tongue and didn't think me able enough."

"Well, at least you tried." It struck the Captain that this handyman had been received no more courteously than he himself. "Now give me your trowel."

From where she stood Anne thought how cleverly Ridley had fooled the officer, but now, as the trowel was handed over, she held her breath and knew that Ridley was as tense as she. The Roundhead dug the point of the trowel into the wet plaster and scraped it away here and there to make sure no secret door was being concealed beneath. When the inspection narrowly missed the King's plaque and the trowel was returned to Ridley, she felt nauseous with relief and had to withdraw from the Long Gallery to lean against a wall, waiting for the spasm to pass.

A thumping sound somewhere in the house was echoed closer at hand as the soldiers went through the routine of banging their fists against the panelling in the Long Gallery, listening for a hollow ring that would tell them there was a cavity where valuables might be hidden away. She put a hand to her head, a throbbing in her temples seeming to keep tempo with the banging. This was the method the Roundheads had used when searching for the treasure of Chichester Cathedral. Eventually it had been located behind a panel in the bell tower and the priceless medieval gold and silver crucifixes, chalices, candlesticks, and alms dishes had been seized and melted down.

The Long Gallery had become quiet, and Anne realised that the Roundheads had left by another door. Supporting herself with a hand against the wall, she went back into the beautiful gallery. Ridley had sunk down into the nearest chair, his tools discarded, his hands hanging over the ends of the wooden arms.

"You did well," she said in a cracked voice.

He raised a haggard face, looking older than was normal to him. "It were a narrow shave, madam. If they'd found me out it would 'ave been a whipping for me and Sotherleigh would have been wrecked for the deceit we practised on them narrow-minded bigots."

"I'm most grateful for your loyalty."

He gave her a grin. "It was a pleasure to give 'em what amounts to a kick up the"—here he amended what he had been about to say—"in the backside."

The thumping had been resumed in the west wing and as Anne went downstairs it was also resounding from the east end of the house. She pressed her fingertips to her throbbing temples, longing for the sinister din to stop. There was no sign of anyone in the hall within the entrance, but she could hear by the subdued chattering that the maidservants were tidying up the Great Hall after the Roundheads' clumsy searching and were pushing the furniture back against the walls.

To reach what was known as the Queen's Parlour she had to pass through an oak archway that led to a passage only twenty feet long with a door on each side, one on her right leading into a cupboard and the other on her left giving access to the library. The door that lay ahead stood open and she could see Katherine and Julia seated side by side on the day-bed. To keep themselves occupied they had taken Julia's sampler out of the box where it had been kept with its silks and wools since first begun on her fifth birthday.

Anne recalled vividly how difficult that early tuition in embroidery had been. There had been tears and tantrums and constantly unpicked stitches until the top band appeared pock-marked. It was a long while before a result that was up to standard was achieved. Being told that to embroider well was a necessary accomplishment for any lady had left Julia unpersuaded. She still sighed with exaggerated heaviness whenever she sat down to her sampler at set times each week, long wistful looks at the window being ignored. Now she and Katherine were counting the num-

ber of different stitches she had already mastered in bands of varying
depth across the nine-inch-wide strip of linen which, when unrolled from
the ivory rods attached to each end, was three feet in length. By the time
it was finished Julia would have entered young womanhood.

Neither noticed Anne's quiet approach and she took in the sight of
them, thinking they looked like figures in a painting in the setting of the
lovely and yet simple room. South-facing, it was a favourite place with
the family, being neither too large nor too small, with panelling descrip-
tively known as linenfold and a large fireplace topped by a ceiling-high
overmantel where in winter logs blazed, and at this time of year fresh
flowers filled the hearth.

Most of the furniture had been new when the house was built in the
last years of Elizabeth's reign and was of heavy oak on bulbous legs. The
seats of the high-backed, carved chairs had been embroidered by Katherine during her betrothment in a vigorous, formalised pattern worked in
uninhibited colours and trimmed with a gold fringe. The cushions were
also of her handiwork, embroidered in silk in tent- and cross-stitch, some
in the Elizabethan tradition of pictorial story-telling by means of trees,
flowers, windmills, castle, and house with a solitary figure on the brow of
a hill and a cheery, nimbused sun among fluffy clouds in a blue sky. These
glowed like gems on the day-bed and on the chairs standing against the
walls, the dyes unfaded by time. Seeing no evidence of the Roundheads'
search, Anne guessed the servants had tidied here first.

"There's satin stitch and stem, which makes the total ten so far." Julia's
forefinger was hopping from band to band on the sampler. "Here's tent
and feather and—" She broke off as a floorboard creaked under her
mother's approaching step and looked up. "Mama?"

"All is well in the Long Gallery," Anne said at once to Katherine.

Julia sprang up and ran to her excitedly. "Grandmother says I needn't
worry about Starlight and that he and the other horses are safe in the
woods with the stable-lad, and the groom has gone to them."

Anne tapped a finger warningly against the child's lips. "That's a secret
we must keep from the Roundheads."

"Oh, I know. But what of Sotherleigh? Are they taking anything
away?"

"I saw one soldier smash a Venetian crystal bowl for its silver rim, but
they'll have poor pickings this time."

"What of my apartment?" Katherine asked the question without expression as if she dare not let her suspense show. "Have they been there yet?"

Anne suddenly remembered that Katherine kept something valuable concealed there. It was so long since she had been shown it that she had completely forgotten about it. She was thankful that she had, for it had enabled her to answer the Captain without seeing it dancing in her mind.

"No, they're not there yet. Do you want me to be present when they are?" She dreaded a bidding to go there, for she was feeling weak and dizzy, not sure how much longer her legs would support her. All she wanted at the moment was to sit down and embroider some ribbon. The delicate work was her bastion against turmoil of all kinds. Even worry about Robert, which often destroyed her sleep at night, could be changed into quiet, loving thoughts and memories of happy times together as soon as she took up her needle and stitched away, whatever the hour.

"No," Katherine said stoically. "It's better that we all stay here together." Then she prompted her granddaughter. "Finish your counting."

Anne took her favourite seat, which was her wedding chair, the carved back incorporating Robert's initials and her own, together with the date of their marriage, the cushions on it embroidered by her own hand. By her chair was her crewel-covered needlework box, neither of which was ever moved away from the window, which gave such good light for her work. Fortunately Sotherleigh was blessed with an abundance of glass that allowed sunshine to flood every room and nowhere was gloomy. The panes held the faint greenish tinge of all glass made at the time the house was built, but none of the windows were marred by thickened circles, known as bulls' eyes, which formed during manufacture. Normally these were relegated to less important windows, such as the kitchens, but there had been such pride in the construction of Sotherleigh that nothing blighted its beauty anywhere.

"That's done!" Julia had completed her counting in as many seconds and she began rolling up her sampler, anxious to get it out of the way in case she should be told to take a needle and thread to it.

"My! That was quick," Anne commented vaguely, one hand on the domed lid of her needlework box to raise it. She always thought of it as being Pandora's box in reverse, full of good things to flood over her instead of evil as in the myth, but today that comfort was to be denied her.

"No stitching now, Anne!" Katherine rapped out authoratively. "There's a book of mine over on the sidetable. Read to us."

Julia fetched the book for her mother and then took her seat again at her grandmother's side. Anne was beyond asserting herself at the present time. Standing up to her mother-in-law took a measure of willpower that had temporarily deserted her. Obediently she opened the book at the pages divided by an embroidered bookmark, which had a Biblical picture in silk stitches of Ruth and her mother-in-law. Anne wondered whether, in spite of the good relationship shared by those two women, if there had been times, such as she herself was experiencing now, when Ruth had felt oppressed by filial duty.

She began to read. It was automatic, for she could scarcely take in the meaning of the words in her high-pitched state of nerves. The sun rays through the window behind her made an aura about her neat head and slanted her shadow in the diamond pattern of the panes across the Persian rug at her feet. Light and shade played on the carved ceiling. To outward appearances all was tranquil in the Queen's Parlour.

It had been so called for half a century to commemorate the day when Queen Elizabeth had sat talking to widowed Katherine on her one and only visit to Sotherleigh. Usually on tours of her realm she stayed many days at mansions of her choice, but Sotherleigh was too small to accommodate the large retinue of those of her household that travelled with her and their innumerable servants. Never fewer than three hundred carts carried royal and palace baggage, each with four horses in the shafts, and so with saddle mounts it meant that at least two and a half thousand horses had to be stabled, an impossibility in itself for Sotherleigh. So the Queen had come solely to enjoy a banquet under its roof and to view every corner of the house that had been built through her munificence to Katherine's husband. Elizabeth had been genuinely charmed by the house and expressed regret when it was time to leave. It was said she took a backwards look as she rode off in the direction of Parham House, which was no great distance away, to visit her goddaughter there.

When the heavy tramp of soldiers' feet passed across the floor of the room above, Anne looked distractedly at the ceiling. Julia also glanced upwards, but with a glower. Katherine did not flicker an eyelid.

"Keep reading, Anne," she instructed calmly.

Anne bent her head over the book again. She had finished two chapters when Captain Harding returned from a long and extensive search. Her nervousness returned at the sight of him and she rose to her feet, clutching the book to her as though it were a talisman against anything he might say that boded ill for those at Sotherleigh, quite apart from the property itself. Katherine's gaze, shot covertly at him under her lids, was more discerning. She was able to tell from his disagreeable expression that he had failed to uncover anything of special value, for which she breathed a silent sigh of relief. He was just a disappointed man with no vengeance on his mind.

"Have you finished here, Captain?" Anne inquired, her throat tight.

"Yes, Mrs. Pallister." He regretted the time he had wasted.

"Then do not let us delay your departure." She thought the clamps about her head might crush her brain if he did not go soon.

"Before I leave I'll relieve you of your pearl ear-bobs, which I see are set in gold."

Julia flushed angrily and would have shouted her outrage if her grandmother had not grabbed her wrist and frowned warningly. Katherine was exasperated anew by Anne's foolishness. Why had Anne not hidden the ear-bobs away? She herself had not noticed them under her daughter-in-law's curls, but the officer had better eyesight. Anne, who had put on her ear-bobs automatically that morning when she was almost too scared to know what she was doing, dropped her book onto the chair and fumbled at them, close to panic that the Captain might change his mind about her wedding ring. She thrust them into his out-stretched palm. "Here you are!"

His hand closed over them and he glanced again at Katherine to check she wore no jewellery except her marriage band. "I'll take my leave now, ladies. My sergeant is in the kitchen organising the gathering of enough food to sustain the men for the rest of the day. Then we'll trouble you no further. I bid you good day."

Anne's natural courtesy made her incline her head, but Katherine did not speak and Julia looked away in case he should single her out for a special word of farewell. As soon as he was gone from the room Anne turned to watch through the windows for the soldiers' departure; Katherine and Julia joined her. Three wagons, each with four horses in the shafts, were lined up by the steps, one loaded from previous hauls. In single file the Roundheads left the house. The sergeant carried a canvas sack that appeared to be only half full with the spoils from Sotherleigh, while the men bore white laundered flour bags crammed with food, which were either slung over a shoulder or carried between two of them. Everything was loaded onto the wagons and the troopers stood ready to march away. Captain Harding was the last to emerge from the house. He remounted his waiting horse and rode ahead out of the courtyard into the tree-shaded drive. As the last of the Roundheads disappeared from view beyond the elms Anne moved away from the window as if to return to her chair. Then she paused and swayed as she put the back of her hand to her brow. Before Katherine could reach her she tipped forward onto the floor as if pole-axed, engulfed by the deep faint that had been threatening to return ever since her first swoon from tension in the early morning.

Julia uttered a shriek of alarm. Katherine, taking charge, gave her a thrust in the direction of the marriage chair. "Fetch that cushion for your mother's head—she must have bumped it hard as she fell." When the cushion had been placed in position, Katherine gave the child another directive. "Run upstairs to the Long Gallery and tell Ridley to come down here and lift your mother onto the day-bed."

"Yes, Grandmother!" Julia was already making for the door.

"Wait! Before you come down again go along to my bedchamber and bring down the flask of lavender water from the table beside my bed."

"I'll do that!" Julia ran from the room in a flurry of ribbons.

On her own Katherine lowered herself with difficulty down to the floor beside Anne, who lay with her arms tumbled and her knees slightly bent. Katherine's age-mottled hands adjusted the cushion. She was fond of her daughter-in-law, who had never resented her widowed presence in the house, had nursed her tirelessly when she was sick, and had shown her more kindness than could ever be counted. Moreover, Anne had never given her a cross answer and Katherine was well aware of having a sharp tongue. Massaging her daughter-in-law's wrists she shook her head, muttering to herself under her breath. "No backbone. The most amiable nature any woman could have, but no iron in the spine. My! If I had been as weak as this one in my early widowhood it would have been a dismal outlook for Robert and Sotherleigh. God grant that I survive until he comes home for good to cosset her again. Otherwise there's no telling what might befall her." Then she added the concern that was never far from her mind in her son and grandson's absence: "Or Sotherleigh either for that matter."

She looked up as Ridley came hurriedly into the room, Julia with him. He lifted Anne up without much difficulty, for she was light in weight, and placed her on the day-bed. He then turned to help Julia in getting Katherine off her knees.

When Anne continued to remain deep in unconsciousness, Katherine became extremely worried and sent for some acrid-smelling herbs from the herb-garden. She wafted the sprigs to and fro under her daughter-in-law's delicately shaped nostrils for some time before the closed lids began to flicker. Both she and Julia sighed with relief.

"Have they gone?" Anne's grey eyes opened wide. She had forgotten momentarily that she had seen the Roundheads depart.

Julia flung an embracing arm about her mother. "Yes, they have! Grandmother says they'll not be back and soon Starlight and the other horses can come home from the sanctuary of the woods."

Katherine put the herbs aside. "We can be thankful that everything went as well as it did."

"Due in no small part to my little daughter's brave and honest answers." Anne, still propped against cushions, smiled at Julia and raised a maternal hand to touch the child's curls. "I will dress your hair if you will fetch a brush and comb."

"Not yet," Katherine stated firmly. "You must be still for a while." Then she patted Julia on the shoulder. "I think you should leave your mother now. Why not go up to your bedchamber and see if anything has been taken."

Julia kissed Anne and then ran from the room, suddenly fearful for her little doll's house, a country mansion with four rooms and a hallway, which came next to her pony as her dearest possession. Christopher had made it for her during one of his sojourns at Sotherleigh and it was designed to be the home of a tiny wax doll in a blue taffeta gown.

Reaching her bedchamber she burst into it and then halted with dismay. The mattress of her bed had been hauled up, throwing the bedclothes to the floor, shoes from her closet had been strewn about, and the contents of her drawers tipped out. Her trinket box had been upturned and the doll's house, which always stood next to it, was nowhere to be seen.

Then she saw that it had been swept to the floor from the top of the clothes press, together with her hairbrush and comb and other small things that had been lying there. She rushed to it and dropped to her knees, relieved it had not been taken, for it seemed impossible to her that others should not value it for its craftmanship as she did. At the same time she was full of distress at the damage it had suffered. The chimneys had been knocked off, the glazing of two of the windows was smashed, and the whole frontage, which opened like a door to reveal the panelled rooms within, was hanging on its hinges.

She held it gently as if its wounds could be felt and set it back on top of the clothes press. Not expecting to find the tiny inhabitant in one piece, she dived carefully into the tumbled furniture and picked out the four-poster. To her joy the little doll securely tucked into the bedclothes had escaped all harm.

"At least you're safe, Susan Wren." She had named the doll after Christopher's older sister. The choice of the lady's maiden name had been deliberate. It had seemed to her that any doll who lived in such a charming house should have some link with its builder and so the surname of Wren had been appropriate. Twitching the doll's taffeta skirt into place as she did every morning, for it always retired at her bedtime and normally rose when she did, she placed it carefully on a shelf. Then she began to assess the damage to the Wren house and hoped it would not be long before Christopher and Michael took a vacation from their studies at Oxford to come again to Sotherleigh. Christopher was the only one who could repair it as it should be done. She did not feel confident about putting it into Ridley's hands. Much later in the day she discovered that a gold brooch, which had been given to her at her christening, had been looted from her trinket box along with the silver buckles from her shoes.

Anne and Katherine took account of all that had been done to Sotherleigh. They also had lost shoe buckles and a trimming of semi-precious stones had been torn from one of Anne's ballgowns, leaving it ruined. She regretted the loss, for the gown had evoked memories of happier times that she hoped would soon come again.

Silver handles, knobs and inlays overlooked by previous looters had been taken, but the few remaining pieces of good porcelain had been left as before, for such wares smashed all too easily on bumpy army wagons. The most valuable jewellery owned by the two women, including their betrothal rings, had been concealed in a silk purse pinned to Katherine's petticoats and these items were returned to jewel-boxes again. Katherine was annoyed that Julia's brooch had not been included in the purse. Privately she blamed her daughter-in-law for the oversight, for no one of her great age could be expected to think of everything, but for once she refrained from voicing her displeasure to spare Anne from further distress. Much of Katherine's own jewellery, as well as her daughter-in-law's, had been given long since in vain support of the late King's cause, but she had kept back a few heirloom pieces that would be for Michael's bride, who-ever she might be, and for Julia one day. To make up for not contributing these items, she had sent money constantly and drained her resources considerably.

The Roundheads had torn down some fine tapestries, which lay tumbled and trampled on the floor. Two paintings had suffered the same fate, but a collection of valuable books, although tossed from shelves in the search for hiding places, remained intact. That lessened the importance of smashed doors and drawers, which had either been locked or proved slow to open to impatient hands. On the whole Sotherleigh had escaped relatively lightly.

That night when Katherine went to bed she felt exhausted. She needed her maid's help more than usual to get into bed. When she was left alone on her pillows with a single candle flame burning, her thoughts went to the child sound asleep on the other side of the bedchamber wall. The time had come for her to entrust a treasured keepsake into those hands that were younger and more able than hers. Her own failing health and the upsurge of the war again decreed it. All she had to do was to wait for the right moment.

# THREE

*A* FEW DAYS LATER the horses came home. Julia was waiting for them with some pieces of sugar from a block that the cook had broken up especially for her. The old coach horses seemed particularly glad to be back, putting on an unusual burst of speed to reach their stalls and the feed that awaited them there. Starlight snorted and tossed his head while she clapped his neck and welcomed him. She rode him for the rest of the morning and it added to her pleasure that her mother instead of a groom accompanied her on horseback.

On her own she was allowed to ride only short distances within the park. She missed her rides with her father, but she and her mother had happy times together. Always they had gone on their own for wildflower gathering when Anne wanted some new blooms for her embroidery motifs. They took with them a small, locally made trug, which was a flat-bottomed wooden basket peculiar to Sussex. When lined with damp moss it was the perfect receptacle in which to lay the garnered blooms. Anne would never take more than she needed for her embroidery, except in springtime when the woods were so full of bluebells that it was impossible to put a foot down without treading on them, or in summer when the Downs were as golden with cowslips as if a king's mantle had been flung over the slopes. Then they would return with armfuls and fill vases all over the house.

Anne liked to ride, not only for the exercise but to be among the beautiful trees of Sussex with which the county abounded and to look upon its vistas from its softly curving hills. It also gave her a sense of freedom that revitalised her. For although lip service was paid to her as mistress of the house, it was impossible not to feel Katherine's unchanging possessiveness towards Sotherleigh or to ignore her domination of it through the sheer power of her personality. Away from the house in its tranquil environs, Anne felt she became her own person, her true self rising to the surface, and she was light-hearted and carefree as she never was indoors in her husband's absence.

Within a week the good weather broke in a storm, and heavy rain became a daily occurrence. Julia, bored and querulous at being house-bound, missed her riding more than anything and made dashes through the rain whenever possible to commiserate with Starlight in his stall. He did at least get a gallop in the paddock, but whenever the weather eased it was usually when she was at her lessons or during mealtimes, as if the rain-clouds were carrying on some special vendetta against her.

Unable to tolerate it any longer, she decided one morning to make a special request at dinner, which by established custom in their circles was always eaten at two o'clock. In the absence of the men of the house, the two Pallister ladies and the child did not eat in the Great Hall but in a chamber leading off it. Although the room appeared to be of moderate size, it was possible to make it the same length as the Great Hall by sliding a false wall back into the panelling, thus supplying a supper room when entertaining on a grand scale. Since Robert's departure the larger section of the room had been permanently shut off to lessen housework for the diminished household staff and only opened again by a maidservant de-tailed to that purpose during the various Roundhead raids in case it should be detected and damaged in the belief that something of value was hidden beyond it. In any case, none of the maidservants liked to clean the windowless section of the long room, always nervous of being shut in.

They were unaware of a secret door leading out of it, for that was known only to the adults of the family. Ned and Katherine had seen too much of the intrigues at court, apart from the rise and fall of various religious persecutions, not to make some provision for an emergency at Sotherleigh. It had been Robert's way into the house on several occasions when he needed to make sure no Roundhead trap had been set for him.

Julia particularly enjoyed her dinner before she came to the moment of making her request. It was the best time of year for vegetables from the kitchen garden and there was venison pie with a feather-light crust, new potatoes, peas and beans picked only an hour before, crisp salad, and a strawberry syllabub to follow.

"I think the weather is clearing up," she announced optimistically, spooning up the last of her syllabub, "so may I go riding this afternoon, Mama?"

Anne happened to be seated where she could see the raindrops running down the window panes. She never liked to refuse Julia anything, but she had her own rules on how to be a good mother and it included preventing her child from catching a chill.

"I'm afraid that is out of the question. It's still raining and the sky does not look any brighter to me. We must wait and see what tomorrow brings forth. I'm just as eager as you that we should go riding again."

Julia opened her mouth to argue, caught her grandmother's warning eye, and closed it again. There was no chance of getting her way when Katherine gave backing to her mother. After the meal she went upstairs to her room for half an hour during which she fed Susan Wren with wax food on a tiny pewter plate and set her bigger dolls, three of wood and one also of wax, on the bed beside her rag-doll, changing their hats and switching their clothes. Then she saw that the rain had diminished to a drizzle and left the dolls to hasten downstairs to the Queen's Parlour.

Anne was in her customary place by the window embroidering minuscule poppies on a cream silk ribbon. She looked up as the door opened and Julia entered, bright as a flame in her gown of tawny taffeta, her chestnut hair almost fox red in the curious greenish light of the dismal afternoon. Smilingly, Anne put a finger to her lips, nodding to where Katherine sat deep in an afternoon doze.

Julia went swiftly to lean on her mother's lap, her expression eager. "May I go riding now?" she asked in a whisper as if there had been no break in the conversation at table.

"This drizzle would soak you and Starlight in minutes," Anne whispered back. "At the first fine morning we'll go off for a ride together."

"I could wear my thickest cloak and hood."

Anne shook her head in gentle rebuke at such persistence and mouthed her final refusal. *No.* With a huge sigh, Julia turned to the window and began to drum the fingers of both hands against the panes. Seagulls, driven inland by some stormy turbulence at sea, were wheeling like wind-blown petals against the bruised sky. She longed to be out there with them, to be one with the elements and to gallop her pony far across the park.

"Rain, rain, go away and come again another day," she chanted in a low and monotonous tone, mischief in her rising on the hope that if she was exasperating enough she would get her way. Out of the corner of her eye she could see that her mother was beginning to be wearied by it and she pretended not to hear the whispers for her to hush.

Suddenly Katherine's voice shot across the room at her. "That's enough!"

She jumped and yet was impishly glad at having created this diversion. Nothing was ever dull when her grandmother was about, no matter that she was probably going to receive a sharp slap. She spun about and faced Katherine down the length of the Persian carpet. "I woke you, Grandmother."

"Indeed you did." There were many reasons why Katherine loved her granddaughter, and the child's straightforwardness in never trying to evade responsibility for her own actions was one of them. She beckoned with a bony finger. "Come here to me."

As the child approached Katherine noted how confidently she came, even though punishment was expected. Knots of embroidered ribbons danced around her hems, emphasising the lively step. Not for the first time Katherine thought how much better it would be if Anne dressed the child a little less elaborately. It was more usual for children to wear simplified versions of adult clothes, but in a larger size this gown could have been worn by any lady to Court. The reason probably lay in Anne's own childhood of simple garments devoid of all ornament and in sombre colours, for by her own account she had neither worn nor owned any fripperies until her marriage to Robert. For an artistic and sensitive person it must have been a deprivation to have had no outlet in the wearing of lovely hues.

Julia had come to a standstill by a footstool. "Yes, Grandmother?"

"You were making a nuisance of yourself to your dear mama."

"I know I was."

"Nobody likes rainy days and you're old enough to behave."

Anne spoke up from her chair, wanting to prevent the punishment she could never have inflicted herself. "Julia has missed her riding for three days now because of the rain."

"That's no excuse."

Julia prodded a finger into her own chest. "*I* haven't made any excuses."

Katherine frowned. "No pertness is called for." Then she relented and reached out to draw the child into the circle of her arm. "Maybe I can think of something far more entertaining for you than your pony ride, which you take often enough. It happens that I have a treasure upstairs that I've been waiting to show you since you were born."

"A treasure!" Julia was agog, her eyes stretched wide. "Has Michael seen it?" Always she tried to keep abreast with her brother's achievements at her age. He had always been able to out-run and out-ride her, but she was resolved that one day he should be the one left behind.

"No, Michael has never seen the treasure I've been saving for you."

"For me! Oh, Grandmother!" Julia jumped up and down, clapping her hands with excitement.

Again Anne spoke up. "Surely, madam," she protested mildly, "Julia is too young as yet to appreciate either the keepsake's history or its value."

"I disagree. She is doing well at her lessons and this is the chance I've long awaited to teach her all that she should know of Sotherleigh."

Katherine did not intend to be swayed now.

Anne contemplated carefully before she gave a nod. "In this case I agree with you." She always used this phrase when giving in on some matter to her mother-in-law. By a play of consideration before concession, she attempted to emphasise her position as mistress of the house.

"That's good." Katherine set both hands on the arms of her chair and levered herself up to take her cane, which Julia handed her before turning on a skip of anticipation to take her free hand. Anne, watching them go from the room, noted as she had done many times before the similarity in the proud way they both held their heads. Then there was the colour of the hair. When Anne had come as a bride to Sotherleigh Katherine's hair had still shown traces of a wild chestnut colour. A portrait of her in the Long Gallery proved that once it had been as luxuriant and rich in hue as Julia's seemed destined to be.

In the hall the child matched her pace to her grandmother's as they crossed the marble floor to the Grand Staircase. On the first landing Katherine called a halt in front of the portrait of Queen Elizabeth.

"Tell me what you know about this royal lady."

Julia realised immediately that this was to be some kind of test for her. She tilted her head back to gaze up at the chalk-white face with the high intelligent forehead and the long, pointed nose, the thinly plucked brows and those clear, direct eyes. The frizzed red hair was topped by a demi-crown of diamonds and four drop-pearls, more pearls studding the full sleeves and the bodice of the russet satin gown with its huge standing ruff that made a frame within a frame for those arresting features.

"She gave Grandfather Ned the gold to build Sotherleigh and the land on which it stands."

"Go on."

Julia thought carefully, wanting to be sure of getting her facts right from her history lessons. "Our new King, Charles II, is the grandson of James, the Scottish king who came to the throne after her."

"That's right. What else?"

"When England was threatened by invasion by the Spanish Armada, she made a great speech to her soldiers to show them she would be with them in spirit. She said that although she had the body of a weak woman she had the heart of a king of England."

"Correct. That is how you must be, Julia. Keep a stout heart at all times and nothing will ever prevail against you."

"The Queen must have been a kind lady. Was Sotherleigh given to Grandfather Ned at Yuletide or on a natal day?" These were the only times she received presents herself.

Katherine smiled to herself somewhat wryly. Elizabeth had liked to be generous to good-looking men at all times, having an eye for a handsome face, however much she kept them at arm's length, jealously guarding her royal power. Ned, the fourth son of a noble but impecunious family with his own way to make in life, had been extremely personable, with the dashing air of a privateer, which in some ways he was, for he had plundered ruthlessly many foreign ships to bring home the spoils to lay at the royal feet. Katherine, raw with love, had seen that he was enthralled by Elizabeth, although she was old then in a red wig, her face painted white and her lips scarlet over bad teeth. Yet still she had enchanted him. He had spoken of her with a glow in his eyes and something close to awe in his voice. Katherine recalled how difficult it had been for her to share even a small part of his heart with another woman, in spite of knowing that his devotion to the Queen was no threat to his love for her. There had been many times during her years at Court when she had witnessed the effect of Elizabeth's intense personal charm on her nobles and ordinary people alike. It was no wonder that many men had fallen in love with that strong and vibrant woman.

Then she had seen that same charm dawning in this firework of a granddaughter almost before the first toddling steps were taken. It lurked in the eyes, the smile and the tilt of the head, exactly as she had seen it before. When it became obvious that Anne was innocently set on spoiling the child, Katherine was determined that such a mistake should not be made or else the gift of charm could be used to the wrong ends, greed and selfishness prevailing. Having been well tutored herself, she had done everything in her power from that time forward to mould the child's character into reason and good sense, to instill a desire for learning and a respect for heritage in all its forms, a pattern set by Elizabeth. On a gentler aspect there had been plenty of help from Anne, who in herself set an example to her daughter of consideration for other people and their feelings, something Katherine knew was not one of her own strong points.

"Sotherleigh was neither a Christmas nor a natal gift," she said in answer to the child's question, "but a reward for loyal services courageously rendered from the days of the Spanish Armada when your grandfather fought in an armed merchantman attached to Vice Admiral Sir Francis Drake's command."

"Would it have been very bad if the Armada hadn't been defeated?"

"Oh, yes. England would have been governed by the Spaniards and they would have brought their terrible Inquisition with them."

Julia shivered. She did not know what it meant, but it sounded frightening. Katherine's thoughts were still with her husband. "The Queen's real gratitude stemmed from later years when Ned was commanding his own ship, sailing, trading and exploring in the Far East. The Portuguese were already established in those parts, but he saw that there were great opportunities for the English to form settlements and trade in many countries from India to the little-known lands beyond. It was due to his persuasion and his arousing of the Queen's interest that she was moved to give support to her subjects endeavouring to increase England's wealth and power in those far distant places."

"Did you like serving the Queen, Grandmother?"

"Oh, yes. She could be stern and quickly angry, but she was just and had a wonderful sense of humour. I was her ward and became one of her ladies when I was fifteen. It was at Court that I met your grandfather."

That had been at the Palace of Whitehall during an evening of music and dancing, the Queen leading the measures. Katherine recalled the impact across the room of Ned's blue eyes and a clear-cut face tanned dark by sea air and hair bleached to a pale gold. She had felt her heart and her bones melt. When he had come to partner her she had trembled like an aspen leaf as he took her hand. In the bussing of the lips, which always ended that particular dance, his kiss had been bolder than was customary, but it had been the heralding of their union.

"Did you leave Court when you married?"

Katherine shook her head. "No, I continued to serve the Queen after Ned and I were wed, because it would have been very lonely for me when he was on long voyages of two years or more. He received the Royal Grant towards the end of the old century and I recall how we came down from London to view the acres of land known as Southerly meadows. On the documents the scribe had spelt it more imaginatively, so we kept it to Sotherleigh in future. The master builder met us on site to discuss the plans drawn up to our specifications." As she talked she could see the day clearly in her mind's eye. It was high summer and there was nothing but flower meadows and waving grass and larks singing. "The master builder became difficult and stubborn when I said I wanted the house to face south."

"Why was that?"

"He thought it should look northwards to the nearby Downs, which gave the better view, but even more important in his opinion was the danger of infection drifting across the Channel from the Continent. Most people building within range of the Sussex coast at that time would have thought the same as he. I pointed out that evil vapours could enter even if the house had its back to the sea, but he insisted that the danger was less. He expected Ned to over-ride me and follow his advice, but he had put the wrong argument to a sea-captain. Your grandfather declared that salt air was always pure and only good could come from facing the sea, no matter that it was some miles distant. Sotherleigh was to be exactly how I wanted it."

She had never loved Ned more than at that moment. He had turned to her with dancing eyes and she had flung her arms about his neck, laughing in her triumph at the victory he had handed her, careless of the defeated master-builder looking on. After the man had ridden away, they had gone still farther from their coach waiting in the narrow lane that was to become the drive. Together they had lain to make love in the warm grass under the flutter of butterflies, stripping each other half-naked and kissing all that was uncovered. He had smothered her ecstatic cry with his mouth or else the sound would have carried in the sweet air like notes from a flute to the lane where their coach waited.

A month later the clearing of the site for Sotherleigh was done and the digging of the foundations begun, but after this initial flurry of activity there were various delays. Mostly these hold-ups were due to the winter weather and the master-builder's refusal to deal with anyone but Ned, who was away at sea.

"Master Pallister must decide," he would say every time she wanted to settle a matter, his hatred of her thinly disguised. She was certain he was neglecting the building of Sotherleigh through taking on work he considered more urgent. The walls had scarcely begun to rise when Ned came home the following autumn. Progress had been made by the time he left again, but the house was still no more than a shell when his ship was wrecked in a storm at sea, going down with all hands. She had been left a broken-hearted widow and pregnant with Robert.

Although Ned had bequeathed her all his wealth, it was generally expected that she would sell Sotherleigh as it stood, for there were many would-be buyers, but it was a link with him that she would not let go. She gained permission from the Queen to absent herself from Court and with her newly born son she moved into a small house in the village. From there, leaving a nursemaid in charge, she sallied forth every morning to the site and fought many verbal battles with the master-builder, who had thought to pass off shoddy workmanship now that Ned was gone. She caught him out in trickery and various deceits, realised he had been swindling all along, and to his fury dismissed him and his workforce together.

As the men left, their carts and wagons trundling off down the lane in the wake of their irate master, she had entered the doorless entrance hall and shouted aloud to the house, throwing out her arms as if to embrace it. "Nothing is over! This is just the beginning."

She hired in London a youngish man named Henry Colchester, who was a master-builder calling himself by the new term of architect. He employed good craftsmen, had the position of the rafters changed, saw that walls were taken down and rebuilt, and returned panelling and frames and anything else ordered by his predecessor that did not come up to his standards. Had she been less frozen by grief she could have taken him as a lover, or even as a husband, for he was soon in love with her, but she wanted no man other than the one she had lost. Sotherleigh was all she craved as a balm in her bereavement. She watched its graceful chimneys rise to touch the sky, and its windows were so tall and fine that when they caught the sun they made Sotherleigh appear to be a house of dazzling glass.

When it was finished the Queen was her first visitor. There was talk between them of her returning to her duties as lady-in-waiting at Court, but at that time she was reluctant to be parted from her young son, who she felt should remain in the country for his health's sake. The option was left open, but was never to be taken up, for in March the following year of 1603 she was suddenly sent for and rode in an escorted coach to the Palace of Richmond where the Queen was dying.

It was hoped that Katherine could persuade Elizabeth to take to her bed, for with the courage that Henry VIII's daughter had always shown she was attempting to meet death on her feet. Without a wig, wisps of white hair hanging from her pate and her face devoid of paint, she still presented a majestic figure. Katherine had curtsied and spoken to her. Elizabeth had shown recognition, a corner of her mouth twitching as if in a smile that her loyal lady of Sotherleigh had come back to be with her to the end. Yet she would not move from where she stood. None dared touch her, not even her doctors, and she was beyond food and drink, closing her eyes in refusal when once Katherine would have put a crystal goblet to her lips. As the hours went by some of the ladies fainted from exhaustion, for none could sit while the Queen stood, and Katherine was thankful for the stamina that enabled her to keep vigil during the last hours of a woman who had always been gracious and kind to her. Finally the Queen had collapsed, slipping down to the floor without a sound. At last she could be lifted onto the bed and Katherine herself had bathed the white brow with a clout soaked in cool rose-water.

"Thank you again for Sotherleigh, madam," she had whispered for the Queen's ears alone. Whether the whisper was heard there was no telling, for she was thrust aside by Lord Cecil, who was fearful the Queen would die without naming her successor. But all had gone well. She had accepted the name of James of Scotland and her death was peaceful.

London had never seen such public grief as when the Queen was carried to her last resting place in Westminster Abbey. Katherine had stayed in London until that day and had watched from one of the windows lining the funeral route. Then she returned to Sotherleigh and had never since spent a night anywhere but under its roof.

There had been plenty of social life in Chichester and the surrounding countryside and at that time Katherine was never short of proposals from men, honourable and otherwise; it had been obvious to her since first losing Ned that men considered widows to be fair game. With the passing of time she might have considered marrying again if it had not been the case that upon marriage any woman, whether spinster or widow, forfeited everything she owned to her husband. She did not intend to lose control of Sotherleigh, especially as Robert, having been born after Ned's death, had not been mentioned as the eventual heir in his father's will.

The one man she had loved just as much as her dear Ned was married already and had children. He was Sir Harry Warrender of Warrender Hall, father of the objectionable colonel who had slighted her grand-daughter in Chichester. She recalled how strongly she had been attracted to Harry with his mature good looks and flashing dark eyes. They had begun to meet secretly, possessed by passion and love, but when she realised that whispers about them might soon increase to outright scandal, she became alarmed. Nothing must taint the future of her son and his good Pallister name. After much painful heart-searching she had forced herself to end the affair. She had seen Harry age overnight as if some kind of physical sickness had afflicted him. But it had been a malaise of the spirit, for he had continued to live an active life to the age of ninety, riding to hounds every week in season until his heart failed him. His longevity had been galling to his ill-tempered son, who had been long waiting to step into his father's shoes as Master of Warrender Hall. It had been Harry's misfortune that his heir had proved to be a throwback to some distant ancestor, for in temperament, John Warrender was totally unlike either of his parents.

After that period of violent attraction to Harry, Katherine had fol-lowed the example of the late Queen by continuing to endure a lonely bed. As a result she understood Elizabeth better than anyone else. They had both suffered sexual deprivation by their own choice: the Queen to maintain her mighty rule free of male domination and she herself to retain control of her own heart and property. Yet in her son she had a blessing that had been denied the Queen.

Although Sotherleigh was Robert's now and Anne its mistress, Kather-ine secretly felt herself to be still as much the head of it as she had always been in the past. Why else had Sotherleigh not been sequestrated by Parliament when the majority of the neighbouring Royalist estates had suffered the fate of confiscation?

She believed the exemption to be the late Harry Warrender's bequest to her, an intercession by him with powerful Parliamentary friends to ensure that she should end her days in the house she loved and that her family would continue to live there after her. She and Harry, by reason of their opposing loyalties, had never met face to face once the war had begun, but when fortune had turned against the Royalists at the Battle of Naseby, he must have been convinced then that Parliament would prevail and one of his last acts on this earth had been for her welfare. Most surely he would have known that she would guess what he had done for her, and that her gratitude would be boundless. She had never disclosed this supposition to Robert or anyone else, fearing explanations would have to be given and the past was a closed book.

Julia tugged at Katherine's sleeve. "Is there anything else you wanted to ask me about the Queen's portrait, Grandmother?"

Katherine collected her thoughts again. One of the weaknesses of old age was in letting one's mind run away at a tangent. She smiled down at her granddaughter. "No, you did well. We'll go up to my apartment now."

As she moved to take the next section of the stairs, Julia went to her side, one small foot in a white shoe put down on successive treads at the same moment as black silk ones, stretched over painful bunions, until they reached the first floor. They had to pass the screen before turning into the west wing and at their slow pace Julia had time to play her game of identifying some of the carved flowers, giving them the country names her mother had taught her.

"There's Shepherd's Purse and Heart's Ease. Up there is Lady's Smock, Jack-by-the-Hedge and Cat's Ear." She chatted on about every one of the plants, giving the reason through shape, colour or location for being so called. Did her grandmother know that pretty little Self-Heal had been known for its curative powers since time began? Together they paused to look up to where it was entwined with some Black Medick. "That's yellow in bloom and black in seed. By it is a spray of Traveller's Joy. That would lift anyone's spirits on a wearisome journey."

"I'm sure it would," Katherine agreed and, not having minded the short rest, went plodding on again. It had been her idea to have such a screen, preserving in wood that special day that she and Ned had shared among the flowers of Sotherleigh. He had secured the royal wood-carvers for the task, for they were the best in all Europe. He had seen a section of the screen finished, and been highly pleased with it, before the sea took him from her.

When they drew near the door of the apartment, Julia sprang ahead to open it into the parlour through which she had run on the morning the Roundheads came. It was here that her grandmother was content to be alone sometimes. A comfortable domain, its walls were lined with book-fold panelling, which had the appearance of the backs of volumes, and her marriage chair, its legs far more bulbous than those on Anne's chair downstairs, stood by the hearth, its velvet cushions in tulip colours. As Katherine entered the room in her granddaughter's wake, she glanced as was her habit at the portrait of Ned above the fireplace. It showed him in the short ruff and padded doublet of the era, the drapery behind him drawn back to reveal the largest and most renowned of the ships he had commanded, painted against a background of a palm-fringed coastline, a tribute to his part in the founding of the East India Company. She had made and embroidered the ruff he was wearing, tracing the design in black on white in double running stitches with speckling like minuscule stars. The so-called black work gave the snowy ruffles the look of being overlaid with delicate lace.

Julia skipped across to one of the windows to look down at the Knot Garden, which had always fascinated her. It lay stretched out like a very large carpet, the pattern made up with blossoms and fragrant herbs and shrubs. There were rosemary, lavender and thyme, hyssop and gillyflowers, sweet-williams and germander, violets and primroses, and many more according to season, everything kept low or close clipped to add to the multi-hued petit-point effect, delighting the eye from a raised view and the nose at close quarters. Every fancifully shaped bed was clearly defined, some in the love-knots that had given this type of garden its name, some in swirling arabesques, stars and crescents and concentric circles, the intervening spaces filled with different-coloured earths. The sanded paths, along which she loved to walk, were part of the design and were bordered with large, round white pebbles, an edging that had been an innovation at the time this Knot Garden had been laid out. Beyond it, set at the end of a lawn, was the maze, which was made up with high box-hedges and stood dark and green in the misty rain.

When very young, Julia had hoped to discover the secret of how to get out of the maze by standing on a chair in front of this very window. By being higher she had imagined she would see it laid out as clearly as the Knot Garden below. To her chagrin she had discovered she could see no more than from the floor. In clambering down from the chair she had toppled it, cracking her head against the sill as she fell. There had been panic in the household when she had been discovered lying unconscious, but she had recovered with no ill effects.

"Did you ever lose yourself in the maze when it was new, Grandmother?" she asked. She had ventured into it alone one day and lost her way, but she had managed to keep tears at bay, Michael's words always with her. It was dusk before her shouts were heard and by then servants with lanterns were combing the park and her mother was quite frantic. She had blinked in the lantern light, white-faced but determinedly dry-eyed when the head gardener had brought her out. Her mother had embraced her and wept with relief. Her grandmother had merely given her a long, steady look that was meant to be stern, but which had something more kindly in its depths.

Katherine came across to stand looking out at the maze with her. "No, I never did. Ned with his clever mind worked out the plan, although he never saw it planted. I studied the diagrams until I had memorised the lay-out and knew the secret of escape."

Julia twisted round to look up at her. "When will you share the secret with me? Mama doesn't know it and told me that she doesn't want to know either, because she hates to be in closed-up places and she has never been in the maze. The head gardener wouldn't tell me, saying it wasn't his secret to tell."

Katherine smiled, cupping the child's chin in her hand. "That is right. He took over from his father before him and nobody else has ever trimmed the hedges within the maze."

"But why?"

"Because a maze would be no fun if everyone could walk in and out of it at will."

"But you told the secret to Michael. Why not to me?"

"He is older than you and is to be master of this house one day. You'll learn it in good time." Katherine smiled again. "Now come with me and see what I have to show you."

She drew the child with her into her bedchamber. Julia liked this room. Whenever there was a storm or she had a nightmare, she would run from her own bedchamber near by and tuck in beside her grandmother in the cosy warmth of the four-poster caparisoned in embroidered silk. There was plenty of room in the bed, but it was narrow compared with the huge four-poster that her parents shared whenever her father was home. Her mother slept badly without him. That was why she and her grand-mother had an understanding that her mother's rest was never to be disturbed unnecessarily.

To Julia's surprise Katherine went to an ancient black chest set against a wall. As far as she knew nothing was kept there except clean linen for her grandmother's bed and the alternative hangings for its canopy, which were changed for the seasons of summer and winter. She had seen a similar chest in Chichester Cathedral and another in the local village church, dating back to what she thought of as "castle times" when knights rode off to the Crusades. She knew the ecclesiastical robes had been kept in these chests in holy places before the Roundheads had made bonfires of the rich garments.

"Open the chest for me, child," Katherine said, sitting down on a nearby chair.

Julia went across to it. She knew it was never locked, for the maids went to it constantly during bed-making, and she set the balls of her hands against the lid. It lifted easily on its much-used hinges. The sheets and pillowcases lay within as usual, tidied again since the looters' hands had rummaged through.

Katherine spoke again. "Take all the contents out and put them neatly on the floor."

Julia obeyed until there was nothing left; the chest was empty. "Have you made a mistake, Grandmother?" she asked tentatively. "Perhaps you put the treasure somewhere else."

Katherine smiled and rose to her feet. She came to rest a hand on the rim of the chest as she leaned forward and hooked a fingertip into an indentation in the ancient wood. The whole middle section of the chest's apparent base swung upwards on concealed hinges to reveal something covered over with fine lawn.

"If I had kept this chest locked," she said, lifting away one layer of lawn to reveal another underneath, "the Roundheads would have been suspicious immediately and without doubt would have smashed the chest to find out what was hidden in it. This is how it has escaped discovery every time."

Julia was peering eagerly into the chest. What was going to be there? Perhaps she was about to see Spanish doubloons and other gold coins captured by Grandfather Ned on the high seas. Or would it be ornate silver plate? Then abruptly Katherine whisked away the last layer of lawn like a magician in the market place.

Julia gasped. It was as if suddenly the chest was filled with light. Creamy satin like pale sunshine glowed out of the darkness of the ancient chest with multi-hued areas of embroidery and the gleam of pearls. It was a gown out of a fairy tale.

"Did it belong to a princess?" she asked in awed tones.

"Better than that! To a queen who let me choose from her wardrobe a gown for my wedding day."

"Queen Elizabeth?"

"Yes, it was hers and then mine. One day it will be yours." Katherine reached into the chest and took hold of one end of the gown. "Help me lift it out and we'll take it over to the bed. Your hands are still clean, aren't they?"

"Yes." Julia wiped them down her skirt to make sure and then leaned over the edge of the chest to gather the satin folds into her arms. Together they carried the precious burden over to the bed and laid it down carefully.

There Katherine straightened it, so that it lay directly across the bed, the bodice and sleeves spread out, the skirt cascading down over the side where she and her granddaughter stood. Still it glowed, none of its magic diminished in the child's eyes, although it was in a fashion of long ago. The neckline was square and hung with beautiful drop-pearls that shimmered as if fashioned from moonlight. The bodice with its stomacher, which ended in a long point below the waistline, was covered with scrolling flower embroideries worked in silk in marvellous colours and glittering gold and silver thread. The sleeves, which puffed high above the shoulders and narrowed to the wrists, were similarly embroidered, the cuffs of needlepoint lace. The gleaming skirt had isolated slip flowers like small nosegays cast in lovely profusion all over it with tiny round pearls shining like dew-drops on the petals. The hem was encrusted with gold braid to the depth of four inches, which must have given a graceful weight to it when worn.

"What do you think?" Katherine asked with satisfaction, able to see the child's reaction by the rapt expression on the young face.

Julia's deep blue eyes, shining like sapphires on the thrill of the moment, looked up at her. "It must be the most beautiful gown in the world!"

"That is my opinion."

"Did my mama wear it on her wedding day?"

"No. I offered it, but it was too out of style. In any case the gown of her choice was already in the making." Katherine gestured in the direction of the ancient chest. "You'll find more adornment for this royal garment in there."

Eagerly Julia returned to the chest and unearthed a box. It was large and unwieldy, but not particularly heavy. "May I open it?" she asked excitedly.

"Yes, child."

Julia removed the lid. Within were layers of lawn and in the midst of them a stiffened ruff edged with the same exquisite needlepoint lace as the cuffs on the gown, light and delicate as if woven out of spiders' webs. She set it carefully on the bed. Then she dived into the box again and brought out a thin, silk-covered bolster suspended by ribbons to a waistband. "What is it?"

"A farthingale. It gives fullness to the top of the skirt. Give it to me and I'll show you how it was worn."

Katherine put on the waistband, tying its ribbons at the front and the farthingale itself encircled her hips. "Under the gown it would have given a circular shape to the skirt, which had been the mode at that time." Julia eyed it doubtfully.

"Surely it made ladies look fat?"

"Not if they had small waists like the Queen's and mine. The stomacher was stiffly boned as were bodices, as you can see for yourself from the gown on the bed, and these circular skirts were extremely pretty. You should have seen the scene when we were dancing, all these wheel-shapes in every colour made the whole floor seem to rotate."

"Didn't those farthingales make skirts sway about?" Julia's modesty had come to the fore. As with adult women, the stockings of little girls were gartered just below the knee and no female wore anything else under her petticoats. "I wouldn't have wanted to wear a gown that swung up and down like a bell."

"Our petticoats were well weighted down."

Katherine, removing the farthingale again, thought how close the child had come to the truth. Some of the dances popular at the Elizabethan Court had been very vigorous. The Queen herself had been very fond of a lively dance called the Volta, during which a man would take his partner by the waist and lift her up and around him before setting her on her feet again. Ned had always danced the Volta in the manner expected of any gentleman, and if Katherine had been the Queen herself he could not have been more careful to see that her hems swayed very little. Yet if a man should be careless or seeking to entertain lascivious male friends among the spectators, the lift would be designed to give them a flash of the woman's bare thighs and buttocks. That sight would have given the present-day Puritan Parliament something on which to pin their aim to abolish all dancing from the land. As it was, the Volta and other dances like it had gone out of fashion long since, and it was beyond her to comprehend how anyone could see sin in people's enjoyment of music and the putting of innocent dancing measures to it.

Julia had gone again to the chest and returned with a pair of gold satin slippers with gilded heels and white rosettes. "These were the last things in the chest."

"My wedding slippers," Katherine said nostalgically. She moved away from the side of the bed to sit down in the chair again and rest them on her lap.

Julia thought it sad that her grandmother's feet had become too swollen to wear the dainty footwear. "Did the Queen give you those too?"

Katherine shook her head. "My sister gave them to me. They had not been worn, although she had had them made for herself. There would have been no time for me to get a new pair."

"Why not?"

"Because Ned and I brought our wedding day forward. We were to have remained betrothed for a year, but we were desperate to become husband and wife before he sailed again and when a voyage became imminent the Queen gave her permission for us to wed." Katherine paused. "You see, she knew what it meant to love someone very much. Once she had to sign the death warrant of a man who meant much to her when he was found guilty of treason."

Julia fingered the creamy satin thoughtfully. "What made you choose this particular gown for your wedding day. Was it just for its beauty?"

"Not quite. Neither did I choose it for its value, which now lies in those perfect drop-pearls." Katherine smiled as Julia reached out a hand and touched each of them reverently. Little did the child know that one of them, taken temporarily from the gown at the time of her birth, had been placed in her clasp when she was less than an hour old. "They were not on the gown originally, but after I had made my selection the Queen gave me a set of them with the exception of four, which she kept for herself; she had two pairs of ear-bobs made from them. She loved pearls and always wore them in her demi-crowns and in ropes about her neck and on her gowns, because pearls symbolise virginity. She knew what these particular drop-pearls would mean to me. You see, Ned had brought them home from one of his voyages and as Elizabeth had invested money in his expeditions a portion of all treasure was rightly due to her."

"What was your reason for choosing this gown then, Grandmother?"

"The Queen had worn it on only one occasion. It had been a happy one for her and I thought that a good portent for my choice. Otherwise it would have been a difficult decision to make, because she owned many beautiful gowns."

"How many?" Julia asked with a child's pedantic interest in detail.

"Well, I can't say what number it was at that time, because I was not Mistress of the Robes, but when she died she left many hundreds of gowns in her closets and chests."

Julia's mouth dropped open. "All those!"

"They were in every kind of glorious fabric. Brocades and velvets, silks and satins and taffetas. Some were so stiff with gold and silver thread and jewels they could have stood alone. One was draped with rust-red silk embroidered with eyes and ears, showing that she saw and heard everything that happened in her realm."

"Where are the rest of the gowns now?"

"You may well ask!" Katherine exclaimed, thumping her fist on the arm of her chair as her outrage over the fate of those garments came to the fore as fiercely as if there had been no span of years between. "When King James came to the throne from Scotland he was married to Anne of Denmark. She was a frivolous, empty-headed woman with no thought in her head except to lead a merry time with masques and theatricals and such-like festivities. And what did she do?" Katherine threw up her hands in furious exasperation. "She engaged a fellow, whose talent I don't deny, named Inigo Jones, who excelled in designing fine costumes for such pastimes, and she had all of Elizabeth's gowns cut up to supply the rich fabrics and trimmings that he needed to costume that decadent Court!"

It distressed Julia to see her grandmother in such a state. She rushed forward and flung arms about her. "I'll guard the gown always! Nobody shall ever cut this one up! And I'll wear it on my wedding day!"

Katherine was moved by the child's fervent promise. There were even tears in Julia's eyes. Putting the slippers on the floor, she drew her granddaughter down onto a little stool beside her, putting an arm round her shoulder and clasping one small hand in hers. "May it be as you say, my little one. May it bring you the bridal joy it brought me, and may your happiness never be cut short, but last the whole of your life through."

Julia's head was pulled close to her grandmother's side and she closed her eyes contentedly as a hand stroked her hair gently. She relaxed blissfully, feeling full of love for her grandmother; for her father and mother; for Michael and Christopher far away in Oxford; for her pony and the horses and the new kittens in the stable. And for Sotherleigh. As for the Queen's gown, one couldn't love a garment, but she had the strangest feeling that it had already become an integral part of her life.

Katherine stroked a wayward curl back from her granddaughter's forehead. How different the child's reaction had been to that of the mother. It was unfair to compare Anne Pallister with Anne of Denmark, for their characters were entirely different, and yet their attitude had been much the same. She recalled how proudly she had shown Sotherleigh's new bride the treasure from the chest, although whenever she had looked at it after Ned's death it had brought back distressingly poignant memories. Robert's marriage had signified a new beginning, for she was eager for grandchildren and saw in the lovely, sweet-faced young woman he had chosen a whole new era of happiness for Sotherleigh. In those days she had been active and vigorous still, and she had lifted up the gown triumphantly to hold it against herself for her daughter-in-law to see.

Anne had shown mild surprise and then polite interest. Being a needle-woman she had murmured admiration in a close scrutiny of the fine stitches, but the spell of the gown had not touched her. She had not sensed its historical importance as the one surviving gown of a great queen; its link with a past age of courage and triumph when England had staked a claim to share the mastery of the seas and oceans of the world. There had been nothing in her of Julia's acclaim, no brilliant sparkle of the eyes, no commitment to its preservation.

Looking across at the gown, Katherine wondered again if she could have done anything to stop the destruction of all the rest of the royal wardrobe if she had stayed on at Court after Elizabeth's demise and become lady-in-waiting to James's queen. It was a question she had asked herself many times, although she had had no foresight of what was to happen and had left London before the new King had arrived, his queen following still later. In any case it was virtually certain her voice of protest would have made no difference.

Katherine looked down fondly at her granddaughter. The time had come to end regrets about what had happened in the past. The future of the last remaining gown was ensured. Although Sotherleigh would be Michael's when the time came, Julia would have a special keepsake to hold in trust for those who came after her.

And Julia, content at her grandmother's side, knew that for some reason she might never understand, her strange and lovely dream had become one with the gown. She would never be mystified by the dream again. Why then did she feel that this was only the beginning? Was it that her wish to share her dream with Christopher meant that it had yet to be fulfilled?

# FOUR

*J*ULIA, COME HERE! Such a surprise!" Anne's voice reached her daughter in the library. "Michael has come from Bletchingdon. Christopher is with him."

Julia flung down her pen, heedless of the ink-blots splashing across her set-work. Why were they here? The plan had been that they should go straight back to Oxford from Christopher's home and Michael had not been expected to return until Christmas. Excited, she ran from the library and by the time she reached the porch outside, Anne was being greeted by both young men at the foot of the steps, a groom leading their horses away. Suddenly Julia was overcome with shyness at seeing Christopher again, not knowing why, and she hung back unnoticed in the shadows of the porch. It was two years since she had told him about her dream and he had visited again last summer, but she had never felt self-conscious before in his presence and it was all she could do not to run back into the house again.

"How I wish Robert were here to see you both," Anne was saying to the two young men, clasping her slim hands together and releasing them again expressively. "But he has gone to join the King! He took nine men with him, all re-armed and looking brave. They made a proud sight." Her voice faltered.

Michael nodded seriously. "We know, Mother. I've seen him, but I'll tell you about that later." Then the expression on his still boyish face lightened again. "Meanwhile it's good to be home again. That doesn't mean Christopher and I haven't been marvellously well looked after during our stay with Dr. and Mrs. Holder. While we were there we had cause for celebration. Christopher is now a Bachelor of Arts. He achieved this distinction in two years while I and the rest of my fellow undergraduates have another two of the four-year course to complete."

Anne exclaimed with pleasure. "How splendid, Christopher! My felicitations on such a wonderful achievement."

Christopher looked acutely embarrassed. "A fluke, madam. It was no more than that."

Michael laughed. "Don't listen to him. He's already working for more examinations to make him a Master of Arts and the devil of it is that he could do it on his head and be asleep at the same time."

Grinning, Christopher made a mock swipe at Michael's chin. "Enough, my friend! Or else—"

Anne, much amused, held up her hands. "Stop it, both of you! Let us have a little order now. Did you achieve all the study you had hoped for in your time at Bletchingdon?"

"We did indeed," Christopher replied. "Susan and my brother-in-law both sent their compliments to you."

"I thank you. And what of your father? Is his enforced retirement from the Church of England still causing him much sorrow?" She was full of sympathy for the elderly churchman, Dean Wren, who had held the high ecclesiastical position of Dean of Windsor, which also entailed being Keeper of the Royal Treasure House, until the Roundheads had ransacked his home, plundered the Crown jewels, and turned him and his young son out to take refuge where they could. When Dean Wren, a clever and artistic man, had taken up another living at a little church, he had been banished once and for all for making a beautiful altar piece that the Parliamentarians had denounced as Papist. All this had had a disruptive effect on Christopher's early years, but the stability of school under a brilliant headmaster had done much to settle him into the steady young man that he was.

"My father will ever miss his ecclesiastical duties," Christopher replied, "but my sister takes good care of him and he spends his days reading and writing."

Anne nodded compassionately. "I sent him a letter a little while ago. Do you know if he received it?"

"No, I'm certain he hadn't or else he would have given me a reply to deliver to you."

"It should reach him soon." Anne had never met Dean Wren, but they had kept up a correspondence ever since her son and his had become staunch friends, being the same age, during their first term at Westminster

School. She was a strong advocate for the mild and salubrious air of Sussex for anyone in poor health and it was the reason why Christopher had spent a deal of his school vacations at Sotherleigh. She made a little bustling movement with her hands. "Come now. We have plenty of time to talk later. I'm sure you must be hungry after your journey. Let us go into the house without further delay."

"Allow me, Mother." Michael smilingly offered his arm and Christopher did the same. Happily she put a hand into the elbow of each as they strolled towards the flight of stone steps.

"I am sure," she said, glancing assessingly up at her tall son, "that you've grown a full three inches since you were last at home."

"I'm not the only one who has grown," Michael replied with amusement, having spotted Julia standing to one side in the porch. "Who is this young maiden that I see?"

Julia giggled at his teasing. He was always the same. She sprang forward to leap down the steps and greet him exuberantly. To her enormous delight Christopher bowed with a flourish and kissed her hand for the first time as if since last seeing her she had become as grown-up as Michael had declared her to be. She curtsied as she had been taught.

"Shall you be here a nice long time, Christopher?" she asked him hopefully.

"I can stay a little longer than your brother, who is only here on a flying visit." He glanced at Michael. "Is that not so, friend?"

Anne's pupils dilated momentarily as if in shock at this information and she looked questioningly from Michael to Christopher and then back again. "Do you really have to make it a short sojourn?"

"It has to be." Michael tried to ease the disappointment for her. "But all being well, I should be home again before long."

She summoned up a smile. "That's something to look forward to." Then she appeared to recover her original joyousness at their arrival. "We shall make the most of the time you're here."

Julia moved to Michael's side as they went up the steps. "How is Father?" she asked eagerly. "Where did you see him?"

It seemed to her that he hesitated slightly before replying. "I'm going to give Mother all the details first, but I will say he looked fit and well."

"Did he send his love to me?"

"Of course he did. He also sent you this." He dived into the pocket of his jacket and brought out a necklace of small blue beads such as pedlars sold, obviously purchased by Robert at some wayside. She exclaimed with pleasure and dangled the gift in front of her as she ran ahead to show Katherine what she had received.

"I've something for you, too," Michael said to his mother as he drew a letter out of his pocket for her. "It comes with Father's fondest felicitations."

Anne's eyes were misty as she took it from him. "You couldn't have brought me anything more welcome."

As soon as they were indoors Anne went to see about extra dishes for dinner before retreating to read her letter privately and the two young men went to greet Katherine. She was sitting in a high-backed chair in the Queen's Parlour with Julia perched on the footstool, preening in the new necklace. Christopher let Michael converse with his grandmother first after they had both kissed her hand.

"I trust you are in good health, Grandmother," Michael said with his cheery smile.

"I'm perfectly well, I thank you." Katherine was aware of being cantankerous at times, but she prided herself on never moaning about her aches and pains. "Your home-coming is most welcome, but very unexpected."

He shrugged easily. "I decided that a visit of twenty-four hours at home would be most agreeable."

Under her wrinkled lids she observed him closely, reading behind the relaxed air and the smile the serious purpose of his coming home. Her heart contracted on the pain of it. She felt sure he was about to enlist and was here to say farewell before he went to join the King. She loved him no less than Julia, this hard-working, good-humoured and determined lad with so much of his father in him. He had never lacked courage and would serve the King well. If he had a vulnerable streak in his nature it was that of sentiment that he had inherited from his mother, his heart coming before his head at times, particularly when faced with someone's tale of woe. As a boy he once had given away his brand-new jacket to a beggar child and on another occasion he opened the cellar door to a horde of thieving gypsies, who had pleaded hunger, and they had stripped it bare of its winter stores.

"You did well to come home," she said in a tone softer than was normal to her. Then she gestured to Christopher to come forward while Julia sprang up from the footstool to chatter to her brother as they went together from the room. Katherine nodded approvingly. "It is good that you came too, Christopher. I can see that Oxford continues to suit you."

"It does indeed, madam." He was in his element there and had dedicated himself to keep opening new doors into knowledge and above all to make the world a better place for it. He had a deeply religious faith and although the reading of the liturgy was forbidden by Parliament, he listened to it at a private meeting place of Anglican worshippers every Sunday and was devout in his prayers.

"Perhaps you could stay a little longer than Michael," Katherine suggested hopefully. She had a strong affection for this thin, short, bright-eyed young man, whose lack of physical strength had been compensated for in his remarkably brilliant brain. There could be no military service for him.

"I thought by two or three days. I have a deal of work awaiting my return to Oxford."

"More inventions?"

"Yes, in addition to my research and studies."

She reached a hand to him and when he took it she drew him closer to her chair, looking up earnestly into his face. "I think my daughter-in-law would appreciate having your company for as long as possible since Michael is set on a speedy departure for reasons of his own."

He saw by her whole expression that she had guessed her grandson's intention and that Anne would be in need of comfort when Michael left. He did not hesitate in his reply. If his presence would help Anne Pallister in any way it was the least he could do for this family that had shown him such warm hospitality over the years. "In that case, I'll be glad to extend my sojourn to a week."

"Good. I know Julia will be particularly pleased as well. During the Roundhead raid we suffered recently her doll's house was damaged and she will trust only you to mend it."

"That shall be done."

Dinner was a merry meal. It was traditional that all troubles should be set aside when sitting down to meat and in the Great Hall that day the custom was fully upheld. Christopher was particularly partial to a dish, virtually unique to Sussex, which in poorer homes was served first to help fill the belly and enable the spit-roasted joint of the day to go further, but in homes like Sotherleigh it was served as an accompaniment to meat. Known as "drip pudding," the suet and flour mixture was first boiled in a cloth in the shape of a roll and then thick slices of it were placed in a pan beneath the spit that collected the drippings. There it fried, rich and golden, soft in the middle and crisp on the outside. Christopher's immense enjoyment of it in boyhood had soon taken its place with the family jokes, and so on these days a dish of this Sussex specialty was always brought in with ceremony and placed in front of him. There was laughter and applause as he bowed his head to all at the table and then plunged his three-pronged fork into the nearest slice.

After dinner Katherine went to take her customary doze while Michael drew his mother outside for a stroll. They made their way to the Knot Garden, chatting about things generally until they came to a seat. There they sat down, turning to face each other.

"Where is Christopher?" she asked, remembering their guest and straining her neck to look for him.

"He and Julia were going to fetch some items from Ridley's workshop."

"Oh, yes." She settled again. "I heard her ask him if he would mend her doll's house. Quite a few things were damaged in the Parliamentary raid."

"I want to hear about that. When we came through the village someone called out that troopers had been here, but had failed to find the horses they sought. I haven't asked any questions before now, because I didn't want to spoil the happiness and merriment of our unexpected visit and also because I wanted to hear a quiet and steady account from you without others interrupting."

She smiled slightly and then gave him a brief description of all that had happened, but almost as if it were of little interest at that moment. "That's over and done with, but now you've something important to tell me, haven't you?" she said discerningly, the suspense she had been enduring revealed at last in the quiver in her voice. "I think I can guess what it is."

He did not take his eyes from hers. "Father met me as he had arranged on his way north. There was a nasty moment when two soldiers asked to see his travelling permit, because everywhere they're on the lookout to stop anyone they suspect of being on the way to join the King. Fortunately the papers showed Father to be just a good parent checking on his son's studies."

She gave a nod. "He has forged papers for every stage of the journey. Go on."

"We ate together in a tavern and talked for quite a while. Then he had to leave. I wanted to ride with him then to the royal standard. I've been practising my swordsmanship daily ever since I heard our new monarch was on Scottish soil, but Father insisted that I come home to see you for twenty-four hours before I rode to enlist."

Her head dropped like a rose on a broken stem and she covered her face with her hands. "I knew it from the moment Christopher said that this was to be a short visit."

"Don't weep, Mother," he implored. "The King needs every sword and mine must be among them or I should feel I had failed in my duty to him and to my country."

She raised her head again. There were no tears on her cheeks, but her eyes were bright as jewels with those unshed for the anguish within her. "Surely there has never been a war as pointless as this one or as cruel!" she burst out. "Political and religious differences have split families apart, setting brother against brother and even father against son. It is only by lucky chance that you and Robert are on the same side, because there are hundreds of wives and mothers less fortunate than I in that respect."

She broke down at that point and he put an arm about her. "Listen to me, please," he said. "I'm not denying that the late King made grave errors during his reign and that there was cause for grievances, but now tyranny has taken over and the rest of the civilised world has drawn back in horror at the regicide committed on the scaffold at Whitehall. Only the sick should stand back at this time."

She knew he was thinking of Christopher, whose lungs were unable to take any undue exertion. Once at school and again during the early part of a sojourn at Sotherleigh he had seen his friend gasping for breath and had been in terror of his dying. Anne dried her eyes with her lace-trimmed handkerchief and blew her pretty nose. Then she looked up at him again, knowing that her eyelids must be swollen and red-rimmed.

"I can't go back into the house as yet looking as I do. It would cause distress to Julia and your grandmother, whom I believe to be less well than she would have us suppose."

"Shall we take a turn down to the fountain?" he suggested. They rose from the seat and she took his arm as they went up the steps out of the Knot Garden. "It's always shady and cool there."

She was grateful to have a little extra time on her own with him, understanding Robert's insistence that he should come home to see her before going into battle. The young believed themselves to be inviolate to death, but Robert had seen too much of war not to know that the youngest and the bravest were often the first to fall before enemy fire. There had been no mention of such a possibility in his letter, no word about the war at all, only loving words about what she meant to him as his wife. Yet the very air was charged with the unspoken knowledge between her and her son that these few hours he was to spend at home constituted a special farewell. All she could do was to hope and pray that he and his father would both be spared.

Two hundred yards away from the Knot Garden, Christopher sat at a garden table in the shade of an oak tree, the doll's house in front of him amid a selection of paints, clay, tools, small pieces of wood and a giant pot of glue. Julia's elbows were resting on the table, her chin in her hands, as she sat watching him shape some tiny slates to replace those missing from the back of the roof.

"There's nothing here that I can't fix," he told her reassuringly.

She heaved a satisfied sigh. "I was sure that was what you'd say. Can I help?"

"You can scrape the old glue off the bottom of those chimneys that were knocked off."

For a few moments she worked at her task in silence. "One day I'd like you to build me a real house to live in," she said suddenly.

He shot her a smiling glance. "You told me once that you were never going to leave Sotherleigh."

"I was younger then and didn't understand it could never be mine. My father will leave it to Michael and it will be his son's after him."

By the exaggerated carelessness of her tone he guessed it had been a painful lesson for her to learn. "Just because I drew up the plans for this little house before I constructed it doesn't mean that I'm making a master-builder of myself at Oxford. Far from it! If that were all I wanted I would have apprenticed myself to one of the new architects when I was still in London. Mathematics are, and always will be, my particular field."

She wrinkled her nose incredulously. "How could you ever like *sums?*"

He chuckled, slotting the first of the little tiles into place. "It's far more than that. Do your arithmetic well and maybe one day a wider outlook will open up to you as it did to me."

"Impossible!" she declared adamantly. Yet she made a mental note to try harder with her reckoning, which she did not find difficult if she applied her mind to it. She had no aim to reach his exalted state, which in any case was denied to her since she was not a boy, but she respected his advice as she did Michael's.

With a small hammer and some tiny tacks he fastened each of the tiles securely. He enjoyed any task that needed care, even something as simple as the one in hand. "If you've finished the chimneys you can start cleaning the glazing that I removed."

She did not immediately move to take up the little windows that were laid out on the table. "If you are not going to be able to build me a house," she said earnestly, returning to the earlier thread of their conversation, "will you promise to design me one?"

He was amused by the fervour of her request. "What makes you think that my plans for it would be better than anyone else's?"

"It's not just because of the doll's house being so splendid." She was gazing intently at him. "You see, I *know* you."

It was impossible for her to express the inner feelings that she had, for her vocabulary, extensive though it was for her age, did not extend to a full range of aesthetic terms. She knew only that there was goodness in him as there was in her mother, a purity of spirit that nothing could taint. Therefore, it stood to reason in her view that anything he designed or made or created would reflect that quality in him and be beautiful, just as her mother's embroidered ribbons were often so lovely it seemed as if the flowers themselves had come from the gardens and meadows to blossom there.

"I'm not quite sure," he acknowledged with a smile, "but I think you have paid me much honour. If ever you wish it I'll design a house for you."

"Let's seal our agreement in the way of Sussex country folk."

"Very well." He spat lightly on his palm and she did likewise. Then they slapped their palms vigorously against each other's. He did not laugh, for he saw she was treating the ritual seriously.

She returned her elbows to the table and her chin to her hands. "I've made up my mind where I shall live. It won't be too far from Sotherleigh, but not too close either. I don't suppose Michael would want me walking in every day and that is what I'd do if I were too near."

"You're showing wisdom beyond your years," he remarked dryly. "But you are making a decision about the location of your future abode much too soon. Your husband might have entirely different ideas from yours about where to live and you'll have to follow his guidance."

"That's one of the reasons why I'm not going to marry. I don't want to be told what to do all my life. In any case I don't see anything special in being a wife. Grandmother was left a widow years ago and my parents have been separated by war yet again. I think I'll have a place of my own as soon as Michael marries. Perhaps after all I will be in London. Somewhere near Whitehall where from my windows I'll be able to see the King ride by. Because he'll be at the Palace by then."

Such loyal convictions from a child touched him. None could be more Royalist than he, although he deplored war and the futility of it. Nevertheless it was a bitter pill that he was neither fit nor able to serve the King, for his sickly childhood had prevented him from being trained in more than the rudiments of sword-play. Totally academic, he had always combined relaxation with reading and thus never missed the pastimes more common to youth of hunting, shooting, and engagement in mock duels in readiness for the defence of honour or for war.

"I'm sure it would please His Majesty greatly to know of your faith in his ultimate victory," he said quietly.

She appreciated his comment and then continued in a matter-of-fact tone as if some important business had been well concluded between them. "That's settled about London, then."

"I suggest we don't anchor your abode yet. Let London be a possibility."

"I thought you liked the city."

"I do. It's exciting and stimulating and the busiest place in Europe."

She flung her arms wide. "Then that will suit me too."

In the morning everybody in the house gathered on the steps to see Michael ride away. There was food in his saddlebags and gold from Katherine in his purse. He bade farewell to his mother last of all. Anne was brave, shedding no tears and waving him off with a smile, but when he had gone and she turned back into the house the smile seemed stuck on her face, for she went on smiling for the rest of the day.

Christopher did much to appease the gloom that would otherwise have settled on the house. He took Anne and Julia fishing with him in a nearby river and another day the three of them climbed to the top of one of the Downs, he carrying the picnic. From there they could see the Channel lying in the distance like a strip of blue glass and Chichester nestling within its Roman walls, the Cathedral at its heart clearly visible. Julia made daisy chains for both her mother and Christopher and entwined another like a garland about her head. Not wanting Katherine to feel left out, Christopher hired a hackney coach to take them all into Chichester, it being too risky to use the Sotherleigh coach-horses, and they dined at the Dolphin by the market cross. Katherine was able to go into neighbouring shops without too much walking and there were many purchases to be piled into the hired coach when the time came to go home again.

Anne gave a party for Christopher, inviting local Royalist families, and among them a pretty girl whom he had met on a previous visit. He gained a few kisses from her before the evening was over.

The days of his sojourn ran out. When he left Sotherleigh he was as well provisioned as Michael had been, and he received the same family send-off from the steps of the house.

"Come back soon!" Julia entreated, having run down the flight to stand by his horse and look up at him.

"At the first opportunity," he promised from the saddle, "but I can't say how long it will be. Work hard at your lessons, Julia."

Then he rode away down the drive, turning to give a last wave before the elms hid him from sight.

Julia went up to her room to take another look at the doll's house he had carried there that morning, having finished its repairs, including some furniture that had been damaged. She saw there was a square of folded paper on the tiny table at which Susan sat propped in a chair. She reached in and took it out to unfold it carefully. It was a minuscule plan of a house. She knew it was meant to be a forerunner of the plans he would draw up some day for the house she had asked him to design for her. He was not a man to forget a promise.

LIFE AT SOTHERLEIGH settled down again to its usual routine. No letters came from either Robert or Michael, but none were expected for a while, mail being unpredictable, particularly in troubled times. News of the King's advance into England did filter through, but rumour was rife and it was difficult to discover the facts. Locally it was known that Colonel Warrender had ridden off again under Parliament's standard to meet what was being called the Royalist insurrection by those against the King. Several Cavaliers in the vicinity of Chichester were too impoverished by the previous conflict and subsequent heavy penalties imposed upon them to be able to give Charles II any much-needed support. It was the condition of many Royalists throughout the country. Robert had had to sell some land twice during the war to meet his obligations and had sold another parcel of meadowland before he left. There was also a general resentment on both sides against the Scottish army with whom the King had marched into England, for by long tradition the Scots were the enemies of Englishmen, no matter that both countries had been united with Wales and Ireland under James. Oliver Cromwell, who had engineered the execution of Charles I, had been harassing the Scots on their home ground, but had now turned his large army about and was following the King as he advanced southwards. It was only a question of time before there would be a decisive battle between them.

Whenever any information reached Sotherleigh it was shared immediately, whether it was received in the kitchen or the parlour. Anne did not find it easy to give depressing news, but it became her duty one afternoon when all the domestic staff had gathered in the Great Hall for her to address them there.

She told them first that she had heard that many of those Scots marching with Charles were dropping out to return home, the numbers depleting every day. "What is more," she continued when the murmurs of consternation had died down, "it appears that not enough Royalists are coming forward to take their places, some because of circumstances beyond their control, as has happened in our own district, and some because their own foolish pride prevents them from fighting alongside those Scotsmen who are remaining staunchly with the King. There is also the fact to be faced that we have become a war-weary nation and the prospect of a fresh onslaught of many battles and the loss of countless lives has caused many to subdue their royal allegiance for the sake of peace at any price." Her voice took on a stronger note. "All of us here can be proud that our menfolk have not shirked their duty or ignored their consciences and are with His Majesty."

To Anne's surprise there came a little burst of applause from Joe, the kitchen scullion, who was, as usual, the only male present. The women servants then followed his example. Anne left them and returned to the Queen's Parlour, somewhat overcome by the effects of the speech she had made. It was only when she awoke in the night, always restless when Robert was away, that the disturbing thought came to her that she might have inspired the lad to enlist, which was the last thing she wanted. In the morning she went straight to the kitchen to reassure herself.

"Where's Joe?" she asked quickly, not seeing him there.

"Gone, madam!" the cook declared between annoyance and distress. "I thought he'd overslept and sent one of the girls to wake him. But he wasn't in his bed and it now appears that he hasn't been seen by anyone since yesterday evening."

"We must look for him!" She ran herself to the stables to send the groom after him. It was a risk to let the saddle horse go beyond the gates, but a boy's life might be at stake. The groom shook his head pessimistically.

"I'll go if you wish, madam," he said to her, "but I could comb the lanes and byways for a week and not find him. He's unlikely to take the London road in case he's levied into service by passing Roundheads and finds himself on the wrong side in this new war."

"Time is being wasted. Go!"

The groom was away all day. Anne waited anxiously. When he reported back to her that evening, telling of his lack of success, he was moved by the distress in her face to offer some reassurance.

"Don't worry, madam. Joe is a sensible lad with a good head on his shoulders. He'll take care of himself."

Her eyes went to the pinned sleeve where his left arm had been before the Battle of Naseby. "I pray to God that he comes back safely."

THREE MILES AWAY Joe was hiding in the stable loft of a Royalist house, Holly Manor. He was enjoying a good supper smuggled in to him by Henry, a stable-lad there and his friend from the days they were in a Chichester orphanage together. It had been Henry's good luck to get work looking after horses and his own misfortune to be landed in kitchen drudgery.

He had never liked Cook. She was permanently as red-faced as the fire in the hearth and always finding extra chores for him when he had thought his work done. No wonder he had slipped away to the stables at every opportunity, helping with the tasks there and learning to ride. His hope had been to be transferred there as he grew older, but Cook had him in her thrall and did not intend to let him go, wanting to teach him bread-making and so forth. The only way out had been to volunteer to accompany the Master of Sotherleigh to war when the call to arms came, for he thought that showing how well he could groom and care for horses on campaign would ensure stable-work when they returned home again. Then by ill luck he had contracted measles when Colonel Pallister, as the Master now was, had departed to join the King without him, putting an end to his hopes.

It had taken him a while to recover his strength. Then he had heard on the servants' grapevine that the eldest son of Henry's Royalist master was off to war too, taking volunteers with him. It was his second chance to meet up with his own master and prove his worth with the Pallister horses.

As he had known, Henry was willing enough to conspire with him. Intuition had told Joe that Mrs. Pallister would never allow him to go within range of warfare at his age, and so he had made plans to leave by night in order to escape any pursuit she might organise out of concern for him. Her little speech about duty and conscience had fired a rush of patriotic feeling in him, but mostly it had convinced him that he could be certain of her forgiveness when he returned. It was this prospect of pardon as much as anything else that had caused him to clap enthusiastically.

"What time do we leave in the morning, 'enry?" he asked, mopping up with a chunk of bread the last drops of gravy in his wooden bowl. His belly was comfortably full, something he had appreciated ever since his orphanage days.

"At dawn. You'd best be 'idden amongst the baggage in the cart until we meet up with another Cavalier and his party near Arundel. Then you can come out. Nobody with us will give you away and the two gentlemen will each think you belong to the other's party."

Joe stretched out lazily on the straw. "I'm ready for some shut-eye now after missing last night's sleep."

"I'll wake you in good time," Henry promised, taking away the empty bowl and a tankard drained of its ale. Joe was snoring before he reached the ladder leading down from the loft.

Everything went smoothly and according to plan. The eldest son from Holly Manor was a haughty fellow who would not have recognised any one of his father's servants out of their normal environs. Nobody questioned Joe's presence when he emerged into sight after the link-up with the other party was made. He enjoyed every minute of the long journey, proud of being given a pike to use in the event of a surprise attack being made by Roundheads out to prevent loyal men reaching the King. When danger was suspected the travelling was by night, but much of it was through the quiet countryside with only the birds and grazing cattle to observe their progress.

The euphoria that had held sway over him since leaving Holly Manor lasted to the gates of Worcester. It was a fair city dominated by a beautiful Cathedral and holding a good defensive position, but the news to be learnt there was all bad. The King's army was dispirited and exhausted by their long trek of twenty-three days and even with those who had joined them on the way their numbers were left at only sixteen thousand. Nobody knew how many Cromwell would set against them, but it was likely to be double that figure. Reinforcements for the King had been defeated at Wigan, and many cities had failed to give him the support he had expected. To add to his troubles, hundreds of Royalists, who would have been with them, had been betrayed by Parliamentary spies and some of the best and most experienced commanders and officers had been taken into custody.

Joe and Henry, riding on the baggage cart, gaped at the marchers who were relaxing now as they ambled about the streets and went in and out of the taverns. Most were in tattered uniforms and many were barefooted, having worn out whatever footwear they had started out with. In contrast, those coming from other destinations were well clad and there was an abundance of vivid-hued hat plumes and handsome coats and trimmings of silver and gold. Joe began to think about where he would find his master. As soon as he had helped Henry and the grooms stable the horses he set out on his search, asking here and there for Colonel Pallister. He tracked him down after about an hour to a small medieval house, which turned out to be the King's lodgings with two guards on duty by the door.

"I'm Colonel Pallister's servant," he explained.

They allowed him to enter and within the hall a gentleman asked him his business. "You can't see him yet," he was told. "The Colonel is with the King. You may wait by the wall."

He stood in the place indicated, his mood one of amazement, and looked about at the modest surroundings. Who would have expected to find a king staying here?

He did not have long to wait. A door opened and the King appeared, several gentlemen with him. Joe stared. He knew his monarch's features from the plaque that had been plastered over in the Long Gallery, but nothing had prepared him for the height and drama of this black-haired young man with the swarthy complexion, the twinkling dark eyes in a romantic setting of long lashes under brows as thick as a tom-cat's tail, and a thin moustache above the sensual mouth. No wonder he was known as the Black Boy, it being the custom to give such nicknames to those with remarkable hair colour, but Charles could just as easily have been the Yellow or the Red Boy had he not inherited a strain of Italian and French blood from his mother.

"That's settled then, gentlemen," Charles said in a deep, velvety voice as he paused, pulling on his gloves. He was wearing a buff-coloured coat, the sash crimson as were the plumes adorning his wide-brimmed black hat, and from his neck in sparkling jewels hung the insignia of the

Knights of the Garter, depicting Saint George slaying the dragon. "And may God be with us."

"Amen to that," was the general response from his company. Then the King strode out of the house, the rest following him, and the Colonel would have been gone with them if Joe had not stepped forward quickly.

"Sir! I've come from Sotherleigh to 'elp with the 'orses!"

Robert halted in astonishment, narrowing his eyes as he sought to recognise the upturned face of the lad standing before him.

"Your name, boy?"

"Joe Berry, sir. I'm the scullion and would have been the assistant cook if I hadn't come away."

Robert had not been in to the kitchen quarters of his home since childhood, but he knew this boy who was often to be seen hanging about the stables of Sotherleigh instead of being at his duties in the house. "I know you now. Give me Mrs. Pallister's letter then, Berry." He held out his hand for the expected correspondence. "And those you are doubtless carrying from Mistress Katherine and my daughter."

Joe gaped at him. "I don't 'ave no letters, sir."

An anxious expression contracted his master's face. "Are the ladies not well?" he demanded harshly.

"Oh, yes. In good 'ealth, sir. But you see nobody at Sotherleigh knew I was leaving."

Robert stared at him in furious disbelief. "You set off without having the wit to realise what it would have meant to your mistress and my mother to send a note to me, or me to receive it?"

"I didn't dare tell 'em, sir. They would 'ave stopped me from coming."

With difficulty Robert suppressed his rage and an urge to strike the lad for his thoughtlessness, but his sense of justice prevailed. It was true that Anne would never have allowed the boy to come to war. He heaved a heavy sigh. "You'll find my horses in the stables of the Red Fox tavern. If you know anything about grooming, now is your chance to prove it because Whitington, the groom you knew from Sotherleigh, became a turncoat two days ago. You can have his accommodation, which is in an attic room at the tavern. I'm busy now, but later you shall give me the latest news from Sotherleigh and tell me how you came here."

Joe's freckled face was one big grin from ear to ear as he went to tell Henry of his good fortune. Just as his appearing went unnoticed when he joined the travelling party, so did his leaving it again. At the tavern he met the servants he knew from Sotherleigh, all of them armed and wearing a regimental colour in their hats and as eager as their master had been for news from home. That evening, when he went to give an account of his journey to the Colonel, he found Michael Pallister there too, both gentlemen seated with their pipes at a table in the tavern, tankards in front of them. They heard him out, asked questions, and were amiable towards him.

"I should think all that talking has given you a thirst, Berry," Robert remarked when the interview was concluded, and put a coin into Joe's hand. Michael did the same. They watched the lad walk jauntily away to another tavern where the ale was of rougher quality and cheaper. Then they looked at each other in shared amusement.

"That artful little devil is aiming to be head groom at Sotherleigh," Michael commented with a chuckle.

"I could tell that too," Robert agreed with a grin. "Well, he showed initiative and that's to his credit."

When morning came father and son watched from the city wall as Cromwell arrived with thirty thousand troops and strong artillery. A brilliant military strategist, he proceeded to virtually encircle the city, his intention obvious. The King was to be caught in a net.

Preparation for battle began. Charles was cool-headed and determined, less experienced than his enemy, but not lacking in ability as a leader and soldier. At his orders four bridges leading into the city were put out of use and regiments under the command of Robert and three others were set to guard the fields west of the city at the confluence of two rivers Cromwell was likely to cross with the boats he was known to have waiting. Before taking up his position to defend that area, Robert entrusted a letter, written to Anne, into Joe's charge. He was certain the lad was wily enough to survive and get back again to Sotherleigh again no matter what happened to anyone else. Michael did likewise with his letter home. He and Robert clasped hands before they parted to take up their respective posts.

"May God protect you, my son."

"You too, sir. We'll celebrate the King's victory when we're back at Sotherleigh."

Robert gave a serious smile. "I pray it will be so."

Michael watched his father ride away and then returned to the foot-soldiers under his command.

The bombardment of Worcester by the Parliamentary cannons began almost as soon as they were in position. Women within their houses screamed and gathered their children to seek shelter in the cellars. Windows within the Cathedral were shattered, but its richly hued glass had been destroyed by the Roundheads several years before when they had pillaged the city and it was only plain glass that fell to the ground. Charles rode about the city doing everything in his power to cheer his men in readiness for the assault when it came, but such misfortune had dogged him all the way from Scotland that few had any hope of its changing in the face of the overwhelming odds in full preparation outside the city walls. Under the orders of their officers, Michael holding the rank of lieutenant, the Royalist soldiers drilled on the College Green, cleaned their muskets, sharpened swords, polished pikes and checked that their powder was dry, but there was little heart in any but the most optimistic and those more resolute than the rest who would not contemplate defeat.

A three-columned attack came on the third day of September. The King went with a spy-glass up to the top of the Cathedral tower and, seeing Cromwell's men to the west crossing the two rivers on bridges of boats as well as beating back the defenders of the bridge there, decided to launch a surprise counter-attack to the south-east where the enemy forces would be reduced in number. If he could capture the enemy artillery there, the day would be his! He leapt down the tower steps and ran out into the sunlight to lead a charge out of the Sidbury Gate, the crimson plumes streaming from his gold-crested helmet, his gilded breastplate shining.

A torrent of men and cavalry burst out of the gate with him under a forest of multi-hued banners, their armour, helmets and weapons gleaming. Michael was among them, yelling and swearing, half deaf from the din of the covering Royalist artillery. The cannons created so much smoke that at times he and his men appeared ghostlike in the greyish swathes as they pressed on uphill all the way. It was out of this smoke that he came suddenly upon the enemy and for the next three hours knew nothing but the clash of steel, the explosion of muskets, the whistling of balls past his head and the screams of the wounded and the dying. The King was in the midst of the whole affray, his courage and tenacity rousing spirit and hope in men untouched before. He took a cavalry horse that had lost its rider and rode from regiment to regiment to fight alongside, charging again and again upon the enemy, and giving aid in the saddle or on foot wherever his soldiers were particularly hard pressed. When ammunition ran out, the butts of muskets were used by both sides, often the struggling men too closely packed in the general melee to gain enough elbow room to thrust with a pike.

Briefly it seemed that victory was with Charles as the enemy artillery was captured and the Roundheads fell back. But Cromwell had received word of what was happening and sent reinforcements that arrived in such numbers that the Royalists fled in defeat back into the city. Michael, running for the Sidbury Gate close on the heels of the King, felt the Roundheads closing in on them and the way ahead was blocked by overturned and damaged wagons, dead men, horses and oxen. Then Charles clambered through the wheels of an upturned wagon just as a Roundhead snatched at his coat-tails and hung on to haul him back. Michael, his sword still in his hand, swung it wildly to save the King. The coat-tails were released and the soldier's head spun away like a thrown ball. Michael dived through the wheels himself and with lungs bursting reached the safety of the Sidbury Gate only seconds after the King.

Leaning against a wall, he gasped to get his breath back. Sweat was running down into his eyes and his shirt was sticking to him beneath his slashed coat, parts of it hanging in ribbons. It was as he lifted his hands wearily to unbuckle his helmet that he realised he had received a sword-cut to the left arm. In his state of exhaustion the pain surprised him and he saw that his sleeve was lying open, the wound running blood down his arm to drip from his fingers.

"Mr. Michael, sir!"

He raised his drooped head and saw Joe offering him a shoulder to lean on. "I'm not that weak," he said with a grin, "but you can find some linen to bind me up."

"I have it ready at the Red Fox, sir."

"Have you seen my father?"

"Yes, he's there too. A musket-ball skimmed his ribs, but it's not serious. He was brought in with the other wounded half an hour ago while you were in the field."

In spite of the reassurance, Michael was concerned. As he and Joe made their way to the tavern they saw Charles in the saddle of a fresh horse. He was riding round urging his soldiers to take heart, but they had collapsed everywhere in exhaustion, casting aside their armour and their weapons, the Scots among them wanting nothing more than to be back in the land of their birth.

"Why not shoot me?" Charles roared at a group of them. "I have no wish to live and see the terrible consequences of this day if we do not stand firm again now!"

They would not listen and made no move, continuing to lie where they were sprawled or sitting with drooped heads, blood-stained and dirty. Charles jerked on his reins, making his horse rear as he swung about to try to rouse others elsewhere.

When Michael and Joe reached the Red Fox, Robert was not there. The tavern-keeper's wife had bound up his wound and she told them that nothing would make him rest.

"He refused to take my advice, sir. Now he's gone to the King's lodgings."

Michael was somewhat relieved to know that at least his father was fit enough to be mobile and resolved to go to the house himself as soon as his wound was dressed.

That was not to happen. Some of Charles's soldiers were so set on surrender that they had made sure the Sidbury Gate was not closed. Cromwell's men stormed in and once again Michael found himself in the midst of hand-to-hand fighting, but this time in narrow streets, in and out of doors, on steps and under archways. Many who had turned away from the King rallied again to defend him and the wounding and killing went on until it was reduced to the slaughter of any Royalist fighting beside dead comrades. Already the King's men had begun to scatter and flee by whatever escape route presented itself.

Robert, searching for the King, heard a clash of blades in a side-alley and found him engaging two Roundheads. Immediately he plunged in with his own sword. Together they felled their adversaries and when Charles would have rushed to find fresh conflict, Robert seized him by the arm and thrust him back against a wall, protocol disregarded.

"You must leave, sire! Now!"

Charles thrust him off, both of them breathing heavily from exertion. "My life doesn't matter! If I'm killed I have a brother safely at The Hague to continue the monarchy! Then there's Harry as well."

"But the day is lost! There's nothing more to be done and if you are captured, sire, you'll give Cromwell all the bargaining power he needs! You'll be a political pawn!"

For a matter of seconds Charles stared at him. Then he gave a bitter nod. "There are a few things in my lodgings I must collect. Let us go."

They were not far from the house and they met three senior officers all anxious to get him safely away. In the lodging house the Cavaliers discarded distinguishing Royalist colours and the King stripped himself of all that marked him as Cromwell's prime quarry. He was downstairs putting the last of what he wanted to take with him into his pockets when one or more of the enemy began forcing a way into the front of the house. A window smashed.

"Quick, sire!" Robert stood indicating the way. "Out the back door!"

Charles ran and the rest followed, ready to stand and fight to cover his escape if necessary, but they all emerged into a small yard, the last man being Robert, who locked the door after him to cause some small delay. Once out of the gate they found themselves in such a melee that they were able to make their way through it without being noticed. There was shouting and shoving as townspeople tried to protect their property from looting, prisoners being hurried along and pockets of fighting still in progress. All the gates in the city walls had been opened. One of the four bridges Charles had ordered to be destroyed had been patched up by Roundhead engineers and was adding to the flow in and out of the city.

Robert looked about him as he went, hoping to catch sight of his son, but it was in vain. The escape party went undetected through St. Martin's Gate, but the danger was still with them. Beyond the city walls Roundheads were spreading out to round up Royalists who had fled and once it was discovered that the King was still alive and missing, the whole country would be combed for him. Whatever happened, nothing must delay the King in his escape from Cromwell.

In a derelict shed not far from St. Martin's Gate, Michael lay unconscious. He would have been taken prisoner, senseless as he was, if Joe had not been following him at a safe distance during the fighting in the streets and finally dragged him out of sight into the ill-smelling refuge. Michael had been engaged in a sword-fight when another Roundhead saw that his comrade was getting the worst of it. He came from behind and knocked Michael down with the butt of a musket. The resulting cut was small due to the protection given by his helmet, which Joe had removed from his head at once, but there was a swelling large as a duck's egg that was going to cause him discomfort when he was himself again.

Joe did not know much about nursing, minor accidents in the kitchen being his only source, but he remembered how a maidservant had been treated after she had fallen and cracked her head. So he had taken off his own coat to cover the unconscious man with it, even though the day was mild. With strips of linen brought from the tavern he had given the young man's arm a fresh dressing and placed a wad against the cut on the head, which he had secured with a hat he had been wearing himself. Satisfied with what he had done so far, he realised he must get some transport to convey his charge out of the city while getting away was still possible. He recalled that the maidservant had been groggy on her feet when she recovered consciousness, which meant that the heir to Sotherleigh would be in no condition to walk for a while.

Cautiously he slipped out of the shed. It was in a street of warehouses, everything closed by reason of the city's turmoil, and there were no inquisitive eyes to peer at him from windows as he ran off on his errand. When he returned he was leading the same horse and cart that had brought him to Worcester. He had found the stable deserted, no sign of Henry, and in the noise and confusion prevailing all around the stable nobody had noticed him backing the horse into the shafts. He scavenged a few items in the streets that he thought would be useful as a disguise for his young master and tossed them into the cart.

Back in the shed the unconscious man groaned as his Cavalier coat was removed and he was pulled into a scarlet one taken from a dead Round-head officer, the left sleeve slit to the shoulder to enable his wounded arm to be more easily accommodated. An orange sash filched from another of the enemy was wound around his waist. Into it Joe tucked a Roundhead officer's baton of office, which he had found in the gutter in the midst of several fallen men. He stood back and regarded his efforts critically. To all appearances the Cavalier had gone and a wounded Roundhead lay in his place. There was still a helmet in the cart, its lobster tail and some kind of insignia on the front showing it belonged to a Parliamentarian, but his master's head was too tender for the pressure of anything hard and the hat was softer for him.

"Come on now, sir." Joe looped Michael's arm about his neck. "You and me 'ave some travelling to do. It's my bet you'll be as glad to get back to Sotherleigh as I will be."

Although he was a strong lad he was hampered by Michael being a dead weight, and he had to haul him somewhat ignominiously into the cart. Then with his heart in his mouth he set off for the nearest gate. The horse was nervous, alarmed even before leaving the stable by the noise and musket shot, but Joe talked quietly to it and apart from a couple of delays reached St. Martin's gate without much difficulty. They passed through it only a matter of minutes after the King and the Master of Sotherleigh had gone through similarly unnoticed.

Once beyond the bridge Joe climbed into the cart's driving seat and urged the horse to a good speed. The road was full of people, military and civilian, but after a while, when he turned at a crossroads to take the road south, he had the highway more or less to himself. The sun was setting when he heard the fast beat of horses' hooves coming behind him.

"You, there! Halt in the name of the Commonwealth!"

He had not expected the enemy to be scavenging the countryside yet for fleeing Royalists, but as he drew up and looked back over his shoulder he saw in the gathering dusk that several prisoners under guard had come into sight from a side road, some Scottish plaid to be seen. A Roundhead sergeant was riding up to him.

"Yes, sir?" He tried to hit the right note to show he was neither nervous nor afraid, but his stomach was churning.

The sergeant had seen the orange sash. "Who's this?" he asked more leniently, looking down into the cart.

"Captain Praise-to-the-Lord Fotheringill," Joe replied glibly, using a Puritan name he had heard one day in Chichester. "I was given payment by a senior officer to transport this wounded gentleman to his home near here where he can be attended." He produced from his pocket a gold coin that he had taken from Michael's purse to cover any emergency. It had seemed to him that such a task would not be worth less in the eyes of anybody questioning him.

"Where is the Captain's home?"

"The village of Amberley," he replied, taking a chance that the sergeant would be no more familiar with the county of Worcestershire than he was himself.

"Is it far?"

"No. I'll get there by nightfall."

"Here." The sergeant turned in his saddle and unbuckled a blanket-roll, which he tossed down to Joe. "Cover the Captain with this. Then make haste. The sooner he is in good nursing hands the better."

He rode back to the men and his prisoners. Joe tucked the blanket around Michael and then drove off at speed, but only until he came to a side lane, which he could see led through a slope of thick woods. There he took the cart well into the seclusion of the trees before returning to watch the road from some bushes. He had to be sure that he had not inadvertently created any doubts in the sergeant's mind.

He did not have long to wait. Twenty minutes later the sergeant and another Roundhead on horseback went galloping past in the direction he had been taking, hot in pursuit of a lying boy and a Cavalier in disguise.

Joe grinned and thumbed his nose at the soldiers as they vanished into the dusk. Then he returned to the cart and peered into it at his charge. Where had he made his mistake? What had rung a bell of suspicion afterwards in the sergeant's mind? Perhaps a Roundhead Captain would not have carried that particular baton while wearing that colour sash. Or maybe the helmet lying there was a colonel's? It was just possible that the sergeant had asked the location of Amberley and learned it was in Sussex and no village of that name was to be found anywhere near the city of Worcester.

# FIVE

*D*URING THE NIGHT Michael recovered consciousness. He was desperately thirsty and drank several cupfuls of water that Joe brought him from a stream. Then he slept again to wake with a throbbing headache to find that he was sitting in a cart, half covered by a blanket in the midst of a wood and wearing an enemy coat. He shut his eyes again, struggling against the intense ache behind them, the soreness of his arm nothing by comparison. Unaware that he had brushed a hat from his head during the night, causing it to become a pillow, he reached up a hand and felt dried blood and the large bump on the back of his head.

"Ouch!"

"Drink this, sir."

He opened his eyes again to see a lad he recognised handing him a mug of milk over the rim of the cart. "Joe Berry! What are you doing here?"

"A musket knocked you out and I got you away, but I'll explain everything later. There's a farmhouse up this track." Joe indicated the direction by jerking a thumb over his shoulder. "I've been doing some business there and come back to tell you about it. They sheltered a Royalist last night and 'e's died from his wounds. They're scared stiff of 'im being found there and they're going to carry the body down through the woods to the village church and leave it to the Parson to find out who he was and anyway give him Christian burial." He saw the stark look Michael turned in the direction of the farmhouse and hastened to reassure him. "It's not the Master, sir. This was just a youngish fellow. They asked me if I knew 'im." That was not strictly true. It had crossed Joe's mind that some strange quirk of fate might have brought the two male Pallisters close to each other at this traumatic time and he had requested to see the body. "Nor did I see the Master among the wounded or the dead yesterday, sir."

"God grant that may be as true today as it was then." Michael had been holding the mug of milk and now he drank it down without pause. It was warm from the cow and seemed to him the most delicious drink he had ever had in his life. "What was this business that you mentioned?"

Joe refilled the mug from a bucket of milk that he had set down on the ground and handed it over again. "These farm folk are left with the Cavalier's 'orse at the moment. They can chase it off easily enough, but we can't wait for 'em to do that. I suggest you let me buy it from 'em." His expression was cocky. "I reckon on getting it at bargain price."

Michael had drunk down the milk as thirstily as before. "Buy the animal," he said at once, giving back the mug. Then he would have reached into his pocket for money only to remember that his own coat had gone. He looked anxiously at Joe. "Did you—"

"Yes, sir," Joe broke in reassuringly, producing the leather drawstring purse from his own pocket and bouncing it on his palm with a jingle of coins. "I didn't want you robbed when I weren't with you, so I took charge of your money."

"I should say that was an unlikely possibility here in the safety of these woods," Michael commented dryly.

"I don't mean you were likely to be robbed 'ere," Joe said, "but yesterday when you was in that shed in Worcester."

"What shed? I don't understand."

Joe shook his head impatiently. "I'll tell you about that when I've bought that 'orse."

As he went off again, boots thudding up the rutted track, Michael climbed slowly out of the cart, careful not to jerk his painful head in any way. It was worse than anything he had endured after a carousal. He went to relieve himself and in reeling back to the cart he saw a little stream. Kneeling down on the bank, he dashed the cold water into his face. He thought he felt a little better until he got up again and then he had to find a fallen tree-trunk on which to sit. There he supported his wounded arm by the elbow. He would have liked to discard the enemy coat he was wearing, but he was still as weak as a baby and disinclined to do anything more for the time being. He had seen his sword lying in the cart, but if the enemy should come upon him now through the trees he could do nothing to defend himself.

Yet it was good to be alive and the cool ferny silence of the woods, broken only by the twittering of birds and the sudden rustle of some unseen little creature in the grass, made the noise and horror of the previous day seem like a nightmare and something that could never have been. But the reality was there, images stamped on his memory that he would never be able to forget, even though his mind was blank as to the shed that Joe had mentioned and how he came to be here. He saw again the flying head of the soldier he had killed and, although there had been other men who had fallen to his sword that day, he wept on a rush of emotional reaction for that one man. The tears dropped from his eyes to the grass at his feet for he was leaning slightly forward with his arm balanced across his knee. His shoulders heaved in his sobbing. If that Roundhead had been his own brother his grief at that moment would not have been worse. He understood now why no soldier returning home after warfare ever spoke of what he had seen or else the guilt of living on when others had fallen would be a yoke impossible to bear. It was only when veteran soldiers grew old and became nostalgic for past comrade-ship-in-arms that they were able to let the dead whom they remembered in their hearts finally lie in peace.

He heard Joe returning with the horse and hastily wiped his eyes with his sleeve. The lad noticed nothing, proud of his purchase of the black animal, which lacked any sign of breeding but was sturdy enough and, apart from a slight graze across the neck, appeared to have been unharmed in yesterday's battle.

Joe had also brought food from the farmhouse, enough to last through the day, with two clay mugs and plates, some wooden utensils and a knife for their journey. Immediately Michael was aware of being ravenously hungry, realising he had not eaten since the same hour the previous day. Joe tucked in with equal gusto and in a voice muffled by mouthfuls of bread, cheese and meat recounted all that had happened from the time Michael had lost consciousness.

"You saved me twice from being taken prisoner," Michael said grate-fully when Joe had concluded with the outwitting of the sergeant. "When we get back to Sotherleigh I'll see your days in the kitchen are over."

Joe wiped the crumbs from his mouth with the back of his hand. "What'll I do then, sir?" he asked tensely. "Plants wouldn't grow if anyone tried to make a gardener out of me and Ridley won't let me in 'is workshop 'cos I'm clumsy."

"I was thinking to make a groom of you, Joe."

The boy's face flooded crimson and his eyes sparkled. "Yes, sir! That's a good idea of yours if I can say so. I like 'orses. You won't regret it, sir."

They washed down their food with the last of the milk in the bucket and made ready to leave. Michael threw off the sash he was still wearing and changed his coat for another, which had been among Joe's purchases. It stank of cows, but Michael was in no mood to be particular and it was roomy enough for him to slide his arm into the left sleeve without too much pain. Both he and Joe realised the importance of his having no apparent connection with the previous day's battle. The sash and coat, the baton and the helmet were all thrust down by Joe into a hollow and covered with dry leaves.

"I'll make you a sling for that arm, sir," he said, folding into a triangle his own neckerchief, which had not been washed since he left Sotherleigh, "but it's best you take it off and shove it in your pocket if we meet anyone."

The sling did relieve the aching, but when Michael would have swung himself into the saddle of his new mount, his head swam to such a degree that he was forced to lie down again in the cart, and the black horse was hitched to the rear of it. With Joe once more in the driving seat they set off up the track away from the road, the farm folk having given him directions that would lead them past their house and southward on a route little used by any except local people, where it was unlikely that any Roundheads would be encountered. If it should happen, Joe was confident the two of them could pass as a journeyman and apprentice going about their business. If the need arose they could say they were brothers and if Michael was still confined to the cart he would have to pretend to be drunk.

The day went without a hitch. They passed from Worcestershire into Gloucestershire and that night they were able to sleep in a barn. Joe thought the farmer's price was high for the loan of some straw for a bed until he realised it included supper as well. He had told Michael from the start to mumble whenever it was necessary for him to speak, for otherwise his gentlemanly voice, being at odds with his rough attire, would arouse curiosity and there was no telling who was friend or foe. The farmer was a hard-eyed, uncouth fellow and the kitchen where they ate supper with him was filthy, the food less appetising than that given to the dogs at Sotherleigh. They were waited on by the man's wife, who looked completely downtrodden, and there were several daughters who scurried about every time the farmer shouted for something. Just as the two travellers were settling down to sleep, one of the girls came to keep Michael company. He had neither the strength nor the least wish to avail himself of her offer and sent her away again. Joe would have followed her, eager for initiation into sexual experience, but Michael ordered him to stay where he was and he obeyed.

The following two nights cost them nothing, for they slept by hayricks in fields, covering themselves with hay and resting well. By then Joe had reached the limits of the local directions given to him by the farm folk, having come to the end of them during the second day, and they were having to take busier roads, but they were more relaxed, knowing that every hour took them farther from danger. They would have dumped the cart if it had been possible, but Michael continued to have spells of giddiness and was unable to be in the saddle for more than an hour or so at a time. He concluded that his condition came more from loss of blood than from the blow on the head, but his wound was clean and showed signs of healing well. At least retaining the cart helped to keep up the illusion of their being workmen locally employed, and they became increasingly jubilant as they rode through villages and towns without attracting undue attention, stopping only to buy food.

When they came to a place where a market was in progress, Michael bought new clothing for himself and Joe. Everything on sale was well suited to their supposed station in life, locally made and home-spun, fit for hard wear over a long period. He bought a coat and hat for each of them, the colours sombre, the headgear bare of plumage, as well as breeches, hose and change of linen. Later that day they bathed in a river, Michael having to keep his bound arm out of the water. Afterwards they donned their clean garments with relief while the river carried away everything they had cast off.

That night they stayed at a hostelry, where they had the luxury of jugs of hot water and Michael barbered himself with the new razor he had bought in the market. They ate well downstairs at a table in the tap-room. There were plenty of Roundheads coming in to swill down the ale, but they were laughing and talking among themselves or flirting with the barmaids. It was the first time Michael and Joe had entered anywhere that might have turned into a trap for them and, having passed the danger successfully, they became completely confident that nothing could delay their home-coming now. Already Gloucestershire was behind them and there was only a road, long though it was, to take them through Wilt-shire, down through Hampshire, and bring them finally onto Sussex soil.

Their cart now held several empty barrels which they had found dumped by the wayside and they were often greeted by carriers supposing them to be transporting ale. Joe became adept at returning these greetings, which were made by a tilt of the whip. They had almost no news of what was happening in the country, avoiding conversation whenever possible, although in one village they found bonfires lit and church bells ringing to celebrate the King's death. A Parliamentary trooper was being fêted and given all the ale he could drink in the tavern, claiming he had killed the King at Worcester.

"This is the Stuart's coat that I'm wearing!" he informed his avid listeners, who had invited him to step onto a table in the forecourt in order for everyone to hear his tale at first hand. "I ripped it from him myself!"

Michael and Joe, who had drawn up to listen on the outskirts of the crowd, moved on again. "The King was not in a coat of that colour," Michael said quietly and with relief. "If circumstances had been different it would have given me great pleasure to have exposed that lie being perpetrated."

They had been seven days on the road when they reached Winchester and in the light of a street lantern read the first of such posters as they were to see elsewhere.

*By the Parliament. A Proclamation for the Discovery and Apprehending of Charles Stuart and Other Traitors, His Adherents and Abettors!*

It went on to state that after being defeated with his forces at Worces-ter this dangerous son of the late tyrant had escaped. Parliament charged all officers, civil as well as military, and the good people of the land to do everything in their power to bring him to justice, a reward of one thou-sand pounds being offered for his capture.

"So he is alive," Michael breathed thankfully. "We'll have a celebration at Sotherleigh as soon as we get there."

They were only a day or so's journey from home now and would have carried on through the night if it had not been for the horses having had enough travelling for the day. All along they would have made better speed if they could have changed horses, but nowhere would it have been wise to become linked up in the chain that existed for the benefit of travellers.

It had become their custom always to drive through a town or village to the most outlying hostelry for the night. This gave them a good start on the road in the morning. Michael, whose money was dwindling, had to make sure of keeping enough for bribes or anything else that might prove necessary in an emergency, but on what might be the last night he decided to have a room to himself. He was wearied of sharing with Joe, but when they arrived at the hostelry beyond St. Cross there was only one attic room left with two truckle beds. He had no choice but to take it and it was an uphill climb, with a rickety flight rising from the third floor to their accommodation under the eaves.

He did not sleep well. The bed was uncomfortable and he stirred at every sound. He was half awake again when he heard the tramp of marching feet. Instantly he dived from bed to the dormer window. Because it was dark when he and Joe had arrived, he had not seen what was clearly visible now through a gap in the foliage of the roadside trees. Their room was on the side of the tavern giving him a direct view across the river of a row of gibbets standing on the verge of the road that he and Joe would shortly be taking. Quickly he leaned from the window and was able to see going past the tavern a Parliamentary officer on horseback riding at the head of a band of troopers marching in the direction of the bridge leading to the gibbets. They were escorting three prisoners, who were walking one behind the other, their wrists tied behind them. The first two were middle-aged men, but the third was a fair-haired girl with long loose tresses soft as silk, no more than sixteen years of age, dressed in a plain grey gown such as a maidservant or one of modest background would wear. To judge by her lowered head she was weeping. Drawing up the rear of the procession was another soldier leading a horse in the shafts of a light army wagon of the type used when a moderate load had to be carried at a fast pace. Michael knew immediately what its purpose was to be that day.

He leaned a hand against the wall as he waited for the condemned to reappear beyond the trees. It was usual for gibbets to be outside a town and they were a common sight. Hangings were to be seen in London and other cities at almost any time; there was nothing remarkable about them unless the condemned were people of fame or notoriety, in which case large crowds would assemble to listen to the last words from the scaffold. It was obvious that these hangings were of no local interest, for he could see that nobody had gathered to watch, which meant it was likely that the three prisoners had been brought from elsewhere to be more conveniently despatched.

Now the procession was in sight again, coming to a halt at the first gibbet. Michael pushed the window wider. He would not have stayed to watch if it had not been for the girl. She had a look of springtime youth in the midst of that grim scene. He was filled with compassion for her, no matter who she was or what she had done.

At a barked order from the officer the soldiers jumped into action. The first man had a noose placed about his neck and was shoved unceremoniously up into the wagon, which had been drawn up exactly under the gibbet. It was obvious that all three prisoners were to be despatched with a minimum of time and no allowance granted for a condemned man's right to make that last speech. The reason was either that these people had to be silenced as soon as possible or, more likely, that the soldiers found the task abhorrent and wanted it over without delay. The fate of the two men would not have touched them, used as they were to seeing death in battle, but as they were only soldiers and not professional hangmen, the girl was a different matter. They were showing her a strange kind of mercy by despatching the men first, giving her a few breaths longer of the fresh morning air.

Despite the haste with which the soldiers were carrying out the executions, the first man managed to shout a few words with his last breath. Michael heard them clearly as they rang across the water. "God Save the King!"

At the second gibbet the girl fainted and did not see the other man meet his end, proclaiming the same loyalty to the King. It was clear to Michael that the soldiers knew she was not shamming, for they stood around her in attitudes of consternation, hands on hips and shuffling their feet. A sergeant knelt and scooped his hand through the dewy grass to wipe the moisture over her brow. She revived almost immediately and shrank away from his touch, struggling to her feet without assistance. Then a trooper stooped to tie her skirts about her ankles with a length of cord, a customary concession to the modesty of those women who feared exposure of their nether parts after death as much as the rope itself. The noose was placed about her neck and she was lifted bodily onto the wagon. Michael felt protest rising in him to such an extent that his hand had balled against the wall and the tendons tightened in his neck.

"No!" His roar shut out to his own ears whatever last cry the girl made before the rope jerked.

Joe threw himself up from the pillows, sleep flying from him, and leapt from his bed. "What's up?" he yelled. "Are we trapped?"

Michael moved away from the window, shaking his head. "There's been a triple hanging. Royalist conspirators against Parliament. Poor wretches. There was a girl too. Very young."

"What 'ave you done to your right 'and?"

Michael saw the knuckles were bleeding from the force with which he had slammed his fist against the wall at the moment when the girl died. "My futile act of protest," he pronounced bitterly.

Joe went to his stock of linen, replenished at the market-place, and proceeded to bind up his master's hand. He thought to himself that it was as well that his employer's son was still handicapped or heaven alone knew what misguided chivalry the young man might have attempted.

"I've had enough of this place," Michael exclaimed irritably as Joe tied a knot to finish off the binding. "Let's get on our way. We can breakfast somewhere else along the road. I've no stomach for more food here."

When they were ready to leave, Joe hurried ahead to the stables while Michael went to the office where he settled his bill with the landlord's wife, who sat there at a high desk.

"I trust everything was to your satisfaction, sir," she said amiably.

"Yes, indeed. Er—who were those who were hanged just now?" he inquired casually.

"I don't know. There's hangings all the time for one thing or another."

"Doesn't it interfere with your business?"

"No, sir. You see, nobody is left swinging there as in some places, so there's no whiff after a while, if you get my meaning. There are a couple of doctors in the town who have opened a hospital for the sick, and they have a number of medical students there. These young men take the hanged away real quick. They'll be at the gibbets already I shouldn't wonder." She leaned an arm on the desk, cheerfully confidential. "As a matter of fact, it does a tavern a power of good to be as near to gibbets as we are here. We get large crowds coming on special occasions."

"It was a military hanging of civilians today," he persisted, hoping to jog her memory about anything she might have known and momentarily forgotten.

"Ah." She sat back in her chair, tapping a finger against her cheek. "It comes back to me now. My husband came late to bed last night when I was almost asleep and he said something about hearing there was to be a hanging of some folk suspected of sheltering the late tyrant's son."

"I saw by the posters last night that he is still on the run."

"We'll get him. No fear of that. He's surely in disguise by now, but nothing can hide his height. I'm told he's two yards high and a few inches over."

"I've heard that too." He picked up the change she had taken from her desk drawer and placed in front of him.

"You can't be far off the same." She cocked her head to one side, looking up to the crown of his hat.

"Two yards exactly," he replied. "Good day to you, madam."

"Good day, sir." She craned her neck to watch him leave. Could he possibly be Charles Stuart? He was dark and spoke like a gentleman in spite of his ordinary clothes. But no, that was not possible. No such fugitive would stay in a tavern where someone might recognise him. She had no idea what the Stuart looked like, but there were many who did. As she continued doing her accounts she thrust the suspicion from her, but it continued to dance at the back of her mind.

On the road Michael and Joe had crossed the low bridge over the river before finding the gibbets directly ahead of them. The soldiers had gone, but the medical students were there as the landlord's wife had predicted. All three of the hanged had been taken down. Since only the corpses of felons could be legally used for dissection, the eagerness of doctors and their students alike for fresh cadavers was notorious, but as yet only the two dead men had been loaded on to the waiting hand-cart. The students were in a close and talkative group around the female corpse, which was lying on the grass.

Wanting to know what was happening, Michael spurred his horse and rode to the spot. He reached it in time to see the students propping the limp form into a sitting position against a tree. One of the young men was bare to the waist, having wrapped his shirt about the female's neck, and was putting his coat on again.

"What do you think you're doing?" Michael roared in outrage. "Have you no respect for the dead, you vultures!"

Their animated conversation stilled at once, all of them tetchy about their reputation, and they turned to regard him with marked hostility. One addressed him belligerently, thumbs looped in belt, feet set apart.

"We've no cause to account to you for our actions, stranger, whoever you may be. But since you have chosen to thrust yourself into our affairs I will tell you that when we came to this girl we denoted signs of life still in her."

"Alive!" Michael gasped incredulously. "But surely that's impossible? I saw her hanged with my own eyes."

"These were slow strangulations. A man has to leap from the cart if he wants a really quick end. Haven't you read how one of the conspirators of the Gunpowder Plot did that to hasten his demise?"

"Well, yes, since you mention it. Do you mean that you cut her down in time?"

"We did. Maybe she fainted a second before the vital moment and a lack of struggling saved her. Remember that there were no kind friends or relatives present to jerk the legs of those hanged today and shorten their last sufferings, which again was her good luck. If you want another reason, perhaps she is a witch and used her arts to protect herself until we should do the rest!" The student's eyes narrowed mockingly as he watched for a superstitious drawing back by this stranger, but no movement was made. "As you can see for yourself, we succeeded in reviving her and have sat her up to help her breathe more easily."

Michael dismounted and moved quickly to the girl as if having witnessed her death he had the right to be first at her rebirth. She was making faint breathy sounds and he could not begin to imagine the agony, both physical and mental, that she must be suffering. "You must get her to a hospital bed at once! Unload the hand-cart and lay her on it. I'll help you."

The students exchanged significant looks, impatient with this stranger who had chosen to interfere. Although they were supporters of Cromwell and the Commonwealth themselves, they had no truck with fanatics. Their mutual guess was that the intruder was a soft-headed Puritan out to concern himself with everybody else's business.

"She'll recover, given time." The student who had given his shirt for her neck had stooped to remove the cord from her ankles.

Michael went nearer and leaned over her to smooth back some of her hair, which in its disarray half covered her ashen face. "What's to become of her?"

At his touch she opened green eyes stark and unfocused in pain and shock and fear. Briefly her gaze cleared enough for her to see a stranger's face, full of concern, looming over her. Then all faded again. There was such torture in her neck that she felt maddened by it, all thoughts in turmoil, every nerve screeching. It seemed to her that shadows were moving away from her and she could hear men's voices. Why, then, could she not hear her own screams of agony, which she believed herself to have been uttering ever since she realised she was still alive and lying on the grass. Someone at hand shouted out clearly. She supposed him to be the one who had brushed back the hair from her eyes.

"Wait! Where are you going? You can't abandon her here!"

The students, trundling their loaded cart from the grass onto the rough road, laughed among themselves and shouted back at Michael. "We're only authorised to take the dead. Not the living."

"She needs nursing."

"Not by us. Make arrangements yourself!"

"What about your commitment to the sick?"

"She's still a condemned felon. We'd be breaking the law."

They went jovially on their way, well pleased with what they had achieved, even though it meant one cadaver less for the dissecting table. By now Joe had drawn up by the verge and had witnessed the latter part of what had been happening. He had been ill at ease ever since he had seen his master being drawn into some kind of dispute and now he was positively frightened.

"Come away, sir! Now! At once! Them students will be boasting about what they did 'ere today as soon as they gets into company. We don't want you talked about."

"We can't leave her here! Throw out those barrels from the cart and then come and help me lift her into it."

Joe forgot himself completely. "Are you balmy?" he yelled in fright, getting red in the face. "We got away from that sergeant and kept out of trouble all the way! Now you want to plunge us into fresh danger when we're almost within sight of 'ome! If we're caught with 'er, they'll only string 'er up again and us with 'er!"

Michael swore. "Get down and do as I say. If you don't I'll knock you from that seat and leave you here!"

For the first time since starting the perilous journey from Worcester Joe's spirit almost broke. Just when he was almost able to see Sotherleigh's stables on the horizon, buoyed up by the priority claim he intended to make over the charge of the two horses he had acquired for his master through his own wits, everything had been put in jeopardy. He was sorely tempted for a brief, head-spinning moment to whip up and drive off, making his own way and leaving Michael to do as he pleased. But common sense prevailed. His master had the swifter horse and would catch up with him at once.

He jumped down from the cart and rolled the barrels into the ditch on the other side of the road. Then he ran to help, not because he was any more willing, but because it was a case of survival in getting away as quickly as possible. He took the girl's feet while Michael leaned down to pick her up with his good arm about her waist. Supporting her with his left hand, he made sure her head and shoulders were resting against his chest, his chin helping to hold her head steady. It was an awkward way to carry her, but one that should cause her less pain in being moved. Joe had taken an instant dislike to her for the new danger into which she had plunged them. He had always liked the parable of the Good Samaritan, attendance at Sunday church being compulsory under the Commonwealth, and had imagined he would play the same role should such circumstances arise, but he knew that was not the case now. Helping his master to escape was one thing, but risking one's neck for another that had been stretched already was a different matter entirely.

She made rasping sounds in her throat as they laid her down in the cart. Michael folded his coat to make a cradle for her head and save her from some of the jolting she would have to suffer. Then he covered her up to the chin with the same blanket that had been used to cover him when he had been lying there. He saw she had fainted from the ordeal of being moved, but there was no time to try to bring her round. In any case, oblivion would be more merciful considering the rough ride for her that lay ahead. As great a distance as possible in a short time had to be placed between her and the gibbets. It was fortunate that nobody had come by after the medical students had departed, so that there had been no witnesses to their placing the girl in the cart.

He remounted and set off at as fast a speed as he dared attempt, Joe whipping up behind. They soon met people on foot and a farm wagon here and there. Women gossiping over a garden gate were among those who turned to watch them passing by; where children were playing in the road their mothers would run out and snatch them onto the grass verges, fearful that the little ones might run under the hooves.

Michael was no longer on unfamiliar territory. His mother had come from this part of Hampshire and a framed map showing her childhood home was on one of the landing walls at Sotherleigh. Not only had he looked at it countless times for as long as he could remember, having always had an interest in maps, but many times his mother had traced with a finger the villages and lanes and meadows that she had known in childhood. During the time he had been at home waiting to go up to Oxford, he had accompanied her several times on visits to a great-aunt who lived hereabouts. Now that every village was being sign-posted, he knew exactly where to turn off this road into a tangle of side lanes. He explained this to Joe while still keeping to the road.

"Then why aren't we turning off?" Joe shouted, still hovering on rebellion.

"I have to get to an apothecary. That girl will need something to ease her pain when she comes round or else she may start screaming involuntarily. That's the last thing we want quite apart from it being our moral duty to relieve her pain as much as possible."

"*Our* duty! Yours, you mean, sir! I'm having nothing to do with this." After thus disclaiming all responsibility, Joe did not speak again, thinking he was not far from screaming himself in fright and exasperation, for he was still in the high state of terror he had experienced at the first mention of rescuing the creature from the gibbets. When getting away from Worcester he had been in charge and then it was a case of pitting his wits against others and getting the better of them, but now he felt as helpless as a hare being coursed by hounds. If it had not been for this girl they would have been jaunting happily along this road instead of fearing discovery from every passing traveller. They were not even able to seek evasion from pursuit down side lanes until they had run the gauntlet of riding through a town with anyone able to glance into the cart and wonder why that creature was lying there.

It was not long before they came to a large village. Michael, who had had little hope of finding what he sought, was delighted and surprised when told of an elderly man who had once been an apothecary in Winchester. His son, now the owner of the shop, paid his father fairly frequent visits, leaving him a small supply of physics and ointments to enable him to deal with local accidents.

Following the directions he had been given, Michael located the place he wanted in a narrow cobbled street. In the dark, aromatic interior he told the old apothecary that his sister had had a fall and was in need of something strong to take away the pain.

"Perhaps she has broken some bones," the old man suggested. "I'll set them for a fee."

"That's been done," Michael assured him hastily. "It's the aftermath that is causing her suffering." He came out of the shop with a bottle of syrupy anodyne.

To Joe's relief, when they left the village it was to branch into a side lane, which Michael seemed to know like the back of his hand, pointing out the landmarks of an ancient oak and a curious rock formation. Although he led the way, he frequently dropped back to ride beside the cart, keeping an eye on the girl. Suddenly she opened her eyes and her hand flew to the shirt wound about her neck as if for a moment she thought it was strangling her.

"Stop, Joe!" Michael ordered, dismounting. As the cart slowed to a standstill he sprang up into it and dropped to a knee beside her.

"Don't disturb the binding!" He caught her hands and held them within his own. "It's giving your neck some support and that must do until we can get something better." She obeyed him, but was wild with pain, gasping and twisting. He uncorked the bottle of anodyne and poured some into a spoon. "Drink this. It will help you."

He trickled it into her mouth; her eyes bulged as she swallowed and she almost choked. Raising her up, he let his arm act as a splint for her neck and she held her jaw with both hands as if in some vain attempt to ease the weight of her head on its injured stem. Her face was grossly swollen, her eyes bloodshot and barely visible in the pouching of her affected lids. Although it was obviously torture for her to swallow she took two more spoonfuls with a desperate eagerness, trusting in the relief it would bring her.

Joe twisted round in the driving seat to look down at her. He thought her hideous and that her face in its puffed state was like those cut out of turnips for scarecrows. His loathing of her grew inside him like a blown-up sheep's bladder and he turned away to munch stale bread and cheese, which was the first food he had had since the night before. Again if this wretched turnip-head hadn't thrust her company on them he would have been enjoying a good roast dinner in a hostelry, for his master was not tight-fisted and they ate the same food. He had never been more homesick for Sotherleigh and never had it seemed farther away.

"Are you able to tell me your name?" Michael asked the girl as he recorked the bottle. She made no sound, but from the way she pressed her lips together he made a guess. "Mary? Is that it?" It appeared he had guessed correctly for she did not make a second attempt. There was no point in asking her surname. That could come later. He helped her to lie down again and put the blanket over her once more. The anodyne did its work swiftly. She was in a sound sleep within minutes, her agony already half drugged away until the next dose should become necessary.

They followed many winding lanes and passed the house where Michael's great-aunt had once lived, but it had been sold long since to strangers and they could not look for hospitality there. They crossed into their home county at dusk, hours later than if nothing had happened to delay their journey. Mary was kept sleepy with the anodyne and since she could not be left when they drew up at a hostelry, Michael went in to purchase a couple of hot meat pies and had a mug filled with broth. He had hoped to feed Mary with a little nourishment, but she could only take sips of water. When he and Joe had eaten the meat pies and shared the broth between them, they rode on again by the fitful glow of the cart-lamps. Joe continued to be jumpy at every hoot of an owl or anything else that disturbed the silence of the dark countryside. Michael tried again to reassure him, convinced that their detour would have thrown any pursuers off the scent.

"Listen, we are now well into Sussex and I'm sure we've had almost a day's head start in any case," he said confidently. "Those medical students would almost certainly have gone straight back to the hospital and begun their dissections immediately, which means it was probably not till about a couple of hours ago that they dispersed to a tavern and their boasting reached military ears. The Roundheads would not start an extensive search with darkness falling and by the time they set off in the morning there will be no trail left."

It would have been exactly as he had said if it had not been for the wife of the landlord of the St. Cross hostelry. At noon she had been gossiping in the tap-room and mentioned what had increased in her imagination from an impression of his height and dark hair to a marked resemblance to Charles Stuart. Two Parliamentary officers happened to be having dinner there at the time and overheard what was said. They sprang up from their table, cross-questioned her and then rushed out to set up a hue and cry. Within a remarkably short time soldiers were riding out in all directions and rumours ran through Winchester like a forest fire. The tyrant's son had been there and nobody knew! Then suddenly people thought they remembered sightings themselves and more rumours were set in motion. One reached the hospital, borne there on the active tongue of the doctor's housekeeper, and even the medical students began to wonder about the tall young man who had expressed such an interest in the survivor of the hangings and his insistence on the girl being taken away and nursed. By nightfall, with the landlord's wife passing on everything she had heard and exaggerating her own tale for the benefit of the crowded taproom, all Winchester knew that Charles Stuart had whipped away a Royalist girl in his coach, assisted by Cavaliers armed to the teeth!

The Parliamentary Colonel investigating the case considered, on adding up all the evidence, it was highly improbable that Charles Stuart had been anywhere near Winchester, let alone deliberately drawing attention to himself in a hostelry. He knew there had been innumerable "sightings" all over the country, especially since the enormous reward had been offered. Nevertheless, it did appear a Royalist had been involved. The missing girl was a seamstress named Marion Moore, who had been condemned for conspiring with two relatives, both watch-makers, to lead Parliamentary forces astray in their search for Charles Stuart. The three of them had professed to know where he was and had led the soldiers far from the house where the royal rogue was hiding and where he would otherwise have been found. It had all taken place in another part of the country where a certain commander, not wanting the word spread that he had allowed himself to be fooled, had insisted on the execution taking place where the three condemned were not known locally.

Now the responsibility was the Colonel's to track down the two new quarries and the female escapee in order to bring them to the gallows and to ensure that there was no bungling this time.

MICHAEL AND JOE arrived home at Sotherleigh the following evening. Their pace had been slower than they had anticipated due to the torment of the girl. Whenever the effects of the anodyne wore off, her agony appeared to have increased a thousandfold, every lurch of the cart making her eyes roll up with pain, her hand clutching the blankets until the knuckles showed white. She had to be kept sedated most of the time. Towards the end of the journey they took woodland lanes that Michael had known since boyhood and they met nobody. It was dusk when they came to the rear gates of his home and found them locked, although a smaller gate in the wall, used by the servants, was not yet bolted and Ridley could be expected at any time to perform that duty. It meant leaving the cart and horses temporarily tied up by the gates. After wrapping Mary in the blanket, Michael picked her up in his arms to carry her through the gate, Joe holding it open for him.

"Go into the house," Michael instructed, "speak to my mother and tell her to meet me at the Queen's Door." It was the code word for the secret entrance to the house, never before mentioned to anyone outside the family, but this was an emergency. "Prepare her for my having an injured girl with me, but no more than that. She is to send Julia with a closed lantern to me at the orangery as quickly as possible. I know the domestic staff is trustworthy, but Mary's life may depend on no word of her neck injury being released. When you've done all that, get the keys to the gate and take the horses to the stables as quickly as you can. The cart will have to be chopped up and burned later."

When Joe entered the kitchen by way of the servants' entrance into the house, he welcomed the familiar sight of its spacious proportions and copper pans, its glowing hearth and those he knew sitting at the long scrubbed table or busy at some task. For a matter of seconds nobody noticed him. Then one of the maidservants gave a shriek and leaped forward to box his ears before he knew what was happening.

"You wicked boy! Where have you been all this time?"

He shoved her off. "You silly 'apporth! I've been to the war." Then seeing Cook approaching him with a bellow, he dodged to the other side of the table. "I 'ave to find the mistress. Where is she?"

"With company in the Queen's Parlour. Mr. and Mrs. Townsend have called," the youngest maidservant informed him.

He grabbed her by the wrist. "Come with me. You've got to tell 'er she's wanted urgent and Miss Julia too!"

Anne, enjoying the neighbourly visit, excused herself and Julia from the visitors' presence and left them with Katherine to go out into the hall where Joe was waiting. She asked him the same question as had been put to him in the kitchen but without abuse, only showing relief that he was back.

"I've come home with Mr. Michael, ma'am."

"He's safe! Is Colonel Pallister here too?"

"No, ma'am, but there's no bad news of him." Then he gave her the message and the letter from her husband that had been entrusted to him.

Julia was excited about the task she had been given and with a shawl about her shoulders she ran to where her brother was waiting in the gathering darkness with an unknown young woman in his arms.

"Good girl!" he exclaimed as soon as he saw her. "Now don't ask any questions. In fact, I don't want you to speak at all. You'll understand why in a minute."

She nodded, clamping a hand briefly across her mouth to show that she was obeying him already. He set off by a path that went by the maze and she hurried after. As yet the lantern was closed, for there was still just enough light to see where they were going. She was bursting with curiosity about the silent person in his arms. The blanket had been pulled over the young woman's head and hung down over her face like a monk's cowl, which was making it impossible for her to be seen. Yet she did not complain, only making odd little gasps and sighs.

To Julia's astonishment her brother did not turn towards the house as she had expected, but went straight into the nearest entrance of the maze. Now she kept still closer to his heels, fearful of being left behind. In and out and round the box-hedges they went, she losing all sense of direction. Then when they were close to the centre of the maze he laid his burden down.

"I'm leaving you here for a few minutes, Mary."

Then he beckoned to Julia and they went together into the heart of the maze where a central octagonal stone seat awaited those needing rest after their achievement in reaching it. To Julia's further amazement, Michael put his hands to the edge of one of the sections and it rose with barely a sound of its well-oiled hinges like the lid of a box. Drawing Julia forward, he whispered that she should go down the steps that were revealed and then light them for him.

She opened the lantern and went down into the darkness. There was a rail in the wall to hold on to and when she reached the bottom of the flight she saw that there was a strongly constructed passage with stout beams leading away into the distance. She was thrilled to have been initiated into this closely held family secret. No wonder her brother had kept the girl's face covered and made sure she had no chance to see him open the entrance.

There was almost no time to wait until he reappeared with her. As soon as he was down the flight he laid his burden down again, this time on an ancient elm bench set against the wall. Then he darted back up the steps to pull the slab closed by a ring handle on the underside of it. "Lead the way, Julia," he said as he picked the girl up again.

The lantern beam danced ahead and their footsteps echoed strangely on the stone flags. Julia guessed they must be at the level of Sotherleigh's cellars and supposed it was there they would emerge, but this was not the case. They came to a series of short flights, each divided off at the landings by a stout door and finally they came to one showing a faint chink of light. Michael told Julia to tap on it. Immediately it slid back into the wall and Anne stood there with a lighted candlestick in her hand. They had reached that section of the supper room that was kept closed off by the false wall.

"Thanks be to God that you're home!" Anne exclaimed at the sight of her son.

He leaned forward to kiss her cheek. "Did Joe tell you that the last time Father was seen he was on his feet and active?"

"I was told there was no bad news, but that does not mean you know him to be safe." Her anxious face hoped for contradiction.

"Everything was so confused after the battle. He had every chance of getting away. I have good reason to believe he is with the King." It was a conviction he had formed since his own escape.

"Pursued like an animal!" she cried in distress.

"Just as it's possible this young woman is being hunted, although if that should be the case I believe the Roundheads after her will have lost all trace by now. Only yesterday, by mere chance, she escaped their efforts to end her life for being suspected of attempting to help the King. Hence the condition of her neck. As yet she is unable to speak, but she gave some signs of assent when I asked her if her name was Mary."

"The poor girl!" Anne was all compassion. "Should your father be with the King, and the accusations made against this girl be true, we shall have a debt owing to her that we can never repay. Anything she may have done to aid Charles has also aided Robert."

"My thoughts are on the same lines. There's no danger in its being known that I'm home. The Roundheads will be too busy searching for the King to trouble about those of us who are home again, but Mary must stay out of sight for the time being. I have to get her upstairs without any of the servants spotting her. Gossip about her condition could easily cost her life at the present time."

Anne nodded and went ahead to make sure the coast was clear. To Julia's chagrin she was sent back to rejoin the company in the Queen's Parlour, her mother returning briefly to explain to the visitors that one of the household was indisposed and she would be with them again as soon as possible. When Anne came back again into the hall, Michael was already at the top of the stairs. She bunched her skirts and flew up to him.

"Bring Mary into the east wing. We'll put her in the bedchamber next to mine."

There Mary was laid on the bed and the blanket removed from her. Anne thought she had never seen eyes more stark with suffering. "I'm going to look after you and get your neck well again," she said gently, showing none of the shock she had experienced at the sight of the girl's badly swollen face, black bruises having seeped up, grimly colouring the cheeks. "Michael shall stay with you while I fetch my basket of liniments and bindings."

When she had gone Michael smiled down at his mother's patient. "You're in the best hands in England now. My mother is in her element when caring for people. Nobody will find you here and all you have to do is to rest and get your voice back again. We'll have lots to talk about."

Anne had collected her basket from a cupboard when she heard the visitors departing and hurried downstairs. They had been on the point of going earlier and had taken no offence at her absence, inviting her and Katherine to dinner the following week. As soon as the door had closed after them, Anne sighed with relief and shooed Julia back into the Queen's Parlour. "Go and tell your grandmother all that has happened. Despite her outward control she is suffering from intense anxiety."

Upstairs she summoned Sarah, her personal maid, who was her own age and had been with her since she had first come to Sotherleigh as a bride. Sarah had long since proved both loyal and trustworthy. She explained the situation and Sarah echoed what Anne had said earlier.

"I'll do anything I can for someone who has suffered in the King's cause and more than likely helped the Master, however indirectly it was done."

"I knew I could count on you," Anne said gratefully.

When they entered the guest room the girl's wild gaze was fixed on Michael and followed him as he left the bedside, almost as if she were silently calling him back. No sooner had he gone than strange sounds, almost like inner sobs, came from the girl's throat. Having learned from Michael that it was at least three hours since Mary had last had a dose of the apothecary's anodyne, Anne poured out a spoonful and gave it to her.

"This will take away the pain while Sarah and I make you comfortable and dress your neck."

On going downstairs, Michael was relieved to find the visitors had gone and went first to see Katherine for a few minutes, promising to return soon and give her a full account of all that had happened. He then went to the kitchen to give the household staff such news of their menfolk as he had been able to glean and finally ordered Joe to bring two jugs of hot water to his room. When the boy arrived, Michael made sure the horses had been stabled and fed and once again impressed on Joe there must be no word about the young woman.

Joe, happy and thankful to be home, reassured of being allowed to work in the stables, and the possessor of three gold coins given in thanks for all he had done, was only too willing to swear solemnly he would never tell a soul.

When Michael brought one of the jugs of hot water to the guest room, Mary was asleep again, undressed beneath the bedcovers and with the makeshift binding removed from her neck. He stared in horror at the grotesque swelling, the bruises purple and black. "Will she ever be right again?"

"If it lies in my power she will be," Anne said firmly while Sarah poured the hot water into a Delft basin and put towels ready.

When Michael had gone, they bathed the girl from head to toe, put her into a nightgown and finally treated her neck. A soothing herbal ointment was smoothed on first to reduce the bruising, followed by a soft cambric layer and then a linen bag tight with wool to give a firm support with a final binding to hold it in place. Anne did not leave Mary alone that night but after reading Robert's letter many times over she slept on a day-bed in the room. It was always Sarah who woke her in the morning so she did not have to fear anyone else on the staff finding her absent from her bedchamber. She tended her patient several times in the night and when she went back to her own room to prepare herself for the day, she saw that Sarah had ruffled the bedclothes to make it appear that the four-poster had been slept in when the maidservant came later to see to the room.

It did not prove as difficult as Anne had feared to keep Mary hidden. Always it had been her custom during the last months before Christmas to keep locked that particular guest room where she would sew Yuletide gifts for the family and servants. Therefore the pretence that there was no other purpose than the annual one made it easier for her. The family had always been allowed to enter, if their gifts were shut away in a closet, and so the procedure went on as usual.

Anne did sew and embroider at the bedside and was thankful that the care of Mary kept her extra busy, for every morning she hoped the day would bring Robert's return and every evening she went to bed disappointed. The village sweetheart of one of the maidservants came home from Worcester, having escaped capture, and Anne gave her time off to be with him. A week later the father of another returned. He was Sotherleigh's coachman and was much changed by all that he had been through. Of the nine men who had ridden off with Robert only two more returned, both of them gardeners at Sotherleigh and, like those who had come back before them, they had endured great hardships on the way. They were able to fill in the final gaps as to the fate of the others who had been with them. Three of the four footmen had been killed, the fourth taken prisoner, and as Michael already knew, the groom had changed sides when he realised the odds would be against the King's chances of victory. None of the survivors were able to give Anne any more news of Robert than she had received from her son already, although they gave her eye-witness accounts of his courage at the forefront of the defence of the bridge before he fell from his horse and was carried from the field. Had Michael not given her reassurance that Robert's wound had not been fatal she would have feared the worst.

Mary made steady progress. She was still unable to speak but communication with her was active. From the start Anne had instigated one-sided conversations, by telling her to raise her right hand for an affirmative answer and the left for a negative. In this way, by trial and error, some picture of her background had been built up. At the first opportunity Anne offered her paper, pen and ink, but she made it clear that she could neither read nor write. So the original method had to suffice and in time it was learned that it was her widowed uncle, who with his wife had fostered her from birth, and his brother who had lost their lives that day and her grief, overwhelming at first, resurged from time to time, her eyes frequently sad and far away. She had no other family and nobody to whom she could return.

Her loneliness among strangers was a factor in bringing about the close friendship that developed between Julia and her. While she was still immobile Julia read to her and when she was able to sit comfortably against the pillows Julia taught her to play draughts and backgammon. Anne's anxiety about Robert was infectious, pervading the whole house, and Julia became increasingly fearful that she was never going to see her father again. It was something she could not confide to either her mother or grandmother, but she told Mary, who tried by miming and facial expression to urge her to keep up hope.

Although Mary was always glad to have company in her room whether it should be lively Julia, Anne with her sewing or Katherine, who related long stories of her days at Elizabeth's court, sometimes telling the same tale over and over again, it was Michael's visits that meant the most to her. Her eyes lit up at once when he appeared and she was transparently happy.

Anne went into Chichester to purchase underwear, hose and shoes for Mary, who was slimmer and taller than she, and a warm cloak with a hood for the coming winter days when it was to be hoped that the need to keep the girl hidden would be at an end. Four gowns, ordered previ-

ously for the girl from a dressmaker, were delivered in boxes to Anne's
waiting coach. While in the city Anne took hot chocolate at the Dolphin
with a friend and heard that Roundhead activity in Sussex was intense.

"They're searching for the King everywhere," her friend said in a
whisper. "It's rumoured that he's already safely abroad. Let's hope that to
be so."

Anne knew it could not be. If Robert was with the King he would
never leave England without seeing her first.

Mary was delighted with her new clothes, all the gowns able to be
fitted with the be-ribboned and lace-trimmed collars that Anne had made
for her, which came to her jaw-line and hid the supporting collar underneath. As yet she could not, and dared not, dispense with the padded one
either by night or day. Pain never entirely left her and at times she still
needed the anodyne to give her some ease. She could not sit and sew for
any length of time, although she was eager to help with the making of the
fancy silk purses, shoe rosettes and petticoat trimmings for the servants'
Christmas gifts. The skill of her fingers with a needle was proof she was
indeed a seamstress as she had indicated herself to be, and she was familiar
with every kind of stitching.

All looking glasses had been kept from her room until the swelling of
her face subsided. She proved to be quite a pretty girl, her remarkable
green eyes set wide apart, her face round with a little dimpled chin and a
very fair complexion. As soon as she was able to dress her own hair she
used a style that overcame its fineness, drawing it back farther than the
current mode and letting it fall in long silky ringlets instead of curls, the
rest gathered up into the fashionable top-knot. When Michael complimented her, saying how much the style suited her, she blushed with
pleasure.

He happened to be with her when it dawned on her that she was never
going to be able to speak again, her vocal cords damaged beyond any
repair of time or rest. She was sitting opposite him as he talked of what he
had done that morning, seeing to matters of the estate in his father's
absence, when something he said happened to draw a comparison in her
mind with the place where she had lived, and she wanted to tell him. All
along she had planned that he should be the first to hear her voice. When
her first attempt failed, she tried again, convinced that it would return this
time. He saw the horror and anguish flood her eyes as she mouthed in
vain what she wanted to say, rising slowly to her feet as if every physical
effort must be made to project her voice out of its silence.

He stood up at once and took her by the arms, able to see what she was going through. The possibility of her remaining mute had been discussed out of her hearing, but they were all hoping it would be otherwise.

"Don't be afraid," he urged. "It's early days yet."

No tears came into her eyes, but her face contracted pitifully into such a mask of torment that it tore at his most sensitive feelings.

"Mary! Don't lose heart! Not now when you've been so courageous and endured so much."

Her eyes were full of him as if he were all that stood between her and an abyss. She crumpled, reaching out, and he caught her in his arms, aware that she was shuddering with despair. He cupped her head in his hand, her forehead against his lips, and said everything he could think of to make her see that life could still be rich and fulfilled.

"This is your home. You'll never have to leave Sotherleigh until you marry and that will be by your own free will or not at all. We've made so many plans for you. We'll teach you to read and write. Julia wants you to learn all the stately dances with her when your neck no longer pains you. We want you to be happy and to look upon us as the family you have lost."

After a while her shuddering ceased and she became calmer and seemingly resigned. When he would have returned her to her chair she suddenly caught at his jacket and pressed a long kiss to his cheek, her eyes closed. *I love you!* she cried silently to him, the clean, young, outdoor smell of his skin in her nostrils. Then she drew back, abashed by her own boldness until she saw that he had taken her impassioned kiss as an expression of thanks and nothing more.

It was becoming increasingly apparent to him and his family that she should soon take her place publicly as a member of the household. So far the smuggling of food to her had been a combined effort. When she had first arrived liquids had been all she could take, and Anne had gone every night to the kitchen when the servants were asleep to sieve broth and make possets to keep hot in a hay-box in Mary's room. Later, daily portions had been taken from the family meals, but there was always a danger of this being spotted. So preliminary plans were laid and it was decided to choose a surname for her, for since she did not know the alphabet there was no way of finding out what her own name was. Various suggestions were made but Mary did not seem to care for any of them. Perhaps she was hoping they would alight on hers by chance.

"What about Twyat?" Michael asked her at last. "That's my middle name, and a family one as well, coming from a distant ancestor. Since we are going to tell everyone that you're a cousin, it would be appropriate. What do you think?"

She smiled her approval, raising her right hand. Katherine, watching her, thought to herself that the girl would have accepted anything that had links with Michael.

ON THEIR OWN, Anne and Julia decided that Mary should have a little gift to commemorate her new surname and they went off to Chichester together the next morning to see what they could find. Julia also needed new shoes, and a call was to be made at the shoe-maker's in South Street to choose both silk and leather for some new pairs. When this was done a pretty hand-glass was purchased for Mary.

While in the city they met many people they knew and all spoke of Colonel Warrender's having taken command of the search for the King in this part of Sussex, just as there had been officers appointed in other counties for the same purpose. Hundreds of Cavaliers, who had served in the Battle of Worcester, had fled to the Continent, although these were mostly of high rank or with some other special reason for evading arrest by the Parliamentarians. Those who returned home did not escape close interrogation, even if they were wounded, and when cleared of aiding or concealing the King were usually fined and often imprisoned on some pretext. This was already known at Sotherleigh, for Michael had been among the first to be questioned, summoned to Warrender Hall for the interrogation since his father and the Colonel were neighbours of long-standing, albeit on opposite sides of the conflict and with no liking for each other, not even in their boyhood days. Michael, who still needed the relief of a sling for his arm in its healing, had been questioned by Colonel Warrender as to the seriousness of the wound. Slight though it was, the Colonel had dismissed him as having been physically incapable of giving any help to the Stuart and said as much, adding strict orders forbidding him to go beyond the bounds of Sotherleigh's estate.

Nevertheless, Michael was left with the impression that his father's prolonged absence, as well as the name of Robert Pallister failing to appear on the lists of those dead, wounded or captive, was highly suspicious as far as the Parliamentarians were concerned. He was certain that a Roundhead raid could be expected at Sotherleigh whenever his father should return, and had discussed with his mother how Mary should be concealed in such an emergency.

That same evening, after the excursion to Chichester, conversation was interrupted in the Queen's Parlour when a sealed letter was handed to Anne. She recognised the hand-writing. With a qualm she knew it to be from the same friend of the family who had warned her of Captain Harding's coming to take the horses. Michael and Katherine watched her as she broke the seal and silently read the letter.

*Be on your guard*, it began. *I have discovered there is a double hunt afoot. Not only is the King being sought on all sides, but also a Cavalier, a young woman and a boy, a trio rumoured to have been seen in this area. You will understand why I am communicating with you when you view the enclosed document bearing their recent likenesses. Take warning. There is no time to waste.* It was signed with the initial G.

All colour drained from Anne's face and wordlessly she handed the letter to Michael before unfolding the enclosed document. Then she gave a faint gasp of alarm at what she saw on the printed sheet. It was headed *Top Secret* and was obviously issued only to those in command, for it stated that the three felons, whose faces had been reproduced, were to be arrested with the least possible delay and taken immediately to the nearest Parliamentary headquarters. The printed visages were roughly drawn, but Michael's face was so clear in all his features that he might have sat especially for the artist. Joe's was equally unmistakable and his hair, shown rougher and spikier than he now wore it, was exactly as it had been on the journey. As for Mary, she was the least recognisable, her tresses hanging in the disarray caused by her attempted execution, such fear in her face as to give her features a witch-like appearance and there was little to connect the drawing with the re-blooming girl she had become. Anne's hand shook as she passed the document in silence to her son.

"What is it?" Katherine questioned anxiously from her chair. Julia was not present, being upstairs reading to Mary.

Michael looked up from the drawings. "Bad news, I'm afraid, Grandmother. It looks as if the Roundhead net is closing in on Mary, Joe and myself." He noted that Mary had been named as Marion Moore and realised how he had misunderstood her first attempt to tell him who she was. "We appear to have been sighted somewhere in the environs of Chichester and probably Joe and I were recognised, but who would have seen Mary, wrapped up as she was at the bottom of the cart? Unless, of course, we were viewed from an upstairs window." Turning the paper over, he read what Anne had overlooked in her distress. "What's more, from this report the Royalist concerned seemed to have his left arm in a sling, but what really puzzles me is the sketches of our faces. I can only imagine that one of the medical students with whom we were talking for several minutes at the gibbets near St. Cross was something of a draughts-man and drew our likeness from memory when being questioned by the authorities." His solemn gaze went from his mother to Katherine and back again. "I fear that as soon as Colonel Warrender receives his copy of this document he will be heading for Sotherleigh to make his arrests."

"There's no doubt about that," Anne declared despairingly.

"Mary must be moved to a safer place of hiding. As for Joe and myself, we must ride for the coast and escape to France." He went to his mother as she gave a stifled sob and put an arm about her shoulders. "I'm afraid there's no alternative. I'd take Mary with me if I could, but she can't ride with her neck in need of support. She must be transferred immediately to the underground chamber and kept there until all danger is past."

Katherine interrupted from her chair. "No!" she expostulated angrily, rising to her feet as swiftly as if the force of her outrage had given a renewed mobility to her stiffened joints, all pain forgotten. "It would mean revealing the secret of the Queen's Door to an outsider! You kept it from the girl when you came home with her, but to house her there in this new crisis is out of the question. I forbid it!"

Michael addressed her quietly but sternly, his arm still giving Anne support. "In my father's absence I am master here. It is my word that shall be obeyed. We can't keep the secret to ourselves when a human life depends on the knowledge of the Queen's Door. It shall not be denied to Mary, who wasn't able even to tell us her true name when she came here."

"Why ever did you bring that creature to Sotherleigh?" she flung at him madly, her voice high-pitched.

"If I had my time over again I would do the same."

Katherine crumpled. "What are we to call her now then?"

"She will have to keep the name of Mary Twyat to remove any possible suspicion when eventually she can take her place as a member of the household. Now I'll go and tell her what is to happen."

Anne nodded. "I'll come with you."

Katherine had sunk down into her chair again. For the first time ever she felt control of Sotherleigh pass from her hands. It had not happened when she signed it over to Robert, seeing it as no more than a gesture, while knowing privately that as long as he was away at sea it was she who was the beat of Sotherleigh's heart. Later, during his absence at the war, she had played lip-service to Anne as mistress of the house, but she had had the secret knowledge of what she had thought of as Harry Warrender's bequest and knew that nothing had really changed. Now, suddenly, she had a vision of Sotherleigh slipping away from her and the family into nothingness and it filled her with despair.

She felt Anne's hand descend comfortingly upon her shoulder, sensed her daughter-in-law's uncertain hovering, and then heard her depart in a rustle of skirts, following Michael who was already on his way to Mary's room.

For what seemed a long time Katherine gazed unseeingly into the fire. She had heard the expression often enough of the ground being cut from under one's feet and she understood its full meaning now. When the door creaked again she thought Anne had returned, but it was Julia. Abruptly she turned in her chair and gripped the child by the shoulders. "Promise me that you will keep Sotherleigh as securely as the Queen's gown!"

Julia frowned, puzzled by what had been said. "But Sotherleigh is not mine and never can be. In any case Michael and Joe will only be taking refuge on the Continent for a little while. Just till it's safe again."

In spite of the tumult of her feelings Katherine spared the child her certainty that it would be years instead of months before Michael would be able to return. She gave Julia a sharp little shake to emphasise the importance of her words.

"If anything untoward should happen, promise me that you'll be the keeper of this house for your brother and his heirs!"

Julia had never seen her grandmother in such a state. There were tears glinting in the old lady's eyes and her whole face was working. While upstairs, she had heard all that had happened and how Michael and Joe must flee abroad while Mary was hidden, but although she knew she should make the promise her grandmother asked of her, instinctively she baulked at it. She wanted to live in her own house when she was grown up, that magical abode that Christopher was going to design for her one day. She had come to see herself as growing away from Sotherleigh, always loving it as her place of birth, but looking out on wider horizons from windows that were hers.

"Julia! Answer me!" Katherine's cry of appeal was so distraught that Julia could no longer hold back.

"Yes, Grandmother! I'll keep Sotherleigh safe! Never fear!" She flung her arms round Katherine's neck and they hugged each other tightly. Clasped as they were, Katherine did not see that the child's eyes were troubled. Julia was hoping that she would never have to make a choice between Sotherleigh and the Wren house that somehow symbolised her freedom. For she knew as the daughter of a Cavalier that one's word once given remained a bond for ever.

# SIX

*I*N THE STABLES Joe was saddling up three horses. They were all recent purchases, for the end of the fighting meant that the Roundheads were no longer on the prowl to commandeer any good mounts that came their way. He was heart-sore at having to leave behind the black horse that had done such good service on the journey from Worcester and the brown one that had pulled the cart, for he had come to think of them as his own, but neither was as speedy as those he was making ready for departure. There was no need for excessive stealth in what he was doing, the head groom and the coachman being at supper in the kitchen. It was as well, for he was in a furious temper, kicking things about and occasionally thumping a fist against the side of a stall in livid frustration.

"It's all the fault of Turnip-head!" he raged to the twitching ears of the horses. He had not seen Mary since the night he and Michael had arrived home with her and he still pictured her as she had looked then. "This is all 'er fault! I don't want to leave 'ere. With time I'd 'ave been top man. But oh, no! You-know-who 'ad to ruin everything for me. I don't want to live with foreigners. They won't catch me eating frogs!"

He swung a lady's side-saddle onto the third horse. It was of padded velvet with a high back and had been used by Anne many times. Into it was to be placed an effigy of Mary and he turned to where it was propped against the stall, looking remarkably life-like. The mistress, her lady's maid and Miss Julia had constructed it from a bolster, a ribbon tied near the top to give the effigy a head and neck, and then they had clothed it in garments from a chest of amateur theatrical and charade garments. A dark green cloak with a cowl-like hood concealed the lack of features while a yellow wig revealed sufficient hair to be noticeable, the gown in plain blue wool over petticoats. To give backbone to the figure and keep the head upright Michael had constructed a fixture of wire and wood.

"Come on, Turnip-head," Joe growled savagely, lifting up the effigy and settling it in the lady's saddle. It had to be strapped into position and the high back of the saddle gave excellent support. The arms, which were white stockings padded with soft linen, had sleeves to the wrist where gauntlet gloves hid a lack of fingers. These were tied to the reins. Apart from the final adjusting of a piece of black cord to the horse's bridle, which he himself would hold at the other end, everything was ready, even his saddle-bags and his master's packed and in place. It would not be long now. He sniffed a great deal as he completed all his tasks, telling himself he was getting a cold, but that did not explain the watering of his eyes. Rage and misery and fear of the sea that he would have to cross gripped his guts until he had to retreat again to the privy behind the stables.

As soon as the servants had settled to supper in the kitchen Julia, at Michael's bidding, led the way with a candle as he carried Mary downstairs and through the Queen's Door. At the foot of the steps leading to the subterranean passage was a chamber where she would stay for the time being. It had proved necessary to let Sarah in on the family secret, which had increased Katherine's anger, but Anne knew that her lady's maid would be invaluable help in the weeks to come. They had gone ahead together to clean the room, make up the bed and see that everything was made as comfortable as possible for its new inhabitant.

When Mary was set down on her feet she looked around as far as she could in a daze. The room was square and, according to what she had been told, had some kind of ventilation out into the shaft of a disused well. For that reason a charcoal burner could supply her with heat and it was already aglow in its deep alcove, which was, like the walls, built of stone. In addition to the bed, which was hung with freshly unpacked velvet bed-hangings still showing some creases, there were two chairs with cushions, a table on which Sarah was setting out some supper, and a cupboard into which Anne was folding away clothes that Mary knew to be hers. A smaller cupboard was open to show her that she had been supplied with bread, preserves and pickles beside some jars holding other foods. On the floor two rugs, obviously brought from the house, made muted patches of colour. Half a dozen pikes, a rack of muskets and some swords in their scabbards were by the door into the passage and another door leading off the chamber led to a closet where there was a jug and ewer on a stand and a necessary closed stool. When this refuge had been planned, thought had been given to the comfort as well as the defence of whoever might need to hide in it.

Mary forced herself to indicate it was all to her liking, knowing that the best was being done for her in the circumstances. When she had heard she must go into deeper hiding her immediate reaction had been an inner rejoicing, believing that Michael was to share it with her, but upon hearing he was about to depart across the sea she had become stunned by misery.

*I'll go with you!* she had mouthed desperately, but he had shaken his head.

"Joe and I will be riding to the coast for our lives, Mary. This time there can be no cart or any moderation of speed. In any case, you'll be far safer here. Within a few weeks the plan we laid will be carried out and you'll be a free girl again. By taking an effigy of you with us all will believe you and Joe and I left together. There'll be nothing to connect you with the past ever again."

*When shall you be back?*

He had become adept at understanding her, as had the others. "As soon as it is safe. With luck, exiles will be pardoned one day and then I'll return, have no doubt about it."

Anne's gentle voice broke into her unhappy reverie. "I hope you won't be too uncomfortable here, Mary. You can be sure that Julia, Sarah and I will keep you company as much as possible. In the daytime you can go out into the middle of the maze for fresh air, except when I let you know that the head gardener will be clipping the hedges there. Otherwise there is no risk of you being seen by anyone. I advise you most strongly not to venture into the paths or else you would lose yourself very quickly." Her expression was considerate and concerned. "You won't mind sleeping here on your own, will you?"

*No,* Mary mouthed. What did it matter where she was or what happened to her when Michael was going away? She turned to him and he gave a nod.

"Yes, it's time to say farewell."

Anne, seeing the tragic expression on the girl's face, took Julia with her from the room and accompanied by Sarah they went back into the house. On his own with Mary, Michael said many things to cheer her and encourage her to look to the future. His own feelings at having to leave his home, his family and his country were too agonising for him to think of much else. In no way did he blame her for being the cause of his having to take flight. As he had said to Katherine, he had no regrets about saving her and what had come afterwards was no fault of hers.

"There's something you can do for me," he said, fully aware of how much she had come to depend on him. "It's not going to be easy for my mother and grandmother and even for Julia if my father should be captured or forced to go into exile too. Do whatever you can to cheer them in their darker moments. Try to keep their spirits up." He saw that she was grateful for this charge, not realising he thought it would help her as much as the others to have some small duty to perform on his behalf. "Now I must go. Wish me well, Mary Twyat."

Her eyes, glittering like sea-pools, gave him his answer. He bent his head to kiss her cheek, but she drew back slightly to indicate he should kiss her lips, for she could not tilt them upwards as any other girl would have done due to her stiffened collar. Acceding to her request, he kissed her lips softly and would have drawn away again, but she flung her arms about him as if she would never let him go, kissing him back passionately. His lusty nature was stirred and he held her hard to him, moving his mouth against hers and discovering her in a new light. He had to force himself to break away and knew regret that this revelation had come too late.

"Time is running out, Mary. I can delay no longer. I wish you a speedy recovery from your injury and all the happiness you deserve."

*God be with you! My only love!*

Whether or not he noticed what she tried to convey to him it was impossible to tell, for he went swiftly from the room. She remained standing where he had left her long after his footsteps had ceased to be heard and all was quiet. Tears coursed down her face. She could not even bow her head to cry, trapped as she was in the hateful supportive collar she could not do without. No matter how long Michael should be away, she would go on loving him until the day came when they would meet again.

In the house Michael had parted from his family and hastened to the stables where Joe awaited him. Anne was addressing the servants, who had been summoned from the kitchen to the Great Hall as they always were for important announcements concerning the whole household.

"After the Battle of Worcester," Anne said as evenly as she could manage in her agitated state, "my son and Joe Berry gave assistance to a Royalist young woman who had helped save the life of the King and thus flouted Parliamentary law. Her name is Marion Moore and she has been hiding with sympathisers. Now there's been a new development and she and Mr. Michael and Joe are in danger of their lives and must take flight for France. Without doubt, we can expect a visit at any time from Colonel Warrender and his troopers, but there's no need for any of you to be afraid, or to hold back from saying anything as you did when the Roundheads came for the horses. Speak openly. The more you tell them of my son's departure the less likely we are to be troubled by further futile searches. Is that understood?" As she scanned the nodding faces, Anne knew that the strength sustaining her could only be heaven-sent, for how else could she have faced Michael's departure with no knowledge of when he would be able to return, let alone make this speech? "Good. Now it has always been the custom at Sotherleigh for the household to see off any member of the family about to set out on a long journey and I see no reason why this time should be different from any other."

She led the way and the servants followed, whispering among themselves at the thought of Joe being involved in such an adventure. Katherine, wrapped in a cloak, was already waiting by the door, her face deeply sad from this parting with her grandson. Outside, the usual formation fell into place with the family on the wide top step and the servants on either side of the flight. The shadows of all fell across the courtyard in the rectangle of light thrown by the candle glow within.

After a few moments there came the clatter of horses' hooves from the direction of the stables and the three riders came into view just beyond the candle-range. The lantern on the wall gave enough light for them to be seen, Michael riding in front with Joe and the third party riding alongside. The servants strained their eyes at the female figure, but as they said to one another afterwards Miss Moore could not have been acquainted with the ladies of the household, for she neither turned her head nor waved as Mr. Michael did. Joe, too cast down by his departure, could not bring himself to glance at those on the steps out of fear of blubbering like a baby. As the three riders turned into the drive the servants glimpsed the white frills of Marion Moore's petticoats fluttering and that was the last to be seen as the darkness swallowed up the departing escapees.

Colonel Warrender did not come that night or the next day. Anne was certain that it had been his document of notification to arrest that the family friend had intercepted and sent to her. When another day passed she felt as if a cloud had been lifted, for it was almost certain that no news was good news and that Michael and Joe were surely safely on their way to France. Had they been arrested it would have become known by now.

That night Colonel Warrender and twenty armed soldiers descended on Sotherleigh. The women servants screamed, running about panic-stricken in their night clothes, for there had been no knocking on the door for admittance but a smashed entry through the library windows to take the house by surprise.

Only Katherine had not been in her bed. Since Michael's departure she had been prepared for this intrusion and had dozed each night in her marriage chair by the fireside in her parlour, a warm violet robe over her nightgown, for she was intent on maintaining her dignity. She was aware of being an imposing figure as she stood grandly by her chair when Harry Warrender's son burst into her apartment, his drawn sword in his hand.

"Your father would not have approved of this rough invasion!" she declared scornfully in her most cutting tones as if he were still the snivelling boy she had despised for his bullying ways.

"This is Parliament business, madam!" He was square-jawed and granite-featured with a crimson colour in his cheeks much heightened by the tension of this raid. "You'll not hide your traitorous grandson from me!"

He went plunging about her rooms, snatching at hangings and throwing doors open. Julia appeared and came running to her in fear.

"Do not be alarmed, child. These intruders will soon be gone." She sat down again, cuddling her granddaughter to her protectively. Later when the search had proved fruitless, interrogations took place and every servant gave a full account of having seen with his or her own eyes the departure of Michael and Joe with a young woman. Imagination took flight and details of her appearance were added that left Colonel Warrender in no doubt at all that the three quarries had slipped the net. He also questioned Katherine and Anne closely about Robert's possible whereabouts. Both took hope from this unwitting confirmation that he was still alive and well, and undoubtedly with the King.

When morning came, Anne, still pale and shaken from all she had been through, went to see Mary to tell her of all that had happened in the night. The girl conveyed her thankfulness that Michael was safely away and Anne was momentarily overcome. At once Mary poured her some hot posset, which had been heating on the charcoal burner. Anne sipped it and grew calmer again. Mary liked having the facilities to prepare drinks and some meals for herself. Not only did it ease the family's problem about keeping her fed, but it gave her something to do. She had also been practising the first letters of the alphabet which Julia had taught her and she showed them to Anne, who nodded with approval.

"Well done. One day I hope you will be able to tell us, either in your own words or on paper, of your years of growing up and of your own family."

*I hope so,* Mary's lips replied silently.

After Anne had gone Mary put on a cloak and went at her slow pace along the passage to the steps that would lead her up into the heart of the maze. She could not walk with any speed for fear of jerking her neck and had all unconsciously adopted a gliding step, which, unknown to her, was very graceful. She did not mind her incarceration; there was nothing frightening about her underground quarters. In fact, she felt extraordinarily safe there, and had Michael been able to share her seclusion she would have thought it paradise.

She stepped into the open air and breathed in deeply its crisp, autumnal aromas. For exercise she strolled to and fro past the octagonal seat and then around it. In her thoughts she tried to follow Michael on his journey, wondering if he had landed yet in France and what that country would be like. She hoped that he would miss her and think of her often. He had said that with time he would try to send a letter home and that would be a milestone along the way to his return.

She had never received a letter in her life. Until she and her uncles had been instrumental in saving the King from capture she had never moved out of the little Worcestershire village where she was born. Orphaned at fourteen, she had moved into the nearby home of her mother's brothers, both kindly widowers with a carpenters' shop. She had kept house for them and taken in sewing, her mother having trained her to be a seamstress. It was her first experience of living in a Puritan household, her parents having been Anglicans, and the peaceful, orderly life suited her quiet nature. Her uncles had had many anxious days under the religious bigotry that had marked Charles I's reign, but neither could they tolerate the extremist methods of the present Puritan government. They had pinned their hopes of full freedom of worship on the new young King and for him they had given their lives.

A long sad sigh escaped her. Now all who had been most dear to her had gone, but she would cling to the hope that with Michael it would not be for ever.

. . .

DAILY ROUTINE settled once more on Sotherleigh. What had become apparent to everyone was that Katherine had deteriorated sharply since the night of her grandson's departure. She had had to be helped up the stairs to her apartment that night, having always managed them unaided before; since then she had not come down again. Although still mentally alert, no less observant than before, her strength seemed to have ebbed from her body and she spent most of her time in her marriage chair by the fire, or tottering about her apartment in a determined attempt to keep mobile.

Anne, beside herself with worry about her son as well as her husband, found succour only in her embroidery, which she took up either to Katherine's room or to Mary's. The one bright spark in the overcast lives of the women of Sotherleigh was that with every passing day it became more certain that Michael and Joe had slipped safely away to France. They were sure that Colonel Warrender, being the man he was, would have taken satisfaction in letting them know if the Master of Sotherleigh's son had been apprehended.

On the morning of the thirteenth of October, when Anne was visiting Mary, there came a knock on Katherine's door. Julia entered and presented herself with her customary bob of a curtsy. She had checked in her own room that her hair was tidy, her gown neat and her fingernails clean, for the old lady had keen eyes and she wanted nothing to distract from the purpose of her visit.

"I have a request to make, Grandmother," she began, standing with her back straight and her chin uptilted.

Katherine, sitting in her marriage chair, a rug over her knees, regarded the child quizzically. "Oh? What might that be?"

"Now that Michael has gone away for what everyone fears will be a long time, I feel I should be told the plan of the maze."

"Do you indeed?"

"I'm ten years old tomorrow. That means that I'm almost grown up and I'm ready to shoulder a third responsibility. I've two already. You've made me custodian of Queen Elizabeth's gown in time to come and the same with Sotherleigh, if the need should arise. If I knew the way in and out of the maze I could visit Mary without having to dodge servants to get through the Queen's Door without being seen."

"But Mary should only be in hiding for a little while longer if everything can be worked out soon."

Julia dropped her formal manner and flung out her hands in appeal. "Please, Grandmother! I don't want to be kept in ignorance any longer."

Katherine chuckled. "You're an impatient young miss. As it happens I have a plan ready to give you on your birthday morning, but it must remain here in my apartment where you may study it to your heart's content. At other times I shall keep it under lock and key."

"Oh, thank you, Grandmother!" Julia kissed Katherine on the cheek and then went dancing from the room to tell her mother about it. She did not think it strange that she had not told Anne about the promises made about the gown and Sotherleigh, for somehow she had accepted without question that these matters were entirely between her grandmother and herself. It was wholly instinctive, no thought or discussion given to it, simply a natural development of the bond that dispensed with the age gap between them.

It was the morning when her tutor was due to give her lessons and she just had time to tell her mother about the plan of the maze being promised her when he arrived. The Reverend Oswald Garner was a thin, scholarly-looking man with a gift for teaching that would never have seen the light of day, beyond his own children, if he had not been cast out of Chichester Cathedral by Parliament.

"Good day, sir," Julia greeted him. "My lessons are prepared."

"I'm pleased to hear it. Await me in the library."

She scampered off and he took a letter from his pocket which he handed to Anne. It was he who delivered all the communications that came from the family friend and she thanked him for it. Leaving him to follow Julia to the library, she went into the Queen's Parlour and opened the letter. Its message was brief: *Take coach for the sign of the George and Dragon at Houghton. R. will be there tomorrow.*

She caught her breath. It could only mean one thing. Robert was coming home! Light-heartedly she sprang up the stairs and went to Katherine.

"I've had a message that I'm to meet Robert tomorrow! Read this communication for yourself." She handed the letter to her mother-in-law. "Is it not wonderful news? The coach is to bring him home in secrecy."

Katherine lowered the message to her lap and removed her spectacles. "If Robert is with the King, as we have believed all along," she said in a thin, tightly controlled voice, "he will be on his way abroad. Should he stay, it would mean the Tower for him. Perhaps even the block."

Anne clutched the back of a chair for support. "We could hide him! The underground chamber is there."

"To conceal him for years?" Katherine shook her head. "It was only ever meant as a temporary refuge and a route of escape. The risk is as great as it would have been for Michael."

A barrier came up in Anne's mind. She had always supposed that Robert would find some way of reaching the house to say goodbye if he had to flee abroad. There would have been a day or two, perhaps even a week to be with him once more. She refused to believe she had mis-read the message. Robert had wanted transport home and she would provide it.

"Forgive me for saying it, but I'm sure you're wrong in this matter." She was smiling, unaware that there was a look as brittle as glass about her that was giving her mother-in-law cause for concern.

Katherine could cope with her own frailty, accepting it as a natural outcome of old age under stress, but she feared for Anne, having observed previously how the strain of everything had been taking a heavy toll on her daughter-in-law. Anne was not one to sway compromisingly to the winds of misfortune, but was conditioned by her whole upbringing to stand rigidly in the hope that all would soon be calm again. The danger was that she might easily snap with an increase of pressure.

"I shall set out this afternoon," Anne continued. "The hamlet of Houghton is not many miles away, but I want to be there overnight and ahead of time in case Robert should arrive earlier than expected. Watch for our return tomorrow."

"What if pursuit is closing in on him? Remember that Houghton is on the route to the coast. There may be significance in that. I am sure that Robert's instruction that you come by coach is for your protection. In fact, I am going to write a letter addressed to my cousin in Steyning that you can show as proof you are on your way to visit her should you be stopped and questioned by those searching for the King."

Anne took little notice. "Thank you for your consideration," she said, "but Robert will be safe at Sotherleigh for a while at least. He would never leave before coming home first. I've known that all along."

"Take Julia with you," Katherine urged. If Anne's optimism should be doomed to disappointment, the child would prove a stabilising influence and in any case Julia had a right to see her father again before he went farther afield. For herself, Katherine yearned with all her being to see her son once more, well aware that time was against her for any future meetings, but she knew she could not get downstairs, let alone ride any distance in a coach. "Julia would enjoy the outing and be company for you," she added to emphasise what she had said.

"On this point you are right," Anne agreed after her usual little show of consideration to assert her position. "Robert will be so pleased to see Julia that it will help to soften the blow when I tell him that Michael has left England. It will also be a great treat for her to meet her father again on her birthday, making it an occasion she will always remember."

That afternoon both Anne and Julia came to see Katherine before they set out. Julia admitted to not having been able to eat her dinner for excitement and Anne was like a girl again, a flush to her cheeks and eyes sparkling with anticipation. It seemed to Katherine that her daughter-in-law had become as blinkered as any cart-horse, refusing to see, or even contemplate, anything but a pleasing outcome to the forthcoming meeting with Robert.

Katherine reached out and cupped Julia's animated face between her hands. "Give my dearest love to your father." Something of her seriousness and depth of emotion reached her granddaughter, for the froth of frivolous high spirits melted away and the lovely little face became almost adult in its wisdom, showing that the child had grasped the fact that coming events might not prove to be the holiday her mother expected.

"I will, Grandmother."

At the door Julia, following in Anne's wake, paused on her own to give a backwards glance at Katherine in an exchange of perfect understanding. "Take care of your mama," Katherine implored in husky tones. The child nodded and went out, closing the door behind her.

The road to Houghton lay through some of the county's loveliest countryside amid the rise and fall of the slopes of the Downs. Along some stretches of the narrow lanes the branches of the trees mingled overhead to form caverns of russet, crimson and gold while fallen leaves fluttered up from the horses' hooves and the coach wheels like bright butterflies. Drawing near to the hamlet of Houghton the road climbed high, making the horses strain on their traces. There were sweeping views of soft meadowland and the chequered fields of small farms, clusters of thatched cottages and stretches of rich woodland, all tinselled by the late rays of the afternoon sun.

Then the sharp dip down the hill to Houghton began, the coachman applying the brakes. Julia, putting her head out of the coach window, saw the tavern lying ahead where the road eased out to level ground again. It was huddled close to the roadside, a deep-thatched, black-timbered and rosy brick building of good size. Its sign hung from an iron bracket and was newly painted, St. George's armour gleaming and the Dragon puffing clouds of shining grey smoke and a scarlet tongue of fire.

"We're here, Mama."

The coach drew up outside the door. Anne and Julia alighted to enter the low-beamed taproom where a cheerful fire blazed on the open hearth. The landlord made them welcome and his wife showed them upstairs to a bedchamber, assuring them that accommodation would be found for their coachman above the stables.

"Have you many travellers staying at the present time?" Anne asked as she glanced about the room, which was simply but adequately furnished, a cosy warmth prevailing from the chimney breast that passed through into the roof.

"No, madam. You and your little girl are the only ones. But we can be very busy at times."

Anne was certain this was a Royalist household, or else Robert would never have come near. "I'm expecting to meet my husband here. Would you let me know immediately if a gentleman arrives?" She hesitated briefly. "He may not be using the same name as mine. These are troubled times for Royalists."

The woman smiled reassuringly. "Have no fear, madam. We're loyal to the Black Boy here. Every night behind locked doors we drink a toast to His Majesty."

"I should like to partake in that little ceremony."

"You are more than welcome to do that."

In the taproom, tables for meals were set at one end, and when Anne and Julia ate their supper within the seclusion of high-backed settles they kept an eye on the door for whoever entered. Mostly the customers were local farm workers and a game warden or two and nobody paid them any attention. Afterwards they sat by the fire until Julia fell asleep and had to be woken for Anne to take her up to bed where she slept again as soon as the covers were over her. Downstairs again, when the tavern closed for the night, Anne was invited into the innkeeper's own parlour where he poured out five measures of sack: one for himself, the rest for his wife, his two grown-up sons and Anne. Together they stood in a circle and he proposed the toast.

"Here's health to His Majesty, God bless him!"

They all raised their glasses high and then drank. The Spanish wine was strong and although the others knocked theirs back quickly, Anne took longer until the last drop was gone. She had not expected to sleep that night, but as soon as she lay in bed the sack acted like a sleeping draught and it was bright morning before she woke.

Nobody had arrived in the night and after breakfast Anne sat by one of the taproom windows to watch the road. Julia went to the stables where there was a litter of puppies to keep her amused. After a while Anne strolled a little way up the hill, hoping to meet Robert on the way, but although some traffic went past and a local squire on horseback doffed his hat to her there was no sign of the man she awaited. It was nearly noon and she had gone upstairs to fetch a shawl, feeling increasingly shivery with nervousness, when she thought she heard horses. Her hopes had risen at the sound so many times already during the morning that she did not rush back to the stairs as she might otherwise have done. Then the voice of the innkeeper's wife came calling up to her.

"Mrs. Pallister! Come down! The King is here!"

She flew down the narrow flight in time to see the innkeeper carrying four large foaming tankards outside to the road. Rushing after him, she saw the King and three gentlemen on horseback, one of whom she recognised but the other two were strangers to her. Disappointment struck at her heart. Robert was not with them!

"Sire!" She curtsied deeply to the King where he sat in the saddle. He looked travel-worn and weary, thin in the face and sunken-eyed with his hair cropped as short as a Roundhead's, his clothes plain and his hat far from new. "May God be thanked for keeping you safe from harm."

He gave her a serious smile of enormous charm. "We thank you, madam. Your pardon that we are in great haste and need to be on our way as soon as possible." He raised his tankard to her while helping himself to a thick slice of bread with good yellow cheese from the platter that the innkeeper's wife was holding up for him.

"I am Mrs. Robert Pallister and I had hoped to find my husband with you." She saw a serious look come into his eyes and knew immediately that something was wrong. Close to panic, she turned to the other man she recognised, who had been dismounting as she came outside. He was Colonel Gunter, the old friend of the family who had sent her the secret messages, and his face was grave. "George! Where is Robert? What has happened? You said he would be with you!"

"So I had believed at the time I sent word to you. He is still coming here, but at his own pace. He has been acting as scout for the King and late yesterday he ran into trouble. Colonel Warrender and his men shot at him in what appeared to have been an ambush. At first his wound did not seem to be serious, even less severe than that which he suffered at Worcester, but he took a turn for the worse this morning some while after we had started the last lap of the King's journey to a ship waiting to sail for France. We had to leave him back along the road when he could not keep up."

"Dear God! Is he alone?"

"No. By sheer good luck we met a squire of my acquaintance and he volunteered to see that your husband gets here."

Vaguely she remembered the man who had greeted her an hour or more ago. "I'll take the coach and find him!"

"Do that, Anne. I fear he must be bleeding internally."

One of the other two gentlemen in their saddles spoke up. "His Majesty is ready to leave, Colonel. We cannot delay."

George kissed Anne's hand and then swung himself back into the saddle. The King had a last word for her.

"You and your family can be proud of your husband, madam. He is a brave man and should be remembered for it."

He wheeled his horse about and rode away, his companions with him. She saw that half a dozen people had collected and they gave him a cheer as he went. Her coachman was there and she did not have to give him any instructions. "I'll have the coach out in front of the inn in a jiffy," he said at once.

Julia was among those present, having come at a run at the King's arrival. She had heard most of what had been said and had drawn close without Anne being aware of it. "Let's get ready, Mama," she said starkly. "There's no time to waste."

Earlier that morning Anne had repacked the few things she had brought with her. She had paid the innkeeper and was outside with Julia as the coach appeared, others having lent the coachman a hand in the circumstances. Later Anne did not remember anything of this departure in her daze of fright. All she did recall was the coachman's shout when a few miles farther on Robert was sighted.

She sprang from the coach. He was slumped in the saddle, watched over by the squire riding close at hand to support him by the arm when necessary. He looked up when he heard her call and managed a smile.

"My dear," he said weakly, "how glad I am to see you. I'm in a sorry state, I'm afraid."

"Don't talk. There'll be plenty of time later."

She watched anxiously as the coachman and the squire eased him down from the saddle and together lifted him into the coach. He sank back into her arms where she had seated herself to support him and reached a hand to Julia, having just seen her. "I didn't expect to find you here, my child."

"We're taking you home to Sotherleigh, Father," Julia said tremulously, taking his hand into both of hers. "You'll soon get better there."

"I'm sure I will." His voice was weak. "I know there's no place I would rather be."

"Grandmother sent you her most loving greetings."

He gave a little smile again. "Is she well?"

"Yes."

"Good. Why is Michael not here with you?"

Anne intervened. "Hush, dearest. Rest for a while."

He obeyed without protest, exhausted by the brief exchange. Sotherleigh. He was to be there at last. It came into his mind's eye with a new-built look to it as he first remembered it in childhood and then the nightmare of the past weeks swept away that bright glimpse. He and Charles and the others who had been with them from time to time had been hunted relentlessly. They owed their lives to ordinary people who had risked all manner of dangers to help them. The King had endured much, once being hidden for a whole night in a cramped space behind a panel, a terrible ordeal for a tall man, for he could neither sit nor stand; on another occasion he had had to perch for hours in an oak tree while the Roundheads looking for him had passed to and fro under the branches. In addition, the King had been disguised as a woodman and then as a servant; he had starved in hedgerows and been drenched by rain, chased as an intruder by a miller and spent nights without sleep. Worst of all the discomforts were the borrowed shoes, never large enough for his feet, and the royal heels and toes had been rubbed raw and bleeding.

Robert felt Anne smooth his brow as he lay propped in her arms. There had been times when he thought he was never going to see her again. He had shared many of the King's hardships and had eventually adopted the role of a scout, which had plunged him into constant danger. It was he who had summoned George Gunter from his Sussex home to help him locate a ship for the King. But that was all fading away. He was going home to Sotherleigh where the windows vied with the flints in the walls in catching the sunlight. Why had he been away? His thoughts were becoming confused. It could only mean he had been to sea again. But it must be his last voyage because Anne was with him now. So young. So gentle.

For Anne the journey seemed endless. The coachman was being careful not to jolt the wheels too much, and when the road was rough he maintained a crawling pace. It was to her huge relief that she saw the coach was passing through the gates of Sotherleigh.

"We're home, my darling," she said softly to Robert when the house came in sight.

"Father is asleep, Mama," Julia whispered.

Anne, bending slightly to look into his face, saw that he would never wake again.

# SEVEN

*T*WO DAYS before the funeral a fisherman from the hamlet of Bognor arrived to see Anne. He had landed Michael and Joe in France and had been paid, not only for the voyage but to let her know that all was well with them.

"I'd have been here before now," he explained, "but the herring shoals were keeping me busy."

She was only grateful that he had come in the midst of her sorrow and saw that he was fed, for he had walked all the way, and rewarded him again for what he had done for her son and her servant.

Many people attended Robert's funeral and afterwards at Sotherleigh Anne received them. It had become widely known that her husband had been on the King's business and that Colonel Warrender was responsible for his death. This did not stop a few Parliamentarians from being at the funeral, for they were men who had known Robert as a friend and neighbour in happier times and wished to pay their last respects to him at a personal level, only refraining from calling at the house. Christopher Wren was among those notified of what had happened, but Anne knew there was little chance of her letter reaching Oxford in time for him to attend the funeral, and this proved to be the case. Several cousins came from Steyning and others from places no great distance away and they stayed overnight.

The presence of these house-guests caused Anne's maid, Sarah, to use her initiative for a certain purpose. Anne and Katherine could not be consulted in their grief, and yet a chance had presented itself that should not be missed. She took some black clothes of her own down to Mary in the underground chamber.

"Put these on quickly now," she instructed. "I'm going to get you into the house among the mourners and make it appear that you are a relative come for the funeral. Then you'll stay on."

Mary, supposing Sarah had been sent by Anne, obeyed. Michael had had another plan that involved smuggling her out of the grounds and then, since by that time he was bonded to keep to his own land, she was to return riding pillion behind Joe on horseback, supposedly collected from a stage-coach that had brought her to Chichester. With his and Joe's hasty departure this plan had been shelved indefinitely and Mary could see that Sarah's was a good one, even though the means of bringing it about were the last she would ever have wanted. The black gown fitted her well enough, but she realised as soon as she had it on that the neckline would not take any of her fancy collars that covered her neck support. Sarah, busily packing Mary's clothes and other possessions into a piece of baggage she had brought with her, saw the girl's dilemma.

"There's no help for it but you will have to remove your neck collar."

When Mary made a show of vehement protest, Sarah lost patience. "Do you want to help the family who have been so good to you, or don't you? This scheme will save putting them into extra danger on your behalf, because it's simple and straightforward."

*Let me wear a shawl,* Mary mouthed, miming at the same time.

"You don't have a black one and neither have I. You'll have to do as I say." Sarah took pride in being nearer to her mistress in the hierarchy of the household than any other servant, there being no housekeeper or butler as there had been before the outbreak of war, and so felt entitled to order Mary about in these special circumstances. "There can't be anything wrong with your neck now. It's almost seven weeks since Mr. Michael saved you, and bruising and swelling doesn't last for ever. Hurry! There's no time to be lost!"

There was less need for urgency than she made out, but she could see that Mary would have to be rushed into discarding the collar or panic would take over and the girl would not budge. As soon as Mary's trembling fingers had unfastened it, Sarah whisked the collar away.

"There! You have a pretty neck! Not a mark on it. The gown's falling collar suits you well." She took Mary's hand firmly into hers to save any drawing back at the last moment. "Come along. Pick up that candle to light the way. We have to be quick!"

Carrying the baggage in her other hand, she led Mary up the steps and through the Queen's Door into the section of the room presently closed off by the false wall. She opened it to let them both slip through and Mary blew out the candle, setting it down on the small dining table. From behind the double doors leading into the Great Hall there came a muted buzz of voices from those who had come back from church and the interment and were about to sit down to the dinner prepared for them. Sarah gave Mary final instructions.

"Go in there. Nobody will notice you. They'll all be busy finding seats. Meanwhile I'll take your baggage up to one of the guestrooms." She gave Mary a little push. "Now!"

Mary, shaking with nervousness and feeling naked and unprotected without her collar, made an inconspicuous entry into the Great Hall. It was as Sarah had said it would be. She blended in, just another mourner going to the table. When she sat down by Julia not even those close at hand observed the child's start of surprise.

"Your neck, Mary! Is it well now?"

For a while afterwards Mary did continue to wear her support collar within the privacy of her room until her confidence increased as her condition continued to improve. Although she was always to have some discomfort at certain angles of her head and neck, her collar, once thrown away, was never needed again.

All the servants assumed, without even discussing the matter, that Mary Twyat had arrived when the other mourners poured into the house. When it became known that she would be living at Sotherleigh permanently, having been bereaved herself quite recently with no other family to care for her, she did become a topic of conversation in the kitchen, especially since the fact that she was dumb was of exceptional interest. Cook assured them all authoritatively that it would have been an affliction since birth.

"That's when it 'appens. I've 'eard of other cases."

"She walks a bit stiff, don't she?" one maidservant remarked.

"Proud, most likely."

Another maidservant sniffed. "She better not come any fancy ways with me."

"Where's she been put?"

"In the bedchamber next to Miss Julia's."

"That's a nice room. She'll be comfortable there. But no chest or any travelling boxes came with her. I think Sarah had only one piece of baggage to unpack."

Again Cook supplied the explanation. "I wager she's a poor relation. All the best families 'ave 'em. Trust the mistress to take 'er in."

Anne, although thankful that the problem of getting Mary absorbed into the household had been solved, was too distressed to be more than vaguely aware of what was going on around her as daily routine took over again. She spent more time than ever at her embroidery, not making mourning ribbons, as would have been expected, but designs in the brightest flowers of all. Poppies and tulips, cornflowers and buttercups were among those that predominated. Katherine approved of this emotional outlet in the lovely work, not censoring the choice of colours, for Anne's face was calm whenever she had a needle in her hand. It was easy to guess that with the most brilliant of silks her mind was full of contented memories, the agony of bereavement thrust away.

Julia's grief was very deep and private. She could not allow herself to cry in the presence of either her mother or her grandmother, fearful of starting their tears afresh, and when she was alone the sorrow clamped painfully in her chest, leaving her anguished and dry-eyed. It was not something she could share with Mary either, for although they were friends it was not a relationship of long standing. There was only one person who would understand her feelings.

He came. When Anne's letter finally reached Oxford, Christopher closed his books and left his studies, shut the door on his experiments and took horse the same day. After staying overnight at an inn on the way, he reached Sotherleigh the following morning. Julia was alone in the library, packing up her books after her lessons with her tutor, when the door opened and Christopher stood there.

She flew to him, bursting into a torrent of noisy sobs. In silence he guided her across to a carved bench-seat, sat her down and took the place beside her, ready with words of comfort when he had a chance to speak. She flung her arms about his neck and soaked a dark patch on his velvet coat with her tears. Patiently he waited until her sobbing eased and then he took a blue silk handkerchief from his pocket and handed it to her.

"I thank you." She sat up straight, looked into his good kind face full of concern for her and knew she had in him her best friend in all the world. Surely nobody else had ever had such a special friendship as she shared with Christopher. Vigorously she dried her eyes until not a trace of her tears was left, except for the swollen state of her eyelids. "I haven't been able to cry before."

"I guessed that. Do you feel better now?"

"Yes, but I'm still sad."

"It would be unnatural if you weren't. But now your grief should begin to heal, which is what your father would have wanted above all else."

"Have you seen Mama yet?"

He gave a nod. "I went to her first with my condolences. She told me the bad news of Michael having to leave. I hope most sincerely that he won't have to be away long, but at the present time not even the best lawyer in England could get him acquitted of the charges against him. Parliament has decreed that it is treason to give aid to the King or to help those who have assisted him. When I went upstairs to see Mistress Katherine the young woman in the case was with her."

"We're afraid that Mary will never be able to talk again."

"Surely she should by now?"

"Michael said her vocal cords must have been damaged."

Christopher looked sceptical. "I doubt it from what I was told of her fortunate escape from the noose. A temporary swelling of the throat would make it difficult for anyone to speak, but on a permanent basis that is most unlikely. There was a similar case in Oxford not all that long ago when a poor, half-demented woman was hanged for supposedly smothering her illegitimate baby. It did not affect her vocal cords, for she cried out her gratefulness to the medical students who had brought life back into her, saying her innocence had been proved."

"What happened to her?"

"Fortunately for her, the authorities took the same view. There was a complication with the hospital, which had already paid for her body in advance, but the money was refunded."

"Maybe Mary could be pardoned too?"

"Hers is an entirely different case, not only for being a political one, but because from what she has been able to make known to you there was definite proof of her involvement with those seeking to mislead the authorities who were hunting the King."

"They're still looking everywhere for him, you know."

"So I have heard. There was a recent report that he was dead. At least now I've spoken with your mother I can be sure he is safely abroad, no matter what rumours fly about."

"I think Mary is pretty, don't you?"

"Yes—and talented too. She was playing the lute when I arrived at your grandmother's apartment."

"The lute?" Julia was astounded.

"That is right. Your grandmother said that you had left it there and this morning the young woman picked it up and began to play. From what I could hear before I knocked on the door she plays well. Naturally she stopped as soon as I entered."

"She has never played before."

"Perhaps the opportunity had never arisen."

Later Mary managed to make it clear that her aunt had been musical and had taught her. That same evening she played again in Katherine's parlour, her audience increased by the presence of Anne, Julia and Christopher. Her repertoire included the tunes of old folk songs and Christopher, a tenor, sang the words, encouraging the others to join in the choruses. A maidservant, who had come upstairs to prepare the bedchambers, paused in astonishment at hearing such singing in a house of mourning. Then she thought it was as well, for life had to go on and Mrs. Pallister looked almost incapable of doing anything at the present time and needed cheering up. As for the old lady, it was clear she would never get downstairs again, for the loss of her son coming hard on the departure of her grandson had reduced her to physical frailty while her mind remained seemingly as alert as ever. A little singing would be good for her too.

Never had Anne been more grateful for Christopher's presence than when, two days later, she received an official document. Previously when wishing to discuss financial matters she had been handicapped by being unable to grasp anything the lawyer had tried to explain, but with Christopher she could rely on a sympathetic attitude. He would have none of the impatience with her that the lawyer, a turncoat to Parliament after the King's defeat at Worcester, had so thinly veiled. She knew only that everything to do with Sotherleigh was left to Michael and his heirs or, if he died childless, to Julia. She herself was allowed to draw an income from the estate until Michael came of age. After that a sum was to be set aside annually for her.

"Christopher," she said shakily, holding out the document to him, "the Government is demanding the payment of a large fine because of Robert's and Michael's involvement with the Royalist cause. What am I to do?"

He studied the paper slowly and thoughtfully. "Yes," he said finally, "it is heavy indeed, but if possible it must be paid or you will risk Sotherleigh being sequestered. Can you raise the monies?"

Anne looked distracted. "I think . . . I'm not sure . . . It's hard to say . . . but there is money which might suffice. You see when Robert left the sea he kept a financial interest in three of the ships in his company and the share accruing to him was handled by a merchant friend in London. But when war was seen to be inevitable, Robert collected these monies in gold coins and brought them here to be hidden in a secret place and drawn upon only when necessary. I brought the bags out of hiding when Michael was leaving and they are still concealed in my room, but if all that money has to go I don't know how I shall manage."

They fetched the bags from Anne's room and then sat opposite each other at the library table while he counted the gold coins and then went through all the papers and documents in the deed-box she had brought there for his perusal. Afterwards he jotted down figures at a lightning speed and made some calculations while she sat watching him, grateful for all he was doing. Finally he put down the quill pen, glanced over what he had set down and then turned the paper about on the table to push it towards her.

"Put your mind at rest about the fine. It can be paid. As you will see, I have worked out your financial affairs, allowing for a small income that the new Master of Sotherleigh may expect to draw from the estate to keep him from starvation abroad. There are means by which money can be conveyed to exiles, although it's often a costly business. Sooner or later you will receive an address from him."

"We sent a bag of gold with him when he left and my mother-in-law turned out some jewels I had known nothing about, saying they had been meant for his bride, but he could sell them if he found himself in dire straits."

"Then he should be all right for quite a while."

"Perhaps indefinitely. He was hoping to find some employment, being fluent in French."

"That's all to the good. It will put less of a burden on you."

"If ever he should be in need I can always sell a piece of land to help him, or even to help ourselves if it should prove necessary. Robert did that once or twice."

"But that was wartime and he had no choice but to raise capital where he could without resorting to money-lenders. At least you have been left free of debt, unlike many wives whose husbands have gone into exile. I've heard of some sad cases." Then he returned to the subject of Sotherleigh land. "I advise you most strongly not to sell any part of the estate. Once you have paid this fine the land will be virtually your only asset. At the moment the price per acre is at rock-bottom and likely to stay that way with so many Royalist estates being bankrupt and on the market. More important still is to remember that you have a duty to keep Sotherleigh intact for Michael."

"I'll do anything you say."

"With regard to the farmland and its tenant-farmers, leave everything as it is. Your bailiff has proved himself to be a reliable and competent man and I know from what Michael has told me that he is also trustworthy and won't try to cheat you in your widowhood. However, you should rent out to your Royalist neighbours all the rest of the Sotherleigh land that is lying fallow as far as bringing in money is concerned. Even the park itself could be rented out as grazing land. It would be easy enough to draw a line along the wall that runs south of the maze and divides off the lawns and the flower gardens from the greater part of the park."

"What you suggest is impossible," she cried distractedly. "You don't realise how much things have changed in this district. My neighbours are all Parliamentarians now. Every one of the old Royalist families had to move elsewhere when their property and estates were sequestered."

He wondered why Sotherleigh was the exception and thought it had probably been overlooked or, more likely, that it was too small for the grandiose tastes of some Parliamentarians who were less committed to Puritan ideals than others. "The war is over now," he reminded her, not wanting to hurt her sensitive feelings, but knowing that for her good he had to be firm. "As I remember, the boundaries of two estates, other than those of Warrender Hall, border Sotherleigh to the east and to the south. I will go myself to negotiate with the two new owners, playing one against the other to get you the highest rent possible. I'll take your lawyer with me and also the necessary papers drawn up in readiness for signature. Is that agreed?"

He was giving her no option and she knew it was from the best of motives. "I agree," she said faintly, twisting her hands on the table before her.

He leaned over to still them with his own sympathetic clasp. "It's only a temporary arrangement and can be cancelled when times change for the better. In my reading of history I have learned that no reign or regime lasts for ever, although no doubt Attila the Hun and the Romans once thought that nothing could ever gainsay them. Take heart! Nobody can fill the gap that the loss of your husband has left in your life, but you have Julia and I predict that in mellower times Michael will be here at Sotherleigh again."

She inclined her head. "You give me comfort, Christopher. It shames me that I'm such a weak creature."

"You have more courage in you than you realise, madam. That is why now you are going to cope with the necessary economies I have mapped out for you." He then went on to advise her how to keep secure the money she had and also gave advice on other minor matters. When he suggested she should shut up part of the house and reduce the staff drastically, she was aghast.

"I can't do that," she cried out in protest. "They've all been so loyal! Every one of them." She straightened her back. "In fact, I will not do it!"

He was pleased to see her speaking out. Before his arrival he had feared to find her collapsed completely in the face of her tragic bereavement, for in the past he had seen her bewildered by trouble and quite distrait. Yet somehow she was struggling against herself to keep going and he admired her immensely for it.

"Very well," he said, "I'll speak to the staff myself and explain the situation. If they should all be willing to take a reduction in their wages until such time as they find other employment, they may stay on here indefinitely. And now, one other matter. I think you should tell Mistress Katherine of all that has befallen this household, or would you prefer that I should see her?"

Anne could cope with no more and Christopher went upstairs and told Katherine of all the problems that were threatening her home and his plans for meeting the difficulties.

As he expected, she took the information calmly, remarking only, "Colonel Warrender is behind this. He couldn't be content with killing my son, but must do his best to reduce us to penury as well."

"At least he hasn't tried to have Sotherleigh sequestered," Christopher said. "You have been more fortunate than most of your friends."

"No," Katherine said, slowly turning her gaze towards the open window, "that I think he cannot, or dare not, do." There was a movement of her lips that was almost a smile and Christopher sensed there was more behind the statement than he was likely to be told.

When he had gone, Katherine looked across the room at the ancient chest and pondered awhile. "No," she said to herself at last, "not unless everything else fails. They were the Queen's and my dear husband's gift to me and I must do my best to keep them for Julia!"

Christopher met with a better response from the servants than he had expected. Katherine's maid was ready for retirement, having a sister to live with in Chichester, and Sarah was willing to look after both the Pallister ladies for the same single wage. The coachman was quite eager to go, because his brother-in-law had taken an inn and offered him a job there. Two of the housemaids wanted to leave by Christmas anyway, to be married, and the family of a third was moving away, this new situation at Sotherleigh making her decide to go with them. The gatehouse keeper's wife, who had always done the laundry for the house, volunteered to do some cleaning daily, being fearful of having to move from her comfortable home. Her husband, spurred by the same reason, offered to act as coachman whenever Mrs. Pallister should wish to go out. Lastly Cook, having only the day before kicked out a new scullion for stealing, said she would manage on her own, for she had done it before and could do it again in the light of Sotherleigh's present difficulties.

With the voluntary withdrawing of five of the staff and others doubling up, the financial pressure was slightly eased and Christopher was able to keep the remaining wages at their original level, which was far more satisfactory for both sides.

He stayed at Sotherleigh a little longer than he had intended and during the last days of his sojourn he contracted good rents for Anne, taking advantage of the rivalry between the two new neighbours, who were anxious to score over each other in acquiring still more land to allow them to increase their herds and flocks. He felt he was leaving her well organised. She was resolved to make small economies wherever possible and would be helped by keeping to the organised pattern of her days. Before he left she had moved out of her marriage bedchamber into another near Katherine, allowing the east wing to be closed up, and the Long Gallery was similarly shut away in dust-sheets.

When he returned to Oxford he threw himself back into his work. Life there continued to suit him in health and in every other way. A new coffee-house had opened and at times of relaxation he liked nothing better than to sit in good talk there with intellectual companions, coffee on the table and a pipe in his hand. Occasionally in the street or at a social gathering a girl's pretty face would catch his eye, but the normal urge would pass, nullified by work and more work. The universe was full of wonders yet to be discovered. He was particularly fascinated by the planet

Saturn and through his telescope, which was one of his own design, he had been able to discover and record information about it not known before.

He made another break in his work when Dean Wren was taken ill. He went home and stayed a week. By that time his father was recovering after a minor crisis common to old age. While there Christopher told his sister and her husband of his visit to Sotherleigh and the tragic reason for it.

"I'll write to Mrs. Pallister," Susan said, full of pity, "and send our condolences. I've been thinking for quite a little while of taking up Father's correspondence with her on his behalf, now that his strength and his eyesight are fading."

She kept her word. Her interesting letters became a source of cheer to Anne while Julia appreciated the news sent about Christopher's achievements, which would never have been learned from him.

SEVERAL MONTHS had elapsed since Christopher's visit when Julia wrote to tell him that a letter had been received from Michael. It had been brought to Sotherleigh by the servant of a merchant who had met him in Paris and had promised to see it was delivered.

It was a sad letter, for her brother had heard of their father's death from a Cavalier come recently from England to escape Parliamentary retribution. He expressed the wish to be at Sotherleigh to help console them all in their grief. He wrote little of himself, his thoughts too concerned for his family, but reading between the lines it was easy to guess that things had not gone easily for either him or Joe, and it was clear that the King in exile was faring no better. Michael explained that France was generally unsettled due to a struggle for power, referred to generally as the Fronde, between the French nobles and the young Louis XIV, which was making life difficult for everyone. Michael gave no address, promising one at a later date, and Julia closed her letter to Christopher with a promise of her own to keep him informed when anything more was heard from her brother.

At Sotherleigh Michael's letter was read aloud by Anne a good many times, its contents dissected and discussed with Katherine and Julia, conclusions being drawn from this sentence or that. Mary hugged to herself the fact that he had included her by name in his fond greetings to all at Sotherleigh. Perhaps he was thinking about her a lot in his exile, recalling her improved looks after her recovery, the kiss they had exchanged and her last clinging embrace to which he had responded. When the chance came she would write to him. It was expensive to send a letter in England and far more expensive to get one delivered abroad, but she was saving up. These days she had a little money of her own, for she had volunteered to become the dressmaker for the family and to make the working garments supplied to the women servants, wool in winter and cotton in summer. She had not wanted to be paid, but Anne had insisted, saying that she must have some remuneration since she would be saving Sotherleigh money in any case.

Mary was making steady progress with her reading and writing and had set down in simple words the details of her early years and her involvement with her uncles' plot and its aftermath for the Pallister ladies to read. Julia told her of the woman at Oxford whose voice had not been silenced by the noose. This had frightened her, making her think the Pallisters might become impatient with her or wary, but that had not happened. Anne had said the woman had been exceptionally lucky and nothing more on the subject was mentioned again.

Secretly living for Michael's homecoming, Mary always watched out to ease the spells of overwhelming sadness that came upon Anne at times. Being by nature a kindly girl, Mary would have done anything she could for Michael's family even if he had not requested it. She had taken the trouble to find out the folk tunes and other pieces within her range that Katherine liked best and, if they were not already known to her, she would pick them up by ear when Anne or Julia played them on the spinet. Frequently she would sit on her own with Katherine, playing for the old lady's entertainment and unaware that she had a true musical talent.

Katherine suspected that the girl had had a good singing voice before her ordeal on the gibbet. Then one afternoon Mary opened her mouth and strained to bring forth the lyrics of the folk song she was playing. No musical sound came, but one word and then another came through, husky but articulate. For months past she had not dared to try to speak again, unable to face another disappointment, and now she sat stunned, the lute silent in her lap.

"I spoke," she exclaimed wonderingly. "Did you hear me, Mistress Katherine?"

"I did indeed." Katherine was smiling with delight and nodding her head.

"I'm not mute for ever after all!" The girl's face was suffused with joy.

"Don't strain your voice by raising it to make me hear in my deafness." Katherine beckoned to her, indicating the footstool. "Come and sit near me."

Mary rushed to the footstool, breaking down on the way. She sat sobbing tears of relief and happiness, her one thought being that she would be able to talk to Michael and tell him of her love when next they met. Katherine drew the girl's head onto her lap, patting her shoulder and smoothing her hair until she became composed again.

Until that day Mary had always been a little afraid of Katherine, not at all sure that she was liked by the old lady, but now that had changed. She felt herself to be fully accepted into the family. And her voice could finally be heard!

She did not realise that, whereas Katherine had never had anything against her personally, having pitied her most profoundly for all she had been through, it was her devotion to Michael that had been and still was a barrier. Katherine's concern was that Mary might win her grandson through sheer compassion on his part and nothing else, which she did not consider to be a sound basis for marriage. There was also the question of their different social backgrounds to which Anne would give little consideration, but which Katherine, brought up in Court circles, felt to be of utmost importance.

Much as Katherine missed him, she thought some good must come of Michael's being away, for he had left before his sense of responsibility was able to trap him into a commitment he would surely have secretly regretted for the rest of his life. Through spending time abroad he should return with more wisdom and experience in emotional matters, saving himself and Mary from an irretrievable mistake.

MARY'S LITTLE HOARD of savings did not increase as much as she had expected, for in these hard times it was more patching and mending than actual dressmaking that took place. Katherine wanted nothing new, having an extensive wardrobe from which she could draw for variety, and Anne continued to keep to black in her widowhood, having had four good gowns made in Chichester at the time of bereavement, which she rotated for equal wear. Neither did the women servants expect replacements as frequently as before. Yet the general parsimony was not through lack of available fabrics or a need to purchase, for Sotherleigh had begun as a house of plenty and large stocks of most things had been maintained, including enough sewing silks and threads for years ahead as well as linen and woollens for embroidered bed-hangings and coverlets and every other household need. It meant that nowadays when funds were particularly low, the stores could be tapped and, if it should prove possible, replacements made later.

There was one storage chest, its surface covered with Elizabethan cross-stitch from Katherine's days at Court, that contained only finer fabrics. Originally it had held the rich Oriental silks and gossamer fabrics from the Indian continent that Ned had brought home from his voyages; afterwards Katherine had always bought and lain away sumptuous materials for whenever she should need a new gown. Anne had done the same, being obedient to all the traditions of Sotherleigh. Yet the lid was never lifted in these penny-pinching times, the fear being that there would be no money to buy more of the same quality should family gowns be needed for special occasions, such as a wedding gown for Mary and later Julia with trousseaux as well.

Consequently Mary's most frequent task was to lower hems for Julia, who was growing fast. When there were no hems left she resorted to adding deep bands in a contrasting colour taken from a box of left-over remnants from gowns made for Katherine and Anne and even Julia herself in more affluent days. The joins were disguised by a simple braid or feather-stitching. Anne would have liked her ribbons to be used, but in this new Puritan England, fripperies of adornment were frowned upon. Women who dared to appear frivolous in dress were labelled as whores and in some cases rubbish and dung had been thrown at them in the streets. As a result most of Anne's lovely ribbons were rolled up and stored away when finished, for she had no wish for her innocent daughter to be shouted at for having too many loops and ribbons dancing on her outer clothes. Her own gowns, which had not seen the light of day since Robert's death, constituted a source of material that could be used when wanted. So when Mary, who had become a little plumper, split armholes beyond repair, or seams wore out through sheer wear, she was allowed to unpick one of these gowns and cut it to a new pattern for herself. After a while, when the box of scrap materials could no longer supply suitable additions to Julia's garments, another of Anne's gowns was made over for her. Whenever Katherine saw this work in progress she was reminded of Queen Elizabeth's wardrobe, which had been similarly disassembled, although for a far less useful purpose.

Julia still had to spend an allotted time at her sampler each week. It was a task originated in a previous century by needlewomen to record various types of stitches before books on needlework appeared. She was presently embroidering a strawberry, which symbolised Perfect Righteousness, in a feather stitch, which had been brought back from the Crusades. Her sampler was growing band by band of embroidery, the work done rolled up around its ivory rod in her lap while she sewed, enough leeway left for easy movement. Her chatter entertained Mary, who sat sewing beside her.

"Next to the strawberry will come a lily for Purity and then a rose for Divine Love." She chuckled. "Michael wouldn't be able to believe his eyes if he could see me stitching placidly like this, because he remembers my tantrums over it in the past. How he would laugh if I admitted that I enjoy the work now!"

From Julia's talk of her brother Mary had learned much about him, including incidents from his childhood, which his sister did not remember personally but which came from what she had been told. The Pallisters were like all families in having amusing accounts of younger members' activities in childhood that were related often, and Mary never tired of any stories that involved Michael.

His second letter had arrived more than a year after the first, much battered in transit where it had been passed from hand to hand, and it had been written three months before. It appeared that two previous letters sent during the past year had failed to reach Sotherleigh. In contrast to the first one received, this letter was cheerful and optimistic in tone. He was still in Paris. The Fronde had finally been settled with the young Louis XIV in power and the Court back at the Palace of the Louvre. Michael wrote that his ability to speak French had stood him in good stead, for he had obtained a post as a clerk with prospects of promotion. Joe was working in the royal stables and had become fluent in all the curses in the French language and little else!

*Our own King Charles,* Michael continued, *is still living gloomily in poor accommodation at the Louvre with his mother. Since she is French it no doubt suits her to preside over her son's exile, but she keeps him short of money, although in all charity she may not have any to spare. He has a meagre wardrobe and no horse of his own. Joe tries always to supply him with one of the best in the stables whenever he rides out. Mostly he is in the company of fellow Englishmen of noble birth, all homesick and as impoverished as himself. The French courtiers are a haughty lot and show no friendliness to an exiled English King and his shabbily dressed companions.*

Michael went on to assure all at home that his own lot was much better. He had a room and board with a good French couple who kept a bakery and lived above the shop. Paris was a city of narrow streets and ancient buildings, the majority dating back to medieval times, the more magnificent being, among others, the Louvre and the Cathedral of Notre Dame. Most of the houses and shops had outside shutters, the clattering of which in the mornings was the equivalent to the dawn chorus of the birds in the trees at Sotherleigh. Joe had accommodation at the Louvre stables, which he shared with thirty other grooms, and the two of them met at least once a week. Michael closed his letter with a request that his mother should write with all speed, for his only worry was to know how those dearest to him were faring at Sotherleigh. As before he sent individual greetings and Mary blushed when her name was read out.

At Oxford Christopher received a full report of Michael's letter from Julia with the greetings that had been sent to him. He was relieved to know that things were going better for his old friend. His own life continued to be extremely busy. He had become a Master of Arts by the time he was twenty-one and was a Fellow of All Souls. In between his lectures he continued his research with a zest that made twenty-four hours in the day far too short for him. He continued his study of the planet Saturn while his inventions and scientific experiments continued to bring eminent people from far afield to see the work he had in hand and he was, as ever, eager to share his knowledge. In addition to everything else, he had made a large and very beautiful sundial for the south wall of the Chapel of All Souls. His sister and her husband were invited to its dedication.

Susan, gazing up at the sundial gleaming like the face of the sun itself, saw it as a token of her brother's thanksgiving to God. Although extremely proud of his artistic and scientific achievement, she held back the praise she would have given him, knowing that nothing made him more uncomfortable or embarrassed, and spoke only of its practical use to him, which he was pleased to discuss. That same evening she talked of him to her husband.

"Since he sees his talents as God-given, which indeed they are," she remarked meditatively in their room at the hostelry where she and William were staying, "he will take no credit for anything himself. He is the most modest and retiring of men and ever will be."

"All the more surprising when one realises he is a genius," William replied, leaning a shoulder against the wall as he watched his wife putting a final touch to her hair with a comb before a mirror. They were shortly to go downstairs to meet Christopher for supper.

She twisted on the stool where she sat to look up at him. "You were impressed by all he showed you of his latest work this afternoon, were you not?"

"That is putting it mildly. There were mathematical devices beyond ordinary understanding and then ingenious inventions such as a pen with two nibs for writing or copying two documents at the same time, which he uses himself for his records. Another gadget is for measuring the mileage covered by a coach wheel. He is experimenting to find out how to navigate under water, how to raise water levels by engines, better means of rock mining, new ways of printing and so forth. He has even devised a method by which a man who has lost excessive blood might be given it in a vein through a needle and a syringe."

"Mercy!" Susan exclaimed, putting down the comb.

"That's not all. He believes that a tincture of opium could be similarly infused to induce a stupor."

Her eyes were becoming wider. "A stupor? For what purpose?"

"The possibilities are endless. Before surgery it would save a patient all that pain under the knife. The hopelessly insane could be quieted in their ravings."

She was a sensible middle-aged woman who had been married a long time to a clever man, and she did not dismiss these theories as impossibilities. "If ever it can be done, I'm sure Christopher will do it. When we were in the crowd looking up at the sundial this morning, people all around were talking about him. I heard him referred to as 'that miracle of a youth, Mr. Wren.'"

"I would compare him with one other."

"Who could that be?"

"Leonardo da Vinci. Christopher will match him yet."

Christopher was waiting for them when they went downstairs. Susan surprised him by kissing his cheek when she reached him. "What was that for?" he asked merrily. "You greeted me upon your arrival yesterday."

"It's for being my young brother," she said fondly, "and I do not see you very often."

Over supper there was family talk about their father's health and how their uncle, who had been Bishop of Ely until arrested by Cromwell, was faring in the Tower. He was an old man and although he had books and writing materials his incarceration was telling on him. They spoke about

the Pallisters and exchanged the news they had, which reminded William
of a recent incident at Cambridge that he believed to be indirectly concerned with the Sotherleigh family.

"Didn't you tell me at the time that a Colonel Warrender was responsible for Robert Pallister's death?" he asked Christopher.

"That is correct. Why do you ask?"

"It happened that I was in conversation with some undergraduates two
or three weeks ago. One of them said he was from Sussex and his name
was Adam Warrender of Warrender Hall."

"That would be the Colonel's only son. What was the occasion of your
meeting?"

"I had delivered a lecture during which I mentioned having talked at
length with Oliver Cromwell. Warrender was among those who shared
my enthusiasm for the man's political acumen."

Although Susan had always been staunchly Royalist, William had been
a supporter of Parliament from the first challenging of Charles I's auto-
cratic behaviour and his implicit belief in the Divine Right of Kings. Yet
it had never caused any awkwardness between husband and wife or with
any of her family, for he was a wise and moderate man. It was the
principles of just government that he was upholding and not the excesses
that had been committed in the name of freedom. He had been horrified
by the beheading of the King and the many acts against the established
Church, having been a sub-deacon himself at Windsor when he and Susan
had met. But his faith in Oliver Cromwell remained firm and he foresaw
only good coming from that man's leadership. Christopher, who always
enjoyed a lively discussion, slipped naturally into talk with William on
recent events at Westminster and the name of Warrender did not come up
again. Even from opposing sides they were able to approve Cromwell's
ending of the Long Parliament.

It had been so-called for having sat without elections for well over a
decade, having been originally elected in 1640, and now it had become
violently quarrelsome, incompetent and thoroughly corrupt. Cromwell
had taken matters into his own hands by marching into the House of
Commons with a band of musketeers. There he shouted at the Members
that they had sat far too long. He ordered the Speaker of the House to
dismiss them and had them driven out at sword-point. A new Parliament
had been formed. As for Cromwell himself, he had taken the title of Lord
Protector of England and was addressed as His Highness. In addition he
had taken up residence amid the royal trappings of the Palace of White-

hall and the other palaces, as if in some oblique way he had gained the inheritance of the Throne.

Piety remained the rule with Sunday church attendance still compulsory and devoid of organ music since Cromwell considered that it drowned the words of hymns. Opera escaped his censure by being performed unadorned and without the trappings of the theatre, which he abhorred as sinful. He had both acting and its viewing punishable with flogging and imprisonment. Even strolling players, who had never walked the boards of a London stage and had once brought laughter and drama to villages and market towns, were destitute on the streets. Maypoles gathered more layers of dust in country barns and the caps and bells of the Morris dancers were kept hidden away. Christmas came and went and came again, the festive eating of plum pudding banned and the decorating with evergreens strictly forbidden, the carol singers silent and all wassailing outlawed.

AT SOTHERLEIGH economy continued to be the rule as another year went by. This did not mean there were no treats. When a ragged fellow begging at the kitchen door turned out to be an actor, he was not only fed but invited to give a performance for which he was paid. Sotherleigh was a safe house for performers and the entertainments were held in Katherine's apartment in order that she should not be left out, and family and servants sat together. The programmes ranged from bawdy songs and caperings to speeches from *King Lear* and *Hamlet*.

Christmas was celebrated as it always had been with traditional fare and the giving of gifts, Cromwell's rules ignored. Neither was anyone's birthday overlooked, either in the parlour or the kitchen, something extra always found. It was on Mary's nineteenth birthday that she was given a book. Having learned to read and write had opened a whole new world for her and to possess a book of her own was a wonder to her. It was a small treasure bound in vellum, its contents devoted to cosmetic receipts, herbal cures and how to sugar violets and such novelties, all of which interested her. It was a proud moment for her when she wrote her name in it. *Mary Twyat, her book.* Her other self had gone forever and she wished only that her adopted surname might be changed to Pallister one day when Michael should come home again.

She was embroidering the cuffs of a pair of gloves for him, for although it had been Anne's idea that this should be done, either to await his return or until some means were found later to send them to him, she had volunteered to do the work. Her offer had been taken up, for these days she excelled at embroidery. She had done little before coming to Sotherleigh, her experience limited to practical sewing, but Anne had only to demonstrate a new stitch to her once, twice at the most, and then her needle would be flying away at it.

In the three years of Michael's absence Katherine's aching bones had slowed her down still more and she merely shuffled about her apartment, sometimes having to pause and draw breath before she could take another painful step. Yet it was only from the hips downwards that she was badly affected, and although she was also plagued by aching in her back and stiffening of her fingers, she still managed to do some wool-work for a chair if she sat in a good light with spectacles on her nose. She also read a little every day and whenever the weather permitted she would have all the windows open and sit looking out at the Knot Garden and the distant maze, the plan of which Julia now knew like the back of her young hand.

Katherine still thought of her granddaughter as a child, but at thirteen Julia was fast approaching womanhood and there were times when she waved up to the window from the Knot Garden that her slenderness and grace made her seem to have reached that state already. Maybe the plainness of her garments these days added to the illusion. Katherine recalled how once she had thought fewer ribbons on her granddaughter's clothes would be a good thing, but she would never have wished it to come about as it had.

Another year went by and life at Sotherleigh continued at the same slow pace, but changes were taking place. Katherine dozed more in the daytime, Mary's yearning for Michael consumed her at times with such restlessness that she took on many tasks with which she need not have burdened herself, and Julia became more adult in her attitudes. Yet the one in whom the change was most marked was Anne.

She had never regretted moving out of the bedchamber she had shared with Robert. It had held too many cherished memories that could only be borne when she was at her embroidery. Then she was able to recall the joyous times when she had woken during the war years to find that Robert had returned secretly for one of his flying visits and was taking her into his arms again. There were nights when she still started from sleep at the creak of floorboards, Robert's name on her lips. In opening her eyes to another room there was less anguish, even if the sense of loneliness was not abated and never could be.

She had never guessed before experiencing widowhood herself what utter emptiness to everything it would bring, no matter how close family and friends might be. In fact, the sense of loneliness was often more acute in company, especially if married couples were present. But the time to face up to it was long overdue, and she must do as Katherine and countless generations of women who had loved their partners had done before her. She had been more fortunate than many in having a purpose to her existence in keeping Sotherleigh financially stable for Michael's return, quite apart from having her daughter and mother-in-law to care for. It had been her lifeline and now she could broaden out into wider spheres, taking one step at a time.

She began by lifting the long-closed lid of the fabric chest. From it she took a length of dark violet silk, which she handed to Mary, who made it up into a new gown for her. It was not more than a few weeks before others in silver-grey, lavender and smoke-blue were added to her wardrobe. Eventually, to the relief of the household, she stopped wearing black altogether.

In the meantime Mary had finished the gloves for Michael. They had been entrusted to someone known to the family who was going to France and would deliver them to him. With the gloves went a letter from Anne, who had left enough space for Julia and Mary to add a few lines. Katherine also added a greeting to her grandson in her shaky hand.

Julia reached the final stage of her sampler in what was known as stump work. This was a type of raised embroidery in which padding was used to plump out motifs ranging from figures and animals to clouds and trees and flowers to give a three-dimensional effect. She found it fascinating to do and put the last stitch in the whole sampler shortly before her fifteenth birthday. Already she had planned to make a border of stump work for a mirror that would hang in her bedchamber. Snapping the silk, she tossed aside scissors and thimble in triumph.

"It's done, Mary!"

Unrolling the sampler completely, she sprang up to send it whipping out like a banner. Mary left her own sewing to snatch up the bottom end of it just before it reached the floor, holding it by the ivory rod that had been attached to it ten years before. Immediately Julia stepped back a few paces to stretch out the full three feet of the sampler between them.

"It looks very fine," Mary said with approval.

Her gaze travelled down the sampler from the top bands of simple stitches down through the alphabets and the numerals, the fantastic beasties and the more recognisable wild and domestic creatures. Following were the bands of drawn threadwork and the cut work, the latter filled with delicate needlepoint lace, this section being known as "white work." Then came the "black work," no less intricate, for the designs in minuscule black stitches on a white ground had to be equally perfect on both sides of the ruffs and frills it usually adorned. Next was the encrusted embroidery in metallic threads and glittering beadwork, and finally the stump work. Apart from the white and black work and the wide bands sparkling with gold and silver, the sampler was a closely covered stretch of coppery reds and bright pinks, brilliant blues, mustardy yellows and clear greens, almost stiff with its multitudinous stitchery.

Julia heaved a satisfied sigh. "It will please Mama, I know."

It was natural that she should have thought of having an ornamental mirror, for over the past months her appearance had become highly important to her. Gone were the days when she had never glanced at her reflection and found her be-ribboned garments such a bugbear to wear. Now she would have loved those be-flowered ribbons looped about her neckline to enhance the increasing swelling of her bosom. She thought that in shape, if not yet in size, her breasts more than matched the cleavages in the portraits of female ancestors in the Long Gallery when she held aside the dust-sheets to view them.

Spring came again to Sotherleigh. In the woods the windflowers showed in pale, blush-like hues among the carpet of the previous autumn's rusty leaves until the bluebells rose in a thick haze to be gathered in armfuls once again.

Mary had a suitor, a hard-working and steadfast young merchant who was both prosperous and charming. She liked him well, which all at Sotherleigh could see, approving him at the same time. Then, just when everyone thought she was on the point of accepting him, a long-overdue letter came from Michael, part of it written to her, and the next day the courtship was ended.

Katherine was the only one not surprised. None of the others connected Michael's letter with Mary's refusal, for her section had been slotted in with everybody else's on the same single sheet of paper and written in the same friendly tone.

His news was good. He had gained a much better position as chief clerk to a rich merchant who dealt in fine silks. Joe was still at the royal stables. He had been promoted to the charge of the horses kept solely for Louis XIV himself and was quite a dandy in his blue livery. Michael added that

Joe's command of the French language had become so authentic that few took him to be an Englishman these days and he continued to be a favourite with the maids in the palace kitchens. Michael had made some good friends of his own among the French and in all he seemed as content as he could be away from his homeland.

At the end of the letter he gave the latest that he had heard of King Charles. Now in Cologne, the unfortunate man was frequently in a state of penury as bad as when he was with his mother in Paris. Although most of the exiled Cavaliers had accompanied the King to his new place of abode, Michael had felt no obligation to leave France with them since he did not move in the King's circle.

*Time enough,* he concluded, *when I can follow him back to England under a newly raised Royal Standard. May that day be not far distant.*

Never once had Michael asked for money to be sent to him. Unlike those hapless noblemen with Charles, who continued their same role of gentlemanly leisure in exile, existing on whatever could be smuggled to them by their families and friends, Michael had used his intelligence and his skills to carve a living for himself without being a burden on those at Sotherleigh. Since he was as much a gentleman-born as any nobleman, it was all to his credit and Anne was proud of him.

She received news of another kind when visiting a sick tenant to whom she had taken special foods to aid his recovery. When she returned to Sotherleigh she went, still in her outdoor clothes, to Katherine and told her what she had heard.

"Colonel Warrender is dead! Of apoplexy. It happened yesterday."

When Katherine made no immediate reply Anne thought at first the old lady had not caught what was said, having grown quite deaf. Yet Katherine had heard. Her eyes, sharp and bright in the wrinkled lids, turned in the direction of one of the windows that was half open, almost as if she were stretching her gaze to see beyond the countryside with its woodlands to the old Tudor mansion of their late enemy.

"So he's gone, has he? Well, there's a new young Master of Warrender Hall now. I wonder if he is as tight-fisted and bull-necked as his father was."

Anne turned away, clasping her hands restlessly. It was the first time she had spoken the name of Warrender or heard it in this house since the tragedy of losing Robert. In a gush it had released the stored-up anguish in her. She had to hold herself back from rushing downstairs to her embroidery and the refuge it had become to her. There were times when she feared for her own sanity and this was one of them. The words burst from her.

"At least those of that fearsome name have done their worst to us here at Sotherleigh. There can be nothing left for them to do."

"Pray God that may be so."

Had there been a note of doubt in Katherine's voice? Anne did not dare ask in case some kind of scream of protest might rise up in her throat. "Amen to your prayer, madam," she whispered fervently. Then she left for her own room to toss her hat and gloves on the bed before hastening downstairs to her chair in the Queen's Parlour and her embroidery box.

Julia, carrying her stump work for her new mirror wrapped in white linen, found her there. "I've come to ask your advice as to whether I should take the foliage right to the edge of my border."

"Show me." Anne had had almost an hour at her favourite pastime and was composed again. She went to a side table under a window where her daughter spread out the border on its protective cloth. It was embroidered on a ground of ivory satin with a garden motif, flowers intermingling with birds and hedgehogs, peacocks, butterflies and a lake with a swan in a rectangular shape, the central space allotted for the mirror, which would have a door closing over it. The panel for the door was arranged separately and on it Queen Elizabeth stood in the gown kept by Katherine. Julia had been granted access to copy it in detail, and tiny pearls and beads gave accuracy to the embroidered version. She had wanted real red hair for the Queen's tresses, but her own was too chestnut, for all its bronze lights, and Joe, who could have provided the right colour, was not available. So she had settled for orange-red silk and the result was effective.

"I don't want a gap left along the edge when it's mounted," she explained.

"Has Ridley finished the frame yet?"

"No. He said it wouldn't be ready until the end of next week."

"Then if I were you I should wait until you can try it against the frame before you decide."

"I'll do that."

Ridley had expected to deliver the frame to the house when it was polished, already guessing the Pallister ladies would want to see it first before committing the girl's work to it, but Julia forestalled him. He was having an afternoon nap in the chair he kept in his workshop, his feet up on the bench, when the door of the workshop crashed open, flooding him with sunshine, and she came bounding in.

"Did I wake you? Oh, I'm sorry," she exclaimed.

He dropped his feet with a thud to the floor and stood up quickly. "Wake me? No, Miss Julia. I was thinking with my eyes shut for a few moments. Did you come for your frame?"

"Yes. Is it ready?" Her wide smile was eager.

It struck him as he reached for the frame on a shelf that she was turning into a real beauty, this downright girl with a mind of her own. With her creamy, unblemished skin, those sparkling dark blue eyes and the glorious sheen of her hair she was transformed from the moderately pretty child she had once been. There was still the same unconscious, haughty poise of the head, which was so much like the old lady's that he grinned to himself at the resemblance.

"Here it is, Miss Julia," he said, handing the frame to her. "Its door is still separate. Do you want to take that too?"

"Yes, please. This frame looks splendid. How clever you are!"

She left as spectacularly as she had come, darting out and away, holding the frame and the little door above her head as she danced in wide circles away from the workshop. It might have been a May Day garland that she held and he could hear her singing when he began work again, his rest over.

Skipping, dancing and twirling, she continued on her way, her saffron skirt and petticoats swooshing up and out to reveal her white-stockinged calves, her garter ribbons engaged in a dance of their own. Her exuberance was due to everything's being particularly wonderful that day from the weather to a happier atmosphere at Sotherleigh, as her mother had at last turned the corner of sorrow and become more herself again. If there had been a slight setback some days ago it had gone away.

To add to this joy there was another. Christopher, whom she had not seen for a long while, had had a great honour bestowed on him by Gresham College in the City of London. He had been offered and had accepted the greatly esteemed chair of astronomy there. That it should have been given to such a young man was proof of the high regard in which he was held. Julia could not help wondering how he could tear himself away from his beloved Oxford until she remembered he had once said that London was the most exciting city in which to live. What was most important to her personally was his written promise that as soon as he had organised his routine in London he would visit his good friends at Sotherleigh.

On and on she danced, taking a short cut across a lawn to return to the house by way of the drive. Carefree, she sprang through a gap in the elms and bushes to land, bright as a butterfly, in the cool green shade and right in the path of a spirited horse scarcely a foot away.

The stranger in the saddle reined in instantly with a jingle of bridle and a rattling of gravel under hooves. Alarmed, she had darted back to a safe distance, clutching the frame and its door to her chest like a shield. For a matter of seconds she and the horseman stared at each other as if mutually transfixed by the danger that had only just been averted, his eyes dark and piercing. He was clothed in creamy velvet with a wide-brimmed plumed hat as black as his hair and his splendid thoroughbred, which stood sixteen hands high with a tetchy flare of its snorting nostrils and a gleaming eye. She thought it as fierce-looking as its rider, but for the moment she could not place him. Who was this young man with the handsome and yet daunting countenance, the forceful nose, the clear tanned skin and the bold chin? Whoever he was, she judged he would not be easy to cross.

"Allow me to present myself, Miss Julia." His voice was deep, his speech that of a gentleman. He had swept off his hat and held it against his chest. "I am Adam Warrender of Warrender Hall."

The blood drained from her face with a speed that was painful, making her skin tingle. The last time he had spoken to her was eight years ago from the saddle of his pearl-white pony. She knew him now, although she had scarcely seen him since that day in Chichester. He had been almost permanently away at school during his late father's military activities and, from what she had heard, was presently studying at Cambridge, which all along had been as staunchly for Cromwell as Oxford had been for the King. Shock, fury, hatred and terror exploded in her simultaneously like a gigantic firework. Crimson gushed into her face and her eyes glittered. That he should come here after all that had happened was insupportable. She wanted only that he should be gone.

"We'll not receive you here at Sotherleigh, Adam Warrender! I speak for my brother in his absence!"

He redonned his hat with a frown. "I'm not prepared to accept your dismissal. It is Mrs. Robert Pallister whom I wish to see."

Her mother! He dared to hurt the one person she would die to protect! Something seemed to snap in her. "You'll not go near her!" she cried out. "You and yours have caused enough misery in her life. I'll not let you insult her with your company. Turn back! Go away! Now!"

Seized by panic that he might ride past her, she hurled the frame she held at him. But it was not an easy object to aim and to her horror one corner of it drove like an arrow-head deep into the horse's shoulder, hanging for a matter of seconds before it dropped. She heard herself scream as if suffering the horse's pain herself. The spirited animal, maddened by the unexpected onslaught, had reared up with a loud whinny of pain, hooves plunging and eyes rolling while its rider, livid with rage, fought grimly to stay in the saddle. She would have rushed forward to help soothe the animal, but Adam Warrender bawled at her to stay clear.

"Use your wits! Do you want to risk injury a second time?"

She glowered, blaming his pride on his refusal to let her do what she could. Nothing would please her more than to see him fall from the saddle and she guessed that he knew it. Taking better aim, she flung the frame-door directly at him, making sure that she would avoid the horse this time. It went spinning through the air and would have struck him harmlessly on the arm if his mount had not careened at that precise moment. The edge of the frame-door caught him across the cheekbone. Blood spurted.

"You wild cat!" he roared at her furiously.

The horse had glimpsed the skimming object and its haunches swung towards her as it gathered muscles as if to bolt. Adam Warrender was using all his strength to master the situation and it was unlucky chance for him that a bird should swoop across the drive with a flash of wing. With a snort the horse took a great leap forward and was off at a gallop down the drive, bearing its irate owner out through the gates and away from Sotherleigh.

In the silence that followed Julia remained standing where she was, her arms at her side and breathing deeply. It was the first time she had ever tasted vengeance, but it was overshadowed by the torment she felt over the horse. She had never harmed an animal before in all her life. Admittedly she did not think any permanent damage had been done, but that did not change how she felt. She was less sure about Adam Warrender's cheek, for it had looked a gaping cut, but firmly she told herself that it should serve as a reminder for a long time to come that Sotherleigh would always be barred to him.

The frame lay in splinters on the drive where the frantic hooves had trampled on it. She retrieved the little door, which had fallen free. In a sober mood she retraced her steps at a slow pace back to Ridley's workshop. She found him working with a plane, curls of wood floating everywhere. He paused in surprise at seeing her again so soon.

She spoke quietly. "I'm afraid you'll have to make me another frame, Mr. Ridley. The other one is broken."

"What! Did you fall over with it in your larking about?"

"No. I threw it at the new Master of Warrender Hall and made his horse bolt."

Ridley's mouth dropped open and he looked aghast. She had dreaded that he would laugh, but his expression was one of complete dismay.

"Miss Julia! What have you done?"

"More than just that. I clipped his cheek with the frame-door and it bled."

Ridley groaned loudly and shook his head. "The late Colonel Warrender was the most powerful Parliamentarian in this county. He had friends in high places. All that power and all that goodwill will be with his son now. If the Colonel was a bitter enemy of Sotherleigh, just think how much worse the son might prove to be in view of what you did today."

His dismal words set a terrible qualm churning in the pit of her stomach, but she stood her ground. "I admit I mismanaged everything, but as a Pallister I had to deny entrance to a Warrender."

He heaved a heavy sigh and took the frame-door from her. "I can see this is scratched, but it's easily polished up again. I'll start on the replacement frame tomorrow."

She followed the same route as before away from the workshop and back to the house. The drive was deserted and the gates closed.

# EIGHT

S ALWAYS Julia went first to Katherine, full of distress about what she had done to the horse. After she had calmed down she gave her grandmother a full account of all that had happened, including Ridley's warning.

"The horse was not seriously harmed and take no notice of Ridley," Katherine said confidently. Out of perverse curiosity she would have liked the opportunity to see Harry's grandson. Since he appeared to share the same insensitive ways of his father, it would have given her pleasure to have dismissed him in her most freezing manner, for she would have insisted that she and Anne receive him together. She could not reprove Julia for her impulsive behavior, for in all honesty she knew she would have reacted in the same way at her granddaughter's age, given such circumstances. "However, say nothing to your mother. We do not want to worry her unnecessarily."

In spite of Julia's conviction that Adam Warrender would not return after his ignominious departure, Katherine sent her with instructions to the gatehouse keeper that he should not open the gates again to that enemy of Sotherleigh. The gatehouse keeper took his orders literally. When a letter addressed to Anne came from Warrender Hall he refused the servant admission and would not accept the missive through the bars of the gate. The servant rode away with his mission unfulfilled and no further attempt at delivery took place.

This second insult coming hard on the first was not overlooked by the Master of Warrender Hall. Full of anger, he penned his bold signature to a letter destined for Westminster. Then he finished settling his late father's affairs and made ready to return to Cambridge and complete his studies. Changes lay in wait for Sotherleigh. When he was home again he would view them at his leisure. There should be no one to bar his entrance next time, least of all the girl with passionate beauty in her face and hair that blazed like the Slindon woods in autumn.

Ridley finished a new frame for Julia and mounted her stump work. No mirrors were entirely true, not even the Venetian one that Ned had once brought home from a voyage for Katherine, and hers, which had been cut from a large looking-glass that had been broken, gave a good reflection only when she stood close. Yet that did not detract from her pleasure in it and when its door was shut it became a colourful picture on her panelled wall. The figure of Elizabeth in the ivory gown stood proud, tiny beads twinkling like the diamonds they represented, and tiny seed pearls trimmed the front of the square neckline to portray the precious drop-pearls. Much painstaking work had gone into the embroidery on the sleeves and skirt.

When Christopher sent word that he would be paying a visit the mirror's door was never closed for a week before his arrival. Julia studied her appearance constantly, trying new ways with her hair and deciding which ear-bobs to wear. It was a long time since she had seen him and she wanted her good friend to see that she was a grown woman now.

The day before he was due she went riding for the whole morning and arrived home late for dinner, dishevelled from a final gallop. She ran into the house to go skidding through the Great Hall and enter the adjoining room where she knew her mother and Mary would be at table. She intended a swift apology for her tardiness and then a flying trip to her room to make herself ready to eat with them.

"Forgive me for being late! I—"

Her voice trailed away. Christopher was there with them, rising from his chair with a smile to greet her, and for a timeless moment they saw each other with new eyes. Everything registered. He had not been prepared for the change in her, never supposing that she would have left childhood so completely behind to become this lovely girl with the flushed open-air look to her and the glorious mass of hair that had grown more luxuriant and richer in colour, full of reddish-gold tints that set off her creamy skin.

"I found I had time to visit Sotherleigh before my London lecture and thought I would give all here a surprise." He had reached her and kissed her hand and then her cheek.

"How long have you been here?" She felt she was absorbing the sight of him into her whole body. Never before had such a feeling come upon her. He was twenty-four now, no longer the youth she had known, his cheeks less hollowed, his nose appearing larger with the long, straight nostrils more pronounced. For the first time she realised that his mouth was the most handsome she had ever seen, with a sensitivity of movement and those amiable, curling corners that were so quick to smile. And the way he was looking at her! Drinking her in!

"A couple of hours, I suppose," he answered her.

Anne spoke from where she sat at the head of the table. "More like three, I should say." She was in excellent spirits, gladdened by the presence of a surrogate son.

Julia could scarcely bear the thought of having missed even a minute with him. For the first time in her life she considered that her morning ride had been time thrown away. "Then I'll be extra quick in changing to join you at dinner."

"Don't let the remainder of your soup get cold, Christopher," Anne urged mundanely, missing the instinctive, coquettish glance Julia threw over her shoulder at him as she whirled from the room. But Mary noticed it and saw how his gaze lingered after her for a matter of seconds before he returned to the table.

When Julia appeared a quarter of an hour later, she attracted even her mother's attention. She had donned one of her best gowns, a cornflower blue silk, and during the time she had been upstairs had restored to it the rose-embroidered ribbons that had been removed in keeping with the austere rules that governed present-day dress. Around her neck was the blue bead necklace that had been her father's last gift to her and narrower ribbons had been plaited into the top-knot of her hair with streamers left floating down her back.

Christopher, observing the astonishment of both the older woman and the younger at the table, rose to hold Julia's chair for her. "What a pleasure to see a young lady attired fit for the King's Court—as once it was."

A deep blush ran over Julia's cheekbones at the compliment as she seated herself. Her mother took up the subject of the King and his small, impoverished Court, who had been jostled from pillar to post on the Continent, politically unwelcome wherever they went. He was presently in Bruges where, according to what Christopher had heard recently, the

Flemings had shown him more kindness than he had received anywhere else.

"He has formed the Royal Regiment of Guards, raised from our fellow countrymen who have followed him into exile," Christopher said. "It is only the nucleus of the vast force he will need to make any attempt at a return, but hope is stirring."

That afternoon Anne wished to discuss her financial position with Christopher. As he was only staying overnight and would be away soon after midday on the morrow, they went without delay into the library. Julia waited impatiently, bewildered by the excitement she was experiencing at his presence in the house. It had never been like this before. When eventually he emerged with her mother again, she felt her heart turn over with joy at the sight of him once more.

"We're going for a stroll," Anne informed her. "Christopher wants to take a look at our neighbour Hannington's herd, which is grazing on our rented-out parkland. Come with us."

Julia had every intention of accompanying them, although she could have wept with frustration at not having him to herself. Yet it was bliss that he took her hand as the three of them left the house and held it all the way. At the same time realisation dawned on her that she had fallen in love with him.

That evening she sat beside him when, with Anne and Mary, they played cards with her grandmother, who was still a skilful player. Katherine had noticed the change in her granddaughter from the moment she entered the room. There was a new radiance in the girl's face and those sparkling glances directed at Christopher could have only one interpretation. He seemed equally fascinated by her, but whether it was because of her newly blossomed beauty or anything more was impossible to judge.

When it was nine o'clock, which had become Katherine's hour for retiring, they left her in Sarah's care and went downstairs to the Queen's Parlour. Mary picked up her lute and began to play a country dance. Christopher, noticing Anne's toe tapping, took her by the hand and led her into the lively steps, dancing her out into the hall where there was more room. Julia, following with Mary, was pleased to see her mother enjoying herself. The dance ended with the laughter of the two dancers and the thrumming of the lute strings, Julia applauding.

"Play again, Mary," Christopher urged.

Anne shook her head merrily. "I'm too out of breath after that romp for any more exercise. Take another partner now."

Julia whipped the lute from Mary's hands and gave her a little thrust forward. Mary had learned all the old country measures and went gladly to partner Christopher while Julia played a tune that was as lively as the first. There was such delicious anticipation in her of when it would be her turn to dance with him that she was willing to prolong it and struck up a second time for them.

When at last he held out his hand to her she had the sensation that her feet were not touching the ground. To her surprise Mary chose to open with the sprightly notes of an old Elizabethan dance.

"Do you know the steps of the Volta?" Julia asked him.

"Your grandmother taught me when I was nine or ten. There were always summer dances on the lawn here in my boyhood." He remembered well that it had been during a summer vacation when the good Sussex air had done its healing work and he had lost his cough and regained much of his energy. The joy of dancing with a pretty girl his own age was a memory he was never likely to forget. With the dance ending in a kiss it had been his first experience of a girl's soft lips.

"Grandmother taught me too."

They whirled into the dance. When he set his hands on her waist and lifted her high and around, he was careful that her skirts did not sway unduly, something that Katherine had impressed upon him during his instruction. Anne had come to sit on the bench seat beside Mary and she clapped her hands to the rhythm. She thought what a splendid couple Julia and Christopher made, the daughter who was her joy in spite of many ups and downs of temperament, and the clever young man with the masterly mind who was another son to her.

It was as the dance ended that she saw in a moment of revelation what Katherine and Mary, who had never communicated their knowledge to each other, had been aware of for a long time. Anne alone had failed to connect the fondness with which Julia had always spoken his name with anything more than sisterly affection. For the same reason, during the past few weeks after word had been received of his coming, she had not identified the girl's spurts of despair over her hair and her complexion with anything more than the agonies of adolescence. Now as the kiss that concluded the Volta was exchanged, she saw her daughter's eyes close, the look of bliss on the lovely young face, and the instinctive straining forward of the slim, lithe body. And Christopher, his hands still on her waist, made the kiss longer than he should have. It was to Anne as if she was seeing it all in a curious slowing down of time and motion. Yet it was all over in a matter of seconds, only the intense joyfulness of Julia's expression and Christopher's smiling sidelong glance at her showing that it had ever happened.

Next morning Anne went to tell Katherine about the conclusions she had drawn, never supposing that her listener would not be in the least surprised at what had taken place.

"I had never thought before of a possible match between Julia and Christopher," Anne said speculatively, immensely pleased by what was to her an entirely new development. "I cannot think of anything to make me happier or a union that would have pleased Robert more."

"My dear Anne, dismiss that idea," Katherine advised firmly. "It will come to nothing."

Anne was taken aback. "How can you say that?"

"He is attracted to her. I saw that for myself yesterday evening during those games of cards. After all, she was a child when he last saw her and now, seemingly overnight to him, she is a nubile and quite beautiful young woman. It is as if he is seeing her for the first time. He may fall in love with her. Being the man he is, he will never forget her, simply because she will always be associated in his mind with Sotherleigh and old friendships. It is also possible that his path and hers will cross until the end of their days." Katherine paused deliberately, wanting to emphasise her point. "But he will never marry her."

"Why not?" Anne was bewildered.

"Julia is too volatile for him, too demanding of those she loves. He has his research and endless ventures to take up his concentration and his time. The little he has told us about his work is enough to give an insight into his intense absorption, even if his sister had not kept us more fully informed. Julia would never be content to play a minor role in his life."

"But she is an intelligent girl. She would understand."

Katherine sighed heavily, thinking how little Anne knew her own child. "Julia will want to be her husband's equal on many planes, to be able to match her wits against his. With Christopher that would be impossible. He would always be far ahead of her and that would set her battering against a door that could never be opened." Katherine paused again to let her words sink in. "He will marry a gentle, docile and loving woman who will make him happy as Julia never could. If she had been more like you in temperament and less like me, she would have stood a chance."

During the short silence that followed Katherine could see that her daughter-in-law had taken some heed, but was reluctant to relinquish a new-born hope that appeared to be the answer to everything. She watched Anne rise slowly to her feet and cross thoughtfully to the nearest window where she stood looking out. There was a certain wistfulness in her voice when she spoke.

"I had hoped for a betrothment before he returned to Oxford. Julia is old enough. I was married at her age now and Robert was thirty. She will be sixteen in October and Christopher's twenty-fifth natal day is a week later."

"Where are they at the moment?"

"She has taken him into the maze." Anne's gaze was focused on it. "He accepted her challenge to find his way out again if she led him in blind-folded."

Katherine saw through her granddaughter's ploy. The maze. No chance of interruption. There they would be alone, making it a lovers' play-ground. "Julia will not be expecting a proposal yet, so you can put your mind at rest there."

"I suppose I should warn her not to lose her heart to him." Anne spoke uncertainly. The hope persisted that a match was possible and she could not dismiss it.

Katherine thumped a fist on her knee. "You'll do no such thing. She's in love for the first time and to give a girl of her age that sort of advice would make her more resolved to have him. In any case, you're too late. She's been devoted to him all through childhood."

Anne swung round to face her. "That was no more than hero-wor-ship."

"Agreed. Had he not come back into her life when she was ripe for love some other young man would have become her target. As it is, their early friendship sowed the seed of what she feels for him today, and it will be more difficult to dislodge because of that."

Anne's face came as close to an expression of defiance as was possible for her. "In that case, madam, we will await events. Forgive me for being outspoken, but you cannot always be right. People who truly love each other are able to overcome many problems. Who is to say that Julia and Christopher could not do the same?"

"I cannot argue with that, except to point out that the odds against their achieving happiness is greater than you appear to comprehend."

Anne went from the room in a swish of dove-grey silk. She did not exactly stalk, but her shoulders were set far enough back for Katherine to

see that she intended to cling tenaciously to the hope of gaining Christopher as a son-in-law.

IN THE MAZE Julia was laughing as she took Christopher by the sleeve and
turned him twice around to disorientate him. His own silk handkerchief
covered his eyes, knotted securely at the back of his head, and he made
grinning protest.

"When I took on your wager you didn't tell me that you intended to
use these tricks."

"Just be glad I don't keep leading you to and fro along the same path
for a spell," she retaliated merrily, "because that would have deprived you
of any chance at all of deducing the way we have come."

"Hmm." He cocked his head in the birdlike manner that he had never
lost. "Don't be so sure. I give you permission to try it."

"I may or I may not do that. You'll get no clues from me."

She took his hand and led him on again. It was wonderful to be on her
own with him amid the high green box-hedges with the blue spring sky
above and their shadows together on the sunlit gravel paths. Last night it
had been hours before she slept, for she had relived the kiss they had
shared, his firm lips on hers, their breath intermingling. In the candlelight
she had studied her reflection in the stump-work mirror, almost as if she
had expected to see some visible effect of that kiss on her mouth. All she
saw was her own radiance and the sparkle in her wide-awake eyes. Before
going to her room she had whispered her thanks to Mary for choosing to
play a Volta, knowing that her friend had deliberately done her a good
turn in playing a dance that ended in a kiss.

"We're almost at the heart of the maze now," she announced mischievously. "Find the rest of the way by yourself." Releasing his hand, she
darted along the path and through the last archway into the circular space
with the octagonal stone seat.

"Wait! Where have you gone?"

She ran to be level with him on the opposite side of the hedge, full of
giggles and expecting him to be blundering about. The close-cut foliage
was too thick for her to see through, but she could tell he was standing
perfectly still. She held her breath, but it was too late.

"You're not far away," he said with a chuckle in his voice. "I judge
you to have run about ten paces before you went through a gap in this
hedge. Am I allowed to remove this blindfold when I reach it?"

"You are."

When he pulled the handkerchief away, blinking for a moment or two in the sunshine, he was standing framed in one of the four archways that stood at the points of the compass. She sat on the seat, leaning back slightly and supporting her weight on her hands, her face merry and as beautiful as the day.

"Now you're my prisoner, Christopher. You'll not get out of here for a thousand years!"

"What will happen to my work?" he joked.

"We'll make time stand still and you'll be as young as you are now when I release you."

He laughed. "It would suit me well to see this land of ours a thousand years hence. No doubt many of the problems I struggle with will be solved. I have a friend and fellow astronomer who believes that one day men will find a means by which to reach the moon and I see no reason to disagree with him."

"Oh, no!" she cried out in protest. "The moon belongs to lovers—not to explorers."

"The romantic in me accepts your view, but the astronomer in me prevails." His eyes were dancing as he sat at her side and turned towards her.

"Your head must always be full of puzzling notions," she declared, "but here in this maze you can relax and be happy with me."

"You say that when you have taken my freedom from me?" he teased.

She sat forward, making a little face at him, and rested both her wrists on his shoulders. "Nobody loses freedom in a magic place."

"Is this how you see the maze?"

"I did when I was little. I always thought there must be something very special about it when it was such a secret. Once I tried to find out what it was on my own and became lost."

"I remember hearing about that, but I never knew the reason why you were in the maze alone."

"I've never told anyone before. Just as I once told you about my dream."

"Do you still have the dream?"

"If I do I don't remember it when I wake." She had become more serious and drew her wrists away to settle her hands in her lap. "I do like to come here. I will be honest and admit to finding some magic in its atmosphere even though all its secrets are known to me." In her thoughts were the subterranean passage-way and the hidden room as well as the lay-out of the maze, which she could have followed even if she had been wearing Christopher's blindfold. "If you will just listen for a few minutes with me you will understand what I mean. I'm sure you never sat to listen when you and Michael ran through here as children."

That was certainly the case. In boyhood an occasional game had been played there, but Michael was conscientious about keeping the solution to the maze to himself, having been entrusted with it. Knowing how Christopher excelled at mathematical and geometric problems, he was not entirely sure that his friend would not work it out. For that reason Christopher could count on the fingers of one hand the times he had been into the maze, the last occasion when he and Michael were young schoolboys.

Yet the lack of sound amid the high box-hedges had been recalled from those days past when he had entered the maze again with Julia. He realised it must be due to location and perhaps a by-passing of air currents that could not penetrate the thick, close-cut foliage. Being blindfolded had not been any great disadvantage in registering the lay-out of the maze in order to beat her challenge. One section of his mind had been counting paces, and additional clues were received when turning a corner made the yellow silk binding across his eyes lose light in the resulting shadow. There had been no lowing of cows from the parkland, no bleat of sheep or the bark of a dog. Neither had there been any echo of activity in the distant stables or around the house. What he was aware of now in the encompassing silence was her soft breathing, his own pulse and the whisper of her petticoats beneath her apple-green linen skirt. Maybe it was simply that one's senses became heightened by isolation, for being in the middle of a maze was akin in some ways to being in the eye of a hurricane. Then nearby, in one of the hedges, there came a lively twittering, surprising him by the effect it had of shattering the stillness.

She gave a nod. "The birds love it here. Their songs are all that is to be heard in the maze. You should hear the nightingales in May. I've often sat alone on this seat at night to listen to them. They sound sweeter in this place than anywhere else."

"I have realised that here in the centre of the maze there seem to be certain acoustics that would enhance such sounds heard at close range."

"Maybe the birds know that," she commented quizzically.

He smiled. "I'm sure they do." Even as he spoke a thrush gave full throat and they listened in silence until with a rush of wings it was away.

"That thrush sang yesterday or tomorrow, but not today," she decreed firmly. "As I told you, present time has been terminated."

"Why is that?" He thought to receive one of her impish, amusing answers.

Unexpectedly she turned her dark blue eyes on him in a long and melting look that stirred him deeply. "Because I want this morning to last for ever and for you never to leave Sotherleigh."

He understood that she had substituted Sotherleigh for herself and a wave of tenderness towards her swept over him. "None of us can make the clock stand still," he replied quietly, "but we can be thankful for good times and for meetings and for friendship."

"And for love."

"For love above all else."

"Do you have a sweetheart whom you love?"

An image came into his mind of a shy, self-effacing girl he had known since childhood: Faith Coghill. She was the daughter of a Bletchingdon family he had known as neighbours to Susan and William for many years. He saw her whenever he visited her home, but she was shy and left talking to others. For all he knew he was in her thoughts no more often than she in his. Yet it was odd that Julia's question should have spurred a memory of her. "No," he answered truthfully. "My work leaves me no time for the pursuit of ladies."

She had not taken her gaze from him. "In this maze you have no work and I am here."

If any other woman, young as she or older, had spoken such words to him they would have been a blatant invitation, but she had uttered them out of her heart. He put up his hand and lightly cupped the side of her face, intending to defuse the situation with some distancing remark, but at his touch she shivered sensuously and cradled her cheek into his palm, her eyes closed as if she might swoon. His voice caught harshly in his throat.

"Julia—"

Her eyes flew open and she flung herself passionately across his chest, her arms wrapped about his neck, her mouth on his. Her kiss was innocent, her lips closed, and he struggled with himself to let her mouth remain uninitiated as by her very weight she bore him down over her until her back rested across the broad stone seat. His senses reeled. He knew he could take her and she would fall to him like a ripe peach, but because of who she was, every principle he had ever upheld and even his love for this girl held him back from making the first moves to possess her. Then she took one arm away from him to seize his hand and press it to her firm young breast, the nipple raised hard and true. Unable to stop himself, he began to fondle her. He saw her eyes close languorously and heard her quickened breathing, her moist lips parting. His own mouth was magnetised in the direction of hers and almost imperceptibly the distance between them shortened as he reached out to stroke her thigh, ripped through by a pounding desire for her. But abruptly he checked himself, summoning up all the willpower he possessed, and his hand shook with effort as it remained suspended over her thigh and did not descend. With a great gasp of effort, he hurled himself away from her and the seat where she lay in willing abandonment.

The curious hush of the maze hung in the air. He stood with his back to her, breathing heavily, and dashed the back of his hand across the sweat that had gathered on his brow. When he had recovered himself he turned about to look at her. She was lying exactly as he had left her, her untouched skirts hanging decorously to her ankles, her arms at her sides and silent tears running from the corners of her eyes down the sides of her face as she gazed skywards. He went and sat beside her again, looking down into her face. Her swimming eyes, like sapphires under water, met his.

"Am I wanton?" she asked him tragically, her voice barely audible.

"No," he reassured her softly, wiping the tears from her face with his fingertips. "To be wanton is to show passion without love. Your heart ran away with you and mine would have followed if circumstances had been different and we were husband and wife."

She wanted to ask him if that would ever be, but she had been too bold already and dared not set him drawing back from her again. "I broke every rule that I've been taught with regard to my virtue."

"Not every one."

"Well, almost."

As her tears continued to flow, he took from his pocket the yellow silk handkerchief that had bound his eyes and mopped them up gently. "I'm glad it happened with me and no one else."

She looked at him pitifully, fearful that her behaviour had set a breach between them. "Are we still friends?"

"More than that. We are dear and loving friends." At all costs he wanted her to have no sense of shame. "I'm the one to bear the blame for what occurred."

She sat up and was grateful that he put an arm about her, letting her rest against him as she dried her eyes completely with his handkerchief. It was a hard lesson she had just learned. If she wished to win him she must learn patience, discover how to endure waiting until such time as he, committed only at present to his precious work, was ready to take a wife into his life. She would be that woman. Briefly she had glimpsed his love-face when she had caused him to lie across her and had had an insight into the sensual power she could have over him. He was hers, claimed by her love, and nobody else should have him. She had only to wait.

"I think everyone will start wondering if we are both lost." She wanted to close the episode gracefully. "What time is it?"

He took his watch from his pocket. It was housed in two pouches, the outer one of thin, soft leather to protect the inner one, which had been embroidered by Anne on satin. It was typical of a richly embroidered item that it should often defeat the purpose for which it had been made, simply by turning into a work of art which itself needed protection.

"The hour is almost noon," he said.

"Then we must go back to the house." She spoke briskly, hiding the ache in her at the imminence of his leaving again. "But we shall see first if you can find our way out of this maze as you boasted you could." Teasingly she waved his silk handkerchief to and fro in front of his face. "Remember that this is mine if you fail."

"And your new embroidered bookmark belongs to me if I win," he reminded her with a grin. "Just follow me."

He could have found his way out easily. Even in boyhood he had almost mastered it. Yet he would not spoil a triumph for her. He took one wrong turn and then another until she was in fits of laughter. Once she fell against him in her mirth, leaning against his chest, her face only inches from his. For one dangerous moment he almost crushed her in his arms and then there would have been no retreat for either of them. But unwittingly she saved the situation, skipping away from him and fluttering the yellow handkerchief tantalisingly. Eventually, as he had expected, she declared she would take pity on him or else he would be blundering about the maze for ever. With his hand in hers, she led him along the exact paths he would have taken had he not kept up his harmless pretence to please her. When they emerged from the maze she looped the silk handkerchief around her neck, delighted at having won her wager.

Yet when he was in the saddle of his horse and about to depart she ran forward and pressed her bookmark into his hand. "Take this!" There was a look blended of love and laughter in her eyes. "I don't believe the great mathematical genius, Mr. Wren, was quite as lost as he made himself out to be."

He laughed as he tucked the bookmark into his coat pocket. "How did you find out?"

"Twice you turned from the right path into the wrong one when you need not have. In any case, I was expecting you to play that little trick on me."

He chuckled as he smiled down at her. "How well you know me."

"Better than anyone else in the wide world!" She could have added that was because she loved him as no one else ever could, but the time for such declarations was not yet. As he rode away she waved the yellow silk handkerchief until he was out of sight. Then she folded it carefully and took it up to her room where she placed it among lavender bags on her cupboard shelf. She would keep it for ever, together with her Wren doll's house.

SUMMER ROLLED BY as one warm day followed another. Hay-making was early and soon the crops stood high and golden. Julia had her final lessons with her tutor and closed her school books. As a young woman near her sixteenth birthday her education was over. She had not been her tutor's only pupil, for her mother had recommended him to other Royalist families, but he and his family would have missed the good produce given from Sotherleigh's kitchen garden if it had not been arranged that he should call once a month to fill his basket with vegetables and fruit. No doubt he would also get a joint of meat from the estate farm that supplied the house.

Julia had become interested in gardening ever since her success at stump work. She had always loved the colour and variations of the Knot Garden, and it seemed to her that gardening there was not unlike carrying out raised embroidery in the choosing of plants and the allotting of pattern. The old gardener was only too pleased to leave it to her care, having more than enough to do himself, and now that she was free of study she had plenty of time for what she thought of as her hobby. Whereas the Knot Garden had become somewhat ragged and neglected, it now took on its neat appearance again in Julia's charge. No flower was allowed to protrude above the rest, not a weed permitted to grow, and straggling plants were replaced with new cuttings that she had taken and raised herself or carefully pruned back into shape. The paths came in for the same care, the gravel raked and wayward grasses plucked out and thrown away.

It was a relief to Anne to see the Knot Garden in order again. Much as she loved flowers she was no gardener herself. Yet it was Katherine to whom Julia's gardening was of most benefit, for she could look from her window now and see the Knot Garden just as it had been in happier times. She would nod and wave to her granddaughter, miming applause when Julia stood with arms outflung in mock conceit at the results achieved.

On the farms the harvest had been safely gathered in and the warm weather remained unabated on the afternoon that a maidservant came running to the Knot Garden where Julia knelt weeding.

"Miss Julia! There's a visitor and Mrs. Pallister isn't home yet from Chichester!"

Julia sat back on her heels, brushing a tendril of hair back out of her eyes. "Who is it?" Then she saw that the woman looked anxious. "What's wrong?"

"Nothing that I know of, but it's a stern Puritan gentleman. He gave his name as Mr. Makepeace Walker."

Julia felt a qualm. It would not be a social call. Was there to be another fine imposed on Sotherleigh? There had now been two since her father's death and she did not know how her mother would be able to meet another one so soon. She stood up and pulled off the gloves she used to protect her hands, dropping them into the trug that held her gardening tools. "Where is he?"

"I showed him into the Queen's Parlour."

Julia went round to the front of the house. The groom had led the visitor's horse away, which showed it was not to be just the delivery of a document of demand such as happened before. She crossed the sun-streaked entrance hall and entered the Queen's Parlour. It was deserted. Surely another maid had not been foolish enough to disturb Katherine's afternoon rest and take him up there?

She hastened back to the entrance hall, prepared to dash up the stairs, when she heard someone moving around in the Great Hall, the door of which stood open. She went swiftly to it and paused on the threshold. The stranger, a thick-set, powerful-looking middle-aged man, was running his hand over a tall, magnificently carved cupboard that stood against the north wall. Many had admired it, but nobody outside the household had ever opened the outer doors without invitation to examine the half dozen smaller and equally splendidly carved doors within. She gasped at the impertinence of this man as he opened one of them.

"What are you doing, sir?" she demanded.

He replied without turning his head. "Examining some of the contents of this house since it is to be mine."

She thought for a moment that her knees would give way. "I don't think I heard you correctly."

"I am sure you did." He closed the doors and moved on to finger a tapestry depicting David slaying Goliath. "Very fine. French, is it not?"

She could endure no more. Sweeping forward to the long table, she picked up one of the pewter candlesticks and banged it down with all her force on the dark oaken boards, making the echoes ring against the beams overhead. "Get out or I'll have you thrown out!"

He did turn then to face her across the length of the great chamber and an expression of contempt settled on his broad, square-jawed visage. She judged him to be in his mid-forties, his brown hair still free of grey but thinning back from the wide forehead and worn with a middle parting to hang straight to his shoulders. His nose was beak-shaped and large, his skin pale as if he spent little time out of doors, and his mouth fleshy. He also had the strangest eyes she had ever seen: round and clear as a fresh herring's and as sea-cold.

"I'm not accustomed to impudence from any one," he said in deadly tones, "least of all from a slip of a girl who needs to be taught good manners."

"How dare you!" Her hands were clenched at her sides. "I represent my mother in her temporary absence. I'm Julia Pallister, daughter of the late Colonel Robert Pallister, who died in the service of the King. Tell me by what right you intrude upon this house and make your outrageous claim!"

He ignored her demand. "There is an older woman in this house. I will see her since your mother is not here."

"No!" She flung herself in front of the door to bar his way as he made a move from where he stood. "My grandmother is old and physically weak. Sotherleigh is her life-blood. Should you say to her what you have said to me her death from shock could be in your hands."

"She will have to know sooner or later that Sotherleigh Manor has been sequestered and that I am the new owner."

"Sequestered?" she echoed with white lips. "We've had no notification."

"I have all the papers with me." He patted his pocket. "But you will not find me unmerciful. I shall allow all in this house forty-eight hours' grace in which to pack up and leave."

She was staring at him in stunned disbelief, unable to accept that this should be happening. "We are four in family," she said tonelessly. "My brother is abroad."

"I know all the details. Everything is in the records about this house. You had a distant cousin come to live here about six years ago, did you not? A mute who learned to talk after she came here?"

"Yes." Then her temper, which could explode without warning, lashed out at him. "Since you know so much about us, you should also be aware that we are not people to give in to anything we do not believe to be right! There are Courts of Appeal. We'll fight you to the end!"

He patted his pocket again. "In this case your appeal would not reach any court. The sequestration order bears the signature of His Highness himself."

"Cromwell!" It was as if she had heard the gates of Sotherleigh slam behind her and she clapped her hands to her ears.

He did not like what he took to be a show of dramatics. "I want no more talk with you. If you wish to make yourself useful, inform the servants that their service to this house is at an end and break the news to your grandmother in any way you wish."

She had lowered her hands again and she clasped them in front of her, further shocked that the servants were to suffer. "But our servants are good workers! For several of them Sotherleigh is the only home they have. They are loyal and true."

"It is for that very reason that they are to be replaced by my own staff. I want no Royalist sympathisers serving me."

He made her gall rise. She could no longer endure to be in the same room with him and she took a few steps in the direction of the door. "I shall do nothing until my mother returns." She thought she heard a whisper of departing petticoats and guessed that the maidservant who had alerted her to his coming had been listening. Normally she would have been furious, for the rule against eavesdropping had always been strictly upheld, but servants seemed to have a sixth sense about anything that involved them and in less than a minute the kitchen would be buzzing with the dreadful news. All she could feel was intense pity for their plight. Her own, and that of those dearest to her, still seemed as unreal as if she were caught up in a nightmare from which she would soon wake.

"For all I know, my mother may have some document of dispensation since Sotherleigh has been left undisturbed with its rightful owners until this false claim."

His bushy eyebrows met as he glowered at her. "It is fortunate for you that you're not remaining under my roof. I should soon punish your tongue into respect and humble that Royalist pride of yours."

With her hand on the door she looked over her shoulder at him. "The roof of Sotherleigh will never be yours nor any other part of it. This house was built by a Pallister and will belong to Pallisters long after you and Cromwell are no more."

He shouted something after her as she swept from the room, but she did not listen. Instinctively she turned for the stairs to make her way to Katherine's apartment. Ever since childhood she had turned to her grandmother in moments of crisis and this time, apart from her own need of Katherine's company, she wanted to be sure that Makepeace Walker was kept at bay if he should try to approach the old lady.

As she drew near the apartment she was not surprised to see the door to it standing wide. In summer Katherine liked to keep a flow of air through her rooms from the open windows, providing there was no resulting cold draught. Then Julia caught the noise of sobbing, interspersed with what sounded like a high-pitched pleading. She dashed to the door and entered, aghast at what she saw. Katherine was sitting in her marriage chair, her back to the door, and kneeling down in front of her and quite hysterical was the maidservant who had admitted the Parliamentarian to the house. Any doubt as to who had been listening was gone.

"Think what are you doing!" Julia cried out in distress. "Come away!"

The distraught woman gathered up her skirts to run from the room with her head down, sobbing and knowing she had done wrong to give the old lady the news as she had done. As she came level with Julia, she looked up with eyes streaming.

"Mistress Katherine took the news bravely! She said she had been half expecting it ever since the new young Master of Warrender Hall was turned away from Sotherleigh. All I wanted was her promise that I'd not be left high and dry, because where would I go?" Then she bolted on her way.

Julia shut the door and leaned her back against it, hugging her arms in shock. Ashen-faced, she shook with uncontrollable trembling from head to toe as the full implication of what had been said sank into her. This terrible situation was due entirely to her headstrong, thoughtless actions.

Makepeace Walker would not be in the house at this moment if she had not offended Adam Warrender and driven him away from Sotherleigh. Her head bowed under the weight of her remorse. How could she go forward and face her grandmother now? How could she face any of those who were going to suffer through what she had done?

"Come here to me, child," Katherine said quietly.

"I'm too ashamed!"

"Do as I say."

Scarcely knowing what she was doing, Julia went slowly forward to the footstool and sat down by Katherine's chair as she had done countless times before. She twisted her hands in her lap. "This is all my fault," she declared brokenly in a voice raw with anguish.

Katherine's lips were tremulous and nervous little twitches played around her eyes from the shock that had been dealt to her so bluntly by the maidservant, her expression as tortured as that on her granddaughter's upturned face. "It is a terrible thing that has happened, but in what way should it be your fault?"

"If I hadn't lost my temper with Adam Warrender he would never have taken this awful revenge."

"There is rarely a time when we don't wish afterwards we hadn't lost our tempers, but we still do. Old age has mellowed me, but when I was younger I was fiery enough at times." Katherine rested her thin hand on the girl's head, smoothing back the burnished hair. "You wanted only to protect your mother, to keep this new Master of Warrender Hall from distressing her by his insensitivity in thinking to call on her. We agreed between us that what took place should be kept from her and that agreement must stand, because I wish it. Is that understood?"

"Yes, Grandmother."

"I tell you now that I feared in my own mind there would be repercussions to your treatment of the young man that day, but I expected nothing on the scale of what he has set in motion. My hope was that he would have had enough charity in him to overlook the incident, but that was not to be."

"Then you are not angry with me?"

"Why should I be angry now when I approved what you did at the time?"

For a few moments Julia was unable to speak for emotion. Then she took the frail hand with its gold wedding band into her own and kissed it. Surely there was no one anywhere as good and just as her grandmother.

She could not absolve herself from the responsibility of her action, but Katherine with her unique understanding had not wanted her to have regrets about what could not be undone. Her spirits soared again.

"We'll not let this sequestration take place! I'll fight Adam Warrender again! Nobody shall take Sotherleigh away from us, no matter what evil conspiracy has brought about this attempt. Do you have any documents that would help us make a case? Of course, a deed showing there had been a royal grant of the land, in spite of Elizabeth being queen then, might even go against us. Does Mama have anything among my father's papers that would stand us in good stead?" Julia waited hopefully for an affirmative answer, but Katherine had leaned her head back against the chair's tasselled cushions and seemed far away in her thoughts. Supposing the old lady was trying to remember, Julia exercised patience, but then she was not entirely sure that Katherine was not close to falling asleep. "Grandmother! Are there any papers?"

For some reason the prompting caused Katherine to blink and she spoke in slurred tones as if momentarily she had dozed. "Papers? There are none. There was never any need. Neither should there be now. Harry never meant to let anyone turn me out of Sotherleigh."

Hope soared again in Julia. "You know someone who could help! That's wonderful! I'll ride to him at once wherever he is and tell him of our desperate plight. Who is Harry? Where shall I find him?"

Katherine gave a faint sigh. The tremulousness of her lips had developed into erratic little spasms. "At the Hall, of course. The Warrenders have lived there for generations."

It had become difficult to understand what she was saying and Julia felt a cold finger of fear run down her spine. "Are you speaking of Sir Harry Warrender, Grandmother?"

There was no reply, but Katherine turned her head and looked at her quite helplessly. Julia smothered a cry of alarm. It was as though those alert hazel eyes had retreated behind opaque glass, seeing her only from a far, unfocused distance. Without letting go of her grandmother's hand, Julia half rose to lean across and jerk the bell-pull that would summon Sarah.

"I don't think you're very well, Grandmother. We'll sit quietly together."

Then something of all that had been said seemed to have penetrated Katherine's consciousness again, for she struggled to sit forward with a childlike grimace of sorrow contorting her features and her words came in a slurred torrent. "Never let anyone make me leave Sotherleigh!"

"Nobody ever shall!" Julia promised wildly, putting both arms around her and gently easing her back against the cushions.

At that point Sarah arrived and instantly summed up the situation. "What happened?" she asked, peering anxiously at Katherine, whose eyes were closed. Julia explained and they had a whispered conversation during which Sarah remembered to tell her that the mistress of the house and Mary were back from Chichester. Then together they raised Katherine slowly to her feet and between them they guided her, one slow step at a time, into the bedchamber.

"That's right, madam," Sarah said encouragingly to Katherine. At the bedside she nodded to Julia that no more assistance was needed. Still talking to the old lady, Sarah began helping her to bed.

Julia ran from the room. She met Anne on her own coming slowly up the stairs. One look at her mother's stricken face was enough to tell her that the bad news of the threatened sequestration had been received.

"I've heard!" Anne exclaimed, shaking her head as if unable to believe such a catastrophe.

"I've something else to tell you. Grandmother has been taken ill! I fear it was the shock. I'm going to send someone for the doctor."

Anne gulped with dismay, gathered up her skirts and rushed past her daughter to take the rest of the flight. Reaching Katherine's apartment, she tossed her straw hat and summer gloves aside and went at once to help Sarah tend to the old lady and get her settled. A groom went galloping off on horseback to Chichester.

Anne was coming out of the apartment when her daughter returned. "I think your grandmother has had a slight stroke. Probably rest is all she needs, but the doctor will determine that." She reached for Julia and they hugged each other tightly. "Oh, what a sad day this is!"

"How did you hear about Sotherleigh?" Julia asked as they drew apart again.

"I was petitioned by the gatehouse-keeper's wife as soon as her husband had driven us into the courtyard where the gardener also met me," Anne explained tautly. "When I came into the house the rest of the staff were waiting. They all want to come with us when we leave."

"We're not going to be dispossessed! There must be a way out of it somehow."

"Pray God there is. I was on my way to see Mr. Walker and I must find him now. Downstairs I was told he was inspecting the Long Gallery, but by now he is probably in the east wing. He asked for the keys when he heard it was shut up. Does he look like a man with any pity in him?"

"No. He's arrogant and aggressive and, I would say, as hard as nails."

"That's what I feared," Anne sighed despondently.

"Do you want me to be with you?"

Anne shook her head. "I think it is best that I see him alone." Absently she patted her daughter's cheek. "Your temper does get the better of you at times and I intend to use all the tact I possess."

"I've already crossed swords with him." Julia was painfully conscious of having committed another folly that had back-lashed against those she loved.

Anne's expression did not change. "I heard that from the servants. Mr. Walker has reduced the time allotted for our moving out from forty-eight hours to twenty-four because of it."

"He has no right to penalise everyone else because of me!"

"When he has a document of authority signed by the Lord Protector of England he has every right to do whatever he wishes." Anne was exceptionally calm. She felt as if she had been thrust to the edge of a precipice and if she panicked there would be no hope of saving a situation that had gone from bad to worse. "I shall try to persuade him to reverse that decision. We need all the time he will grant us, especially now that Katherine is ill."

"Stop talking about our going as if there were no chance at all. Let's send for Christopher! He would petition Cromwell on our behalf. He managed to gain a pardon for his uncle in the Tower, even though the old man was too proud to accept it. I'll go myself to fetch him—the groom could escort me and Sarah as well if I have to be chaperoned."

"I forbid it!" It was so rare for Anne to put her foot down that she was almost as taken aback as her own daughter. "Christopher came to mind immediately when I received the first of several garbled accounts as to what had befallen us. First I'm going to see Mr. Walker and hear from his own lips what the situation is. There may be the chance of some reprieve."

"Mama! That man has his hand on this house and nothing you can say or do will make him relinquish it. Our chance lies elsewhere."

"I can try."

Anne walked back down the corridor along which she had rushed such a short time before. She passed the carved flower screen and entered the

Long Gallery. There was no sign of Mr. Walker, although the dust-sheets had been pulled away from the furniture and also from some of the paintings as if he had wanted to assess everything. As she advanced to a door at the far end, which led to the east wing, she wondered how many times she had had to put a shield over her timid heart, for she was terrified of this man she had to face. She knew he was in an ugly mood already through her daughter's behaviour, but in no way did she blame Julia. Youth invariably spoke its mind and it was not in the girl's bright nature to be submissive to injustice. When she reached the door she hesitated for a minute in order to summon up her strength of will. She had not been into this part of the house since the early days of her widowhood. Then, taking a deep breath, she pulled open the door and went through.

Makepeace Walker was in the master bedroom. He had seen at once by its good size that it should be his place of sleeping. When he had folded the shutters back at the sides of the windows, which he had then set wide, he had turned to view the room in the sunny afternoon light. A massive four-poster, marvellously carved as was most of the furniture he had seen, stood caparisoned in hangings of heavy green satin with gilt fringe, a coverlet of the same satin, and all embroidered magnificently in the style of the Elizabethan period when it was most surely made. Tudor roses, flowers and foliage gave the general theme, but most marvellous of all was the deep pelmet that hung from the carved canopy, so stiff with stitchery that it could have stood alone. He moved nearer to examine it more closely and then he frowned censoriously at what he saw.

The pelmet was a frieze depicting every kind of merry pastime. Men and women cavorted in dances, kissed in bowers of roses, followed one another in procession playing musical instruments and rode horses with streaming manes in the chase. Boars and stags and even exotic wild animals were to be seen among the trees, every leaf of which was portrayed in the same delicate detail as was everything else. Cleavages and codpieces were much in evidence since this frieze had been made for a marriage bed. The Elizabethans had had a realistic outlook on life, with a bawdy sense of humour to match, and the little jokes in the frieze, which would have made them laugh heartily, offended Makepeace Walker to the depth of his narrow-minded nature. There was even a bathing scene, the nipples picked out in what he believed were called French knots.

Yet he could not take his eyes from the frieze, although he knew it was tempting him to lascivious thoughts, and he was lured to look for a man and woman coupling, but there was nothing of the kind. A husband and wife, their marital state symbolised by looped rings, did lie decorously in a bed, smiling at each other from their pillows, the bed-hangings a cleverly executed representation of the very ones Makepeace Walker was examining. Garlands of flowers led from this embroidered marriage bed to cradles and then to children playing, growing up, and finally skipping hand in hand into the same dance that commenced the frieze. He returned his gaze to the nude female bathers, who were voluptuous in breasts and buttocks. Lost in salacious contemplation, he failed to hear the whisper of lavender taffeta as Anne entered the room.

"Mr. Walker, I believe."

He started as if he had been caught in some immoral act and turned such a glare on her that she quailed visibly. "Yes, madam!"

"I am Mrs. Pallister." She came farther into the room.

He made a slight bow and with his senses heightened by the frieze took note of her slim yet well-shaped figure, the waist as narrow as a girl's, the elegant length of neck. As for her face, she had remarkably fine eyes, large and grey with curling lashes as dark as her hair, which had a wing of white at each temple, much as if a feather had been laid there for ornamentation. In all she was a good-looking and attractive woman, who was wasted in widowhood. He had buried two wives himself and loathed the role of widower with its sexual deprivation and lack of a well-managed household, for he had been singularly unlucky with housekeepers, having no mother or sister to manage such domestic appointments for him.

"If you have come to argue your right to retain ownership of this house, Mrs. Pallister, you will be wasting your time. His Highness, the Lord Protector of England, has granted Sotherleigh to me for loyal services rendered and even if I should wish it I could not spurn such a gift." He took a folded paper from his pocket and held it out to her. "Read the document for yourself."

She took it from him and read it through carefully. It was all as she had been told. She refolded the paper and returned it. "Since I cannot dispute your authority to be here, at least I can appeal at a humanitarian level for an extension of stay for myself and my family. When I returned home about twenty minutes ago I found my mother-in-law had suffered what I believe to be a slight stroke. I have sent for the doctor."

"Indeed?" he remarked sarcastically. "I suppose you are about to say that she cannot be moved for many weeks. Then your Royalist doctor will connive with you by confirming the nature of this unexpected attack."

She flushed. "We are honest people in this house, sir! Do you imagine that I should pretend such a dreadful thing as the sickness of my late husband's mother, for whom I have the deepest affection?"

He inclined his head, for this was obviously a woman without duplicity, a ring of truth in all her words. "Maybe I did speak too hastily, madam, but I was warned to expect every kind of trick to cause delay."

"You'll meet none here."

"Good. However, I can make no decision until I have seen the sick woman for myself and received the doctor's report. You must remember I was insulted by your wayward daughter when I was barely over the threshold."

"She loves this house."

He noted there was no apology. Anne Pallister had some spirit in her in spite of her acute nervousness, which revealed itself in her voice and in the rotating of the lace handkerchief that she held in her hand. During the war years it had been his experience that often on the battlefield the mildest and seemingly meekest of men would perform the bravest deeds. No doubt facing up to him was the equivalent for her.

"Who keeps the accounts here?" he asked, turning to more practical matters.

"I keep both the household and the estate accounts. You will wish to see them. I will set them out in the library, which is downstairs."

"I have already been in there. After I have been through them I shall want you to be on hand in case of any query."

"Am I allowed the furniture and the trappings of Sotherleigh?"

"No, madam. Only personal effects. If there is any stored furniture in the attics or cellars surplus to the house's requirements, you may take that. However, should there be something of special sentimental value that does not come into either of these two categories, I would be prepared to consider whether it could be spared." He expected thanks, but none came. She merely cast a distraught glance about the room as if at a loss to find anything that was not treasured by her. It reminded him of the decision he had made about his sleeping quarters. "I shall take this room and its attendant facilities for my use. Send maidservants to make up the bed and change these hangings for something plainer."

Her gaze lingered on them. "Then I will ask to keep possession of them."

"I regret that cannot be permitted. They shall go from here into a bonfire."

She was aghast. "Those hangings were embroidered as a marriage gift for my mother-in-law by Queen Elizabeth's ladies. Mistress Katherine never slept in that bed, because she was widowed before the house was finished, but that frieze, together with the carved flower screen, are the two most revered works of art in the house."

"That frieze, madam, is only fit to ornament a brothel."

In bewilderment she stared from him to the frieze and back again. "I see nothing but the joy of life in it."

"Then you must be as innocent as a babe not to realise that it was designed to raise lust in those that study its theme. Had I not known that you have two grown children I would have believed you to be a virgin still."

He saw he had embarrassed her with his straight talk as much as if he had torn open the front of her gown. High colour soared into her cheeks and receded again. It made him want to fondle her nakedness and watch the expression on her face struggle between anguished modesty and pleasure.

"I will send maidservants to replace the hangings and everything shall be as you wish," she said with dignity. "There are a few of my gowns left in the closet and they shall be removed at the same time. After I have put the account books in the library, I shall return to my mother-in-law's bedside. She and my daughter as well as a cousin of the family and myself all have rooms in the west wing. When you have spoken to the doctor I will conduct you through them myself. In the meantime I should appreciate it if you would leave that part of the house uninspected."

"I have no objection to that."

He watched her leave. The top-knot at the back of her head was encased in a little net of plaited silken threads. It was a frivolous fashion and not to be approved any more than the excess of ribbons that had adorned her daughter's gown. He recalled that she had mentioned some garments of hers in the closet. He crossed the floor and found the closet in the anteroom. When he opened it he saw three gowns on wicker frames. When he lifted the lid of a chest he saw more. Almost of its own volition his hand reached into the chest and snatched up the top gown. He buried his nose in the soft satin folds and his nostrils were filled with the sweet fragrance of verbena. It was to him the bouquet of Anne Pallister herself.

# NINE

*I*T WAS OWING TO JULIA that the treasured embroidery was not burned. Upon hearing from Anne what had occurred she instructed the maidservants as to what was to be done. Although they put the frieze and the bed-hangings into linen bags for the bonfire, Julia switched these for others containing rags, to which she added her sampler for good measure. When Makepeace went to check that his instructions had been carried out the charred remains of the sampler with its glint of silver thread and fancy stitches convinced him that Anne had been prompt in obeying him and the frieze was no more. She went up in his estimation as a result. Obviously she recognised a master's hand when she saw it. No doubt her late husband had been a man to stand no nonsense, as he was himself, and had taught her early on how obedient and submissive a wife should be.

He went to see Katherine before the doctor left her apartment, but she was too ill to know he was there. Anne invited him to hear the doctor's diagnosis and as she had expected it was confirmation of a slight stroke.

"This is not her first," the doctor said, taking Anne by surprise. "She has suffered several little flutterings of the heart that have caused dizziness and momentary black-outs, but she made me give my word not to tell you until such time as she might be more seriously afflicted." His amiable face, set like a rosy cherry within his grey, shoulder-length wig, was unusually grave, not so much for his patient's condition, for he fully expected the tough old lady to rally to a degree, but because he had been told why this Puritan stranger was at Sotherleigh. "This is the worst attack so far and each one has weakened her, but she should pull through with good nursing and a lack of anything to worry her."

"How long should that take?" Makepeace inquired cynically.

"I cannot say, Mr. Walker, but it would be benevolent of you to allow four weeks at least for her recuperation. Even then I cannot guarantee that she will be fit to move."

"I thought as much." There was a sarcastic edge to Makepeace's voice.

The doctor's face darkened angrily. "I do not like your attitude, sir. Although I have the welfare of this family at heart, I would give the same advice had Mistress Katherine been a Parliamentarian in this household that is now yours."

Makepeace made a slight flick of his hand to show he took back any error he had made with regard to the doctor's honesty. "In that case I will allow Mrs. Pallister four weeks in which to get her mother-in-law fit to move, but not a day more, whatever the condition of the patient when that time comes."

Anne's natural good manners compelled her to acknowledge what he considered to be a munificent concession on his part. When the doctor had left by a side door, for only gentry arrived and departed by the main entrance, Makepeace told Anne to show him which bedchamber she and the two girls occupied. Finding that all three were in the west wing he allotted one less to them.

"Your daughter and your cousin can share," he said when the short tour was done and they stood by the carved screen. He saw her brows contract on her thoughts and guessed she expected trouble from her wilful daughter, but she accepted his decision meekly. It was as if gaining a reprieve over leaving had drained all her strength and she would submit uncomplainingly to anything else.

"I'll see to it," she said tonelessly.

"During the rest of your time in this house," he went on, "you and your family will keep entirely to the west wing and use a side door for your comings and goings. In that way there will be less interference with my arrangements. I suppose you will wish to retain your lady's maid, but she cannot take up a room that will be needed by my servants and you must accommodate her within your quarters as best you can." He paused, but no protest came. She stood docilely, looking down, her hands linked in front of her. "Now, if you will be so good, madam, as to send your housekeeper to me I will be in the south-facing room to the west of the entrance hall."

She looked up then. "We call that the Queen's Parlour. Elizabeth herself once came here."

"Did she? In future it will be known as the South Parlour." He turned for the stairs and her voice followed him.

"We have no housekeeper. I have managed the household ever since the war disrupted Sotherleigh. It will not be as a favour to you but out of concern for my own family that I will continue with those duties until a housekeeper of yours arrives to relieve me of them."

He stopped, clasping the staircase hand-rail, and looked back at her, guessing what it had cost her to rally her spirit and let him know the circumstances in which he would be served. She stood in the pattern of sunlight and shadow thrown by the screen, dark hair gleaming, her slenderness causing her to look younger than her years. She stirred him physically again, proof in itself that female beauty was the bait of the devil. He was also more than a little inclined to the theory held by some extremists that women had no souls, having been created solely for men's convenience. It would not have been hard to convince himself it had been ordained that a suitable third spouse should be provided for him along with the gift of Sotherleigh. Then he took a grip on himself. A Royalist woman! Never!

"In that case, Mrs. Pallister, you will want to instruct your servants yourself on what there is to be done to make all the house open and habitable again. Let them have their forty-eight hours' grace before departure. I also give you leave to direct my servants to your wishes when they take over."

That evening he sat down at the head of the long table in the Great Hall and was served a good supper that he could not fault. Two maidservants waited on him with hatred in their eyes, but there was no slapping down of plates or dishes and he guessed that Anne had given them strict instructions. He liked that. It showed that she did not tolerate slovenliness even in the most stressful circumstances. When he went to bed he slept well in the massive four-poster with its replacement hangings of olive-green velvet. Life at Sotherleigh was going to suit him. His rooms in London had never been to his liking and his ancient stone house in Cumbria where he was born had more draughts inside than out. Moreover his land there, although possession of its acres had enabled him to stand for Parliament some years before, had never been productive, its soil poor whereas that of Sotherleigh's farmland was as rich as plumcake.

When morning came he made a tour of the house before partaking of the hearty breakfast that awaited him. There was not a dust-sheet to be seen or a speck of dust. For all her meek and mild ways, it appeared that Anne Pallister knew how to run a home.

His tour of the house completed from cellars to attics, he went outside to inspect its environs, pausing on the steps to fill his lungs with the good Sussex air. The late Colonel Warrender had told him that his father, old Sir Harry, had lived to be over ninety, evidence that if one avoided gargantuan eating and wine-swilling, in which the Colonel had indulged himself, it was possible to make very old bones living here. He had served with Warrender until a wound in a skirmish with the Scots had put an end to his military activities. His convalescence had been long, but his leg had healed well and did not handicap him, although it ached badly at times.

He had thought to return to a seat in the House of Commons, feeling that no other choice was open to him, for the chills of Cumbria would have played havoc with his leg. Yet his political ambition had waned, for his aim had been achieved in seeing an established Commonwealth in a Puritan England with the monarchy eliminated for ever. Also he was not as young as he had been and somehow he had lost his appetite for the intrigues and bickerings of politics that had been the spice of life to him in the past. Maybe his leg wound had affected him in mind and body more than he had first realised.

Then, no more than a month ago and totally unexpectedly, the Lord Protector had rewarded him with Sotherleigh and settled the question of his future. No more politics. An end to living in London and travelling out to Westminster by coach or by ferry-boat on the Thames. Instead of the stinking city he had the fragrant countryside. What a multitude of gifts all in one! Who had been responsible for bringing the long over-looked Sotherleigh to the Lord Protector's notice he had no idea, but that was not important. It had been given him not only for the routing of the Scots on the day of his wounding, but also for other deeds of valour in war combined with his staunch political support of the Lord Protector from the start.

As Makepeace made off to stroll in the park, he knew how much he was going to enjoy being a prosperous landowner. One of his first acts would be to take back the land presently being rented to two fellow Parliamentarians, but it should be done amiably. It did not pay to be on ill terms with neighbours, for he wanted to be invited to hunt and to voice his views in conversation with congenial male company. He would pay

Warrender Hall an early call, for Adam had formed the Warrender Hunt, the young man himself able to say yea or nay as to who might join, and it would be galling if he were left out. There would be reciprocal hospitality at Sotherleigh, for it was too good a house not to be used to its limits, and in any case he liked to model himself on the Lord Protector, whose Puritan beliefs did not stop him from living in rich surroundings and enjoying a good table. At the first opportunity he would invite the Lord Protector to Sotherleigh. It would be fitting to have that pleasant south-facing room renamed Cromwell's Parlour.

ANNE WROTE TO CHRISTOPHER setting out the situation at Sotherleigh and asking him to present an appeal to the Lord Protector on their behalf. When it had been despatched she sat down with Julia to discuss the next move, Mary sitting with them, for Anne considered her to be possessed of sound good sense and her opinions were always welcome.

"We have to make emergency plans," Anne said tautly. She was sitting in her wedding chair, which with her needlework box had been brought to Katherine's parlour from downstairs. "It might take more than our allotted four weeks for Christopher to get an appointment with Cromwell even if he should communicate with Whitehall at once. I have also written separately to Robert's three cousins at Steyning to see if any of them, with their wives' agreement, of course, would accommodate us indefinitely."

"I'm not going there!" Julia declared, dismayed by the suggestion. "They all sat on the fence during the Civil War, turning whichever way the wind blew, and you can be sure they'll all be for Cromwell now."

"They are family," Anne pointed out in distress, "and would not turn us away."

"We'd end up in the servants' quarters—just as we're being cramped up here in our own home. As I've said before, I'm not leaving here and neither is Grandmother even if she and I have to lock ourselves in this apartment!" Julia's face was intractable. "I've given her my word and I'll die before I'll break it!"

Anne turned distractedly to Mary. "Have you anything to suggest? There is no reason in Julia. I cannot appeal to George Gunter, because when I last heard, he was in trouble with the authorities and feared it might come to the point when he would have to flee to the Continent. It could weight the scales against him if a Royalist family connected with the escape of the King landed on his doorstep. To others it would be a less sensitive matter, but now almost all our old friends are scattered and I have no relatives left in this country. The last left several years ago to join others of my family in a place called Plymouth in the New World."

"There is an empty house in the village in Briar Lane," Mary said.

Anne's face cleared. "I had forgotten it. It was never relet after old Mr. Jackson went to live with his daughter." She turned hopefully to her daughter. "That is on Sotherleigh land."

Julia bounced to her feet. "No!"

She flew from the room and would have banged the door after her if she had not had the invalid in mind. By the flower-screen she leaned her forehead wearily against a carved cluster of hawthorn blossom, full of anguish. She thought what a bitter turn of fate it was that the one person who would have backed her in the fight for Sotherleigh was lying help-less and ill. Much as she loved Christopher and knew he would move heaven and earth to save Sotherleigh for them, she had come to realise that his chances of influencing Cromwell this time were nil. His old uncle, the Bishop, had been incarcerated too long to be able to harm the Com-monwealth and so was a very different case from the forfeiture of prop-erty belonging to a Royalist in exile. Michael was not only the son of a Cavalier who had defied Parliament, but had done the same himself. Somehow she must work out a plot to compel Makepeace to leave of his own accord. How that was to be done she had no idea as yet, but it would most surely come to her. She had four weeks, all but a day, in which to bring a plan to fruition. A ride should clear her head and help her to concentrate on her important project. She fetched a cloak and went down the grand staircase and out through the main entrance now forbidden to her. The effect of her defiance was lost since Makepeace did not see her, but she felt the better for it.

At the stables the groom saddled up her horse, delaying her with his pithy views on what had befallen Sotherleigh. He was like the rest in accepting defeat before the battle had even started and she was glad to get away. She had outgrown Starlight long since and rode a long-tailed bay, whom she had named Charlie after the King. Her pony had gone to the children of Royalist friends, who had given their word that he should never be sold and would end his days in their care. She was full of hope as she rode Charlie out of the stableyard. Makepeace should never win over her!

Anne, still sitting in Katherine's parlour, had bowed her head in de-spair, a hand over her eyes. She recalled how her mother-in-law, the most strong-willed of women, had also urged Julia to follow the Tudor Queen's example and hold fast in the face of adversity. It was apparent now that there had never been any need for urging. Queen Elizabeth, Katherine and Julia herself appeared to have been cast in the same mould. Never before had Anne felt more keenly her own inadequacy in time of trouble. She had only just remembered that the house in the village was part of the Sotherleigh estate and they were dependent on Makepeace's consent as to whether they could move in there.

IT WAS A ROUGH DAY and the wind blew hard into Julia's face when eventually she emerged from the woods onto the brow of a hill that gave her an open view of Warrender Hall. It was as if in her need to defeat Makepeace she had to take full account of enemy territory.

There was no denying the Hall was a handsome house. It was older than Sotherleigh, having been built of stone, now mellowed by time, early in the sixteenth century when Henry VIII was newly come to the throne and Elizabeth still many years from being born to the ill-fated Anne Boleyn. The old oaks and firs of its deer park veiled it in part from her gaze, but she could see that its terracing and flowerbeds were as originally laid out, although the enclosed Knot Garden would have been added in the latter half of the previous century. According to Katherine, the family there had always been loyal to the Crown until dissatisfaction had crept in with Sir Harry, first in James's reign and then the outright break coming in the time of Charles I with such dire consequences resulting eventually for Sotherleigh.

Absorbed as she was in contemplation of the house and with the wind carrying away sound, she failed to hear the approach of horses through the trees behind her. The first indication that she was no longer alone was in the sudden jingling of a bridle as the hoof of one of the horses jerked down into a rabbit hole. She looked round sharply, holding her wind-tossed hair back from her eyes, and saw that a phalanx of young men on horseback, at least a dozen or more, had emerged from the woods, blocking the bridle path that she would have followed homewards. They showed amusement at their discovery of her there. One spoke up at once.

"I'd know those bright curls anywhere! The little Royalist bird from Sotherleigh has flown far from the nest today!"

The majority of the riders were strangers to her, the rest known only by sight since, without exception, they were the sons of Parliamentary families. The one who had caused the laughter was of the family that had

moved into the property of Royalist neighbours after it had been sequestered.

"Let's make a new nest for her," one of the others suggested, rising in
his stirrups to beckon the rest forward. Then to her dismay they peeled off
with battle yells and enclosed her in a moving ring of their horses, not
giving her a chance to wheel away. She glared at them, not at all sure that
they did not intend her some harm, for young men whatever their backgrounds were exhilarated by a sense of power. Her father had said once,
not knowing she was within hearing, that it was to his regret that as many
heinous deeds of rape and pillage had been committed by Royalists as by
Roundheads.

"Stop behaving like schoolboys," she said angrily, hiding her alarm.
"Break the circle and let me leave."

Another band of horsemen, fewer in number, had also emerged from
the woods and she saw that Adam Warrender was among them. His look
of surprise at seeing her changed to a smile of satisfaction at her predicament. Those with him grinned at the game being played and took their
horses forward to form a second sparser ring, circling in the opposite
direction, adding their voices to the din of shouts and laughter already
created. She began to feel more frightened than she showed, her temper at
pitch. As for Charlie, he was thoroughly fidgety, snorting at a clamour he
did not like. Only Adam remained stationary, his hands with the reins
resting on the pommel of his saddle as he watched alertly.

She was well aware of being on part of his estate and did not expect
him to lift a finger to extract her from this unpleasant situation. Turning
Charlie about, she appealed again to the riders for release. She thought it
unlikely that Adam would have told them how he had been treated at
Sotherleigh and hoped to persuade someone in the rotating ring to give
way to her. But the way he was keeping out of it made her afraid he
might be thinking up some devilish means to take further advantage of
her folly in being caught there.

"Enough! Let me pass!" She made as if she would force a way through
with Charlie, but the grinning horsemen reached out as if they would
grab her and several drew swords to flick the tip of a blade in her
direction.

"I suggest we slit a few of those Royalist ribbons," one swordsman
roared, whirling past. "I've a mind to see this errant dove without her
feathers."

A deafening cheer went up. She turned cold with fright. It had been an old Roundhead taunt about Cavalier finery that had been thrown at her, for she had only two plain bows on the front of her bodice today.

She drew in a deep breath and steeled herself, glancing about with hostility as the young men dismounted riotously and advanced in a predatory manner from all around her. What had started out as a piece of boisterous fun, inflamed to a certain extent by the good wine imbibed at Warrender Hall, had shifted to far more dangerous ground. She knew it and so did they. The majority of the faces were lustful and even those who looked somewhat uncertain over this turn of events had excitement in their eyes. An air of lecherous anticipation emanated from them.

Warily she watched them approach. She was gripping her whip, ready to lash Charlie forward through a gap in the now dispersing rings of horses that were taking a few steps to stand waiting or to crop the grass. But she had no chance. The whip was snatched from her hand and Charlie's bridle was seized, keeping him fast. It was only a matter of seconds before she would be hauled from the saddle.

"Let none of you dare to lay a hand on me!" She spat the words at them, her temper as high as her fear. "As one of you said, I am of Sotherleigh! Not some pitiable drab trapped for your pleasure!"

"You were of Sotherleigh," someone mocked her. "I've heard there is a new owner now."

She felt nauseous at their laughter. It was the first time that anybody outside her home had emphasised the terrible truth to her and the pain of it was excruciating, bringing a sting of tears to the back of her eyes. Makepeace Walker had not been in the house more than twenty-four hours and already it was public knowledge, surely spread by Adam Warrender himself. She kept her gaze rigidly away from him.

"A theft doesn't make an ownership," she cried out bitterly.

They tumbled her from the saddle then and gripped her by the shoulders to set her on her feet. The point of a sword sliced through the ties of her cloak, which the wind had blown back over her shoulders, and aimed for the bows now visible on her bodice. Yet the swordsman hesitated, a wide grin spreading across his face.

"I have an idea. Why not let this sharp blade persuade our Royalist dove to disrobe herself? If you all draw back and give her space everyone will be able to see and nothing missed."

"Never!" she shrieked amid the roar of agreement.

Adam's voice cut through. "The jest is over. There'll be no dishonouring of a lady on my land." He had ridden up sharply and was looking down on them all. His note of authority and his severe expression defused the whole situation. "One of you make a step for Miss Pallister to remount."

She wished she could have mounted without assistance, but she had to get away as quickly as possible. Settled in her side-saddle, she held out her hand for her whip and it was returned to her with her cloak. As she swung her horse round to leave she gave Adam a look of such hatred that his lids narrowed, his eyes glinting with an expression she could not define.

"I'll never trespass here again!" she assured him wrathfully. "You and your friends are barbarians!"

"Neither you nor I have been well received on each other's land," he replied dryly. Then he half turned his face, enabling her to see the ragged scar across the side of his cheekbone. For the first time she realised how narrowly her missile had missed his eye.

"At least you've extracted full vengeance for that mishap!" she flared out, "but I'm still left with a heavy score to settle!"

Urging Charlie to a gallop, she thundered away back through the woods out of his sight. Then he saw that his friends were again in their saddles. His set expression deterred any from quipping about his terminating the sport they were having with the girl. A few were relieved it had ended the way it had, not quite sure how they had allowed themselves to be influenced by the ring-leaders, something they discussed among themselves out of Adam's hearing as he led the way back to Warrender Hall.

The circle of churned-up turf remained for a long time on the brow of the hill. Adam never rode by it without being reminded of that certain afternoon. At first he had been amused by his friends' encirclement of Julia, seeing it as a just return for his reception at her hands. He had expected their sport to end after a few minutes, letting her go free, and had not foreseen that the situation would suddenly blaze out of hand. In a matter of seconds his smiling mood had changed to a cold, murderous wrath when he saw she was being offended and mishandled. His first shout had gone unheard. If any had defied him after he had ridden up he would have drawn his sword with savage intent. The three main culprits had not re-entered his gates that day, for he had turned them away before they could do so, their invitations to the Hall at an end. Yet even then he believed that none had suspected he had marked Julia for his own, all doubtless thinking that his honour as a gentleman would have caused him to defend any one of her sex in those circumstances.

It was strange that he could remember the first time he saw her. It had been on his tenth birthday and he was riding a new pony. In seeing her adoring appreciation of the lovely animal, he had felt an overwhelming urge to share his joy and pride. His cold, hard father had admittedly chosen a sound, well-bred mount, but neither he nor anyone else at Warrender Hall was interested in his enthusiasm and pleasure. His mother had been having one of her tantrums that morning and Meg, his last unmarried sister, the only one to whom he was close, was locked in her room. At the age of thirteen she was refusing to marry a wealthy baronet older than their father, and was beaten twice a day by their mother to force her to submit.

Two days after he had seen Julia there had been a fresh development at his home when his sister had been shut up in a cellar cupboard. Meg had always been terrified of the dark and her screams still echoed in his memory down through the years. He had been frantic to release her, trying to shake the door of the cupboard open when his desperate search for the key had failed. His father had found him there and wrenched him away to throw him halfway across the cellar floor. It was after that that he had been sent to St. Paul's School, and he had been glad to go, for Meg had given in. His grandfather, who would never have allowed such treatment of her, was just a memory of kindly eyes, broad old hands that were well used to horses' reins and that could always find a sweetmeat in a jar for a child, and a wide knee on which a small boy could sit and hear exciting tales of long ago.

It was odd how he had never forgotten Julia. Maybe that mop of distinctive curls had consistently jogged his memory each time. Once he had seen her through the shop window of a Chichester tailor. He was being fitted for new school clothes. Nothing could have been more severe than those garments, for his father had seen the Cavalier taint in the simplest type of trimmings. There was a similar outfit in the shop window to that for which he was being measured. Julia was in the company of her girl cousin, and must have made some derisory remark about the plainness of such garb, for they both giggled as they went from his sight. For some reason he had felt extremely angry as if she had mocked him and his whole Parliamentary background.

There had been other sightings too, but if she noticed him she never showed it. Once they had met riding in opposite directions along the road, but they had ignored each other as those of differing political views did, although neither of them was old enough to be actively involved in the war raging at that time. His visits home were rare, for it was possible to board at school all the year round and his mother preferred him out of her sight. It was not a personal dislike; it was simply that she was not maternal and children bored her. He did not doubt but that she had been fun-loving as a girl, but an arranged marriage with his father had soon crushed that out of her. All her frivolous instincts had had to be channelled into sober tasks and conversation, souring her outlook and bringing forth all her worst qualities of spitefulness, greed and selfishness, which a gentler and more loving union would have tempered. His two older sisters had grown up much like her, but happy marriages had made pleasanter people of them and they were good mothers to their children. Meg alone had suffered and was still suffering. He saw her as often as he could, and when at Cambridge he had been able to meet her every week, for the great mansion where she lived in splendour and misery had been little more than a stone's throw away.

Now he was alone at the Hall, his parents gone and his sisters far distant. Locally he had many amiable friends for company and was never short of a pretty woman to bed, and the husbandry of his land was of intense personal interest to him. He liked to think that no blade of corn came up or cow calved without his knowledge. If he had wished it, he could have eaten dinner and supper out at a different house every day without retracking, while marriageable daughters were being dangled at him by hopeful matrons at every opportunity, but his liberty was too important to him at the present time for it to be dashed away.

As for his stables, he had inherited some of the best thoroughbreds in the country, for he had the same eye for good horseflesh as his father, who had given him his first lessons in what to look for when he was barely old enough to sit in a saddle. The white pony had not only been a birthday gift but also a reward for showing intelligent judgement, exceptional in a boy of his age, over a number of horses for sale. Pegasus must have been the most handsome pony ever born and it had ever been linked in his memory with Julia.

At present there were seemingly insurmountable barriers in his path to her, the incident on the hill having added another. It was a horrific situation that his father should have fired the bullet that had resulted in her father's death, albeit that both men would have seen it as a continuation of the conflict in which they had fought with such energy. Robert Pallister had fired back and it was by the merest chance that they had not both been fatally injured, for Adam had seen the bullet hole in his father's hat. At a personal level he felt the deepest regret over Robert Pallister's death. No one of any conscience could do anything but mourn the passing of a brave soldier whether Royalist or Parliamentarian. It was abhorrent to him that his father had celebrated the death of a long-standing enemy.

Julia had much to learn about him, many deep-rooted prejudices to overcome, for it was easy to see she had tarred all Warrenders with the same brush. He could have offered her and her family a well-built, spacious house on his land. Apart from the fact that he knew Julia would sleep under a hedge before she would shelter under any roof belonging to him, it was the refusal of the gatekeeper to accept his letter, which could only have been on the orders of Mrs. Pallister or her mother-in-law, that convinced him it was useless to offer assistance in their present plight.

But one day he would have Julia in his own bed. Sooner or later she must come to realise that. If he was like his father in any other way than being an expert on horses, it was in his intractable determination to get what he most wanted.

JULIA TOLD NO ONE of what had occurred on the hill. She felt too foolish over allowing herself to be ensnared. Almost by the same token Anne had not mentioned the question of moving from Sotherleigh when, with Julia on one side of her and Mary on the other, she said farewell to the servants. She had a special word for each of them as well as a purse from a stock embroidered by herself, which contained money and a letter of reference. It was a harrowing occasion, for all the women were in tears. Cook forgot herself, embracing Julia as if she were still the child for whom there had always been a extra baking of gingerbread men on Saturday morning, and was hugged soundly in return. The old gardener had a last worry about his duties that were now finished.

"Who will clip the hedges of the maze?" he asked. "Mistress Katherine won't want no stranger let into its secrets."

"I'll do it," Julia reassured him.

"But after you've left 'ere—"

"Don't think of that."

"No, miss. But it's 'ard not to."

When the servants had all gone, trailing off down the drive with their belongings, Anne stiffened her shoulders. "Come with me, girls. Mr. Walker's domestic staff is lined up in the entrance hall."

Julia and Mary followed her. Thirty men and women with two scullions, one a girl about ten years old and the other a boy slightly older, stood waiting. Julia noted the different expressions, some severe and hostile, others curious about this Royalist family about to be displaced and a few who might have smiled if their Puritan shyness had not been so acute. Both sexes were sombrely dressed in dark olive green with starched cape collars, the hose of the men cream, the women with snowy aprons and caps with a fold back from the brow that covered their pinned-up hair. Anne gave them clear outlines as to their individual duties and then dismissed them, several assigned to unpacking Makepeace's household effects that had come with them in boxes on a wagon.

Anne suppressed a sigh as she and the girls returned to the west wing apartments. "I could see that several despised me for having no housekeeper, but I should say they were the ones equally unsympathetic towards our Royalist loyalties and our plight."

Outwardly Sotherleigh changed little with Makepeace's occupation. Apart from the frieze, he had objected to nothing in the furnishings. Some tapestries of his own were hung and a portrait of Cromwell, whom Julia thought an extremely ugly man, replaced to her chagrin the one of Elizabeth on the stairs. The royal portrait was rehung in Katherine's parlour.

He also possessed several fine paintings of scenes from the Old Testament. Julia saw two of them being carried to his bedchamber, one of David watching Bathsheba bathe and the other of Susannah naked before the Elders; both were women whose stories Katherine had not allowed her to hear until she was old enough to be enlightened in sexual matters. She drew her own conclusions over his casting of the frieze into the flames like a prophet of old and his tolerance of these pale-fleshed, seductive beauties. Makepeace was a hypocrite.

Katherine made a little progress. She recognised those at her bedside and one day questioned the identity of one of Makepeace's maidservants cleaning the room. The girl, willing and obliging, and one other equally amiable, had been selected by Anne for the domestic chores of the apartment. She had briefed them both as to the possibility of such an enquiry.

"I'm new here, madam."

"What is your name?" Katherine asked in her weakened voice, propped against her lace-smothered pillows.

"Elizabeth, but everyone calls me Bess."

"You are well named for service in this house, Bess." Katherine smiled and closed her eyes to doze again.

It was her longest lucid conversation since her attack and Anne took it as a promising sign. She thought this marked improvement would be welcome news to Makepeace when she put the further appeal to him that had become necessary after the replies she had received from Christopher and from the cousins in Steyning.

Christopher had acted with the swiftness characteristic of him when his friends were in trouble. He had gone to Whitehall immediately and had had only half a day to wait before the Lord Protector received him. His letter had been written the same evening from the Gresham college where he had accommodation. He had to relay the bad news that nothing he had said could persuade Cromwell to change his mind. The argument was that both Robert and Michael had committed treason against the Common-wealth, which made the sequestration of Sotherleigh and its reallotment to a staunch Parliamentarian long overdue.

"In any case, Mr. Wren," Cromwell had concluded, "no gift once given can be taken back again, a principle which any gentleman would uphold, and this aspect alone should have saved you from rearranging your lectures."

But Christopher was not leaving his friends in the lurch. He wrote that his sister, who by good fortune was at Oxford the day Anne's letter arrived, was ready to welcome the Pallister ladies most heartily to her home where they might stay for as long as they wished. Later on, when Katherine was stronger in health, there was a most pleasant house next door that could be rented when the time came and Anne could be assured that Susan and William would be ever her friends and the most helpful of neighbours. The warmth and compassion of Susan's offer dissolved Anne into tears. She consulted the doctor as to what she should do, but he stated categorically that Katherine would not be able to survive such a long journey now or in the future. This information Anne penned in her reply, while also expressing her immense gratitude for the invitation.

The letters from the cousins in Steyning arrived later when Makepeace had been twelve days at Sotherleigh. The servant of one cousin came with the correspondence from all three, showing there had been a family con-ference. One offered to take Anne and Julia; another would take Mary on condition she did domestic work in the house since she appeared to be a distant relative of Anne's toward whom they had no real obligation; while the third knew of an impoverished widow with a cottage who would nurse Katherine and care for her in her dotage. Anne had thrown all three letters into the fire, a foolhardy act since the servant waiting to carry back an answer had seen her do it. After he had left empty-handed she realised she had burnt more than the letters. All her boats had gone up in flames as well.

Now she had to make a definite approach to Makepeace and ask him if he would rent a house in the village to her. It was her opinion that, in spite of his original stipulation, he would never turn her out with a desperately sick woman in her care. She believed he might be presently troubled by the prospect of having to relent and let her stay on, for nobody would want outsiders at variance in every way under the same roof for long and she wanted to relieve his mind. Julia would never give him credit for such charitable thoughts, but it was often impossible for Anne to attribute to another person deeds that would have been inconceivable to herself. Again, unlike her daughter, she did not loathe him for the good fortune that had befallen him. It was merely their own misfortune that was to be bemoaned. Had victory at the battle of Worcester swung the other way, it would have been Parliamentarians' property being sequestered instead of Royalists'.

She and Mary kept to the section of the house allotted to them while Julia flouted the restriction constantly. The only time Anne had ventured out of her terrain had been at Makepeace's summons when he had a household detail to query or wanted to question a point of administration by the former bailiff, who had been dismissed with the rest of the Pallister employees and replaced with one of the new master's choice. Even now, wishing to speak to him, Anne sent Sarah with a note of request for a meeting that same evening. In return she received an invitation to have supper with him, which she accepted. She decided to say nothing to Julia, knowing there would be a tempestuous scene of fury that she should consider sitting down to table with him. But Anne was desperate for his goodwill and to snub him now might shatter everything.

It was a long time since she had given thought on how to array herself in order to look her best for a man. She decided on a rich apricot satin, one of those that had remained unaltered in the clothes chest, and she adjusted the bodice seams herself not to let even Mary know to what extent she had committed herself. When it was done she spent the rest of the day attending to Katherine.

Sometimes after a long spell with the invalid Anne would retire early and neither Julia nor Mary, who were playing backgammon, was surprised when she bade them good night at eight o'clock instead of staying for supper.

Sarah was off duty until ten and Anne was thankful to be able to dress without any silent disapproval from her maid, who would have guessed her purpose. The apricot satin gown had a low-cut neckline. When she had donned it she added a gauzy bertha, something she had never worn with it before, which she fastened with a moonstone brooch, a piece that had escaped seizure during the Roundhead raids, having been in the purse pinned to Katherine's petticoats. Makepeace had already proved how easily shocked he could be and she did not want to start off by offending his sensibilities with her décolletage.

She added matching ear-bobs to her lobes and then picked up a hand-glass to study her facial reflections critically. Her eyes were pools of nervousness. She blinked twice as if it were possible by that means to banish the timidity she saw there. What a coward she was! But she would get permission to move her family to the house in the village if she had to go on her knees to Makepeace. Their shelter and well-being came first, and her pride was a small price to pay. Leaving her room, she took the back stairs where she could be sure of not meeting Julia, glad for once of her daughter's rebelliousness. Explanations as to her absence from supper in the apartment could come when she was upstairs again with, she hoped, her mission accomplished.

Makepeace awaited his guest in the Queen's Parlour. His black clothes were relieved only by his shoulder-wide white collar. Although he could have modified his style, even chosen sombre shades of brown, dark green, grey and blue as many Puritans did, he kept to black attire as a form of self-discipline. It might be safe enough for the Lord Protector to have braiding down his sleeves, deep lace cuffs and fringe at the hems of his breeches, but for himself the change of a plain bone fastening on his coat to one with a self-pattern could be the first step towards the sin of vanity. That in its turn could lead to many more pitfalls. He would have liked a glass of wine while waiting but that in turn, if taken too often, could lead to self-indulgence and drunkenness. He glanced at the clock. One minute to eight. He could not endure tardiness, for it preceded laziness, and he hoped Mrs. Pallister would not be late.

He strolled into the entrance hall as she appeared by way of a corridor, which he saw as strict obedience to his wish that she and her family should not use the main stairs, and she was exactly on time. She looked remarkably fine. His inborn appreciation of colour took in the splendour of her gown, but filling his gaze more was her delicate beauty, the soft grey eyes and, through the gauzy bertha, the pale shoulders and the shadowed cleavage.

He bowed. "Good evening to you, madam."

"And to you, sir." She rested her hand on the wrist of the arm that he raised to escort her in to supper. As she entered the Great Hall with him it caught at her heart to see the long table laid again with silver plate after years of pewter replacements of all that was looted. She noted some tapestries that he had had put up, new only to Sotherleigh, for they were medieval and quite exquisite. Makepeace was a man of taste. At least Sotherleigh would never be vandalised by alterations during his charge.

She sat in a chair at his right hand, he at the head of the table in what she had always thought of as Robert's place since Michael had never had the chance to preside there. His cooks were skilled, which she knew already from the meals served in the apartment, and she had the feeling that he had personally selected the dishes for this supper.

In that she was correct. Makepeace, since receiving her note, had been looking forward to entertaining her. There was nothing worse than eating alone and her request for a meeting had opened the way for him. As yet he was not even on nodding acquaintance with his neighbours, for the estate occupied all his time. He thought the ample compensation he had instructed his lawyer to offer to those giving up the parkland should sweeten the business with them, but until that was settled he did not expect any social exchanges.

"Where was your birthplace, Mr. Walker?" she asked him after they had discussed the weather, the Knot Garden and a fire in Chichester that had burned down two houses.

He told her, adding that the family estate was smaller than Sotherleigh and was being managed for him. He visited it once a year.

"You have no children, sir?"

"None survived infanthood. You are fortunate to have a son, even though he did not keep to the right path."

"That is your opinion and not mine," she stated with quiet firmness.

He eyed her thoughtfully for a few moments. Even the mildest of women became tigresses in defence of their children. There was the question of her daughter's disobedience that he intended to raise, but he decided to leave that until later. He was enjoying her company too much to want to spoil the atmosphere. It pleased him to see her taking generous portions from the dishes offered her. He could not abide fussy eaters and his second wife had always picked at her food, leaving most of everything on her plate until he kept a riding whip by his own and compelled her to eat what he deemed the right amount. She had gagged, but she had had to learn that food should never be wasted and there was a limit to the amount of scraps he was prepared to give to the poor.

"The bell-ropes all over Sotherleigh are very colourful in design and finely worked. Who embroidered them?" he asked her.

"I did."

She had given him the answer he had expected. "They must have taken a great deal of time."

"I never notice the passing of time when I am embroidering. My mind draws on many contented thoughts and memories." She was not quite sure why she had told him that. She supposed it was because the frieze had been a bone of contention between them and, since he believed it to have been destroyed, she was embarrassed by even an oblique reference to embroidered items in the house. To change the subject she went on to say she also liked to ride and read and listen to music. As soon as she mentioned music she wondered if he considered it to be a sinful waste of time. But it appeared he did not, for he asked her if she played any musical instrument herself, a certainty with any lady whether talented or not, and at her affirmative answer asked if she would play the spinet for him after supper.

"How was Mistress Katherine today?" he inquired when they had both helped themselves from a dish of Sotherleigh asparagus. It was the best he had ever tasted.

"I'm thankful to say that my mother-in-law makes a little progress every day."

"You believe she will recover?"

"Not to any strength. Tomorrow she will be sitting out of bed for the first time. Naturally when it comes to moving out she will have to be carried downstairs, because in any case it is a considerable time since she has been able to go up and down the stairs on her own."

"My servants will oblige you there. A stretcher can be improvised."

"That is obliging of you."

"Have you decided where to go?"

"Not yet." There was a difficult pause.

"Were you from this county of Sussex originally, Mrs. Pallister?"

"No, I was born in the neighbouring county of Hampshire. My parents moved to Chichester when I was twelve."

She talked on and he listened, relieved there were to be no more awkward moments in their conversation. With a sharp rise of interest he learned that she was of basically Puritan stock and saw at once that this lovely woman had been corrupted away from the path of righteousness by her husband into the Anglican Church. She had not heard for a long time from her relatives who had gone to the New World and he was able to enlighten her as to how their lives would be in Plymouth, for he was acquainted with a sea-captain who had sailed his ship to Cape Cod many times. This set him on a still firmer footing with her and they were still in a good flow of talk when they left the table to retire to the Queen's Parlour.

"Captain Crowhurst shall come to dine next time he is in port with some days to spare," he said, leaning forward in the chair where he sat opposite her. "You will be able to meet him. He may well know your relatives."

It gave her the opening for which she had been waiting and it had come when she judged him to have reached a mellow mood from the wine and good supper. "Nothing would have pleased me more, but I think you are forgetting I have barely two weeks left here at Sotherleigh."

This reminder that any further evenings with her were limited jarred him through. "Of course," he said somewhat abruptly. "Momentarily it had slipped my mind."

"Nevertheless, it is an opportunity that I would not want to miss and there is a means left by which I could meet the sea-captain."

He sat back in his chair, watching her warily. There should be no more extensions. "What might that be, Mrs. Pallister?"

"There is an empty house in the village." She managed to keep her voice steady. "It is the brick one in Briar Lane. If you would rent it to me, it would solve all my problems for the time being."

He did not answer her at once as he considered what her possession of that place would mean. There was not a house or cottage in the village that did not stand on Sotherleigh land and he had visited them all, occupied or empty. The Puritan preacher, living in the rectory, had met him by arrangement at the little Saxon church and given him information about the villagers. Most of them had been Royalist in the war and the preacher's milksop attitude towards them had not been to his liking. The soft-hearted fellow would have to go. He himself had no patience with those Puritans—and there were many—who thought of all men and women as their brothers and sisters. In common with many Parliamentary land-owners and business men, he was wary and watchful of the rising radicalism of the lower orders and their sects, fearing a state of social anarchy. Even if such ideas had not reached rural Sussex, to have the Pallisters in the Briar Lane house would give a monarchist rallying point to local people who might resent him as their new master and landlord.

"Why should you prefer that house to accommodation in Chichester?" he wanted to know.

She saw how his eyes and jaw had hardened, but still pressed on. "There are important reasons. It would ease the break for my mother-in-law to remain on Sotherleigh land and the same applies to my daughter. The rent is modest and I have to admit I shall be in impoverished circumstances with no income at all. To obtain the same kind of property in Chichester would be out of the question."

This time he did not hesitate before he answered her. "What you ask is impossible, madam. I have no idea how long ago the Sotherleigh rents were set, but I have raised them all to an economically acceptable level. Briar House is too good a property not to be extended and sold at a handsome price to a gentleman while retaining the freehold of the land. There must be a number of vacant cottages scattered about in isolated areas that you could obtain for a peppercorn rent."

She knew those cottages. There would be thatch in need of repair, poorly glazed windows and nowhere to stable Julia's horse, which should not be left behind. In more prosperous circumstances she could have taken the coach and the other horses, but she would not be able to afford to keep them and they would have to remain at Sotherleigh. Robert had drawn what gold he had needed before riding off to join the King prior to the battle of Worcester and a generous quantity had been given to Michael when he had been forced to leave the country. She had what was left and Robert had left untouched the valuable plate still buried in the kitchen garden, having expressed his hope that one day it would grace the table again in the Great Hall. But both the remaining gold and the plate were legally Michael's. She had no right to draw more than was absolutely necessary, although she knew he would not begrudge anything to her or to those in her care.

Any thought she had had of pleading with Makepeace was gone. It was useless. His mind was made up. She rose to her feet, scarcely able to focus her thoughts on saying good night to him. "It has been the most pleasant evening." She spoke automatically, unable to recall afterwards what else she had said.

"Your taking supper with me has cemented my coming to Sotherleigh in a charming manner I shall not forget, madam," he said as he saw her to the foot of the grand staircase.

As she took the first tread she remembered something that had been left undone. "I forgot to play the spinet for you."

"I know, but I'm counting on that for another evening if you would be so obliging."

She nodded vaguely. "Good night to you, Mr. Walker."

"May you sleep well, madam."

It was as if her feet had heavy weights to them as she dragged herself up the stairs. By the flower screen she rested her hand on a carved rose and let her forehead droop into her arm. She had failed. If it were just for herself she would not have cared. She had never quite belonged to Sotherleigh, and all the happy, loving hours it had given her were not confined by its four walls, but would go with her wherever she went. When she had come to Sotherleigh as a bride it could not have been easy for Katherine to be usurped as mistress of the house by a simple girl from a strait-laced background that did not match her son's in any way. Yet Katherine had been gracious and welcoming. It was owing to her training and encouragement that Anne had felt herself blossom into a wife fit to hold the social and domestic reins of Sotherleigh. The only flaw was that Katherine had never really let go of them herself, no matter how much she believed she had. It would have taken her counterpart, which Julia was, to have made Sotherleigh subject to a new personality and a fresh authority.

Anne thrust herself away from the screen. The house would let her go as if she had never been and her portrait, which came under personal effects, would be taken from the Long Gallery, to remove the last trace of her ever having been there. But her guilt at having lost Sotherleigh would linger on in its history, down through the centuries, whether anyone ever knew it or not.

She trailed away to her bedchamber. There she lay awake all night and did not sleep until dawn. Only Sarah, who through her duties as lady's maid had brief contact with the new servants, heard the next day that Makepeace had had company for supper. When Anne did not mention it, Sarah had no cause to reveal that she knew, but she wondered how Julia would have reacted if she had known that her mother had sat at table with the enemy.

• • •

THE PACKING of the Pallister goods began. Anne went into Chichester and began the depressing search for suitable accommodation. She would not impose on the kindness of the few friends left in the vicinity, for Katherine's condition in itself would be a burden on any household. She did ask a Royalist couple of long acquaintance if she might store surplus chests of goods in their stable loft and they willingly agreed.

From an upper window Makepeace saw her return from her expedition. One of his own grooms had driven her. She alighted at the side door and he, looking down, caught a glimpse of her downcast face before the width of her hat hid her visage from him. With the last sweep of her skirt, she vanished under the portal into the house.

He turned away from the window. Supper had been a lonely affair yesterday evening after having her company. He would hold her to her promise to play the spinet for him before she left. After that he should be better acquainted with his neighbours and could expect the social side of his life to be pleasantly settled.

Because Katherine was slightly better, it was proving difficult to keep her from being aware of the packing up that was taking place in the rest of the house. Her possessions were to be removed on the last day when the news could no longer be kept from her. Julia was in a permanent state of distress as Makepeace's servants packed Pallister portraits, pewter tableware, cushions, hangings, Ned's Chinese bowls and other such items in readiness for the family departure.

What upset her most of all, overwhelming everything else, was the effect that the upheaval was having on her mother. Anne's face, taut and strained, seemed to get thinner and paler every day in her search for accommodation in Chichester, the location on which she was set. Desperate to lift the burden from her mother's shoulders, Julia rode out daily on Charlie to comb the city's outskirts, but beyond the walls any of the suitable cottages were tithed to local farms while other available property was beyond her mother's purse. Refusing to be daunted, she went much farther afield. Had her mother not been so busy and preoccupied, her absence would have been questioned, but as it was she could come and go as she pleased.

She was overjoyed when in the village of East Lavant she finally tracked down a thatched cottage that was in the process of being vacated. A daughter was taking away her elderly mother, who was no longer capable of looking after herself or living alone. The whole place was in a filthy condition, but there was nothing that soap and water could not put right. The daughter, who looked harassed, was thankful to find a prospective tenant so quickly for her mother's property.

Julia returned to Sotherleigh, eager to talk to Anne about the cottage's views, its access to a little shop, and the good-sized rooms. Katherine would still be able to see the sweeping Downs, and the garden, presently overgrown, presented a challenge that Julia was eager to meet. She arrived home just after Anne had returned from Chichester. Before Julia had a chance to speak Anne broke her own news, her voice dull and listless.

"I've taken a house in Chichester, Julia. It is in a row of ancient properties just off West Street. I fear it is in a dilapidated state, but it does mean that we will have a place to ourselves and I managed to secure it at a low rent."

"But, Mama! I have found a good place for us in East Lavant!"

Anne looked dismayed at such a prospect. "I wouldn't think of going that far out."

"But it's no distance!"

"It is when we have to walk everywhere."

"We have Charlie."

Anne's gaze shifted. "All I can say about that is we shall keep him as long as we can, but he may prove to be a greater expense than I can maintain." Her eyes filled with tears at her daughter's stricken face. "I hope it won't come to getting rid of him, but I have to think of everything."

Julia nodded, beyond speech for a few moments in her distress. Then she managed a wobbly half smile. "I understand. But we would find him a good home, wouldn't we?"

"Of course!" Simultaneously they reached out and hugged each other in wordless comprehension of the courage they needed for the uncertain future ahead of them, not knowing what sorrows they might have to face.

The next day Julia went with Anne to see the house. Her heart sank. It had all the gloom of a prison after light-flooded Sotherleigh. The windows were of thick glass, the rooms small with low ceilings smoke-black from the open hearth. As for the stairs, they were so narrow and twisting that Katherine's bedchamber must be a narrow room on the ground floor behind the kitchen with no view but walls outside.

Seeing how anxiously Anne was watching for her reaction, Julia feigned cheerfulness as she looked around. "It will all be very different when the ceilings are white-washed and we have moved in our furniture and rugs from Sotherleigh. Most of the year I'll be able to gather wild flowers and plants to brighten Grandmother's room. If I fixed a trellis on that wall outside her window I could train some greenery and roses to give the feeling of a garden being there. Ridley would make it for me."

Anne felt weak with relief that she had her daughter's support and encouragement in this venture. She knew it was a dreadful house, but it was the best she could do in the circumstances and it had a shelter of sorts in the rear that would make a stable for Charlie. This was the first time in her life she had had to face alone a crisis of such dimensions, and she could carry on with more heart now that Julia had shown a way by which Katherine might gain some comfort away from her beloved Sotherleigh.

THERE WERE ONLY three days left when Makepeace invited Anne by a written note to have supper with him and she accepted. Only the night before she had enlisted Julia's help in digging up the Elizabethan plate after midnight by the glow of a lantern. It was now concealed in a chest in the underground chamber, ready to be brought out secretly on the eve of departure. Then the chest could be placed inconspicuously with other boxes ready for the transport wagons without the risk of inquisitive servants questioning its sudden appearance in her bedchamber.

Anne's spirits were low as Sarah helped her dress for supper with Makepeace. The house in Chichester seemed to look worse every time she went into it and even with the ceilings white-washed it remained a depressing place. The truth was that she loathed it, but the fear that haunted her was how Katherine would be when confined to such dismal surroundings. Suppose the old lady should give up the will to live? It was a thought that tormented her.

"Your pink beads?" Sarah asked, fetching the jewel-case that held so little of value these days.

Anne nodded. That necklace went well with the smoke-blue silk she had chosen to wear. It had no décolletage and the collar was interlaced with some of her embroidered ribbons depicting irises and forget-me-nots and several other blue flowers, which made it suitable for evening wear on this occasion.

When ready she opened her door cautiously and listened in case Julia should be about. Taking a chance, she sped past the apartment door and ran like a girl eloping to the grand staircase, for this time she felt entitled to descend by that route. Makepeace, waiting in the hall, saw her shadowed figure pass along by the flower screen and smiled to see how eager she appeared to be in coming to join him on time.

Supper passed off well. He was proud of a particularly fine wine he had obtained and poured it himself for them both. His eyebrows remained raised inquiringly as she sipped it, not realising that she was wondering why her best Venetian glasses had been overlooked in the packing of her goods by his servants. She was forced to conclude it was by his instructions, for they were particularly beautiful examples of the craft of Venice. When she nodded approval of the wine he appeared as pleased as if it were some vintage of his own.

In the Queen's Parlour afterwards she played the spinet for almost half an hour and he applauded her performance heartily. He rose from his chair to lead her to where she had sat opposite him the previous evening she was there.

They had talked for a while before he broached the subject that he had had in mind to ask her. "Tomorrow half a dozen women are coming as applicants for the post of housekeeper here. May I ask if you would be obliging and interview them for me?"

"Yes, if that is what you want." She was about to ask him if there were any special qualifications he deemed necessary in the applicants when, with the force of revelation, she saw a way ahead free of all the troubles that had been mounting up with awful steadiness. "Have you been satisfied with the way Sotherleigh has been run since your arrival?"

"It has been admirable. You have managed my servants well and you surely realised that many were not well disposed towards you when they came."

"I did indeed." She was feeling curiously calm as she always did when finally brought to the edge of an abyss. Since she knew from what he had said during their last evening together that money was all-important to him, she had a signpost to what she should say.

"Then allow me to stay on as your housekeeper. I'll ask for no pay. If you should wish me to move with my family out of the west wing into the attics I would be agreeable. Julia could take on the gardening of the flower beds, which would save the wages of one gardener, and Mary would make shirts for you—she made two that were sent to my son recently—and deal with the linen and all the mending, again without payment. As you have no competent linen-maid on your staff, she has already carried out some tasks I deemed necessary on your behalf. As for Katherine, I ask only that you let her draw her last breath at Sotherleigh."

He put the fingertips of both his hands together in an arch, his elbows on the arms of his chair, as he considered what she had said, looking at her in speculative silence. When he did not dismiss her suggestion immediately, as he had done when she had asked for the house, she allowed a glimmer of hope to begin rising in her. Then that was shattered as slowly he began to shake his head.

"No, madam, that would not be acceptable to me."

He had expected some undignified bursting into tears at the thwarting of her brave attempt to salvage what she could of a situation he could see was unbearable for her, but that was not forthcoming.

"Please forget I ever made that request. I was foolish enough to forget for the second time that you do not want Royalists in this house."

She was struggling hard against tipping into her personal abyss, able to see Katherine suffering a further stroke upon being removed from Sotherleigh, for the old lady would know instinctively, despite her confused state, that she was being torn from her roots. Pity and despair were threatening to split her heart asunder from its slight healing in recent years, releasing grief and loneliness anew.

"Mrs. Pallister."

She realised she had been gazing unseeingly down at her hands folded in her lap and she raised her head. "Yes, Mr. Walker?"

He shifted forward in his chair, resting one thick hand on his broad knee. "Although I'll not have you for my housekeeper, Anne, it would give me joy to take you as my wife."

She stared at him. He saw the pupils of her eyes dilate until the grey iris was no more than a rim and all colour went from her face until even her lips were pale and bloodless. Then, as if from far away, she found her voice.

"Katherine may stay in her apartment with Sarah to tend her?"

"Agreed. She shall live out her days here."

"Mary may sew what she will?"

"Yes."

"Julia shall again hold her position as the daughter of Sotherleigh, free to come and go about the house as she has always done?"

"If you will be my wife she shall be my daughter with all the privileges that entails."

She drew in a long shuddering breath. "Then I will marry you."

He went to her at once and raised her hand to kiss it. "I shall be a good husband to you."

He truly intended it. All day long he had been looking forward to this evening with a boyish excitement he had not felt for years. When she had passed so swiftly by the flower screen he had been touched by her haste. Without realising it, he had been falling in love with her, a sentimental term with which he had never before held any patience. When she had been offering herself and her family to serve him in this house, he had been weighing up her virtues, knowing her to be honest and reliable and transparently malleable. What was most important, he would be able to draw her back to her Puritan roots. With that she would lose her Royalist fancies, which were no more than a simple loyalty to a wrong cause, and the day would come when they would rejoice together at her salvation.

She inclined her head. "I shall do my best for you, too."

He raised her to her feet. "I do not doubt it, my dear Anne."

She thought for one horrified moment he was going to kiss her lips, for she was not ready for that, needing to adjust her thoughts and her whole attitude to this new state of affairs, but instead he put his lips to her hand again.

She went upstairs in a daze. At the apartment door she drew a deep breath and entered. Julia and Mary paused in their game of backgammon and stared in amazement at her dazzling evening attire. Sarah, closing the door of Katherine's bedchamber after checking that she was asleep, showed by a sudden change of expression as she looked at Anne, that she was aware something dramatic had happened.

"We're going to stay at Sotherleigh after all!" Anne announced shakily. "Everything can be unpacked tomorrow. I've agreed to marry Mr. Walker."

The silence in the room was almost tangible. Then Julia uttered a despairing cry.

# TEN

ANNE AND MAKEPEACE arrived at the civic office of the registrar of marriages in Chichester. Church weddings no longer took place, abolished with all other ecclesiastical rituals that were abhorrent to the extremist majority in the government. At Anne's request, Mary was attending as witness with a gentleman acquainted with Makepeace. Julia followed the wedding party into the bleak panelled room where there was not a flower on show to mark the occasion. Sadness and anger were churning within her. If only she could have thought of a practical plan to prevent this awful day! She recalled the dozens of ideas she had turned over in her mind, even in sheer desperation considering how she might lock Makepeace up in the underground chamber, but she had had to dismiss it as being the most foolish of all. An important man could not vanish from the face of the earth without a thorough investigation taking place. The way Michael and Mary had been tracked down had showed her how intensive the Parliamentarians could be.

How little and slight her mama looked beside Makepeace's hulk as they stood side by side facing the Registrar in his straight-dressed wig. Julia's heart melted with pity. Not by a single disloyal word against Makepeace had Anne revealed why she had made this decision to be his wife, but the truth was now digging like a knife in Julia's chest. All the time there had been some hope that a miracle would happen, such as Makepeace going away or a new plan proving practicable at last, so she had not dwelt too deeply on what this new role of wife instead of widow would mean to her mother. Since the announcement of the betrothal she had simply done what she could to be a friend and companion as well as a daughter to

Anne, not wanting Makepeace to be the cause of the slightest breach between them. Now the realisation of her mother's self-sacrifice came home to her with full force.

It was not her strong-willed grandmother who had saved Sotherleigh, or young and vigorous Michael, or even she herself, who had made a vow about it, but this tender-hearted, self-effacing woman whom Katherine had once accused of not being able to say boo to a goose. Anne, who had loved Robert devotedly and kept his memory alive for others who had loved him as a father and as a son, was surrendering her privacy, her quiet hours of reminiscence, her contentment with the freedom that had always been hers and her closely guarded modesty. An inward cry of anguish seemed to rend Julia and she learned how it was possible to weep inside at circumstances that could not be changed. None of this would have happened if she hadn't lost her temper with Adam Warrender. The least she could do was to support her mother in every way in the future. No more rebelliousness! No more defiance of Makepeace! It had to be.

The brief marriage declaration was over and the names were signed. Julia was the first to step forward. "God bless you, Mama!"

Anne accepted Julia's kiss and loving embrace with gratitude. Although she knew how much her daughter opposed this match, there had been no recriminations, no stormy scenes. Julia had shown a new maturity out of the torment that her eyes revealed. Anne knew the girl understood that she herself could bear anything as long as this marriage did not create a gulf between them. To her immense relief and comfort they had drawn even closer to each other.

"May you be happy, Anne." Mary had come forward to show her affection to the woman who had always been so kind to her. It was her most sincere wish that some good could come out of this marriage. Perhaps Anne's gentleness would have some effect on that bigoted man. It was easy to see by the way he was looking at his bride that he had some fondness for her.

Anne returned Mary's kiss and moved on to receive the good wishes of the gentleman who had acted as witness. She felt in a whirl. The joining of her life with Makepeace's had been so quick that it was over almost before she had realised.

She thought how different everything was from the deliriously happy day when she became bride to Robert. In contrast to the groom at her side in his sombre black garments and tall steeple-crowned hat, Robert had been attired in yellow slashed satin with trimmings of gold and silver lace, cherry-red plumes floating from his hat. She had been ashimmer in silver tissue, a gown that was far removed from her present plain rose silk. Instead of the hollow ring of an office there had been the paeans of trumpeters and smiling faces all around. Wine had flowed during the feasting at Sotherleigh and there had been the traditional gift of a pair of scented gloves, jasmine-coloured that day, made in softest leather, for each guest. At the gates money had been distributed to the poor. Makepeace had not even asked his acquaintance to return to Sotherleigh with them and dine. It went against all her hospitable instincts, although she supposed that to these two men even a simple dinner invitation on this day would smack distantly of the roistering that followed Royalist weddings.

Her groom was offering her his arm. "Let us go home now, my dear."

She hesitated by the coach, Julia and Mary waiting to enter after her, and she looked towards Makepeace's acquaintance walking away down the street. "Surely we should—"

Makepeace anticipated what she was about to say and guided her firmly into the coach. "He lives locally. Had he come a far distance it would have been a different matter, because then he would have been a traveller to be fed. Remember that from now on all decisions will be mine and made with the best judgement."

Mary, taking her seat opposite the bride, wondered if Anne had caught the hard note in Makepeace's voice. Obviously he had started as he meant to go on. In the time that had passed since Anne's announcement of her forthcoming marriage there had been no disruption in their secluded life centred on Katherine's apartment, but from now on the family was to be integrated into Makepeace's household. She hoped that for both Anne and Julia all would go well.

Upon arriving home Anne went to remove her hat and cape before looking in on Katherine. The old lady was dressed, as she was each day now, and seated in her wedding chair, a rug over her knees. Julia was already with her.

"Grandmother is asleep," Julia whispered.

"Then you can leave her to come down to dinner," Anne said. It was no longer necessary to have Katherine constantly under supervision, for she was more aware of everything and content to sit in her chair for hours, unable in any case to move without assistance.

"I'd like to eat dinner with her when she wakes. Do you mind?"

"No. You stay here." Anne understood what it meant to her daughter to see her wed to Makepeace. Julia needed a little time of adjustment and where better than in the company of her grandmother, with whom she shared such a bond.

Downstairs again Anne went into the Great Hall. Makepeace and Mary were just taking their places. No sooner was she seated than a servant came forward with a dish of oysters. Makepeace held up his hand to halt the serving and asked Anne where Julia was. She explained tactfully. He frowned, looking sternly at her.

"We are a family now, madam. From this morning Julia became my stepdaughter. It is my duty to see she eats properly. Young girls get fanciful notions about their figures and I should be amiss if I did not consider her well-being in every way." He turned to another footman standing by the sideboard. "Inform Miss Julia that dinner is being served."

As Anne expected, the footman returned unaccompanied and delivered Julia's explanation that she had already been excused. To her relief Makepeace said no more and dinner continued. Afterwards on his own in the Queen's Parlour, he sent for Julia. She noticed as soon as she entered the room that her mother's needlework box had been placed by another window on its stand and not where it was before. Neither was Anne's wedding chair beside it, although both items had been brought downstairs together by two footmen. An ordinary chair, covered in bright wool Turkey-work, stood in its place. No other changes were apparent.

"You wished to see me, Mr. Walker?" she said evenly.

He was standing with his broad back to her, hands clasped behind him, and his gaze set at some distant point outside. "You will address me as Stepfather in future." Then he turned and looked fiercely at her from under his brows. It was the first time they had been face to face since before the night of her mother's *fait accompli*. "Out of consideration for your mother, whose wedding day this is, I overlooked your breach of good manners today. It must never happen again. You will take your place at the breakfast and dinner table on time. Punishment will be inflicted if you are late—confinement to your room, the cancellation of a ride or some social appointment. I do not tolerate tardiness in any form and my clerk has written out some rules that you are to obey without question. I suggest you have the list in your room where it will be a daily reminder. Don't you think that would be sensible? No answer?" He waited until her stilted agreement came.

"To return to the subject of mealtimes. You will come to the Great Hall for supper only by invitation. I have taken a liking to eating that last meal of the day with Anne on her own. I expect to be entertaining a great deal before long. There will be evenings when gentlemen only are invited and on these occasions neither you nor your mother will be present. Is that understood?"

She nodded, determined to be polite to him in her new resolve to do nothing to upset him for her mother's sake. "Yes, Stepfather."

"There is another thing for you to remember. There are no Royalists in this house now." He made a sweeping gesture of contempt as if waving away through his own power all the loyalty to the Crown that Sotherleigh had harboured throughout the years. "Take your grand-mother, for example. She is too old and sick to know whether it is today or yesterday, and Mary knows better than to talk of matters beyond her comprehension. And you, a slip of a girl on the brink of sixteen, I know that you would dither about which way to go if let out of the gate. As for your mother, all that was Royalist in her past came to an end today in her marriage to me."

"You're wrong!" It was a heart cry. "She'll never forget!"

"She'll retain memories. I'm not denying that, but it is well known that the female brain has limited powers of assimilation, which cuts out any political understanding. Women follow as they are directed by their male superiors in such matters."

"I have heard that one of Cromwell's own daughters does not share her father's views and takes pleasure in less Puritan company."

"That daughter is a natural-born rebel, as I believe you to be. She lacked his correction through his absence at the fighting and no doubt much of your wilful behaviour is due to similar reasons. This simply confirms what I have already said to you. The weaker sex has no sense of its own beyond that for which it was created—housewifery and child-bearing. Now are you prepared to be obedient in future?"

She answered him straight-forwardly. "To my conscience, yes."

"Then yours had better be in accord with mine, because I'll give you no second warning on your behaviour. I will have obedience in my house. There shall be no more flouting of my orders. I had enough of that from you when Sotherleigh first became mine. I'm not one to make idle threats and I warn you that if you digress again I shall not have the slightest hesitation in marrying you off to the first man who asks for you."

Fear chilled her. She could see that he meant what he had said and as her stepfather he had complete authority over her. None could gainsay him if he made such a decision, and it would be a personal struggle between the two of them, because she would never give in. Somehow she managed to hide the effect his words had had on her.

"My mother would never allow me to be married against my will!"

"There is nothing she could do to stop me," he said complacently. "I cherish her feelings, but I will be master here. If I have to cause her distress through getting rid of you, so be it." He had become bored with the interview, having finished all he had to say, and he flicked a hand at her in dismissal. "Go now and mull over my warning. I shall expect to see you at supper."

On her way back upstairs she gritted her teeth, seething inwardly at the terrible threat he had made. At least she had not lost her temper, which was surely a sign that she had made a little progress along the path of keeping the peace that she intended to take. Yet there was no guarantee that she would not err at some point. What a sword of Damocles to be set hanging by a thread over her head! She had heard of girls being forced to marry against their will, beatings and starvation methods used to make them submit to a parent's will. She did not think Makepeace would use such means, for he knew how stubborn she could be, but there were distillations that for a short time could make a person malleable enough to do anything or sign any document put forward. She shivered.

Then as she was about to pass the flower screen she paused, looking towards the doors of the Long Gallery. Her face cleared and a little smile crept into the corner of her lips. Opening the doors, she hurried through to run the gallery's length and back again, releasing her tension and blowing a kiss from her fingertips to the place where Charles II's profile was hidden beneath the plaster. Makepeace thought there were no Royalists of consequence under his roof, and yet the King himself was here! Suddenly everything seemed brighter again.

ANNE SPENT PART of the afternoon writing to Michael. She had waited until today before breaking the news to him of Sotherleigh changing hands. It was a letter she had hoped would never have to be written, but at least it should soften the blow for him a little to know that his family were still there and that as Makepeace's wife she was able to care for the property. She did not dare write "I see myself as your caretaker" as she could never be sure into whose hands the letter might fall, but she knew Michael would read between the lines of her hopes that one day the Pallisters would again be the owners of Sotherleigh.

It was several months since she had last heard from Michael, but he had risen to a position of buying and selling for the merchant who employed him and, except for a yearning to be home, was finding life agreeable. The same went for Joe, who had become the young French King's head groom. It was a prestigious appointment, bringing more gilt braid to his ceremonial livery, and he had perfected a proud strut that any French musketeer would envy. Anne always enjoyed these snippets of news about Joe as did Julia. He fitted well the old adage that if he fell in the gutter he would come up with a mouthful of diamonds.

When the letter was sealed and despatched on the first stage of a long and uncertain journey, she went to the east wing where another bedchamber, smaller than that where Makepeace now slept, had been prepared. It had the advantage of being linked by connecting doors to the room that had been her own parlour before the wing was closed. Out of this, aligned with the doors to her new bedchamber, were those into the master bedchamber. She could not, and would not, share with Makepeace the bed in which she had lain with Robert, but he would come to her in the other bed whenever he chose with nobody else being any the wiser. For the present she had shut out of her mind what the forthcoming night might bring. Time enough when the hour came. The physical side of marriage had always been joyful to her in the past, but to endure such intimacy with a man she did not love was another matter. She took heart from the fact that he had shown her nothing but respect from the start, even when they had not been in agreement.

When she went down to the Queen's Parlour prior to supper, she wore the apricot satin with the gauzy bertha. Makepeace complimented her on her appearance.

"But, my dear, that bertha is too transparent for true modesty. I had no right to point this out before, but as your husband I have. There's no need to change the bertha now, but wear a concealing one in future."

"Yes, Makepeace." She felt uneasy and snubbed, but reminded herself that as a Puritan he was bound to frown on many of her ways and also that he had expressed his wish with a smile in a most courteous manner. Nevertheless, it was a welcome diversion when Julia and Mary arrived just then. Anne, knowing nothing of what had passed between Makepeace and Julia, smiled warmly at her daughter, who had managed to come to terms out of her own free will with the new order in the house. There was no décolletage to Julia's gown; the scallop-edged collar spread out like large petals, each trimmed with a bow of embroidered ribbon too small, she had thought, to offend the most astringent taste.

"Now we shall all go in to supper together," Anne said brightly. She took Makepeace's arm and the two girls followed.

Julia did not find supper as much of an ordeal as she had expected. She had only to think of the King's image in the Long Gallery and then everything Makepeace said or did became endurable. There he sat, pompous and satisfied at the head of the table, not knowing that his ownership of Sotherleigh could never be completely fulfilled, as he supposed it to be, as long as the plaque remained safely behind its plaster covering.

Conversation was not fluent over the meal, but it did not drag. Nothing untoward was said and once there were smiles all round when Anne recounted something that she herself had done as a child. It was when they all left the table and the two girls stopped by the Grand Staircase to say good night that Makepeace corrected both of them as to their attire.

"No bows on your gowns in future, Julia. Neither should you wear such flamboyant adornment, Mary," he added, pointing to her thin string of beads. "These and all such frivolities on women's garments are symbolic of Eve's apple. I appreciate that you have worn your adornments in all innocence, which makes it my duty to remind you that women have always been the temptresses. To wear such symbols in male company other than mine would be to stir up evil in their minds. Now good night to you. Sleep well."

Julia thought the effort of controlling her tongue would cause her to burst, and she ran upstairs with her skirts bunched in her hands to rage out of earshot, but no sooner had she glimpsed the doors of the Long Gallery again than she slowed her pace, allowing Mary to catch up. A smile played on her lips. As soon as they had reached Katherine's parlour she told Mary how she had remembered the King's plaque and her father's words to her, and what a joke it was on Makepeace. They laughed together over it, and Mary was thankful that the release of mirth would stand Julia in good stead in the months and perhaps even years ahead.

Then, in the midst of laughter and without warning, Julia felt the full weight of the day's happenings descend on her. She was sitting in her grandmother's wedding chair and suddenly she flung her arms over her head to rock to and fro in misery.

"My poor mother!" she cried out in anguish. Mary, guessing what was in her mind, drew up her own chair to reach for Julia's hand and hold it comfortingly. They sat there for a long time as if keeping vigil. It was far into the night when they went into their own rooms, unaware that Katherine had been lying awake and that her door was slightly ajar.

In the east wing there was no sleep for Anne, although Makepeace snored at her side. She lay looking up at the canopy of the bed in which she had never slept before. Each of its four posts had a bulbous curve a foot in diameter and the headboard behind her pillows was richly carved with many niches. Into each one Makepeace had fixed a candle before proceeding with what had been an even greater ordeal than she had expected it to be. It was as if he could not have enough light thrown down on her and had set candelabra on either side of the bed with the curtains looped back. Then he had rolled her nightgown up to her chin and started his fondling with a thoroughness that was entirely for his own gratification, for by Puritan standards marriage was only for the procreation of children. To share sensual pleasure with one's wife was sinful. Yet in spite of lacking any finesse as a lover, he was not rough or hard-handed with her, for which she was thankful, and was at times quite tender, but his one-sided enjoyment of their mating had had moments she had not known how to endure. Worse, far worse than anything else, had been his gloating, salacious gaze, which returned constantly to her face as if by catching any change in her expression he gained some devious satisfaction. She kept closing her eyes to shut out the sight of him and what he was doing, but he coaxed her constantly to look at him. It was not a rape of her body that took place, but an attempted rape of her mind. She drew on her trick of withdrawing from the present as she did when at her embroidery and fixed her thoughts far from him. By this solid defence he was unable to possess her as wholly as he had clearly intended.

All the candles had been snuffed before he slept and she did not think he would draw on such an excess of light again since her body no longer held any secrets from him. For a long while there was a restful darkness before dawn began to flood the room with pink and gold. Makepeace woke with a snort, remembered where he was and reached for her again.

"It's to beget a son, my dear," he muttered as if needing some excuse for his desire. She had succeeded in keeping from him the precaution she had taken against conceiving. Childbirth was dangerous to any woman and whereas she had never considered that aspect before, she dared not take the risk now. She would be jeopardising the security of those dependent on her, because she was certain Makepeace would not hesitate to banish them from Sotherleigh if anything should happen to her. Then she heard him repeating what he had said many times in the night in his silkily persuasive tones. "Look at me, wife. I want your eyes on me, my dear."

His coaxing was loathsome to her, but with time she would perfect her mental withdrawal until she could obey without seeing him.

JULIA'S SIXTEENTH BIRTHDAY came and went in that October of 1657 without any celebration to mark the occasion. Makepeace had forbidden it. But in Katherine's apartment she received gifts from Anne, Mary and also her grandmother, who was well enough that day to observe the event and to wish to take part. From her mother Julia received a grey velvet muff; it was lacking trimming since otherwise Makepeace would have forbidden its use. From Mary, whose pride in being able to read and write had never abated, there was a book on astronomy.

"I thought you might like to know more of Christopher's great studies," she said.

"Nothing could please me more!" Julia replied enthusiastically, leafing through it. "I'll be well informed when I meet him again."

Katherine had one of her own fans to give, which had been tucked away in its box for a long time. It was a rigid one with pale green feathers shaped into the form of the fleur-de-lis, which was appropriate since it had been made in France, and its ivory handle was beautifully worked.

"I know you've always liked this fan, child," Katherine said when she had been thanked and kissed for it.

"It's so pretty." Julia stroked the feather tips across her palm, thrilled as much by her grandmother's awareness of her birthday as by the most welcome gift itself. She was glad Katherine did not suspect there was an interloper under Sotherleigh's roof who would confiscate and destroy the lovely fan if he should ever glimpse such frivolity. She thought of concealing it with the be-jewelled Pallister silver, which had been taken from the blanket chest and hidden in the secret underground passage leading to the maze. But she could not bear to have the lovely gift out of her sight and decided it would be safe in her room, as Makepeace never went there.

Now that Katherine was more alert again it was hoped that she would not realise she was the only one still wearing lace collars and trimmings on her garments. At Makepeace's orders Anne, Julia and Mary had had to remove everything decorative down to the smallest ornamental fastening on their clothes. All low necklines had been filled in, starkly plain collars the rule, and petticoats, shifts and nightgowns had been stripped of lace and embroidery, all replaced by bands of linen. Only gowns of silk, wool or cotton could be retained, Makepeace being of the opinion that the heavy rustle of taffeta was seductive to men and satin on the female form too inviting. Makepeace himself emptied a drawer of Anne's fancy garters, some of which had been given her by Robert, and threw them away. Mary and Julia were supposed to do likewise with theirs. Mary obeyed, but Julia kept the best and continued to wear them like hidden banners.

Makepeace began to entertain. His first guests were those neighbours from whom he had taken back the land. Since wives, sons and daughters were invited as well, Julia and Mary were present. One of the sons, Lucas Hannington, had been in Adam Warrender's company when Julia was encircled on the hill. He had not been among those who had manhandled her, but to her annoyance he gave her a wink when the other guests' backs were turned.

Julia soon found herself enjoying the occasion, for the Hanningtons, although Puritans, were not extremists and exuded goodwill and kindliness. Anne felt greatly at ease with them, for they were akin to the good folk she had associated with in her youth and as pleasant as she knew the majority of ordinary Puritans to be.

The Hannington offspring numbered ten in all, with ages ranging from seven to twenty, all given to lively chatter. In contrast the other family was strictly controlled, the two Thompson sons in black, their three sisters in grey. The girls were docile enough, eyes downcast most of the time, but there was spirit in the boys, who made sure they sat well away from their parents at the long table in the Great Hall and talked of football and cricket with enthusiasm.

After dinner the older people withdrew to the Queen's Parlour, only the three Thompson girls accompanying their mother, while the rest donned cloaks against the cold and windy November day and went outside. They were supposed to take a walk, but they all knew of the Sotherleigh maze and Julia allowed them to get hilariously lost in it until she, intoxicated by so much lively company after being bereft of it for so long, led them out again. Then the Thompson boys made a football from rags scavenged from the stables. Although Lucas would have preferred to dally on his own with Julia, she treated him with such indifference that he joined in the game with everybody else.

It became very noisy. The intention of all was to keep well away from the house, but in the excitement of the game the flow of play took them onto a lawn within full view of the lower windows. Julia, giving a hearty kick that fluttered her petticoats, sent the ball soaring before falling flat on her face. Lucas, grinning at the glimpse he had had of her knee-high garter with its dancing scarlet ribbon, ran to help her up.

"Are you all right?" he asked with his arms around her.

In her mirth she forsook the grudge she had held against him and did not push him away. "Yes! That must have been a goal!"

It was then that she and all the rest saw a row of outraged faces at the windows of the Queen's Parlour.

The Hannington offspring did not receive a second invitation to Sotherleigh, being deemed a bad influence on Julia, and the Thompson boys came into the same category. It was not that Makepeace disapproved of football, having played it himself when younger and it was known to have been a favourite sport of Cromwell's in days past, but to see his stepdaughter kicking up her petticoats among the equally riotous Hannington girls had shocked him to the core. Fortunately for her he had been too far away to see the show of her garter. Since all the young people were involved, he did not pick her out for any special punishment, but he warned her severely against any such immodest displays in the future. He remained on good terms with the parents simply because it was to his advantage, and encouraged the dull wife of the strait-laced Mr. Thompson to call as often as possible with their three equally dull daughters, for he thought their company entirely suitable for his womenfolk. Anne, Julia and Mary spent many tedious hours with them as a result.

When Christmas came it was the most austere that Sotherleigh had ever known. Nobody was allowed to mention its coming and the room where Anne had once secreted herself, making gifts for the entire household, had not been entered. At dinner on Christmas Day there was a special menu ordered by Makepeace, but it was broth and black bread as if he wanted to ensure that those who had previously enjoyed feasts in the Great Hall at the festive season should do penance for it. By chance Katherine was poorly during the spell of Christmastide, or else she would have queried the lack of holly and greenery festooning her parlour and become suspicious over the broth and black bread.

By the spring of 1658 Makepeace was able to take stock of his position at Sotherleigh and realise he had achieved much. He had been invited to become a local magistrate, to hunt, to dine and to sup, the social invitations having snowballed. The exception was Warrender Hall. He had called on the young man there and been courteously received, but there had been no invitation to join the most important local hunt. The call had been returned when the ladies of Sotherleigh were in Chichester and

Adam Warrender had gone by the time they returned. Since then there had been no more contact, except when meeting by chance or when hunting with others. Adam always made a point of enquiring after Anne and Julia and seemed keenly interested in the Sotherleigh estate, ready enough to give advice on crops and cattle. If the young man had not possessed an equally fine estate, Makepeace would have almost believed Adam had a mind to the place himself. The lack of an invitation to join the Warrender hunt continued to rankle and Makepeace pondered as to how the oversight might be amended.

Makepeace had treated Anne to some new gowns in the Puritan mode of sombre-coloured silks with the type of collars he had stipulated, but which she regarded as over-large until it dawned on her that he wanted the shape of her breasts hidden from the sight of other men. It was apparent to all that he was deeply in love with her, but he had been seized by an overpowering jealousy as a result. He watched her constantly in mixed company. Any gentleman who lingered in conversation with her could expect Makepeace to come and clap a hand on his shoulder with some comradely remark to divert attention away from her. At table in other houses, if he was seated some distance from her, his eyes would be forever drifting in her direction.

She was not quite sure when she first realised he was beginning to resent her attention to her own family, but whenever he was in the house he tried to keep her away from Katherine's apartment and seized any excuse to send Julia off on some errand if the two of them happened to be together. Neither did he like Mary sharing her time.

"Surely the young woman has someone else with whom she could live, Anne," he remarked testily one day. "Where is her home, anyway? Devonshire, I was told. Whereabouts? I could probably arrange for her to go back to her roots with a small income."

"No." Anne was adamant. "I promised her a home after she was bereaved and nothing shall induce me to break my word."

He left the matter there for the time being, returning to it occasionally, but was unable to prise much more information out of Anne. He tried questioning Mary, but she was equally vague, saying all she knew was that her father had been concerned with seafaring matters in south Devon. She had been orphaned very young and had been cared for by various friends and relations, mostly elderly, until the last one was too old to have her; then someone had contacted Anne on her behalf. Makepeace began to

scent a mystery and intended to solve it if that should prove possible. The
few facts presented had been so pat, so—rehearsed.

He began his investigation by going through all the papers and correspondence in Anne's desk when she was absent. There was nothing of
interest, although her son's letters reeked of royalism and he would have
burned them if he had not wanted to keep his search from her knowledge.
He went systematically through every room as he had never done before
and a number of unexpected things came to light. There was a chest of
rich fabrics, which he locked again and pocketed the key, and others of
every kind of sewing materials, including yards of plain silk ribbons
awaiting the embroidery that he had now banned and which he left
untouched since they were not important any more. He searched for
secret panelling, but could find nothing. The false wall invited suspicion.
He pulled it from its slot where it was housed permanently since he now
used the whole room for entertaining, but no hidden cavities were revealed.

Finally he decided that since he had left nowhere unexplored, apart
from Katherine's apartments, he would let the matter rest for the time
being. Meanwhile he would write to his friend Captain Crowhurst, asking him to make enquiries at Dartmouth, at which port he always berthed
for a few days on his voyages to and from the New World.

Anne was thankful when he stopped his persistent nagging about
Mary's presence in the house, but then there came a further onslaught
from him on the question of her needlework. From the first he had
interfered in every aspect of it, starting by not letting her have her needlework box where she had always had it in the Queen's Parlour, insisting
that the light was better from another of the windows there. It had upset
her when he had her wedding chair removed to the attics, although she
had accepted his explanation that it was not seemly he should be reminded
daily of his predecessor by the initials on the chair. Over and over again
she had given in on what would have seemed mundane matters to him
and others, but were important to her. Early on he had forbidden the
embroidering of ribbons, the work she had always loved best, by pointing
out it was a waste of her time since the end product could not be used in
any way. She had been obliged to accept this decree and turned to other
forms of embroidery, but gradually he had exerted pressure on that too.

"Put that stitchery away, my dear, and read to me instead," was one of
his ploys. At times he would want her to discuss some trivial matter with
him or draw attention to a domestic affair that he thought she should

investigate, or to go a stroll with him in the garden, whatever the weather. It was any pretext he could think of aimed at making her put away the work that was such a comfort to her in her life with him. She believed he would not give up until he had driven a wedge between her and her work for ever. It was not difficult to guess the reason. The first time he had invited her to take supper with him she had told him how she could lose herself in contented memories as she stitched. It had been a foolish confidence, for he was set against that last link she kept with the past.

Day by day she put up with his petty tyrannies. She had always enjoyed riding, but he had forbidden that too, expressing concern that she might take a fall. When she went shopping in Chichester a certain maidservant, instead of Sarah, was always detailed to accompany her at Makepeace's order, and she believed a full account of everything she did, and whom she met, was reported back to him. If one of her old friends called, he would hurry from wherever he was to ensure that she should not be alone with her guest, reminiscing about times past in which he had had no part. She tried to find excuses for him in her own mind, aware that jealousy affected people like an illness they could not control, but it was becoming as if she could not breathe without his knowledge.

Then the day came when she went into the Long Gallery and found that Robert's portrait, which had been painted on his thirtieth birthday, just before their marriage, had been removed to the attics. Something seemed to snap in her. She gathered materials for her ribbon work into a basket and went up to the attics herself. These consisted of a series of rooms that stretched the length of the house, each cluttered with discarded furniture, ancient chests, old bed-hangings and boxes of papers and receipts that probably dated back to Ned's time. Her wedding chair and Robert's portrait had been dumped in the first room nearest the door, showing that the servants concerned had not wanted to penetrate farther into that dark and dusty place.

She went to the room at the far end. The window there looked down on the courtyard and she'd be able to watch out for Makepeace's comings and goings. The panes were grimed and hung with cobwebs, which she cleaned away with an old cushion cover that came to hand. Then she fetched her chair, which she placed by the window. Next she took Robert's portrait from its wrappings and hung it on a convenient nail exactly opposite where she would sit. Some of his old sailing charts were stored on a shelf there and she dusted them off after taking them down. They were hand-drawn on vellum stuck to panels of wood for easy folding. She opened them and propped them up in a semicircle at a short distance from her chair, anticipating how she would follow those past voyages with him in her thoughts. Lastly she kissed his portrait on the lips before sitting down to embroider under his keen blue gaze for almost two hours, utterly at peace.

When she heard hooves in the courtyard heralding Makepeace's return, she locked the door of the room after her and sped back down the stairs to the narrow corridor at the east end of the house. From there she slipped through a door into the east wing and reached the safety of her bedchamber in no more than a minute. There was some tell-tale dust and cobwebs clinging to her skirt-hems, and she decided that at the first opportunity she would clean up the section of the attics she would be using.

Two days later this was done. Unbeknown to Julia or Mary, or to anyone else in the house, she began to slip away to the attic and embroider whenever it was possible. Sometimes when she could not sleep at night she would leave Makepeace snoring in their bed and go up there, for by now she had candles and a curtain for the window to keep the light from being seen outside. She was always back in bed well before dawn at which hour Makepeace sometimes woke.

As he increasingly denied her the relaxation of embroidery downstairs, she felt herself becoming more exultant in the knowledge of the haven she had created for herself with Robert, away from her dominating husband. She was often forced to sit with idle hands or read a book that was never one of her own choice, for Makepeace selected editions of Puritan sermons or volumes on the principles of Puritanism in his effort to hammer into her his beliefs and intolerances. She thought how he was corrupting her instead of uplifting her, for she had turned to deceit by hiding her embroidery in the attic.

That her secretiveness came from sheer desperation did not allow her to excuse herself in her own eyes. In atonement she put her ribbons aside for a while and made a chalice veil of finest linen. After delicately marking out what she was to embroider on it, she used silver and white silks in hem and satin stitches for the main work. In the middle of the chalice veil were the words *Unto God Be Praise.* Then along the border on four sides she put her own prayer. *O, Lord, consider my distress. With speed erase my sin's deface and my fault redress, Lord, for thy Great Mercy's Sake.*

When it was finished she folded it away in a small box and put it on the shelf of an ancient cupboard in her retreat where she also stored her newly embroidered ribbons. She added to them the many rolls she had worked in happier times from boxes in what she thought of as the "Christmas Gift" room, which had escaped Makepeace's notice. Then she became like a magpie adding the bows and streamers from her gowns and those of Julia and Mary that had been discarded but never thrown away. When she remembered there were more boxes in the closet of the bed-chamber she had occupied in the west wing, it was like discovering gold. By now the cupboard in the attic was full and she had to make use of a chest there. It troubled her sometimes that she was like a miser hoarding money, but it did not stop her rising from her bed at night if she remembered suddenly where another length might lie; more than once she had hurried in from the garden when she thought where several other rolls might be found. It did not occur to her that she was holding on to these symbols of love and freedom like a life-line.

The day came when Makepeace successfully eliminated any chance she had to stitch downstairs. "I think you might as well put that old needle-work box right away," he said smilingly to her. "You have no need of it any more."

"Whatever you wish, Makepeace," she said, her lashes lowered to hide the flare of exhilaration in her eyes.

Her needlebox was thrust inside the door of the attics by a servant's hands. That night she was up there to carry the stand and then the box to her retreat. When she sat in her wedding chair and lifted the lid she thought that if it had not been for Julia, Katherine and Mary, she would have been content to stay in her attic haven until the end of her days, never again to share a bed with Makepeace.

MAKEPEACE was holding one of his all-male supper parties. Anne had followed her usual pattern of discussing the menu with the housekeeper before leaving everything in the woman's capable hands; then, on the evening itself, she checked the table to see that it was all to her husband's liking. When wives were present he left the seating arrangements to her, but these male occasions were less formal and guests settled themselves where they pleased at the well-laden board. This meant she was able to be upstairs before they arrived and did not have to appear at all unless Makepeace asked her or Julia, sometimes both, to provide a little musical entertainment in the Queen's Parlour when supper was over. It was to Mary's relief that he never suggested that she form a trio with them. She was always nervous of being present in his gatherings, never forgetting there was still the chance of her being recognised by a former Roundhead officer among them.

Anne always welcomed these gentlemen's supper parties. It meant that she was left free to be in Katherine's apartment, secure in the knowledge that he could not trump up some excuse to call her away. She believed half the reason for his wanting a musical interlude was to make sure she did not have too long on her own with her family and thus forget him temporarily. He had forbidden all games of chance with the exception of chess, which he considered an intellectual exercise, but this did not stop merry games of cards and dice and shove-halfpenny being played in Katherine's parlour. The old lady was much better again and although she did not play she liked to watch and applaud the winners with gentle clapping.

"Well done!" she would exclaim.

On this particular evening Anne and Julia had been ordered to attend Makepeace and his friends at ten o'clock. Katherine retired early enough for Sarah to see her into bed and then return to make up a foursome at the card table again for a hand of Triumph.

In this Royalist nucleus remaining at Sotherleigh, there were no false barriers. Sarah had her duties but it was unthinkable to either Anne or Julia that such a loyal woman should not be included in the simple pleasures that passed the evening away.

They had played two lively games when Anne suddenly noticed the clock and sprang up in alarm. "It's a quarter past ten! Fetch your lute, Julia! You and I should have been downstairs fifteen minutes ago to time our entrance to the second. We're terribly late!"

They hastened downstairs, checked each other's appearance in the hall and then Anne led the way into the Queen's Parlour, Julia following. Chairs scraped as Makepeace and his thirty guests rose to bid them good evening. Anne acknowledged their courtesies with a gracious nod left and right, but her vision was dominated by Makepeace. She could see he was extremely annoyed over her and her daughter's tardiness. The smile with which he welcomed her was solely for the benefit of his guests. She knew she would be severely reprimanded when she was on her own with him in her bedchamber later. She feared these sessions. He always lectured her for an hour or more, making a sermon of it, and at the end she had to apologise humbly, admitting how wrong she was and how right he was in everything. She had learned early on that to voice anything else at that point was to bring a resurgence of the upbraiding, interspersed with reminders that it was entirely for her own good. During these ordeals he never varied from his fond tones, but his voice and all he said created crushing bands around her brain until she withdrew her thoughts from him in a means of escape that she was using more and more. Even when he finally fell silent all was not over. As if to make up for having had to be severe with her, he made love to her afterwards with an adoring passion to which her body frequently responded of its own volition while her mind remained shut away behind her eyes that had to be turned on him.

"Take your place at the spinet, my dear," he said, bowing her to it. "We have all been waiting impatiently for this treat that you and Julia are to give us."

It was a veiled barb, a hint of what was to come. She put her hands on the keyboard and saw they were shaking. As she began to play, the sweet tinkling notes had a soothing effect and she became calmer. After two pieces it would be Julia's turn. Her opening song was to be one of Makepeace's favourites, being in praise of the countryside, for he saw himself now as a fully fledged Sussex squire as if he had been born in the county.

As her mother played Julia sat unobtrusively on a stool by the wall. She let her gaze travel over the middle-aged audience, noting who was there. Many of the faces were flushed with wine and she guessed that an older guest here and there would be hard put not to slip into a doze during the recital. She picked out two gentlemen a few seats apart whom she did not know. Normally Makepeace would have presented any newcomers to her mother and herself upon their entry to the Queen's Parlour, but he had been so rattled this evening by their failure to appear on time that he had not adhered to the good manners he was accustomed to show in public. Her glance went to her stepfather. Makepeace's doting gaze was fixed on Anne, a smugness of possession on his face as if that sensitive, lovely woman were a prize he had won through his own virtue.

Sickened, Julia let her eyes wander back to his guests again. At least two-thirds were Puritans, but only an extremist here and there was in black or grey like Makepeace, the rest dressed in rich colours with some conservative braiding. Most wore silver-buckled shoes and several were in deep-cuffed dress boots, but only one man flaunted a pair of bucket-tops in a pale creamy leather. She could see only one of his boots and just his blue velvet-sleeved elbow, for some large gentlemen in high-backed chairs blocked her view and also prevented any clue to his identity.

Unlike all the other guests and Makepeace himself, the unknown gentleman was wearing the new straight-cut breeches that flapped at mid-calf
instead of the fuller, knee-length breeches such as had been worn for as
long as she could remember.

Applause broke out again as Anne finished her second piece and bowed
smilingly from her seat in acknowledgement. Makepeace courteously
turned the chair for her in order that she could more easily watch her
daughter play. It was as Julia rose from the stool to move into a more
central position that she met the glittering, onyx-black eyes of the wearer
of the bucket-topped boots. It was Adam Warrender.

Lightning seemed to sear across the room between them, scorching and
eliminating everything else in its path. All sound melted away as though a
vacuum had been created in which only the two of them remained. She
did not escape that unseen violence, for she felt it burn through her,
making her flesh throb and activating every nerve in her body to a
trembling awareness. It was fiercely pleasurable, in spite of her will being
wholly set against it, and instinctively she knew it was the same for him.

Then as abruptly as it had happened the extraordinary encounter was
over, no more than seconds having passed, and the room closed in on her
again. She sat down quickly on the chair that had been put ready and
automatically settled her lute against her, ready to play. Her mind was
racing and such a volcano of wrath was building up in her at Adam's
presence under Sotherleigh's roof that she thought she must choke. She
had been tricked! Her mother had yet to learn, with the inevitable subsequent distress, that a Warrender was in the same room with her. Julia
almost ground her teeth. Makepeace, now glibly announcing the first
song she was to sing, must have had his own deceitful reason for not
presenting the newcomers that evening, for he could not have given the
names of two and left out the third and most loathed name to those who
once owned Sotherleigh.

The colour was running up her neck and she breathed deeply. For a
moment she remembered her resolve to keep the peace and even her
regrets of her past treatment of Adam Warrender, but when, under her
lashes, she glared at the gathered guests, every one opposed to the King
and thus the enemy of her late father, her brother in exile and to
Sotherleigh itself, her earlier intentions were forgotten. There were no
individuals in this audience any more, not even Adam, since now that she
was seated again she could no longer see him. She wanted vengeance for
this violation of her home. Makepeace had behaved traitorously to her

mother and to herself. But she had to swallow her pride once again and play the role of meek stepdaughter that went against her whole nature.

Everyone was waiting. Her heart was pounding and rage gripped her throat, making her wonder how she would sing. But it had to be done. Somehow she must struggle against this tumult of fury. Much as she loathed Makepeace she would never have thought him capable of inflicting such an insult upon her gentle mother.

She struck the first melodious notes and could hear the faint tremour in her voice as she began to sing a verse of an old song in praise of the Sussex countryside. Then Adam's face came into her view again. He was staring hard at her, conveying his awareness of the effect of his presence.

It was the last straw! For a second she hesitated at the chorus of her song and then, before there was time for second thoughts, she switched to another. It was a rollicking drinking song of the Cavaliers.

"Here's health to the King! God bless him! Let the name of Charles ring! God bless him! And let every loyal Englishman in the land—"

She was almost tossed from the chair by the force with which Makepeace hurled himself from his seat to wrench the lute from her hands and smash it across his knee. In the pulsating silence that followed he threw it with a clatter to the floor. Anne made a despairing little whimper, but he silenced her with a furious gesture. His face had contorted to purple and, not taking his livid gaze from Julia, he pointed to the door with a forefinger shaking with temper.

She rose with dignity, tilted her chin in her Katherine-like way and took a few leisurely moments to smooth a crease from her skirt. Makepeace's finger shook in dismissal again. She appeared not to notice and as if by her own wish entirely she began to thread her way with a rustling of silk through the seated guests, whose glowering expressions followed her. Still nobody spoke or moved.

Then, without warning, Adam, who had been struggling with his sense of humour, burst into hearty and uninhibited shouts of laughter, shattering the dignified setting of her leaving. Everyone turned in their chairs to stare at him, unable to see wherein lay any cause for amusement in what had taken place.

Julia paused to stare at him. His head was thrown back, showing that his back teeth were as white as those in front, and he was possessed by a paroxysm of rib-straining mirth that he could not control. She clenched her fists. Whether he intended it or not, by his laughter he had lessened the impact of what she had done. There seemed to be no end to the harm that he could do to her whenever their paths crossed. She swept to the doorway, where she turned to look back into the room, only avoiding her mother's tragic eyes as the volcano within her finally erupted.

"Regicides!" she hissed. "There is Stuart blood on all your hands!"

Uproar broke out but she did not stop to listen and ran for the Grand Staircase. Adam's amusement had been wiped from his face and he sprang to his feet as angry as the rest. It took a little while before voices subdued to a normal level again. By that time Anne had slipped away to her daughter, but Julia had locked herself in her room and would not open the door.

"Please go away, Mama. What happened is between Makepeace and me. I will not let you be involved."

Eventually, after receiving a brief explanation through the door, Anne, realising there was no moving her daughter, did as she had been bade and left.

Downstairs the guests had departed. Makepeace returned to the Queen's Parlour and sat with his head in his hands, thinking over all the harm his stepdaughter had done to his good name and the reputation he had built up as the new master of Sotherleigh over recent months. It was not just her show of royalism or her flagrant impertinence to him as her stepfather, but through her having drawn attention to the fact that his signature had been among the long list of those who had signed the death warrant of Charles I.

Although all the gentlemen with whom he was acquainted knew of his Parliamentary and military career and it was possible some were aware it had culminated in his having put his name to that death warrant, he had managed to keep Anne in ignorance, as far as he knew, of his having been a signatory, not wanting any more barriers between them. He believed Julia had remained similarly in the dark or else she would have directed her denunciation at him alone. It was an unlucky chance that she had chosen to highlight an action he had most wanted to keep out of the public eye since coming to Sotherleigh. He had no regrets about what he had done, and would have signed again to bring the same end to that royal tyrant's three sons if such a chance had come his way, but the local gentry were moderate folk politically, few diehards among them. However strongly they had been for the Parliamentary cause, and however staunch their present loyalty to the Commonwealth, it troubled many men's consciences here in Sussex and throughout the land that such a violent act as regicide should have been perpetrated in their cause. The outrage shown by his guests this evening was indicative alone of that unease. It was quite likely that a few would not come to his house again after having received such an unwelcome reminder of the role he had played.

He sat back in his chair and set his hands on the arm-ends. His chest rose and fell as he drew in deep breaths. This evening could be lived down and he would do it. Tomorrow he would mete out punishment to Julia and remind her of the warning he had given her and that now would be in force. In command of himself again, he went upstairs.

When he entered Anne's room in his nightshirt, she sat up from her pillows anxiously. She had learned from an acquaintance in Chichester, some of whose relations had been Parliamentarians, that the new owner of Sotherleigh was the one and the same Makepeace Walker whose name was among the signatories on that notorious death warrant. She remembered the immediate sensation of drowning in aversion for him, not knowing how she could endure living with such a man. Then there had come the realisation that she had no option. She could not abandon Sotherleigh and her son's interests or the safety of the family. So somehow she had slammed the door on the knowledge she had gained, refusing to dwell on it, and had managed to survive once more. Now she had been propelled into facing up to it again and must summon up her strength. Endeavouring to keep her voice steady, she spoke quickly.

"I realise that what Julia said downstairs must have caused embarrassment to you. I've always known you were a signatory, but please don't punish her, I beg you! You should have realised what a shock it was to have a Warrender here."

He climbed into bed beside her. "Are you blaming the son for what the father did?"

"Indeed not!" Anne's sense of fairness flared. "It was simply the question of the revival of painful memories that could have been overcome if you had only presented the young man to us in the first place."

"Had you been on time, madam," he replied bitterly, "I would probably have done so."

"Please don't start upbraiding me!" she cried out defensively. "I cannot endure it tonight."

"I have no intention of doing that at this late hour." He took her by the shoulders and bore her back into the pillows, leaning over her and looking down into her face. "You have a most wilful daughter. It's high time I had a son to amend her presence. Do not suppose I have been totally unaware of how you have kept my seed from your womb, but there'll be no more of that deviousness. The sin is entirely mine, because I wanted to enjoy your beauty to such an extent I did not wish a pregnancy to keep me from you. Now the time has come for you to do your duty and bear me an heir."

Panic possessed her. A child was a gift and she would have loved another if only it could have been Robert's! Not one by this crude, insensitive husband prepared to force conception on her. She sought vainly for excuses.

"But I'm no longer a young woman! Changes are almost upon me. My doctor would never advise—"

He cut her short. "My impression of your doctor is that he is a country fool. When the time comes you shall have the best midwife available. I love you, Anne. I never thought I should say those nonsensical words, but that is the case." Suddenly a wave of white-hot jealousy overwhelmed him at the thought she should have conceived by another husband before him. "You shall give me a son!"

The further protest she would have uttered was cut off as his mouth swallowed hers. He entered her without any preliminaries, except ensuring that her womb was open to him.

JULIA WAS SILENT throughout the tirade that Makepeace let fly at her next morning, enraging him still further by her calmness when he informed her that she was now as much up to offer as a slave in a foreign market-place. It sweetened his mood later when he heard her despairing cries upon discovering that her horse had been sold. When Anne suggested that her daughter should stay with William and Susan Holder at Bletchingdon for a while he agreed. He had had enough trouble for the time being and it would be good to get Julia out of his sight.

Julia, although overjoyed at the thought of visiting Christopher's home, did not like parting from her mother or her grandmother. Mary had been invited to accompany her, but had declined, always nervous of going into the presence of strangers.

"Send for me immediately if I'm needed," Julia insisted to Anne when the day of her departure came.

"I will, but I'm sure that won't prove necessary." Anne embraced her fondly. "I want you to have a happy time. I was grieved to read in Susan's letter that Dean Wren is dead and, of course, she and her husband will be in mourning for him. However, she has assured me there are plenty of young people in the village with whom you can mix."

Katherine had been prepared for Julia's going. She was seated in her wedding chair when her granddaughter came to sit on the footstool and say farewell. "Shall you be seeing Christopher?" she asked.

"Yes!" Julia's face shone at the prospect. "I wrote to him upon his bereavement and in his reply, which I received today, he tells me that lecturing twice a day at Gresham College, in Latin in the morning and in English in the afternoon, has palled. Those who attend are older men and the City Fathers. Admirable though it is to further the education of adults, he has to admit that Oxford calls him."

Katherine nodded. "I can well believe it. Now I want to give you a little present." She reached stiffly for a purse worked in the Florentine stitch on the table beside her and gave it to Julia. "Buy yourself a new gown and some pretty gewgaws to wear. That husband of your mother's wants to make you all as plain as pikestaffs, but he can do nothing about your lovely young face."

Julia sat straightbacked with astonishment, clutching the purse with both hands. "How did you know of the marriage? We thought we had kept it from you!"

The wise old eyes were grave. "Since I've been better many things have come to my notice. Firstly a complete change of staff. Then a man whose voice about the house I did not recognise and then seeing this stranger out in the Knot Garden. Your own whispered conferences with Mary when you thought I was asleep. From two gossiping maidservants I learned Makepeace Walker's name, and that he has property in the north and no children, and that Sotherleigh was sequestered by the Commonwealth Government and given to this man by Cromwell himself."

Julia shook her head in self-reproach. "What fools we've all been! We should have known we couldn't deceive you indefinitely."

"I have weighed everything up and I'm convinced your mother married that man for all our sakes and to allow us to remain at Sotherleigh." Katherine's voice was weak these days, but although she still kept her forthright manner, an unexpected catch in her speech told that she was deeply moved by what she had to say. "She has sacrificed herself for us, Julia. It shames me that I always thought her too gentle for her own good, but she is the frail bough that never breaks, no matter how ill the winds may blow. She has been the heart and the guiding light of

Sotherleigh ever since she came here, and I was too proud to see it until now."

Tears streamed from Julia's eyes. "My conscience has troubled me too. Many times! I realised on the day of her marriage to Makepeace that Mama was doing what she least wanted to do and it was for those of us whom she loved. She took everything onto her shoulders and yet I was the one who had made you a promise to keep Sotherleigh secure."

"Your mother fulfilled it on your behalf, even though she knew nothing of what had passed between us. For all we know Fate had decreed that it was not your turn yet to protect Sotherleigh. That may come. In the meantime we can appreciate what Anne has done for us and be thankful for the rest of our lives."

"I will! Always."

"There is something more I have to say to you." Katherine took Julia's right hand into both her own and held it in a clasp that quivered from her age and physical frailty. "It's to do with your going to Bletchingdon. If you think to waste your hours and days yearning after a young man unsuited to you, the visit will bring you no benefit and nothing but misery will await you if you continue along the same path in the years ahead."

"I hope you're not thinking of Christopher," Julia said uncertainly.

"I am. I know that when you were younger, the advice I'm going to give you now would have set you after him like a bolting horse and nothing could have held you back. That is the way of youth. But you have been through a great deal of sorrow and heartache in recent weeks, and no matter if you have acted in a headstrong manner at times, it is all behind you. Learn from the mistakes you have made. This will help you to guard against another that would be totally disastrous for you and that clever young man, who is in love with knowledge and beauty of another kind, which he finds among the stars in the firmament."

Julia bent her head. "You're asking too much of me, Grandmother."

"I think not. I can't see you being content to be just another planet."

"Would you sooner see me wed to whatever husband Makepeace picks out for me?"

"Is that what he has threatened?"

"Yes. He said he would stop at nothing to make me obey."

"Bah! He doesn't know your mettle as I do. Not even Queen Elizabeth could have made me marry anyone other than Ned. I'd have gone to the Tower first."

Julia looked up at her then. "I've told Makepeace I'll never give in and I mean it."

Katherine smiled fondly at her. "We've always been two of a kind, child. You'll recognise the man who is right for you when the time comes. In your own heart you know that the genius of Oxford and Gresham is not for you."

"I'll love Christopher until the end of my days."

"There is love and love, Julia. You'll find what you are seeking in a man who'll let no obstacle stand in his way to win you."

Julia tried to thrust away the memory of Christopher turning from her in the maze, but it persisted. For the first time she saw it as the rejection that it had been, not just his sense of honour coming between them, but a division of their whole lives. If they had been destined for each other would not a truly loving passion on his part have swept all else away?

"It's a long time since we've had a good talk together like this, Grand-mother. I'll remember what you have said, but this is something I have to think about and decide for myself."

"I haven't the least doubt about your good sense, Julia. But now surely you must go. Have a merry time at Bletchingdon. At your age I was dancing every night."

They made an affectionate parting, Julia turning back at the door to kiss her grandmother's cheek once more. When the door closed after her, Katherine put a shaking hand over her eyes. She had had to speak out for there might never be another chance. It was much in her mind that despite her health rallying at the present time, there were many little signs that her days were fast running out.

JULIA TRAVELLED in the Pallister coach with a Mrs. Reade, the mother of one of Anne's Chichester friends, who was seizing this unexpected chance to visit another daughter in the city of Oxford itself. The coach was to deliver Mrs. Reade after leaving Julia at her destination and then go back to Sotherleigh. It would return to collect them when they were both ready to go home again at some date presently left open, neither being restricted by a time limit.

Bletchingdon proved to be a picturesque village and the Holders' fine rectory was set amidst trees and flower beds. Susan welcomed Julia as if she were a home-coming daughter.

"I can't begin to tell you how much I've been looking forward to your visit, Julia."

"I'm so happy to be here."

Julia was shown to her room, which had a view of the countryside and where a maidservant waited to attend her. William had returned home when she went downstairs and he welcomed her as warmly as his wife had done.

"We want to try and give back a little of the wonderful hospitality your family have shown to Christopher in the past," he said to her. "But that would take many years to fulfill and so we must do our best with as much time as you can spare us."

She thought them a most kind and friendly couple. William's stiff and scholarly appearance was no doubt daunting to Cambridge undergraduates at such times as he lectured at their University, but he had a broad smile that lightened his whole face. As for Susan, she was plump and charming with a birdlike way of holding her head that reminded Julia of Christopher.

From the first evening Julia was drawn into many enjoyable occasions. There was little Puritan element in Blētchingdon, for together with Oxford this area had been staunchly Royalist. The Parliamentarians who lived in the village were like William in having nothing against people enjoying themselves. The law imposed restrictions here as elsewhere in the land, but if private parties were merrier, games more lively and company less abstemious than Cromwell would have allowed, nobody reported a neighbour, not even when the floor was cleared for the forbidden dancing.

Julia soon learned more of the general restlessness that was pervading the country. She had heard rumours at home, seen news-sheets that wrote of the crushing of subversive activities, but through conversation with William and hearing general talk she realised the full extent of the unrest. Much of the trouble came from ordinary folk resenting the restrictions and curtailment of the old customs; moreover, promises made to countrymen that they should own their own acres when the King was defeated had not been kept; many other workers had found themselves in bad straits through the changed conditions due in some cases to the banning of certain luxury trades, and payment to the army and navy was in arrears. At the outbreak of the Civil War there had been innumerable citizens uncertain whether to support King or Parliament, and many who had chosen the latter were becoming steadily convinced they had made a mistake. Pockets of Royalist activists, who had never given up the struggle, were working on the discontent and flare-ups that were continually occurring. To Julia this information was like a breath of hope.

She had become a frequent visitor to the house of Sir Thomas and Lady Coghill, having struck up a friendship at first meeting with their daughter, Faith. Susan was delighted this should have happened although, as she remarked to her husband, no two girls could be less alike in looks or temperament. Julia's beauty was flamelike, sparkling and volatile, whereas Faith was reserved and composed, and considered plain by many. Her pale oval face verged on thinness, the brow high with soft, straw-brown hair growing back from a peak, the eyes green and wide-set, with a longish nose and a small chin. She responded to Julia's warmth and gained confidence in her company, while Julia admired Faith's quiet wisdom and dry wit.

"I wish you had come to Bletchingdon long ago," Faith said one morning when they were returning on foot from a shopping expedition in the village. Neither wore capes for the day was warm. "Mrs. Holder told my mother she is willing that you should stay permanently if it suits you."

"That's because she knows from my mother's letters that Makepeace and I do not get on together." Julia had never had a close friend other than Mary, who was seven years older, and it was natural that Faith should have become her confidante. Nobody in Bletchingdon except Faith knew of Makepeace's threat. "I wouldn't want to stay away from my family too long, even if Makepeace is there. As I told you, my mother urged me to attempt a new beginning with him when I return and I shall try for her sake. I've already accepted that he has the right to ask whomever he likes to the house, even Adam Warrender." She sighed. "What worries me most now is having discovered from Dr. Holder that Makepeace's own hand signed King Charles's death warrant. Walker is such an ordinary name, I never made the connection. And in any case it happened when I was seven and that terrible event isn't anything people like to talk about."

"Your mother must have known."

"I expect she did. That makes her sacrifice in marrying Makepeace all the greater. Somehow she had come to terms with it. If only the clock could be turned back to the day of King Charles's trial and matters arranged as Dr. Holder and others like him wished them to be. It would have been so simple. Exile for the King and a reformed monarchy for his successor. Then Charles the Second would be reigning in London now instead of trying to raise an army abroad and Michael would be Master of Sotherleigh."

Faith put a hand on her arm. "Don't go back to Sussex except on visits. Let's you and me choose a husband out of this district and then we can be friends and neighbours for the rest of our lives."

"But I've never doubted that I'll see our present King ride by one day in London," Julia answered absently. "I'm going to live in a house there that Christopher will design for me."

Faith looked puzzled. "How could that be? He's not an architect, but an astronomer and a mathematician first and foremost."

Julia laughed awkwardly. "I really don't know why I said that. It was something Christopher promised me years ago when I was still a child. It suddenly came back to me."

"I suppose you and I have known him about the same length of time," Faith said meditatively. They proceeded to work it out together and discovered there was little difference in how long each had thought of him as a friend. It did not occur to either that the other might have a special reason for cherishing the bond of time. Julia wanted no one, not even Faith, to know of her love for him, which now seemed under threat. As for Faith, she loved him without the least hope that he would ever look at her with more than a mild and polite interest in his eyes.

Julia had been two months at Bletchingdon when Christopher returned to Oxford and then came home. He was to arrive in the early evening and Susan planned a supper party with many of his local friends, Faith and her parents among them. Julia was still hesitating before her bedchamber mirror when Faith arrived and joined her there.

"Why aren't you downstairs and waiting?" Faith wanted to know. "Christopher will be looking for you when he arrives."

"Yes, I suppose he will." Now that the time had come Julia was nervous, longing to see him again but with none of the wild joy she had previously experienced at his coming. She had had plenty of time to mull over her talk with her grandmother, and rising against the romantic in her was her own acceptance that in her relationship with Christopher the love had always been heavily on her side. She gave a start as a chorus of greetings floated up from downstairs.

"He's here!" Faith clasped her hands excitedly together. "Do come now, Julia. You look lovely in your new gown."

She led the way hurriedly to the head of the stairs and waited for Julia to catch up with her in order that they might go down together. As Julia reached her friend she looked down into the hall where Christopher was in the centre of the gathering, smiling and greeting everyone in turn. Her heart seemed to somersault with love. Then, as she and Faith set off down the stairs, he looked sharply up over his shoulder and saw them. His smiling mouth spread still wider into a merry grin.

He went to the foot of the flight. His gaze had been drawn first to Julia, gloriously beautiful in amber silk with ribbons in her hair. Then his eyes switched to Faith and lingered on her. No ribbons, but pale green taffeta the colour of her eyes and there was a cool yet glowing look about her. He realised that Julia's vivid loveliness was highlighting Faith's serenity of expression and the quality of stillness that hung like an aura about her even in these crowded surroundings. The astronomer in him compared the two girls to the sun and the moon, one no less beautiful than the other. He greeted them from the foot of the flight, throwing his arms wide.

"Julia! Faith! Now my home-coming is complete!"

Everybody laughed and applauded, the mood for the evening set. Julia, gaining confidence again, swept down to meet him and Faith followed slowly.

After supper, when he was dancing a slow Courante with Julia, he looked across at Faith, who sat conversing with a trio of older women. The glow had gone from her as with an eclipse of the moon to which he had compared her, and she was once again the quiet, unassuming girl with the shy presence. Yet none knew better than he that the moon never lost its radiance, even when it could not be seen. Then Julia spoke to him and once again he forgot everything else.

Next morning he drew Julia out to a seat in the garden where they could talk undisturbed. There was the same fierce tug on his senses in being near her as there had been in the maze. For a long while after that encounter, thoughts of her had come between him and his work. In spite of his determination not to be similarly affected this time he feared that resolve was lost.

"Now tell me," he said, keeping to the purpose of bringing her out of the house, "how were things at Sotherleigh when you left and what news of your mother and grandmother since?"

She told him everything except Makepeace's threat to marry her off by his will and not hers. Knowing Christopher for the man he was, she was certain that his sense of duty would compel him to step in and offer for her, but that was not what she wanted. If they had been back in the maze, she would have had no compunction in using any means in her power to become his wife, but she was no longer an impulsive girl trying to make everything go her way. If he wanted her he must take his own steps to win her. It was what she yearned for above all else and it would be the hardest task she had ever faced just to wait and see.

"It's a sorry case," he said when she had concluded her account of all that had taken place. "But do you remember my telling you once that no regime lasts for ever? I can see the present rule cracking like ice in the spring. Cromwell goes daily in fear of assassination. I have heard that he sleeps in a different place every night. Those at Westminster are well aware of the increasing unrest in the country. The day may not be far distant when Sotherleigh is in Pallister hands again."

"If only that could be," she breathed, cheered by his words.

On another day, when they were at a picnic in the company of others, their talk turned to Oxford. "I would like you to see that ancient seat of learning while you are here at Bletchingdon," he said, lounging back on the grass beside her. "I'd show you round the whole university."

"I should like that so much." Her face was eager. "Would you allow me to look at the stars through the telescope you invented?"

"Yes, indeed. I'll leave the matter in Susan's hands and she shall bring you at the first opportunity."

Throughout the rest of his stay she revelled in being with him. It filled her with bliss just to see him at the table at breakfast time or when she caught his smile across the room when they were being entertained by the Coghills and other hospitable people. In readiness for her visit to Oxford he agreed to show her some of the many early drawings and diagrams of his experiments and inventions that he kept stored in his room at the rectory. At a convenient hour he brought out two files and set them on a table for her to leaf through in turn. What struck her immediately was that his detailed drawings were works of art in themselves. There was one of a left hand drawn palm up which she recognised as his own. With numbers and lists it demonstrated the sign language he had invented for the deaf and dumb.

"Would it be difficult to learn?" she asked wonderingly.

"Not at all. It could be mastered in an hour." He leaned close to her as he pointed out how each finger and the thumbs played a part.

"Please teach me. At least Mary could hear when she couldn't speak, but I have met others who have been born deaf and have been laboriously taught some speech and to read. With them I could communicate with your sign language."

"You shall learn it this very day."

She turned over the drawing of the hand and studied all the rest in turn. There were precise anatomical drawings. Some showed the injection of blood into human beings; these would have made her turn squeamishly away if he had not pointed out how beneficial it could be in the field of medicine. On a similar category was his drawing of an artificial eye, which could relieve many who had lost an eye in battle or by other means. There were diagrams of instruments for grinding glass, illustrations of the lenses of telescopes, and other inventions for pneumatic engines, embroidering by machine, a variety of musical instruments and a weather wheel. He told her that some of his inventions had been put to use over the years while others were still only working models. His years in London as a boy seeing ships on the Thames had borne fruit in an invention for strengthening the hulls of ships of war and many ingenious aids for those at sea, such as a new and better way of reckoning time-away-longitude, how to stay long under the surface, submarine navigation and much more.

Diagram after diagram was turned over. Then she came to one showing the mechanism of an unusual loom. "What's this?"

"It's an idea of mine that would enable several lengths of ribbon to be woven at the same time instead of singly as they are now."

"My mother would like to see this."

He promptly picked it up and rolled it up. "You shall have it to show her when you go home."

The final papers in the first file composed a small section on astronomy. He explained that almost all his work on that subject was at the University, but she was able to see at a glance that her study of the little book on the subject, given her by Mary, was laughable in comparison to this mathematical approach to the galaxies. It was almost a relief when she turned to the second file, which was devoted to strength and beauty in buildings, much of it dealing with new materials. She would gladly have framed any one of the sections of houses illustrated, the porches and cornerstones and suchlike, as a true artist's work. He explained several things about it all before they reached the end of the file.

"Now I've seen for myself that you will be well prepared when it comes to building the London house for me one day," she said teasingly.

He grinned widely. "Build? I thought I only said I would design it."

"Ah! But you surely would have to see that the builders had the benefit of all your knowledge in erecting such a fine residence."

"I suppose I should do that," he agreed.

Throughout his time at home he did not kiss her, but at the moment of parting his eyes went to her lips as if it were hard to restrain himself. Yet the moment passed, other people being present, and she felt bereft when he was gone. The matter of her visiting Oxford had been left in Susan's hands, so she did not have a definite date to which she could look forward to seeing him again.

The summer rolled on, one warm day following another like breakers on a seashore. Susan had so many engagements and pastoral duties as the wife of the Rector that it never seemed convenient to go to Oxford. Then one afternoon when Julia returned from a walk with the rectory dogs, Susan met her in the hall, her very serious expression filling Julia with sudden alarm. "Have you heard from Sotherleigh, Mrs. Holder? Has anything—?"

"Calm yourself, my dear. All is well there. An hour ago I received a letter from Anne, which you shall read and to which your grandmother has herself added a few shakily written words. There is something else for which I have to prepare you." There was a moment's pause. "A young man, who graduated at Cambridge while my husband was still lecturing there, has come to see you all the way from your neighbourhood in Sussex. He is Adam Warrender."

Julia drew back, her face hardening. "He and I have nothing to say to each other."

"Forgive me, but I think you have. William and I have been talking with him for an hour. Nobody could regret more than he that moment of conflict in which your father was fatally shot."

"I don't lay that at his door. It's all he represents and there's something about the sequestration of Sotherleigh that I haven't told you."

"Do you hold him responsible for that?" Susan asked perceptively. Then, when Julia made no reply, she gave a firm nod. "If that is what you think it would be better to bring the matter out into the open with him and hear what he has to say. How do you imagine that William and I could have stayed in harmony with each other if he had stuck stubbornly to his Parliamentary views without discussing anything with me or I did likewise with my Royalist loyalties? War could have split us asunder for ever, but we bridged the gap with understanding."

"That was different. You and William were married." She made for the stairs, but Susan's next words halted her, sending a chill down her spine.

"As you and Adam might well be. He has offered for you and Makepeace has agreed."

# ELEVEN

*A*DAM WAS STUDYING a painting, his back to her, when she entered the room. His blue-black hair curled down to his broad shoulders, his wide collar was of lace, his short jacket and straight breeches were of fox-red velvet and his boots bucket-topped. As she closed the door behind her he turned slowly and their eyes met across the length of the oak-panelled room. Instantly, like a flint spark to tinder, there was a resurgence in her of that frightening awareness of the magnetism in him that had affected her at Sotherleigh on the evening of her Royalist outburst. She had thought afterwards it was due simply to the shock of suddenly seeing him in her own home, but now it had swept back again to burn mercilessly into her, making her flesh quiver.

"I wanted to see you," he said without preliminaries. Those few words covered everything from the long ride he had made from Sussex to the marriage settlement arranged with Makepeace.

Her voice was dangerously soft and even. "When a good friend made an appeal to Cromwell on my mother's behalf against the sequestration of Sotherleigh, he was told he had been wasting his time. I'm saying that to you."

He took a couple of steps forward. "We need to clear the air between us and put old feuds to rest."

"Impossible." She was not heated, simply cool and distant, "You should never have come to Sotherleigh that day. Sheer basic common sense should have told anyone in your position that to come blundering in without announcement would cause a widow much distress."

"Yet I came out of concern for your mother: It was to warn her of the forthcoming sequestration, because I had had confirmation of it that same morning. My first thought was to see what I as a neighbour might do to help." He moved nearer again as he continued what he had to say.

"But you made the feelings of the Pallisters towards my family clear enough and when afterwards I wrote to Mrs. Walker—or Mrs. Pallister as she was then—my letter was refused at the gates. At that point my hands were tied. I did write once more to the Lord Protector to ask that the sequestration should at least be postponed, but it was to no avail."

She had been listening with subtle changes of expression passing across her face, ranging from initial disbelief to the realisation that every word he was saying showed clearly that in her headstrong way she had made a grave error about him.

"Once more?" she queried uncertainly. "Had you tried before then?"

"Yes, I had." He gestured for her to sit. She moved slowly across to a window seat while he continued to stand, watching her. The sun through the thick panes made golden threads of her wayward curls and shot streaks of light across the rose silk of her sleeves.

"Why should you wish to intervene when there has been such enmity between our two families on a personal as well as a political level?" she asked soberly.

"For one thing, when I heard my new neighbour was likely to be a regicide it made my gall rise. But far more than that, when I went through my father's papers after his death some interesting facts came to light." A corner of his mouth twitched in private amusement as he took a chair by its back and swung it forward to sit facing her. "I don't quite know how to tell you this, but I believe your grandmother and my grandfather were lovers in their younger days."

She stared at him, her eyes widening. Katherine had spoken of Sir Harry in the past, and during her mental wanderings after her stroke his name had come to the fore sometimes, but this information was startlingly unexpected. "Whatever led you to that belief?"

"There were no love letters. Nothing of that kind. But there was wartime correspondence between my grandfather and several powerful Parliamentary politicians whom he counted as old friends, in which he requested their word that whatever punishments were inflicted on prominent Royalists at the end of the conflict, at least the Pallisters of Sotherleigh should be spared the loss of their house and land. A document bearing the signatures of those politicians gave my grandfather the promises he wanted in the last days of his life." He saw the unspoken question in her eyes and shook his head reassuringly. "None of those names were later on the royal death warrant."

She considered what had been said. "Maybe Sir Harry took that action out of sheer kindness. I know from what my grandmother has said of him that he was a good man."

"I think it was more than that. To one old friend he wrote twice that it was for the sake of his dear Katherine."

"But if that document exists, why did the sequestration take place?"

"When that paper was signed none of the six signatories was young. Now three are dead and two are retired. The last one is still in the government, but has no influence on his own." He drew in a deep breath. "I regret to have to tell you that shortly before my father's death he deliberately reversed all that Sir Harry had done by bringing the exemption of the sequestration of Sotherleigh to the Lord Protector's notice. After that, a new order had Cromwell's seal on it and the fate of your home was settled beyond any further intervention."

She saw clearly that he had had the choice of letting his father's ill deed go unchallenged or taking up his grandfather's goodwill. "So you did what you could for us out of respect for Sir Harry's wishes."

"I did." He recalled again his disgust at his father's senseless vengeance against the helpless family of a dead enemy.

She was silent, her gaze directed unseeingly out of the window, her long lashes flecked with the same golden light as in her hair. It was impossible to turn back the clock, but if only she could stand again in Sotherleigh's drive at the moment of meeting Adam she would have found a friend instead of making him an enemy in her own mind. It might have been possible for him to use his influence in such a way that Sotherleigh could have come under his jurisdiction and Makepeace need never have appeared on the horizon. Adam would have allowed life to go on at Sotherleigh undisturbed. It was all her fault. Every bit of the mayhem caused could be laid at her door. Such despair welled up in her at all her past foolishness that she trembled from the force of it. What a wild, headstrong girl she had been! Was there any way in which she could ever make amends to those who had suffered through her actions?

She turned and looked Adam full in the face. "I offer you my most sincere apologies. I have made many terrible mistakes and misjudging you through my Royalist prejudice was surely the greatest of them all."

"You were not to know that I came to Sotherleigh in goodwill. One of the tragedies of war is that it leaves bitterness and suspicion where none should be." He drew up a chair and sat close to her. "Let us put that day behind us."

"But I gave you no chance to speak and I scarred you for life." Then she remembered something else. "I didn't mean to hurt your horse. That grieved me deeply."

"I understood that, although I must admit that at the time it made me angrier than anything you had done to me."

"I should have felt the same."

The atmosphere had become more relaxed and yet he knew that she still had barriers up against him, although that could be as much from the powerful sexual attraction between them as anything else. Had she been of a Puritan family she would scarcely have known the shape of her own body, but Julia had the poise of a woman fully conscious of her lovely face and figure. There were untapped depths of passion in her that released silent signals instantly recognisable to any lusty and observant male. The impact of those signals had hit him harder than the frame she had hurled at him when she had stood defiantly before him in the drive at Sotherleigh.

"I can't let that incident on the hill go unmentioned," he said determinedly. "I have to admit that it all went much further than I had supposed it would."

She shrugged. "Your friends behaved foolishly. Let us leave it at that."

"I still have a grievance. Say you take back your taunt of regicide that you threw at me together with that sour-faced company at Sotherleigh."

"I take it back, but you goaded me into it with your laughter."

The atmosphere had tautened again and they eyed each other like wary adversaries. He realised that this was how it was likely to be for a long while to come. "I'd only gone there in the hope of seeing you. I had nothing in common with any of the gentlemen there, Makepeace Walker least of all."

"They were all Parliamentarians. You should have felt at ease in such company, apart from the fact they were all older."

His hands tightened over the arm-ends of the chair and he shifted his weight forward as if prepared to leap from it at the slightest slur she might cast at him. "I'm as much for Cromwell in peace as my father was for him in war. That doesn't mean I can't see that his grip has slipped, but he brought law and order and reforms when they were most needed. Moreover I'm not a bigot or an extremist or a hypocrite, and you'll have to judge me on my own merits, Julia."

She wondered if his mentioning the term "hypocrite" meant he had seen through Makepeace as she had done. "I would if we were going to spend any time together, but that's unlikely. I intend to stay at Bletchingdon for as long as I can."

"But I have a special reason for wanting us to be on good terms and to get to know each other."

"I'm aware of it," she answered frankly. "But neither am I a hypocrite and I can't let you hope for what can never be. I happen to love someone else. Whether I shall marry him or not is uncertain at the present time, but that doesn't mean I'll ever wed someone that my stepfather has chosen for me. That in itself would put an end to anything before it should start." She held up a hand as if he was about to protest, although he had shown no sign of interrupting her. "I know I'm legally under Mr. Walker's control and guardianship, which can reach me wherever I am in England, but I can slip that net whenever I wish."

He answered her with equal frankness. "What makes you think I'd want you except by your own free will?"

She thought of the naval expression about the wind being taken from one's sails and it applied to her now. "I suppose I've become so accustomed to Mr. Walker's rigid will that I thought you'd be no different." She sighed with relief. "So I have nothing to worry about after all. You may tell Mr. Walker upon your return to Sussex that you have accepted my decision."

"You're putting words into my mouth. I'll do no such thing."

"But you said—"

He rose from the chair and stood over her, looking down into her face. "You've given me no chance to say any of the things I planned to say to you. I thought when we had swept away all that was dividing us we should have entered upon a time and an experience that comes to one couple in a million. But you have introduced some lovesick nonsense that has not begun to touch the passion in you or else this wavering talk of perhaps a marriage or perhaps not"—here he spread his hand and waved it like scales in the balance— "would never have entered your head."

"You're wrong!" She sprang up and drew away from him. "Once all I felt for this man made me forget modesty of every kind!"

He regarded her piercingly. "But still he did not take you!"

She felt the hot colour run across her cheekbones. "Not before marriage! He is an honourable man."

"You would not have received honour from me in such circumstances."

"That would not be expected from a Warrender."

Too late she realised she had undone all the good achieved earlier by her words. His arm shot out and he caught her about the waist bringing her hard against him, trapping her as if in a snare.

"I'll remind you we are betrothed, Julia." His angry face was only inches from hers. "One day you'll be a Warrender too, upholding its strength and its reputation for all that is trustworthy as it was in times past and is again today." Then his mouth took hers with a force that she felt would have broken her neck if he had not been cupping her head in his hand. His kiss broke like a warm tidal wave over her lips, her teeth, her tongue and on and on down into her whole body, leaving no part of it untouched. If her arms had not been clamped to her sides by his iron strength she might well have driven her fingers up into his hair to gain some grip against the sensation of being totally swept away. She believed she cried out at this revelation of how a kiss could be between a man and woman, but his total possession of her mouth smothered all sound.

When the kiss ended he brought her head forward to let her cheek lie against his chest as if he had no wish that she should see his expression and she felt his lips rest lightly against the middle parting of her hair. She trembled within his tight embrace, knowing that she should utter some protest or make all the foolish show of indignation expected of a woman kissed against her will, but she and Adam had been honest with each other earlier and that was the better way. To pretend she had not enjoyed the experience would not have deceived him in any case. He would also know that she would be wishing that such a kiss had been given her by someone else.

He put her from him quite gently. His face gave nothing away. Whatever his reaction had been to the kiss he had mastered it now. "When you return to Sotherleigh, Julia," he said with a touch of a smile, "I shall court you relentlessly."

"I may never return."

"You could not stay away from Sotherleigh indefinitely. Then one day, when you are ready, I shall take you as my wife to the Hall."

"You're forgetting you said it would have to be by my own free will."

"That's how it will be."

"The stigma of Makepeace Walker can't be erased."

He took up his wide-brimmed grey hat. "I'll overcome that somehow. Farewell for the time being, Julia. I'll be waiting."

He was almost out the door when he turned back. "I was forgetting to tell you. I bought your horse Charlie from your stepfather, so you need have no fears as to his well-being."

She stood stupefied and speechless, but before she could grasp what he had done for her he was through the door and had closed it behind him.

She returned to the window-seat, which faced the rear lawn, and so she did not see him leave. Voices in the hall were clear enough. He declined most courteously Susan's invitation to supper and had a final word with William before the front door closed and she knew he had gone. Nobody intruded on her privacy for the next hour, giving her plenty of time to think over the whole encounter. She did not intend to marry him, but she was thankful that the situation between them was mended. Moreover, she felt as if her mind had been opened—all old prejudices banished. She had been as guilty as any extremist, whether Royalist or Parliamentarian, in making hasty judgements without investigation and tolerance. At least she would never be like that again and she owed it to Adam, who had shown himself to be fair and just as she had never been. He was also kind, a quality to commend him yet further in her estimation.

But in one way he was still dangerous. She had also discovered in being with him what it was like to be violently attracted to a man without loving him. That came in the category of wantonness, which she would have to guard against most staunchly.

Life at Bletchingdon rectory drifted on peacefully. Julia continued to receive letters at intervals from Anne and Mary. Then there came one from her mother which filled her with sadness. Michael, full of concern for Anne and the change of situation at Sotherleigh, had written that he himself had married. His bride was the only child of the silk merchant by whom he was employed. Her name was Sophie Brissard, and it distressed him that in the midst of his own happiness in this marriage there should be so much misfortune for those dear to him at home.

Folding the letter up again, Julia thought how devastated Mary must have been by this news. Unwittingly Michael had ruined the chances of any other man winning her love, for she had been patiently waiting, pinning her hopes on his return. It was not that she had ever disclosed this in so many words, but she had given herself away many times. For a matter of seconds Julia drew a comparison with her own love for Christopher and then dismissed it. Her case was entirely different. Christopher did care for her whereas Michael had never shown by a single word in his letters that Mary held any special place in his affections, although he always included her in his fond greetings. In addition, she herself was being totally realistic. No matter what Adam had said, it was not lack of passion that had made her uncertain about marriage with Christopher. There was no lack of love on her side, and if that should never prove to be the case with Christopher she would get on with her life and carve her own future. Nothing should ever make her go under. Not even losing the man who would always mean the most to her.

After receiving a letter from Sotherleigh Julia would suffer a bout of homesickness, but she would remind herself of Adam waiting for her and that dashed away any thought of return. At these times she was particularly grateful for Faith's friendship. Steadily each girl's character was influencing the other's, Julia becoming quieter and Faith more confident.

In August the Lord Protector fell ill and in September he died. A whole era of his masterly handling of the war and his stabilising control afterwards had come to an end. There was an impressive state funeral in London, but little or no show of public grief. The cost of his imperialistic ventures abroad and his rigid Puritan restrictions clamped on the lives of ordinary people had caused his popularity to wane over the years. Some people were no longer afraid to speak of him openly as having been a tyrant. The fact that his son Richard, a thoroughly inadequate person, had been appointed as his successor brought further doubts about the wisdom of letting England's rightful king remain in exile.

Julia, expecting to spend her seventeenth birthday in Bletchingdon, was overjoyed when Susan received a letter from Christopher in which he insisted she put everything aside and bring her charge to Oxford on the fourteenth of October.

"He's underlined the date with four strokes of his pen," Susan declared with exasperation. "It is not convenient for me to leave just then, but I will do as he wishes."

The journey was not far and it was mid-afternoon when Julia caught her first glimpse of Oxford. The ancient seat of learning with its medieval buildings and narrow streets was bathed in autumnal sunshine that gave a gilded warmth to the grey stone and every tree was afire with red and orange hues. Christopher was waiting at the hostelry where she and Susan were to stay and greeted her with good wishes for her special day.

"I thank you! Coming to Oxford is a wonderful way to celebrate," she answered while her hands carried out the same words in sign language to show him she had been practising and had forgotten nothing.

He nodded admiringly. "Well done!"

They entered the hostelry and he went with her to the large room that she and his sister were to share. While Susan bustled about, telling the porters where to set down the travelling chests, Julia hurried across to the window to see what view she had of the University. Then she turned and was about to pass some excited comment when Christopher, standing near the door, spoke to her in sign language. It was a message that caused her to smother a happy exclamation with her hand clapped to her mouth. She glanced around quickly to see if her action had been noticed but Susan was now instructing the chambermaids about unpacking.

"Would you mind if I went out with Christopher for a little while?" Julia asked cautiously.

"Not at all." Susan sat down on the edge of the bed. "I've no intention of chaperoning you all round Oxford and anyway I'm going to rest for a while. I always need to do that these days after a journey."

Julia hastened out of the room to join Christopher, who had withdrawn to the corridor. "Where is he?" she asked eagerly, on tiptoe with suspense.

He frowned slightly to warn her against eavesdroppers and replied in sign language. She nodded and sped along the corridor to a room at the end where she entered immediately. The young man waiting there sprang forward to catch her outstretched hands as she darted to him.

"Michael!" she exclaimed joyfully.

"It's been a long time, Julia!" Then brother and sister hugged each other exuberantly.

"You look more French than English!" she declared when she had congratulated him on his marriage, standing back to study him. "That thin moustache suits you and your clothes must be Parisian. We don't see gentlemen in such elegant style these days."

"You have confirmed that my disguise as a French silk merchant on business in England is deceiving enough. But more of that later. What a transformation in you, little sister, since I left! You've grown up to be slightly better-looking than I dared to hope."

She laughed at his teasing. He had not been changed by his years in exile as the King was said to be. Then they had so much to ask each other; such a lot to tell. They were both able to fill in details that had had to be left out in letters owing to fear of possible confiscation of their correspondence en route, he fearful of drawing down trouble on their heads and they withholding anything slanted against Parliament for the same reason.

"What made you start out on this dangerous visit to England?" she wanted to know.

He told her he had been approached in Paris by a representative of King Charles to ask if he would risk his life by taking some papers to a nest of royal activists in Warwickshire, the last spy sent having been killed. "I've long wanted to see you all at Sotherleigh again and I seized the chance of getting the necessary forged travel documents. Monsieur Brissard made no opposition to my going. Since gaining an English son-in-law he has taken up our Royalist cause. He was always in our favour, having told me many times how appalled he had been by King Charles's execution and how nothing like that could ever happen in France."

Then Michael went on to explain how he had made brief contact with Christopher on the journey through Oxfordshire into Warwickshire, not wanting to lose this chance of seeing his old friend again. Then, upon hearing that Julia was at Bletchingdon, he had asked Christopher to arrange a meeting for him on his way south again with his mission accomplished. The intense secrecy was to spare Susan the obligation of having to keep the knowledge of his being in England to herself and also to avoid chance recognition by anyone who knew or had served him during his Oxford days.

"Now tell me more about everyone at Sotherleigh," he urged.

When it was her turn to question him again, she was eager to hear about her French sister-in-law. "What is she like? Pretty, I'm sure."

"You may judge for yourself." He dived into his pocket and drew out a pouch embroidered with white fleur-de-lis on a green silk ground from which he removed a gold-rimmed painted miniature. "Here she is."

Julia took the oval miniature and held it in the palm of her hand. A pale French face looked out at her with a seductively hooded gaze that would intrigue any man. Her skin was flawless, her Gallic bones exquisitely formed and her mouth small and pink with a glisten to the lips. In appearance she could not be faulted, but Julia could detect no warmth or generosity in those almost perfect features, although that could be blamed on the artist's inability to capture anything but the surface beauty of the young woman. "You have a beautiful wife," she declared sincerely, returning the miniature to her brother. "Where did you first meet?"

"The very day I was taken into Monsieur Brissard's employ. It was not a case of love at first sight for either of us. She simply came to her father's office by chance and I was presented to her. That was that, except that I had been struck by her haunting and unusual beauty as people always are.

I saw her occasionally when she came to the business premises, but we
never spoke. Then when I was eventually promoted to manager I was
invited into the family circle and that's when it all began. Her father gave
me permission to court her since I was now socially of the standard
required and six months ago Sophie and I were wed."

"I'm sure you had many rivals for a hand such as hers."

"I believe I did."

As with the miniature she felt that in his reply there was something
that had not quite fallen into place. He looked smiling enough at this talk
of Sophie, but knowing her brother's exuberant, outgoing nature, she
would have expected him to burst into lively talk about his exquisite wife
as soon as initial news had been exchanged. Instead he had waited until she
extended her information beyond the family circle to tell him that George
Gunter had had to flee abroad and that the old head gardener's son, Titus,
had managed to get taken on as one of Makepeace's outdoor staff and kept
the maze trimmed. Michael had even heard her out, still without mention
of Sophie, when she had told how Makepeace had demanded a plan of the
maze and Anne had taken it from Katherine's drawer and given it to him.
Even as this was in her thoughts Michael spoke of the maze himself.

"Does Makepeace ever go into the maze?"

"No. He went once, I believe, but that was all."

"Then he doesn't suspect the secret entrance there?"

"Not at all. You'd be able to enter Sotherleigh as freely as Father did
sometimes in the war."

"I'll have to go in by night to make contact. It will have to be with
Mary or Sarah. Then during the day Mother can come to see me in the
underground chamber."

"If Grandmother isn't too well, Sarah sleeps in a truckle bed in her
room. So Mary is the one you must awaken." Julia thought of what it
would mean to Mary to start from sleep to see him at her bedside. The
poor girl would think that some dream had come true. "Don't let her cry
out in surprise. It's unlikely that anyone would hear, but you can't be too
careful."

"I may have to put my hand over her mouth until she realises who I
am. Where shall I find her?"

"She has the bedchamber next to mine in the west wing." Julia then
told him everything else she could think of that would eliminate danger
for him when he entered Sotherleigh again. He had had the foresight
before leaving for France to take the key to one of the side gates and she

told him to leave his horse tied up out of sight in a copse there. Mary would contact Titus, as much a Royalist as his grandfather had been, and he would take care of the animal until it was needed again.

Two hours passed by like so many minutes. He gave her a gift of azure Lyonnaise silk and then had to go. Julia was left to discover the marvels of Oxford under Christopher's guidance and to view the stars by telescope in his observatory.

As Michael rode away he thought what a blessing it was that his country was no longer at war. With his dangerous assignment behind him he could travel quite freely, and when staying overnight at a hostelry the French accent and Gallic gestures he adopted caused curious glances but no suspicion or hostility.

It was a bright moonlit night when he slid back the Queen's Door and entered Sotherleigh after more than seven years away. He inhaled the house's mingled fragrances of oak and lavender and candle wax as if he were in a flower garden. Throughout his time away he believed he had adapted to life in France, that nothing there was as alien as it had first appeared, but he knew now it had been a myth, an opiate to sustain him in a place where he did not belong. Back here in his birthplace, he felt his torn-out roots assert themselves to go snaking down invisibly from his feet to lodge fast in the good Sussex soil on which Sotherleigh stood. How was he ever going to be able to leave again when the clock came round to this hour tomorrow?

It was not as if Sophie's arms would be waiting to welcome him back. If that had been the case a second parting from Sotherleigh would have been easier to bear. He had been deeply in love with her when she became his bride and he loved her still, but she had married him for reasons of her own and if she loved anyone it was herself. It seemed incredible to him now that he had not perceived how it was to be between them. Chaperonage in France was even stricter than in England and until their wedding night he had had only five minutes alone with her in which he asked her to be his wife, well aware even then that her mother and two aunts were listening at the door. Upon her acceptance he had seized the chance to kiss her and he had smiled over her chaste response, thinking her inhibited by those unseen eavesdroppers and that all would be different when they were married and under their own roof.

But she had not wanted to leave her parents' home. On the same evening as their betrothal she had pleaded with him in her soft, coaxing way, her fascinating amber eyes looking up at him under those deep lids.

"Why should we move elsewhere until it is time for you to take me to Sotherleigh? I want it to be our first real home together. Anywhere strange here in Paris would spoil that special dream of mine."

He had agreed to her whim, charmed that already through her love of him, Sotherleigh meant so much to her. Their betrothment was purgatory for him. He scarcely knew how to stop himself from whisking her away. To him her long-lashed glances and air of mystery suggested erotic discoveries once they were wed. He could not have been further from the truth. Those lidded looks had hidden a wariness of life and what he had taken to be mysterious was only a cool defence against any close relationship with others.

Slowly he ascended the Grand Staircase and with a frown saw a portrait of the late Lord Protector where the Queen's visage had been. The stairs creaked and he paused now and then to ensure that nobody stirred. The moonlight touched the flower screen with silver and he remembered how once in boyhood he had climbed it to the ceiling, risking his neck and getting a box on the ears from Katherine when he came down again.

He was passing the screen when suddenly there came a dull thud. Immediately he froze, listening intently. It had come from above him in the attics and he had the extraordinary feeling that someone up there had become equally motionless, fearful of having been heard. But according to Julia the servants were still in the old quarters, the women in rooms leading off the kitchen passageway and men in accommodation above the coach house. If someone was in the attic, prying about, it added to his danger, for at any time he might meet that person when he or she came down again. He changed his direction and went silently to where he could stand concealed by a cupboard and watch the narrow flight that led up to the door that shut away the attics.

Someone was coming down from there. Candle-glow danced ahead on the lower treads and there was a swish of a silk robe. Then to his astonishment he saw his mother appear. At first he thought she must be sleepwalking, but her actions were as stealthy as his and she glanced about nervously.

"Mother!" he whispered. "It's Michael. I'm here!"

She put a hand to her chest as if her heart had lurched with shock and she swayed. He took the candle from her as she fell against him, weeping with joy.

"My son! I can hardly believe it. What is happening? Are there Cavaliers with you? Has the King returned?"

"No, Mother. I'll explain everything. Let's go down to the Queen's Parlour where we can talk."

"I can't." She became extremely agitated. "It's almost dawn and I must get back to my bed before then. Let's go somewhere nearer. To Mary's room! That's it." Her maternal instincts came to the surface. "You need to be fed. She will prepare something for you and find you fresh clothes from those we have kept for your return. I'll have to meet you later underground."

He peered into her face. "Why are you so frightened? Is your husband ill-treating you?" His voice hardened. "If he is I'll—"

She shook her head wildly. "No, but I don't want him questioning me about why I should not be in my room if he wakes. When I can't sleep I like to—wander about."

"In the attics?" he exclaimed incredulously, keeping up with her as she almost ran in the direction of Mary's bedchamber.

"It's peaceful there," she answered vaguely. They had reached Mary's door. Anne opened it, peeped in and then beckoned that he should follow, taking the candle from him. "Shut the door quietly and stay in the shadows. I'll prepare her." Crossing to the four-poster she touched the sleeping young woman on the shoulder. "Mary. Wake up."

Mary stirred and then sat up abruptly, pushing a wave of hair back from her face, the candleglow full on her. "Oh! What's wrong?"

"Nothing. Quite the reverse. Michael is here."

He was watching her, seeing instantly that she had the same vulnerable look about her which had first touched him when he had seen her passing on her way to the gallows. Yet now she was twenty-three and good-looking where once she had been only mildly pretty—her features full of character as if she had laughed and cried much in the interim since he had last seen her. Neither was her figure any longer that of a slip of a girl, her breasts full against the soft lawn of her nightgown. Then, as she grasped what had been said to her, her whole face became suffused with such yearning that it was dazzling. He experienced an echo of the way she had suddenly roused him seven years ago in the underground room.

"Where is he, Anne?" she whispered tremulously.

He left the shadows then to go to the foot of the bed. She sprang from it and then seemed transfixed, unable to take a step towards him, hands clasped in front of her. "It's good to see you again, Mary," he said smiling.

"I can talk now. My voice is healed."

That information had been sent to him long since in letters both from her and his mother in carefully guarded language that spoke of her having outgrown a certain injury, but he understood this was something she had long wanted to say to him personally. He had already noticed that her voice was soft and husky in tone, pleasing to the ear. "So I can hear." He kissed her cheek. "I wish I'd been here when your voice returned."

Anne had fetched a robe for her from the closet and she put her arms into it automatically, finding it impossible to take her eyes from him. She thought it fortunate that he was busy telling of his seeing Julia and Christopher in Oxford, Anne full of busy little questions, and did not notice her hungry, unswerving gaze.

He looked older, all the more attractive because of it, and the French-style moustache gave him a dashing air. Yet it might have been yesterday that he rode away beside an effigy of her on horseback, Joe at the other side. She still loved him as much now as then. Perhaps not in quite the same way because of the years between, for she was now more his equal, accustomed to elegant manners and a standard of living that she had never known before he had brought her to Sotherleigh. If he had still been single, she would have been strong enough in will to refuse to be left behind this time. That thought alone crushed agonisingly all her most tender feelings for him as she accepted that it could no longer matter to him either way.

He had taken a miniature of his wife from his pocket to show Anne and her. It was like a knife-thrust when his mother had declared Sophie most lovely and then handed the miniature to her. She had to force herself to study the face of the woman that had captured his heart.

Anne, loath to leave her son but frantic to get back to her bed, promised that she would see him at the first chance later. Then she fled away. He re-pocketed the miniature.

"When did you last eat?" Mary asked on a safe and practical note.

"I had a late dinner yesterday and nothing since. I was eager to get home and so stopped as little as possible on the ride from Oxford."

Mary took a candle and lighted the way down to the kitchen. There was an hour yet before the servants stirred. In the large pantry she found a cold game pie, bread, butter and pickles. He did justice to the impromptu meal while she sat on the bench opposite him at the table.

"Your good health, Mary." He raised the tankard of ale she had poured for him and drank thirstily. "The French may have the best wines in the world, but nothing can beat a good English ale when a man has a parched throat."

She had expected him to talk incessantly about Sophie. Surely that was what young men did when they were in love? Instead he spoke of his work in Paris, of his trips to Lyon to select and buy the silks for which France was famous. He told how Joe continued to thrive and recounted several amusing anecdotes about him that made her laugh.

"Whereabouts in Paris is your home?" she asked when his vivid descriptions of the city had enabled her to picture the flowing Seine, the water traffic and the narrow streets virtually unchanged since medieval times.

"For the present time we are continuing to live with Monsieur Brissard. He has a large house that was once part of an old palace and until I can bring Sophie to Sotherleigh that is where we shall remain."

Nothing in his face or voice gave the least indication that this arrangement was not entirely to his liking, yet with the high-pitched sensitivity of a woman in love she knew instinctively that she had come close to touching a raw nerve in him. Perhaps Sophie was so used to luxurious surroundings that she would not move into a small place such as he could presently give her and must wait for the grandeur of an English mansion. Yet she herself would have lived in a garret or a cellar with him and thought it paradise.

Suddenly she knew she hated this Frenchwoman who had not given him all he deserved. Just because she was quiet by nature did not mean she was submissive like Anne, or that her feelings did not run as deep as Julia's. At the news of Michael's marriage she had lain on her bed and privately writhed with jealousy, making no sound, the old habit of silence having returned to her in her stress, and she had wept oceans of soundless tears. Yet then his wife had been totally unknown to her and in the midst of her despair she had wanted only that Michael should be loved as she had loved him since he had first taken care of her long ago. Now that she had seen the miniature, Sophie had a face, one that was cool and calculating behind a mask of beauty, no heart to the eyes, no smile to the lips. Such a loathing of the shallow creature welled up in her that she feared she might suddenly cry out with rage and frustration.

She pulled herself together as she saw he was looking at her with a worried frown. "There's something I have to ask you. How long has my mother been wandering about at night?"

"What do you mean? I know nothing of it."

"I met her coming down from the attic. She told me it had become her habit to move about the house when she can't sleep."

Mary was astonished. "I did not know she ever went near the attic by night or day. At least not since the time when we thought we should have to move and I went up there with her to see if there was anything we could take with us."

"Do you think she is well?"

Mary thought carefully. "Yes. I have noticed she is often completely withdrawn in Makepeace's presence unless he happens to be speaking to her. It's as if she has slipped far away. Where once she was always busy with her embroidery she never touches it now. It's as if she had become like the lady in the children's rhyme that lived on strawberries and cream and sat all day on a cushion sewing a fine seam, except that in her case her hands are idle in her lap."

"She sounds desperately unhappy to me."

"I fear she is, but she keeps it to herself. Partly it's to spare the rest of us worry about her, but also because Makepeace is her husband now and she shows him the respect that is expected of a wife, no matter how much she may be suffering privately." Then she repeated what Julia had said during a similar discussion. "I think Makepeace is a detestable man, but he does care for her and at times is quite insanely jealous of anyone who takes her attention from him."

"Perhaps she regains a sense of freedom when she goes about the house by night," he suggested meditatively.

"Yes, I should think that is the case," she agreed. "But now it is time you went down to the underground chamber. Take a pitcher of water with you while I get some bedclothes and follow in a minute."

When she had taken an armful of bedding from a cupboard, she paused for a moment and laid her cheek against the sheet on which he would soon be resting, his powerful limbs sprawled, his eyes closed in sleep. A tremour of long-pent-up desire went through her. Then she straightened her shoulders and composed herself as, carefully watching and listening to be sure she was not observed, she made her way down to the Queen's Door.

He had lit candles in the underground chamber and came to take the load of bedclothes from her, but she held them back. "These are not heavy. Tell me more about France while I make up the bed. You've mentioned Lyon in your letters. What is it like there?"

He told her how the silk-weavers worked in their humble homes that were adapted with lowered floors to take the height of the looms, and how whole families worked together as a unit in producing their quota for the merchants, who sold it to buyers who came from all over France and beyond to buy, himself among them.

She listened dreamily, more to the sound of his beloved voice than to what he was saying, although images passed through her mind's eye of the clanking looms and the little children crouched beneath to mend the broken threads. She gave a last smoothing touch to the fold of the top sheet and then turned to find him holding a glorious length of silk threaded with silver across his arm.

"This is Lyonnaise silk. I brought a length for each of you at Sotherleigh. Julia received hers when I saw her at Oxford. It seemed to me that this would suit your fair colouring. I have learned such things since I entered the silk-trade."

She came slowly across, her robe and nightgown billowing lightly, and then fingered the soft silk. Her face was radiant. "For me? Oh, Michael!"

He draped one end of it over her shoulder and they both turned to the mirror on the wall for her to see her reflection. The neckline of her nightgown was low-cut, her robe only tied at the waist, and the silk gleamed against her skin. She was as speechless as if once again her voice had deserted her. It did not matter that he had brought for the others too. This had been his personal choice for her. His gift for her alone.

"You like it?" he asked her. His gaze had lowered to her cleavage. The bouquet of sleep from which she had been awakened still hung about her, a feminine fragrance of warm flesh and hidden places. He felt dangerously stirred, his feelings for her rising rapidly.

It was at that moment she looked up over her shoulder into his face and saw in his eyes what the distorted glass of the old mirror had not revealed. The words of thanks for the silk faded from her lips. She turned towards him and put up her hand to the side of his face, raising herself on tip-toe to kiss his mouth.

Instantly his arms were about her, passion flaring up between them. The silk slipped unnoticed to the floor. The hunger of his mouth met what he wanted from hers, her response unrestrained, giving and utterly loving. Their need for each other overwhelmed them. They moved simultaneously to the bed, he pulling her robe and nightgown from her on the way and then tearing off his own clothes and throwing them aside.

They churned the bed into furrows and she climaxed again and again as if her body, released at last from its long-held virginity, had become insatiable for love. When at last they lay still, all verbal sounds silenced, they looked at each other in a kind of wonder.

"I love you," she whispered. Why should she hold back this confession when she had been totally uninhibited about everything else that had taken place between them? "I've loved you ever since the day you brought me to Sotherleigh and I was suddenly terrified when you went from the room, leaving me alone with Anne and Sarah."

"I know now that I should never have left you at any time," he said ruefully.

"Circumstances were both for and against us. We met and then because of that same meeting you had to go alone to France."

"Now we have met again and history is about to repeat itself." His voice was hoarse with regret and he put an arm about her waist to draw her to him and kiss her again.

After they had made love once more he slept, and she slipped from the bed to re-don her nightgown and robe. Then she tidied up the tell-tale scatter of his clothes and piled them neatly on a chair. Pausing only to kiss his closed eyelids, she left the underground room. She had to use extreme caution in getting upstairs without being seen, because it was eight o'clock and Makepeace as well as the servants would be about, breakfast being at a quarter past the hour. Twice she had to dodge into doorways until she was in the west wing where fortunately she met nobody. Never before had she bathed and dressed and arranged her hair with such speed. Even then she arrived five minutes late at the table and Makepeace glared his displeasure.

"If you wish to stay in my house," he said with emphasis, "you will not come late to this board."

Anne glanced at her in sympathy at the barked command and then looked down at her plate again. She had noted with increasing anxiety how he never missed an opportunity to let Mary know that she was at Sotherleigh on sufferance. It was apparent that if the right excuse came his way he would banish her immediately.

That day Michael saw Katherine. She had been told of his coming and her cheeks were pink with anticipation. He went to her apartment at an afternoon hour when Makepeace was out and the servants were gathered in the kitchen regions, their earlier duties done. Her reunion with her grandson was a tonic to her. In addition, she was delighted with the prospect of a new gown out of the length of ruby silk he had brought her. She was animated and talkative, having much that she had long wanted to discuss with him about Sotherleigh and what he should do when it was his once more.

"The day will come when the King is home again and all the trespassing Parliamentarians like Makepeace compelled to surrender their ill-gotten gains."

"I'm sure you're right, Grandmother. We just have to be patient."

"I fear that virtue does not run in Pallister veins. We want what is our due without delay when we know it is our right."

"I agree with you there." There was a wry note in his voice that she did not quite catch.

That night Mary came to his bed at midnight and left before the servants were about next morning. He postponed his departure yet another day, not knowing how to leave Mary with her loving heart and body. When they made love her little sighs afterwards were of sheer contentment and not of relief that it was over as his wife never failed to utter. No rigid submission from Mary, no distaste for a man's body with averted gaze, but a passionate eagerness and a demonstrative glorying in his strength and prowess.

Yet he had to go. His danger increased with every hour he lingered. Anne, much as it meant to her to see her son during the day hours, innocently implored him to depart, imagining it was for her sake and Katherine's that he was staying on. Finally he told her the predominant reason.

"I'm in love with Mary. I've made the greatest mistake of my life in marrying someone else, but I have to live with the consequences."

It was typical of Anne that she should feel compassion equally for the three people involved in this unhappy triangle. "Yes, you must, Michael. You have hurt Sophie whether she should ever know it or not, as much as Mary. I shall do what I can for Mary while you try to make amends with your wife." Her eyes were full of pity. "Leave today, Michael. When you return with the King and bring your wife with you, I know Mary will want to be far from Sotherleigh."

"I fear she will, but the loss will be mine."

That night he and Mary made love for the last time. They knew they were parting for ever. He could not hope to be sent to England on a royal mission again. His role as a French merchant had worked once, but a second time might stir suspicion with fatal results, as had befallen the spy before him. Should he ever return as master of Sotherleigh, Sophie would be with him.

In the early hours of the morning he made ready to depart. He put his arms about Mary as they went along the subterranean passage and up into the maze. They had agreed they should say their farewells there. The gardener would be waiting by the side gate with Michael's horse and she did not want their final words overheard by anyone else.

"I'll remember these hours we have had together until the end of my days," she said softly, her eyes searching his face in the glow from the lantern that he had set down on the octagonal seat.

He realised she was memorising his face anew in these last seconds and he held her close to him. "Nothing will ever be the same for me, my dearest. I should have realised it was not mere chance that I took you from the gallows that day. Fate had given me the woman who should have been my wife and I failed to realise it until I saw you again."

"I'm going to be thankful for what we have had. If you hadn't risked your life in coming to England, even that time would have been lost to us."

"I love you," he murmured in the need to tell her once more, and he kissed her with a fierceness born of his despair at losing her. Then he broke away to disappear through the south archway into the path that would take him from the maze.

She picked up the lantern and stayed above ground until she could be sure that he had left the park and was galloping for the coast.

BY THE FOLLOWING FEBRUARY Richard Cromwell, a worthy man in his own way, less Puritanical than his father, had shown himself to be a weak leader and had made enemies across wide sections of the populace for a variety of reasons. As a result he had been nicknamed Tumbledown Dick.

Julia was abreast with all that was happening through the intellectual and political talk that prevailed at Bletchingdon rectory. It was suspected that certain powerful army officers at Westminster were more attracted to taking control for themselves than considering a return of the monarchy as an alternative to Richard's government. There were also some men, according to William, who were secret Royalists in that same government, and thus it was possible the King had more friends than he knew to counteract that danger.

Interested though Julia was in all she heard, looking for hope wherever it showed itself, her thoughts were never far from Sotherleigh and had become directed recently with increasing anxiety towards her mother, from whom she had not heard since shortly before Christmas. Then Anne had insisted she remain at Bletchingdon. Much as she longed to see those dear to her at Sotherleigh, she had been glad to stay on with the Holders. Christopher had come for Christmas Day and made other occasional visits. Everything was still the same between them, his affection for her noticeable, his glances ever on her. He saw for himself that she had plenty of local young men eager to hold her hand and dance with her, or to have a seat next to her at table and offer to accompany her on walks, but if he was jealous he was too sophisticated and mannerly to show it. She told herself he was so sure of her he knew he had no cause for anxiety while others courted her. At times when he did exchange a restrained kiss with her in a game or a dance, or in rare, delicious moments on their own, she sensed the desire vibrating in him. More than once Adam's vow of what he would have done in Christopher's place returned to her, making her wish that the man she loved would set aside honour to hold her as she wished to be held, wildly and in total abandonment. Then she despaired of her own wayward yearnings.

Although Christopher had left Gresham College, he returned once a week to give lectures on light and refraction there. He was at Bletchingdon on the eve of one of these London visits when Julia received a letter from Mary. He saw her look of pleasure at hearing from home fade with her colour as she began to read.

"What's happened?" he asked, going to her.

She looked at him with frightened eyes. "My mother is not well. She is three months on the way to having a baby. I must go home. Now! Today!"

"I'll get two horses saddled up. It's late in the day to start for you, but we'll ride until dusk and start off again at dawn. We'll be at Sotherleigh tomorrow."

When Susan heard what was happening, she insisted that the maid who had been attending Julia should go with them. It was not that she doubted Christopher in any way, but convention demanded a chaperone. "Keep Phoebe with you at Sotherleigh if you wish. I can spare her and as you have no maid of your own there she would fill the gap."

"That's most kind of you, but it all depends on my stepfather."

Susan stood at the gate of the rectory and waved the three riders out of sight. It concerned her to think of Anne pregnant at the age of forty-four.

When the journey ended at the steps of Sotherleigh, Julia did not wait for assistance to dismount and went running into the house. Makepeace stood at the foot of the Grand Staircase, his scowling expression showing it did not please him to see her again. She remembered Anne's wish that she should make a new beginning with him whenever she should return home and she would try to keep to that.

"Good day, Stepfather. I've come home to care for my mother in her pregnancy. Where is she?"

"Resting," he said coldly. "She can't be disturbed now."

"I should like to see her without delay since I've been told she is not well."

"I've said that you must wait. Have you learned nothing of obedience to your elders in your absence?" Then he looked beyond her to the doorway. "Who is this?"

She presented Christopher, who had entered after her, Phoebe behind him. The change in Makepeace's attitude was remarkable. He was smiling and benign as he went forward to greet Christopher, unaware that he immediately said the wrong thing. "The famous Mr. Wren! What an honour to meet you, sir. Praise of your marvellous inventions is to be heard everywhere. I read a paper only recently on your approach to navigation through mathematics, science and astronomy. Brilliant!"

"I am only one of many seeking to find a means of establishing longitude accurately at sea," Christopher replied. "There are others far more advanced than I. But I'm afraid I have no time to stay and tell you of them. I should like to see Mrs. Walker before I leave, although I think I heard you say she was resting."

"But she is not asleep. I will escort you to her myself and you must at least take something to sustain you before you go again."

"Perhaps Julia and I could share some refreshment with your wife when we sit with her for a little while?"

Julia noted Makepeace's thinly disguised annoyance at having to grant her admission to her mother's room through the wishes of this eminent man, but he led the way. She gave her cape to Phoebe and told her to ask the footman on duty at the door to direct her to Sarah. Then she hastened on up the stairs in the wake of Makepeace and Christopher. Dearest Sotherleigh! She was home again.

# TWELVE

*A*NNE COULD TELL she was about to receive visitors by the footsteps approaching her bedchamber. She was fully dressed and lay propped against cushions on a day-bed in her comfortable room, a good fire blazing in the fireplace. She had never been robust, but she was not ailing unduly during this pregnancy and her original fears of not surviving another childbirth had gone. It suited her that everyone wanted her to rest, because it meant she was able to catch up on her sleep, the lack of which was caused through still longer nocturnal embroidery sessions.

Her maternal instincts had always been strong and she longed for the baby she would hold in her arms. Had someone reminded her that Makepeace was the father she would have been caught off guard, because she had chosen to think of the forthcoming child as Robert's. She had succeeded in withdrawing her mind from anything that upset her and had reached a point where she could shut herself away with whatever she wanted to believe was true. She had even perfected a way of not quite looking at Makepeace's face at table or about the house, and at night she slipped into her void completely while he persisted in his fetish of wanting her to gaze on him. She supposed her lowered lashes and the shadows cast by the single candle-flame hid from him the fact that her inner self was never there.

The door opened and Makepeace entered, unaware that the ends of her lashes drooped to make a mist of his face. "Anne, my dear." He rarely spoke without the familiar endearment, even when he was angry. "You are in for a little surprise. The eminent Mr. Wren is here and—er—your daughter is back."

She thought she must collapse with joy. "Let them come in!" she cried.

Then Julia was in the room and rushing to her. "Mama! How are you?"

"I'm well, dearest child! Don't think otherwise. I'm just being a little lazy, that's all. Oh, how glad I am to have you home again."

Then Christopher joined the happy reunion, taking the hand that Anne outstretched to draw him close. Makepeace watched from the other side of the room, knowing himself to be forgotten, shut out from this charmed circle. Never once had Anne looked rapturously at him as she did now at the two arrivals. Not for him the spontaneous outburst of delight or expressed gladness for his presence. He was tortured by jealousy. It seemed to scorch the back of his eyes. His obsessive love for her gave him no peace, and although he had done everything he could think of to concentrate her affections solely towards himself, he had failed. There was one weapon left and he would use it. All along he had hoped it was something she would do by her own wish, showing that her Cavalier husband was forgotten and at last he was first with her, but that had not happened. Now he would make it happen.

When Julia went to see Katherine she observed a great change in her. No doubt it had been so gradual that it had not been as marked to Anne and Mary as it was to her. Her grandmother was still alert, but it was as if she had shrunk and was far more frail in appearance, her eyes deep-sunken and her movements feeble. Yet her greeting had its usual blend of pith and love.

"You've come home then? I suppose you thought I missed you."

"Why should I imagine that?" Julia's eyes twinkled as she settled herself on the footstool. At least Makepeace had never changed anything in this room and it was still the sanctuary of the Pallisters.

"Christopher came to see me before he left. Have you come to your senses over him?"

Julia's cheeks hollowed and she answered soberly. "At the present time he is in love with his scientific work and whatever he feels for me takes second place. If ever he should look at me in such a way that I know I've won over everything else, I'll be his."

"What if that should never happen?"

Julia did not flinch. "Somehow I'll survive as you did when you lost Ned in another way."

Later that day Julia asked Mary why her letter had emphasised Anne's need of her return instead of Katherine's. "I can see that my grandmother has entered the last lap of her life and I'm thankful to be here with her again."

"It isn't your mother's physical health that worries me. She is up each day and attends every mealtime. In between, Makepeace insists that she rest and fusses that she has a footstool, enough fresh air and much more. In that respect he means well, but I fear that without realising it he is steadily driving her out of her mind."

Julia stared at her in disbelief. "That can't be true. She was perfectly all right when I saw her and we had a long talk together."

"Did she do most of the talking or did you?"

"I suppose I did and Christopher talked as much before he left."

"That's it. She listens more than she ever speaks now, and if it's something she doesn't want to hear or see her eyes go quite blank."

"That can happen to anyone losing concentration or becoming bored."

"It's far more than that. Makepeace rules her completely and she is too gentle and sensitive to retaliate in any way."

"Mama is incapable of hatred. Go on."

"After you went to Bletchingdon she spoke often about you, wondering what you were doing and so forth, and I saw how Makepeace resented it. When she was excited over getting a letter from you he had a face as long as a fiddle. It's as if he can't bear to share anything she says or does with anyone else. Gradually he began to impose tighter restrictions on her. There was much more I could have told Michael when he was here, but I did not want him to go back to France with extra worries when there was nothing he could do about them."

"What restrictions did Makepeace impose?"

"He began by not letting her go shopping unless he was with her and never allowed her to call on anyone she had known before his coming to Sotherleigh. She is permitted to visit Mistress Katherine only once a day for a quarter of an hour and not a minute over, which makes her watch the clock most of the time she is there. I no longer dine in the Great Hall and I believe I was banished after Anne talked more to me than to him during meals there. Now they have all their meals alone together unless there is company of his choice for her and that is usually dreary. About three months ago a certain sea-captain spent the day here, a man called Crowhurst, who was big and jovial."

"Mama mentioned him in a letter to me. He acts as a courier sometimes with papers connected with a business interest Makepeace has in America."

"According to Sarah, who heard it through the servants' grapevine and then told me, Anne enjoyed his visit far too much for Makepeace's liking. The sea-captain made the mistake of flirting with her and paying her compliments. It was all harmless and Anne was her usual dignified self the whole time, but after he had gone Makepeace gave vent. I heard him shouting at her in the east wing. You know how the Long Gallery can echo sound. The next day it was as if he had shocked her into a trance. For twenty-four hours she did not seem to see or hear anything."

Julia anguished over what she had been told. "Nobody has ever raised a voice to my mother, not even Grandmother, who has shouted at me often enough in the past. Trouble always confused and upset Mama, but never once have I seen her succumb to such a state as you have described."

That evening at supper Julia observed her mother closely. All was not well, although perhaps this was what Makepeace wanted. Anne had become utterly docile and subdued. Gone was the spark that had given such charm to her sweet nature. It was no wonder that she wandered about at night, which Mary said Michael had discovered. Her state of stress beneath that outward calm could only be guessed at. Julia felt doubly thankful to be home, able to give Katherine more company and to do whatever she could for her mother.

Anne was already in bed when Makepeace, who had been reading late in the Queen's Parlour, came into her room. The fact that he was still fully dressed showed that he would be sleeping in the master bedroom that night, for he was always in his nightshirt when he intended to stay. She sighed inwardly with relief. It meant she could get to her embroidery with less risk. Yet whether or not he shared her bed at night he never failed to give her a good night kiss. As he approached the bed she sat up in readiness, her mind ready to slam the door on his wet lips. But he took up her hand from the coverlet instead.

"Come, my dear. I think it's high time now that you shared the master bedchamber with me. I'll take this room when you are nearer your time. After the confinement I shall return to you in the great bed."

Her eyes regarded him with horror. "I can't sleep with you in Robert's bed!"

He did not intend to lose his temper. That had happened only once with her and he had regretted it ever since. All she had done throughout his tirade was to speak once, saying that Captain Crowhurst had intended no harm. He had known it and yet still had been unable to stem his jealousy. There was every reason to suppose that in seeking to atone afterwards he had made her pregnant. As for the present matter, he had been lax in not putting his foot down earlier, but no second husband wanted the ghost of the first to share a marriage bed. For that reason he had let her take another bedchamber for herself where he could go to her. That had been his mistake.

"It is my bed in my house and you, my dear wife, are going to move into the great bedchamber with me."

She tugged against the pull of his hand clasping hers. "No! I can't! I won't betray Robert!" He had his arm about her and was drawing her inexorably from her bed. The pressure of the bands about her brain was becoming more than she could bear. "His baby is in my womb! You shall not touch me!"

In her panic she was not quite coherent or else he would have realised the extent to which he had lost her. "Calm yourself. You will be fulfilling a duty long left undone. The past will stop haunting you once and for all."

She was screaming inside, but aversion to him was smothering all sound. Suddenly she recalled a time when she had been willing to kneel to him, had it been necessary, to implore that she and those dependent on her should not have to leave Sotherleigh. As he levered her free of the bed she dropped to her knees and clawed at his velvet jacket.

"No! Let me stay here! I beg you!"

He reached down, put his hands under her armpits and hauled her upright, but the strength seemed to have gone from her legs, for as he held her suspended her feet hung down and her toes dragged. Murmuring endearments to her, he scooped her up in his arms and carried her, her head lolling against his shoulder, away through the intervening parlour to the master bedroom. Her mind had escaped into its void before he was through the door.

AFTER BREAKFAST next morning Julia had a short, sharp interview with Makepeace in the library from which he conducted the business of the estate and other matters. The marriage settlement, signed by Adam and himself, was on the table before him. She realised she had given Adam little thought over the past weeks, except to recall his kiss occasionally, and it startled her to be brought face to face again with this betrothment that she had long since dismissed as something she would escape somehow.

"As you know, your future has been agreed," Makepeace said bluntly. "You can consider yourself fortunate that Mr. Warrender is willing to take you without a dowry, although he did ask for an acre of land where his boundary and mine meet and I'm letting him have it."

She knew that acre. It jutted awkwardly into a Warrender field. They might as well have bartered a cow or two for her. "I have always intended that a man should marry me for my worth and not what I brought with me."

Makepeace looked at her suspiciously, but made no comment. "No date for the marriage is set yet and Mr. Warrender will wish to discuss it with you and your mother, although naturally the ultimate decision will be his. He knows I have no objection to a wedding date in the near future. That concludes all I have to say to you now."

On her way to her mother's room, Julia thought how far she had advanced in keeping control of herself under enormous provocation. She found Anne dressed and lying on the day-bed just as she had been the previous day. A dullness cleared from Anne's eyes as she looked into her daughter's face.

"You're really here, Julia. I thought I might have dreamed it."

"No, I'm here to stay, Mother. Why not come down to the Queen's Parlour? You can have a chair by the window and I'll find some embroidery for you."

Anne shook her head wearily. "I've been stitching for hours. That's why I'm tired and need to sleep."

Julia smiled. "Indeed you have been dreaming, Mama. But never mind. Rest now. I'll come back to see you later." As she made to move away, her mother reached out to catch her sleeve.

"Michael brought me a length of Lyonnaise silk garlanded with flowers, a little like Elizabeth's gown that your grandmother possesses." Anne's face worked with distress. "I had to hide it away."

"I know," Julia said compassionately. Then she stayed quietly beside her mother until she slept.

Julia had left the east wing when a servant informed her that Adam had come to see her and was waiting in the hall. An unbidden flare of excitement rose up from the pit of her stomach. When she reached the flower screen she looked down at him through an aperture in the foliage. He must have heard the whisper of her skirts, for he turned his face up to her at once.

"How are you, Julia? I've come to ask you to go riding with me."

She breathed a soft laugh. "You've wasted no time in getting here. I only arrived home yesterday. Who told you?"

"Mr. Walker promised to keep me informed. I've just gained his permission for you to dine *al fresco* with me."

Her face grew taut. He and Makepeace were conniving together over everything! But at least he was being honest about it, even though he would know that anything remotely connected with her stepfather was anathema to her. "Have you forgotten that the first day of spring isn't for three weeks yet?"

"I like winter picnics best. There are no wasps or flies. In any case it's very mild today and unlikely to rain."

She hesitated no longer. "I'll fetch my cloak."

"Julia!"

"Yes?" She turned back to the screen.

"No chaperone today. I've gained permission for that too."

She was glad he could not see her bite her lip on a grin. There was nobody to accompany them in any case, Mary being with Katherine and Phoebe having contracted a cold on the journey from Bletchingdon. Probably Makepeace thought to get her compromised into a quick marriage, but Adam should never get her by those means. It was lucky that neither her mother nor her grandmother knew of the liberty she had been deviously granted.

He came to the foot of the Grand Staircase as she descended. "Let's ride to the Downs," she requested, pulling the hood of her scarlet cloak up over her head and tying the strings. "It's so long since I was last there." She went ahead of him out of the house and he caught up with her to go down the stone steps with her.

"I've brought your betrothal present with me."

She stopped to look at him in mild exasperation. "I'm not accepting a ring or anything else from you, Adam. I thought I made that clear between us at Bletchingdon."

"Not as I understood it. In any case, it's not time for a ring yet. I'm not forcing one on your finger, although I don't doubt Makepeace would hold your wrist for me. No, it's something else today. If what I've chosen for you isn't to your liking, I shouldn't expect you to accept it." He looked away from her to signal with a nod to the waiting groom, who passed it to a second groom out of sight. Then that man appeared, leading Adam's black horse and a bay she recognised instantly.

"Charlie!" She flew to her horse and it tossed its head, its nostrils flaring as she clapped its neck and smoothed its soft nose, talking affectionately. "You've not forgotten me! To think that once it seemed I should never see you again."

A groom handed her some roughly cut sugar pieces and she held them out on her palm to the horse. When all were taken she went nimbly up the steps of the mounting block and settled herself in Charlie's side-saddle. Adam, who had mounted during the reunion, came riding up to her.

"By what name did you call that horse?" he questioned incredulously.

She eyed him with merry defiance. "You've been keeping a royally named bay in your stables, Adam. You couldn't have expected me to call him Cromwell."

"I understood from Makepeace that he was called Starlight."

"That's right." She laughed. "Charlie-Starlight. I once had a pony with that second name and Charlie was for the King, although Makepeace never knew about that! If you had known the truth, would it have made any difference?"

His eyes were amused and he shook his head. "You know what Shakespeare said about a rose smelling as sweet. You never fail to surprise me, Julia. Shall we go?"

She thought to herself that he had done his fair share of surprising her. He had kindness in him, but he was also extremely astute, which meant she must always be on her guard. If proof was needed it showed in the way he had selected the one betrothal gift he believed she would find impossible to refuse. As they rode side by side down the drive in the direction of the gates she broke the news to him that she was sure he would not want to hear.

"Naturally I can't keep Charlie."

"Why not? When Makepeace delayed me from leaving on the night of your Royalist sing-song to offer to sell me your horse, I only purchased it with the intention of returning it to you one day. From what he said I could tell you were attached to it. Now that you and I are betrothed he raised no objection when I told him a few weeks ago that I intended it should be yours again whenever you came home." He grinned widely. "I daresay he would have stipulated a change of name if he had known."

"But don't you see? You said Charlie was a betrothal gift, which makes it impossible for me to accept him. I'd buy him back if I could, but I can't at the present time."

"He's not for sale and so it's pointless to think that way. Take him on permanent loan. Will that satisfy you?"

"No. I'd still be under an obligation to you. Keep my horse. Charlie has been well cared for and is in perfect condition. That's what matters most now."

"Then you shall ride the animal whenever you wish."

"I agree to that."

He rolled up his eyes in exaggerated relief. "I can hardly believe that we've come to an amicable settlement. May it be a stepping stone to many more."

"I can't endorse that wish," she replied wickedly. "I think it will be more fun to remain at daggers drawn with you."

He did not respond with amusement as she had expected. "That time is over, Julia. Let's aim for friendship now."

She saw he was making it clear there was to be a solid foundation to their relationship. Friendship on its own would suit her well, because she would miss all the young company she had had at Bletchingdon, but marriage was another matter. "I spoke thoughtlessly," she admitted. "This is a time for amending past mistakes, both between us and the country as a whole."

He gave her a serious sideways glance. "Ever the Royalist, aren't you? I suppose you subscribe to the exaggerated belief that Charles I was a martyr and Cromwell a tyrant. Has it never occurred to you that there is a way to draw the good from both sides to form a new path?"

"When I can worship as I please, dress as I like, eat what I wish at Christmastide and dance around a maypole without anyone accusing me of being a pagan or a Papist, I'll know that the King is home and England is herself once more."

"You're confusing extremist ideas with the original Parliamentary ideals that I hold. Our country would be equally free if it adhered to them."

"The gulf between us is wide," she pointed out meaningfully.

"But friendship can bridge anything." He smiled kindly. "Let us call a truce for now." Bringing his horse closer to hers, he pulled off his gauntlet to reach out his hand to her. "Agreed?"

She nodded, giving him an answering smile. "Gladly." She put her hand into his to seal their pact. "Now we can enjoy our day together."

They rode for the Downs. The countryside was a spread of mellow browns and greys with the eternal green of the rolling hills and the air fresh with the scents of damp grass and dark earth. Pale sunshine lingered on the bark of the trees. When they followed a path through the woods last autumn's leaves were trampled down into the soft mud by their horses' hooves, leaving a shining trail behind them. Snowdrops clustered within the shelter of roots and he dismounted to pick a small bunch of the fragile blooms for her. She shared them with him, threading hers through an eyelet in her bodice while he tucked his into the band of his hat.

On the open brow of a hill they rode hard, clods of turf flying up in their wake, colour stung into their faces. When they rested their horses he produced a picnic from his saddle-bag and they sat on a fallen tree-trunk in a sheltered hollow to eat. Their view spread over the meadowland and the fields and far beyond the smudge of Chichester with its Cathedral standing proud, to the pale green stretch of the sea. They bit into roasted capon drumsticks accompanied by diet rolls, which were so named for providing extra nourishment to any meal, being thick and rich and buttery, tasty with herbs. There was wine to drink, which he poured into silver travelling cups and when only the capon bones remained, they tucked into preserved plums and apricots, which left a sugary coating on their lips that they wiped away on linen napkins.

"This is much better than dining at home today," she said contentedly. "I'm so glad you thought of it. My mother is probably too exhausted to go downstairs and it would have been dreadful to eat alone with Makepeace. He doesn't like my being home again and can't wait to be rid of me."

"I can guess what he wants you to do," he drawled lazily, leaning back against a tree to gaze seawards, his long legs stretched out in front of him, booted feet crossed at the ankles. He was sipping the wine from his silver cup.

She glanced sharply at him. "Makepeace showed me the signed marriage settlement this morning. It's pointless, you know. I've told you before I'm waiting for someone else. If my stepfather starts getting persistent about it I shall go back to Bletchingdon." Then she drooped her head and put her hands against her eyes. "What am I saying? I can't leave either my mother or my grandmother now."

"Warrender Hall isn't far away," he reminded her, taking another leisurely sip of wine.

"It's a thousand miles distant as far as I'm concerned."

"Not at all. When the boundary wall is changed to square off that acre of land I'm getting as your dowry, I thought I'd have a gate set in and a path laid to join up with another near the Hall. Then you could ride to Sotherleigh whenever you wished, because it would cut the distance by half."

She scarcely listened. Letting her hands drop into her lap, she looked at him in appeal. "Help me with this problem. Show me that you meant it when you said you wanted us to be friends. If Makepeace starts pressing for a wedding date, find excuses to postpone it; that will make it easier for me to stay on at Sotherleigh caring for those who need me."

He sat forward and for the second time that day regarded her with disbelief. "You're asking me to do that? I want our marriage. I'd let it take place tomorrow if it didn't mean twisting your arm. You've lost us time already. There'll come a time when you'll regret every hour wasted in procrastination."

She looked at him incredulously. "You're impossible! You and Makepeace are two of a kind!"

He hurled aside the silver cup he had still been holding, the red wine spraying out in an arc, and grabbed her by the shoulders to shake her, his face livid. "I told you before! Never mention that man's name in connection with mine! I'd never allow myself to be under the same roof with a regicide if there were any other way by which I could see you!"

"I apologise for that!" She was struggling frantically to free herself from his iron grip. "I thought that as my friend—"

He shook her again. "Friend! Lover! Husband! That's what I'll be to you, but not necessarily in that order!"

She lunged backwards, seeing he was about to aim his mouth at hers, and they fell together from the tree trunk onto the grass. His hold on her was loosened and she struck out with her arm, scrambling to her feet to rush for her horse, which was only a few yards away. Still on the ground, he hurled himself forward and caught a handful of her skirt-hems. She swung round to try to snatch them free of his clasp and then he was on his feet with his arms round her. In trying to escape him again, both of them gasping in the struggle, she stumbled on the slope and they went crashing down. Immediately the weight of his body trapped hers and he cupped her head in his hands, holding it steady to plunge his mouth down on hers, forcing her lips open and kissing her with intense passion. She was possessed by a delicious fear and her fingers dug into the soft turf, her arms pinioned by his elbows, which seemed anchored to the ground. His heart was pounding against her breast, almost as if it were seeking her own, and one of his long legs lay between hers, her petticoats tumbled above her garters. All was fire and darkness in his kiss and she was lost in it.

When eventually he took his lips from hers, it was to raise himself slightly and to draw one hand from the side of her face down to caress her breast through the soft wool of her bodice with, what was to her, almost unbearable tenderness. Her fear of him changed into alarm at the sensual abyss into which she felt herself slipping. She turned her head sideways, the turf against her cheek and disguised the surge of desire in her by speaking with all the coldness she could muster into her voice. "Take your hands from me. You'll never seduce me into a marriage."

He caught his breath as if she had struck him, although for a matter of seconds his hands lingered on her as if magnetised there. Then he rolled away to sit with one knee updrawn, his arm resting across it. He spoke with steel in his voice. "You certainly know how to be viperish, Julia."

She had risen to her feet and was brushing bits of grass from her skirt. He had unwittingly given her an outlet and she seized on it, although not without sympathy for him. "My grandmother has told me more than once in the past that I have the making of a shrew in my temper and my stubbornness. It's as well that you've found that out. No man wants those characteristics in a wife. Now you can look elsewhere."

"You forget that I'm bound to an agreement."

She tossed her head, her impatience directed at Makepeace and not at him, although he did not realise it. "That marriage settlement isn't worth the ink of your signature."

He watched her as she knelt to pack up the remains of their meal, wrapping everything in napkins to be put back in the saddle-bag. "I want that strip of Sotherleigh land and if it means taking you as part of the bargain, shrew or not, I'll have it."

There was such anger in his voice that every word was clipped. She felt a shiver of apprehension run down her spine. In him she had an adversary far more dangerous than Makepeace, because he had the power to stir all the pent-up sensuality in her by his very nearness. She half wished she could love him, which would solve everything, but physical excitement was not love as she knew it, perhaps from the time long ago when she had shared her dream with Christopher.

Making no reply to what he had said, she sat back on her heels, the packing-up finished and rubbed her arms, looking at the sky. "It's getting colder and the best of the day has faded. We must be getting back."

They rode in silence for most of the way. The snowdrops had wilted in his hat and she had lost every one of hers in their struggles. When they were almost in sight of Sotherleigh he spoke as if after much deliberation.

"You need not worry about a wedding date in the near future. I'll find reasons for postponing it as you asked. Your mother in her present condition and Mistress Katherine need your care."

She looked at him gratefully. "I thank you. That means more to me than you can possibly know. In that case we'll not be seeing each other for a while."

"On the contrary," he replied wryly, "this morning I accepted an invitation to take supper with Walker this evening."

"I may not be included."

"You will be. I believe he thought all would be settled between us today."

In her bedchamber, when she was changing out of her riding clothes, a single half-crushed snowdrop fell to the floor. Somehow it must have slipped inside her bodice. She picked it up and put it in water, not through any sentimental attachment to the earlier and better half of the day's outing, but because she cherished all nature's beauty. When she passed the flower screen later on her way downstairs, she paused for a moment by a carved snowdrop and traced its delicate curves with a finger.

When she reached the Queen's Parlour Makepeace was there and Adam had already arrived, attired now in crimson velvet. Their eyes met and all the events of the past hours on the Downs seemed to tumble between them as they bade each other a formal evening greeting. Makepeace was in full flow on the subject of pheasant-shooting and the pair of exceptionally good retrievers that he had had this winter. When it came to a few seconds to eight o'clock he showed he had not forgotten the time, for he glanced at the clock twice, awaiting Anne's arrival.

It was exactly on the hour when there came scuffling sounds in the arched passageway leading from the hall to the Queen's Parlour. Makepeace strode across to the door and flung it wide. Then he took a step back as if unable to believe his eyes. Anne entered with her usual grace, but she was attired in the dazzling Elizabethan gown. The scrolling flower embroideries on the bodice and the isolated slips on the skirt gleamed like multi-coloured jewels, the wrist-length sleeves so encrusted with stitchwork that they held a lovely ballooning shape. Around her neck was a filmy ruff edged with needlepoint lace while the extremely low décolletage, enhanced by its ornamentation of the swinging drop-pearls, pale and gleaming, revealed the white mounds of her bosom almost to the aureoles of her nipples, for she had not fastened the bodice properly at the back. Behind her in the passageway Mary and Sarah hovered aghast, having glimpsed her from a distance and been too late to prevent her entrance.

Makepeace uttered a bellow like a bull about to charge. "Out of my sight, madam! You have dared to garb yourself like a bawd in my house!"

She did not seem to hear, continuing to advance into the room in a state of dreamy abstraction, the soft grey eyes unfocused. Julia thought her mother had never looked more beautiful or more vulnerable. In a flash of understanding she recalled Anne's distress that morning at having to hide away Michael's gift of the Lyonnaise silk. The Elizabethan gown had been mentioned and it must have remained in her confused thoughts all day.

Adam, having grasped the situation, was bowing to Anne. "How elegant you look, madam."

In a flicker of her mind like a swaying curtain letting in light, she recognised him and gave him her hand to kiss. "I'm delighted to see you here, sir. All feuds should end in harmony as between your family and mine."

"Anne!" Makepeace roared, maddened above all else that her bosom should be thus revealed to another man's eyes. "Go and clothe yourself decently!"

He reached forward to propel her from the room himself, but Adam held him back by the arm. "No, sir! Don't touch her! She's in some kind of trance. Let your daughter and womenfolk see to her."

Julia took her mother about the waist. "We'll go and show your finery to Grandmother," she said emotionally.

Anne looked pleased by the suggestion, forgetting already that there was a guest in the house. "Yes, she will like to see her gown worn again."

She went eagerly from the room, stepping lightly ahead of her daughter, and Makepeace saw to his further dismay that the back of her bodice was completely unlaced. Before she disappeared from sight the single ribbon in the eyelet holes at the nape of her neck, which would have been all she could manage to tie unaided, slipped apart and the whole of her back almost to the base of her spine was revealed to him and his guest. He wanted to choke the life out of Adam for having seen what belonged to his pleasure alone.

Adam's voice broke in on the maelstrom of his wrathful jealousy. "I think I should leave, sir."

"No." Makepeace gulped down his rage and managed a grimace he hoped was a smile of apology. "I invited you to sup this evening and it would disappoint me greatly if you failed to let me fulfil my duties as a host. I've heard tell of pregnant women having strange fancies and I fear my dear wife has fallen prey to one. I ask you to forget what you have seen."

"You don't have to ask me, Mr. Walker. That was already my resolve."

In the hall Julia halted Anne while Sarah retied the loosened ribbon to prevent the whole gown falling from her. "How did you take the gown without Grandmother's knowledge?"

"She was dozing in her chair," Anne answered simply, "and I didn't want to wake her. I knew she wouldn't mind." Taking hold of her skirt to raise the hem slightly, she went on up the Grand Staircase, Julia at her side, Mary and Sarah following. Then she surprised them all again by running to the flower screen and swirling around beside it, exulting in the splendour of the embroidered satin as the skirt swayed out. "Look! See how the same flowers are all over this gown, which is such a happy garment to wear." Her face was quite radiant. "I think it must have magical qualities."

Then she turned and sped on to Katherine's apartment, the others following after her. The old lady's astonishment was equal to Makepeace's, but her reaction was entirely different as Anne swept towards her and then curtsied as deeply as if at Court. Katherine held up her thin hands in delight.

"What a wonderful surprise to give me! Thank you, dearest Anne. I thought never to see that gown worn again until Julia's wedding day, and since that may prove to be too far distant for me I'm grateful for what you have done."

Julia, watching the happiness of the two women at this time, thought it would be easy to believe that the gown had the power to cast good spells. Maybe it was just that any lovely garment could make a woman feel beautiful and other women, knowing that bewitchment themselves, could share vicariously in the experience. Proof of this was in the smiling faces of Mary and Sarah, who had forgotten momentarily that it was Anne's confusion through sheer misery that had prompted the putting on of the gown in the first place. Even Julia herself, conscious as she was of it, could not help but be warmed by the glowing look on her mother's face. It made her realise how long it was since she had last seen Anne truly happy.

MAKEPEACE QUESTIONED JULIA about the gown. He had tried to get an explanation from Anne, but all he could gather was that it belonged to

Katherine and was sixty years old or more. Why she had made such a display of herself she seemed neither to know or care.

"My mother isn't well in her mind," Julia said firmly. "It's because she has no freedom any more. If you would let me take her shopping or calling on—"

"No!" He thumped his fist on the library table to emphasise his refusal. "It would not be seemly for her to appear anywhere in public from now until after her confinement. I want your word that your grandmother's flamboyant garb is kept under lock and key in her apartment and that Anne does not gain access to it again. If not, I'll go myself to fetch it now and put a flame to it."

She knew he would not find it now that it was back in its secret compartment, but she could not risk his upsetting Katherine by turning the apartment upside down. "I'll see that my mother doesn't displease you over the gown again."

When Julia had gone he rose from his chair to pace up and down in the library, punching his fist into the palm of his hand. Something was amiss with Anne. He had noticed it increasingly, but since she obeyed him in everything he had dismissed her bouts of vagueness as nothing more than absorption in her pregnancy. Yet maybe he should consult a physician. He would call the best man in London down to Sussex without delay.

When Dr. Broadcourt arrived Anne was having what her daughter would have termed a good day. He asked Makepeace to allow him to present himself to her and not to come into the room until called for. Anne was pleased to have such an agreeable visitor, for he was a charming man with silken manners and she was touched that Makepeace should have shown such concern for her health. While he questioned her in a conversational manner she poured him a cup of fragrant Chinese tea.

"This is delicious, Mrs. Walker," he said, taking a sip from the porcelain cup.

"I thought coffee was proving more popular to date with all the coffee-houses springing up everywhere."

"I believe these two drinks will always be rivals, madam. I defy anyone to declare one better than the other. You mentioned earlier that you drink a cup of tea in the evenings sometimes. Does it keep you awake? In fact, how well do you sleep?"

Instantly she was wary. Was Makepeace suspicious of her whereabouts at night? Had the physician come to trick her into revealing where she went? She looked down at the brown liquid in her cup. "I get plenty of sleep," she answered truthfully, totting up the hours she dozed during rest periods.

He was satisfied with her reply, but he noticed that she was no longer relaxed with him. Somehow he had disturbed her. She was on edge, her eyes opaque and distant, a trembling in her hands. Their previous easy talk was at an end. "Are you looking forward to your baby, Mrs. Walker?"

Her face became utterly blissful. "It is the greatest blessing. My husband has always wanted another child and so have I."

He was puzzled. "But I understood from Mr. Walker that he has no children."

She did not answer him, her thoughts on their own trail. "My daughter, Julia, and Mary Twyat are busy sewing and embroidering garments for the new infant."

"Don't you sew yourself?"

Instantly panic flooded her eyes. This physician *was* here to trick her. "Mr. Walker doesn't like to see me with a needle and thread."

Dr. Broadcourt drew his conclusion there and then. This sensitive, gentle woman was frightened of her husband. He had seen it when sleep had been discussed and again now. He talked to her a little longer and then at his suggestion she tugged the bell-pull to summon a servant to ask her husband to come to the room. He watched her closely as Makepeace entered and saw her face lose all expression like a flower closing its petals. She answered her husband slowly as if she had drawn away, and she forgot to pour him a cup of tea until he reminded her.

Dr. Broadcourt gave Makepeace his opinion when they were on their own. "Your wife is absorbed by her pregnancy. Many women in her condition are the same. I also suggest to you that her marital duties have become repugnant to her at this time, again a common enough development, but everything will return to normal after the birth. You have nothing to worry about, but I advise you to resign yourself to celibacy for the remaining months. Cosset and cherish her, sir. She is of nervous disposition, which will only worsen if you are not extremely patient with her at the present time."

Makepeace was annoyed by what he saw as the slurs that the physician had made against him. He knew himself to be a monument of patience as far as Anne was concerned. No husband could be more devoted or more eager for the son she was to bear him and through whom he would found a new dynasty at Sotherleigh.

Not long after the physician's visit Anne felt the baby quicken. It happened one morning when she was taking a stroll for exercise with Makepeace. She would have liked to wander through the Knot Garden, but this man, who had somehow thrust himself into her life as another husband, always steered her away from it, although she had explained that it held romantic memories for her when she had come as a young bride to Sotherleigh.

"What is the matter, Anne?" he asked, for she had halted as they were halfway along one of the long paths bordered by shrubs and spring flowers.

She was in a state of supreme happiness at the tell-tale flutter in her womb and stood with her face tilted skywards, pressing both hands to her stomach through the layers of her skirts. "Our child has life," she breathed to Robert.

Then the man at her side, whose name she could not always remember, gave a kind of strangled shout of exultation. Hastening her out of sight behind a box-hedge, he violated her modesty by thrusting his hand up under her petticoats, his palm pressed flat against her belly to feel that movement for himself. But the babe was resting again after that first kick and he felt nothing. Wave after wave of aversion for this man went through her to such an extent that she fainted and did not recover consciousness until she opened her eyes to find herself in the house with Julia waving astringent herbs under her nose.

That night, in her impatience to get to the attic to be alone with Robert at this special time, she did not wait to make sure that Makepeace was soundly asleep. Normally he slept as soon as he closed his eyes, but since coming to bed he had felt the butterfly stirrings of his child and that had excited him. His hand was still on her when she slid from the bed while he was only on the surface of sleep. He supposed she was going to the closed stool in the garderobe, but when the door closed almost soundlessly on the opposite side of the room he knew she had gone out into the corridor.

"Anne?" He raised himself on an elbow, thinking she would hear him and return. When nothing happened, he flung aside the bedclothes, stuck his feet into slippers and pulled on a robe. In the corridor, lit by a single candle-sconce, there was no sign of her. He went to look in the direction of the stairs, again without seeing her. Then he opened the doors into the Long Gallery, but that was still and silent. He looked doubtfully towards the north end of the corridor, unable to think of any reason why she should have gone that way, for the door there was little used, only giving access to the attics, the servants' back staircase and a secluded entry into the west wing.

Suspicion suddenly flared. Had she gone to see her relatives secretly? He had interpreted Dr. Broadcourt's advice about cossetting by keeping Anne on her own in the east wing if not in his company. It was his duty to see that nobody tired her and since it distressed her if Katherine was poorly, which the old woman was most of the time now, he had forbidden any further visits to the west wing. "The welfare of our unborn son must come before the old and senile," he had said, full of hatred for all those who had been part of her life before her marriage to him.

Now he truly believed she had found a way to defy his will. He rushed to the far door and flung it wide as he charged through. The glow of a single candle, which she must have paused to light somewhere, illuminated her like a pale wraith halfway along the narrow passageway. She was almost level with the attic stairs and, to his mind, bound for the west wing.

"Wait!" His strong voice burst upon the silence like a cannon's roar to echo and re-echo against the panelled walls. She gave one terrified look over her shoulder, the candle dropping from her nerveless fingers to the floor, snuffing out the flame. Then she bolted past the attic flight to the sconce-lit servants' stairway.

Her one thought was to lead him far from her attic room. She felt like a mother bird fluttering ahead of a predacious enemy to divert notice away from its young. Down the winding stairs she flew, handfuls of her nightgown grabbed up to leave her feet unhampered, her damask silk robe billowing out behind her. She knew he was pounding along in her wake and she could think of only one place where she could be safe from him. And Robert would be there! Hiding from the Roundheads on a secret visit home, while she, fleeing from the same danger, was on her way to share his sanctuary, his arms and his love!

She took the last tread of the flight in the kitchen regions. On she ran, losing a slipper while the flagged floor of that part of the house struck icy cold to her feet. Then through one door and another into the entrance hall and across to the Great Hall. She could hear the Roundhead close behind her. She dodged the long oaken table and rushed into the adjoining room, breath tearing from her lungs. The dividing wall was in its socket and she had no obstruction in her way as she threw herself towards the Queen's Door. Her hand was shaking violently as she slid it sideways and darted through into the darkness beyond. She was safe! Swinging round, she slid the door back into place and it had almost closed when to her horror her pursuer's foot slammed down in the remaining aperture. She set her weight on the handle inside the door, hoping the pain would make him withdraw, but his big hand, with a far greater strength behind it, began forcing it back.

"Robert!" she screamed, knowing he would rush to her assistance, but in the same instance there came a sword-thrust of pain up through her body that knocked her to the floor.

ANNE DID NOT LOSE HER BABY, although for a while it seemed she would. She had forgotten her midnight flight through the house and Makepeace did not remind her. When the danger of a miscarriage was past another physician was summoned from London, Makepeace not wanting to see Dr. Broadcourt again. Complete rest was advised, which meant that Anne was destined to be practically bedridden for the rest of her pregnancy. She became like Katherine in sitting by the open windows of the master bedchamber whenever the weather allowed and was not permitted to leave it for any reason whatever. Although the baby was vigorous in her womb, she became pale and weak, missing the comfort of her embroidery, but conditioned to not stitching away from the attic. There were times on her own when she pretended she held a needle and thread and a ribbon to be embroidered and went through the actions, but it was not the same, for concentration eluded her and before long her hands fell listlessly into her lap.

Her face lit up whenever Julia and Mary came to spend the time allotted to them by Makepeace, and she admired and handled lovingly the baby clothes they brought to show her as if the infant were already in them. There were caps, coats, nightwear and jerkins all in softest linen so fine as to be almost transparent. Everything was white with smocking and the most delicate designs in coral stitch and in thousands of French knots, which formed whirls in patterns so closely and minutely worked they almost appeared to be printed. There were tiny mittens of the same soft linen that lacked fingers but had a thumb for protection during sucking, and were similarly embroidered around the wrists. Anne had saved the robes that Michael and Julia had worn and these were re-laundered to their original snowy whiteness to be laid away in readiness with the rest of the layette.

Her mother-in-law also came once to see her. Four manservants bore Katherine in her marriage chair across to the east wing. They carried her as steadily as they could, but each slight jerk sent daggers through her permanently painful joints. The short ride exhausted her and she could only reply faintly to Anne's appreciation that she had come.

"I wanted to see you so much, dear Anne," she gasped, close to collapse. "Take good care of yourself. I fear I'll not be able to come again."

"At least we have seen each other," Anne replied gently. "My first walk after the birth shall be to carry my baby to see you."

It was that same night that Anne's yearning to get back to her attic room overcame her. She went unsteadily, propping herself against the wall as far as the attic stairs. When she was halfway up the flight her strength gave out and she sank down to lie weeping across them. It was a while before she was rested enough to get back to the master bedchamber and then she had to crawl the last few yards. Fortunately the man who thought he was her husband had removed himself to the other room at the time of her threatened miscarriage and there was nobody to see her struggle to get back into bed.

Makepeace had waited a considerable while before investigating the Queen's Door and then at an hour when he was sure to be unobserved. It had astonished him to see Anne disappearing through the secret door, having been certain there was no such place in this house, for he knew there had been two Roundhead raids, which were usually of exceptional thoroughness, and he himself had searched well. He nodded appreciation of the craftsmanship when he opened the panel, seeing that the sliding door, made on the same principle as the dividing wall, was four times the width of the aperture with another behind it that operated at the same time and prevented any hollow ring.

With a lantern he conducted a preliminary investigation of the underground quarters and was surprised a second time to raise what he thought to be a trap door but which turned out to be a section of the octagonal seat in the maze. He then returned to the underground chamber to examine everything there. The weaponry interested him and he handled every piece. Some of the musketry belonged to the time of Queen Elizabeth, while the rest included snaphaunce and flintlock guns as well as wheelhock holster pistols such as had been used in the Civil War. There was a locked chest that he did not attempt to open, but when he tilted it to try to discover its contents, there was the unmistakable rattle of coins. He left everything as he had found it and gave no indication to anyone that he now knew the Sotherleigh secret way.

His patience with Anne was wearing thin. Increasingly he was irritated by the glazed look she turned on him and at times she seemed confused as to who he was. Yet she would also answer him quite sensibly at times if it was anything connected with the baby or those in the west wing. The main trouble was that he could not find it in himself to forgive her for the mad chase she had led him down to that hidden door. His great fear had been that she would fall and he had shouted to her to stop, to take care and to think of the baby, but it was as if she had become completely deaf. Then to hear her shriek for her late husband for protection against him had chilled his blood. Since then he had found it impossible to feel the same about her, not just for using the name of his predecessor, but for disobeying him by being on her way to the west wing and then in her guilt giving no consideration to the safety of his precious unborn off-spring. During the twenty-four hours when she had bled and a miscarriage seemed inevitable, he knew his love for her was being tested and found wanting. His thoughts were only for the baby, with concern for his wife only secondary. If there should be any complications at the birth through her irresponsible behaviour on that night he would have no hesitation in wanting the child saved before the mother. Wives could be replaced, but not a son and heir.

Otherwise he had little to worry him. He had known some concern when Richard Cromwell had resigned, wondering what the outcome would be, but an orderly state of affairs prevailed throughout the country. Although there were some gentlemen who had never again accepted his invitations to Sotherleigh after Julia had brought his being a regicide into the open, there were plenty of others who came. Among those with a like mind to his, he had had many a laugh over the short-lived Cavalier rejoicing on the other side of the Channel after Tumbledown Dick's resignation. The Royalist uprising that had been expected in England had failed to take place. To add to the joke, Charles Stuart had moved to Calais with his regiment of Guards in readiness to cross the Channel and then had had to return to Bruges when no foreign military support was forthcoming.

JULIA SAW ADAM OFTEN. She had noted his intervention the evening her mother had appeared in the Elizabethan gown. It had spared Anne being hustled away by Makepeace and she had marked it up in his favour. He refrained from asking her to go riding again until the apple blossom had left the trees and lilac was in full flower. Then he included Mary and the result was an enjoyable outing, Julia finding that the presence of an amiable third person eliminated all strain between Adam and herself.

She had decided it was time to present him to Katherine, whom she had told long since of his attempt to intervene in the sequestration of Sotherleigh, although not his main reason. It would not be tactful or kind to let Katherine know that some long-held secret of her romantic association with Sir Harry was now known to his grandson and her granddaughter. Katherine, able to tell that Julia could still be quite irritable about him, had not requested a meeting, but her curiosity was keen, mostly because she wanted to know if he bore any facial resemblance to his grandfather.

When the day of the meeting came, she wore the new ruby-red gown that Mary had made her out of the Lyonnaise silk and felt quite excited by this link with the past. Then at first sight of him she was disappointed, not that he was not a most striking young man, but because he was so much younger than Harry had been when she had loved him. Nevertheless, the black eyes were the same, the strong build and the voice brought back memories and there was something else vaguely familiar she could not place immediately.

"You followed in your grandfather's footsteps by being a good friend to us here at Sotherleigh as far as you were able," she said after they had conversed for a short while on other topics.

"I only wish I could have kept the house in Pallister hands."

"You did your best and that is what counts." It had come to her who he was mainly like; in the portrait gallery at Warrender Hall there was a painting of one of his ancestors, who had been at court in Henry VIII's time. The same dark and handsome countenance, the fierce eyes and the broad shoulders. She had been familiar with that gallery when she and Harry had been in love. At balls and parties when they could slip away for a while without being missed, they had met in one of the alcoves there and given way to the passion that possessed them. But it was no time to recall that now.

Neither would she mention the betrothal that Makepeace had agreed on between these two sitting with her. She liked Adam. He talked to her respectfully, but without making her feel a thousand years old, which was often the fault of those of his age and younger. She felt they would have got on well together if only Julia had given them the chance by relenting towards him. It was not that she thought him a better man than Christopher but one far more attuned to the ways of women. He knew Julia had still to be won and he was after her, his hunter's instincts high.

"I only wish it were possible for you to visit the Hall again," Adam was saying. "I've heard tell of a Guy Fawkes night when the bonfire flared up out of hand in a high wind and set the stables alight. Were you there?"

"I was indeed!" When she had described it all to him she reminisced about other events, but talk soon tired her and her voice grew weaker even though her enthusiasm remained. It was then that her young company made a move to leave. His bow was deep and he expressed the wish that he might come again. As the door was closing after them she called Julia back for a moment, not realising, through being partially deaf, that she spoke louder than she supposed.

"Yes, Grandmother?" Julia said from the doorway.

"That's the man for you!"

Julia went scarlet with embarrassment and retreated hastily, hoping Adam had not heard. Fortunately he had stepped on a few paces, but she was still uncertain and plunged into telling him how it was Katherine who had first taught her to read and sew.

"I only wish my mother could embroider her ribbons again, but Makepeace doesn't allow it. She always loved that work and it would lighten so many hours for her." She went on chatting as if by mere talk she could erase anything he might have overheard from Katherine's room. She did not notice his amused sidelong glance indicating that he indeed had heard all.

A few days later Anne was in possession of a casket that Adam had sent her, which had been his mother's. Julia was with her when she lifted the lid and saw that it was lined with pink velvet and held scissors, thimbles, embroidery silks in many shades and some rolls of plain ribbon that he must have bought in the ribbon-shop in Chichester, for they were brand new. She would have expected Makepeace to whisk the casket away once Adam had left, but Anne had started stitching at once and he had made no objection.

"It can only be due to something you said to Makepeace," Julia commented to Adam. He had come to the house to see her and found her busy weeding and planting in the Knot Garden, a task she had taken on again since her return from Bletchingdon. "He's never listened to me when I've asked on Mama's behalf."

He sat on the stone steps to watch her working with her trowel. "I did let him understand that if his wife could embroider a ribbon for me, which she had offered to do, it would mean an invitation for him to attend the first meeting of the Warrender Hunt in the autumn."

"Ah! You had him there. From what I've heard every gentleman in the county wants to ride with your hunt. What flower did you choose?"

"Mrs. Walker suggested several. I thought snowdrops would please you."

She glanced up at him from under the shady brim of her hat. "Why does my approval have anything to do with it?"

"Because I shall give it to you. I remember how pleased you were with the snowdrops I picked for you on the Downs. I hope these stitched ones will block out the quarrel that came later in the day."

"But that has been eliminated by the improvement in our relationship," she said honestly, pausing in her work to sit back on her heels. "I do think of you as a friend now. Let's share the ribbon. Half for you and the other half for me. I'll wear mine in my hair when the chance presents itself." Her eyes danced mischievously at him. "And you should wear yours looped in a bunch at the side of your hat, Cavalier fashion."

He grinned at her good-humouredly, wondering if she realised that her teasing political taunts were her defence against the erotic game that was played in an undercurrent every time they met; whether they were in harmony or clashing over some difference of opinion, the sparks of passion were never far away.

"I may do that," he said casually. He saw she was puzzled by his reply, having expected him to retaliate. It happened he had his reasons.

Anne chose a green silk ribbon on which to embroider the snowdrops. It was a flower she had embroidered many times before and now she stitched as assiduously by day as she had done by night in the attics. The work did not rekindle her awareness as Julia had hoped, but it gave her utter peace and contentment, her face serene as it had not been for a long time. Makepeace had ceased to exist for her.

He realised it and considered it of no consequence. It was as if he had broken free of his ridiculous infatuation for her that had held him in thrall. First love had never come to him in his youth, assailing him instead in middle age, and it had proved to be as equally short-lived with a grown man as with a boy. After the birth, when she had recovered from the strange state of mind that pregnancy had inflicted on her, they would resume a more conventional state as husband and wife. He would give her the respect and attention to which she was due, while she could embroider all hours of the day if she wished, for he was no longer jealous of those who were important to her now or in the past. Their marriage would be altogether more agreeable. He would have liked a second son to ensure the continuation of his line, but her age was against that possibility. It had taken many months for her to conceive this forthcoming child and it was unlikely to happen again.

When Anne finished the ribbon, two yards of it gleamed green and white, minuscule French knots in yellow making the stamens. Julia made a little ceremony of dividing the ribbon with Adam. He had to measure it exactly and by good luck the scissors cut through one of the tiny stems and not a flower. She rolled up one length and he the other. Then they exchanged the neat rolls.

"We have sealed an act of friendship." She spoke precisely, wanting to emphasise that they had reached all that their relationship could be.

"So we have."

She did not find his smiling acceptance all that reassuring. There was something too explicit and intense in his eyes that she refused to read.

ANNE STITCHED HER WAY through June and July. Then one night in August she went into labour. The midwife and her assistant had been installed in the house a week ahead as a precautionary measure.

"Delivery will be quick," the senior midwife informed Makepeace.

That did not prove to be the case. A breech birth had not been anticipated and difficulties arose. Julia was at the bedside, bathing Anne's sweating forehead with a cool damp cloth, but when the pains became worse the midwife would not allow her to remain any longer.

"Your mother is choking back her cries. It's because you are here," she was told. "It helps a woman to shriek. Go now and don't listen. There's nothing you can do."

Julia would have waited with Makepeace, who was pacing the floor of the parlour adjoining the master bedroom, but he did not want her there. He and he alone should be the first to see and to hold his new-born son. When the midwife emerged from the bedchamber to warn him that all was not going well for his wife, he made a dismissive gesture.

"A purse of gold for you and your assistant if you save the child at any cost."

She looked at him, stony-faced. This type of man was familiar enough, an heir the be-all and end-all of everything. "We aim to save both mother and child," she replied coldly, withdrawing into the bedchamber again.

As the hours dragged by, Makepeace's resentment against Anne mounted steadily. The sounds of her torment meant nothing to him. All he could think of was the harm this prolonged birth might be doing to his child. Then, when she had been twenty-four hours in unremitting agony, he heard the new-born cry.

Unable to wait a second, he threw open the door of the bedchamber and rushed in, impervious to the stench of blood and sweat and soiled linen that met him, the windows being closed. The assistant midwife was holding the baby, the other woman attending to Anne who lay in disorder in the bed, her eyes closed. Both midwives looked at him and the senior of them spoke with a certain amount of vengeful satisfaction in her voice.

"It's a girl, sir."

He gave a rasping groan. For a few moments with fists clenched he glared bitterly at his wife and then lunged from the room, banging the door after him with a force that made the windows rattle. In his rush to get away he ignored the midwife's reassurance that his wife had survived her ordeal surprisingly well.

When Anne was in a clean nightgown and lying between fresh sheets, Julia and Mary were allowed at the bedside and, although weary for sleep, she smiled to see them. She watched the midwife lift the new-born infant from the crib for Julia to hold.

"She's lovely, Mama!"

"Won't your father be pleased to know he has another little daughter," Anne answered blissfully, not noticing the startled glance that Julia and Mary exchanged. "It's so hard this war is keeping him away just when we need him here, but Cromwell has to be defeated."

"Of course he has, Mama," Julia said gently.

"Take Patience to see her grandmother," Anne's voice was drowsy. "Mistress Katherine will be waiting to see her. And be sure to write to Michael at Westminster School and let him know he has a new sister."

Cradling the baby, Julia leaned over to kiss her mother's brow. Then she left the room with Mary, feeling worried. "Perhaps Mama will come back to herself once she has had a good sleep."

"Let's hope so," Mary agreed, but she thought it unlikely. She had been aware of a break-down gradually advancing for many months, and perhaps the ordeal of such a difficult childbirth had tipped the scales.

In the west wing Katherine was relieved to see no likeness to Makepeace in the little red and wrinkled face. The old adage that a child's likeness began as it meant to go on made her hope that Anne's features would always predominate. She knew the name chosen was that of Anne's own mother and should meet with Makepeace's approval, for Puritans liked their daughters to be named for a virtue.

"May this little one know much happiness here at Sotherleigh," she said, touching the tiny hand with a forefinger.

Mary asked to carry Patience back to her crib. She looked tenderly at the infant. This was Michael's half-sister and any link with him was important to her. Her hope was that she would be allowed to care for this child. Her role at Sotherleigh had always been a nebulous one and this would give her a purpose as well as fill a gap in her life.

Makepeace did not go to see either his wife or his daughter. His disappointment was too acute, his distaste for them both beyond measure. The day after the birth he departed on a journey, issuing one order to Julia before he left.

"I want your mother moved back into the room she occupied in the west wing before she became my wife. Is that clear?"

"Very clear," Julia replied coldly.

It was soon obvious that physically Anne would never be strong again. She had been worn down before the birth and the difficult confinement had finally drained her. It was a month before she was able to get about again and take little walks. By then she had been moved into the west wing from the master bedchamber and had made no protest.

"It's sensible to close the east wing when there are so few servants to clean the house in these wartime days." Her mental state was unchanged since the birth.

Anne had been disappointed that she could not breast-feed her baby, a wet nurse having been needed, but otherwise she was utterly content. Nothing troubled her in her confused state and she had started embroidering again, using the needlework box that Adam had given her.

Julia was puzzled as to why her mother should show no sign of anxiety about Robert since she believed he was still fighting under the standard of Charles I. Carefully she broached the subject.

"Do you know where Father is?"

Anne gave a little chuckle. "Still celebrating the great battle with ale and song, you may be sure of that. Well deserved, too."

"What battle was that?"

Anne glanced up from her embroidery with a look of surprise. "How could you forget when the news only came yesterday? The victory at Edgehill, of course. It was bravely fought and bravely won. Even the

Prince of Wales—and he no more than twelve years old—drew his pistol and shouted, 'I fear them not' when a body of Parliamentary horse rode in his direction. The Cavaliers in their splendour routed the Roundheads who fled from their swords and their pikes and their cannon."

"Oh, Mama," Julia breathed. Edgehill had been the first great battle of the Civil War, a victory for the Royalists on a scale that never came again. She herself had been only a year old at the time.

"So now it's only a matter of time before Cromwell and his forces lay down their arms. It may be happening already." Anne lowered her embroidery to her lap and looked out of the window. "Perhaps by the end of the week Robert will be home. Oh, think of it! Then he'll never have to go away again."

Julia realised her mother was lost in the only period during the conflict when her hopes had been high and all had looked well for the future. Little did she know that the twelve-year-old Prince of Wales, as Charles II had been then, was now a king without a crown in an alien land.

MAKEPEACE RETURNED to Sotherleigh after two months away. He arrived when Julia had begun to hope she was never going to see him again. He alighted from his coach just as Mary was coming down the stone steps, having collected his infant daughter to take her out for a little fresh air. He passed them on his way up the flight without a glance.

At the head of the Grand Staircase there was a meeting he could not avoid. Anne and Julia were coming along by the flower screen and they were face to face with him. He flicked the gauntlets that he held in one hand irritably against his other palm.

"I see you are well, madam," he boomed at Anne, his face hostile.

She curtsied gracefully, no sign of recognition in her eyes. "I thank you, sir, but I don't believe we are acquainted."

"What game is this?" he thundered, taken aback.

Julia spoke up, moving slightly in front of her mother. "I need to talk to you about what has been happening here."

He glanced from her to his wife and back again. "Very well. I'll see you in the South Parlour in half an hour."

He stalked on in the direction of the west wing. Anne looked over her shoulder at him. "Who is that gentleman? What is he doing here? I thought him very disagreeable."

"He's staying for a while, Mama. You needn't see much of him."

"That's good."

With some restraint Julia explained the situation to Makepeace, her aim solely to protect her mother from any displays of temper on his part or any kind of distressing scene that would upset still further the delicate balance of Anne's mind. The fact that he was entirely to blame could not be brought up now for that very reason.

"Often childbirth leaves an aftermath and can affect women in different ways. My mother has simply lost her memory for a little while."

He answered her bluntly. "Whether she has or hasn't makes no difference to me. I might as well tell you that I have been seeing Puritan elders about securing a divorce. Unfortunately, after stating my case many times, my grounds were not deemed sufficient since your mother has not been unfaithful and has proved herself fruitful. I'm not a man to shirk my responsibilities, but I want that infant kept out of my sight and hearing. You and Mary can share that duty until your marriage. After that it will be up to Mary to carry it out or else there is no reason why she should continue to make her home here."

"Your daughter's name is Patience."

He ignored what she had said. "When the child is old enough a home can be found for her in the household of a tutor and a marriage arranged from there."

Julia could scarcely believe that any man could be so ruthless towards his own child. At that moment she made up her mind that no matter what he planned, Patience should never be parted from those who loved her.

# THIRTEEN

*I*T UPSET ANNE that Makepeace should occupy what she thought of as Robert's place at table, but Julia settled her by explaining that he was being treated as a guest of honour. Anne still did not like it, but made polite conversation about the weather and music and books she had read. She never noticed that he did not bother to answer her, for Julia spoke on his behalf. Only once did Anne blithely mention the war in connection with Edgehill. Makepeace turned crimson and thumped his fist down on the table, making the cutlery jump.

"We'll have no talk of that under this roof," he bellowed.

Anne stared at him in amazement. She had never seen a guest behave in such a way. Then it dawned on her that he was as sensitive as herself in thinking of the wounded and dying on the enemy's side as well as their own. He would say prayers for all those unfortunate men just as she did. She would take care never to distress him again.

Makepeace had good reason for not wanting to be reminded of Royalist victories, however long ago the battles had taken place. His world was falling apart. When away from Sotherleigh he had followed his fruitless visits to the Puritan elders with a certain amount of time in London. There he had been in touch with people he knew in government and others who were influential in the city, to see if there was any likelihood of support for Charles Stuart that might threaten his own position. There was a possibility of all regicides' awards of Cavalier property being rescinded if milder attitudes began to prevail, but he had returned reassured.

That sense of security had been short-lived. Events had begun to move throughout the land like the first tremblings of an earthquake. Suddenly there was a general fear of anarchy in England, and he threw his weight in locally with land-owners, whether Royalists or Parliamentarians, who as elsewhere were sinking their past differences and acting together to protect their livelihoods.

Merchants were doing the same and army officers were similarly alarmed. As the quakes of that danger increased, ordinary people seemed to be breaking the bonds of Puritanism that had held them in thrall for so long, an urge for freedom coming to the fore whatever the cost, while fear mounted on all political and religious fronts.

Makepeace banged his fist on a table in frustration when a servant returned from Warrender Hall to tell him that the master there was absent from home. Immediately he sent for Julia. "Do you know where Adam Warrender is?"

"I didn't know he was away from home," she replied coolly. "I don't see him all the time and he said nothing to me. Perhaps he is at Westminster again."

"I'll contact him there," Makepeace replied, dismissing her with an arrogant flick of the hand. He had hoped to consult Adam at home where he could be sure of no interruption, a kind of testing the water as to his position as a regicide in the growing hostility towards those forty-one men who had signed the royal death warrant. Adam was now a Member of Parliament, having won a seat in the first free election for many years that had resulted in Royalists' openly gaining seats, the ban lifted from them at last—results Makepeace could only see as the writing on the wall for himself.

He laid the blame for these new political developments at the feet of a Roundhead general under whom he had served in Scotland during the Civil War. Since that time General Monck, who was in his fifties, had been keeping the Scots down with his army, first for Oliver Cromwell and then for Richard, but a few weeks ago, with England practically leaderless, he had marched ten thousand men into London, demanding long overdue pay for them, and had forced Parliament to raise all bans against those long denied the right to sit at Westminster. It had inflamed many things and led to a wave of talk of restoring the monarchy.

Effigies of Charles Stuart had been displayed crowned with flowers in London streets where shouts for the King were said to be heard on all sides. Some places of entertainment had been reopening over past months, including two or three theatres and—most shocking of all to Makepeace —women had been seen on the stage for the first time. He took consolation from the resolve of leading Puritans to check this decadent slide and to ensure that the King should be hamstrung with political conditions if his return did take place. What worried Makepeace most was the general assumption that vengeance would be allowed against the regicides as a concession to Charles, who had never forgiven the execution of his father.

That was why Makepeace knew himself to be in need of Adam's support, both politically and as a future son-in-law. Surely someone who was almost one of the family should do everything in his power to help the stepfather of the girl he was to marry? Makepeace intended to remind Adam strongly of that obligation and of the number of times he had fought beside the late Colonel Warrender. In fact, he did not dare let another day go by without seeing Adam, even though it now meant a journey to London that he would have liked to avoid at the present time.

Julia watched him depart from a window in the Queen's Parlour. "There he goes," she said to Mary, who had brought Patience downstairs after waiting to hear the door close after him.

"I wish he'd never come back," Mary sighed. "It's like playing cat-and-mouse all day long. Even when I take our darling into the park we have to scuttle away behind a hedge when he appears." She lowered her head and smiled devotedly into the face of the nine-month-old baby sitting on her lap. "Don't we, my sweeting?"

Patience showed her dimples and shook the rattle she held, one that had been Michael's. She was a happy and healthy child with her mother's dark hair, which was as curly as Julia's. The only likeness to Makepeace was in the roundness of her grey eyes, but whereas his were an ill feature, hers gave a charming quaintness to her bonny face.

Julia leaned back against the window ledge, gazing at the two of them. The only shadow hanging over the prospect of the King's return was that Mary would have to leave Sotherleigh before Michael and his wife came home. There was no question of her staying under the same roof. At least it was certain that if Makepeace should find himself in dire trouble as a regicide, he would not want to take Anne with him wherever he went and Patience would be a burden to him. The only danger was that he might decide to make those heartless arrangements he had planned for his daughter's future before he left and that had to be guarded against, for nobody could deny his rights as a father to do with his offspring as he willed.

Julia missed Adam when he was not in the neighbourhood. He was fun to be with and they continued to send sparks off each other when they clashed. It was as if one of them was forever trying to dominate the other, refusing to admit that they could balance any scales should it be possible to weigh them in character and willpower. She had been torn when he had been successful in following his grandfather's footsteps into the new Parliament, pleased for him on a personal level while up in arms that a voice against the King should win a way to power.

When Makepeace arrived in London he was astounded to see how much Cavalier finery had reappeared on the streets, frills and bows in abundance and colourful plumes flowing from the hats of both men and women. It happened to be the first day of May and on the way to the city he had passed celebrations of the old May Day that had previously been suppressed. He had shouted his outrage and shaken his fist at such wickedness, but the villagers had jeered back at him from their maypoles. There must have been such a move towards a Restoration that people were starting to imagine it had already come.

He hastened to Westminster to discover that it had indeed come and less than an hour earlier. The Members of Parliament, coming from the House of Commons where a momentous decision had been taken, found many waiting to hear the tidings and Westminster Hall was crowded. From a gentleman he knew Makepeace received the bad news that the Speaker of the House had read out to Members a formal letter from King Charles II—here Makepeace shuddered at hearing this statement of recognised status—in which he expressed his wish to see all future parliaments of England preserved by the monarchy and vice versa. He had called upon the wise and dispassionate Members to raise up all that had been cast down, to avenge and redeem a certain guilt and infamy, which was a reference to his father's execution, and to know that all he himself had suffered in exile would be turned into Christian consideration and betterment for his subjects. Makepeace heard in that letter the unmistakable voice of doom for himself and the rest of the regicides.

"There was also a Royal Declaration from the King," his informant told him. "It was sent from Breda where he is now waiting." He continued with a full account of all that Charles was going to do in the future, which included, through an act of Parliament, a pardon for all men of conscience who appealed for his grace and favour—a generous action for the country as a whole, but again leaving out the murderers of his father. Finally this man described how, when the Speaker had finished reading, a resolution was passed amidst scenes of great rejoicing to request the King to return to his people.

Sickened, Makepeace turned away and happened to sight George Monck in the crowded Westminster Hall. He pushed through, not caring whom he shoved out of his way, to reach his old comrade.

"This is your doing," he roared furiously, shaking his fist in Monck's distinguished face.

"I thank God if it is," General Monck replied, giving Makepeace a look that told him how much he was despised. The General himself had had no part in any way with that notorious death warrant that Makepeace had signed. "I have been in secret correspondence with the King ever since I saw there was no other way to bring unity and stability to this nation again. In view of our past comradeship in arms, I give you a piece of sound advice, Walker. Leave England! Or else when the King has come home on his birthday at the end of this month I'll be seeing your head on a spike at Tower Bridge!"

He moved on and Makepeace stood stunned in the milling throng of several hundred people. There was nothing Adam or anyone else could do for him now. He would have to heed Monck's warning and get out of the country to save his neck. At least he had about three weeks before the King set foot on English soil again.

He went slowly past the spot where Charles I had accepted his death sentence. As people pushed past him to get into that great hammer-beamed medieval hall he paid no attention to the impatient thrusts. The irony for him was that after all that had happened, the King was being allowed to come home without a single condition imposed upon him. Instead it was Charles himself who had declared what he would do and announced the improved path of monarchy that he intended to tread. But kings were only men with weaknesses like everyone else and he should have been given a cast-iron set of rules to clamp on his head with his crown.

Outside in the streets people were dancing. Taverns were doing a roaring trade. Men were even drinking toasts to the King on their knees. Makepeace's stomach turned.

At Sotherleigh Julia realised the long-awaited time had come when at dusk a chain of bonfires began to appear on the Downs, taking up the signal of one beginning to flare high in the village. She rushed outside and stood listening. In the quiet evening a breeze brought the distant sound of the villagers cheering, Royalists and Puritans alike rejoicing in the hope of a return to tolerance and freedom and the stability of the nation. Tears of joy filled her eyes. It had finally happened. In this never to be forgotten year of 1660 the eve of the Restoration was here at last!

She darted back indoors and ran straight to Katherine's apartment. She found that her grandmother, seeing the glow on the Downs, had somehow struggled out of her chair and crossed to the window, which she had opened.

"So it has come, Julia," she said emotionally, still gazing out.

Julia went to put an arm about her and together they saw yet another bonfire flare on the crest of a more distant hill. The message was spreading fast. "Yes! God bless King Charles II!"

"Amen to that. Michael will soon be home again."

"He will, Grandmother."

Katherine turned stiffly, leaning on Julia for support. "Fetch your mother here and Mary and little Patience. Don't forget Sarah. We'll drink a toast to the King."

Anne came carrying Patience, who was warm and towel-wrapped from her bath, damp curls still to be properly dried. Mary was with them and Sarah followed behind. While Julia poured the wine Anne gave the baby a tiny piece of sweetmeat that made her dribble deliciously. Katherine insisted on rising to her feet to propose the toast.

"The King!"

It was echoed by the little gathering. Anne thought they were toasting Charles I and was perfectly content. She was sure Robert would be home soon.

Katherine retired to bed shortly afterwards, completely exhausted by all the excitement. Julia sat at her bedside for a short while and they talked of all the happier times to come. Then when Julia kissed her good night on the brow, Katherine caught her granddaughter's hand in her own.

"This is the day I've been waiting for." Her voice was very weak, but full of calm. "If I should not be here when Michael returns, I want you to remember that. Now, no sentimental protests!" She released her clasp. "Good night to you, dearest girl."

That night Julia's dream, which she had almost forgotten, returned with a force that threw her into wakefulness, crying out. Then she knew what was happening and rushed to her grandmother's bedchamber, her nightgown billowing, her bare feet racing. But she was just too late. Katherine had slipped away from Sotherleigh in her sleep.

•   •   •

MAKEPEACE WENT QUIETLY about making his own preparation for flight in his usual methodical manner. He paid scant attention to the funeral or those who came to it, not attending himself, although he did greet the notable Mr. Wren and his sister, Mrs. Holder, who stayed for a couple of days. Adam, still in London and probably in ignorance of what had happened to Julia's grandmother, was not there. Makepeace considered himself magnanimous in letting Julia have the use of the long room with the slotted wall to receive mourners and have dinner served to them after the burial, but he kept both sets of doors in the Great Hall closed to make them use another way and not come through it. He was still master at Sotherleigh until he left and he intended to maintain his status until the last minute.

When Christopher and Susan left Sotherleigh, sitting side by side in the Holder coach the morning after the funeral, she was very thoughtful. Finally she broached a rather sensitive subject.

"Through the difference in our ages, Christopher," she began, "I've been more of a mother to you than a sister, and therefore I hope you will take what I have to say about Julia in good part."

He was in a serious mood, looking out at the Sussex countryside as the gates of Sotherleigh were left behind. Mistress Katherine would be sadly missed. Anne's grief, in spite of her confused state, had made it a particularly poignant visit. He turned towards Susan, who had her plump pigeon look about her, a troubled expression on her good-natured face.

"Speak on," he said in his amiable way. "What is it you want to say?"

"What are your feelings for Julia?"

"That is easily answered. I'm extremely fond of her. She's an enchanting girl and our friendship goes back to my schooldays and her babyhood. Why do you ask?"

"Do you intend to marry her?"

He smiled a little crookedly. "She'll be wed long before I can think of marriage. I would never expect any woman to wait until I've accomplished even a portion of what lies ahead of me."

"But you're doing precisely that!"

"Doing what?"

"Keeping the girl dangling. She adores you. I saw her face when we arrived. It blossomed like a rose and she flung herself into your arms."

"I've explained the situation. She has always shared her joys and griefs with me."

"Do you never kiss her?"

He laughed. "Really, Susan. There are limits to what even a maternal sibling may ask."

"So you do." She sighed heavily and let her linked hands rise and fall in her lap. "Now I must be blunt. I have seen enough of the intelligentsia in my time to know there is a certain category of men—brilliantly clever in their own field of study—who are blind as bats when it comes to dealing with women."

"Am I to assume you have placed me in that group?"

"You most certainly are. William is another, but I'm not speaking of him now. You like pretty women paying you attention—and what man doesn't! If that were all with Julia it would be harmless, but she has deep feelings and she is in love with you. And all the time that state of affairs continues, she's never going to look at any other man. Do you want to be responsible for her losing all chances of finding happiness with someone else?"

"You're exaggerating."

"Not at all. When she was at Bletchingdon several young men spoke to William and asked their chances, but even though he had to tell them she was already promised, it was obvious to me none of them interested her in the least, except in the pleasure of flirting. It was always you she was waiting to see, although I admit she did not reveal to what extent until this time when her emotional state let her heart show through."

"You misjudged what you saw."

She noticed the stubborn set of his jaw and tried another tack. "I thought you would come home from Oxford less often after I told you that Mr. Walker had betrothed her to Adam Warrender. Did I not say he was a fierce young man, not altogether predictable, but that I believed his love for her to be genuine?"

"You did," he commented dryly. "I see now that was a broad hint to me that I failed to take. When I asked Julia about it at Bletchingdon she said the settlement was not worth the paper on which it was written. Neither is it now, because anything a regicide has ordered or negotiated will be null and void."

"All the more reason for you to propose to Julia or end her hopes of marrying you once and for all."

He turned his head and looked out at the passing hedgerows and flower-flecked meadows for a considerable time before he spoke again. Then she could scarcely bear the starkness of his expression. "You have made me see my own folly. My work is my lodestar. I have to follow it."

She felt no sense of triumph at what she had achieved, only sadness at what she had had to do. She understood more than anyone why his work must always come first. His lungs continued to trouble him periodically and he did not know how much time was left to him in which to gain the knowledge and skills that the genius in him was perpetually seeking.

MAKEPEACE WAS KEENLY AWARE that nobody called to see him during his last days at Sotherleigh. His neighbours were conspicuous by their absence. There were no invitations, no gentlemen coming to chat or take a chance meal or glass of wine with him. He ate alone at all times. Such ostracism was a help in making him more than ready to leave Sotherleigh and start another life in the New World where his long-held business interests would be an asset to him. By being on the spot he could build them up as he had never been able to do from a distance, trusting to a representative there. By good fortune Captain Crowhurst's ship was due in the Port of London any day, having called at several West Country ports during the last month, and he had sent a message for a berth to be reserved for him when the vessel sailed. He had been given to understand this would be on the day the King would set foot on English soil again after an exile of almost ten years. Makepeace wondered if he would be the only passenger anxious to be clear of England by that date!

There was no question of Patience going with him. She would have a home at Sotherleigh until she was of an age to marry, probably in her twelfth year, when he would be legally within his rights to send for her. Installed in his American household she would be there in readiness to look after him in his old age.

He was planning to leave the next day and had just finished his supper when the maidservant, Charity, who was his bedmate, came to him where he sat in the Queen's Parlour. It was not by choice that his lusts demanded the constant presence of a woman in his bed, but he had only to remind himself that women were soulless creatures put on earth to be subject to men and that set his mind at rest. Therefore, according to his logic, it was only adultery if another man's wife was involved, and he had kept himself free of that unforgivable sin. In no way had this young woman threatened Anne's status as his wife, any more than those in the past had threatened his previous marriages. They had needed the one virtue of knowing how to be discreet, aided by a deep threat of what the consequences would be if they failed him, and thus he had kept his sexual life orderly whenever his marriage partner had been indisposed.

"Sir!" the girl exclaimed. "I've come to warn you. It's been whispered that local people in Chichester are coming to Sotherleigh tomorrow to make a civil arrest and lock you up in readiness for the King's justice."

He regarded her calmly. All his arrangements were made and he only had to bring everything forward by a few hours. Luckily it was a bright moonlit night and he would be able to see the roads as if by day. "You did well to tell me, Charity. I shall leave tonight. Go to the stables and tell the head groom to saddle my horse and make ready the two pack-horses that will be carrying my goods." There were some things he had to leave behind, but that had to be.

"Sir! Let me go with you!"

The thought had not crossed his mind before and it surprised him to discover she appeared to have some fondness for him. She was a plain enough creature, but she had a voluptuous body and she did things for him that he would never have asked of a wife. Now it occurred to him that if a hunt was rising against him he would do better to appear as a family man travelling with a wife and baby. She could care for his daughter on board ship and then raise her out of his sight as had been happening at Sotherleigh.

"Very well. Be ready in an hour. Under these circumstances I have decided to take my young daughter with me. Pack a few necessities and whatever baby garments and accessories will be needed on the voyage. I'll go myself to the stables and pick out a steady mare for you to ride."

Her expression was mixed. She had not bargained on being saddled with the baby, but as she feared she was pregnant herself it was to her advantage to go with him, whatever the conditions. "Getting Patience's clothes won't be a problem, but getting hold of her will be, because Miss Mary sleeps in the same room. She'll be like a tigress defending its young."

"What nonsense! She's only a nursemaid. I'll fetch the child myself at the time I have set you."

"Yes, sir." At the door she paused. "Where are we going on the ship? Is it to France?"

"You'll find out when we are on board." He did not want her blurting out something if they should be questioned somewhere along the way.

It was close on midnight when he went silently to Mary's bedchamber. He hoped to remove the child soundlessly from her crib in order to avoid a hue and cry or any kind of scene, pointless though it would be. He glanced first at the bed, but the sheet was still turned down and it was empty. When he looked into the crib it was equally bare. He smiled humourlessly to himself. He knew where the two of them would be.

Mary had been sleeping in the underground chamber every night, for although Makepeace's preparations for his departure had been observed, nobody knew which day he would be leaving or his ultimate destination. Patience slept well in a spare crib brought down from the attics and Mary knew that nowhere else could the two of them be safer from Makepeace.

The Queen's Door only creaked faintly when it was opened, but the hinges of the two inner doors were in need of oiling and squeaked slightly. When this happened, Mary, under too much stress to sleep soundly, opened her eyes at once. The chamber was dark except for a finger of light coming through a gap in the door from a passageway sconce. It was enough to show her the late hour on the wall clock.

She threw back the bedclothes, anxiety high in her, for it could only be Julia coming to warn her that something was amiss. Then she went out into the passage-way and saw to her horror it was Makepeace, dressed for travelling, who stood there. "Go away!" she shouted defensively.

"I'm here for my daughter!" he yelled, advancing towards her and breaking into a run.

She whirled back into the chamber, slammed the thick oaken door shut and turned the key as he reached it. With all her strength she shot the first heavy bolt home as far as she could, ignoring the drumming of his fist as she sent a second one into its socket. Patience had woken and started to cry, but Mary was standing on tip-toe to settle the top bolt and did not go to her until it was in place. Then she snatched her up and held her close, cupping her head protectively.

"Open up!" Makepeace roared, beside himself with rage. The door had been designed for a last-ditch stand against any onslaught and he knew its strength from his previous inspection. Mary's reply, muffled by its thickness, came through to him.

"No! You've never wanted Patience before! She's nothing to you, but she's Anne's daughter and belongs here at Sotherleigh where she will always be loved and protected!"

To him it was all the more reason to wrench his daughter away. These wretched Royalists were getting Sotherleigh back and they wanted the child as a bonus. He wondered about shooting the lock. He did not want to arouse the house, not knowing any longer how many of his servants he could trust. One pistol ball wouldn't do it and the constant rumble of several attempts might stir some wakeful person into the realisation that it

was not thunder being heard but gunfire resounding underground. Then
he decided it was a calculated risk that he should take. There was every
chance that Mary had lacked the strength to send those heavy bolts home
properly and then with his powerful shoulder he should be able to vibrate
them loose again.

"Keep the child well away from the door!" he shouted.

Mary had already drawn back instinctively against the far wall, but
before she could dart with the baby into the closet leading off the chamber, the pistol was fired. She screamed at the explosion and Patience
sobbed piteously. Powder billowed in round the lock. Snatching up a
blanket from the bed, she rushed into the closet, laid it on the stone floor
and sat Patience on it. "Wait here, my darling! Mary will be back in a
moment."

Patience's sobs became even more heart-rending as her clutching hands
were gently unfastened. She continued to hold up her arms as Mary closed
the closet door to keep out the worst of the second explosion as it came.
Terrified, she took down a pistol from the rack of weaponry and with
powder, ball and ramrod she loaded it as she had been taught, for Katherine had always insisted that Pallister women should know how to defend
themselves in an emergency, having once in her young day winged a
highwayman. When Makepeace fired for the third time before she had
finished her task, she thought how his military experience had given him a
speed she could never match.

The door had splintered around the lock and now he was using the full
force of his strength to shake the door. One bolt was already working free
and another was rattling wildly. She put aside the pistol and struggled to
get the bolts back, but the vibrations being created put that beyond her
efforts. Taking up the pistol again, she stepped backwards until she was
standing against the door into the closet. Patience's sobs tore at her; there
was no reckoning the misery the child would suffer in her future life if
Makepeace should snatch her away. She herself would shoot Makepeace
dead before she would let that happen.

The door was going to give! The last of the bolts was loosening. She
could imagine his face contorted with effort and running with sweat as he
lunged his weight again and again. Another few thrusts and he would be
in the chamber. She cocked the pistol. Then the attack on the door
stopped abruptly as Julia's voice rang out somewhere in the passageway.

"Get out and leave, Makepeace!"

Julia had come through the Queen's Door and thrust the inner door open to stand aiming a pistol at him. Being armed was a contingency she had thought of in case Makepeace should try to get Patience by day if Mary was not quick enough to hide with her. What neither of them had suspected was that he had discovered the subterranean hide-away or that she would ever see him in this passageway in his shirt-sleeves with his jacket, cloak and hat thrown to the ground while the seemingly impregnable door was much damaged by his efforts.

"You're breaking the law by keeping my own child from me!" he snarled, well aware she had the upper hand, for although he could have shot her easily enough, the pistol in his belt was empty and he had not stopped to reload it a fourth time. He had thought to do that when the door needed no more than a final push.

"Don't talk to me of the law!" Julia replied angrily. "You're running away from justice and you'll go alone! Patience shall not go with you!"

He accepted defeat, snatched up his jacket to heave it on, flung on his cloak and replaced his tall-crowned hat. He seemed to fill the whole aperture of the passage-way like a black shadow.

Julia drew back to keep him covered with the pistol as he came forward to pass her on his way back into the house through the Queen's Door. He paused when he was level with her, his eyes full of hatred.

"Keep the brat for now. I'll get her later when the time is right."

His cloak swung about him as he made his way out of the house and down the steps to where the two riding horses and a pair of pack-horses waited. Charity was already in the saddle but no longer necessary to him.

"Where's the baby?" she asked.

"They will only hand her over to you," he lied, putting up his hands to help her down. When she hesitated he spoke reassuringly. "It's all agreed. Don't be afraid."

"Where is Patience?" Charity still sounded doubtful, although she let him assist her from the saddle.

"In the west wing. Hurry! We've no time to lose."

She hastened back up the steps and into the house thinking it all very odd. He had only to carry the child downstairs. She had barely reached the flower screen when a terrible suspicion assailed her. Turning on her heel, she rushed down and out of the house again. Her saddled horse stood on its own. Makepeace and the pack-horses were already out of sight down the drive, the sound of galloping hooves fading away into the distance.

She ran forward and shook her fists, screaming after him every gutter name she had ever learned.

In the underground chamber Patience had been rocked back to sleep in Mary's arms and Julia had discovered the Sotherleigh treasure was gone. She knelt by the chest with the forced-open lock. Mary had not noticed it, for Makepeace had left the front side turned to the wall after plundering the contents at some time earlier in the day.

"Everything!" Julia shrieked in fury, banging her fists on the rim. "All the Elizabethan plate and every gold coin. I even moved a few bags of money down here that Grandmother had left, to be absolutely safe! There's nothing for Michael! Nothing! What a homecoming for him! Why didn't I suspect that Makepeace had somehow discovered the secret of the Queen's Door?"

"Don't blame yourself. How could you know? He was a cunning man in every way. Let's go back into the house now. We haven't lost the greatest treasure of Sotherleigh, which is Patience. In any case, if Makepeace is arrested wherever he is on the road, the money and plate will be returned to you."

Julia shook her head, closing the lid as she stood up. "Local people won't catch up with him now, and in any case who would know where to look for him?" She stroked the sleeping baby's cheek. "You're right. Eventually money can be replaced, but not a half-sister as this little one is to Michael and me. We have all that matters in her. I'm so thankful Makepeace didn't close the Queen's Door when he came after her or else I would never have caught the echo of those pistol shots and realised what it must be."

When they reached the Grand Staircase, Julia went up to the first landing and without a word removed the portrait of Oliver Cromwell from the wall and turned it face downwards on the floor. Then, while Mary waited, she fetched Elizabeth's portrait from her grandmother's room and set it back where it had always belonged.

"Tomorrow," Julia said as she straightened it, "I'll get old Ridley to come up from the village and chip away the plaster from the King's face in the Long Gallery. Sotherleigh will soon be itself again."

IN THE MORNING Julia addressed the household staff in the hall as her mother and her grandmother had done in the past. Several of the menservants and three of the women dropped out rather than serve a returned Cavalier, their Puritan or political views still too strong. Phoebe, who had become increasingly homesick for her native village of Bletchingdon, also decided to leave and Julia raised no objection. She was left just enough staff to keep the house, stables and park in order until Michael's home-coming, after which the responsibility would be Sophie's, whom she would help and advise.

Although Mary had acted as nursemaid to Patience, help was needed and Julia promoted the smiling maidservant whose name of Bess had pleased Katherine. The girl was proud to be chosen. Julia then instructed the house staff to begin cleaning throughout. She wanted all traces of her stepfather swept away.

From the library she sent for Ridley and the bailiff. While Ridley commenced his task in the Long Gallery she received the bailiff's report. Whether he should be kept on or not was a decision for Michael to make, but the bailiff showed himself to be one among many in the land whose old loyalty to the Commonwealth was fading before the new Royalist fever that prevailed. He pronounced himself keen to stay on at Sotherleigh and admitted having to put pressure on those tenants who had fallen into arrears with the higher rents that Makepeace had imposed on them, several families having been evicted. This was already known to her, but she had been helpless to do anything about it. Now she could put matters right.

"I know all those people. Some of the families have been here longer than Sotherleigh. My grandmother and then my father dealt fairly with them and I know my brother will do the same. In the meantime the arrears are wiped out. The rent will be reduced by two-thirds of the increase that Mr. Walker set. That should be agreeable to everyone. Find out where those evicted families went and offer them vacant cottages. Lastly, serve notice to quit on the Roundhead gentleman in the house in Briar Lane which Mr. Walker renovated and then rented furnished instead of selling, as he had first proposed. Mistress Mary will be having her own home there quite soon."

It was not an ideal arrangement, but after careful discussion between herself and Mary it had been settled. Mary would inevitably meet Michael from time to time, but she had dreaded having to leave everyone she knew in Sotherleigh and its vicinity.

"I must find a way to make a livelihood for us, Mary," Julia said, closing her account ledger after the bailiff had gone. "Michael is going to need every penny from the rents to maintain his household and the estate.

At least his wife's dowry didn't go on an expensive house in Paris, so he should be able to secure himself against debt."

"I was a seamstress before and I can be one again," Mary volunteered willingly. "I'm sure almost every woman will be wanting new gowns for her wardrobe."

Julia nodded thoughtfully. "That's certain, but any female who can wield a needle will be calling herself a seamstress now. If only we could think of something more original and more profitable, something that maybe we could sell in London where prices would be much higher than in Sussex." She slapped her hand down on the closed account ledger. "I have to make money somehow. No matter what you say, I'm to blame ultimately for Michael losing his fortune. The larger portion of whatever I earn must go to him!"

"There's some sewing I'd like to do as a means of celebrating the Restoration," Mary said wistfully. "Unless you feel I should sell the Lyonnaise silk that Michael gave me."

Julia's eyebrows shot up. "Sell it? Never!" Then she grinned jubilantly. "Mine was never made up at Bletchingdon and the time is now! Let you and me have a new gown each with ribbons and flounces that show our bosoms as gowns did in Royalist days! What's more, we'll go to London and see the King come home to Whitehall with Michael riding after him in the great procession!" She flung her head back, closed her eyes rapturously and hugged her arms. "It's so long since we have had a treat! Mama will have Sarah to watch over her and now Jane, who was head-housemaid since before I was born—until, of course, Makepeace dismissed her —is so anxious to come back and she will be able to help Sarah."

By the end of that first day everything that had been Makepeace's property had been removed and taken by wagon to an auction-house in Chichester to await the next sale. The feather bed in the master bedchamber was replaced by another from storage and the Elizabethan bed-hangings rehung again in all their magnificence. While this was being done Julia sent a manservant up to the attic to fetch down her mother's marriage chair and needlework box, but he returned while she was opening the windows of the master bedchamber still wider to let the breeze blow the last traces of Makepeace away.

"I couldn't find them, madam," he reported.

She turned to him in concern. "But they must be there. Did you look everywhere?"

"In every room except the one that was locked."

"Locked?" To her knowledge there had never been anything up there that had to be locked away. Perhaps Makepeace had made extra secure all those items that Anne valued, which he had been determined she should not have about her.

"I'll go up there myself." She fetched a ring of keys and on her way to the attic called through the flower screen to Mary, who happened to be in the hall. "Would you like to come and help me search for Mama's chair and needlework box?"

"Yes. Can't they be found? I saw them go up there myself."

In the attic rooms they could see how the manservant had made a thorough search, patches of dust-free floorboards showing where he had pulled out furniture and boxes to look behind. None of the keys on the ring fitted the locked door. Then Mary spotted one lying on a ledge quite inconspicuously.

"Try this one," she suggested.

It clicked the lock and the door swung inwards. Both girls stood on the threshold transfixed. In contrast to the dust and cobwebs elsewhere under the eaves, here was a clean chamber with Anne's chair set at the same angle to the light as it had once stood in the Queen's Parlour, her needle-work box beside it. Robert's portrait hung from a nail on the opposite wall, the frame clean and polished. Julia saw how it was in direct line with the chair from which her mother would have glanced up at him from her embroidery. His maps were displayed on all sides and propped on the chests and boxes that lined the walls, except where a tall cupboard stood.

Deeply moved, Julia slowly walked across to lift the lid of the needle-work box. Within all was as neat and tidy as it had ever been. She took up a half-completed ribbon with an embroidered design of May-blossom.

"This is where Mama found solace," she said huskily. "No wonder she wandered up here at night. It was the only place where she could sit and embroider."

She went to the tall cupboard and pulled on one of the two central brass handles. It did not respond and she jerked it harder, causing the cupboard to sway slightly. Immediately both cupboard doors flew open, releasing a cascade of stacked-high rolls of multi-coloured ribbons. They unwound and whirled and rolled out and rippled about her, in the air and over her head, finally coming to rest in ankle-deep mounds at her feet, the thousands of tiny embroidered flowers lying like a meadow of wild blooms. With a sharp intake of breath, she stooped to gather up an armful and hold them close to her as if she embraced the woman who had put them there.

Mary moved swiftly to the nearest chest. "There's more!" she exclaimed, flicking back a piece of protective linen and looking down at the tightly packed ribbon rolls that filled the chest completely. Julia, unaware that one of the falling ribbons had come to rest on her head and trailed down her back, others on her shoulders and dangling from her arms, went to raise other lids. None of the containers were empty. All were full.

Julia gazed wonderingly. "There must be many, many years of work here. I know Mama used a great deal on our clothes and gave away some as presents, but that could not account for one-tenth of what is hoarded here. Now I remember Katherine used to say Mama embroidered as a shield against her anxiety ever since my father first joined the late King at Nottingham, and then later up here it was her way of blocking out her unhappiness with that wretched Makepeace." She was silent for a moment, her eyes moist; then she raised her head and said tremulously, "She has given me the means to restore Michael's fortune in some small way and earn a living at the same time. We'll be ribbon-makers, Mary! Not making the ordinary, every-day kind that will soon be commonplace again, but the rich and expensive and beautifully worked like these!" She pulled two at random from the bunch she still cradled. One shimmered with a galaxy of moons and stars in silver thread, the other had bunches of lilies-of-the-valley tied with love knots.

"I agree it's a splendid idea." Mary was reluctant to cast a damper on the plan. "But neither you nor I could ever work with your mother's special speed with the needle. Those patterns seem to grow by their own volition from under her hand."

"That pace is not so essential if I have a host of embroiderers carrying out these designs at the same time. I'll have cottage workers! The employment will be welcome in the village. I'll supply the ribbons and silks and keep to the Pallister tradition of a fair remuneration. Mama won't mind my selling these for a start, I know. She has always liked others to enjoy her handiwork."

Mary was won over. There were women in the village who did the most fanciful smocking on their men's and children's linen smocks and their clever fingers would make the transition to the more delicate ribbons without any difficulty. As for herself, she loved to embroider and it was work she could do while keeping a constant eye on Patience. "Where will you sell the finished ribbons?"

"In London! There's a market waiting there like a huge whale ready to gulp up whatever I fling to it." She began to pace up and down, hugging the ribbons closer as she worked out details. "I'll have to approach shops and secure orders. The shopkeepers will be mad to get hold of these only days before the King's arrival."

"You'd go to London ahead of that day?"

"Yes!" She twirled around twice like a top in her growing excitement, making her skirts swing out and her ribbons flutter. "We'll go together and take boxes of these ribbons with us." She became quiet and serious again. "Mama has often duplicated many of her favourite patterns—there are plenty of examples of that here. I shall save a roll of every one of her designs and those will never be sold. I'll keep them for my children and all my descendants to let them see what a treasury of stitches was once created by Anne Pallister!"

As soon as they had left the attic Julia resummoned the manservant. He fetched her father's portrait and she saw it rehung beside Anne's in the Long Gallery. Then he and one of his fellows brought the marriage chair and the needlework box to the Queen's Parlour. Julia made sure they were in exactly the same places as they had been in the past and then she went upstairs to the nursery where she knew she would find her mother at this hour.

Anne was tucking a sleepy little Patience into bed. It was something that she never allowed anyone else to do unless there was a special reason. Quickly she put a finger to her lips to warn Julia to make no noise. Then together they went quietly from the room.

"I have a little surprise for you, Mama. Your marriage chair and needlework box are back in the Queen's Parlour."

Anne gave a delighted exclamation. "I wondered where they were!"

She rushed ahead down the stairs, Julia in her wake. In the Queen's Parlour Anne went quickly to sit in the chair, putting her hands over the ends of the chair-arms and leaning back blissfully against its cushions. "I can always feel your father's arms around me when I sit here."

Then she sighed with pleasure as she lifted the lid of her needlework box and looked at everything lying neatly within. There were her silks in all shades wound onto mother-of-pearl crosses and squares and snowflake shapes. Beside her needlecase was the wax and bristle for beadwork, her gold thimble inscribed with words of love that Robert had given her and another of silver that twisted off the top of a little powder shaker for keeping the hands smooth and dry for metal embroidery. She stroked everything in reunion, smiling over her three pairs of scissors in varying sizes, her scarlet velvet pincushion. She could have been greeting beloved friends. Lastly she picked up a roll of ribbon, only half of which was embroidered and mused over it thoughtfully. It was her habit to complete a leaf, or petal, or stem, before putting her work away, but for the first time that she could recall the last motif to be stitched had not been finished.

"I had to leave this because I suddenly realised it was dawn." She spoke in a faraway voice.

Julia crouched by the chair, looking up into her mother's face. "Did you embroider every night?"

Her daughter's voice drew Anne back to the present and her air of faint bewilderment vanished as she laughed. "I've given myself away, haven't I? When I can't sleep in that wide bed with your father away, I do get up sometimes and come down here to stitch for a little while and calm my restlessness." Already she had forgotten that her chair and needlework box had only just been regained.

"There are hundreds of yards of lovely ribbons in this house, Mama. I've come across a great store of them. Would you mind if they were sold? We need funds for Sotherleigh and I want to make money for Michael by starting a ribbon business."

"What a splendid idea! I said to your grandmother that Michael's fortune must not be touched." Unknowingly she had come close to the present again. "May I help?"

"I should be delighted if you would. Nobody in the world can embroider ribbons like you. It means I shall be going to London to sell them. Prices will be higher there."

Anne put both hands on Julia's shoulders. "Go whenever you wish, but please don't ask me to go too. I went to London once years ago with your father and it was far too noisy and busy a place for me."

Julia smiled. "Just embroider for me whenever the will takes you. You need never leave Sotherleigh again."

Before the day ended she despatched a letter to Christopher with a request that he should find accommodation for Mary and her in London for their stay. He was back at Gresham College for his weekly lectures after a break when it had been used as a barracks for General Monck's soldiers. He had told Julia what a pleasure it was that his circle of old friends from his undergraduate days, all renowned names now in the sciences, gathered at the college each week after his lectures to resume their hours of discussion on all that was happening in their particular researches. She knew that if anyone could get hostelry rooms in London it would be Christopher, for otherwise everything would be fully booked for the royal event before she could get there.

On her way to bed she took a candle into the Long Gallery to see again the King's profile. Encircled by its laurel wreath it shone like a white medallion set amid the ornate plasterwork of the wall. Its pristine condition was evidence of the good work Ridley had done in both covering it and uncovering it. Gazing at it, she remembered that she had been a child when it vanished from sight and now she was eighteen. Similarly, Charles II, whom she had seen that fateful day drinking ale at the George and Dragon while fleeing from his enemies, had left England as a young man and would be coming into his own at last on the very day he was thirty years old.

Mary volunteered to do the sorting and measuring and listing of the attic store of ribbons, which had now been brought downstairs to the old gift-making room. Julia checked on the chest of sewing supplies that had always been kept well stocked. There was enough there to keep workers supplied for quite a while, but she would have to start replenishing without too much delay.

She was interested to find that Makepeace had locked the chest of fine fabrics at some time and removed the key, but it was a simple lock and she soon found another to fit it. The fabrics were sumptuous and there would be fine gowns for her mother and Mary as well as herself whenever the occasion arose. If there should be any chance of getting to Court to display ribbons at any time she would not lack the right garment.

That same day she began a round of the village. Women welcomed her in, the older ones having known her mother's kindness to the sick in their households and generosity when times were bad, while the grandmothers had been similarly cared for by Katherine in days gone by. To the younger wives she had already proved herself by readjusting the rents. She met at least one willing needlewoman in each cottage and in fortunate cases as many as three or four where there were daughters of a grown age. She stipulated two rules: the work must be of a high standard and it must be done with spotless hands and with clean aprons and white cloths over a scrubbed table to protect the ribbons from getting soiled. Many of the cottages were dirty, but she understood the problems where the place seemed to be swarming with children and tired men clumping in from the fields and farm-yards with soiled clothes and muddy boots. For those lacking a corner that could be kept spotless and free of cooking smells, she said there would be a room in the house in Briar Lane where they could gather. She saw by their faces that this would be a great pleasure to them, a chance to leave the children with grandmothers and escape for a while to enjoy the fine needlework and a gossip with neighbours.

The next day she returned to inspect the places where those working at home would sit at their embroidery. They had tried hard to get everything right and had an example of a single flower to show her, executed from a design and silk thread and scrap of ribbon she had left with each one. Some of the work was splendidly done, but the rest had to be weeded out. Since most country women knew how to spin and weave, she let those whose sewing was below standard try their hand at her mother's little ribbon loom. Anne had rarely used it in latter years, but had kept it in store. Here many of the women came into their own, happy to be at familiar work and undeterred by its being on a small scale, with finer thread to warp and weave than the linen and wool they wove for hard-working garments and household necessities. It would be much cheaper to have her own weavers and before leaving the village that day Julia ordered from Ridley half a dozen commercial looms, which wove four ribbons at the same time.

In spite of all there was to do Mary cut out and made the new Lyonnaise silk gowns for London. A box of Katherine's collection of beautiful lace, carefully laid between snowy linen, supplied what was needed for cuffs falling from full three-quarter-length sleeves and for edging the drapes and loops that offset the low necklines.

At the auction Makepeace's tapestries, paintings and silverware fetched a particularly high price, some dealers having come from London to bid, for a whole new market had opened up as people set out to refurbish their homes more extravagantly. There was even a buyer for Cromwell's portrait, although the Puritan who purchased it had only to bid a few pence. Julia locked all the proceeds away in a strong-box in keeping for Michael.

Just as she supposed that to be the last link with Makepeace's sojourn there proved to be another. The maidservant, Charity, asked to see her. The girl's freckled face was desperate.

"Mr. Walker left me in the family way!"

Julia considered what she should do about this new problem. Had the father not been Makepeace it would have been easy enough to find the girl a husband locally, for country people accepted such matters philosophically, but this was the baby of a man who had been much disliked.

She wrote to Susan and there was a helpful reply. As a result Charity went to Oxfordshire to wed an agricultural worker, a widower with two small sons. He proved to be greatly to her satisfaction, being both young and virile.

THE DAYS OF MAY were slipping by. The housekeeper of the Briar Lane tenant, who had scarcely used his rented country seat, surrendered the key to the bailiff almost at once. Since it had been kept clean and in good order it was a simple matter to turn one sizeable room at the end of the house into a workroom. Julia saw the women installed, and work on the ribbons began. At the end of the first day she was more than satisfied with the standard produced and Sarah had agreed to be in charge of Briar House during Julia and Mary's sojourn in London, the reinstated maid attending Anne.

Christopher's reply came. He had secured two rooms on the royal route to Whitehall. William and Susan had stayed there several times and found them satisfactory. He would meet her and Mary there in the evening and they would have a celebratory supper together. There was much he had to tell her, having just been home to Bletchingdon again, and both his sister and brother-in-law sent their felicitations.

"What a day the twenty-ninth of May is going to be!" she exclaimed to Mary. "We'll see the King and Michael and Christopher!"

They set off for London in style in the Pallister coach on the morning of Thursday the 25th of May. Boxes strapped on behind contained their new gowns, the ribbons and everything else they would need for their stay. Neither of them had ever been to London before. When Julia had journeyed to Bletchingdon her travelling companion had insisted on a wide detour of the city, for there had been an outbreak of the plague and Mrs. Reade had been nervous of infection, being on her way to a houseful of grandchildren. Julia had been disappointed then, but now she was glad she would be seeing London for the first time in a state of rejoicing.

It was late afternoon when they approached it down St. Margaret's Hill through Southwark where London Bridge offered the only route into the City from the south, except for the heavier traffic of ships and barges coming up the Thames. She knew from what Christopher had told her that the Bridge was a virtual barrier for these incoming vessels, for there was a five-foot drop of water at high tide with swirling rapids there. As a result the shipping kept east of Billingsgate where wharves and quays and the custom house were specially located. Beyond the Bridge and up the river to the west was the seat of government and the Palace of Whitehall, which was now to be the heart of the monarchy again. In between lay the walled City of London itself and therein stood the Tower, St. Paul's Cathedral, the Temple with its Law Courts, the grand Halls of the Guilds and Companies, the Royal Exchange and other important buildings.

Just before the coach reached the Bridge it was possible to see some of the hundreds of little ferry-boats that plied to and fro across the wide sparkling river as far as the eye could see to the east and the west. Then the shops and taverns and other ill-assorted buildings built on the Bridge blocked out all view of the Thames, being as busy as any street and flowing with traffic.

As the Pallister coach rolled off the Bridge and lumbered up Fish Hill Street, there came a great salute of cannon-fire from the Tower, which after a few seconds of surprise sent people cheering on all sides. It meant only one thing. The King had landed at Dover!

"What a moment for us to arrive!" Julia exclaimed excitedly. She and Mary leaned out to glimpse the Tower rising powerfully against the soft May sky, a wraith of gun-smoke drifting across the City. Then there came another booming roar as the salutes continued and they laughed, withdrawing into the coach as their ears rang.

There was so much to see they were glad the crush of traffic imposed a slow pace on the coachman, giving them the chance to look to one side and then to the other. Julia had heard that derisive foreigners frequently called London a wooden city because of the abundance of timber, by far the cheapest building material available, used in its construction, but there was also much medieval stone and rosy Tudor brick to be seen.

Countless numbers of the wooden buildings were covered with pitch and the rest so darkened by the smoke of sea-coal from thousands of chimneys that they were as black. These and houses of better quality rose high, each of the four, five or even six storeys jutting out over the ones below, so that when a street was narrow it was like passing through a tunnel, the top rooms often no more than a handshake apart. Some residences were adorned with painted and gilded figures, one of Queen Elizabeth standing out to Julia's eye, and there was a great deal of beautiful pargetting that demanded a second glance. Pedestrians could walk underneath all these properties protected from rain by the projecting storeys, but there was always the risk of being splashed when pails of slops were thrown out of the windows into the gutter. Only the fine mansions of the nobility, rich merchants and aldermen of the City, which were set in formal gardens, were protected by high walls and gates from the teeming public and never-ending traffic.

There was width to Cannon Street and Watling Street along which the girls were travelling, for these were main thoroughfares; the squalid side streets and twisting passages, which were never swept, were flanked by tall, deformed-looking properties crammed with families on each floor, giving the girls a glimpse of the vast network of such ways that veined the City. With such a throng of people everywhere and such bustle and noise, stenches and fragrances, it was easy to see that three hundred thousand of London's citizens lived within the square-mile radius of the City walls, four hundred thousand more in the Liberties of Westminster and the out-parishes that spread to three points of the compass as well as south of the river at Southwark.

The coach had borne the girls away from the groaning watermills, which pumped water from the Thames into the public conduits, the stinking tanneries, the breweries and the tallow- and soap-boilers, which among other trades made the air so foul in the vicinity of the Bridge. Now they were passing cruciform St. Paul's Cathedral with its square truncated tower, the wooden spire of which had been lost a century before in one of the fires that had broken out here and there about the City. The rose window there had inspired the fashion for rosettes on shoes when installed many years ago.

They reached Ludgate and went down Fleet Street, where there were shops of every pleasant kind taking up the lower floors of the houses. Goldsmiths and haberdashers, drapers and milliners, perfumers, apothecaries and stationers—all their signs competed with those of the taverns and gave a checker-board effect of brilliant colour along every street.

There was plenty to buy as well from street-vendors, the sing-song cries of London as ancient as the City itself heard on every side. "Who'll buy my custard-apples!" cried the custard-mongers. "Lavender, sweet lavender!" came from women with baskets on their arms. "Herbs for the pot!" called another. Vying with them were the muffin-men, the fruit- and flower-sellers and the milkmaids with their yokes and buckets. "Fresh fish, morning caught!" yelled those with creels of fish on their backs.

Everywhere water-carriers obliged from the conduits, their shoulders stooped from the weight of their yoke-bearing buckets, their legs bandy from the number of stairs they climbed.

Everywhere there was traffic. Magnificent coaches with armorial bearings and richly liveried coachmen put the Pallister coach and others in

the shade, while the hackney coaches frequently presented a shabby appearance and outnumbered the rest. There were wagons bearing goods to
many markets, interspersed with cattle and sheep and flocks of geese being
driven to the same destination. Every kind of cart and dray rumbled
along and private sedan chairs carried well-clad and be-plumed passengers,
the feet of the bearers sometimes flashing along the egg-shaped cobbles
when the mission was urgent. Riders on horseback, pack-horses and little
donkeys all added to the colour and spectacle of the City.

Julia and Mary passed the Fleet prison, wherein debtors were housed,
and were borne over the Fleet ditch that was spanned by a bridge. Near
the brick-towered Inner and Middle Temples and gardens the lawyers in
their bushy grey periwigs and black robes darted between taverns and
their chambers and the courts, some with the nosegays tucked in their
pockets that were necessary when prisoners in the dock either reeked from
their cells or were suspected of carrying gaol fever. The Pallister coach
passed through the western outlet of the City at the gates of Temple Bar
into the Strand. After some manoeuvring in the traffic it drew up with a
clatter of hooves into the busy courtyard of the Heathcock Inn amidst its
shouting ostlers, the ringing bells announcing the departure of two stage-
coaches and the scurrying of passengers who did not want to be left
behind.

"We're here!" Julia exclaimed, her eyes sparkling with excitement as
they had been since her first sight of London. She felt she belonged
already and had a strange sense of homecoming.

Mary followed her more slowly from the coach, feeling assailed by all
the noise and bustle. Looking upwards before entering the hostelry with
Julia to take the accommodation that Christopher had booked for them,
she saw it was four floors high with three galleries encompassing the
courtyard, and along which people were going to and from their rooms.
The innkeeper welcomed them with traditional hospitality, the mark of a
good hostelry, and a porter took a key and led the way with some of their
baggage, the rest carried in their wake by one of his fellows. Julia was
given a room that was entered from the second gallery, but looked directly down into the Strand. To Mary's relief, hers was at the end of the
same gallery, but with a view down into an unexpected patch of green
garden with a few trees. She hastily declined when Julia generously offered to exchange rooms in order to give her the better view.

It was too late in the day to think of offering their ribbons for sale, but
Julia took advantage of the lull to buy a map of London, which she

studied during supper. One dazzling smile from her secured the eager help of a young business-man at the next table, who afterwards marked on certain streets the best places for her to sell. He also gave her plenty of valuable information about prices, which were soaring on such goods as hers. After she had shown him some samples of the ribbons he named figures at which she should start that made her blink. He grinned at her surprise.

"The shopkeepers will try to beat you down, but don't budge by a halfpenny. They'll know that if they don't buy from you others will and they won't want to miss the chance."

"But so many guineas a yard!" she gasped.

He fingered a ribbon of red roses. "Look at this, for example. What man or woman wouldn't want to wear the royal rose of England on Tuesday when the King comes? Then there are those with crowns and other royal emblems—they're worth a mint of money at the moment. I'm not in the drapery trade myself, but my brother is and I know something about it. Put a higher price still on anything connected with the twenty-ninth day of May and cash in on that while you can."

"I've four days in which to do it."

"That's plenty of time. If you don't sell out by the first day you will by the second."

"You've been most kind," she said gratefully.

The young man looked hopeful. "May I see you again?"

Before Julia could reply Mary intervened crisply. "Miss Pallister is betrothed."

Julia gave him a length of ribbon for his hat in appreciation and afterwards when he had gone she spoke quite crossly to Mary. "Why did you say I was betrothed?"

"Because you are until all orders and settlements by regicides are officially rescinded. In any case I'm here to chaperone you as if your mother and grandmother had entrusted me with that duty, and I intend to do it."

Julia looked doubtful, but recovering her temper shrugged and laughed.

Early next morning they set out together. On the young man's advice they did not take their produce with them, but before going to bed they had cut off the ends of a number of ribbons to provide a small sample of each pattern. These were pinned to sheets of thick cream paper that Julia had been able to buy in the Strand. All the royal emblems were on one sheet and the floral and sundry designs were on the rest.

Eager curiosity compelled them to look in the shop fronts as they walked to the first place marked on their map. Many were larger inside than would have been supposed by the windows, which with small, thick-glassed panes made it difficult to see the interiors. Sometimes open doors at the rear of a shop created enough light for a cabinet-maker's furniture to be seen, or printing presses at work with books displayed in the foreground on counters. All rooms were dark-panelled and in some cases the gloom enhanced the shimmer of draped fabrics or a jeweller's sparkling wares where a ray of sunlight slanted across them.

Julia experienced a qualm as she and Mary entered their first place of call. It proved to be well founded. The shop-owner was a strict Puritan not yet resigned to the changes taking place and, without looking at their wares, promptly showed them the door. They were no luckier in the next two shops. One proprietor remained at the back, sending someone to tell them he had all the ribbons he needed; in the other establishment the owner was absent that day and there was no one else empowered to buy.

It was hard not to fear another set-back in the fourth shop, especially when they had to wait ignominiously in a corner until a portly man with piggish eyes, wearing a yellow periwig, deigned to appear. Disdainfully he took the samples to the light and peered at them closely. Then contemptuously he tossed the samples back towards Julia.

"I'll take whatever you have of the royal patterns," he said as if granting her an enormous favour, "with delivery today. I'll pay you sixpence a yard and that's generous."

"That's the reverse and you know it, sir!" She began gathering the samples together, shocked by this insight into how hard-working out-workers were treated.

"Wait! What price were you expecting?"

She no longer wanted him to buy from her in any case, her pride bristling over the treatment she and Mary had received, and she doubled the original high figure planned. He turned purple, waved his arms about and asked Heaven if he was to be made bankrupt by the greed of ribbon-makers in this new Royalist era. He then offered her a fifth of what she had voiced. She was already on her way out the door, Mary following. He ran out into the street after them, calling to Julia to come back, but she stalked on with her cheeks an angry red, her chin high and not listening.

"Nobody is going to bargain with me in that way over Mama's ribbons! In any case I didn't like him and wouldn't have let him have them if he had offered double the asking price."

Mary chuckled. "Well, he wasn't offering to do that, but he was shouting that he would meet the exorbitant price you had demanded!"

Julia halted, laughing too and delightedly. "He's done us a good turn after all! He's given me the current market value of those ribbons!"

With her confidence high and her Pallister dignity full upon her, she sailed into the next shop, announced her business and was bowed into an office. There she and the shop-owner, Mr. Denmead, recognised each other's qualities, she seeing an honest man and he a remarkably unusual young woman, fully aware of the bargaining power she had over the ribbon goods that he would give his eye-teeth for. There were woven brocaded ribbons appearing again, but nothing of this originality of design and superb hand-work. Erroneously he supposed she had visited many shops to test the water of her exceptionally high prices, increasing them still further as she went and leaving a trail of willing and waiting buyers hoping she would return. Why else would she have presented samples in such a professional way instead of bringing baskets of finished work as ribbon-makers usually did, mostly taking without question whatever sum was offered. He intended to be the one to culminate this forceful young woman's excursion.

"I'll meet the figures you're asking if we can enter into a contract over the royal ribbons. I want you to agree that I shall have the exclusive right to all those designs, straight through until the King's coronation. After that, unless there is a royal wedding soon afterwards, the sale of them will go down."

"I'm willing to do that, but I should expect you to keep up orders for the floral ribbons as well and such a clause would be included in the contract."

"That, Miss Pallister," he said, rising to fetch a decanter and glasses, "goes without saying."

He sent his own wagon to the Heathcock Inn to collect the boxes of ribbons and he paid her in gold, which she deposited with a banker recommended to her in Lombard Street by Mr. Hannington, from whom she had sought advice before leaving Sotherleigh. For the rest of the day and all through those that followed, she and Mary gathered orders for all the designs not secured by Mr. Denmead. She ended with work for her embroiderers and ribbon-weavers for many months to come, and nowhere, since she had asserted herself with the yellow-periwigged shop-owner, had she and Mary received anything but the most respectful courtesy.

In this walking about the City they discovered that London had many charming courts, yards and steps, flowers blooming in unexpected places and leafy trees extending welcome shade. There were also many fine houses, which were secured by high-walled gardens against the waves of humanity that passed by. Off the Strand, outside the city walls and the tight congestion within, a number of grand residences had open views of the river. Julia, remembering Christopher's promise to build her a house, thought such a location would suit her very well.

As she strolled with Mary back to the Heathcock on the eve of the King's return, London's mood was one of pulsating anticipation. On all sides tapestries and colourful draperies were being hung from windows, giving a bright and festive look here as in the City, and garlands of greenery were being looped over shopfronts and doorways. People had made excursions into the countryside and were returning in wagons with baskets of flowers to strew the royal path on the morrow. The royal arms, unseen in London for so long, were displayed again. News had spread widely of the King's tumultuous welcome at Dover, the same approbation following him to Canterbury where he had held his first privy council and on Sunday had attended a full Anglican service in Canterbury Cathedral. Next he had ridden on to Rochester with cheers echoing round him all the way and now London was poised and waiting to give itself back to the crown.

Julia was conscious of a rising sense of destiny as if something tremendous in her life was to be linked with the royal day that would dawn on the morrow. She began to hope that this sensation had its roots in Christopher's coming and almost without realising it she became convinced that he would say something wonderful to her. Surely nothing else could account for the boundless exhilaration in her? No other reason could be spurring this gush of love for him, which she knew nothing would stop once he held her in his arms again. Tomorrow she would be his. Nothing now existed that could stem his passion and hers.

# FOURTEEN

**M**ARY would have been content to watch the procession from Julia's bedchamber window, but it was not close enough for her friend.

"We must be down there in the street!" Julia declared, giving a final touch to her new azure gown by tweaking the bow of May-blossom ribbon into place at her cleavage. "Right at the front where we can curtsy to the King should he look at us and where Michael can see us and know where to find us afterwards." Then, raising her eyes to the mirror, she caught the reflection of Mary's torn expression and spun round to her. "Don't be sad on this of all days. Sophie won't be with Michael. It's only loyal Cavaliers who will be following the royal party. She might be at Sotherleigh soon but you can have this little time with him with nobody to spoil it."

Mary nodded courageously. "It's not as though Michael and I will be alone at all. By having supper with you and Christopher the pattern can be set for our relationship in the future."

"That's right." Julia picked up her hat by the brim and, turning again to the mirror, lowered it carefully onto her head. Hers was a rose colour with a swirling plume the same shade of blue as her gown. Neither her hat nor Mary's was new, both having been found in Anne's hatboxes in the attic. The plumes each had bought had been their one extravagance since coming to London, for public demand for new finery had sent up the price of feathers too.

They spent the morning hours in the Strand, for here, as elsewhere in London, there was much to see, every street on the royal route now dressed overall for the great moment when the King rode by. Ceremonial arches had been erected and houses were almost hidden in multi-hued tapestries. Flowers festooned balconies that were already full of ladies, their plumes and bright new gowns adding more colour to the scene. Conduits were already running wine being well sampled in the mood of the day. The tallest maypole ever known, and specially made for the occasion, had been erected in the Strand with a multitude of rainbow ribbons that had been wound and unwound since early morning. People danced around it to music, and there were always others waiting to take their places when they tired. Julia and Mary both took turns, young men seizing their maypole ribbons with them, so that they danced in pairs. Afterwards they would have had their partners' company for the rest of the day if they had not managed to slip off on their own, with plenty of other girls to fill the gap.

Morris dancers, forbidden their ancient prancing steps for so long, performed to the whack of their sticks and the jingle of bells on their legs and boots, every one of them in a new smock sewn by a wife or sister, their straw hats encircled by flowers bobbing and shedding petals. Professional entertainers, no longer afraid of whippings or imprisonment, juggled and tumbled, recited poems in honour of the King and enacted everything from Shakespeare to the lewdest comedies. When eventually people began to fill the sides of the streets in readiness for the procession, a large number having taken places since the night before, the entertainment continued, making the time of waiting pass quickly.

By tradition London crowds were orderly and good-humoured on state occasions, and many younger people who were to see a royal procession for the first time conformed with all the rest. Children were given places at the front, their parents eager that this momentous occasion should be imprinted on their memory. When a vibrating salute boomed from the Tower to announce that the King had crossed London Bridge into the city, there was a spontaneous explosion of joy, cheering from every throat rending the air. Church bells had also burst into full chime, which with the thunder of the cannons was to continue until nightfall. Julia and Mary tried to plot the King's slow progress as they waited, their excitement mounting at the prospect of seeing Michael again in addition to the royal return. Then eventually a rise in the cheering in the distance gave the message that was taken up all along the Strand. "The King is coming!"

At last the head of the procession came into sight. First were the heralds, blowing their long slender trumpets, followed by marching soldiers, silver sleeves to their buff jerkins showing that no expense had been spared to bring the King home in style. The Lord Mayor of London, wearing his Tudor-style velvet cap and gold chain of office with his robes, was on horseback, the Aldermen of the City riding after him in their scarlet cloaks. They had ridden out of Deptford to meet the King with an address of welcome and to escort him home. After them came representatives of all the Guilds and Companies of the City, their horses richly caparisoned. There then followed, interspersed with ranks of drummers or bands of musicians, six hundred of the nobility and other gentlemen in saddles studded with jewels, they themselves in newly fashionable periwigs that caped the shoulders of their velvet attire. Beside them on foot were attendants and footmen in liveries of crimson, green or purple. More riders and more musicians went by and then a host of young women who were strewing flower petals from gilded baskets as they came, for behind them was the King! The cheering soared to deafening proportions.

Charles II rode slightly ahead of his two brothers, all three of them in cloth of gold with enormous plumes flowing out from their wide-brimmed hats worn with a dashing air. For a moment Julia was spellbound, gazing raptly at him. She thought he looked every inch a regal figure with his magnificent height in the saddle and his dignified wave. His long curly hair was as black as ever; his face, the sides of his mouth now deeply grooved, was older than she remembered from the brief meeting that had marked her tenth birthday outside the inn at Houghton, and older still than the youthful likeness in the Long Gallery at Sotherleigh. If there was the slightest hint of amused cynicism in his smile it was not to be wondered at, for less than ten years ago he had been hunted out of England like a fox to suffer poverty, humiliation and near starvation in exile, while to all appearances these cheering, jubilant people had never wanted him gone. Breaking out of the spell cast on her, Julia began to exuberantly fling the flowers she had kept for the purpose into his path. His alert gaze fell on her.

"God bless Your Majesty!" she cried out, curtsying.

He inclined his head, his heavy-lidded eyes conveying that it was as much in appreciation of her beauty as in acknowledgement of her loyal benediction. Then he had gone by, leaving her wondering if her neckline had been cut too low after all, for it had been no kingly glance that had travelled from her face to her cleavage and back again. It had been the same as that which she had often caught in the dark, glittering depths of Adam's eyes. She gave a start as Mary clutched her arm.

"Can you see Michael?"

She promptly forgot both the King and Adam in the heightened anticipation of seeing her brother again. "He should be with these Cavaliers."

Riding by now were those who had gone with their monarch into exile, all gloriously dressed for their return, for a chest of gold had been sent to the King in order that he and his Court might come home arrayed as if the years of privation had never been. They waved their hats and their hands to those giving them special approbation. Although Julia and Mary searched the faces, Michael's was not among them.

"How strange he's not there," Julia commented a little uneasily. The procession flowed on, the sparkle of gems, the shimmer of silver and gold lace and the splendour of rich garments seemingly without end. Then suddenly a face did stand out as some gentlemen with their horses caparisoned in red and gold came riding along in pairs.

"Look!" Mary exclaimed in the same moment of recognition. "It's Adam!"

"So it is." Julia gave a little laugh of sheer astonishment.

He was wearing the snowdrop ribbon as a hat band, a large ruby brooch holding in place a crimson plume of loyalty such as many were sporting that day. He was on the same side where she and Mary were standing and his gaze was travelling over the crowds as if he were looking for someone. She took a step forward to stand out as she had done for the King and waited until he should see her. When he did his face cleared.

"I've been looking for you!"

"So you ride with the King at last, Adam Warrender!" Her good-humoured mockery had no malice in it and the happiness in her face showed him that his being won over to the King had made a perfect touch to her day. "I never thought to see such a happening!"

"So I can mark this up as an achievement." His tone was joking as he drew level, but his eyes were serious, showing it mattered to him that this former breach between them had been healed.

"Yes, I'm delighted!" She put her hand into his, which he had reached out to her. Owing to the crawling pace of the procession, she was able to stroll comfortably alongside, looking up at him. "How did you know I'd be here in London?"

He retaliated with a little mockery himself. "You've been such a staunch Royalist all along that it was a natural assumption."

She chuckled. "It's not just that, is it? Where have you been all this month of May?"

"All I can tell you now is that I was abroad on business for the government. When I returned to Dover with the King's ceremonial flotilla a messenger from the Hall was waiting for me, as I had instructed, to give me your whereabouts and other news and information from home." He frowned compassionately and his clasp tightened on her hand. "My condolences on the death of your grandmother. I had not heard before."

She answered soberly. "She lived to know of the Restoration, which was what she wanted most of all." Then she smiled again. "What brought a change of heart in you with regard to the King?"

"I'll tell you later. I know where you're staying and I have a message from Michael."

The anxiety in her came through. "Is he all right? Why isn't he here?"

"I can't tell you now."

"Come to supper at the Heathcock. Mary and I had planned on Michael being with us and Christopher Wren will be coming."

"I may be late. Don't wait to eat. I'll be there tonight whatever the hour."

He released her hand and saluted her with a gallant's Court gesture of a bow from the saddle and poised fingers set lightly against the heart. It was observed by a section of the spectators, who shouted to him with a merry bawdiness, making him laugh, and Julia was applauded as she hurried back to Mary.

When Mary heard what Adam had mentioned about Michael she felt crushed down by disappointment. "It can only mean that he is still in France."

"I fear so." Julia linked her arm through Mary's consolingly. She was puzzled, unable to think of anything that would have kept Michael from coming to England on such a long-awaited day. Mary, remembering the cool, hard face of Sophie in the miniature, could not help wondering if she had played any part in denying Michael's return. Perhaps she had insisted that he should not go home unless she could go with him and that would not have been possible, for the wives and womenfolk of the men who had crossed the Channel in the King's flotilla had had to wait behind.

There was one exception, who was not yet known to Londoners. She was Barbara Palmer, a beautiful married woman who had become the King's mistress in exile and did not intend to relinquish him or the advantages her position would give her now that he was home.

Julia and Mary watched the rest of the procession until dusk fell. It had taken the King seven hours to ride through London. Now at Whitehall he must attend a thanksgiving service in the Palace chapel and afterwards eat a supper banquet in view of all who wished to see him, an old tradition on momentous royal occasions. Glad that their day was to end more peacefully, the two girls returned to the Heathcock, leaving others to rollick and dance in the streets around bonfires.

Christopher had booked a private parlour for their supper. Julia, coming downstairs to it as soon as she had changed for the evening, thought how foresighted it had been of him, for the dining-room and the tap-rooms were full of noisy and roistering customers. Any talk there between Christopher and her would have had to be at the top of their voices. He could scarcely ask her to marry him in that manner!

She no longer tried to check this hope. There were no grounds on which to base her assumption that he was ready to become betrothed, and she could only assume that she knew because she had always been so close to him in spirit. It was as if some invisible current of knowledge had come to her through the air, gradually at first and then with increasing forcefulness. Love and passion were directed at her and this marvellous day was to culminate with a ring on her finger.

She had taken the precaution of asking Mary to delay joining them for a little while. "Come down just before supper is to be served."

Mary had nodded uncertainly. "I suppose that is all right."

It amazed Julia that considering how many times she and Christopher had been alone together in Sotherleigh and Bletchingdon, Mary should think she should accompany them now and also that she should have no inkling as to what Christopher's true purpose was to be this evening. Even a hint of what was to come, and that this would be a time when any couple would expect to be left alone for the asking of the vital question, had failed to get home to Mary. Julia could only conclude she was too wrapped up in thoughts of Michael to be really aware of anything else until Adam had delivered his message.

When she reached the private parlour Christopher had not yet arrived. The round table was laid for four, the linen crisp and the silver cutlery shining, no pewter in this part of the Heathcock. She crossed to a bench by the wall and had barely seated herself when he arrived, bounding into the room in his jaunty way, his brown hair swinging back over his shoulders, his hat and gloves already dispensed with in the hall.

"Julia! What a day this has been! How glad I am to find you alone."

Closing the door after him, he was across to her in a matter of strides to catch up both her hands by the fingers in his and plant a kiss on the back of each. She had no chance to rise for an embrace such as they usually shared and she smiled at his new and formal approach on this momentous evening.

Still without releasing her hands, he swung himself down onto the seat beside her and for a few smiling moments drank in the sight of her. "You become more beautiful every time I see you. How is it possible?"

"You compliment me excessively," she protested happily.

"Nobody could do that," he countered admiringly. Then he wanted to know how she had enjoyed the procession. Being that day at Gresham College, he had walked from Bishopsgate to watch it at a good distance away from where she and Mary had stood. She told him about Michael's non-appearance and how Adam had word of her brother to convey later. She held back from telling him about her ribbon project, for that could wait until Mary was present and they were no longer alone.

He had some good news himself. His uncle had been released from the Tower and had already been re-installed as Bishop of Ely, the position from which the old man had been so roughly snatched all those years before. She pressed him as to his own work at Oxford, always eager to know what he had in hand, and he admitted to having spent many hours over past months furthering his research into the strength, convenience and beauty of line he deemed necessary for buildings of the future. Almost as if in light relief, he had designed a beehive that was both practical and transparent. "As you know," he concluded, his eyes merry, "I've always been partial to plenty of honey on my bread."

She laughed teasingly. "I declare you deserve an extra spoonful if your beehive keeps the bees more contented. Is there anything in the world that has escaped your thought and consideration?"

He smiled ruefully. "A great deal, I fear." Now he looked with great seriousness into her eyes. "Maybe all I want and also an end to my seeking will come with the fulfilment of my half of that dream you once shared with me. I've never forgotten that generous gift. Maybe I felt at the time it portended as much for me as it did for you."

"That's how I wanted it to be," she said very softly.

"Have you ever had the sensation of coming at all close to what it might mean?"

"No. I linked it once to a wonderful gown that Queen Elizabeth gave my grandmother, but that was only a signpost along the way. I've never doubted that there's more to come."

He nodded in agreement. "It has been the same for me. I've thought several times I've been about to grasp it, but always it has eluded me."

"I'm sure there will come a point in our lives when we shall look at each other and know, even without words, that our dream has been mutually fulfilled."

"I believe that too." He regarded her tenderly. "Although our paths are set apart that time will come."

She inclined her head almost shyly. "Why do you speak as if there is a division between us? I know your work will always keep you to a way separated from the one I can travel with you, but they can run parallel."

"I have to tell you that between those two paths runs another and that will be followed by someone to whom you opened a door for me."

Somewhere in her head there rang a warning signal of alarm. "I don't understand."

"Do you remember when you were first at Bletchingdon I came home to a party in that house?"

"Yes." She withdrew her hands from him and folded them tightly in her lap.

"I stood at the foot of the stairs and you nearly made my heart stop when I looked up at you. But you did more than enchant me at that moment. Somehow, and in a manner I could never explain, your beauty gave a candle-flame to Faith's quiet face and I, who had known her as a neighbour's daughter for many years, saw her in this new light. A spark was ignited. A seed was sown. How shall I describe it? I suppose neither she nor I was aware of it at the time, because both of us were encircling you in the friendship you had bestowed on us individually like a blessing."

"So what has happened since?" She held herself quite rigid, having the terrible feeling that if she attempted to move even a finger every limb in her body would begin to jerk convulsively.

"Gradually I made a point of always seeing her whenever I was home. Our relationship grew deeper and warmer. Last week when I was at Bletchingdon we became betrothed."

Was she staring at him in such high-wrought distress that he would have to look away? It did not appear so, for his expression remained serious and composed. She heard herself speaking: "Faith has many good qualities to her character."

"I do agree. She will be writing to you but I wanted to be the one to tell you the news. I know that whatever Faith and I may have in our lives together it will be due to you that evening at Bletchingdon."

She shook her head, managing what she hoped was a smile. "It would have happened anyway. Some things are meant to be." Never would she let him see what he had done to her. Her Pallister pride would not allow it. In love she would have thrown herself at his feet if he had desired it, but now she must guard and keep from him and the whole world the awful hurt that had exploded inside her. She had once boasted to Katherine that should loss of him ever come about, she would bear it bravely. Maybe she had never really believed it could happen, but now she had to live up to her own words.

"Nothing can change our friendship," Christopher was saying, "because Faith and I are most anxious that my ties with Sotherleigh should not be broken."

She wanted to scream that she would not let him thrust her back into the childish and innocent mould of their first acquaintanceship. She did not belong to Sotherleigh in that sense any more, but was herself, whole and complete, adult and sensual and ripe for experience in living and loving.

"When shall you marry?" She tried to associate that coming union with something as impersonal as drinking a cup of chocolate or taking a stroll. If she thought of him making love to another woman she would die, torn to shreds by her own imagination and forgetting that she had sworn to survive.

"That is too far into the future to be settled yet. Financially we could marry tomorrow, but the very nature of my work necessitates a freedom to come and go, to study all night if needs be, and to take whatever journeys are necessary either at a moment's notice or what might soon be the expressed wishes of the King. None of this would be conducive to wedlock. Faith, being the calm and patient girl that she is, knows that we must have a long betrothal."

Many months and even years of remaining in the background was to be Faith's fate. Julia questioned herself as to whether she could have filled such a role and knew that before long she would have set out to change that state of affairs, subtly imposing herself on the path he needed to keep free of encumbrances. Had he known all along that such a love as hers would have been both a glory and a handicap to him? And had the handicap proved more important than the glory? At least let him not suspect now that her yearning for him had not wavered by an iota from the time she had immaturely revealed her feelings for him in the maze. Let him think that only friendly devotion remained. Don't let him know she was drowning in anguish.

"You have made an ideal choice of a wife in Faith." She had always been honest with herself and with him and, although she thought she must be reeling visibly through forcing this admittance into the open, it had to be done.

He should have looked grateful and relieved, but concern was sharpening his gaze on her. "I shall always remember hearing you say that. It means more to me than you can possibly know. What I hope now to hear before long is that you have found someone you love with whom to share your life."

She had to disperse the uncertainty he was showing about her. He must not suspect the torment she was suffering. Nobody should pity her! Not even Christopher out of his kind heart and compassion.

"Surely you're forgetting that I'm betrothed too? It meant nothing to me all the time it had been settled by Makepeace, but already his hand in it is virtually at an end. Adam and I are to begin again." Her bravado was leading her into rash statements, but if she stopped she might break down and that must not happen. "You will see when he comes how well everything is between us."

She saw she had finally convinced him. His face cleared and he shook his head in wonder that such good fortune should have come to her. "Dearest Julia, you've given me the best tidings I could have hoped to hear towards the closing of this Restoration Day."

It was a relief to her that Mary should arrive then and Christopher rose in his vigorous way to greet her. As the two of them chatted together about the events of the day, Julia gained a little respite to struggle frantically against falling apart. How odd it was that she, who never before had had to hide any thought from him, had now entered a new sphere wherein whatever she said or did must be set against his belonging to someone else. Always he had been her Christopher, her confidant, her love and her future. Maybe that was the very reason why he had had to break free and seek out a more tranquil and less voracious partner than she would ever be. If only she could leave this room and find a hidden corner in which to curl up and weep her heart out! She knew now why animals sought havens in which to die of their wounds.

"Shall I serve supper now, sir?" A waiter, hot and harassed through being run off his feet by the unprecedented rush of business in the tavern, had entered the room.

Christopher looked inquiringly at Julia. "Should we not wait for Adam?"

"No, he will be late." She wished he would not come at all. He was the last person she wished to see, fearing his alert eyes that never seemed to miss anything.

When the dishes had been set out on the table, Christopher dismissed the waiter and poured the wine himself. No sooner were their glasses filled when Adam arrived, having managed to get away from Whitehall sooner than he had expected. He and Christopher had never met before, although Adam had drawn his own conclusions a while ago as to this man being the one who stood between Julia and him.

"I'm honoured to meet you, Mr. Wren," he said with complete honesty, for he had the highest respect for Christopher's intellect and famed research.

"Your servant, sir." Christopher returned Adam's bow and then stepped forward hospitably to take him by the arm and bring him to the table. "Let us dispense with formality and be on Christian name terms, Adam. I tell you no one could be more welcome here than you this evening, besides the fact you are the bearer of eagerly awaited news."

There seemed to be such underlying significance in his words that Adam looked fully at Julia, beside whom he seated himself, hoping for some clue to define the reason. She appeared locked in thought, barely noticing his arrival. Then for a second as she cast a wary side-glance at him, he glimpsed with all the love he felt for her a tortured darkness in the depths of her pupils. Then, like a light giving a false brilliance, she smiled with a show of being immensely pleased to see him.

"How gallant of you to leave the King's company early for us!" She swayed towards him, coquettish and enticing, her fragrance filling his nostrils. "Now tell us without delay what message you bring from my brother."

"Is Michael well?" Mary asked anxiously from the opposite side of the table.

"He will be by now and so there is nothing for anyone to worry about, but a slight stomach disorder afflicted him almost on the eve of his departing to Breda to return with the King. He was already getting better when I saw him."

"Was he bedridden?" Julia was concerned. Fevers took strange forms and often the most innocuous symptoms foretold more dangerous ailments.

"He had been, but he was sitting out in a chair when I visited him. He sent his fond greetings to you and to Mary and all those good friends who would be waiting to see him back at Sotherleigh." Adam smiled, having dispensed with the bad tidings. "Now I can give all three of you the news he was most eager I should convey. In a few months' time, unless the baby conceived is female, there should be an heir for Sotherleigh!"

In the midst of her own personal despair, Julia was gladdened by this announcement. Glasses were raised, Mary unselfishly thankful that Michael should have this consolation to his marriage. It was she who forestalled Julia with her immediate question.

"Why were you in Paris?"

"I was on a special mission. The King is completely estranged from his mother now, but it was necessary for some contact to be made with her."

Supper began and the talk was lively over the oysters and the succulent salmon, the Sussex lobsters, the chicken coulis in its cream sauce, the tender roasted duckling, the asparagus, the salads and the tiny new carrots.

Julia had noticed before that round tables tended to encourage conviviality by the very ease with which conversation could be conducted across them and this one was no exception. The candelabrum, set in the middle of it, made an oasis of golden light that flickered on the faces of all four seated there, creating a kind of charmed circle in which the conversation eddied and flowed. She alone remained quiet, taking no part in anything being discussed, for it was enough effort to smile charmingly at Adam every time he turned to her and she only toyed with a taste of one dish or another. Her normal healthy appetite had deserted her. She hoped that after several glasses of wine she would have gained some false courage with which to offer something towards the conversation.

"Why so quiet?" Adam questioned her amiably, topping her glass yet again.

She shrugged, one smooth shoulder almost wholly revealed as the rose satin sleeve slid a little lower, and gazed ravishingly at him, well aware that Christopher was observing her. "I'm listening to every word of wisdom being exchanged." Playfully she pulled Adam's lace cuff. "I may have much to say to you later."

His eyes narrowed cynically. He saw through her. Something had happened before his arrival to shatter her confidence. She was hurt and desperate and playing up to him as some kind of salve to her pride. He doubted she had ever before consumed the amount of wine that she had drunk during this supper and, although in all probability she had used these flirtatious ploys with other men, it was the first time she had attempted to gull him with them. Well, he would retaliate in kind and await the outcome.

"That sounds most promising." He trailed a finger along her bare forearm and saw her knuckles clench as she forced herself not to snatch her hand away. Then he knew her play-acting was for Christopher and by it she had unwittingly put herself entirely in his power. There was nothing he could not coax from her all the time she wished Christopher to be convinced there was a new and amorous development between them.

From then on he lost no chance of paying her special attention. He gave her long looks, sought her hand to hold, paid her compliments and even spooned out the pink rose that garnished his chicken coulis to place on her plate and make it the prettiest at the table. She began to feel herself being overpowered by his unwelcome and lover-like solicitude, which was giving more help to her pretence than she needed. In an effort to break from it she drew on the boost the wine had given her to talk for the first time about her ribbon project and how it had come about through Makepeace's theft of Michael's fortune. Both Adam and Christopher approved her initiative. Although they understood she felt obligated to repay as large a portion as she could ever manage towards her brother's loss of funds, neither felt she should hold herself responsible and both said as much. She shook her head as they pointed out she was not to know that her stepfather would steal from Michael.

"I should have known," she insisted, refusing to excuse herself. "He was wily enough for anything and that in itself should have forewarned me. Also, it must be remembered that he was convinced everything in Sotherleigh was his property from the day he was given possession of the house and estate."

She took up her glass, which Adam had refilled again, and took a sip dreamily. It was her aim to go from strength to strength with her ribbons, but for the time being she was keeping that to herself. Mary thought she had gone far enough in having a country workshop and never supposed she was thinking already of getting one in London. But that extension could only come with time. First of all she had to see how her present arrangement worked out, discover how to erase hindrances to production and be certain of eliminating any loop-holes through which time or even orders might be lost. With that experience behind her she should be fit to compete with those who had been in the business much longer than she had.

She listened to the conversation with half an ear until Christopher asked Adam for his impression of Paris. Then she paid attention, knowing that Christopher wanted to visit that city himself when an opportunity arose, especially after Michael's descriptions to them when they had met at Oxford. There had been enough snippets about it in his letters as well for her to be equally intrigued.

"It's a fine and interesting city," Adam told them, "much of it still many hundreds of years old, the original foundation being on an island in the middle of the river Seine. However I think you, Christopher, would be chiefly interested in the plans the King is making for the embellishment and enlarging of the royal Palaces. Unusual in a monarch, Louis XIV has great interest and considerable knowledge of building construction and architecture and you can be sure that where he leads, the aristocracy and wealthy bourgeoisie will follow. The King is also opening up wide avenues through the city, which will relieve the congestion in the narrow streets and improve the appearance of the capital."

Christopher, with some diffidence, then asked Adam why he was now supporting the restoration of the monarchy. Adam told how over several months after the death of Cromwell and through Tumbledown Dick's well-intentioned blunderings, he had eventually reached the same conclusions as many other erstwhile Parliamentarians in the belief, finally brought into the open by General Monck, that only with the Restoration could the nation settle into a law-abiding existence and strive forward to the full in order and in commerce.

"I have to admit that figuratively speaking I've been detached from politics for a number of years," Christopher said, ringing a small handbell to summon a tavern-maid to clear the table for dessert. "Such matters have no place among scientists set on common goals, but I have been a Royalist in favour of just reforms since my undergraduate days and it is my belief that we shall soon see them come about."

The cloth was drawn and the table set with clean plates. The waiter bore in a large bowl full of oranges, apples, purple grapes and early strawberries, which he placed on the table before adding a shallow dish of sugared violets, almonds and sweetmeats. Then he poured the red wine from the first of two extra bottles ordered by Christopher and left the room.

The dark panelled walls muffled the merry shouting and raucous laughter in the tap-rooms and elsewhere in the hostelry, giving a sense of privacy. Discourse became more leisurely, all four of them relaxed by the wine and the good repast that had been completed with the sweet taste of the fruit. It was then that Adam made it clear he had something of importance to say.

"I think the moment has come for me to tell you all my main purpose in going to see Michael." He was totally at ease with himself and what he was saying. "With Walker gone from Sotherleigh it was important that every other unhappy association with him should be banished too. I asked the true master of Sotherleigh for his permission to wed his sister without contract, dowry or anything else to link the past with the present."

Christopher and Mary followed Adam's gaze as he turned in his chair to look towards Julia. The animated dazzle that she had turned on Adam during supper whenever he had spoken to her had changed to a faint almost disbelieving smile, which to Christopher's mind suggested she was quite overwhelmed by this gallant speech. There was an opaqueness to her facial bones and a shadowed hollowness to her cheeks, which he took to be a trick of the candlelight, while the pang of this final loss of her went painfully through him. Yet he had done what he had set out to do in liberating her and himself from each other, leaving only the links of their original friendship. It was good to find her already drawn into a new love while he had found a haven in Faith's patient and deep-rooted devotion.

"I don't doubt that Michael gave his permission," he said quietly, not to disturb in any way the harmony of this scene.

Adam gave a nod, his gaze on Julia. "He said only that the marriage should be from Sotherleigh."

Helplessly Julia realised she must play up to all Adam was saying or else everything she had declared to Christopher would be revealed as the sham it was, and he would know pityingly that she still blindly and savagely wanted him and no one else. Later she could always explain a drifting apart from Adam as a mutual decision that their marriage should not go ahead because of differences between them.

"How thoughtful of my brother," she said in an empty voice, unable to imbue it with any warmth. Perhaps that lack would be taken for a deepening of the disappointment that Michael could not be here at the present time. She wished Adam would stop looking at her in that curious, penetrating way as if somehow he could see right into her heart.

He had watched her dilated pupils become pin-points, panic overlying her inner torture, and had read her intention as clearly as if she had spoken it. If he let her go now she would take advantage of her new freedom to escape him for ever and ruin his life and hers. He leaned towards her. "I hope for no delay in our betrothal," he said softly, "even if we should have to wait a few weeks for Michael to return before we wed."

She swallowed hard. A stillness had fallen over the table at which the four of them sat, their shadows on the walls behind them. An intimate atmosphere had arisen that was almost tangible. It was one of those rare times that bond people together and made any declaration permissible, any confession tolerable. She seemed scarcely able to breathe.

"Delays are sometimes inevitable," she managed to say.

"There's no need in this case." He used the same soft tone as before, setting his linen napkin down beside his plate on which lay curling ribbons of apple peel, an emerald winking green fire from a ring on his finger. She seemed to be watching in a daze as he pushed back his chair, the legs scraping on the oak floor. The wine she had drunk was creating a golden mist about everything, melting edges and heightening hues as if all four of them in that panelled room had been set into a painted masterpiece. She saw him go down on one knee before her, the plushy velvet of his sleeves rippling from ruby red to crimson in the folds, with a sheen like a cat's fur taut over his knees.

"Marry me, Julia." His voice reached her from far away. "I've long wanted you to be my wife. Before these two witnesses I swear to love and cherish you to the end of my days."

She sprang up so swiftly her satin skirt whipped out and clutching it to her side, she overturned her chair, her only thought being flight, but he was on his feet at once. She gasped out as he crushed her into his arms. His kiss drove into her, sapping her resistance and her hope of any chance of escape. Passion was afire in his mouth and his hand slid down her back to hold her even closer to him. A tear ran from under each of her closed eyelids. What did it matter whom she married since Christopher was lost to her? At least he would never know it was from him she had expected a proposal and such a demonstrative torrent of love.

When eventually Adam raised his lips from hers and looked down searchingly into her eyes, she gave her answer in a strangled whisper. "Yes, Adam, I'll marry you."

Immediately Mary and Christopher were on their feet as well. He, supposing the tears glinting in her eyes were those of joy, embraced her fondly, kissing her on the cheek.

"What a night of happiness this is! It has crowned a day we shall all remember for the rest of our lives." He then congratulated Adam most heartily.

Mary, guessing that the tears sprang from another cause, took advantage of the men's diverted attention to give Julia encouraging words. "All will be well, I know. This is the boldest and best decision you've ever made."

Once more the glasses were filled with wine. Toasts were drunk by Christopher and Mary to the newly betrothed couple and then by Julia and Adam to each other. They all drank to their friendship and once again to the health of the King. It was then that the first crackle of fireworks was heard and the glitter of silver stars showed through a gap in the curtains.

They went out into the courtyard, joining a host of noisy people who had swarmed out of the hostelry to gaze skywards with the "ahs" and "ohs" that always followed the soaring of rockets and the resulting burst of multi-coloured stars. In the midst of the display Adam, standing close to Julia, cupped his hand to her upturned face and guided her lips round to meet his again. It was a tender kiss this time and she responded as the sky turned pink and green and blue from the fireworks, bathing their faces in the rainbow light. To this man she had committed her life and must now strive for an amicable partnership with him. She had known how it must be in the very moment she had promised to be his wife.

ADAM DID NOT ACCOMPANY Julia and Mary back to Sotherleigh, there being too much business on hand in both government and royal matters to allow his return to Sussex. For the time being he would keep the rented rooms he had, but he intended to find more spacious accommodation before the marriage.

"Shall you mind dividing your time between London and Sussex as the wife of a Member of Parliament?" he had asked Julia.

"No, it's an ideal arrangement for me," she had replied. "I'll be able to keep an eye on my ribbon-makers at home and conduct the business side in London."

Before the coach reached Sotherleigh on its homeward journey, Julia alighted at Briar House in the village to see how work had progressed in her absence. Sarah had managed fairly well, but she was unhappy out of her element and thankful that the last day had come. Julia was pleased with the amount of work that had been produced, but her shrewd glance took in a lack of organisation that had nothing to do with Sarah. If she had had more time before going to London she would have settled a routine before leaving, but that could be amended now she was back. She would oversee the workshop herself until her marriage made claims on her time. By then she should have found somebody capable to be in charge.

Anne was overjoyed to hear of Julia's betrothment. She knew Adam had given her the needlework box that she had used temporarily, and he was associated in her mind with kindness and consideration. At the moment she could not recall his face, but she did not admit to it, aware from the glances she sometimes received that she was not remembering things as other people did.

"You're going to be so happy, Julia!" she exclaimed. "My life began when I married your father and I pray it will be the same for you." Then she did remember an echo from the past. "But I always thought it would be Christopher whom you would wed."

"Don't speak of that," Julia implored quickly. "That was never to be." Her mother's innocently spoken words had touched a raw nerve and almost taken her breath away.

The next morning she went early to Briar House, taking with her a pile of clean aprons, which the workers were to don on arrival and leave behind when they left. She recruited a young woman, unable to sew or weave, to keep the workroom floor washed, swept and clean. A routine was organised for taking fresh working materials from the box that did not disarrange any of the contents. To ease conditions for her workers she gave them access to the kitchen where they ate the noon-pieces they brought with them. Julia intended that when winter came there should be a bowl of hot soup for each. No less important was that they should have plenty of light at all times and she made sure that candle-lamps were lit even when the day was only moderately overcast, for the window panes at Briar House were less clear than those at Sotherleigh and diffused all but the brightest sun-rays.

On the whole there were almost no disagreements among the women. They were accustomed to helping one another in time of trouble and not so much in falling out. Any village was a tight-knit, almost isolated community and theirs was no exception. Some of the women could count on one hand the number of times they had been as far as Chichester and all thought themselves fortunate they did not live packed into narrow streets. More or less content with their lot already, they were also of a patient nature, for embroidery demanded that quality before all else. The result was a good-natured, industrious work force with a pride in the lovely patterned ribbons that were produced at Briar House.

Considering how difficult an interchange between villages could be, news spread on an invisible grapevine. It was not long before Julia's ribbon-making workshop was being talked about far afield. As a result women began to make considerable journeys on foot, unless they were lucky enough to own a donkey or managed to get a lift at least part of the way on a farm cart or a drover's wagon. They arrived at Briar House often tired and dusty or huddled and rain-soaked, and asked to see the lady of Sotherleigh.

Julia received them all. Some brought her examples of their embroidery and smocking, having no notion of the delicacy of stitchery that she needed. But, as with her local embroiderers, Julia was able to define the true needlewomen among them, all of whom declared themselves willing to make their individual journeys to collect materials and deliver the finished work. She was not going to tie any one of them to the hardships that would be involved, but she wrote down the names and villages of those she would like to take into her employ, gave them samples to copy and said she would call to collect the finished results herself.

It did not take her long to organise this new round of workers. She hired a trained clerk named John Mather, who had been highly recommended to her as a worthy young man by Mr. and Mrs. Hannington. With him riding beside her she set out a week later to visit each woman on her list, setting out her conditions if the samples showed promise, insisting on absolute cleanliness and leaving supplies. It became Mr. Mather's duty to make a continual round throughout a wide area, collecting work, making payment and leaving fresh materials. He also made sure that the women worked in clean conditions and since they never knew exactly when he would appear there were few cases of slacking, and those he did find were eventually weeded out. Yet other women came forward to fill those gaps and yards of lovely Pallister ribbons bearing Anne's designs and in all widths and colours kept the shelves of the store-cupboards and chests comfortably full. It was a bonus that Mr. Mather had a sensible and steady sister who kept house for him, and she applied for the post of organiser at Briar House. Julia took her on trial and was soon satisfied. Miss Mather knew how to organise and take charge, proving herself a good needlewoman as well.

In the process of these arrangements, Julia went to London with a load of ribbons to fill the orders she had gathered just prior to Restoration

Day, Sarah going with her. She had expected London to have settled down again, but it was as if people had found it impossible to shake off their initial jubilation and a merry atmosphere still prevailed with banners fluttering in the streets, garlands of greenery renewed and musicians gathered at street corners to fill the air with lively melodies to which younger folk would sometimes join hands and dance. She was told by Mrs. Needham, wife of the landlord of the Heathcock, that whenever the King rode by, Londoners left whatever they were doing to rush out into the street and cheer him.

"It's as if London has become a gigantic fête from morning till night," the woman exclaimed jovially, "and there's no sign of it ending yet."

Julia had asked for the same bedchamber at the hostelry as she had had before. She liked the view of the Strand and also the bedchamber had a communicating door at the rear into an adjoining room for Sarah, which Mary had previously occupied. The Needhams had seven sons, who were employed in various duties at the hostelry and in its stables. She hired two, whose ages were fourteen and fifteen, to carry her boxes of ribbons when she made her deliveries, but they had to wear a livery of her choice.

She had them rigged out in cream velvet jackets and breeches braided at the seams and Cavalier hats with tossing crimson plumes. Mary had made her a new gown of striped cream and crimson silk taken from the storage chest of rich fabrics, and she caused heads to turn as she set out in her spectacular attire and her own fine plumage. Sarah walked in front as her chaperone and she followed a few paces behind with the two boys in her wake, bows of crimson ribbon adorning the velvet-covered boxes that they carried. When a delivery meant riding by coach she always made sure that enough distance was left for her to be seen approaching on foot whatever shop happened to be her destination. Her aim was to make London aware of Pallister ribbons and she believed this would be a way of drawing attention to them. Sooner or later people would start asking who she was and what it could be that was so grandly borne along in such fanciful containers.

That evening Adam was coming to the Heathcock to take her out to supper. When getting ready she stamped her foot impatiently at Sarah's expectation to accompany her as chaperone.

"No! I'm going to marry this man and so surely I can be on my own with him for a little while. It's different by day when I need you to accompany me to the shops and in the streets, but Adam and I will have much to talk about and say to each other that would be stilted in a third person's company."

Sarah accepted defeat huffily. Julia thought that Mary would have been far more difficult to shake off, simply because she was a friend and not a servant, but there was little likelihood Mary would ever leave Patience to come to London again. Before Julia left the room she coaxed a smile out of Sarah by promising not to be late. Then, feeling she was on the wings of freedom, she hastened down the stairs to the hallway to await Adam.

He was a few minutes late when he came hurrying in and swept off his plumed hat to her. He explained that he had been at the House of Commons for most of the day and had left to meet her only at the hour previously arranged by letter. With the House of Lords restored again, Westminster had become a hive of old acquaintances greeting one another after long absences and he had been further delayed by a garrulous old earl who had known his grandfather.

"At least you're here now." She felt a little strange meeting him for the first time as her accepted betrothed.

As the evening was balmy they went by ferry-boat along the river to the re-opened Spring Pleasure Gardens at Vauxhall. To the accompaniment of music they ate at a table for two on a terrace under branches hung with coloured candle-lamps. Pavilions of entertainment shone brightly amidst similarly illuminated trees. People from all walks of life, richly adorned or simply clad, strolled the paths between the flowerbeds, taking in all there was to see.

"I have heard from Michael," she said, anxiety in her expression. "He wrote that he is still not well enough to travel even if he could leave Sophie during the last few months of her pregnancy, but he insists he will be at Sotherleigh for our marriage in September, by which time the baby will be a month old. It's taking far longer than I expected for him to recover. Did you think it would take all this time when you saw him?"

"He did look very thin and white, but was in good spirits at seeing someone with news of you and Sotherleigh. I've a feeling he'll never ail again once he is away from France. At present he's a homesick Englishman."

"But that's just it. He says he will be returning to Paris afterwards as Sophie can't travel with a small baby and he must be with her."

Adam, twirling his wine glass by its stem, raised an eyebrow. "Can't or won't?"

"What do you mean?"

"Am I allowed to give you a frank opinion of your brother's wife, who will soon be my French sister-in-law too?" he asked. When she nodded, he spoke thoughtfully as if recalling every detail about Sophie that had impressed him at the time. "I had barely had time to introduce myself to Michael and explain who I was—we had not met for many years and I thought recognition was unlikely—when Sophie came hurrying into the room. My impression was that she wished to miss nothing that I might say to him, because after we had exchanged courtesies she sat down on a chair between us, her head going to one and then the other of us like a spectator at a tennis match. I gathered that her English is not particularly good and she needed to watch as well as listen in order to catch all that was said."

"Why should that be unusual?"

"Only in that Michael had known from my first words to him that I had come on a matter important to me and suggested to her that she should go and see about some refreshment for me. Anyone else would then have retired tactfully, but she said it was all arranged and actually moved to stand by his chair to hold his hand and show that she intended to stay."

"You mean she has some power over him?"

"It was that of a nurse over a helpless patient."

"You didn't like her. I can tell."

"She is a handsome, fascinating woman and was most solicitous in seeing that his cushions were comfortable, keeping his rug warmly over his knees and smiling into his face a dozen times or more. He praised her to me for her care, whereupon she smiled with pleasure and looked triumphantly at me as if I had come to drive a wedge between them and failed."

"Could she be as possessive about him as Makepeace was over my mother, do you think?"

He meditated before he replied. "Only to suit some purpose of her own."

"She doesn't want him to come home?"

"I think that in spite of being distressed over his illness, it had its consolation for her since it saved the upheaval of her having to leave France with him. I met her father afterwards at dinner, an astute, sharp-eyed widower who spoke of Michael both as a beloved son-in-law and the king-pin of the business. Monsieur Brissard himself is getting older and would like to retire before long. I would say that neither father nor daughter wants Michael to come back to England. They would favour his being the absent owner of Sotherleigh, especially if the coming baby should be a son to follow him into the silk trade."

"Poor Michael! He must be torn between loyalties. I know how much he respects his father-in-law, who had the foresight to see his potential and promote him in the business before there was any question of a marriage with Sophie. I shall be thankful to see him again and hear what he has to say. Sotherleigh needs him now. It shouldn't have to wait until he comes home as an old man to live there."

"If he should remain in France would you like us to make Sotherleigh our country seat after we're wed?"

She looked at him incredulously. "You would close Warrender Hall?"

He shook his head. "No. I would offer it to my sister Meg and her children, who are now near Cambridge. She has been unhappily married there for some years and now her elderly husband is in his last days. Until she was forced into marriage by my parents she had a contented childhood at the Hall, whereas I was away at school most of the time and have fewer memories to tie me to it."

"What about Pegasus?"

His eyes smiled at her mention of the white pony. "The ownership of that little steed constituted one of my best memories—and seeing you in Chichester that day."

She looked amused. "Don't tell me that. When your father said that Warrenders had no truck with Royalists you looked at me with such hostility that I can remember it vividly now."

"You're wrong," he contradicted, equally amused. "I was angry that your family had made a Royalist of you and not with you personally. Yet I think in a way it was more than that. I was furious with the whole world for putting barriers between the pretty Pallister girl and me."

"At least there are no political differences to divide us now."

He reached across the table and closed his right hand over hers. "I look forward to our marriage when everything that has ever come between us will be gone."

It was too soon yet for her not to think instantly of Christopher in any mention of the future, but she hoped with time to overcome that clawing at her heart, which she had discovered could come without warning at any time. She chose not to dwell on what Adam had said and took up the subject of former divisions between others. "At our wedding breakfast there will be an equal number of guests from the old side of your fence as

there will be from my Royalist side. I think we should seat them alternately and then anything lingering from the past will be amended and
forgotten in the good wine and general merriment."

If he had noticed that she had shied away slightly from the hope he had
expressed, he showed no sign and grinned at her suggestion. "Let's see that
that is done."

She then told him more of the arrangements being made for the wedding ceremony, which was to take place in Chichester Cathedral since her
family and his had been generous benefactors in times past and he had a
bishop among his ancestors whose tomb was there. The latest Pallister gift
had been the beautiful chalice veil that Anne had embroidered and which
had been gratefully accepted.

When they had finished supper they joined the throngs of people
enjoying themselves. They watched a play in one grove and a display by
tumblers in another. Coming to a pavilion where country dancing was in
full swing, he swept her into it. They kicked up their heels and whirled
and twirled until with linked arms they escaped laughing and breathless
into the night air again. He guided her at once to a secluded rose bower to
sit on a bench there. When they had rested awhile and recovered their
breath, talking together, he took her left hand into his. Then from his
pocket he drew out a sapphire ring set ornamentally in gold and slid it
onto her third finger.

"Now we are truly betrothed, Julia."

Slowly she drew her hand from his to bring it close to her as she
looked down at the ring. The beautiful jewel had such depths of blue that
it was like looking forever into the limitless skies. It struck her forcibly
that she had given no thought to having a betrothal ring, which was such
a highlight to all the girls she had ever known who were to marry. For
them it had been a romantic token while for her it was simply a seal on a
promise given that would be kept.

"I have never seen a lovelier ring," she said with perfect truth.

"It can't compare with your eyes."

She was moved by his words. Whatever happened she would be good
to this man who cared for her. He was even prepared to relinquish his
home since he knew she had an aversion to crossing the threshold of the
house once owned by the man who had killed her father. Never should he
know that someone else blocked the way to her feeling for him as fully as
he would wish. Katherine had warned her that she would ruin her life if
she yearned after a man she could never have, but she knew now there

was such a thing as compromise. Had she not always been practical and clear-thinking in most matters? Therefore she accepted her loss, but would not, and could not, discard a bond that had always been part of it. Pallister women understood their responsibilities. Katherine had never disclosed to anyone her affair with Harry. Anne had kept from Makepeace her unswerving devotion to Robert. Why should she herself not follow that precedent? If a true and secret love was hidden away within the recesses of the heart, no hurt was caused to anyone. Adam should not be stinted. He should have all else that she had to give.

He was gathering her into his arms and she swayed against him where they sat, her lips parting to receive his kiss.

SHE MADE SEVERAL TRIPS to London in the ensuing weeks. There were those who had begun to look out for her with her box-carrying retinue. Sometimes she was in crimson from head to foot, at others in cream or her striped gown and she kept to these variations for the effect. On her second visit she had added the Needhams' six-year-old son to her procession. In cream and gold Oriental silk with a plumed turban, he walked in front of her with a posy from which floated streamers in the distinctive colours that denoted the Pallister ribbons.

It was on her third visit that she engaged one more person. She had noticed several times a mischievous little girl with a mop of red curls dancing barefoot in the courtyard for whatever pennies were thrown to her. Julia, arriving at the hostelry from Sussex one afternoon, saw the child again. Sending Sarah upstairs to unpack, she beckoned the sprite-like dancer over to her.

"Come here. I want to speak to you."

The child skipped across to her. "Yes, madam."

"What is your name?"

"Nell Gwyn." The heart-shaped face was impish, the eyes sparkling and merry, the mouth controlled by smiles and laughter.

"I'm Miss Pallister. How old are you?"

"Ten. Eleven on the second day of next February."

Julia thought her small for her age, but there was the knowingness of the street urchin about her that belied her being any younger. "Where do you live, Nell?"

"With my ma, who pulls pints at the tavern in Russell Street, and my sister, Rose."

"But what is your address?"

"Coal Yard Alley off Drury Lane."

"That's near here. Would your mother be at home now?"

"I expect so." The little bare feet were dancing on the spot as if of their own volition. "She's on evening work and don't go no sooner than she has to."

"I'd like to call on her. Show me the way, Nell."

She took the grubby hand of the child who skipped along beside her. In a way Nell reminded her of herself at that age when it had been more natural to dance and run and leap than to walk normally. Nell chattered all the way.

"My pa was a captain in the King's army. Then when the war ended he and Ma lived in Hereford where he became a brewer. That's where Rose and me were born. When old wart-faced Oliver Cromwell died, my pa thought the King would come back the same day and celebrated a mite too soon. He was clapped into prison and there he died. Poor Pa." She heaved a big sigh and let go of Julia's hand to mimic the expression and stately tread of those who carried a black plume at the head of a funeral cortège. It was a cameo performance done as a mark of respect and within seconds she was her merry self again while Julia still had eyebrows raised at the perfect little enactment.

"Is that when you came back to London, Nell?"

The red curls nodded vigorously. "Ma was born in the same house where we are now. She was glad to get back and Rose and me like London better than anywhere else."

"Except for one special place in Sussex that is my home, I would agree with you, Nell. London is a wonderfully exciting place."

The name of Coal Yard Alley was well suited to the filthy, narrow place flanked by ugly timber-framed tenements. Nell released Julia's hand and jumped down some stone steps to a door at cellar level and opened it to bawl to her mother that there was a lady visitor. Julia, whose hems were heel-high, gathered up her skirts to avoid contact with the dirty stone steps as she followed the child into the house.

The room in which she found herself neither looked nor smelt at all clean. It was crowded with furniture, including some finely carved pieces which spoke of more prosperous days in Hereford. There was a half-emptied bottle of strong spirit on the table and a used glass. Beyond an archway there came the sound of footsteps hastening down some creaking stairs.

"There's a lady in here, Ma!" Nell called. "Her name is Miss Pallister!"

Mrs. Gwyn appeared, looking flustered. She was plump with high colour in her cheeks, her hair a darker red than her daughter's and some remnants of an earlier prettiness in her round face. The sight of Julia, well dressed in travelling attire, made her mouth drop open, but she recovered herself immediately.

"Pray sit down, Miss Pallister." She had an excessively genteel manner of speaking. Nell sprang forward to wipe the dust off a chair with a swirl of her ragged petticoat and then stood back for the visitor to take it.

"Thank you, Nell," Julia said smiling.

Mrs. Gwyn had just spotted the bottle on the table and she made an involuntary flutter with her hands as if she would have liked to hide it away somehow. "To what do I owe this honour, Miss—was it Pallister that Nell said?"

Julia then explained the way in which she was trying to draw the attention of London to her ribbons and asked if Nell could join her retinue. "I thought she would complete the little procession with her dancing feet."

A greedy look came into the woman's eyes. "What would you pay?"

When Julia said what it would be, Nell, who had perched herself on a chair and was swinging her legs, uttered an exclamation. "Cor! A bob a day for being dressed up like a lady. I only get that for a week's work at Mrs. Ross's place."

"Be quiet, Nell," Mrs. Gwyn admonished testily.

Julia was surprised. "I didn't realise that Nell was already employed."

"She only dances in her spare time," her mother replied, "but her job has adjustable hours and I'm sure Mrs. Ross would have no objection to releasing her whenever you are in London."

"Mrs. Ross keeps a whorehouse," Nell piped up. "I don't have nothing to do with what goes on upstairs. I serve watered wine to the girls and strong liquor to the gentlemen, who have to pay the same high price for both drinks. When there's a bit of strong liquor left in the bottles I pour it all into another that I bring home to Ma."

Mrs. Gwyn's fingers twitched as if she yearned to slap Nell into silence and she managed a ghastly smile. "It's very hard for a widow left almost penniless to find honest work for her daughters these days, but, as you heard, Rose and Nell are simply waiting at the tables."

"I'm aiming to open a ribbon-making and embroidery workshop in London," Julia said, thinking that the sooner Nell was out of Mrs. Ross's establishment the better it would be for the child. "I could offer both your daughters work there."

Again Nell spoke up irrepressibly. "Ma gets commission on the country girls she sends to Mrs. Ross when they come asking at the Russell Street tavern for work, always telling them that her own daughters are employed there, and so we've got to stay. In any case, Rose and me don't know one end of a needle from another, but I do want to be your carrying maid."

It was settled. At her mother's nod of the head, Nell made a pot of hot chocolate and brought it from the kitchen with three pretty cups taken specially from a shelf and which, although chipped and cracked, again hinted at a better life known in Captain Gwyn's lifetime. Mrs. Gwyn poured the chocolate. She had become more relaxed now she knew that Julia, for all she was a lady, was in trade, no matter how elegant her ribbon wares.

"You mentioned having a ribbon-making workshop. Where did you plan on opening it?" she asked.

"I've had no real chance to look at much property yet," Julia replied. "What I have seen hasn't proved suitable."

"I know of some premises to rent in Carter Lane. An old seamstress who used to sew for me has just given them up. If you stepped in quick you might get the place at the same rent."

"That sounds interesting. I've been told that once I have premises I'll only have to put up a notice offering work and I'll get all the embroiderers and weavers that I'll need."

"That's right. Many needlewomen doing fancy work have been on hard times throughout the Commonwealth years and you'll get the pick of the best workers if you don't delay. Would you like me to take you to that workshop in Carter Lane?"

"I'd appreciate that very much."

Mrs. Gwyn, excited by the prospect of an outing, put on her hat and gloves, sent Nell off to Mrs. Ross's establishment and then she and Julia rode in a hackney coach to Carter Lane. It was near St. Paul's and was not a lane such as Julia knew from home, for over a century or two it had become a busy street, lined with shops and workshops. Mrs. Gwyn collected a key from the hosier next door to the old seamstress's former domain and she and Julia entered the premises. It had been left rubbish-littered, with cobwebs that would have been there in Cromwell's time shadowing the ceiling corners and hanging from the old beams, but there was an upper floor with some solid tables of smooth planks on which fabrics would have been cut and with windows on three sides that would give plenty of light once the broken panes were replaced.

"This would suit me if the rent is right," Julia said when she had inspected everywhere. The fact that she was shortly to marry a rich man did not come into it, because this was entirely her project. In any case she would never have allowed Adam to contribute to ease the amount she felt she owed her brother. This she had already made clear to him and he had agreed to place no hindrance in her way.

The landlord's address was on a label attached to the key and Julia found him a few streets away. He was a wine cooper and there was a rich and heady aroma of wines when he showed her through to his office. When she pointed out that the roof of the property in Carter Lane needed repair and the stairs were unsafe, he agreed to put everything right by the end of the month when her tenancy would start. He saw in her appearance and her elegant home address a new and potentially profitable customer, especially as she spoke of being married in the early autumn and then living in London herself. For that reason he did not put the rent up, but let her have it at what it was before, knowing he could always raise it later once she was established there and would not want to move.

By the time her wedding day drew near she had fifteen experienced ribbon embroiderers and five weavers at her London workshop and planned to take on more hands in the country as well as the city to meet an increasing demand. Shopkeepers already came out into the street to bow her into their shops when she came with her deliveries, knowing that customers would follow her inside out of curiosity or because they had already heard of the Pallister ribbons. Gentlemen doffed their hats to Julia in the street when she passed with her retinue, which had been made more eye-catching since Nell now preceded her dressed in a replica of whatever gown and hat she was wearing that day.

Nell loved these days of delivery. Julia had introduced her to a new existence of being clean with spotless petticoats and lovely gowns to wear. Sometimes she just had to break into a little dance with the small gilded box that was hers to carry. The boy in the gilded turban who paraded ahead of her had sulked at first when she took attention away from him, but she never liked to have enemies and pointed out that Miss Pallister was the one everybody really noticed. Then she had consoled him with the gift of a toffee apple to eat when the day was done. After that there was no rivalry between them and she bought him and herself a toffee apple whenever her mother gave her back a halfpenny to spend after pocketing all else that she had earned.

Although Julia's days in London, usually a week at a time, were spent in deliveries or at her workshop where she had a competent woman-embroiderer in charge, her evenings and her Sundays, unless she happened to be travelling to or from London, were reserved for Adam. He showed her over Westminster Hall and St. Stephen's Chapel where the Commons sat. They went down the river to Greenwich and upstream to Hampton Court where during the day they watched a tennis match being played by courtiers where once Henry VIII had wielded a racquet.

At the Tower she saw the steps by Traitors' Gate where Elizabeth, only a young princess then, had been landed by boat and where she had crouched weeping for hours, refusing to move and believing erroneously that her half-sister, Queen Mary, had the executioner waiting with his axe for her. Yet there were those in the Tower, somewhere out of sight as Julia and Adam strolled with other visitors in the grounds, who were awaiting trial and possible execution. These were the regicides, only a few having managed to escape arrest. The bodies of Oliver Cromwell and two other prominent Parliamentarians had been disinterred from Westminster Abbey and hung gruesomely in a cage on the Tyburn tree to stay there until they rotted away.

This was the only dark spot in a London that continued to be possessed by gaiety. Foreigners were swarming into the city for the entertainments and jollity, and when a cynic remarked that there was a greater variety of clap in London than anywhere else in Europe nobody listened and the brothels continued to rake in money. Innumerable taverns had been re-named the Black Boy after the King's long-held nickname, or else the choice was for the Royal Oak or the Oak Apple to commemorate his escape after the Battle of Worcester, and all did a roaring trade. There was drunkenness in the streets such as had never been seen during the Commonwealth when flogging was a deterrent, at least to reeling about in public if not within the privacy of the home. It was the same with bull-baiting and cock-fighting, which had been carried on secretly in spite of Cromwell's ban. Since these were now permitted openly again, Adam made sure that Julia never glimpsed the arenas, for she had an unfashionable respect for animals and could not have tolerated such sport.

She was fascinated by the theatre and he took her to dramas and comedies. They would have supper afterwards where there was a hospitable atmosphere and he knew the food and wine would be good. If they walked back a shortish distance to the Heathcock a link-boy showed them the way through the unlit streets or ran ahead of the horses if they rode by coach. These bobbing golden lights were a feature of the London scene and took on a new dimension when the link-boys escorted folk in ferryboats to the other side of the river, filling the Thames with reflected, shining spangles.

Once on her own Julia went to Gresham College, knowing that Christopher would be lecturing there that day. She sat for a little while on a seat within the gates, refusing to admit to herself that she hoped he might glimpse her from a window and come hurrying out of the building to her in his smiling, eager way. Lots of people came and went without giving her a glance. After a time she left again and sought refuge in a small, deserted courtyard. There she leaned her forearm against the trunk of a tree, rested her brow on the back of her wrist and wept desolately. It was a private moment, known only to herself, and she knew such tears were useless since nothing could bring Christopher back to her.

Adam taught her to play pell-mell and they competed against each other with mallets, wooden balls and hoops among other players in St. James's Park. Bowls was another game in which she matched, somewhat inadequately, her skill against his, for he had an eye like a needle and could direct a bowl unerringly. They went riding together and once, when on foot, resting their horses, they saw the King on his daily morning ride in the park. His eyes and his smile were on Julia when he acknowledged from the saddle her deep curtsy and Adam's bow.

Throughout the times they spent together Julia and Adam discussed many matters, argued over more, laughed, quarrelled and kissed. If Sarah had not been in the room adjoining her bedchamber, always with the door ajar, Julia knew he would never have left her on its threshold, night after night with his eyes saying many things before once again he went clattering away downstairs. Once, as he was leaving, she crossed the landing to look over the banisters at him. He must have heard her hastening footsteps, because he paused on the way down and looked up at her, his dark eyes narrowed and he grinned slowly.

"Just wait, my lovely lady," he said between a threat and a promise.

She chuckled softly and threw him a tantalising kiss from her fingertips before darting back into the safety of her room in case he should come chasing after her. When she had closed the door she leaned back against it, smiling to herself. At least with Adam nothing was ever dull or boring. How he would be as a lover and husband was beyond her experience to imagine, but she did not think she would be disappointed.

# FIFTEEN

SOPHIE gave birth to a healthy boy. He had been baptised Jean-Robert after his French and English grandfathers and was four weeks old by the time the news reached Sotherleigh.

"An heir for Sotherleigh," Julia exclaimed jubilantly to Adam and Mary, who were both with her when Michael's letter arrived. "There must be a glass of wine for us and all the staff, both indoors and out!"

Adam did not spoil the moment for her with a reminder that the child was also heir to the Brissard silk business, but as he raised his glass with everyone else, he wondered which country Jean-Robert would come to think of as his homeland. He hoped the child would grow to honour both lands equally, for there had been and still were too many divisions keeping people apart in the world. He had this in mind when he discovered from the completed list of acceptances from the invited wedding guests that the Steyning branch of Julia's family had not been included.

"I didn't want them to come," she explained. "They were so miserly with their offers of help when Mama turned to them in her time of need."

"Didn't you say they had sons and daughters around your age and mine? Are those of our generation to be left out through the selfishness of the parents?"

"But they'll all come if they're invited," she protested. "It's always those who are asked out of a sense of duty who never refuse and turn up."

"Then ask them all! Young and old! The time for rifts is over."

"I suppose you're right," she acquiesed on a reluctant sigh.

The last-minute invitations were sent and were accepted by return. It then meant that since there were so many coming from Steyning every guest room in Sotherleigh would be full, for it was accepted generally that priority was always given to relatives even if it meant that close friends had to stay elsewhere. Accommodation had already been bespoken at hostelries in Chichester, for the Hall was to be full of Adam's relatives and more rooms now had to be reserved. Fortunately Mr. and Mrs. Hannington offered to accommodate William and Susan as well as Christopher and Faith.

As the wedding day drew near all the rooms were made ready at Sotherleigh. Special attention was given to the master bedchamber in the east wing, for it was here that Michael would sleep for the first time as Master of Sotherleigh. Julia could guess what it would mean to him to be coming home again, even though it was to be for no more than ten days this time. Mary, full of her own loving thoughts about him, made sure that the best Pallister linen was on his bed. The narrow strips of linen that made up sheets and pillow cases always had their seams covered by embroidery to give the effect of lace, but for him she selected those worked in black, red and gold silks, which looked magnificent. It was also she who made sure the day-covers for the pillows were the most sumptuous at Sotherleigh; with the coverlet of her choice, they reflected in a floral pattern worked in gold and silver the ornate Elizabethan bed-hangings that again gave such splendour to the room.

When Julia awoke on her wedding morning the house was full of the Steyning folk, who had arrived the evening before, but Michael had not appeared. She and Mary had watched for him in vain, for he had been due for the past week. Throughout that time there had been fierce gales blowing along the Channel in some of the worst weather for years. Sea defences had been flooded, moored fishing-boats smashed to smithereens, and from wreckage washed up it was feared several vessels had been lost. It was her hope that his ship had stayed safely in Calais harbour and had not ventured out. Yesterday the wind had eased and now the morning had dawned with brilliant sunshine. From her pillows in the bed where she awaited Sarah's arrival with her breakfast tray, she could see a late September sky of such a clear blue that it seemed to be pretending it had never shed the torrents of rain that had accompanied the rough weather.

Normally she was always up for breakfast, but this was a special day. She had spent her last night in this bed, for she and Adam were to have Katherine's apartment for their own until such time as Michael came home for good. Then she would have to resign herself to being at Warrender Hall whenever she and Adam were not in London. Such an aversion to that house had built up in her that she did not know how she would be able to cross the threshold, but she would meet that obstacle when it came. In the meantime Katherine's rooms, always fresh and airy from the handsome windows, had been refurbished throughout and the old wedding chair and footstool returned to the place they had first occupied in the Queen's Parlour. Ned's portrait had been removed to the Long Gallery where it hung side by side with Katherine's.

Julia put her feet to the floor, pulled on a robe and padded across to the open window. She set her elbows on the ledge and rested her chin on her hands, her face turned to the sunshine. She wondered how much Adam regretted having to stay with her at Sotherleigh instead of her going with him to the Hall. He had made light of it since he would still be master there and would be keeping his horses in its larger stables, only a few riding horses and Charlie being brought to Sotherleigh. He would also continue to conduct affairs of the estate from his own study, even though his recently widowed sister, Meg, had moved in with her five children.

"In any case the London house will be our main home together for the time being," he had said. Before settling on a property, he had taken her to see those he preferred and let her decide which it should be. Both of them had wanted spacious rooms, a garden for privacy and a house of pleasing appearance. He also wanted to be close to Westminster and Whitehall, while she had never forgotten her childhood wish to have a window from which she could see the King ride by. In complete agreement they chose a house on the south side of the Strand that looked out on the river and had high garden walls that kept at bay the street cries of those selling wares and the endless rumble of wheels. She had put from her that ideal of having a house built by Christopher. It belonged to the time when she had been able to love him and neither Adam nor Faith yet stood between them.

William Holder had agreed by letter to give the bride away should Michael be delayed by any whim of circumstance. By rights it should have been one of her father's Steyning cousins, but although she and Anne had received the head of that family and the rest courteously, she did not want to go up the aisle on his arm. Those of her generation were a jolly bunch, only one sobersides among them, and she was glad Adam had insisted that she should invite that branch of the family. As soon as she had had breakfast she would send a note to William confirming that he would fill Michael's role.

It had been typical of the Hanningtons that they should offer hospitality. She would miss them if they had to leave, for the original Royalist owners had applied for a desequestration order to regain their property. There were countless numbers of landless Royalists putting in these applications and Michael had had to send signed legal papers to ensure that Sotherleigh reverted to him automatically; because Makepeace had been a regicide there had been no delay in his claim, and he promptly received the royal seal granting it back to him.

Others were less fortunate. All the leading regicides, after trials of meticulous fairness, had been hanged, drawn and quartered. Others had been imprisoned and a few pardoned. It was not in the King's nature to be vengeful and after his father's murderers had been dealt with he was reluctant to penalise former enemies by uprooting them from properties now their homes, even when it meant that those who had been loyal to the Stuarts had to suffer. He had granted pensions to those persons who had helped him to escape after the Battle of Worcester, but the great rewards and honours that had been expected by many had not been forthcoming, only a few titles being bestowed. In certain cases where the holder and all his heirs to a title had been killed, some concessions were made. It was apparent to all that he had turned his back on anything that reminded him of his exile and wanted only to look to the future.

There came a tap on the bedchamber door. Julia looked over her shoulder, mildly surprised that Sarah should announce herself, for normally she came quietly at this hour to awake her. "Come in."

The door opened, the breakfast tray appeared and Michael was carrying it. Julia gave a cry of joy and ran across to him. "You're here! Welcome home to Sotherleigh."

He put aside the tray, which bore breakfast for both of them, and they hugged each other. "Nothing was going to make me miss your wedding!"

"Have you seen Mama? She's like a happy child as I wrote you."

"I went to her first. I'm glad she has grasped that I'm living in Paris."

She stood back, holding him by the arms and looking anxiously at him. "Are you completely well again?"

"I've never been fitter than I am now." His healthy colour and the extra weight he had put on since she had last seen him confirmed his words. "It's lucky I don't suffer from sea-sickness or else I might have been in a sorry state after yesterday's crossing. I stayed last night at the George and Dragon at Houghton and made an early start before dawn this morning to get here in good time."

"I'm so thankful to see you. How is Jean-Robert? Is he a handsome baby?"

"There's never been another to match him," he declared with pride. "I only wish I could have brought my wife and son with me, but naturally it wouldn't have been wise to expose him to infection on a ship."

"I agree." She hesitated for a moment in a change of mood. "I want you to prepare yourself for some bad news about the Sotherleigh fortune. Try to steel yourself."

The skin seemed to tighten over the bones of his face. "Did Makepeace take it when he left?"

She nodded miserably. "I didn't realise he had discovered the Queen's Door. The blame is entirely mine. I can't hope to make it up to you now, but I have devised a scheme by which over the years I can at least return to you some part of what was yours."

"Come now, Julia." He spoke in a kindly manner although the shock of his loss still showed in his face. "Let's have breakfast while you tell me about it. I must say I need a cup from that pot of coffee on the tray and I'm sure you do too. But tell me first, how is Mary?"

In answering, she also enquired about Sophie and he said she had had a difficult pregnancy, having ailed most of the time. "That is the reason why I have to return to her as soon as possible. She was quite distraught at my coming away, although the baby is doing extremely well." He thought to himself how his wife had changed towards him as soon as it became clear that the Restoration was to become a certainty. She began to show a passion in his arms of which he would never have deemed her capable. It was almost as if she feared losing him to his roots at Sotherleigh, for when he talked eagerly of going home she had revealed a sudden panic at the prospect of moving to an alien land, needing his most firm reassurance.

Yet in spite of all he had said to her, promising her return visits to see her father, he believed his illness on the eve of his intended departure to join the King's followers at Breda had been a blessing in disguise for her. She had been the most devoted nurse by night and day, not letting anyone else care for him, although already pregnant from the nights *extraordinaires* they had shared beforehand. Then, as he had convalesced to a full recovery, she had virtually collapsed from the strain of her unselfish nursing. He could not in all conscience have left her at that time to come home to Sotherleigh, and had to wait until she had had the baby.

It had not been easy leaving her to come to the wedding. He thought it must have been a nervous reaction to her distress at his going that he had a recurrence of the stomach pains that had heralded his illness before. But he had hidden his condition from her and had been thankful that the few days of waiting for calmer weather in which to cross the Channel had given him a chance to recover and he was wondering why, if these pains were of nervous origin, he had not been reafflicted now. It was astonishing, for the theft of his fortune was an enormous catastrophe beyond even his sister's comprehension for reasons he would have to break to her presently.

Over breakfast, which they ate at a table by one of the windows, Julia explained how she had wanted to tell him face to face about the loss of his fortune instead of letting him know in the letter she had written to describe Makepeace's hasty departure. Then she spoke of her ribbon business. "You are my silent partner in the business, because I take out only the expenses and all the profit is banked for you."

He shook his head slowly. "That I will not allow. I can't see that Makepeace's thievery lies in any way with you. Were you supposed to have eyes in the back of your head? Also, I consider I was equally at fault as I knew when I was last here—hiding in the secret room—that the treasure was concealed in the old chest. I should at least have suggested it should be split up and concealed in different places, or maybe buried again."

"But he must have spied on someone going through the Queen's Door and it was likely to have been me."

"You have no proof of that. How do you know he didn't just make his own investigations and chance upon the secret?"

"Whatever happened, I was in charge of Sotherleigh in your absence. No matter what you say I shall continue to do as I have told you." She refilled his cup with coffee and then her own. "Don't think it is going to be a burden to me. I'm keenly interested and I'm giving employment to a lot of women in need of it."

"If good is coming out of it, then I'll no longer try to stop you, but your stalwart intentions won't fill my coffers to the extent I'm going to need from now on."

"What do you mean?"

"Sophie has extravagant tastes. I could not turn her into a poor man's wife here at Sotherleigh. I know Sophie. She would never stay. For the sake of our child the two of us must remain united even if it means I have to stay in France."

Julia struggled with her disappointment. "This makes everything so much worse. I agree that you must do what is best for your baby. Nobody knows better than I what it meant to have Father away at the war and then to lose him. There's a dreadful lack for a child when one parent is not there. What will your plans be now?"

"The partnership you offered me in your ribbon business was the second proposition put to me in little more than a week. Just before I left Paris my father-in-law invited me to be his partner with full control of the Brissard silk business, enabling him to more or less retire. It was something few men would have been able to resist, but I gave him no hope of my acceptance then. Now I shall take it up and trust to recoup the losses Makepeace inflicted on me until such time in years to come when it will be possible to come home to Sussex one day."

"I hoped that Sophie's dowry would help you at this time."

He smiled wryly and shook his head. "Her dowry was shares in the business. I have been very neatly trapped in one way or another."

"Makepeace has much to answer for!" she exclaimed jerkily, deeply distressed.

"Don't upset yourself, Julia." He reached across the breakfast table and took hold of her wrist. "This is your wedding day. Let's count our blessings. Sotherleigh could easily have passed out of Pallister hands for ever if any Roundhead other than Makepeace had staked possession here. I'm home now and in future I'll be able to visit on a fairly regular basis to see to the estate. The bailiff's reports and the copies of the accounts you've been sending show that at least everything is running moderately well, although naturally I aim for changes and improvements. There's also great cause for celebration in your marrying a neighbour whose family was close to ours before the rift of the Civil War. I wish you all happiness and let it begin now. No more sad thoughts on this special day."

When Michael left Julia he approached Mary's door and had almost reached it when she emerged from the bedchamber, holding the hand of Patience, who was toddling beside her. She turned pale when she saw him and for a moment neither spoke as they drank in the sight of each other.

"I've missed you, Mary, my dearest."

"It's good that you are here." She had to establish a more distant footing immediately. "Does Julia know?"

"I've breakfasted with her." His gaze went to Patience, who immediately closed in shyly against Mary's skirts. Dropping to one knee in order to bring his face more on a level with the child's, he smiled at her.

"Greetings, my little half-sister. Now you shall see what I've brought you all the way from Paris." He put his hand in his pocket and drew out a wooden doll dressed in the cap, apron and bright blue gown that were worn by the stall-keepers of Les Halles where he had purchased it.

Patience's eyes widened and she reached for it eagerly. "Dolly! Me!"

He drew her to him and kissed her round cheek as he handed the doll to her. As she amused herself with it he straightened up again. Then Mary saw such love for her in his eyes that her assumption that he had made a new beginning with Sophie through the conception of their child was swept away. He was about to reach for her when the clatter of footsteps and the clink of pewter jugs warned that maidservants were approaching with bath water for the bride.

"Patience and I will see you later," she said, snatching up the child. "We're going to have breakfast now."

She almost fled from him, alarmed by the powerful feelings that had swirled between them like an invisible current. This was not as she had intended it should be and their desire for each other must be stemmed throughout his visit.

The cloud that had fallen over Julia since hearing that Michael must remain in France did not disperse during her bath or the drying of her newly washed hair afterwards. Sarah, in attendance, was in her element. To dress a bride was the pinnacle of the career of any lady's maid and she had taken the greatest care in the preparation of all the garments that were to be worn. She had personally supervised the laundering of the undergarments, pressing the lace frills herself as well as every ribbon which she had removed from the eyelets to re-thread. The Elizabethan gown was free of any creases, having been arrayed on a wicker frame for days. It was now laid out across the coverlet of the bed and on the floor were the gold satin shoes with the white rosettes that Katherine had worn on her wedding day.

Julia sat in front of her mirror, the original frame of which had once been hurled at the man she was about to marry. Almost half-heartedly she emphasised her eyes with a line of kohl, then touched her lips with a coral salve prepared by Sarah. Like all the cosmetics that Sarah made, it was from floral or herbal ingredients that were harmless, unlike many cosmetics that were offered for sale. A light dusting of powder over her face and neck, her shoulders and breasts completed her beautifying. Lastly she added a few drops of rose-water to her wrists, behind her ears and at her cleavage.

Then as Sarah dressed her hair into shoulder-length ringlets bunched on either side of her face, she pondered sadly her brother's plight. He had always been kind and loyal. Katherine had said many times he was too soft-hearted for his own good, but she had used an affectionate tone, showing that although he exasperated her, she did not condemn him for his charitable nature.

"There, Miss Julia! Your hair is done. Do you like it?" Sarah held up a hand-glass to enable the bride to see the reflected back of her head in the mirror. Julia saw that her hair went smoothly up to her top-knot, the wisps at the nape of her neck formed into kiss-curls.

"Yes, indeed." She tried to sound enthusiastic. It was a perfect coiffure, but nothing could shift her gloom. Standing up, she slipped off her robe and stood naked for Sarah to lower an undershift over her head without disturbing her coiffure, and then she tied the ribbons herself. Her six waist petticoats were stepped into and fastened at the back. Then she sat down again to pull on her white silk stockings to the knee, where she secured them with the blue silk garters that Mary had made for her and had embroidered with hearts and love knots. Next came the shoes. Her spirits lifted as she raised one foot and then the other to inspect them, the gilded heels shining as she rotated her ankle. She thought, as she had done when first seeing the shoes in childhood, they were like fairy footwear that would enable the wearer to dance on air.

The moment had come for the gown itself. When she had tried it on previously for Mary to inspect for alterations it had fitted her faultlessly. She would not be wearing the ruff, for Adam had given her a necklet of pearls as his wedding gift and she wanted to display them. Neither would she wear the farthingale, for it would have lifted the hems quite high, whereas without it the skirt fell softly from the waist to the merest fraction from the floor. She had experienced a sensuous pleasure in its satin softness against her skin and anticipation rose in her as Sarah lifted the gown reverently from the bed to hold it for her. As with the petticoats, she stepped into it and drew it up to put her arms into the sleeves. Sarah went behind her to draw it over her shoulders and began lacing it up at the back. A long mirror of Venetian glass, one that Robert had brought back from a voyage to the Adriatic as a present for Katherine, had been moved into Julia's room, but she avoided looking in it, not wanting to see herself until all was done.

Again the satin was like a caress and the thickly embroidered elongated centre panel of the bodice, which reached to a point below her waist, was not in the least stiff or uncomfortable. If she had been a cat she would have purred; instead she stood stroking the gathers of the skirt, a smile on her lips. Three women before her had found happiness in this gown: Elizabeth and Katherine and then her own mother, distraught and fey, had known a respite of joy by dressing up in it.

Someone tapped on the door and then it opened. It was Anne, fully dressed for the day in a gown of shimmering rose satin and a wide-brimmed hat cocked up at the side that set off her still lovely, if thinner and older, face and her same sweet smile. She brought the wedding posy that Julia would carry and exclaimed at the sight of her.

"How exquisite you look! Not even in her youth could Elizabeth have matched you in her gown!"

"I thank you, Mama. You look beautiful yourself." They kissed each other.

Watching was another lady's maid named Molly, who had come with Anne and was bearing on a tray of damp moss the floral coronet for the bride, both it and the posy having been made up from Sotherleigh blooms by one of the gardeners' wives, who excelled at the craft. Molly was Julia's new lady's maid, it being the first time Julia had had her own personal maid since Phoebe had attended her. Since she was to be away from Sotherleigh most of the time now she could no longer share Sarah with her mother. She suspected Molly was feeling put out at not being able to dress her on this special day, but Sarah would have been hurt not to have had the privilege after so many years with the family. So for today, Molly had dressed Anne instead.

Sarah picked up the little velvet-lined silver casket that held the bride-groom's gift and opened it. Julia took out a pair of pearl ear-bobs to fasten them in her lobes and then the necklet, which she held against the base of her throat. Sarah hooked the clasp.

"Now it's your turn, madam," Sarah prompted, seeing Anne was still gazing raptly at the bride.

"Oh, yes." Anne took the coronet from the moss and raised it high to place it on Julia's head. Then she stood back admiringly. "Now look in the mirror, dearest child."

Julia turned and saw reflected her own radiance. She barely recognised herself, feeling transformed by the gown's magnificence. Every embroidered blossom might have been freshly plucked to lie on the shimmering satin. A tiny diamond here and there simulated dew. The low neckline showed how much of their bosoms Tudor women revealed, but since her breasts had the roundness and fullness she had wished for in early adolescence she saw no reason to cover herself. The trimming of the wonderful drop-pearls was rivalled by Adam's gift and yet each could have been deliberately made to enhance the other, stirring the memory of her childhood dream with its atmosphere of beauty and happiness.

The late rosebuds of Sotherleigh, gathered only that morning, were in the same creamy tint as the gown and nestled on the shining chestnut of her hair. When her mother had married it would have been unthinkable to wear the garment as a wedding gown, even if it had belonged to a Queen, for the style would have been considered old-fashioned to the point of dowdiness, no matter how splendid the fabric. But now the gown had come full circle and what would have been regarded as quaint by the previous generation had become charming, and what had been despised was now to be praised.

A question came to Julia's lips without any previous thought. "Will Adam find me beautiful?"

There was a chorus of assent from Anne and Sarah, Molly joining in, although as a newcomer she knew her voice should not be heard. Plain, sensible and conscientious about her duties, she intended to prove herself as capable as Sarah. Hearing a tap on the door again, she admitted Mary, who was to attend the bride. Holding her hand was Patience, who came toddling in, her peach-coloured silk gown fluttering with ribbons embroidered with harebells. There was chatter and laughter and praise for one another's appearance.

Patience, who had been gazing wide-eyed at the bride's finery, stretched out a finger to touch the shimmering skirt. Julia stooped down to her. "If you wish, this shall be your wedding gown one day."

Then Mary reminded Anne it was time to leave. "All the guests have gone from the house and we should make a start ahead of Michael and Julia."

Anne's face suddenly clouded anxiously, bewilderment in her eyes, "Why isn't Robert here to give his daughter away?"

Mary, who had become Anne's close companion during Julia's absences, answered her in a simple, reassuring manner. "He was here until he rode off to Edgehill."

Immediately Anne's expression cleared. "So he was. His Majesty must be needing Robert's advice on how to deal mercifully with Cromwell, because nothing less important would have taken my husband from Sotherleigh today." Completely satisfied, she kissed Julia, who embraced her, and then guided Patience from the room, chatting happily to the child as they went.

Julia looked gratefully at Mary. "You have become a rock to us all at Sotherleigh and especially to Mama."

"If it lies in my power," Mary replied firmly, "nothing shall ever hurt Anne again, even if I do have to invent a little tale sometimes to put her poor mind at rest." She glanced at the clock. "I must join her and Patience now. I'll be waiting at the Cathedral door."

"Tell Michael I'll be down in a moment."

Mary nodded and left. Sarah made a final check that the bride's appearance was perfect. Then she stood aside. "The master is waiting for you in the Queen's Parlour, Miss Julia."

It pleased Julia to hear Michael referred to by his rightful title. Sotherleigh had been without its rightful master for too long. She was sure he would come home as often as possible and perhaps with time he could persuade Sophie to come with him. Then their son could be introduced to his heritage. She hoped for children herself, an heir for Warrender Hall and a daughter who would play with the doll's house that Christopher had made and which she still had standing on a chest here in her bedchamber. She glanced across at it. Somewhere in the distances of her heart there was a pang, but as ever, the gown was working its magic. She was conscious only of feeling beautiful and composed, all troubles temporarily subdued.

She took the posy of Sotherleigh flowers that Sarah handed to her. It was tied with a bow of Anne's snowdrop ribbon, streamers flowing. "Now I will go downstairs."

She went slowly down the Grand Staircase. By the portrait of Elizabeth she paused and it seemed to her that those eyes, dark as olives, were looking approvingly at her this day, just as Katherine would have done.

She found Michael in the Queen's Parlour, looking more like a French courtier in his rather fanciful Parisian clothes than an English gentleman. He nodded with enthusiasm at her appearance.

"You look very grand, Julia. I'm proud to be your brother today."

"Only today?" she retaliated, jokingly.

"No," he replied seriously. "You're a true Pallister woman. I can't think of a greater compliment to pay you."

"Or one I'd rather receive." There was a catch in her voice. "I do wish Father could still have been here for this day and Grandmother too."

"I'm sure they are in spirit," he answered her comfortingly. Then he offered her his arm and she rested her fingers on his raised wrist as he led her out of the Queen's Parlour.

The door of the entrance hall stood wide to the sunny morning. From the Great Hall where the wedding feast was to be served, the servants there had taken a few minutes off to watch the bride go through. The household staff had been increased for Adam's coming at his expense, and with the extra hands hired for the festivities a small crowd bowed or bobbed to her, the women sighing over the gown. On the steps outside more servants lined the way down to the waiting coach, which was decked with garlands. She waved to them when she had taken her seat and continued waving down the drive to the groundsmen and gardeners, their wives and children, who had gathered to wish her well on her wedding day. Beyond the gates and down through the village, tenants and other inhabitants waved while all her workers from Briar House had brought their brightest ribbons to flutter in salute as she rode by. Then it was on through the countryside until the coach reached Chichester and drew up at the steps of the Cathedral. Michael helped her to alight, spoke to her encouragingly and then led her through the great west doors.

The organ, which had been silenced during Cromwell's rule, thundered forth as they advanced up the aisle of the Norman nave. Faces were turned to them on each side, many having gathered for the joining of two respected families. Julia looked straight ahead to where Adam awaited her with his groomsman, a friend from his Cambridge days, at his side. In keeping with tradition he did not turn to watch her approach, although she kept her gaze on him. He was in cloth of gold, and the sunshine, pouring through the high windows to pattern the floor, set his attire ashimmer as it did hers and struck blue lights in the blackness of his hair. The bishop waited, framed by the medieval stone screen. The choir, fresh-faced boys angelic in their robes and solemn men, filled the ancient stalls. Beyond was the presbytery and the bright gleam of the altar. Then as Michael brought her level with Adam he turned to look at her with smiles and love in his eyes. He reached for her hand and she linked her fingers with his. The organ softened away to silence. The marriage service began.

Certain moments stood out in her mind afterwards. The gold ring sliding onto her finger. The surprising tenderness of Adam's kiss in the vestry before they signed the register there and the fragrance of her Sotherleigh posy when Mary, who had held it for her during the service, handed it back to her. Then walking back down the aisle with her fingers on Adam's wrist while everyone smiled and nodded and the organ made the air tremble. Among the sea of faces only Christopher's stood out, but she did not allow herself to meet his eyes. This was Adam's day and in the compromise she had arranged with herself she could not fail him in what was rightfully his. Her golden shoes bore her on her way out into the sunshine with the man she had married.

It was a light-hearted ride home and from the village onwards there were petals in the path of the coach. Near the gates she and Adam threw showers of silver coins and were cheered and applauded right to the door of Sotherleigh. When they stood next to Michael as he began to greet the long line of guests and they received everybody's good wishes, Julia wondered how it would be when Faith and Christopher congratulated her. She knew of a bride who, when faced with the man she had wanted to marry, had burst into hysterical tears to the embarrassment of all. That would not occur with her, but it would be a difficult few moments.

Yet all went well. She and Faith were so pleased to see each other again and then, by lucky chance, her bridegroom happened to put his arm about her waist just as Christopher stood before her. She was reminded again of her obligations and was able to sustain a friendly attitude towards Christopher, as was expected of her.

Sotherleigh had not seen such feasting and merriment for many years. Wine flowed and dish after dish was borne in to replenish the long table in the Great Hall and the extra tables that had been added. Speeches were made and toasts drunk while musicians played in the gallery, sometimes barely to be heard above the chatter and the laughter. In a meadow that lay the same distance from both Sotherleigh and Warrender half an ox was being roasted, and mutton turned on spits as the tenants of both estates celebrated the marriage, barrels set up to supply them with all the ale they could drink.

Adam and Julia led their guests into the dancing in an adjoining room. When Michael partnered her they exchanged a glance as the measure took them past the Queen's Door.

"If only I had known," she said on a sigh, referring obliquely to their talk at breakfast.

"Hush," he replied with a slight shake of his head. "Think no more about it. This is a time for rejoicing, not for regrets."

She was not entirely sure about that, but then he did not know of the emotional turmoil she had been through and which was not yet over. Fortunately it was proving easy to enjoy herself. Even with Christopher as she whirled in a country dance, her merriment was spontaneous and her laughter full of delight. He had heard that he was to be appointed the Savilian professor of Astronomy at Oxford, the most tremendous honour to be bestowed on a man as young as he.

"You're turning upside down the custom of having greybeards in high places," she declared teasingly.

"It will be a few months before I take up the appointment and maybe I'll have turned grey myself by then," he joked, holding her hand high as she danced under his arm.

"You'll always be young, even when you're old in years," she insisted, half seriously and half in jest.

"How can you be sure of that?" he asked in the same vein.

"In this gown and my golden slippers I can be sure of anything today." Playfully she kissed the tip of her finger and placed it against his mouth. Then the shifting pattern of the dance swept her away as another partner claimed her and he continued the measure with Anne, who skipped light as a feather.

Time, speeding by, brought the supper hour when every guest found the traditional gift by the places set at the tables. There were elaborately cuffed and scented gauntlets for the men and white kid gloves perfumed with a floral fragrance for the women. Again the feasting was prolonged, noisy singing increasing among those getting drunker than the rest.

Julia, chatting to those sitting opposite her at the head table, failed to notice when the singers were hushed and an amused and expectant silence began to fall on the jovial company. Every head was turned in her direction. With a start she saw that Susan with Mary and Faith had come to her chair. It was time for her to be escorted upstairs by her ladies. A blush flared into her face and then she recovered herself. As she rose from her chair Adam, sitting beside her, was the first on his feet and the whole assembly followed suit. With dignity she acknowledged the cheers and raised glasses as she began to proceed from the Great Hall. She took in good part the bawdy remarks and lascivious compliments shouted out to her by the more drunken among the gentlemen, for wedding celebrations gave licence to such talk and it would be worse for Adam when his turn came.

In the bedchamber of the apartment that had been Katherine's, Julia was suddenly assailed by a rush of panic as Mary began to unlace the back of her gown. Sarah, assisted by Molly, had spread the linen sheet on which Julia stood to prevent the Elizabethan gown from coming in contact with the floor when it fell about her feet. But she was reluctant to disrobe. She had not minded when Susan had removed the coronet of roses, faded now, from her head or when the pearl ear-bobs and the necklet had been replaced in the silver casket held by Faith, but the gown was another matter. It had sustained her throughout the day, given her a light heart when otherwise her earlier melancholy could have stayed unrelentingly with her.

She crossed her arms and held the gown by the sleeves as the released lacing at the back caused it to slip down from her shoulders. She wondered what these five women in the room would say if she said she would not care how she was ravished in the night if she could keep this gown on her body.

"Step out of your gown now," Susan said quite firmly, seeing that she delayed. "It will not be long before Adam is escorted here."

Julia obeyed and felt the gown slip from her like a farewell caress, leaving her vulnerable and armourless. Sarah picked it up while Molly gathered up the discarded petticoats and stockings, removing them with the sheet after they had both bobbed to the bride and wished her a good night. Faith helped Julia into her nightgown.

"What a pretty garment this is!" Faith, modest to the extreme, thought such a soft cambric would be too revealing for her own choice, for the lace frill at the scooped neckline fell so low it almost revealed Julia's nipples, which could be clearly discerned. "Did you sew it yourself?"

"No, Mary did," Julia answered absently, sitting down before the mirror at her toilet table. "I've been too busy dealing in ribbons."

Faith was amazed. How could any girl be too busy to sew her own bridal nightgown? She had not realised quite how seriously Julia was taking her ribbon business. Christopher approved of the venture, admiring any initiative that brought the benefit of honest work to people, and therefore Faith approved it too. She had seen for herself at Bletchingdon how strongly Christopher had been attracted to Julia, but it had been in the sexual way that men were drawn to such beauty of face and figure. Not at all as Christopher loved her. He had looked at her and said, "I love you, Faith, beyond all other women." She had known then that he spoke from the heart, and that she would always be the one to whom he would turn and in whose arms he would always lie. She wished deeply that this could have been her wedding night too.

Mary had finished brushing Julia's hair from its coiffure into the curls that danced down her back. Then it was Susan who saw her into bed and brought the sheet up over her breasts for concealment as she sat up against her pillows. From the distance there came a rising tumult of drunken voices raised in lewd songs and bursts of cheering.

"The bridegroom is on his way," Susan announced, glancing about the room to make sure that all was in order. The approaching din grew louder.

"Don't let all those people in!" Julia appealed urgently.

Susan nodded and guided Faith and Mary out into the parlour beyond where they formed a phalanx in front of the bedchamber door. It was to no avail. As the crowd of young men swarmed through into the apartment, all the older ones and the ladies remaining downstairs, the first to reach the three women simply picked them up with battle yells and, ignoring their protests, carried them forward into the bedchamber where they were set down on their feet again. Julia lost sight of them as the prancing, yelling mass spread out around the foot and sides of the bed, every face elated and excited and flushed to all shades of crimson by wine. She did not have to be told that Christopher would not be among them. He had been imbibing, but this leering behaviour would never have been his. In the din nobody could have heard another speak. At least five different ribald songs were in full throat and there were bottles being waved about and passed around.

She looked for Adam and could not see him. Then there came a ripple through the gathering as those who had not yet managed to get into the bedchamber helped Michael and the groomsman push Adam through the jam at the doorway. For a few minutes he was wedged with the rest and then he was seized to be shoved and jostled towards the bed, people well-meaning but rough in their eagerness. He reached the foot in a dishevelled state with his dressing-robe torn and his nightshirt ripped from one shoulder. Leaning a hand against the carved bedpost, his grin was resigned as he recovered his breath. But he was to be given only the briefest respite. He was pounced on again, hands snatching the remnants of his robe from him as he was pushed through to his side of the nuptial bed. As jokers grabbed his nightshirt, intending he should go naked to his bride, he exerted his strength and flung them back, making them topple against others. Then he threw himself into the bed beside Julia. It was the sanctuary that forbade further horseplay, although it did not necessarily bring about the speedy departure of the well-wishers from the bedchamber.

Turning to Julia, Adam cupped the back of her head in his hand and she tipped helplessly against him as he kissed her long and hard. The

raucous approbation might have brought down a ceiling less well constructed than that of the Sotherleigh bedchamber. Still holding her head
when the kiss ended, he put his cheek against hers and whispered in her
ear. "That is what they wanted to see. Now they will go."

He was right. At last Susan was able to be in command again with
Michael to assist her, although even then it took time before they were
able to shepherd the last merry-maker out of the apartment back to the
celebrations downstairs. Then Anne, who had been awaiting this moment
that was solely for parents, arrived to bid the newly-wedded couple good
night.

"God bless you both."

Then she left the room with Faith and Susan. Mary, the last to leave,
was about to close the bedchamber door after her when Julia called out.

"Mary! Wait a moment!"

As Mary paused, surprised, Julia sprang from the bed to take up her
bridal posy, which had been placed in a vase of water on a table. Careless
of the drops spattering her nightgown, she rushed with it to Mary and put
it into her hands.

"May you know joy in time to come!"

Mary's eyes filled with tears. Too choked to speak, she hugged Julia in
gratitude and hurried away, forgetting to close the door. Slowly Julia
pushed it shut. Then she stiffened. Without turning she knew that Adam
had left the bed and was coming soundlessly towards her on his bare feet.

"That posy was well given, Julia."

Still she did not turn. "She is in love with my brother."

"I know."

"How?"

"She talks about him with shining eyes at the least excuse."

"Such is the weakness of lovers."

"Not with all, or else I should have shouted my love of you from the
pinnacles of Westminster." He drew aside the curtain of her hair to place a
kiss on the nape of her neck. Then, from behind her, his hands came
forward to close over her breasts and hold her lightly against him, the
back of her shoulders resting on his chest, the muscles of his thighs pressed
to hers. She could tell he had discarded his torn nightshirt and was naked
and proud. As his palms caressed her nipples she caught her breath on a
delicious tremor and he felt it pass into his own body. Moving his hand
down to her waist, he gently swivelled her round to face him and then
kissed her, loving her mouth. To his joy her arms slid by her volition

round his neck and he held her close, a new harmony created between them by the natural hunger of their young and healthy bodies, the fierce magnetism that had long been between them and his love that sought to find an answering chord in her.

When their kiss ended she laid her head against his shoulder. "I'm sure our marriage mended many feuds today."

He stroked one hand down her back. "There were new beginnings for quite a few people and especially for us."

"I think ours began when I put on my Elizabethan gown this morning. All day I saw it as the safeguard of happiness, a talisman without which everything would fade away again. It made me reluctant to discard it when my ladies brought me up here, but I need not have feared. What it ignited is still with me."

"Maybe it's because I have taken over its charge to be the protector of that happiness."

She raised her head and they looked deep into each other's eyes. "I want more than anything that we should fulfil each other's lives, no matter what is against us," she said quietly.

"There is nothing that we can't defeat together."

He kissed her again and she clung to him, hoping his words would prove true, for if their marriage failed to reach the heights the fault would be hers, of that she was sure. She wanted an end to being torn apart and for the compromise she had made to be a bridge to this man, although if it would take years or a lifetime she could not estimate. Love could not be driven out, but had to take its own time. Not even a new love had the power to banish the old completely if a wilful heart stood its ground.

"Take me to bed," she whispered.

"I will, my love and my wife." He took her face between his hands and with great gentleness kissed her eyes, her brow, her temples, cheeks and mouth. Then he released the bow at her neckline. As the ribbon slipped away through eyelets he slid the nightgown from her shoulders and kissed them. Then, gathering the soft folds of the garment as it descended, he followed its progress with his lips, lingering at her breasts, her ribs, her firm belly and the chestnut haze at her loins. She trembled at the exquisite sensations he was awakening in her. Her fingers buried themselves convulsively in his hair, her head back and her eyes closed. When the nightgown became a white circle about her feet, not even her toes escaped his kisses. Then, as he straightened up again, he clasped her about the hips with his arms and lifted her as if they were dancers in a ballet of love and she rested her hands on his powerful shoulders, gazing down into his up-turned face, which was taut with desire.

Supporting her back with the spread of one hand he laid her down in the middle of the bed and then came to lie beside her. There began for her a night of passion and sensual delights such as she had never known could be possible. He murmured such loving words to her that she arched with pleasure, even as she did involuntarily in response to some erotic touch of his that made her gasp blissfully, there being no part of her that did not exult at the caressing of his hands, his lips and his tongue. When eventually he plunged magnificently into her the seconds of pain were lost in the welcoming leap of her body to meet his to the full, such a surge and flow of rapturous movement following that she felt delirious with passion. When he broke like an ocean within her they both soared gloriously to such a mutual peak of ecstasy that it was as if they were welded together for ever. Time ceased to exist.

Dreamily she felt him move his weight from her and she opened her eyes. He had propped himself on an elbow and was looking down at her. She put a hand to the back of his neck and he bent down to kiss her again.

"I love you," he said with a smile as if he had not told her many times already.

"I never knew that being in bed could be like this," she replied in a gentle jest.

He laughed softly. "I've much more to teach you yet, my darling."

"What could that be?"

"All in good time." He slid an arm about her waist and lowered his head to rest against her breasts. Almost at once he slept.

She stroked his hair, thinking before she drifted into sleep herself that she had known marriage would not be dull with Adam, but what she had not expected was that it should show such early signs of being a most rewarding and even thrilling relationship.

WITH THE EXCEPTION of a few elderly wedding guests who departed after the bedding of the bride and groom, all the rest stayed to breakfast after a night of dancing, singing and general merry-making. Many yawned as they left in the early morning sunshine and some snored before their coaches had borne them away from the steps of the house. Michael saw them all off and personally assisted Susan and Faith into the Holder coach, thanking them again for attending his sister. William took his seat quickly, eager to get back to the Hanningtons' house and to bed. Christopher lingered a few moments to say goodbye to his old friend. During the festivities they had seized a chance to escape to the library for a quiet half hour when they talked together until Michael's duties as a host called him back to his guests.

"I hope it will not be long before you are back at Sotherleigh, my friend," he said to Michael.

"I hope the same, but be sure and visit my wife and me should you ever come to France."

"You may count on it."

When all the guests had gone Michael went back indoors. The house-guests had retired to their rooms and the servants were already starting to clear. He went upstairs himself, but not to the east wing. Instead he went to Mary's room, but she had locked the door and would not open it. He realised she had set the pattern of how their lives were to be from now on, but as he turned away he knew that her anguish at this moment was as great as his.

Dinner had been arranged at the later hour of six o'clock to allow everyone plenty of time to recover from the wedding celebrations. Adam and Julia were expected to make a ceremonial entry and so all were in their places at table when they entered hand in hand. The women looked at her to see if she appeared radiant and the men at Adam to take note whether he looked pleased with himself. But neither gave anything away, both composed and smiling.

None would have guessed that twenty minutes before in their apartment when they were both ready to come downstairs in their finery, a new gown for her and brand-new velvet jacket and breeches for him, that they had made love again. She had been arranging the lace folds at his neck, wide collars having fallen from fashion in the wake of anything that smacked of Puritanism, and seen how he was looking at her.

"Now?" she asked in laughter.

"Now."

"How? I can't lie down in this gown."

"I'll show you."

He did, very effectively, taking her where she stood, although half smothered by her raised petticoats, she as eager as he and as swift in her coming. Their hours had been spent in love-making and sleeping and love-making again, everything as ecstatic between them when their nakedness was bathed in sunshine as when by candlelight. Their only respite from this pleasurable programme had been when breakfast had been set out for them in the adjoining parlour, nobody intruding on the bridal chamber, and in thrown-on robes they had eaten ravenously.

It was afterwards, when he had taken her back to bed, that he gave her his groom's gift of jewellery, as was customary after the wedding night. It was a diamond necklet. He thought he had never seen anything lovelier than Julia, kneeling naked on a tangle of sheets, her back arched and her diamonds glittering as she held her arms high to preen in her delight in his gift.

Later, when jugs of hot water had been placed in the garderobe as the dinner hour drew near, they had bathed together and then, overcome by passion, had made love while still wet and with soapsuds sliding from them.

All this that was secret between them made her wary of meeting his glance throughout the dinner, fearful that just by meeting his eyes she might by a blush give away to others just how perfect everything had been between them, for that was nobody's business but their own.

That evening there were cards and billiards. The guests, having slept most of the day, were in no hurry to retire, although they would be leaving in the morning. It was well after midnight before Julia and Adam escaped behind their apartment door. Then they flung themselves into each other's arms and he bore her through to the bed. This time she did not care how creased her gown became. Later it was tossed onto the floor with everything else she had been wearing. Yet it was still a deliciously long time before they finally slept with their limbs entwined.

MICHAEL LEFT FOR FRANCE a week later. He had been seeing to the estate from morning to night, putting troubles right and setting out an agricultural programme that he had long felt necessary for Sotherleigh. Adam had promised to see that all went as he wished, which made him less anxious about leaving his land. Yet, when he was in the saddle, he took such a yearning last look at the house that Julia raged anew inwardly that circumstances beyond his control and hers had condemned him to exile. She recalled how Katherine had extracted a promise from her to keep Sotherleigh in her care if all should not go according to plan and now, through her husband, she was doing that.

This time there was no bad weather to delay Michael's sea-crossing and he arrived home in Paris the following morning. Sophie, hearing his voice in the hall of the apartment, came to meet him, stately and elegant, her black curls dressed more to the back of the head than was the fashion in England. Although she smiled and kissed him her greeting was petulant.

"Did you have to be away so long? You said you'd come home soon after your sister's marriage."

"I was delayed a week by bad weather at Calais before I could sail. Therefore, I had to extend my time after the wedding. You look well now. How is Jean-Robert?"

"Putting on weight. Come and see him." She liked to encourage his paternal love and interest, aware of the power she held now by being the mother of his son.

In the nursery the infant, sated from the wet-nurse's breast, was about to be replaced in his cot, but Michael took him and walked over to the window to see him better. He had never been more proud of anything in his life than in having a son. Jean-Robert had lost his birth-hair and the down that showed now had the chestnut glint that had every chance of matching Julia's. There were times when Michael caught a glimpse of his father in the baby's features, but supposed it was a family likeness that reflected his own looks. This was the boy he would teach to ride and hunt, to play cricket and football, to shoot arrows at butts and to know that his roots were at Sotherleigh.

"I've something to tell you," he said to Sophie, the wet-nurse having left the room.

She was standing by a table and she clutched the edge of it behind her, full of alarm. Had he made a decision to return permanently to that hateful house that she herself never wanted to see? Her deep fear of his going to the wedding had been that something like this would happen. She had been successful in stopping his return at the time of the Restoration; a few drops from a bottle obtained from an alchemist given daily in his food had incapacitated him. It was unfortunate that it should have made him as ill as it had, but she had been desperate that he should not go. She had risked only a small dose next time and it had not worked at all. At least she had had the baby to ensure he should never leave her. It was the only reason she had allowed herself to conceive, for she was not in the least maternal and had wanted to preserve her figure.

"What is it?" she asked tightly.

"I believe it is what you have wanted before all else." His gaze on her was steady. "I have decided to accept your father's offer to be a partner in the Brissard silk business if he is prepared to make a certain concession."

If he had not looked down again at his son, taking hold of the small hand, he would have seen the triumph in her eyes, because she would never have been able to hide it. Once the partnership papers were signed any threat of her having to live in England would be at an end. He would be in a cage of his own making without a key to it. Her father should see to that.

"I'm very pleased, my dear," she said evenly, moving forward to place a hand on his arm. "As for Papa, you will be doing him the greatest service. He can retire and put all his business cares from him knowing that in you he has a perfect successor. More important even than your keeping the business flourishing is that you will have added years to his life. His health would never have stood up much longer to the strain. What is the concession you mentioned?"

"He wanted me to invest heavily into the business as part of the agreement, but that is no longer possible. I learned from Julia that when the regicide fled from Sotherleigh he took my fortune with him."

Her hand fell from his arm and she stepped back in shock. "Then you must sell Sotherleigh and raise the money that way."

He thought, as he had done many times before, that he had never met a woman more mercenary than his wife. Her demand was not unexpected. "Sotherleigh was entailed by Katherine to the eldest son and cannot be sold. There was some land attached to it that was not tied up in this way, but my father sold most of that when in need of funds during the Civil War and the Sotherleigh monies were still tied up in shipping. What is left after Makepeace took the gold coins and the jewelled plate would not raise the capital that I should need to meet the figure your father wanted."

"Then you are a poor man with a fine property that you can't sell." She was angry and derisive.

"That's it precisely," he agreed calmly. He knew that to be poor was to be despised in her eyes. Her father paid the Brissard employees meagrely and he also knew that the high salary he had received since being married to Sophie had been to ensure that her expenditure could be met comfortably.

"What of the rents and income from the farmland?" she demanded. "You have always said that provided a good income."

"There will be income mounting up in my absence, but at first much of it will go towards improvements that have been long overdue."

She slammed a palm down on the table. "Sotherleigh! Always that place must come first."

"You're wrong. You and our child come first. As for Sotherleigh I've just made my second visit home—the first was in secret for a very short time—since I left nine years ago, so you are exaggerating wildly."

"But you've wanted to go," she snapped irritably, "which amounts to the same thing." Then with a supreme effort she controlled herself. If he should walk out of the house now with the baby in his arms and go back to England, there was nothing she or anyone else could do about it. "I will speak to Papa. He will overlook a lack of investment on your part if I ask him. He'll not be hard on you as he would be to anyone not his son-in-law."

Michael smiled humourlessly to himself as he went to lay the heir to Sotherleigh in his crib. Old Monsieur Brissard would never let him go. The money had not been important. It had simply been another means by which to keep him more thoroughly tied to the business.

"You shall not intervene for me," he said, turning back to her. His tone was the one he used when she knew she had driven him as far as she dared. "This is a matter between your father and myself. I'm going to see him now."

She followed him at a distance out of the apartment and then looked down over the banisters to watch as he descended the three flights curving round the well of the staircase. He was a good-looking man, more so now than when she had first seen him. His years suited him. She had not wanted to marry at all, content to be her father's adored daughter, able to ask and to receive anything she wanted. Men had always been attentive to her beauty, but the thought of the intimacies of marriage had been repugnant to her and she had frozen all her suitors away. Then for the first time in her life her father had asked her to do something in return for all the generosity he had lavished on her for the twenty-four years of her life.

"I want you to marry this Englishman, Sophie," he had said. "He has a flair for the silk business that will guarantee the prosperity of Brissard's long after I've gone. I know from those two slight attacks I've had that my heart is not as it should be. If anything happened to me unexpectedly you, my dear child, would be left on your own and that worries me even more than knowing that all I've worked for would have to be sold. Michael Pallister will be a rich man himself when Charles Stuart regains the throne of England, which to my mind is inevitable since the English are basically as loyal to the monarchy as we in France are to ours. At the present moment his plans are to return to England with the King, whenever that should be, but if married to you and involved in the business to the point where he could not leave either you or the business, your future would be secure."

"Suppose he should sell the business and make me return to England with him?" she had asked. "I never want to leave France—or my home for that matter."

"When has anyone ever been able to make you do anything you did not want to do?"

It was true. She had learned early how to twist others round her little finger, firstly by stamping and screaming in childhood until all feared she would have a fit, and then later by her wits. She had nodded, reassured. "You're right, Papa. I will marry him."

So it had come about. Michael had been as easy to hook as a garlicky escargot out of a shell. Her marital duties had been as bad as she had feared, although she supposed other women would have termed him a good lover. She had simulated a show of passion when she deemed it necessary; it had been based on what she had seen when as still a young girl she had come upon a maidservant and a groom making love in the coach house. They had not known she was in the loft and she had watched everything through a gap in the floorboards, disgusted and yet fascinated.

As she stood by the banisters, remembering how everything had brought her to this moment, she heard a door open and shut downstairs as Michael went through to her father's salon. Then she smiled smugly. Now the trap was closing on him just as she and her father had originally contrived.

She turned back into the apartment. As soon as the partnership papers were signed, she and Michael would give up this section of the house and become integrated with her parents' household again. She would also insist on separate bedrooms. It was inevitable that when a couple slept together love-making would be more frequent than otherwise, men being the way they were. Let Michael take a mistress as any sensible Frenchman would do in these circumstances. As a partner in Brissard, he would be able to afford a second establishment and she would be spared those ordeals. Altogether everything was about to work out extremely well. She wondered if the time had come to throw away the alchemist's bottle with its potent fluid, but then decided to keep it. There was every likelihood that Michael would want to make regular visits home now that there were no obstacles in the way, and there might be occasions when she would have a special reason to prevent them. Suppose he should want to take Jean-Robert to visit Sotherleigh. She was determined never to let that happen!

Familiar now with the dosage, she could always give Michael a harmless drop or two very occasionally to encourage him to believe he still had some slight stomach trouble that flared up now and again. Then she could blame his condition on nervous excitement should he wonder why the pains became more acute whenever he was on the eve of going to England.

She went to the cupboard where she kept the bottle to make sure it was placed inconspicuously among her beauty lotions and the potions she kept for various minor ailments and afflictions, including the devastating headaches that fortunately had begun to trouble her far less frequently.

Carefully she set some of the flasks of herbal tinctures and decoctions in front of the one with an equally innocuous label, which was virtually invisible at the back of the shelf in a corner. Satisfied it would remain undiscovered, she closed the cupboard again and hid the key where only she could find it.

# SIXTEEN

*J*ULIA AND ADAM moved into their London house. They had
furnished it with good pieces from Warrender Hall and new
furniture that had been commissioned from a London cabinet-
maker as soon as they were betrothed. Michael had told her to take what
she wanted of spare bed-hangings and linen embroidered by Anne and
Katherine, since there was enough at Sotherleigh to have fitted out three
or four houses. From shops she chose Persian rugs, Turkish carpets and
French tapestries to give a warm look to the oak-panelled rooms. Not all
the wedding presents received had been to her taste or Adam's, but she put
on display those they had liked and gave special place to Michael and
Sophie's gift of a table set of antique silver Parisian candelabra and to
Christopher's pair of studded leather chairs.

Now that she was a wife of a Member of Parliament, Julia knew she
could no longer parade with her ribbons, but that did not mean she could
not visit her business contacts and her workshops whenever she wished.
She would have to juggle her time, for a flood of social duties would
soon descend upon her. When Adam jokingly offered to spare her the
tedious task of looking for a pretty girl to take her place in the ribbon
parade, they had a merry dispute over it. Yet he hid from her his underlying belief that whatever he did she would never be jealous, because she
did not care enough. If he strayed she would be angry, but his unfaithfulness would never reach the depth of her heart.

He had thought after their wedding night that he had won her to him
and that the invisible barrier of her hankering love for another man had
been vanquished. But he had been in a haze of pleasure himself and had
not realised it had not happened. Frequently she expressed her fondness

for him, praised his love-making and the power of his body, met him eagerly in whatever he wished and whether by day or night showed she enjoyed his company. Yet Christopher Wren stood between them like a solid wall of the building materials that had aroused his special interests. Adam had the uncanny feeling that they shared her. It was as if Julia was giving to him all that was expected of a wife while keeping her innermost feelings for the sweetheart of her childhood. Why he should be so certain of this aspect he did not know, but it was probably due to loving her totally as he did, gaining through it an extra sense that guided him into her most secret thoughts.

He tried to tell himself that he had only to be patient and she would become his as he wanted her to be, a full communication between them with nothing held back of body and soul. It was not possessiveness, for he saw her as his equal in all things except the love she was failing to give him. He was unhappily aware that the jealousy lacking in her had begun to smoulder in him, something he had never known before, and he would have to keep it under control or else it could prove ruinous to all that was right between the two of them.

Julia found the girl she was looking for among her own weavers at the Carter Lane workshop. Her name was Alice Jones, a quiet, smiling Welsh girl with bright eyes, pale yellow hair, a graceful walk and a ladylike look about her that would be a pleasing contrast to Nell's red-headed exuberance. Moreover, she was about Julia's own size and height, which meant that the crimson and cream gowns could be used without an additional expense.

"I'd like to be in the ribbon parade, Mrs. Warrender," she accepted with awe. "When may I start?"

"Tomorrow. I'll rehearse you here and in the morning I'll take you to the Heathcock where you'll meet young Nell and the Needham boys."

Alice proved a most suitable substitute and since she was Julia's representative she received the same courteous attention from the shopkeepers, her lilting Welsh voice pleasing to the ear. There were prettier girls at the workshop, who resented not being chosen, but they were rough-spoken and would not have been able to conduct themselves in the same manner as the country maid from the outskirts of Ponty-Pool. When not on her deliveries, she wove at her loom.

"What brought you to London?" Julia had inquired when first engaging her as a weaver.

"I came to live with my aunt on Cheapside when I was orphaned. She's an invalid now and I look after her."

Julia had come to know the backgrounds of all the girls and older women that she employed in her city workshop, while those at Briar House were already known to her from local association. She noted how her country workers dealt with their own domestic problems, having family and neighbours around them for help, but London embroiderers and weavers were often without such support, having left small towns and villages for work in London which was lacking at home. A community spirit did exist in many streets, particularly in the east end of the city and round the docks, but elsewhere help could be in short supply in certain times of trouble. Julia, aware of such troubles and problems, let it be known that she would always be willing to listen to any of her workers who wished to discuss their difficulties with her. Although she was younger than many of them she had the privilege of birth, and most had country memories or had heard talk of the females of the upper classes that cared maternally for tenants and villagers. After an initial shyness, which could afflict the most loud-mouthed of them, they did begin to turn to her and found a sympathetic ear if they wanted advice or practical help if it was needed. In many cases concern for their children came first.

As a result they were all individuals to her, not just hands at the looms or heads bent over embroidery. She knew of their hopes and their fears, of the husbands who were brutal, drank too much or coughed from lung disease. The younger ones confessed to broken hearts, homesickness and occasionally illegitimate pregnancies, in which case she kept them away from the abortionists by retaining them in her employ, making sure they gave birth in decent conditions and finding good country homes for the offspring where the mothers could visit if so inclined. Her reputation as a good employer spread, for her kind were in a minority. So many embroiderers and weavers applied to her for work that she rented the adjoining premises when they became empty and with the owners' permission had a dividing door knocked through. From doubling her extensive output she now trebled it and looked to further increase before long.

It infuriated her when she discovered that the Pallister designs were being copied on inferior ribbons and sold cheaper. Yet the shopkeepers assured her that those who looked for quality were not tempted away from her wares. Nevertheless she was sure some custom must have slipped away, and realised she should start bringing out new designs to keep ahead all the time. For this she turned to Mary, whose imaginative embroidery had its own charm. The first of these designs was a chain of hearts and love knots that Mary had first produced for Julia's wedding garters. It was an immediate success as were the others that followed.

In the meantime her social life had been gathering momentum. Hardly had the London residence been put in order when the first of the invitations to social functions began to arrive, and they had continued unceasingly ever since. Never to be forgotten in the early batch was one with a royal seal that she had opened first, sharing the moment with Adam. It was an invitation from the King to attend a banquet at the Palace of Whitehall.

"We're going to sup with Charles," she exclaimed, throwing her arms around Adam's neck and hugging him in her excitement.

Laughing, he pulled her onto his knees. "My guess is that all the other Members of Parliament and their wives have been invited too."

"The more the merrier! What an evening it will be!"

Molly, who had adapted to London life very quickly, while still preferring to be at Sotherleigh, was equally excited over the invitation. To a lady's maid, dressing one's mistress for a Court function was second only to dressing her as a bride. She was even more excited than Julia, although nothing distracted her from having everything ready and in order when the evening came.

Adam was in dove-grey and silver brocade and since the gentlemen wore their hats indoors on formal occasions, his was cherry red with a grey ostrich plume that curled around the crown and floated a foot out behind him. Julia in saffron taffeta twinkled with her diamonds, her sleeves and hems looped with gold-embroidered Pallister ribbons. He was looking forward to the evening and confidently expected her to be the loveliest woman present.

Whitehall consisted of early-Tudor buildings with some parts still older. The ruins of an ancient castle that had once belonged to a Scottish nobleman still marked part of the grounds and was known as the Scotland Yard. One notable improvement to the Palace had been made earlier in the century during the reign of Charles II's grandfather, James—a Renaissance building of great size and beauty designed by Inigo Jones, who had been inspired by the work of Palladio in Italy. It was known as the Banqueting House and it was at the steps of its entrance that the Warrender coach took its turn in the stream of equipages disgorging richly dressed passengers. As the coach ahead drew away, Julia recognised with delight the man who had alighted from it.

"There's Christopher going up the steps!" she exclaimed, the radiance in her face giving her away to Adam's knowing eye.

"What a pleasant surprise!" he remarked wryly. Yet it was to be expected that the fellow should be there, for apart from Christopher's fame and his having known the King since childhood, there was another connection in his cousin's having been appointed secretary to the Lord Chancellor.

They entered the richly decorated entrance hall. Christopher, happening to glance back over his shoulder, saw them and returned to greet them with pleasure.

"This is my good fortune," he declared. "These grand occasions are not really to my taste and it's splendid to be with friends. How are you settling down in your new home?"

"Very well indeed," Adam answered.

"We like our house immensely," Julia endorsed. "You will remember I always wanted to live where I could see the King drive by to Whitehall?"

"I remember indeed," Christopher replied. The smiles they exchanged were on the memory of how it should have been in a house designed by him.

Adam sensed some silent message passing between them. "I hope you will dine with us soon," he said courteously. It seemed to him it was better to get to grips with this situation on his own territory than that Julia should be yearning after the sight of her early love.

Christopher bowed. "I should be honoured."

They passed through anterooms and reached the open north door of the long and beautiful banqueting room. Julia knew that Katherine had thought of its architect and designer only as the vandal who had had Elizabeth's gowns cut up for the masque costumes he had created for James's queen, but his marvellous talent could not be denied. Enhancing the splendid lines of the pilastered and gilded rooms were allegorical paintings on the ceiling by Rubens, depicting the union of England and Scotland and the benefits of government under James. Christopher would have given Adam and Julia precedence into the King's presence there, but his name was announced first and he had to go ahead. Then their turn came.

Side by side they advanced up through the gathering to the crimson canopied and carpeted dais where the King sat on a gilded throne. A flicker of recognition showed in his dark eyes as Julia made her first deep curtsy to him and Adam bowed low with doffed hat.

"We have had the pleasure of seeing you twice without speaking, madam," Charles said smilingly to her after a brief word with Adam.

She was astounded that he should have remembered. "Actually it was three times, sire."

"Oh?" He looked intrigued. "How could I have forgotten that third occasion!"

"It was the first. I stood with my mother while you took refreshment on horseback outside the inn at Houghton in Sussex. My father, Colonel Robert Pallister, had been with you until shortly before."

"You are Robert's daughter?" Charles rose at once and came to take her hand and put it to his lips. "We give you welcome at all times to White-hall."

She curtsied again. Then Adam led her away to where they could watch others being presented. He saw her look for Christopher, who appeared to be more important to her than the royal honour she had been shown, but Christopher was engaged in conversation with someone.

"I think after what the King said our names will be permanently on the guest list, Julia," Adam said, drawing her attention back to him.

She looked surprised. "Really?"

"It's certainly what he meant." He spoke quietly so as not to be over-heard.

"I can't think how he could have recalled a single face like mine in the crowd and again through just riding past us in St. James's Park."

"I do." He lowered his voice still further. "There is always the possibil-ity that an invitation will come only for you."

She understood and her whisper was vehement. "I'd never accept."

He had known that would be her answer, but it pleased him to hear it just the same.

During the evening she noticed that a number of people were wearing Pallister ribbons on their clothes. Fashion was taking a most frivolous turn in reaction against the Puritan years, and men and women vied with one another in the sumptuousness of fabrics, the splendour of lace and the abundance of ribbons. She knew that when the King was to be seen with Pallister ribbons on his hat or bunched at the top of his sleeves, her venture would really be crowned with success.

It was not long after the banquet at Whitehall, when she and Adam were at Sotherleigh for a few days, estate matters needing his attention, that Anne handed over a letter that had come to her from the American colonies. "It's about someone called Makepeace Walker," she said vaguely. "It must be one of my relatives there, but I don't remember the name. Whatever money is forthcoming can be Patience's dowry. I don't need it."

Julia opened the letter to discover it was from a lawyer informing Anne that her husband, Makepeace Walker, along with other passengers who had sailed with a Captain Crowhurst, had been lost at sea when the ship carrying them to the colony had foundered on the rocky coast during a storm. Almost all the crew, including the Captain, were also missing and although some cargo and baggage had been salvaged, nothing belonging to him had been recovered. The lawyer explained that he had always handled Mr. Walker's American business interests, which was how he was aware of the Sotherleigh address, and now an offer had been made for the import warehouse his late client had owned. If Mr. Walker had died intestate, for no will had been lodged with the writer, the monies from the sale would go to his next of kin. He awaited Mrs. Walker's reply and instructions.

When she had read the letter Julia sat for a while before sharing its news with anyone. With all his faults she would never have wished such an end to Makepeace, although his demise removed forever all threat to Patience's future. His daughter would grow up at Sotherleigh free of the danger of his ever claiming her as he had threatened. It was not wholly surprising that he had gone to America, for they had known he had business interests there. Few men cared to die without leaving a son, but it was Makepeace's misfortune never to know that the maidservant he had seduced at Sotherleigh had given birth to a boy in Norfolk. As for the Sotherleigh fortune, that now lay at the bottom of the sea.

The next day she gave the letter to the family lawyer for him to deal with. Makepeace had not left a single one of his papers at Sotherleigh, having destroyed what he did not take with him and so, with his will also gone to the ocean bed, Anne would receive whatever was forthcoming from the American sale. Then there was the estate in Cumbria. When all was settled Patience should have a handsome dowry when the time came.

ADAM WAS PROVED RIGHT as to their names going onto a priority guest list. They went to balls and gaming sessions, concerts, suppers and more banquets at Whitehall. It was a court of revelry with the inevitable scandals, intrigues and much drunkenness. Mr. Samuel Pepys, with whom

Adam was acquainted, remarked to him in private conversation that he would never have believed such a lewd and abandoned Court could have come into existence so quickly. But the King had been long starved of merry-making and, when not attending to state affairs, he wanted to laugh and enjoy himself amidst jovial company, which made him more lenient towards the conduct of many of his courtiers and their ladies than he might otherwise have been. He needed to banish forever the melancholia that had afflicted him at dark periods during his exile and which he had hidden from all except those who had known him best. He was thankful his lot was unlike that of his cousin, Louis XIV, whose subjects regarded him with fear and awe, while he knew himself to be respected and well-loved by his people, who flocked to cheer him whenever he ventured out, and even those still his enemies had had to acknowledge his magnanimity.

Of all the entertainments at Whitehall, Charles and Julia shared, quite independently, a particular liking for masques. For these a stage was erected with a very ornate proscenium arch in the Banqueting House, and unlike the theatres where the scenery for the opening scene could be viewed upon entry, a scarlet curtain hung over a rail behind the arch would be dropped to the stage and then whipped away by attendants as the performance began. The surprise impact of spectacular scenery and gloriously arrayed masquers never failed to bring a burst of applause from the equally splendidly dressed audience, Julia always clapping enthusiastically.

Court ladies and gentlemen took part in the plays that were enacted. Professional actors in grotesque masks filled the roles of Disorder, Vice or Murder, which it would not have been etiquette for the nobility to play. Always the emphasis was on spectacle, gods and goddesses descending on clouds, a volcano erupting and once a great Roman procession in which two hundred actors or more took part. Towards the end of the masque, the Court players would descend into the audience and lead people back onto the stage with them for dancing, thus involving everyone in the masque. Once the King, being drawn from his seat by a cherub played by a child actor, took Julia by the hand. Then as the cherub pranced around them he and Julia danced together.

After that she was, now and again, invited to act in a masque, those at Court usually taking turns. She fitted in rehearsals with everything else she had to do and more than once, when the masque was Elizabethan, she wore Elizabeth's gown complete with ruff and farthingale. These were always the times when she felt she gave her best performance whether she had to sing, act or dance.

Through the name of Warrender being on the priority list, two seats were allotted to Adam and her for the Coronation in Westminster Abbey, which took place just a year after the Restoration. Julia was overjoyed to be going. Adam, entertained by her excitement, was glad that the flattering attention she received at Court, including the times the King singled her out for a special few words of conversation, had not turned her head in any way.

On the day itself they had an unimpeded view of the ancient and dignified ceremony and heard all of the superb singing of the choir to the thunderous notes of the organ. The King was in cloth of gold with a mantle of crimson velvet lined with ermine, towering in his splendid height in golden shoes, the bows of which were Pallister ribbons of ivory silk, executed in satin stitch. The design, incorporating the English rose, the Scottish thistle, the Welsh daffodil and the Irish shamrock, had been embroidered by Anne herself, for it had been such a special commission and a design that she had created quite a while ago when she had had the King's father in mind.

As the dramatic moment approached for the Archbishop of Canterbury to place the sparkling crown on the monarch's head, Julia hoped fervently that Charles's future would be brighter than the past months since his restoration had been. He had lost, through smallpox, his brother Harry, who had ridden with him on Restoration Day, and he had seen his most beloved sister married to the homosexual brother of Louis XIV, and his first attempts to bring about religious tolerance among his subjects had not met with any success to date.

"God save the King!"

He was crowned. The whole of the Abbey in its scarlet draperies rang with the shout from many throats. Outside in the streets the crowd took it up. Trumpets resounded. There followed a banquet of forty courses in Westminster Hall after which the King returned to Whitehall in a ceremonial barge. Specially minted coins were thrown to the crowd, having Charles II's head on one side and an acorn, symbol of a new beginning and linked with his escape by hiding in that most English of trees, was on the reverse side. Nell, twelve years old and already nubile, dived through legs and snatched up a coin from the ground. She grinned at her success as she looked at the profile of the King. His was a dear face. It had cast a spell over everyone on Restoration Day, but she thought it must have had special strength when it settled on her, even though he had not noticed her perched on a wall to get a view over the heads of the crowd. There was surely no other explanation for why she often rose early to go to St. James's Park just to see him taking a gallop on his shining horse. Sometimes on cold wintry mornings, her feet warm in the woollen socks that a link-boy had given her, for her mother drank the money for such things, she had held her breath as the thunder of hooves approached through the swirling mist. Then out of it he would come, his black hair flying, and he was past and away in seconds, never noticing her and taking her young heart with him.

She kissed his likeness on the coin before she put it safely away in her pocket. This was one that should not be turned into strong water for her mother. She would keep it for good luck and never part with it in all her life.

THE KING did not grant titles lavishly, but some were forthcoming on the occasion of his coronation. A knighthood went to Adam in recognition of his having supported General Monck and playing a part in the Restoration. Adam was convinced there was an additional reason.

"It's for you, too," he said to Julia. "By your becoming Lady Warrender through my title the King is also acknowledging what your father did for him."

"If it is as you say, the King couldn't have done anything more gracious for us." Julia linked her arm through his and rested her head against his shoulder. There was so much in Adam that had become dear to her. "More and more I believe our marriage was destined."

It did not escape him that she had said marriage and not love.

Julia felt very proud of Adam when she watched him kneel to be knighted by their sovereign. If he should ask her after this day to live with him now at Warrender Hall, she would not be able to refuse, no matter that her aversion to the house had not changed. He had done so much for her, even seeing the award of his knighthood as something to be shared with her.

It was odd that the plain bricks and beams of Warrender Hall could have taken on so much that had been black in her life, for apart from her fondness for Adam she also greatly liked his sister, Meg, both of whom had been born there. Meg always came to call whenever she and Adam were at Sotherleigh, and in their absence always spent a great deal of time with Anne, becoming a friend to her as well as to Mary.

Julia thought it fortunate that since her mother's confused condition could not be changed, it was merciful that she appeared to have shut out everything that had been upsetting to her in her life, which included not only her relationship with Makepeace but all the distress and fright she had suffered from Colonel Warrender and the Roundheads. Most people chose to put the bad things from their minds and remember only the good and in Anne the practice had reached exaggerated limits.

Meg often brought her youngest children with her when she spent a whole day at Sotherleigh. That was always a jolly time for Patience, who loved having others to play with her. She was a sturdy three-year-old with curly dark hair like soft silk, and her gowns were as be-ribboned as Julia's used to be in childhood, the ribbons getting as torn and bedraggled in play in the same way.

"I like my darling to look pretty," Anne would say, tying yet again the hair ribbons that forever slipped from the silky tresses.

Mary, who was at her best with children, was a splendid organiser of games when Patience had young company or if there were parties for them at the Hall. Adam had given Anne a sedan chair as a birthday gift and she was carried there to save her the effort of walking by the short cut he had created between the two properties.

Meg, who had been primed by Adam about Julia's feelings with regard to the Hall, was always tactful when it came into the conversation. Never once did she refer to the future when Julia would be living there, even though she did not attempt to hide her fondness for the house where she and Adam were born.

"It's wonderful to be back in Sussex again," she said many times as if still scarcely able to believe that such a miracle had happened. She made sure that any invitation she issued to Julia did not involve visiting the Hall. Instead it would be an invitation to a play or concert being performed locally with supper afterwards at a hostelry renowned for its good food. In the summer she gave lavish picnics out in the countryside that were evening affairs for adult guests with servants to wait on them and musicians playing in a nearby grove, the whole scene illuminated by flares. Daytime picnics were simpler, family occasions centred on the children and no less enjoyable for that, except that Julia never failed to experience the familiar pang that she still had no child of her own.

Although she waited almost daily for Adam to voice something about its being high time they moved from Sotherleigh to live at the Hall, nothing was said. So during the long periods when Parliament was not sitting, he concentrated on the husbandry of his estate and that of Sotherleigh. It meant he went daily to the Hall, but always on his own.

JULIA'S COMMEMORATIVE ROYAL RIBBONS, which she had had to supply in large quantities right up to the Coronation, were in demand once more the following year as soon as the King's betrothal to Catherine of Braganza was announced. Shopkeepers put in their orders again on the same day, wanting to lay in a good supply in time for the marriage. These days she supplied small round boxes in the Pallister colours of cream and crimson for sale when a customer wished to make a gift of the purchase. She had them made by a box-maker in Chichester, whose prices were lower than those in London, and this unusual novelty added to the prestige of her wares. Normally they were topped by a bow of striped ribbon, but for the forthcoming wedding she was adding a small bell that tinkled.

Catherine of Braganza landed at Portsmouth and she and Charles were married in the Cathedral there after meeting for the first time. Julia was charmed by the Portuguese custom of the ribbons being cut from the bridal gown after the ceremony to be distributed in as many pieces as possible.

Catherine's rich dowry included among other valuable assets the port of Tangier. Christopher, now Dr. Wren since taking his Doctorate of Civil Law, was invited by the King, who knew of his great abilities, to convert Tangier into a naval base. He regretted having to decline this prestigious commission, but he knew from experience that heat and dust, quite apart from sand blowing in the wind, would affect his weak chest. Whenever he was unwell he would recall Julia's prediction that he would live to a great age, while his wheezing chest warned him that it could be otherwise.

Since becoming the Savilian professor of Astronomy he had stopped lecturing at Gresham College, but he still came to London regularly to attend the weekly meetings of the society that he and his circle of old friends had formed. Their aim was to promote, consult and debate physico-mathematical experimental learning. The King, interested in the sciences, had recently granted the society a charter. It was as a member of this Royal Society that Christopher had spent the afternoon before coming to take supper with Adam and Julia at their home as he had done on previous, although infrequent, occasions.

He was one of a dozen guests that evening. Adam, at the head of the table, looked down the length of damask and silver and shining crystal at

Julia, seated at the end, and observed her abundant happiness as she talked to Christopher at her left hand. Jealousy churned in him. There was always something especially deep and warm in her eyes when she looked at Christopher. Later in the evening, after she had sung for the company, accompanying herself on the lute that was a replacement to the one Makepeace had smashed, she sat back on a cushioned seat beside Christopher while someone else played the spinet. Adam, happening to glance across at her, clenched his jaw involuntarily. Julia, holding her companion's hand, had leaned forward to kiss his cheek.

In their bedchamber after the guests had gone, she spoke of what Christopher had granted her. "He's given me permission to have constructed a loom for weaving half a dozen ribbons at the same time instead of only four or five, which is all any other looms can do. He designed it years ago, and I saw the diagram when I was at Bletchingdon. When I asked if I could show it to Mama, he gave me a copy to keep." She was removing her pearl necklet in front of her mirror and she twisted on the cushioned stool where she sat to look up at Adam, her expression jubilant. "Just think what this will mean! I shall be able to employ more embroiderers."

"I take it that your indiscreet kissing of him during Mr. Kirby's recital on the spinet was your expression of gratitude."

He had spoken so harshly that the pleasure faded from her face. Her eyes flashed. "Would you have preferred me to have kissed him behind your back?" she challenged with spirit.

"Don't be ridiculous!" he exclaimed in the same hard tones as before. "It should never have taken place at all. The time has come to end these displays of affection towards him. Our other guests would have supposed you were making a cuckold of me if they had seen that kiss!"

"That's grossly unfair! Nobody who knows me as well as those that were here this evening would consider such a possibility. In any case I checked that they were—" Her voice trailed off and she bit deep into her lower lip.

Furiously he finished the sentence for her. "—watching as well as listening to Mr. Kirby. None had eyes in your direction! You didn't bargain on my glancing across at you at that precise moment."

"Why should I mind that? You know that Christopher and I have been friends since my childhood." She drew in a shuddering breath. "I can see that I've upset you very much. That was never my intention and I regret it more than I can ever say. It won't happen again."

He made no comment, his anger raw. Her actions might be without fault from now on, but she did not know of that revealing quality in her expressive eyes. He wanted to explain that it was more than a putting away of shows of affection for Christopher that he wanted from her, but that curious paralysis of speech which could affect a couple intimate in every other way had descended upon him. He was too full of hurt to be able to talk it out with her, perhaps because he knew there was no solution as yet. He would not have cared about any left-over attachments from her girlhood if she would only stop holding her heart back from him.

They undressed in silence, not exchanging another word. When they were in bed and the candles were blown out they did not say good night and they lay well apart, their backs to each other. But neither could sleep. When, after an hour, he moved across and reached for her in the dark warmth, she turned to him at once in a burst of tears. She sobbed long and desperately, clinging to him, and he knew she wept for a state of her heart that she could not change, no matter how much she might have wished it. When her weeping subsided he made love to her gently and tenderly. It mended the quarrel between them even though the cause remained.

RIDLEY MADE THE SIX-RIBBON LOOM for Julia and was sworn to secrecy. If other ribbon firms came to know of it all her rivals would be copying it illegally. In a side room behind a locked door in the presence of her embroiderer-forewoman, Mrs. Blake, she let Alice try out the loom. For a few minutes all went well and then there came a hitch that could not be solved. As it happened to be a Wednesday afternoon, Julia went to the Temple where the Royal Society met alternately to a room at Gresham College. She sat in an anteroom where visitors were allowed to wait and could hear the rumble of male voices behind the door where the meeting was taking place.

When the members of the Royal Society emerged she was struck by the fact that most of them were around Christopher's age: he would be thirty-one in October, shortly after her twenty-third birthday. No greybeards here, but vigorous, lively men, some fashionably periwigged, others with that disregard for appearance common to many brilliant minds with no time to waste on minor matters. Christopher, with crisp, clean lace and well-brushed clothes of moderate cut, came comfortably between the two extremes. He was arguing cheerfully with a fellow member as they paused to dispute some special point, strolling a few paces and then stopping again. It was as he was gesticulating that his glance happened to fall on Julia.

The sight of her was so unexpected that for a brief, revealing second she saw on his face a similar expression to that which had revealed itself when he had seen her as a grown woman for the first time. Delight, surprise and desire mingled in the look that a man gives a woman he cares for. Then it was gone like a mask discarded as he excused himself from his companion and immediately came across to her.

"What brings you here, my dear Julia?" he questioned with his broad smile.

She explained and he said he would go straight away with her to the workshop. On the way they exchanged news and he asked if there was any word of Michael's making a trip home.

"No, I fear he's not well. Twice he has been coming and then the malady that affects his stomach has prevented him. The bailiff goes regularly to Paris these days to report and receive instructions. Michael seems to have resigned himself to that arrangement for the time being. Adam says we shall go ourselves to visit him one day. My nephew will be three years old now and I long to see him."

At the workshop it was past the hour when work stopped for the day and all hands had gone home except Mrs. Blake and Alice, who had waited. Christopher made a slight adjustment to the loom and solved the problem. Then to the amusement of the three young women he sat down and wove a full inch of six ribbons at the same time with ease and speed. Julia declared her intention of getting Ridley to make more looms for her.

It did not prove a problem to swear her workers to secrecy over the loom. She promised them a special bonus that would result from the increased output, and none wanted to lose the extra money. The new looms were put into action and nobody who was not employed on the premises was allowed beyond the door of the weaving room.

Although Alice was allowed to continue to carry out the ribbon deliveries with the Needham boys, both of whom had grown out of their liveries long since and had had to have replacements, Julia had lost Nell. The girl had grown up swiftly in the unsavoury establishment owned by Mrs. Ross, which with the tavern and the street life were all she knew away from the few hours a week when she danced along with the gilded box. That procedure had not always gone smoothly, for Nell, whose witty tongue had made her an equal in the humorous repartee that prevailed among the stall-holders and the link-boys, had more than once made saucy quips to passers-by that were not at all in keeping with the dignity of the little procession. Yet Nell was so likeable it was impossible to put any sternness into a reprimand, which, in any case, she always took with her unassailable good humour. Then, almost overnight, she was a young woman with a trim figure, her impish charm unsullied by her circumstances, announcing she was going to work longer hours for Mrs. Ross.

"There's no need for you to do that." Julia was most anxious for the girl. "I can have you trained as a lady's maid where you'll be in a good home and be cared for."

"And be bored!" Nell laughed merrily. "Don't worry about me, madam. I don't mean to stay long with that old harridan. I'm ambitious. There's going to be a new playhouse in Drury Lane, only a coin's toss from Coal Yard Alley, and I intend to keep an eye on it. I've a fancy to walk the boards one day."

It was impossible not to believe that Nell would achieve her aim. "I'll come to your first performance," Julia promised, hoping that the girl would never be hurt by life, for she had such a warm and generous nature. "If ever you're in need of help, I'll be your friend."

"I thank you, but I have this." She pulled at a chain round her neck and brought into sight a silver coin that had had a hole bored in it to turn it into a medallion. "It's my lucky charm!"

JULIA DID NOT SEE CHRISTOPHER for a long while after that day at the workshop, although he wrote for her birthday and Christmas as he had always done. Then he was commissioned to build a theatre for the university at Oxford, not for actors and actresses, but for scholastic gatherings of large numbers and the giving of special lectures. First of all he made a model from his own design, which he brought to London to show to the Royal Society and afterwards invited Adam and Julia to see it. When they arrived at Gresham College he was in high spirits, having, prior to coming to the city, successfully carried out a blood transfusion on his dog, which had suffered no pain.

"My good hound was as lively as a cricket afterwards, having no idea why he received an extra meaty bone from the butcher as a reward. I've delivered a lecture to doctors of medicine already in the hope they would see what benefits this could bring to mankind."

"How did the doctors receive it?" Adam questioned with interest.

"Not with any enthusiasm, I fear. They believe more in bleeding their patients than in giving them life's source. A few walked out, taking objection on religious grounds. My hope is that not all will shut their minds to it. At least my fellow members in the Royal Society were far more receptive, but then scientists and thinkers such as they thrive on new ideas." He then opened the door into the next room. "Come now and see my model. I haven't followed convention there either and must leave you to judge whether you like it or not."

It stood on a stand and was reflected in the polished surface. Circular in shape, it was inspired by the Theatre of Marcellus, but whereas the building of ancient Rome stood open to the skies, Christopher had drawn on some earlier research done by a friend and fellow mathematician. He had devised ingeniously a means by which the roofing-in could be done without supporting pillars, which, for a span of eighty by seventy feet, had never been done before. It was to be known as the Sheldonian Theatre and would be as aesthetically beautiful as it would be practicable in use.

"My little joke will be to have the ceiling painted as if curtains have been drawn back from the sky," he chuckled.

"It's going to be a splendid building," she said, peering into the model, for he had lifted away the extraordinary roof.

"I wanted you both to see it," he said, although his eyes were only on her.

He does still care for me, she thought. It had shown in his surprise when she had waited for him at the Temple. Now, inadvertently, he had revealed his feelings again in wanting her to be among the first to know of this project that was so new and exciting to him. She did not doubt that he loved Faith for all her good qualities, but he had not been able to sever that amorous link forged such a long time ago with her. It made her wish it were possible to tell him she knew his secret and he must surely know hers just as she would have done in times past, but it was something neither could ever confess to the other.

THE KING, quite apart from enjoying masques at his own palace, was an enthusiastic playgoer, although he preferred comedy to tragedy, having had enough of the latter in his life. He had presented his coronation robes to the theatre and had encouraged his brother James, Duke of York, to do likewise with all he had worn that day, each having a company of players named after him to whom they gave patronage.

Julia and Adam were in a neighbouring box to Charles for a performance of *Henry V* in which the crimson and gold coronation robes were worn by the actor playing the King of France. She noticed that the Pallister-bowed shoes had been replaced by a red leather pair and guessed the actor did not have such large feet as the King, a fact she was able to observe at close quarters again when she and Adam were invited into the royal box during the interval. It was not the first time this had happened, for they had often been at one or another of the London theatres when Charles had been present, usually with Lady Castlemaine or some other beautiful woman who would be equally elegant with a deep, pale cleavage gleaming in the glow from the stage, jewels winking. All fashionable women wore hats to the theatre, Julia included, and brims had grown still wider since the Restoration, sometimes cocked up at the side as a frame for the face, and she could almost always be sure that any ribbon ornamentation was the work of her weavers and embroiderers. Recently she had begun a line of specially looped ribbons and bows for female headgear and it had caught on immediately.

The new theatre that Nell had spoken about was nearing completion in Drury Lane and it was to be known as the King's Playhouse. Charles had been several times to the site to view its progress. Built largely of wood, it presented a fine frontage with a grand entrance. Within there were three tiers of boxes above which were two galleries, the upper one to be free to coach-servants, personal link-boys and other staff, who would be awaiting masters and mistresses attending performances. The area known as the pit was used as much for strolling about as for sitting on the benches provided. To the rear were the dressing rooms with individual ones for leading actors and actresses. In all it was a jewel of a theatre and much was expected of whoever should act there.

On the opening night the *beau monde* filled all the boxes. In the pit the gallants, many extravagantly dressed, swaggered about, flirting with any attractive women and being as uproarious and noisy as possible. Faith was dismayed when several of these rakes blew kisses to Julia and her from the tips of their fingers and shouted up lascivious compliments. Unused to such behaviour, she drew her chair back timidly to sit closer to her betrothed. Out of the corner of his eye, Adam noticed the reflected pang in his wife's face as she observed Christopher take Faith's hand and hold it reassuringly as if to show that there was nothing against which he would not protect her.

One of the bucks, bold with ale from the nearby Cow and Fiddle tavern, there being no strong waters sold on the theatre's premises, climbed up to the Warrender box to hand Julia a flower. Then he lost his footing and she cried out in alarm as he clung precariously to the parapet, but his friends gathered below to break his fall when he let go. He landed in their midst, bringing them all tumbling about him into a heap to the mirth of everyone. Julia laughed as much in relief that the foolish fellow had come to no harm as she did from the comical sight.

She fluttered her fan, her eyes shining at all there was to see. Part of the roof above the pit was glass and rays of sunshine competed with the sconces and the stage candle-lamps, the performance being as was usual at a late afternoon hour. She acknowledged the bows of acquaintances in the boxes, but the pit was the most fun to watch and Adam leaned on an elbow to look down with her. Comely wenches, employed by the woman who held the licence, moved about the pit selling sweetmeats and oranges as well as flowers, which would be thrown to players at the end for a good performance. Those in the pit and the gallery would have come prepared with their own rotten eggs and tomatoes should any actor or actress disappoint them. It was unlikely that the play itself would fail to please them this evening, for it was *The Humorous Lieutenant,* which was always a favourite.

Suddenly Julia gasped. "Look Adam! There's Nell!"

The girl had a basket of oranges on her arm and must have been selling at a point out of view, for suddenly there she was with her unmistakable red curls, exchanging cheeky badinage with those seated on the benches, although it was impossible to hear what was said in the general hub-bub.

"Try to attract her attention, Adam," Julia urged.

He gave a shout with cupped hands. "Nell!"

She failed to hear him. Gallants had surrounded her, buying her oranges and weighing them in their hands, obviously making lewd comparisons and Nell, with her head flung back, laughed as heartily as they. Then a fanfare of trumpets and a rustle as all seated rose to their feet announced the King's arrival in the garlanded royal box. Julia, who was still watching Nell, saw a transformation come over her as she turned to look raptly up at Charles. Attired in scarlet and gold and a white-plumed hat, he acknowledged the applause of the well-bred and the rousing cheers from the pit and galleries. She looked so absorbed in him that it was unlikely she noticed the Queen at his side, resplendent in oyster silk and pearls. Charles's smiling gaze passed around the theatre, but the orange girl was one in a crowd of upturned faces and went unseen. Then he took his seat and the comical play began.

None enjoyed the performance more than he. He rocked with laughter and slapped his knee at the witticism of the dialogue, interpreted anew by the talented cast. Already he had earned a nickname as the "merry monarch," endearing himself still further to those of his subjects who liked a good laugh themselves and did not condemn him for being less faithful to his wife than he should have been.

This evening the Queen was equally gay. Catherine had not been able to speak more than a few words of English when she landed at Portsmouth, but from the start she had set out to master the language and so the jokes in the play were not lost on her. When the interval came she applauded the first act as vigorously as her husband.

This time Adam went down to the pit to gain Nell's attention. Julia saw him speak to her and she spun round at once to look up with a broad grin. Running forward until she was directly below the box, she took an orange from her basket and threw it up. Her intention was better than her aim and if Christopher, always quick in his reactions, had not caught it like a cricket ball, it would have burst against the box's panelled walls.

"I thank you, Nell!" Julia called down.

"I've made the first step, haven't I?" Nell joked back, sticking a thumb over her shoulder in the direction of the stage.

"Only one more!" Julia gave back in the same vein. "Remember! I'll be in this box when that day comes."

Nell waved appreciation of this encouragement and went back to her selling. She refused to accept payment for Julia's orange, but Adam bought three more from her which he brought back to the box. The juicy fruit was refreshing and Christopher said he could not remember when he had tasted a better orange.

After that Julia always saw Nell when she and Adam decided to go to the King's Playhouse. The girl continued to be hopeful that eventually she would be successful in gaining a part, but she had had no theatrical training and Mr. Killigrew, the actor-manager, was unapproachable towards amateurs, especially as there was such intense rivalry between his company and the Duke of York's players. He had a high standard to maintain.

The Queen discussed with Julia the various plays that they had both seen. Catherine thought it very English to show enthusiasm for the theatre, and in all things she tried to be as much like the ladies around her as possible. It delighted her that her request for a cup of tea, the first words she uttered upon landing on English soil for her marriage, had set a fashion for a drink that previously many had not tasted. She was always looking for guidance in fashion, not wanting to appear at all foreign in her dress. One evening at Court, Julia wore a bow of cornflower-embroidered ribbon in her hair attached to the top-knot with streamers hanging down to her hem at the back. The next day the Queen also wore a Pallister ribbon in the same way and a mode was set that swept through all the ladies at Court and beyond. Eventually even the female street-criers of wares were wearing it; no matter that the ribbons of the poorer women were of gaudy fair-ground quality, it gave a pretty effect that made the streets all the brighter for it. Then gradually the mode was lost, remaining only with lavender sellers, who made it a mark of their trade.

By that time Nell had gained her chance to act. She had finally been noticed, given some training and taught how to dance professionally. Not being able to read or write proved no disadvantage, for she could memorise anything read out to her. An actress born, she made her debut in *The Old Trouper* and, as promised, Julia was at the theatre to applaud her. Then she went on applauding as Nell gained better parts and with astonishing swiftness moved into main roles, some of which were written especially for her, creating situations where it was necessary for her to wear men's attire. These revealed her good legs and it was said that no actress had a better pair of pins than pretty, witty Nell of the King's Playhouse.

The outbreak of war with the Dutch kept Adam many hours at Westminster. His work brought him into contact a great deal with the Clerk of the Acts, Mr. Pepys, at whose home he and Julia were invited to dine or sup on several occasions. These were always jolly affairs with good talk and an excellent table presided over by his wife, Elizabeth, a good-looking woman with fine eyes. Great concern was shared by Adam and Mr. Pepys, among others, when the Duke of York impetuously set sail to blockade the Dutch ports with a fleet that had not been properly equipped or victualled. Julia hardly saw Adam for days when the Fleet did return for the necessary attention of the ships' chandler, and debates about the war in the House of Commons kept him until late at night. She had no liking for the King's brother, who was a conceited, arrogant man, although his personal courage in war could not be denied. He was still heir apparent to the throne, the Queen now believed to be barren, and had been well pleased after the Dutch had surrendered the American city of New Amsterdam that it was renamed New York in his honour. In her own mind Julia was beginning to fear that she was doomed to be as childless as the unfortunate Queen. At least she was spared that royal lady's torment of knowing that her husband had more than a quiverful of bastards.

IT WAS DUE to Adam's preoccupation with the current crisis of the war that he forgot he was to accompany Julia to France on a long-awaited visit to Michael and Sophie.

"It's impossible for me to leave England at this time," he said regretfully when she reminded him that the day of departure was not far distant. "But you shall go. I'll find an escort for you and your maid. Some reliable gentleman travelling with his wife."

"Christopher is going to be there in June," she said immediately.

He sighed inwardly. The mere mention of her early love's name could make her eyes glow. "Is that so? I hadn't heard."

She sensed his displeasure. "I could take Faith with me. When she stayed with us last there was some talk of Paris and she expressed a wish to see it some day."

"I daresay she hoped to make that visit as Christopher's wife." There was a rasp to his voice. Julia had spoken so quickly of taking Faith with her to France. Did she fear the strength of her own emotions should she ever find herself alone with Christopher again?

"They won't marry for a long while to come," Julia remarked casually. "He's far too busy through his venture into architecture. He's building that new chapel at Cambridge and other projects are coming up."

"How can he find time for a vacation in Paris, then?"

She looked at him sharply. It was not like Adam to be sarcastic. "He has heard so much about the modern architecture to be seen in Paris now and wants to view it for himself in relation to his own work. I doubt that Faith and I will see much of him, because, as you know, he becomes obsessed with anything that has captured his interest."

Christopher did not escort Julia and Faith with Molly to Paris, being unable to get away until July. Both young women would have preferred to wait for him, but Adam had made arrangements for them to travel with an elderly earl and his wife, who were going south to Italy for their health and would be passing through Paris. It was planned that Adam should fetch Julia and Faith home again after a few weeks, as Christopher's sojourn would be lengthy.

"I'll miss you, Adam," Julia said fervently in his farewell embrace.

He kissed her ardently. "Enjoy yourself. I'll see you in Paris."

Then she was waving from the coach window as, with the earl and his wife and the nervously excited Faith, she was borne away from him. In the wake of the coach was a baggage train and on horseback were a dozen strong and burly liveried men-servants to protect the earl and the ladies from thieves and highwaymen both on the way to the coast and on foreign shores. A distant rumble of guns like far-away thunder told that the English and Dutch fleets were engaged in battle somewhere at sea. As the coach lumbered over London Bridge, people were to be seen standing to listen solemnly. It was not until their arrival in France that the travelling party heard that eventually the fleets had engaged in battle off Lowestoft and a victory had been won against the Dutch. On reaching Paris they heard the sobering news that it had not ended the war as they had hoped. The Dutch were a tenacious people and did not give up after one defeat.

Four days after his wife's departure Adam was coming along Drury Lane when he saw a sight that chilled his blood. Four of the doors had been painted with a red cross, the dreaded sign of a plague-stricken house, together with the words *Lord have mercy on us*. It was the seventh day of June, the year 1665.

THE MEETING between brother and sister was one of enormous joy. Faith, happy to see Julia and Michael together again, glanced at Sophie to share that pleasure and saw, to her surprise, that her face was set and straight. Her features did relax into a smile as Michael presented Julia and they embraced, which caused Faith to suppose it had been only a momentary shyness that had come over the Frenchwoman.

Jean-Robert had been waiting to greet the aunt whom he had never met.

He bowed as his mother had taught him and kissed Julia's hand in a courtly fashion. Then he looked up at her with a face full of mischief.

"Am I not an English gentleman as well as a French one, Aunt Julia?"

She had been well tutored in French and understood him perfectly. "Indeed you are," she replied warmly in the same tongue.

"I'm nearly six, you know." He was tall for his age and, as often happens with sons, he was most like his mother in features, although there was a look of Michael across the smiling eyes, dark whereas his father's were grey. His curly hair was the colour of Katherine's in the portrait painted in her youth.

"I can see how grown-up you are."

He greeted Faith with the same procedure, but spoke three words of English to her. "Welcome to France, madame."

She could have replied in French, but she thanked him in English and he looked well pleased with himself.

Michael and Sophie had the large Brissard house to themselves now. Her father had died at the end of the previous year and she was still in deepest mourning, wearing her black with all the elegance of a Parisian woman. Her grief was deep and absolute. She had never loved anyone but her father. Her child was dear to her because he had been a joy to his grandfather in the short span the two had known each other. Her only outings were to the cemetery, where she went swathed in black veiling. Now that she had escaped her marital duties altogether, she felt pure and unsullied in her mourning, her life rededicated to the memory of Jean Brissard. It was as if her mother had never existed.

Although her headaches were occasional, her moon-cycle cramps were not. There were times when she could have believed it was justice on her for the poison pains she had inflicted on Michael, except that she had suffered from the same symptoms since she first came to womanhood. She never felt any pity for him. When lying with a hot brick wrapped in flannel against her stomach she was glad that she could strike out at him, a representative of the whole male sex, on behalf of all women for what they suffered through being female at such times, also in childbirth, and at what was expected of them in the marriage bed. One day, when her son was grown up and able to take over the silk business, she would get rid of Michael by giving him a dose that would make him scream for death to take him.

It was when Julia, concerned that her sister-in-law was unwell, took her a warm posset she had found helpful sometimes that she discovered Sophie and Michael slept apart. It was not just having separate bedchambers with a communicating door, for Sophie's was on one floor and Michael's was on another. But by this time Julia had not needed this final proof that all was no better between them than when he had come to Sotherleigh for her wedding. He and his wife were like polite strangers, always courteous but with nothing in common except their child.

Julia wrote to Adam and to her mother of all she was seeing of Paris, the city that the French King was continuing to improve and beautify, not only in buildings but also, as Michael had told her years before, in widening streets and laying down a new roadway that was following the line of a fire-break through the woods of the Champs Élysées. She heard from Adam once and when no more letters came she knew that one day she would come back to the Brissard house from an expedition and find him waiting there. She had even half expected that he might arrive with Christopher in July, but that did not happen.

Christopher had his own accommodation from which he set out daily to view all that he could of the new French architecture with its domes and other specific forms that he had never seen before, sketching them and buying prints whenever possible. He enthused over the ways in which the buildings were surfaced, comparing the enrichment to a living skin, all of it exciting his eye for beauty.

"I've such a file of diagrams, drawing and prints now," he joked when dining one Sunday at the Brissard house, "that I'll be taking half of France back on paper. From Fontainebleau to Vaux-de-Vicomte I've seen much to inspire me towards new designs of my own."

"Have you seen the château of Versailles yet?" Sophie asked him.

"No, madame, but it is on my list. I'm eager to see how King Louis has begun embellishing and enlarging his father's hunting lodge."

Michael spoke up. "Why not join us then tomorrow? I'm taking your betrothed and my sister there. The King is in residence at Versailles at the moment and Julia will have a chance to meet Joe again, the groom who came into exile with me."

Sophie stiffened. "Exile no longer, husband," she said with serene chilliness. "France is your first home now."

The moment was awkward. Christopher smoothed it over. "I thank you, Michael, and I accept." He looked warmly at Faith. "I've seen far too little of you as yet, my dear girl, and the weeks have been flying by."

"I've understood that you came to study," she replied gently.

"At least we shall be together tomorrow in our good friends' company."

In the coach next day he had his arm round Faith's waist all the way, sometimes giving her a little squeeze, which she hoped went unnoticed by Michael and Julia. They were sitting opposite and fortunately Jean-Robert, who was quite a chatterbox, took most of their attention. Christopher was very passionate on the rare occasions they managed to be alone and Faith had hoped he might find a way to take advantage of her being here in Paris, but that had not happened. Men of his nature were always honourable towards women they respected and there were many times when she wished he were otherwise.

At Versailles they alighted by the château's grand gates and walked up the Cour Royale; then Christopher became so interested in how a new palace was being built around the original old hunting lodge that he strayed off, forgetting he was not on his own. Michael then arranged with him where they should all meet later before taking Jean-Robert to see the horses in the royal stable and to find Joe.

Julia and Faith went into the château to look around. There were many sumptuously dressed courtiers and their ladies about and, unlike White-hall at a day hour, they were as bejewelled as if at a great ball. Nobody took any notice of the two Englishwomen, for as with all royal palaces in France the public were free to enter and, if they were fortunate, see His Majesty.

On their way out again they came face to face with King Louis. He lifted his cream-plumed hat to them as they curtsied deeply. The encounter was brief, but enabled them to see a certain likeness between him and his cousin, Charles II, both men being of splendid height with black hair and commanding features.

Outside Joe was waiting. "My lady!"

"Joe! After all this time!" Julia exclaimed delightedly.

When greetings had been exchanged Faith left them and went in search of Michael and his son, who had returned to the park. Joe led Julia to a bench by a fountain where they sat down. He had put on a considerable amount of weight, his face quite fat, but he was as ebullient as ever. Yet he became almost wistful when the talk revolved around Sotherleigh.

" 'Ow's the old place looking, my lady? I'd be back there tomorrow if I could."

"There'll always be a place for you, Joe."

He was sitting with his arms resting across his knees, turning his hat like a wheel. "It's not that easy. I'm wed now with twins and there's another baby on the way. My Parisian wife would dig in her heels if I spoke about going back to England to live. The French are real foreign in many ways, but they're like us English folk in preferring their own country to grow old in." Then he lowered his voice confidentially. "Maybe you don't know and maybe I shouldn't tell you, but Mr. Michael's lady-wife is just the same as mine in wanting to stay put, I can tell."

"I did realise that."

"There's something else." He looked about cautiously to make sure there was nobody within earshot. Then he poked his head forward to be as close to her as possible. "I don't like those pains he gets every time he's due to go home. 'E nearly died the first time. I saw 'im only two days before 'e was due to join up with the King at Breda and then 'e was as right as ninepence. Do you get my meaning?" He cocked his head and winked in a warning manner.

Julia felt her throat tighten with apprehension. "Do you think some evil is at work?"

"Not to kill 'im, but to keep 'im tied. There's plenty of poisons to be 'ad and it's always said to be a woman's weapon."

She recalled what Adam had said about Sophie, but he had not suspected such ruthlessness. "I thank you for telling me. I'll speak to Michael about it at the right moment, giving no hint that you have alerted me."

"You as 'is sister can do that, whereas from me it would 'ave been an impertinence not easily forgiven, 'cos 'e's never said a word against 'er to me and nor would 'e."

"You may have saved my brother's life a second time by alerting me. After all, there's a limit to how much resistance the human body has against such dreadful concoctions."

" 'Ow long shall you be in France?"

"I'm not sure. I've been here seven weeks already and my husband still has not come to take me home. I think he's forgotten there's a limit to how long I can be away from my ribbon business."

"You stay. He wants you to be safe."

"Safe? From what? The war with Holland?"

He stared at her in disbelief. "Ain't you 'eard? London 'as the worst outbreak of the plague since 'eaven knows when. People are dying like flies."

She blanched and clutched the edge of the seat. There had been rumours of the plague in one of the parishes before she left London, but it was common enough in summertime for fevers of one kind or another to flare up and there had been nothing to suggest that this time would be any different. "How long has the plague been in force? Do you know?"

"Since the early part of June."

"Then Christopher Wren would have known about it when he arrived from Oxford in July. His betrothed had a letter from home and it must have mentioned the plague to her. As for my brother, he would most surely know through business, for news travels between countries more by merchants' letters than anything else."

She recalled now how some French guests at the Brissard house had begun talking about the plague, but Michael had intervened and changed the subject. She had thought nothing of it, but now she realised there had been a conspiracy formed with the best of intentions to keep her in ignorance.

"I must say farewell to you, Joe," she said, rising to her feet as he did likewise. "We've spoken on two dreadful topics on which to part, but there can be no delay with either. God be with you."

"And with you and yours, madam."

Christopher saw her hurrying towards him across the Cour Royale. He had put his sketchbook away. To his taste the mixture of brick, stone, blue tile and gold made Versailles look as if it were clothed in a rather vulgar livery. In his own mind he was in agreement with the French architects who had wanted to pull the whole place down and start afresh. The King should have listened to Le Vau, whose Vaux-de-Vicomte was beyond compare.

"Christopher! Why didn't you tell me about the plague in London? It had taken hold before you left England."

So she had found out. It had been bound to happen. He answered gravely. "Adam wrote to me before I left Oxford when it was becoming clear that the situation was extremely serious and asked me to keep it from you. I let Michael know as soon as I arrived, as I was ahead of any mail that would have told him. Adam did not want you to worry about his being at Westminster or that you should take it into your head to return."

"Naturally I will. He might have sickened already for all I know. I shall leave France at once."

"You should do as he wishes and stay on here. The King has acted just as he has done, remaining at Whitehall himself while sending the Queen to the safety of Hampton Court and his courtiers to Oxford."

"My place is with Adam and I have my embroiderers and weavers to whom I have a duty to remove to a safe place."

"Nobody can leave London without a certificate of health from the Lord Mayor and his aldermen. When I left Oxford toll-gates and barriers were being put up on the roads to prevent Londoners without the necessary papers from spreading the infection."

"Whatever you say, I'm going home."

His anxious expression changed to one of alarm and he gripped her by the shoulders. "I forbid you to leave France until the plague has passed!"

Her face softened. She saw that he was afraid she would fall victim to the plague and he would never see her again. "Oh, my dear Christopher, the days when I heeded every word you said went long ago. Let's get to the others and return to Paris now."

Her arms went swiftly round his neck and she kissed him hard. They stood wrapped together, his arms round her, their blended shadows falling across the cobbles of Versailles. Both knew it was the last kiss they would ever exchange.

Within an hour of getting back to Paris Julia was leaving it again, escorted by Michael in a coach making for the coast where she would sail for England in the morning. Molly could have stayed behind and returned home with Christopher and Faith when the danger of the plague was past, but she had insisted on accompanying her mistress.

"In any case I've nothing to fear, because as a child I alone survived in a pest-house when my parents and all those shut in there round me died of the plague," she stated firmly.

"What a terrible experience!"

"It was, but by isolating us the rest of the village escaped the infection. If that had been done at first sign in London all this trouble would never have spread. Country ways are always best."

When Molly fell asleep during the night hours as the coach rumbled on, Julia was able to talk to Michael about his strange pains. As tactfully as possible she pointed out how odd it was that he should always be afflicted on the eve of coming to England. She could not see his face in the darkness of the coach, but she heard him sigh.

"I know what you're thinking," he admitted. "I drew the same conclusions myself after a while, but I was wrong, because I get slight attacks at other times that can only be due to the digestive disorder that the doctor diagnosed just as I have told you."

"Do those times coincide with anything?"

"No, they are entirely without pattern. I blame the stress of business because, naturally, there are difficult periods when all does not go well. Put the matter from your mind, Julia. There is nothing to worry about."

She leaned towards him urgently. "Test my theory! Come to England with me! You can go straight to Sotherleigh and be in no danger of infection. Stay only a day or two if you wish, but do it! Let's see if any pains result from the nervous excitement that supposedly attacks you at the prospect of homecoming! If they don't, you'll know for certain they are induced."

She sensed his hesitation and could guess at the struggle within him. He did not want to believe that his wife was capable of such viciousness—the whole of his nature was set against it—but this was one time when Sophie would have had no chance to do anything, for when leaving Paris with Julia at extremely short notice, there had been no question of his travelling farther than Calais.

"I'll go with you," he said in a hollow voice.

At Calais he found they had five hours before the next ship sailed. While Julia and Molly rested at a hostelry he sat downstairs writing letters to send back to Paris with the coachman. One was to Sophie to explain that he had decided on impulse to make a quick trip to Sotherleigh and another to his chief clerk about business appointments that would have to be cancelled and other matters to be dealt with during his brief absence. When he had sealed both letters and they had been sent on their way, he knew the truth already. Nothing would affect his health this time.

# SEVENTEEN

*A*T DOVER, after having to be strict with well-meaning Molly on the voyage, Julia had made her plans. Her maid had wanted to accompany her to London, but she would not allow it.

"You'll be far more help to me by going ahead and seeing that those three isolated and empty cottages away from the village are prepared for my weavers and embroiderers when I get them there. Make up beds, lay in a stock of food and see that the wells have new buckets. You'll have to be in charge of them if anything should prevent my leaving London."

There would be only one reason for that, which was if she should find Adam too ill to be moved, and she had difficulty in suppressing the anxiety in her voice. She gave Molly more instructions, some of which Mary could help with, and wrote them all down to make sure that nothing was overlooked.

Michael had told her he would be riding through the night to reach Sotherleigh and would leave Molly at a hostelry if she should not be able to keep up with his pace. It suited Julia that he should make such haste, knowing it was Mary whom he was eager to see again, for Julia was able to arrange with him that immediately upon his arrival at Sotherleigh he should send off coachmen with equipages to collect her workers at a given point on the road not far from London.

"I won't know until I get to London exactly how things will work out, but I can always get a message to my embroiderers and weavers that those wishing to leave for Sussex can find the transport there. I hope to manage everything personally, but that depends on how I find Adam."

She was to ride with an Anglican parson and his wife, whom they had met on board ship. The Reverend Thomas Webb, fifty years old, had left his post as tutor to the children of a Cavalier's widow in Paris to answer a spiritual call to minister to the plague-stricken in London. His courageous wife, also fifty, was with him, being of a similar mind.

"My wife and I will be most happy for your sister to ride with us," he had said to Michael. "You need have no fears for her safety. I am armed. Not that I myself wish to shoot a fellow human being, but I have found in the past that firing into the air is enough to scare off any scallywags."

Julia thought that just the look of him might have done that, for he had hawk features and fierce bushy eyebrows that met in the middle, giving him a most threatening appearance. It was only at close quarters that it was possible to see that his eyes were as mild as a child's. Mrs. Webb, tidy, plain and comfortably shaped, had her grey hair screwed back out of sight under a frilled cap on which a felt hat was secured by ribbons tied under her chin. Paris fashions had passed her by and Julia liked her all the more for it. There was something about the woman's practical, no-nonsense attitude that reminded her nostalgically of Katherine.

Horses were hired. Michael helped Julia up into the saddle. Behind it was strapped the small roll of baggage that was all she had brought with her; the rest was to follow with Faith whenever she should return. Among the written instructions given to Sarah was one for any type of clothing, old or still in use, to be sent with the transport Michael would be dispatching from Sotherleigh. Julia herself counted on having the garments she had left in the Strand house.

"God speed you," Michael said to her. "May you find Adam well."

"I pray so," she answered huskily. Then she set off with the Webbs along the London road, leaving her brother and Molly to gallop off on another route to Sussex.

There were no difficulties on the journey towards the capital, although it would have been a different matter had they been coming away from the city. Turnpikes and barriers had been erected at bridges and on the outskirts of towns and villages to prevent refugees from the plague entering the vicinity. Well-meant advice not to go near London was shouted to the three travellers many times.

The long light summer evening and regular changes of horses enabled them to cover much of the distance to London before the Webbs called a halt for supper and an overnight stay. Julia was all for going on through the night. She had never wanted to be with Adam more. Such a yearning for him had possessed her from that moment at Versailles when she had first learned he might be in danger that she could not get to him quickly enough. Yet now, when she was only a few hours away, the landlord of the tavern where the Webbs were seeking shelter had informed her of a hold-up she had not anticipated.

"You'd never get into London now that it's after nine o'clock. London Bridge is barred and there's a curfew everywhere until morning with the penalty of imprisonment for those that break it."

She resigned herself to staying. When she sat down to supper with the Webbs, the landlord himself brought a joint of roast beef to their table and proceeded to give them further information about the capital as he carved. All the theatres and pleasure gardens had been closed by order of the Lord Mayor, who, with his aldermen, was staying stoically in London to ensure that law and order were maintained, the main keepers of which were the watchmen, the women inspectors who investigated houses where it was suspected the plague victims were being concealed, and a small number of troops. Cockpits, bull-and-bear baiting arenas and anywhere else where crowds gathered had also been shut down. So many thousands had died that great pits had been dug in fields outside the city and carts collected the dead by night, public money keeping the collectors drunk, else they would not carry out their gruesome task. Countless numbers of the populace had fled, but thousands more had to stay because of business or personal commitments or simply because they had nowhere to go.

"You'll be getting a glimpse of hell, Sir," the landlord warned, putting slices of the good beef onto the three plates which a waiting-maid, who had brought dishes of vegetables, took in turns to set before each of the three guests.

"Which part of London appears to be faring worst?" Mr. Webb inquired. "I hear that within the walls of the City itself there have not been many cases."

"That was so until recently and then everything changed. Now everybody talks of the Great Plague and indeed it is so. It flared up first in the parish of St. Giles in Holborn and at Covent Garden, whereupon it reached out towards Westminster." He noticed that Julia caught her breath. "You have family there, madam?"

"My husband. Our home is in the Strand."

"Ah!" He shook his head pessimistically to show that he could say nothing to relieve her anxiety there. "The plague doesn't abate in areas that it has attacked. Quite the reverse, even though it is forever sweeping on. Soon all the outlying parishes were in the throes of it. Now the City is beginning to feel the full force of its terrible onslaught." He picked up the dish of beef, ready to carry it away. "I couldn't advise anywhere in London now where you'd be safe, sir."

The parson raised his thatch of eyebrows. "I wasn't thinking of that aspect. My wife and I wish to go straight to wherever the sick and dying are most in need of spiritual comfort and nursing."

Mrs. Webb endorsed his statement. "All that we've heard since landing at Dover has told us we did right to return for that purpose."

The landlord's expression was blended of admiration for such valiant courage and disbelief at such folly. "You'll be much needed. They say many of the doctors have fled the plague themselves and the drabs and villainesses acting as nurses hasten the end of many of the sick to steal from them. May the Lord preserve you all from these many dangers."

Then he left them, shaking his head again. Mrs. Webb noticed that Julia was not touching her food and leaned forward to point at it. "Eat up, my dear. You may be needing all the strength you have and being hungry will only weaken you."

Julia accepted her reasoning. She did not doubt it was a good meal, but she appreciated none of it as gradually she forced herself to clear her plate.

After supper she asked the parson's wife to explain the plague to her and how best to treat it, for she had no guidance. It had never brushed against Sotherleigh and to her knowledge there was nowhere in Sussex that had been attacked in her lifetime. What struck her as most inhumane in dealing with the plague was the old law that decreed that once one member of a household fell sick all the rest living there had to be locked in with the victim to survive or die as fate willed. Although it was intended to check the spread of the disease it meant that many had died who would otherwise have escaped. Usually it broke out in the meanest areas of a city, where the poor were crowded together and the filthy streets were never swept. Maybe the clean sea breezes, which Grandfather Ned was said always to have praised, had much to do with keeping the county of Sussex free of the pestilence.

"What are the first signs I should look for?" Julia had invited Mrs. Webb into the bedchamber she had taken for the night, for Mr. Webb was already in bed and asleep in the neighbouring room.

"You can be sure I know what I'm talking about when I tell you." The woman settled herself comfortably in a chair. "I spent years nursing the poor in my husband's parish in one of the worst areas of Liverpool before Cromwell deprived him of his living and we sought employment abroad.

The plague was a constant hazard, often brought ashore in cargoes. As for signs, there are quite a few and not all immediately discernible."

"Excessive sneezing is one, I believe."

"It is. You know the old rhyme, 'Ring-o-ring of roses'? The mention of roses is the reddish plague-blains or marks on the skin and a pocket-ful of posies refers to the herbs carried to ward off infection. The words 'Atishoo, atishoo, we all fall down' relate to the final fatal symptom before the infected drop dead. Fortunately children in their innocence are unaware of its meaning when they play."

"What else gives warning?"

"Shivering is another symptom. Yet sometimes the only warning is a feeling of immense tiredness when out walking or carrying out some ordinary chore and the victims will need to sit down immediately. Within minutes these unfortunate people expire. Just as if they had dropped off to sleep."

Julia was aghast. "So quickly!"

"It's when the plague-blains have appeared on their bodies without their knowledge. You see, the plague takes two main forms. Firstly there is the spotted fever that produces this particular gangrene of the body. Frequently, the tiredness doesn't come upon them at all and they feel perfectly well, going about their daily business as I have said, and then to their horror they discover the dreadful tokens on themselves. Soon after-wards they will die. Nothing can be done for them." She raised her hands and let them fall again into her lap helplessly. "It has happened that a whole ship's crew has been struck down and the vessel left to drift with no one at the helm."

"I have heard tell of that."

"The second form that the plague takes is far worse, because at least the spotted fever is mercifully quick."

"I know that swellings appear either in the neck or groin or in the armpits."

"The agony is beyond endurance. There are such pains in the head and such torture from the swellings. Many turn crazy from the pain and throw themselves from windows. In such a case you must keep the win-dows shuttered and the door locked. Hot poultices to make the swellings break is the main treatment, but in my experience it is when they are drawn too quickly that they reach the hardness of iron. This is where doctors add to the patients' torment by burning when a sharp knife fails to penetrate, because unless the poison is released it is certain death."

Julia shuddered, but this was no time for squeamishness. She had to be prepared. "Then early treatment with poultices should be cautious. Ideally the swellings should break naturally."

"That's right. I have found a way that has worked well with many although it is entirely unconventional."

"What is it?" Julia trusted instinctively this woman's good sense.

"Well, when I was a child I lived in York and it was half truth and half legend that once the plague was brought to the city in a cargo of silks that came from a ship docked in the Humber. One man was so maddened by the pain of a swelling in his groin that he threw off those who would have kept him restrained to his bed and rushed out of the house to hurl himself into the river. He swam across and back again, getting relief through the coldness of the water on his burning body."

"Surely that killed him? I thought bedclothes had to be piled onto the patient to produce a sweat."

"That's what is always done, but the river had eased his fever and the exercise had loosened the tightness of the swelling, which broke naturally soon after he staggered back home. I keep a patient bathed with cool water and exercise continually whichever part of the body is affected, whether it means rotating the head or the arm or the leg. It is exhausting for the patient and for me. Sometimes a knife has had to be used at the end, but never to such a degree of torture as can be afflicted otherwise, and the patients have been spared the terrible oven-heat of induced sweatings adding to the fever-fire of their bodies." Mrs. Webb leaned forward and patted Julia's hand. "Remember what I've told you. You'll need to be strong to give this treatment, but you look capable to me. Don't be discouraged by anything. I have saved many patients and had greater success than any doctor I've ever met."

"I know whenever my mother visited infectious cases of fever in the village, she always changed her clothes and bathed herself from head to toe before coming into contact with anyone else in the house. Is that how you keep from spreading infection?"

"I do. I go straight into an outside wash-house, throw everything into a tub of soapsuds and then pour a bucket of cold water over my head to douse myself to my feet."

"I have planned something similar for my workers before they reach the cottages at Sotherleigh."

"Well done. When God gave us water to drink does it not seem logical that something so pure should be intended for use in healing as well?"

Before Julia slept she wondered how far Michael was on his journey. There was every likelihood that aided by this bright moonlit night he would be safely at Sotherleigh by now.

IT WAS ON THE BRINK of dawn when Michael roused the servants that slept in the coach-house and stable lofts. Molly had delayed him, refusing to be left behind as she had her duties to carry out for Julia at Sotherleigh too. Lanterns twinkled and yawns were stifled as grooms and stable-boys went about their tasks. When Michael saw that all was in order he instructed on impulse that the coach be added to the three carts that would be going in case his sister should have need of it.

"Be particularly vigilant," he warned the coachmen and the grooms he was sending with each one. "If people fleeing the plague are desperate they might try to take the horses from you."

"I'll see that don't 'appen, sir," the leading coachman answered confidently.

Satisfied, Michael went into the house by way of the kitchen. The cook and the kitchen staff, awakened by Molly, were preparing breakfast for those about to depart and making ready travel food for them and the passengers they were to collect later in the day.

He went upstairs, throwing aside his hat and cloak as he went and making for Mary's room. Since he was not expected her door should not be locked this time. He turned the handle and it gave at once. She did not stir when he entered and only awoke with startled, widening eyes as he sat on the bed and scooped her into his arms, causing her soft hair to swing about her face.

"Michael!" She was panicking at her own yearning reaction.

"My darling Mary, my love and my life!" Then he was kissing her. When he felt the tautness in her melt and her arms slide lovingly about his neck, he knew her door would not be locked against him on this visit. As he was now resolved never to bring Sophie to Sotherleigh there should be no turning of keys between them ever again.

BY SIX O'CLOCK Julia and the Webbs were on the road again with the weather threatening to turn sultry, which was the worst condition for spreading pestilence. They began to meet little groups of sober-faced people on foot or in carts and occasionally a coach with finely dressed passengers, all of them fleeing the Great Plague. In meadows and waste land on either side of the road were make-shift tents of every colour and shape as people rested on their journeys. Others, less fortunate, having been barred from entering a nearby town or village, had to remain there indefinitely. The only sound of laughter came from the children, some of whom would never have been out of a London street before, and they played about and chased one another happily. There were always men and women, as well as their young, who ran to beg as travellers went by, but it would have been impossible to give to all and Mr. Webb advised Julia against giving anything.

"You may be pulled from your horse if they glimpse silver or gold in your purse. I beg you to spare me from shooting anyone and adding to people's misery."

She did lean from her saddle to give a gold piece to a widow trudging along with three children at her heels and a baby in her arms, knowing that at least it would keep them fed for weeks to come. She also gave to other solitary refugees who held out a hand dumbly, despair in their faces. Many simply cried out for a blessing from the parson, dropping to their knees in the dust as he made the sign of the Cross over them as he rode by.

At Southwark Julia parted from her travelling companions, having decided to take a ferry-boat upriver to the Strand. The Webbs gave her an address where they could be contacted and she gave them hers. She waved them on their way to London Bridge and then rode to a tavern at the riverside to leave her hired horse. Travellers rushed out to be the first to hire it before she had dismounted, quarrelling over it amongst themselves. It gave her an insight into the demand for transport to get away from London.

In contrast there was a line of ferry-boats for hire, business being slack, and she could see how sparse traffic was on the river. The waterman took her baggage from her and stowed it aboard, all without the usual quips associated with his trade. Glum and silent, he pulled on his oars, slicing through the shining water while London Bridge slipped away eastwards. The City glided by on the north bank and from it came the doleful sound of church bells tolling for the dead. There was always smoke billowing upwards from commercial and domestic chimneys, but today when she might have expected less there was more, hanging like a suspended wreath over the rooftops and hiding some of the many church spires that gave grace to the skyline.

"Why is there so much smoke?" she inquired.

"That's from the bonfires that are burning night and day to help dispel infection. They're fuelled with fir or cedar for its effluvium of turpentine."

"Some of the smoke looks very dark."

"That'll be from coal bonfires for the sulphur and the bitumen."

"I see. Are they helping?"

"Not that I've noticed," he replied bitterly. "I live in the parish of St. Giles and five hundred died there last week. We was the first to 'ave the bonfires."

She almost quailed, realising he could be carrying the infection on his clothes or be already afflicted in his person, but then she checked herself. From now on everyone she met would have had some contact with the plague. She must simply carry on as normal in times that were anything but normal, which was the way most people would be coping with whatever they had to do.

She stepped ashore at the Somerset steps. With her baggage under her arm, she walked quickly up the street to the Strand. On the way she passed a pair of ornamental gates to a large mansion, red crosses splashed across the stone gate-posts and again within on its great entrance door, showing that the plague took no heed of wealth or rank. A burly watchman stood on guard to ensure that none of the occupants went in or out all the time the sickness prevailed and throughout the period of quarantine afterwards.

When she turned into the Strand she saw more red crosses on both sides of the wide street. Here the watchmen, all rough-looking fellows like the one outside the mansion, patrolled several buildings in a row. They wore a badge of office on their hats and carried thick staves to enforce their authority towards the unfortunate inmates of those houses and shops under their jurisdiction. As with the river, there was none of the customary bustle to and fro along this main artery between the walled City and Westminster. Most of the sparse traffic rolled intermittently westward, carrying escaping families out of London.

Julia increased her pace, her longing to reach Adam overwhelming her now that there was so little distance left. Then it dawned on her that she was the only pedestrian keeping to the side of the street as she hastened along. A new pattern of walking had evolved in which people braved what traffic there was to follow the middle of the thoroughfare and avoid being near any of the infected houses. Suddenly she heard terrible shrieks coming from one of the padlocked houses and was astonished that nobody took any notice. Then she understood that such sounds must have become commonplace.

She hastened along but could not hope to see her destination yet. Shady trees and the fact that some house entrances projected forward, while others lay back behind gates, gave an obstructive view ahead. It crossed her mind that the watchmen had a difficult task on this side of the Strand to ensure that none went in or out of the plague-marked residences under cover of darkness.

Adam! Adam! Adam! Her heartbeats seemed to echo his name as she covered the last stretch of cobbles that would bring her to within a view of their home. And there it was! No red crosses on the gate-pillars! She gave a sob of thankfulness as she pushed open one of the double gates to close it again after her. Because the house faced the river instead of the street, a tree-lined drive led southwards and around to the front. She flung her baggage down on the grass verge, not wanting to be hindered by anything on this final lap of her journey. Gathering up her skirts, she broke into a run as she followed the drive under its leafy canopy. Her hat flew from her head, but she did not stop to retrieve it. Then she burst out of sun-speckled shadow as the drive curved to lie parallel with the house's many-windowed frontage, lawns and flowerbeds sweeping down to the river. The door stood open. With a swirl of petticoats and flashing heels she was up the steps and into the hall.

"Adam!" she called joyously. "I'm here!"

Her voice echoed back at her in a way that told her the house was deserted, neither he nor any of the servants being there. At the same time she saw, although there had been no red cross on the door, that disaster of another kind had struck. Looters had been here! A chair had been over-turned and lay amidst the scattered fragments of a smashed Chinese vase of great beauty and antiquity that Katherine had bequeathed her. It had been the first thing she had found a place for when coming to London. Her favourite tapestry, depicting a knight and a lady in a forest, had gone from the wall, leaving a disarray of hooks that showed how violently it had been tugged down, while the silver salver that was always on a carved sidetable was nowhere to be seen.

Full of foreboding she looked into the Grand Salon and was appalled at the wreckage of the room. What had not been taken had been slashed as if the looters had taken vengeance against the house of those who had left London and escaped the plague, for she was now certain Adam would have sent all the servants to a safe place, even if he should still be at

Westminster and staying elsewhere. The wanton damage proved to be the same in all the downstairs rooms and she supposed the homes of many people from every walk of life would be robbed and vandalised in their absence. There were always vultures waiting to take advantage of a general misfortune. Her guess was that the looters of her home had been there only the previous night, for one had relieved himself against a wall and the floor was still damp.

Although she was certain she was alone, it was with caution that she went up the stairs. As soon as she began to draw level with the landing she saw at once that there everything was orderly and nothing had been touched. Hopeful that at least the upper floor had been spared, she hastened up the last few stairs and crossed the landing to reach her bedchamber door. Entering, she sighed with relief. No intruder had been in here. She could tell by the closed shutters that Adam had shut up the house completely and that those downstairs had been opened by the looters to let in the moonlight, the better to see what they were about. In the light from the door she had left open she could see that the four-poster where she and Adam slept was neat from a maidservant's last smoothing of the coverlet into place.

The shutters went clattering back at her touch. She turned and there, propped on her toilet-table against one of her perfume flasks, was a letter in Adam's handwriting. In a matter of seconds she had opened it. Two slips of paper fell out and she saw they were certificates of health made out in her name and Molly's, bearing the Lord Mayor's signature and seal. Quickly she turned to Adam's letter, noting it had been written five days before.

*Beloved Julia. Today I am closing the house and going home to Sussex. The King has left Westminster to go to Hampton Court and from there he will take the Queen with him to the city of Oxford for greater safety. In addition Parliament has been prorogued for the duration of the plague, which leaves me free of my duties. I intend to set off with the least possible delay from Warrender Hall and Sotherleigh to you in France from where we might travel together and see some of the marvels of Rome, Florence and Venice. In a way I am putting my thoughts on paper, because it is my hope that this letter will be torn up unread when you and I return here when all is well with London again. But always I have to allow for the unexpected with you, my love, and for that reason I have obtained certificates of health for you and your maid in case you should return from France unannounced and expect to find me still at Westminster. If this should happen, leave with all haste for Sotherleigh and let nothing delay you. Your devoted Adam.*

Her disappointment at missing him by a few days was like a knife being struck into her. Her head bowed slowly and she pressed the letter against her breast, her whole being crying out for him. The irony was that he had almost certainly been crossing the Channel to France from a harbour near Sotherleigh while she was on the ship bound for Dover. It might even have been the sails of the vessel he was travelling in that she and Michael had seen in the distance.

She was as far away from him again as she had been during all those past weeks in Paris. If only she had met Joe sooner! But it was useless to dwell on that now. She had to gather her workers together and get them out of London without the least delay, not only for their safe-keeping, but also because as soon as Adam discovered she was not in Paris he would return to England immediately. She wanted him to find her at Sotherleigh when he arrived. Fortunately she had told both Faith and Christopher she would go straight home in the event of Adam's not being in London.

Now she needed water to freshen herself after her morning journey and then she would set out on foot for Carter Lane. Mrs. Webb had warned her not to ride in a hackney coach, because they harboured infection. As she came out of her room she thought she had better check the rest of the upper floor to make sure all the rooms were untouched. She opened one door and then another, satisfied each time. Then she saw that the door to the anteroom of the large guest chamber stood open. Instantly she sensed danger, a chill running down her spine and her heart beginning to thump. There were crossed swords on the wall facing the head of the stairs and soundlessly she took one down. Warily and silently she approached the open door, hearing no movement and yet knowing something dreadful awaited her there.

She reached the threshold. It was dark within, which should have reassured her, but her fear mounted. Pushing the door open wider, she entered step by cautious step. Again she paused, straining her ears for the least sound, but there was nothing except her own fast breathing and the whisper of her petticoats.

The recessed door to the bedchamber lay to her left and it also stood open, but not a glimmer of light reached it from the landing behind her and the aperture loomed like a black cave. On she went, the sword poised and heavy in her hand, and she froze every time a floorboard creaked faintly underfoot. At last she could peer into the bedchamber. Her eyes had become accustomed enough to the darkness for her to see the pale draped bed. The stillness within was absolute. She stepped forward into the room.

Her scream sliced piercingly through the silence as she stepped on an object that rolled away, shooting her off balance, and she crashed full-length over something larger that was lying there, the sword flying from her hand. Terrified that she was about to be grabbed, she hurled herself to her feet and stumbled on her skirt-hem, falling forward to crash her shoulder painfully against one of the two closed window shutters. The force was enough to make the hinges give slightly, letting a bright finger of light penetrate the room and showing her a dreadful sight. Icy horror gripped her and she pressed herself back against the wall, unable to move.

One of the looters lay dead on his back, sprawled across the Persian carpet that had been rucked by his fall. Around him was the plunder he had dropped. A silver-framed mirror, a pair of gold candlesticks and an ivory-topped cane that had slid from under her foot. The man was coarse-featured and unshaven, and mercifully his eyes were closed, but on his neck above his loosely tied, dirty neckerchief, as well as on his hands, were curious reddish markings that she had never seen before, but which she recognised instantly for what they were. He had died of the plague!

Her teeth were chattering from shock and her whole body was shaking as she began to edge along the wall towards the door. He was one of those who had surely been affected by tiredness and, unaware of what was happening to him, not having seen the marks on his body, had probably been on his way to find a chair on which to sit and rest. Instead the plague had claimed him. Perhaps he had come upstairs on his own to gain first pickings, leaving the rest to loot below. She could picture them bounding upstairs at the sound of his fall. Then, upon discovering him, they had turned about and bolted for their lives, taking whatever booty they had already gathered downstairs.

Abruptly she began to gag as bile filled her mouth. She dashed past the plague victim and out to the landing where she leaned weakly against the landing balustrade until the spasm passed. Then slowly she looked at her right hand. Had she touched him when she fell? She could not remember, but her clothes had brushed against him and she must get rid of them.

She ripped and tore at her garments, kicked off her shoes and stockings until she was only in her undershift, which was shorter than her petticoats and would have had no contact. Then she rushed downstairs, much as the frightened looters would have done, and ran through to the kitchen where the indoor pump was located. The water gushed into a bucket on a ledge at waist level as she pumped the handle. She washed her hands, took fresh water again and when the bucket was almost full she scooped up some with her cupped hands and bathed her face several times. Then, heedless of the trickles that ran down her neck, she stood with her hands dangling wrist deep in the bucket, her eyes closed as if to shut out what she had seen.

Her panic subsided. Infection was spread by breath or touch and it was probably her own cloak and not his coat on which her hand had descended in her tumble. Moving from the pump, she opened a drawer and took out a linen towel to dry her face and hands as she sank down onto a bench to review the situation. The kitchen was tidy and undisturbed, the copper pans shining on the walls, every lid closed over containers in the long iron bench that housed charcoal to keep the broad surface hot for food waiting to be served at the dining table. There was something comforting about a kitchen, and the fact that this one was similar to Sotherleigh's was very calming to her.

She thought over carefully what she should do. The corpse would have to be removed tonight when a cart for the dead went by, but if she called to the body-takers from the house the authorities would padlock her up inside it. Somehow she must give word to one of the watchmen without suspicion falling on her as an occupant. She must certainly not look like the owner of the property or suspicion should arise.

She went back upstairs, careful not to touch anything until she reached her room. Then she loosened the ribbons at the neckline of her undershift and let it fall to the floor. Stepping out of it, she took fresh underwear from a drawer, found stockings and garters in another, and when she had donned them she went into the side room where her gowns, shoes, cloaks and hats were kept. She selected a plain gown of striped blue cotton, which was one of the simplest she owned. She then tried to choose a cloak, but in quality they were all like the one she had travelled in, a problem that was resolved when she remembered that the maidservants had an old cloak on a peg in the outer kitchen that they donned in bad weather if sent out into the garden to fetch herbs or a flower-garnish or to take a message to the stables. After a change of shoes into a pair that would be particularly comfortable for walking, she took Adam's letter with the health certificates and went downstairs again to the outer kitchen. The cloak was there. After tucking the papers into its inside pocket, she slipped it on, letting the hood lie back on her shoulders. She had no modish coiffure to give her away for her hair was simply tidy and softly dressed.

She left the house without a backwards glance. All had to be left exactly as it was. Material things were not important in such times as these and if other looters should come—so be it. All that mattered was Adam being safe and well. Had it been he lying in that room upstairs she would not have wanted to go on living. Suddenly, in the midst of so much horror, she realised what his love meant to her and that without it everything would have ended for her.

In the drive she picked up her piece of baggage but left her hat where it had fallen. Her intention to go inconspicuously out of the side gate used by the servants was thwarted by finding it securely locked. Through the bars, and directly opposite, she saw a red cross marking the corresponding gate of the neighbouring house and a watchman was patrolling the narrow passage-way. She drew back quickly, but he had not seen her. Hurrying to the main gates she knew now why the looters had decided to pick the locks there. It would have been easily done in a matter of seconds by cunning hands under cover of darkness.

She slipped out of the gate and joined several pedestrians walking in the middle of the street. Nobody paid her any attention. After going only a short distance she trailed off to look in a jeweller's window. It was bare of goods due to the red cross above the door and she made a grimace of disappointment, catching a nearby watchman's eyes.

"Nothing pretty to look at in there any more," she said, using the inflections of a Sussex country woman in her voice.

"Nor will there be from the hands of the old jeweller again. He's gone and so has his wife. Only the servants are still boxed up in the living quarters."

"Gone? You mean nipped off like the folk in the house over there, leaving a man dead of the plague?"

He did not bother to clarify what she had deliberately misunderstood and glared towards her home. "Why ain't there a red cross there? How can you be sure a corpse has been left?"

"I know the maidservants that worked there. The mistress left in a right old hurry!"

"I bet she did!" he snapped grimly, not taking his glare from the house. "You did right to warn me, lass. I'll see that corpse gets shifted tonight and the house closed." Then he looked at her with more interest, giving her a yellow-toothed smile. "Where do you work then?"

"I sell ribbons."

He looked sympathetic. "Not much call now for that trade, is there?"

"I fear not."

"You won't get no domestic work either. The rich folk are locking up their London houses and turning off their servants left, right and centre, leaving even those of many years' service out on the streets with nowhere to go and at the mercy of the plague."

She was shocked at this information, having been raised always to consider one's responsibility towards those one employed. "You mean they're simply being abandoned?"

"That's it. People are looking after their own skins first these days and the nobs can do it better than most with their coaches and horses to speed them away. What happened to your friends over there?" He nodded in the direction of her home.

"They were all taken to safety."

"Then they were some of the lucky ones." He gave her a sly wink. "Why not make a lucky man of me later when I hand over to another watchman at curfew time?"

"I daren't be out after that hour."

"With me you'll be aw'right. Us watchmen and bakers have special passes."

"The bakers?"

"Didn't you know that? Why else do you think there's always plenty of bread for all? The Lord Mayor has forbade any baker to leave London. People need that staff of life, whether they be sick or well." He reverted to his talk of a further meeting. "You be here just before nine o'clock. I know a place where we can still enjoy ourselves with ale and anything else we fancy."

"I'll see." She began to move on.

"I'll be lookin' out for you," he called after her. Then came an after-thought. "What's your name?"

At that point she was far enough away to mouth the first name that came into her head with no chance of his hearing, for ear-splitting shrieks had broken out again in the same upper room as before when she had come from the ferry-boat. She checked an urge to clap her hands over her ears and rush from the heart-rending sound, certain it would not be the last of what she would hear before the day was out.

Her first task was to hire horses and carts in readiness to transport her workers out of the City in the morning. Remembering the scramble there had been for her hired horse on the other side of the river she wondered what her chances would be. She was sure Mr. Needham at the Heathcock would do everything in his power to oblige her and she could inquire after the family at the same time, but when she arrived there she saw that a red cross stained the hostelry's street door and a chain was looped across the way into the deserted courtyard.

"How fares the landlord and his wife and family?" she asked the short, square watchman leaning his shoulder against the hostelry wall. Her tone was authoritative, the few minutes of pretence necessary for the other watchman over and finished. She could be herself again.

The watchman was chewing tobacco, which was a new habit brought in by the plague in the belief it kept infection away, and he spat a stream of yellow saliva into the gutter before he answered her. "Two dead brought out last night and one the night before." Then a tap came from within the hostelry door and he gestured with his stave for her to draw back. "Clear well away. There will be some errand I'll be required to do or else it'll be to tell me there'll be another corpse for the cart when it comes by."

She moved to a safe distance, full of distress at what she had heard, and watched him unlock the padlock. Then he himself stood well back as the door opened a few inches. She saw a man's hand, probably Mr. Needham's, place some coins on the doorstep, but she did not hear what was said. The door was repadlocked and the watchman gave a shout to one of his fellows as he picked up the coins in a gloved hand.

"I'm fetching food. Back in ten minutes."

Julia was relieved to know it was not more dreadful tidings as she had half expected and she wished the Needham family well as she continued on her way. It was to prove the most harrowing walk she had ever taken, such ghastly screams and shrieks and groans coming from some of the plague-stricken houses that she wept to hear such torment.

She was approaching Temple Bar when there was a sudden commotion ahead. People were scattering in all directions and she was left with a clear view of a stricken woman, demented with pain from a crimson swelling in her neck the size of an apple, who had managed to escape through a window and was running wildly about like a mad dog. Her relatives wailed and cried at other windows of the house, not being allowed to emerge and fetch her in again as she tore her nightgown, her nakedness exposed for all to see, her screaming terrible to hear. Then several men came with homemade pikes, obviously kept for such an emergency, to help the watchman with his stave prod and drive her back indoors, but she seemed unaware of the extra pain being inflicted upon her in her greater agony. An exodus of coaches from the city was being held up and a few coachmen, ordered by their irate masters, came with their whips to see what they could do. It took quite a while before the woman was rounded up and forced near enough to the door for her distraught family to seize her and pull her inside.

Julia was filled with pity for the woman and her kin in their misery. She stood aside as the coaches went rolling on, horses whipped up to compensate for lost time. Out of half a dozen coaches only one had a wagon following with servants.

At the Temple there were no periwigged lawyers dashing about, for the courts were not being held at this dangerous time. Shops and businesses were open in Fleet Street, as they had been elsewhere along her route, but few people went in and out. The markets, normally thronged with customers, were practically deserted. Only the street-criers selling herbs and lavender were making money, their posies being bought to hold to the nose and stave off infection. There were no children to be seen at play, parents keeping them indoors for safety, and even the ragamuffins that begged were few and far between. To Julia's distress, whenever a plague victim began to sneeze, sometimes crying out for help, neither she nor anyone else dared go near. Without exception the afflicted were dead a few minutes later and left where they lay for the death cart to collect them when night came. It seemed to her that the new voice of London was the tolling of bells and the tumult of suffering.

At Ludgate there was a stable that offered horses for hire and stood open for business. All the others Julia had passed had been closed. A man in shirt-sleeves and a leather apron came into the yard to meet her. She asked first if he had any carts or wagons for hire.

"No, I don't," he said, looking at her in such a hostile manner that she guessed he was wearied by such enquiries in the great exodus from London.

"Then I must take whatever horses you can supply. I know they are in great demand, but I'm willing to pay well. If you don't have many yourself I should like you to gather some from elsewhere and bring them to me at an address in Carter Lane at curfew's end tomorrow morning."

"Are you gaming me, madam?" he demanded angrily. "Or perhaps you've had your head in the sand. There isn't a cart or wagon or a horse to buy or hire anywhere in London to my knowledge. My last two nags took my family into the country a month ago. I'm staying on as many tradesmen are just to keep my property from being looted, because I run a harness-making business from here as well."

She was dismayed. "Is the shortage so acute? Indeed I had no idea. I fear I've not adjusted to conditions here yet, having returned from abroad only yesterday."

He looked more kindly at her. "I'm sorry I can't help you. Have you no friends who could oblige?"

She pondered over his suggestion as she left. Most of her connections were with the Court and they were gone. Maybe the Lord Mayor, whom she knew personally, having met him on many social occasions, could give her some advice when she collected the certificates of health for her women, otherwise it would be a long tramp for them along dusty roads to the meeting point with the Sotherleigh carts. At least she could be sure the coachmen and grooms would wait, allowing for any delay. Everything had taken an unusual turn, for when that arrangement had been made she had never expected to be travelling with her party, imagining herself with Adam.

St. Paul's was tolling its tower bell and she could hear its distinctive notes as she entered Carter Lane. Christopher had been asked to see to its much needed restoration, for its spire had fallen down long since and its timbers had been attacked by both damp and the death watch beetle, an insect that could not have been better named in these sad times.

When she opened the door of her workshop she had the extraordinary sensation of time having stood still in these premises and all she had been witnessing had been a nightmare from which she had awakened. Her embroidery hands sat quietly around their large tables, plenty of room for each, and from the weaving room came the clicking of the looms. Within a second all the embroiderers had looked up and seen her and immediately a babble of voices broke out, all relieved that she was there, some springing to their feet while one ran to summon the weavers.

"Where's Mrs. Blake?" she asked as soon as she made herself heard. Immediately a silence fell. Then Alice spoke. "She died of the plague nearly four weeks ago."

Julia swallowed her sorrow. "Who else?"

"Rose and Eleanor among the weavers and Polly from the embroiderers. There's one more who's still alive, but in dire circumstances. That's

Abigail. She is shut up in a plague house with her sick husband and father-in-law with no woman to help her when her time comes."

"When will that be?"

"The baby is already overdue."

"I think I can solve that problem."

"No midwife will step inside an infected place."

"The one whom I know won't hesitate." Julia looked around at the little gathering of women. "I see some faces are missing. Not through sickness, I trust."

Again Alice answered her. "They've all left London to go to relatives in the country." She counted off fifteen names on her fingers and then another four before she was prompted into remembering three more. Most of them were married women with children.

"That leaves just twenty-one of you here," Julia said. "Why haven't any of you left London?"

The explanations came all at once. They knew no one who would take them in; they had no money to leave their work to go elsewhere and all were afraid of falling sick and dying somewhere on a roadside. Alice gave an additional reason that covered them all. "None of us has a certificate of health to leave in any case and it's unlikely we'd be given one as some of our fellow workers have died of the pestilence."

"But none died here or else there'd be a red cross outside," Julia pointed out.

"That's right and all were within a few days of one another."

"Then it's unlikely that by this time any of you will fall sick from that source. If I can get certificates for everyone, would you like to accompany me to Sussex tomorrow morning, even if it should mean walking almost ten miles for the first part of the way?"

Almost without exception they burst into tears of relief, seeing an end to weeks of terror and suspense. All gave their eager assent, many laughing and crying at the same time. She went into her office and wrote a quick note to Mrs. Webb, giving Abigail's address. This was given to one of the weavers, whose home was in the same alley as the house belonging to the Webbs' contact. The young woman promised to deliver it on her way past, for Julia had told them all they could go to wherever they lived to notify those needing to be informed of their absence and to collect only what they would require overnight.

"There will come a point on the journey when you will have to part with everything that is linked with London, so leave anything of value with friends you can trust. If you have no one, those items can be locked up here in a safe place. You are all to spend the night here. It won't be comfortable, but the sooner we become an isolated group the better. We shall leave at dawn."

They poured out of the workshop to disperse in different directions. Only Alice, her calm face framed by her white working cap, remained. "I can't go tomorrow, madam. I have good reasons to stay."

Julia gave an understanding nod. "I know you won't leave your invalid aunt and I've thought of that. When I've seen everybody into the Sotherleigh waggons that will be waiting, I'll bring one of the lighter carts back to fetch you both."

Alice broke down, covering her face with her hands. "I've been so worried about Aunt Henrietta if anything should happen to me."

Julia patted her shoulder comfortingly and thought suddenly of the journey Michael had once made with Mary lying in a cart. The one that she and Alice were to undertake would have to be at a similar slow pace in order not to jog the invalid too much. She put from her any hope she had had of reaching Sotherleigh before Adam.

"Do you know anything about the Needhams?" she asked when Alice had recovered and was drying her eyes.

"No. All I do know is that a groom and two tap-room maids fell sick of the Great Plague about the same time at the Heathcock and it was closed immediately, trapping a houseful of travellers. The three Needham lads were out with me in the ribbon procession at the time, and so they went to an aunt at Islington where I hope they're still safe. That ended the processions, and in any case shopkeepers were cancelling orders everywhere."

"I expected that, but trade will come back when the plague is over. Now I'll go for those certificates." She opened her purse and gave Alice some money. "Meanwhile I want you to buy food and ale for those who will be here overnight."

When Julia came in sight of the Guildhall from which the affairs of London were conducted, she found a vast crowd filling the street and clamouring for admittance. As she reached its outskirts she saw there was an alderman on the steps trying to make himself heard.

"No more certificates of health can be issued on trust. The Great Plague is taking too many lives now. All who require a certificate must present themselves either with a personal doctor to vouchsafe for them or to see our physicians here. That applies to every member of a household."

Such an uproar broke out that he drew back nervously. Shouts that those same physicians should be tending the sick instead of seeing the healthy was the least of the abuse hurled at him. Julia could see that even if she should round up all her women it would take hours of waiting on the morrow, for there was not enough of this day left in which a tenth of those gathered here could get through the formalities.

"Psst."

She turned to see a foxy-looking man at her side and edged from him. "Go away!"

"Do ye still want me to do that when I tell ye that I 'ave forged certificates for sale?"

She did not hesitate. "Let me see one."

He drew her over to a brick porch and took one from his pocket. It was an adequate forgery printed with a blank space for the name to be filled in and a seal that would pass muster. "Well?" he queried craftily, "what do ye say?"

"How much?"

" 'Ow many do ye want?"

She was about to state twenty-one and then thought she should have extra, for she half expected some of her women to turn up with someone they did not want to leave behind. "Thirty."

"That'll be twenty pounds."

It was an outrageous sum, but she could not accuse him of robbery since she was committing a crime herself in buying from him. "I'll have them but you're to hand me each one separately, because I'm not going to get a top one and a sheaf of blank papers underneath."

"Ye're wily, ain't ye?" He scowled at her, obviously thwarted in his intention because he shoved back a wad of papers he had been about to take from one capacious pocket and took a bunch from another. Disagreeably he handed each one to her and then she paid him. It emptied her purse of all except a few shillings, but money was no problem, for she had three bags of gold concealed among her petticoats. Carefully she tucked the papers into her cloak pocket with the two that Adam had left for her. The forger did not leave at once.

" 'Ow do ye know that trick?" he asked between grudging respect and curiosity.

"Something similar happened to my mother once when she bought from a pedlar to do him a good turn and was swindled in the process. I've never forgotten it."

The forger slid away. Julia made for the nearest coffee-house, feeling ravenously hungry and realising that it was now early evening and she had not eaten since before six o'clock that morning. After a simple meal she made a slight detour, harrowed by sights on the way, to reach the place where Abigail lived, being anxious about her. The young woman was one of her best workers, good-natured and merry; and the baby had been eagerly awaited. As she entered the narrow street she found that the house was the fifth one along in a row of timber-framed houses that on both sides seemed to lean against each other for support. The projecting top storeys left only a gap of two feet between the facing houses. Strangely, when the occupants on both the right and the left could have exchanged the proverbial handshake out of their highest windows, only Abigail's row bore the red crosses, proof again of the vagaries of the pestilence. A single watchman patrolled the whole row and at the moment had his back towards her as he slowly paced his beat.

A tapping at one of the small-paned windows of Abigail's home drew her attention. Mrs. Webb was beckoning to her. Julia went near, thankful to see her.

"Where is he?" Mrs. Webb mouthed through the glass.

Julia knew whom she meant. "Going down the row."

The bottom pane of the window had been broken and was blocked with rags and paper. Mrs. Webb managed to pull back a corner of the obstruction and her low tones could be heard outside, though little more than a whisper. "I hoped you might come and I've been keeping a look-out. Listen to me. All is going well with Abigail, but we both want you to do something for her. She's in the final stages of labour and the baby should be here in about half an hour. Go round the back of the house opposite and get in somehow. The family left about three weeks ago, according to Abigail. When she has given birth I'll hand the new-born infant to you through the top window. It's essential to get the babe away from the infection in this house without delay."

Julia nodded and drew away. A life was to be saved and there was no question about it. She went cautiously to the rear of the house to find a cobbled yard that ran the length of the row. Nobody was about. The back door was secure, but she thought it would be easy enough to push in the lead-set panes of the window. As she placed her hand, wrapped in her cloak, against the glass a voice spoke, causing her to spring round guiltily.

"There's no need to do that." A stern-faced woman was looking out of the neighbouring house. "I have a key." She disappeared for a moment to reappear with it and set it into its lock. "I'm minding this house for my neighbours, because I'll not be going myself whatever happens. I've two elderly bed-ridden parents." Entering the house, she looked over her shoulder at Julia, who still hesitated in her surprise. "Come in then if you're going to collect Abigail's infant."

"How did you know about that?" Julia followed the woman inside and the door was shut.

"I saw the midwife arrive and then I watched you in conversation with her. Whether you knew it or not, you glanced up at the top windows of this house. People in infected houses have been handing out little children stripped of their garments to neighbours to save their lives, but this is the first new-born one I know of that is to escape the watchman's vigil. The fellow in this street has eyes in the back of his head, but I'll distract his attention if you like." All the time the woman was talking she was leading the way up the twisting flight of stairs.

"You're a good neighbour indeed."

"I've known Abigail's husband since he was born in that house and when she came here as a bride she proved herself a good housewife, looking after him and his old father. We had a nice chat most days, she and I. What are you going to put the baby in?"

"I'll use a petticoat."

"Do you know how to feed the little one?"

"I'm leaving London in the morning and I'll get a wet nurse as soon as I'm home. Until then it will have to be drips of milk into the mouth."

"Soak a piece of clean linen rag in the milk and let the babe suck. I'll get you some." They had reached the top room. The woman made sure the watchman was still farther down the street and then she opened the window just a crack. "Don't open it wider yet, because he knows this house is supposed to be unoccupied at the present time. Sit down while you're waiting. I suppose you're Lady Warrender. You fit Abigail's description."

"Yes, I am. And you, madam?"

"Mrs. Dealworth. I'll get that rag and I can spare you a small flagon of milk."

"That's most kind."

Julia was grateful for a little time of quietness on her own. She removed one of her petticoats and put it ready. Then she sat looking towards the top window opposite, seeing that it had also been opened slightly ready for the moment when speed would be essential. It had been one of the worst days in her whole life, and if some good could come out of it by saving Abigail's infant she would be more than compensated. She felt as if a hundred years had passed since she had left the Webbs that morning, but with all the crammed hours that had passed it was still only seven o'clock. That left her just two hours before curfew!

When the woman returned she had a bundle with her, a black shawl over her arm and the promised flask of milk.

"I've put some more rags together that'll help you keep the baby dry and this shawl is a spare one of my mother's and should be useful."

"It will. At a happier time I shall tell Abigail of all that you have done."

Mrs. Dealworth flapped one of her large bony hands to show she had done little enough. She was a garrulous talker, obviously one who never missed anything that happened in the street, but good-hearted with it. In a way she was only slightly less boxed in than if she had had a red cross on her door, for she was a widow, tied day and night to the care of two old people. It was no wonder she welcomed any diversion.

Nearly an hour had gone by when Mrs. Webb made a signal from the opposite window, but she had seen, as Julia had, that the watchman was directly below, talking to two men and showing no sign of moving on. No doubt Mrs. Webb was also concerned by seeing Mrs. Dealworth lounging in her open front door as if taking in the evening air. Julia pointed to her and then stuck up her thumb to indicate there was nothing to fear. Cautiously she opened her window and Mrs. Webb did likewise. Mrs. Dealworth was watching and promptly called out to the men, moving from her doorway at the same time. Then she gave a yell as if tripping over her own doorstep and went on shouting she had twisted her ankle.

Mrs. Webb appeared at her window, holding the naked, mewling infant upright. It was a little boy with a mass of black hair brushed up in a cocks-comb and a linen band round his navel. His little legs kicked as she thrust him forward into the open air. Julia reached out and seized him. Within seconds she had placed him on the bed and shut the window. Mrs. Webb had already closed hers.

"Welcome to the world, little man," Julia said softly between laughter and tears as she began to wrap him up in the soft folds of the petticoat. He seemed to be furious at the treatment he had received, his eyes screwed up, his mouth wide on his lusty cry, his tiny fists and feet working. When he was wrapped up, she added the shawl for extra warmth and carried him carefully downstairs, the bundle for him over her arm and the flagon in her pocket. Mrs. Dealworth met her at the foot of the flight.

"The watchman saw nothing. You're safe now."

"I thank you."

"Go now and take care of Abigail's son. London will be in need of such as he when this pestilence has run its course."

Julia arrived back breathlessly at the workshop with just two minutes to spare before curfew. All the women crowded round the baby, who had been asleep on the way. One took him into the weaving room and his loud mewling resounded intermittently as the milk-soaked rag was removed from his mouth for redipping. Julia took stock. Alice had had to go home to avoid being caught by the curfew, but she had brought the food for the rest and knew she had only to wait with her aunt for transport. As Julia had expected, there were a few extra people in the regathering of her workers. One had brought a younger brother, another her two sisters and a third had felt unable to leave her friend from childhood behind. The group of interlopers stood a trifle sheepishly.

"Has any one of you knowingly been in recent contact with a plague victim?" Her strict tones demanded the truth. All shook their heads. "Very well. It is fortunate I have enough certificates of health to cover you. Naturally you must obey the same rules that apply to everyone else on this journey."

The food was laid out for supper with mugs of ale. Julia went into the weaving room and took the sleeping baby from the woman there, telling her to go and eat. It had grown dark and she went to sit by the window with him, not bothering with a candle. Then there came the distant ringing of a handbell. Soon she heard the dreadful shout that had become a new London street cry.

"Bring out your dead!"

Instinctively she cuddled the sleeping baby up against her protectively as she watched the bell-ringer come along the street ahead of two more dead-collectors, all reeling drunkenly and each leading a horse and cart, both of which were half full of corpses, some not even wrapped in a shroud, arms and legs dangling. The watchman on duty unlocked in turn each plague-marked house where he had been signalled that death lay within. The door would open, the light of a candle-lamp would fall across the filthy cobbles and then people appeared carrying their sad burden, and at some houses they would return inside for a second or even a third one. As they wept, some loudly, the watchman would shepherd them indoors again. He would lock up and move on to the next grief-stricken household. Always the awful shout was unceasing and it was a long time before the ringing of the bell faded away into the distance.

In the morning there was excitement among the women that the time of leaving London had come. Several older ones competed cheerfully as to who should carry Abigail's infant, the girls more interested in looking their best for the journey. It was the first time for weeks that any of them had not woken to dread what the day might bring.

It was another warm morning. They streamed out of the workshop in high spirits, their laughter and chatter a bright, unusual sound in any street these days, causing heads to turn almost on a tilt of hope. Men stoking bonfires exchanged badinage with them and there was more from those trundling hand-barrows of fruit, vegetables or creels of freshly caught fish to the markets. London was not going hungry in its torment, the majority of its citizens sticking doggedly to their trades.

When the women had crossed London Bridge they gave a cheer. A few danced a jig. Five miles farther on, some had begun to drag their feet and complain of thirst and tiredness. Only two now took turns with Julia in carrying the baby, whom they were calling Boy because he had no name that they knew. Julia allowed them to rest at the next tavern where, after she had shown the health certificates to the innkeeper, they were served a pot of ale each and some bread and cheese. She asked him about transport and it transpired he had one horse, which she hired, and after that who-ever held the baby could ride. The competition flared up again and once more Boy regained general popularity.

Gradually, by asking at each village and town they reached, Julia gathered a dozen horses. Only one of the women had ever ridden before, but once in the side-saddle all soon felt secure and always another woman led the horse at a walking pace. This chance to rest raised everybody's spirits again and a few of them would look smugly down from horseback at those unfortunate people without health certificates being barred at bridges, or prevented at toll-pikes from entering where they themselves were waved through.

The day passed in mile after dusty mile until at last in the distance on the other side of a shallow river Julia saw the Sotherleigh vehicles wait-ing. Luckily a barrier stopped the women from swarming across it in their excitement. They waited for Julia to show the certificates to the guards, who as elsewhere were local men armed with fieldpieces or muskets once carried in the war.

"I'm not taking the slightest risk of infection being carried in the clothes of my party," she told the guards. "Therefore I'm taking them all down to those trees on the bank. There they will strip, douse themselves in the river and reclothe themselves on the other side where my coach servants are already setting down some hampers of clothes. I'm asking you to be courteous enough to turn your backs during this procedure as my servants will."

The guards guffawed, but agreed. One asked her about the garments that would remain behind and she explained that as she would not be accompanying her party she would burn the garments herself. The guard obligingly offered to supply flint and tinder, which she accepted.

At first the women squealed in protest. "That water will be cold! The guards and those other men in livery will spy!"

"The coach servants have their instructions and know better than to disobey and you're far enough away from the guards in any case." Julia saw how the young brother brought along was also hanging back.

"I'm not taking off no clothes in front of a lotta females!" he declared vehemently.

Julia shouted across the river to a groom. "I believe Molly was including some charade clothes in the hampers. Try to find a coat and a pair of breeches." While this was being done she signalled to the head coachman, who climbed down from the box of the Pallister coach, which she had not expected to see, and came within earshot on the bankside.

"I'll want the lightest of the carts brought across the bridge for me to drive, because I have to return to London to collect two more people, who couldn't come before," she called to him.

"I'll drive you, my lady."

"I'll not expose you to the risk of the plague."

"I 'ad it once when I was a nipper at sea. I ain't likely to get it again. Permit me to drive you. The footman that shared the box with me can go back with the rest. It'll be quicker if I take you."

"It will and I'll not forget that you volunteered."

He jumped back up on his box to drive across the bridge while she went to supervise the women. They were giggling and laughing and saying everything they could to embarrass the young lad, who was still adamant about not undressing.

"You shall go first and we'll all turn our backs," Julia assured him. "Make sure you put your head right under the water to wash any infection out of your hair."

He was persuaded, tossed his clothes onto the spot where the bonfire was to be and splashed into the water. After a few minutes he gave a shout and all looked across at the far bank where he was dressed and drying his hair with a towel. With one accord the women became hysterical with mirth, for the coat enveloped him and the breeches came down to his ankles. He was furious and went stumping off along the bank to where the carts awaited.

Julia held the baby as the women stripped. Considering they had feared to be seen they shrieked so loudly at the chill of the water that they attracted attention they had not anticipated. Four gentlemen sprang out of a coach that had been halted by the guards at the bridge to clap and cheer, and several field workers came at a run to stare. The guards also forgot what they had promised and turned to enjoy the sight of pale female forms dousing themselves under the water and then rising up like a host of Venuses out of the sea. The women's shrieks turned to screams of outraged modesty when they saw they were observed. It speeded up their dressing, for where they might have taken time in selecting and arguing about different garments, they snatched up whatever came first and hid among the bushes to clothe their still wet bodies. When they emerged to dry their hair with the linen towels provided, they were cheered again. Some of the younger ones with well-shaped figures were not so averse to the approbation as they had made themselves out to be. No shoes or stockings had been provided and they walked barefoot along the grassy bank to where the carts waited, Julia keeping pace on the opposite side.

Then, as arranged, one of the older women came across the bridge carrying a soft woollen cape. Since Boy had been only in uncontaminated wrappings there was little risk in his keeping on what he was wearing, apart from the shawl, which had been in contact with the women's clothes, but as a precaution Julia undressed him completely. He was handed, protesting loudly once more, to the woman, who wrapped him up and bore him off to one of the carts.

Julia waited until all were aboard and exchanged waves with the women as they were driven away, staying where she was until a bend in the road hid them from her sight. Then it was as if she had been left in a vacuum, shut off not only from them, but from Sotherleigh and most of all from Adam. She was seized by a dreadful premonition that she might never see him again. A sensation of utter despair swept through her.

# EIGHTEEN

*T*HERE WAS NO TIME left that day to go back to London and leave again before curfew. While the coachman returned the horses that Julia had hired to the nearest post-tavern half a mile away, the guard from the bridge lit the bonfire for her and kept an eye on it to make sure the flames did not spread. The grass was dry from the continuous hot weather, and they both agreed there could be no lull in the plague until that changed. He was more eager to talk than she, for the exercise and stress of the day had caught up with her. When the coachman returned to drive her to the tavern where he had secured accommodation she had already decided on an early night, for she wanted to set off at dawn on the morrow for London again.

It was mid-morning when the Pallister coach arrived at the entrance to the alleyway where Alice lived. It was too narrow for more than a hand-barrow to pass, the wooden houses pressing in on both sides, black-pitched with small windows and narrow doors. The coachman had sprung down from his box, but he looked through the window at her instead of opening the door, his haggard expression showing how shocked he had been by the plague sights since they had crossed London Bridge.

"Let me fetch the two ladies, madam. Don't you step out 'ere. It's a foul place."

She shook her head. "You must stay with the coach and guard the horses. I couldn't aim a pistol as well as you."

"Very well, my lady." Uneasily he helped her alight. There were two pistols in his belt. He would not hesitate to use them.

She had to walk about twenty yards down the stinking, garbage-strewn alley. Each house was joined to its neighbour with no party wall between. Three had red crosses on the door, but as there was no watchman about she guessed that the unfortunate occupants had already perished. It was as she was passing the third of these houses, the side of it adjoining Alice's home, that she paused in compassion. A little girl no more than three years old, dirty-faced with matted curls, was in a downstairs window, huge tears rolling down from the forlorn, frightened eyes, the grubby palms of her small hands pressed against the panes. Julia supposed the watchman had gone on an errand, for there was still life in this house, and she went nearer the window, unable to pass by without some word of cheer to the unhappy child.

"I know it's hard to be shut in on a sunny day, but you'll soon be out to play again."

Through the glass the child's voice was muffled, but it rang with appeal. "I want to play now!"

"So you shall when everyone in your house is well again."

Far from being consoled, the child began to sob pitifully. "All gone away."

Julia's cheeks hollowed. Surely the child could not be alone there! "Who is in the house with you?"

The same answer came. "All gone from Katy." The child let her head sink down on the inner sill, tears flooding her eyes and she patted the window, imploring release.

Horrified, Julia went to Alice's door and knocked. It opened at once, the young woman's face lighting up at the sight of her.

"Good day, Lady Warrender. My aunt and I are ready and have been since first light."

"That child in the adjoining house!" Julia exclaimed as she entered. "Is she on her own?"

Alice nodded sadly. "She is the only survivor in her family. The watchman comes once a day to put a plate of food through the door."

"That's monstrous!"

"I agree. Katy is terrified of the dark and at times she screams. I've tried to talk to her through the walls, which are only partitions in these old properties, but she cries most pathetically for her mother. The parents were the most respectable and hard-working couple and there were several in the family."

Julia leaned a hand on a chair's top rail for support. "I can't endure it. I have to get that child out."

"But how? It's padlocked at the front and there's no rear entrance. These houses were built back to back."

"Could we knock a way through that wall you mentioned? I'd compensate you for any damage."

An elderly voice piped up from a chair in the shadows of the room. "There's a chisel and a hammer in the cellar. The wood is rotten with age."

Julia turned gratefully to Alice's aunt, a tiny woman twisted in her frame by some unidentifiable disease of the bones. "I thank you, madam."

Alice fetched the tools and then showed Julia up a rickety staircase into an upper room and indicated the wall. "I'll help."

"No. You mustn't come in contact with the contagion. Take your aunt out to the coach and tell the coachman what I'm about to do. I'll walk Katy out of London and he can meet me at the river tomorrow. I'll bathe the child here first. Do you have anything I can put her in?"

Alice found a cotton skirt, needle and thread. Knowing Katy's size, she chopped off the top half and gathered up two shoulders, leaving armholes. It was done in a matter of minutes and would suffice. She laid a shawl with it and then went down to the kitchen and set water to heat before she went with her aunt from the house. Their pace was slow due to the old woman's infirmity.

Left alone, Julia began prising out one of the slatted wall boards. Damp played havoc with the timbers of such property, which made them unhealthy places in which to live, but those of moderate means could afford no better and the poor fared even worse. There was a sharp crack and the board, dried out now by summer, split away in a cloud of choking dust and crumbling splinters. She pulled part of it out, gaining a smallish gap that just showed the corresponding room in Katy's house. Through it came a strong stench, the origins of which she could guess at.

"Katy!" she called through, "I'm making a little doorway to get you out!" Then she went on driving the chisel into the rotten wood and jerking off pieces, heedless of her hands. When the gap was large enough she called again. "Come upstairs, little one. There's no need to be afraid. I've made the door and you can come and play."

She listened keenly. At all costs she wanted to avoid entering the infected premises. There was no sound and she kept calling and listening. Finally she heard a faint creaking of stairs as ancient as those in Alice's house. Katy's face peeped through a half-open door.

"See! I'm the friend who spoke to you through the window." Julia held out her arms through the gap. "I've come for you."

The child's lower lip trembled. "I want my mama."

"Yes, I know, but let's keep each other company, because that is what she would want us to do."

Katy was reassured. She came trotting across the floor, barefoot and filthy from head to toe. When she reached the gap she studied it seriously. "It's a nice little door."

"It is, and to come through I think you should leave all your dirty clothes behind. I have a new gown here that I know your mama would like you to wear."

Obediently Katy turned to have the back of her bodice unlaced. This was something safe and familiar. Her mama always changed her out of dirty clothes.

Julia reached through the gap, but the tapes of the child's bodice had become knotted. She took the scissors Alice had left and cut them through. Katy pulled off the garment herself. Underneath she was wearing a petticoat with a neatly embroidered hem that she had torn by catching it on something. Julia snipped her out of it and Katy faced her again to be lifted through. It had been her intention to keep the child at a safe distance until she was bathed, but Katy, suddenly feeling secure, reached out swiftly and hugged her tightly about the neck. The child did not see Julia's expression of fear as the matted curls flicked across her face or notice the automatic tightening of her grip to thrust the innocent embrace away. Yet in the same instant Julia held her tight. This was a child and not a poisonous snake to be flung away. Had Katy been covered with the plague-blains it would have made no difference.

"Your neighbour, Alice, has left hot water in the kitchen for your bath. I expect there is soap too."

Katy leaned back in her arms and nodded solemnly. "I think it'll take lots of soap to make me clean."

Julia gave a shaky laugh. "I'm sure it will."

Alice had relit the fire to heat the water, which was only moderately warm, but Katy did not complain when she sat in a wash-tub and splashed about. Her curls had to be well soaped several times before they showed their natural gold. She was painfully thin and Julia wondered how much she had eaten of the food pushed through to her as if she were an animal in a cage.

The new garment delighted Katy with its bright colours, although she looked quaint in it. Julia tidied herself, her gown soiled from breaking through the wall, and there were small splinters in her hands she would have to remove before she could hold the reins of the horse she hoped to hire for Katy and herself as far as the river.

After putting out the fire she left the house, turning the key Alice had left in the lock and then dropping it in her pocket. She took Katy by the hand and as they reached the end of the alley she saw with mingled relief and anxiety that the coachman had waited for her. He sprang down from the box at their approach and forestalled any reproach that might be forthcoming.

"I didn't quite understand my instructions from the lady passengers," he lied blatantly. "I thought you'd probably like to sit on the box in the open air with me, my lady, and the little girl could sit between us."

She looked steadily at him. "Unless the child is already infected there should be no danger from her. As for myself, that may be a different matter."

"Then I'd better get you home to Sotherleigh, my lady."

"There's nowhere in the world I'd rather be, but Katy and I must be on our own for a while. I'll tell you where to take us after you've delivered the two inside passengers."

Katy slept her way out of London, her head on Julia's lap. When the five certificates of health were shown by Alice at barriers Julia did not experience the slightest twinge of conscience since she had arranged in her own mind isolation for herself and the child. Her premonition of the previous day seemed to get stronger with every mile that was covered and her sense of despair deepened.

The gates of Sotherleigh stood open when the coachman drew up alongside and shouted for the gatekeeper. As always, the view of the house was blocked by trees, but Julia gazed longingly at the drive that would have led her to it. When the gatekeeper appeared she asked him the question that had been uppermost in her mind all the way.

"Has Sir Adam arrived back yet from France?"

"No, my lady."

Somehow she did not feel surprised. His not being here yet seemed to fit in somehow with the conviction that everything was in the process of being turned upside down for them. "Is the master at home?"

"He went back to France yesterday."

"Take a message to Molly. Tell her that I shall be staying for at least three weeks at the cob and wattle cottage in Honeywood dell." She was aware of the coachman turning his head sharply at her and the gatekeeper's mouth had dropped open. "She must see that food, bed linen and all else she knows I will need are left at the gate. I want some toys delivered too, because I have a little girl with me." She nodded to the coachman. "Drive on."

He obeyed and she could guess at his thoughts. He was appalled that she should consider staying at such a humble place, whatever the circumstances. The cottage had been a shepherd's shelter for years until it had been found more convenient to have a covered cart on wheels that could be moved with the flocks. As it was isolated, Katy could run and play in the meadow there. She herself would be able to wander with her for a short distance without the risk of either of them meeting anyone.

The coachman stopped in the lane outside the three cottages her women had occupied. They came crowding out to the gates to greet the new arrivals. Two of the strongest lifted the old woman out, Julia having told the coachman not to come in close contact with anyone until he had bathed and burned his clothes.

"How have you settled in?" she asked one of the older women, whom she had left in charge.

"There 'ave been only minor problems that I soon sorted out. We 'ave everything we need and none of us knew that air could ever smell as clean and sweet as it does 'ere."

"Everybody is well? How is Boy?"

" 'E's bonny and so are the rest of us. A wet-nurse couldn't be found to take the risk of nursing a London baby, so 'e's 'ere with us and a flask with a teat made from a glove-finger suits 'im well. The village midwife 'ad a word with us from the other side of the gate. She says Boy will do better on milk from an ass, and as there's one in the village that foaled recently she leaves a flask of the milk, mixed with a spoonful of flour that's been well baked in the oven, outside every day. 'E's had several feeds of this pap already and didn't leave a drop! Why not come indoors and see 'im, madam? 'E's sleeping in a crib that was brought specially for 'im from Sotherleigh and wearing garments that your little sister wore."

So Patience's baby clothes were being put to good use. Julia guessed it was Mary who had given special thought to the infant. "I should like to see him again, but not now." Briefly she explained the situation. "So I shall not be seeing any of you for a little while. Molly will be the go-between, speaking to me at a distance as she does to you." She gave the woman a final reminder. "Now you do remember Mrs. Webb's treatment that I told you about if anyone should fall sick of the pestilence?"

"Yes, madam. I pray we all got away in time and that you and the little girl will be spared."

"I thank you."

Alice came to look up at her on the box. "I'll never forget what you have done for my aunt and me."

Julia smiled down at her. "You were both instrumental in helping me rescue Katy. She might have died there alone. Even if that had not happened it would have been a life in the poorhouse with a future to follow that I care not to think about. Tell me, have you any idea how long she was alone in that house?"

"I reckon it would be nigh on two weeks since they took the last body away. If it hadn't been for the watchman's food and those of us who talked to her through the window, I doubt the poor mite would have survived."

Julia's thoughts went back to the dead looter she had brushed against in her own house. Surely it was too slight a contact to have done any harm? But she must not risk Katy's being with her for too long. "So in another week there should be no fear of Katy developing the plague. I'll make arrangements for her to leave me as soon as her quarantine time is over."

Katy tugged at Julia's sleeve. "I'm hungry."

Julia opened the box of travel food beside her. She had been letting the child eat a little at a time, for she had been quite ravenous at first. Watching over Katy kept her occupied until the shepherd's shelter was reached. The child spotted it first, pointing a finger.

"There's a little house!"

It looked much like a doll's house perched on its own in a dip of undulating meadowland. Any path to it had been long overgrown, wild flowers sprinkling the grass right to its door. The coachman went ahead to make sure the door was neither locked nor stuck, but it opened with one sharp thrust. He glanced around inside and then stood outside again, looking down his nose at it. There were none so snobbish as the servants of a large house used to the hierarchy created by the domestic staff themselves, prestige allotted to those holding the most responsible positions. He, as head coachman, would not have deigned to spend an hour in such a place.

"Are you sure, my lady?"

With a nod and holding Katy by the hand, she entered the low doorway. The shelter consisted of one room with white-washed walls; a hearth was at one end and a box-bed built in at the other. A table with two three-legged stools upturned on it had been pushed into a corner. A row of pegs, one with a forgotten crook hanging on it, and some shelves completed the furnishings. It was not dirty, but the floor was strewn with dried leaves that had blown in under the door and there were festoons of cobwebs.

"This will be quite adequate. Make sure Molly brings a broom, a bucket and a scrubbing brush."

He rolled up his eyes expressively, but he was plodding off to the coach and his mistress did not see his disapproval.

WHEN MICHAEL ARRIVED back in Paris he met his wife at their own front door. She had returned from her daily pilgrimage to the cemetery and, although her face was thickly veiled, he could tell by the haughty bow of her head and her whole posture that she was highly displeased that he had gone rushing off from Calais as he had done.

"Is Sir Adam Warrender here?" he asked. Before leaving England he had heard that Parliament had been prorogued and it had passed through his mind that it would be an unlucky chance if Adam should come seeking Julia in Paris and miss her on the way.

"No, he is not. Why should he be?" She was removing her veil.

He explained the situation, which she listened to without interest. Then he asked after their son. "The house is quiet. That must mean Jean-Robert is out!"

"Yes. He's gone on a nature walk in the park with Faith."

"He'll enjoy that," he commented, hoping this would be an end to their conversation. But she was not prepared to let the matter of his absence rest there. She followed him from room to room as he sorted through his mail, put travelling pistols away in a velvet-lined box and sat down to a tray of refreshments brought to him by a servant. Her cold polite tirade paused only until the food had been set out and they were alone again. Then suddenly she broke off her disagreeable flow to challenge him.

"What are you drinking?" She had been pacing the floor and now stopped to stare at the bottle he was pouring. "Isn't that Papa's special burgundy? That's only served on celebratory occasions."

"Isn't my homecoming such an event?" he queried, an edge to his voice.

She ignored the question. "It's barbaric to drink it straight from the cellar. It should be presented with finesse and ceremony. Papa never had it otherwise."

"Will you join me in a glass?"

"Not at this hour. Later, perhaps."

He did not intend to leave it where she could gain easy access, for he must be vigilant against any further attempts she might make to poison him at her whim. This was particularly important as far as wine was concerned. It was virtually impossible for her to contaminate his food since she never went into the kitchen and it was brought straight from there to the table. Never again should she pour him a glass of wine and neither would he touch any decanter if she had been in the room with it. He groaned under his breath that things should have come to such a pass, feeling there was little doubt his wife was not quite sane. It increased his commitment to look after her, for her condition might deteriorate as the years went by. All the happiness he had was in his son and the woman he loved at Sotherleigh.

Faith and Jean-Robert were full of talk about their nature walk at dinner. They had spotted a variety of butterflies, which she had named for him in English and he for her in French.

"We're trying to find as many different kinds as we can," Faith explained.

Sophie nodded approvingly. "They are such pretty creatures on the wing."

Jean-Robert paused in his eating, not allowed to speak with his mouth full. "They lay their eggs—"

Sophie held up a hand. "Not at table, Jean-Robert."

The boy looked crestfallen. His mother's cold note of disapproval was all too familiar to him. There was so much that seemed to bore her or raise her ire, and he never knew whether she was going to smother him in affectionate embraces, calling him stupid baby names, or give him an icy stare that was worse than a slap. It was the same at bedtime. He loved to see her come in and sit on his bed to bid him good night and kiss his brow, but if she was tired or cross about something, even when it was nothing to do with him, she would not come near him as if she had to punish him as well as everyone else. His father had spoken his name from the head of the table and he looked up.

"Yes, Papa?"

"It's time I took you to a silk farm. There you will see the full cycle of life for the silk moth just as it is for the butterfly."

"Oh, yes!"

"I have to go on business to Lyon next week and we can ride out to one of the silk farms, where you may spend a whole day if you wish." He glanced smilingly at Faith. "Perhaps you would like to come with us since you are the butterfly expert. I have already offered to escort a Madame Leblanc, whose husband is a mill-owner in Lyon and an old friend of mine. She has been in Paris on family business and has offered us hospitality in their charming home."

She answered him merrily. "I'm not exactly an expert, but I accept with great pleasure."

Jean-Robert was buoyant again, glad to see his mother was nodding permission. It did not strike him as odd that she should not be coming too, because she never went anywhere since being in mourning and never far afield before that, liking best to be with Grandpère. "What fun it will be!"

"It's not just for your amusement," his mother said sternly, "but your first step towards the day when you will be head of your late grandfather's silk business."

He did not dare to remind her that he would also be Master of Sotherleigh. She would not allow him to speak of it to her, but he had heard so much about it from his father that, if the truth could be known, he would have preferred to go there instead of to Lyon, much as he wanted to see the silk moths.

Faith was not sorry to have a few days away from her hostess. Sophie was so withdrawn and solitary, full of courtesy on the surface, but with no warmth underneath. For this reason Faith missed Julia more than ever, but she was enjoying her stay in Paris and did not intend to leave until Christopher went home in the autumn. Her parents had written about the plague, news which she had kept from Julia at Michael's request, and it was due to her mother's nervousness about infection that she was not expecting to be called back when it became known that Julia had returned home. Several cases of the plague had broken out all over England where Londoners had taken refuge in country seats, or humbler folk with relatives, one case not far from Bletchingdon itself.

The fact that Sophie was useless as a chaperone was not important. Michael had introduced Julia and her to many charming French people and she always made sure she was with one of the older married women at social functions.

She was jealous of her good name, not only for herself but for Christopher, and she would allow no blemish to mark it. Undoubtedly he was destined to be a great man and she wanted to be a credit to him. She knew his eye for beauty had found its outlet at last in architecture, revealed in his buildings that had arisen and were arising in England from his designs and direction. Who knew what marvels would result from the inspiration of France? Faith liked to believe that something of his love for her would play a part in every masterpiece that resulted from this visit.

She had the most interesting time in Lyon, Michael taking her and Jean-Robert to the various silk mills, some of which were weaving the most glorious damasks and brocades for Versailles, while the kindness and hospitality of the Leblancs added greatly to her enjoyment. Sometimes she wondered if it disappointed Michael that his son, although fascinated by the cocoons, the caterpillars and the moths at the silk farm, showed little or no interest in the large looms or the process of weaving.

"Now tell me everything about your visit," Sophie said to Jean-Robert upon his return with his father and Faith.

"There was so much, Maman." He did not really know where to begin.

They were all in the salon, where Sophie, wearing one of her elegant black gowns, was seated in an ivory damask chair, crimson silk panels behind her. It was her habit never to enter a room without observing where she would be most set off to advantage. Before going into mourning she would stand instead of sitting if the furnishings in other houses clashed with whatever she was wearing. She smiled at her young son standing before her. "What did you like best? Apart, no doubt, from what you saw of sericulture at the silk farm."

He answered without hesitation. "A cowherd let me help milk the cows when we stayed with the Simond family on our journey home."

"I don't want to hear about that. What about the mills?"

He made a grimace. "Mostly people work in their own homes. The looms fill a room from floor to ceiling. Else it's three or four looms under one roof and no space to spare. At all the places little children have to crouch underneath to mend the threads that break and the weavers kick them when they are slow. They cry, but they daren't stop. I never want *ever* to have anything to do with looms or silk." He stamped his foot in emphasis.

She struck him so hard that he was knocked off balance and his head thudded against a carved table leg. Michael and Faith both sprang to their feet and dashed to the boy, but Sophie did not look at him, her expression furious. With a hiss of her black taffeta skirts she was out of her chair and stalking from the room.

"Is he insensible?" Faith asked fearfully as Michael lifted his son and laid him on a couch.

"No. Just shocked." He looked down into Jean-Robert's white face. "I fear you're going to have a bump on your head as large as an egg, my son."

The boy was tearful. "Why was Maman so angry?"

"She was upset. We'll talk about that later." Michael saw the cut was bleeding and unfolded a clean handkerchief from his pocket. "I'm going to make a wounded soldier of you, and then I'm sure Faith will read to you while you rest here for a while."

When the binding was done and Faith had fetched a book, Michael went to find Sophie. She was not in her bedchamber. It was the first time he had entered there for many months. After she had refused to sleep with him any more, she had had her bedchamber completely refurbished as if to remove any association with his ever having been there. Silk-panelled with a gorgeously draped bed, its canopy gilded and plumed, it would have set harmoniously into the opulence of Versailles. Neither was she in her boudoir. A faint clatter came from her bathing room with its two marble baths where she soaped herself in one and rinsed herself in the other.

"Sophie! Are you there?"

Immediately a maidservant opened the door. "It's me, Monsieur. I'm putting out fresh towels."

She had some over her arm to substantiate her words. At the back of his mind it registered that the girl looked flustered, but no doubt it was due to surprise at seeing him in his wife's domain. "Have you seen Madame?"

"No, Monsieur."

As he left the girl breathed a sigh of relief. Putting down the towels, she returned to the cupboard where she had been helping herself from one of Madame Pallister's flasks of beauty lotion. Carefully she finished pouring a little of the creamy lotion into a flat jar she had brought for the purpose. The *grande madame* never missed such tiny amounts and she was trying all of them in turn to see which suited her skin best. Popping a lid onto the jar, she put it out of sight in her apron pocket and replaced the flask. She had a moment's anxiety as to whether she had put the various flasks back in the same order as they had been before Monsieur's unexpected arrival had caused her to panic. She thought they looked the same and felt reasonably sure Madame would not notice any change in their positions. Hastily she relocked the cupboard with a hairpin. She was not greedy and made the lotion last. It would be another month or two before she helped herself again.

Michael traced Sophie to her late father's bedchamber where nothing had been moved or changed since his last day. She was lying face down across the bed, her arms stretched across it. At the sound of his entry she sat up and glared, her face full of hatred.

"You did that deliberately, didn't you?" she shrieked. "You took Jean-Robert to Lyon with the sole intent of turning him against my father's greatest wish that his grandson should grow up absorbed in the business as he himself was from a boy!"

"That was the last thing in my mind. I thought he would be interested to see the weaving just as Faith was. My fault was in forgetting the boy has tender feelings, young as he is. That is why you shall never strike him again as you did a few minutes ago."

"I'll beat him into obedience to my father's will if needs be!"

It was rare for Michael to lose his temper, but he lost it now. "Grief for your father is one thing, but this unhealthy obsession is another! This is our house—not his any longer—our marriage and our son. Our lives that have to be lived without this unhealthy obeisance to a shrine!" With his arm he swept from a tall chest a pair of hair brushes, a watch and various other items, sending them crashing to the floor. She screamed and flew at him with her fingers like claws. He threw her back across the bed and wrenched its hangings down. Then he hurled away two pillows with such force that the day covers slid from them and one burst into a storm of feathers. Shrieking, she sprang forward from the bed to hang onto his arm. He shook her off, tossing shirts, cravats and collars from a clothes press before snatching out the drawers themselves and throwing them down. When he made for the side room where the rest of the wardrobe was kept she flung herself screaming in front of the door. "I'll kill you before I let you go in there."

He shoved her aside and, when he pulled open the door, he saw to his horror that it was as if his father-in-law stood there, a wicker frame rigged out in a velvet jacket, cape and breeches, one of the late man's periwigs draped over the wooden top and crowned by a plumed hat.

Bucket-topped boots completed the illusion. He gave a roar and knocked the effigy flying. As he turned about he saw her aiming one of her father's pistols at him. He yelled out and she fired, the explosion filling the side-room with smoke.

The ball had missed him by inches, burying itself in the wall. He threw himself on her, clapping a hand over her mouth as he dragged her back into the bedchamber with him. As he had expected, shouts and commotion sounded from the stairs as those of the household came to investigate. Sophie was struggling wildly in his grasp, but he managed to open the door a crack to shout out reassuringly.

"No need for alarm! I was examining my father-in-law's pistols and one went off." As he closed the door again she tried to claw his face, but he gripped her by the wrists and threw her back from him. "I'll have none of that!"

Her face was dark with fury. "This was my sanctuary and you have violated it!"

"For that you would have killed me!"

"Again and again if that were possible!" She spat the words at him.

"Without thought for Jean-Robert? Would you have had him grow up in the shadow of a murder that would have blighted his whole life?" He was maddened by rage. "I've suffered your acid tongue, your rebuffs, your slights and your coldness all these years! I have forgiven and excused many of your devious ways, but the lack of thought for our son is beyond my endurance!"

He struck her with force across one side of her face and then the other before he hurled her from him across the bed. She landed like a twisted rag doll in a tumble of petticoats, blood gushing from her cut lip, and lay with her eyes shut, colour flaring where his blows had struck. Bruises already showed on her wrists from the struggle.

There was a dreadful silence in the room. The pounding of his heart subsided and his head cleared. Never before had he laid violent hands on a woman. Self-disgust rose in him that he should have allowed himself to be driven to such extremities of temper that he should have beaten the mother of his son. He felt degraded by his own action.

Had he stunned her? She was lying very still, her chest rising and falling rapidly. Leaning over her, he took a corner of the sheet to try to stem the flow of blood from her face. Then she opened her glittering eyes and her visage became a gorgon-like mask of hatred as she smiled triumphantly with her distorted swollen mouth. She knew the humiliation was his, not hers.

With a groan he threw himself out of the room.

THE NEXT DAY he had his father-in-law's rooms completely cleared. The furniture was dispersed to other parts of the house and when the clothes were sold the money was distributed to the poor. Decorators were set to work and the whole suite was refurbished. Sophie kept to her darkened bedroom until her lip healed and her bruises vanished, the excuse of having one of her headaches keeping the secret of the confrontation from the rest of the household. Faith was a nuisance, coming twice a day to see if there was anything she needed and bringing her flowers and drinks and suchlike, but she kept well down under the bedclothes and the English-woman suspected nothing.

When eventually Sophie reappeared there was nothing to show of the beating she had received, except a tiny indentation in her lower lip. A touch of carmine concealed it, but she was going to take a savage pleasure in tapping against it as if thoughtfully, especially in company, to remind Michael constantly of his brutality towards her on that terrible day.

She mended the rift with her son in the first seconds of their reunion. The cut on his head had been deeper than had been realised at first and took a while to heal, but he was incapable of holding a grudge and flung his arms lovingly about his mother's neck when she stooped to embrace him.

"Don't have such a long headache again, Maman," he appealed. "I missed you so much."

She never went near the refurnished suite. The atmosphere she had maintained had been destroyed by the husband she loathed and the rooms no longer held any interest for her. Fortunately she had taken possession of her father's jewellery after his death and had left the watch only to add to the impression of his still being there. Michael informed her that it had not been broken in its fall, owing to its velvet case, and he had taken it into his care to be a keepsake for the boy from his grandfather when he was old enough to appreciate it. She listened, but made no comment, for they were alone. She was resolved never to speak to Michael again except when necessary before their son or when others were present, but other-wise she would treat Michael as if he were invisible. She resumed her morbid visits to the cemetery and these were the highlights of her days, more important than anything else.

Then at breakfast one morning Michael received a letter from Adam that had been sent from a place of detention in Dieppe where he had been incarcerated since landing there from England over two weeks before. Michael read it aloud to Sophie and Faith.

*For mercy's sake try to get me out of this hole, Brother-in-law. I was detained when it was discovered I had come from London, such a natural fear in France of infection being brought across the Channel that my certificate of health was discounted. I sympathise with the French, who are as familiar with outbreaks of the plague as the rest of Europe, but that does not help my situation and I have failed to convince the authorities that I should be released. If they should put a new traveller from London into my cell then my quarantine would start all over again. My felicitations to my wife, who by now has surely heard of the plague and imagines me still in London instead of languishing here in Dieppe.*

Michael left Paris within the hour, taking an eminent doctor with him. They arrived at Dieppe to find Adam still on his own in a cell and a thorough examination by the doctor declared him free of infection. He was anxious when he learned that Julia had left for England about the same time as he had set out from there.

"I'll take the next ship home," he said to Michael, after thanking him for acting so promptly. "Julia will be wondering what has happened to me."

"When I left her she was determined to go to London, expecting to find you there, but I'm sure she will have returned to Sotherleigh long since. Come together to visit us another time in happier circumstances."

"I shall look forward to that, my friend."

A ship was leaving on the tide within the same hour as Adam's release and he boarded it at once. He paced the deck in his impatience to be home and watched constantly for the shoreline. At the back of his mind there was unease about the time Julia had been with Christopher in Paris. Admittedly Faith had been there as well and the two of them would never have been alone, but when he saw her again, if her attachment had grown through being in alien surroundings without the restrictions of home, he would soon know.

Once ashore, a swift change of fast horses along the route brought him galloping through the gates of Sotherleigh at sunset; candlelight was appearing in the windows of the house. When he was admitted and had given his hat, cloak, gloves and riding whip to a manservant on duty, Patience came running into the hall holding a younger child with fair curls by the hand.

"Who's this, Patience?" he greeted his wife's little half-sister. "Have you a new playmate?"

"It's Katy. She's come to live here. Julia brought her from London."

"And where is Julia? Do you know?"

Mary had come from the direction of the Queen's Parlour and she hurried forward with a smile as he came to greet her with a kiss. "I can answer that, Adam. Oh, how glad Julia will be to see you and on such a special day!"

He grinned. "What can that be?"

"She comes out of quarantine this evening. Don't look alarmed! All is well. You can go to meet her instead of me. It will give her a wonderful surprise."

"Where has she been staying?" He had a sudden illogical hope that she might have been cared for at the Hall, but that vanished as soon as Mary told him where she was and the reason for her being there. "Why didn't she come home earlier in the day?"

"She could have, but she had worked out her quarantine to the hour, and wanted to be conscientious about it. Katy has been with us for nearly two weeks now."

At the mention of her name Katy took Mary's hand. "I want Julia to come soon."

Adam ruffled the fair curls. "Don't worry, Katy. I'm fetching her now." Then to Mary he added, "I'll take a short cut through the east side-gate and go across the meadows."

"Take a lantern with you. It will be dark on your way home again."

He did not light the lantern before he left, having no need of it to guide his way, for as yet the sky was still bathed in gold from the sunset, the dusk hovering feather-soft. In the meadows the dandelion down flew up about him and clung to his velvet breeches. When he sighted the little cottage it had a candle alight within and he increased his pace, leaping a stream and running on. A curtain was drawn across the window and he could not see in as he made for the door. Then he saw a red cross smeared on it with a carmine lip salve. He sent the door crashing open.

In the candle-glow she sat on the edge of the bed in her petticoats, the top of her undershift about her waist, and she was bathing her neck and breasts from a bowl of water placed on a stool beside her. Her face was flushed and there was a hollow look to her eyes. In her fever she showed no surprise at seeing him.

"Don't come near me, Adam!" she cried out warningly. "The plague is upon me! I have all the first symptoms. My body is burning and full of pain. Just when I thought I was free."

"My love! Do you think I would leave you now?" He set down the lantern on the table and she crouched back as he approached.

"Stay away! Please! I know what to do. I was told."

He came nearer. "Who told you?"

"A parson's wife who has saved many lives. I must bathe myself with cold water and exercise that part of myself wherever the swelling should appear. No poultices until it is full grown."

"I can do that for you."

"No! How can I care for you if I'm sick myself?"

"I don't intend to become ill." He kept his voice low and reassuring, wanting to lull her into submission to his charge without a struggle that could further exhaust her.

"Don't you?" She seemed almost convinced, the fever diminishing her power to reason, her eyes bright as diamonds from it. He reached the bedside and as he took off his jacket some of the dandelion seeds detached themselves and drifted up into the air. A sneeze shook her. She went rigid with terror, closing her eyes tightly and unable to look at herself for dread. "Are the roses appearing on my body?"

"There's not a mark on you."

"Sometimes the blains show first on the inner thighs!" She dropped the sponge and began tearing off her petticoats.

He reassured her. "There is nothing. It must have been a dandelion seed that made you sneeze. Lie back and I will bathe you." He tossed her discarded petticoats and shift into a corner and, after rolling up his sleeves, he retrieved the sponge from the floor and dipped it into the water. Since all the other nursing methods he had heard of seemed to lose more victims than save them, he saw no reason why he should not carry out the treatment in which she had shown such faith.

She sank back against the pillows and spoke in a faraway voice. "When I kissed Christopher at Versailles I must have known I was coming home to die."

"You're not going to die!" he shouted brokenly. Whatever happened between her and Christopher was of no importance now. All that mattered was bringing her through the plague alive. Matters could be sorted out afterwards. If he had finally lost her through that sojourn in Paris it would have to be faced, but in the meantime he had a battle for her life on his hands that he did not mean to lose. "You must fight this sickness with me! Darling! Do you hear me?"

"What are all those circles?" she asked, staring at the ceiling of the box-bed with glazed eyes. Then he knew the fever had overcome her senses and she could no longer hear him. Sweat was running from her body as fast as he sponged it away. He poured water from a pitcher into a glass, which he held to her lips, raising her head at the same time. She drank and then began tossing her head as the fever racked her, and most of the water was spilt. It was not long afterwards when he rested her hand on his to bathe her arm that he saw her wince. Then as he bent her elbow and raised her arm he saw the first redness of the swelling that was to come there. He knew his adversary at last. Keeping her arm bent, he began to rotate it in exercise as she had told him.

All through the night he alternatively bathed her and kept her arm moving. Nobody came near to find out why they had not returned to Sotherleigh together, and he could only guess that Mary supposed them to be having a night of love in this quiet place after all their time apart. He wanted fresh linen and another feather bed, for everything was soaked from spilt water. Now he had mastered the sponging, having used too much water at first, and had acquired the knack of getting her to drink. He was anxious to get some nourishing liquid to spoon into her mouth. A cry of pain had replaced her wincing and, from what he had heard of the plague, it could be days before the swelling broke. At all costs her strength must be kept up.

Nobody came near the cottage until after noon the next day. Then he heard children's voices and went quickly to the door. Tired, he leaned a hand on each post and saw Mary coming across the meadow with Patience and Katy playing about her.

"Don't come any nearer!" he shouted. "Julia has the plague and I intend to bring her through it. But I need food and linen and a change of clothes for myself."

Mary had gathered the two children to her, holding them by the hand. "What else?" she called out in a practical manner, wasting no time in expressing the distress that showed on her face. When he had listed all he could think of, she nodded and hurried away.

There were moments for Julia when the fever made her believe she had been caught up in her childhood dream again, except that this time she felt frightened, unable to find Adam in all the strange circles and patterns that formed and dissolved again in such a bewildering way. Christopher

had never failed her in the past and she called on him to help in her search
for Adam, but he was always walking away from her and out of earshot,
for however much she called he never turned his head. Then such pain
swallowed her up that she had no way of telling whether hours or days or
years were passing.

The supplies for the cottage were left daily where they had been for
Julia and Katy. Wood was also supplied for a bonfire on which Molly
burnt soiled bed linen, his changes of clothing and anything else discarded
that might harbour infection. After her childhood experiences in the pest
house, Molly was convinced she was immune to the plague and insisted
on being the only member of the household to approach the cottage.
Even then she changed her clothes in an outhouse whenever she returned
to the big house and used a hay-rake to move the discarded materials onto
the bonfire.

It was the only chore Adam would allow her to do, although she had
originally arrived at the same time as the daily supplies, advancing upon
the cottage with an armful of blankets in which to sweat the patient and
poultices to be boiled up and applied. He had refused her entry, certain
she would try her own treatment should he leave Julia with her, and he
was determined to keep to that which his wife had wanted.

A truckle bed was brought for him, but although he moved it into the
cottage he never used it. He snatched sleep sitting on a stool with his head
resting on Julia's bed whenever she slept. Sometimes it was only a few
minutes, because she had only to stir and he was wide awake, quick to
exercise her arm again or to sponge her down. Many times the tears
coursed down his face without his knowing, for Julia screamed now with
agony and her head thrashed from side to side as if she fought to escape
from all that was torturing her. In the earlier stages she had cried out for
Christopher so desperately and heart-rendingly that Adam had been torn
for another reason. Never once in her delirium had she called for him. He
no longer felt jealousy. He was beyond that in a sorrow the extent of
which he was not fully aware, for everything had narrowed down to the
terrible treatment that he never allowed to cease.

He was terrified that she would die. It seemed impossible she could
continue to endure such suffering and he was ceaseless in his care, folding
cool damp clouts across her burning forehead, spooning nourishment into
her mouth and trying to appease her endless thirst with sips of barley
water. Then it came to a time when she could no longer take anything,
her physical torment too great, and he knew he must take a knife to the

swelling, whether it was ready or not, if she was to have any chance of surviving.

She was trying to throw herself from the bed, not knowing what she was doing, and her hair whirled about her demented face. He gripped her arm with a force that made a bruise rise and tried to keep the knife steady as he held it poised. Then he drove in the point of the blade, piercing the hideous swelling.

Her whole body convulsed, her knees drawing up and then her legs flying out again as she arched and fell back, blood and pus pouring from the wound until both of them were spattered by it. The scene was like a corner of a battlefield. He did not try to stem the flow, knowing it must drain, and he leaned over to look down at her, smoothing her hair back from her face.

"It's over, my darling. All over."

"Adam?" she whispered, her eyes still closed.

"Yes, my love." He found her hand and held it.

"Why couldn't I find you?"

He could have answered that she had been calling for someone else, but that had been in her delirium when she had given herself away in a manner she would never suspect and which he would never reveal to her. "I was here." Then he saw she had fallen into a sleep of exhaustion and doubted that she had heard what he had said.

When she awoke some while later, she was in a fresh nightgown and lying between clean sheets that smelt of lavender. She tried to sit up, but her physical weakness defeated her and there was an acute soreness under her right arm that was swathed in linen bindings up over her shoulder. From the pillows she could see the cottage was spick and span with the addition of a truckle bed that had not been there before. She supposed Molly had been nursing her. How long had she been here since Katy had been passed into Mary's care? And Adam? Was he home and waiting to see her? Once in her fever she thought she had heard his voice, but that could only have been an illusion.

"Molly!" she called, her voice faint.

Immediately a shadow fell across the floor through the open door and Adam came in. He looked thin in the face and weary across the eyes, but he was fresh-shaven and smiling. "So you are awake."

"Adam!" Joy flooded through her. He was with her. It had been his voice she had heard and he must have been with her throughout her ordeal.

"So you are awake. How do you feel?"

"Thankful to see you." She summoned up her strength to hold a hand out to him, but he did not appear to notice, his thumbs remaining firmly hooked in his belt. Her hand fell back on the bed. "I believe you have been caring for me."

He gave a nod. "I was anxious when I returned from France to find you ill here."

"I don't remember that."

"No matter. All that remains now is for you to get strong again. When you called I was outside watching for dinner to come from the house. I want you to try to eat something."

"I will," she vowed, but slept again in the same breath.

The next time she opened her eyes it was dark and he sat at the table in candlelight, reading a book. Now that she was looking at him again it seemed to her that it was not so much weariness as sadness that shadowed his eyes. It struck a responsive chord in her and her eyes filled with tears without her understanding why. Somehow he was not quite the same. She could not define the difference, but it was there. He glanced across and saw the glitter in her eyes. Instantly he was on his feet and across to her.

"Does your arm pain you?"

"It's sore, that's all."

"I'm afraid it will be for a while." Carefully he propped her pillows to raise her a little. "While you eat a little supper, I'll tell you of my adventures. I heard about your going to London and bringing your weavers and embroiderers to cottages near here."

"Have any of them or the coachman fallen sick?"

"None. Everyone is well, as you soon will be. Molly has kept me informed, although our conversations at a distance have been brief through my not wanting to leave you for more than a minute or two, and not at all when your illness was reaching its crisis. You can be certain that you saved the lives of some if not all of those women, because the plague is said to be worse than ever in London. Carts have begun to collect by day as well as by night due to numbers mounting."

"You have saved my life."

He grinned wryly at her. "It was in my own interests. What would my life be without you?"

"Or mine if you were not with me."

He gave her an indulgent look as if she had conjured up a remark without substance especially to please him. Turning to the table, he removed a linen napkin from a cup and bowl on a tray there. Then he sat on the edge of the bed to feed her with spoonfuls of beef jelly and sips of egg-wine while he told her of his incarceration at Dieppe and Michael's rescue and how he had lost no time in returning to Sotherleigh. "I followed the directions you gave me as to how you should be nursed and they worked well."

"I don't think I caught the plague from Katy's house, but from our London home."

"How could that be?"

She told him about the dead looter and how her garments might have gathered up some infection. His concern was only that she should have had to face such a situation alone and he complimented her on how she had dealt with it.

"You have a fount of courage in you, Julia."

She dismissed his words with a shake of her head, one wish uppermost in her mind. "I pray that you haven't caught the contagion from me!"

Again there was wryness in his expression. "It lies in the hands of fate. We must wait and see."

"I'd never forgive myself if—"

He silenced her jokingly by popping a spoonful of jelly in her mouth. "Let's have no talk of it." His shrug was cynical. "I feel immune. In any case, it fades in importance beside all that really matters to me."

She expected him to elaborate, to speak of love to her, but that was not forthcoming. After giving her the last sip of egg-wine that drained the glass, he wiped her lips with the napkin, kissed her on the brow and bade her sleep again. Her troubled gaze followed him as he took hot water from a cauldron over the hearth and washed up the glass and bowl with some of his own supper things. The same precaution of not returning crockery from the infected cottage was being maintained by him as it had by her while she and Katy were here. When the task was done he glanced towards the bed and saw she was still awake.

"Sleep now, my love."

It was the first endearment he had uttered since she had come to herself again. She turned her head away on the pillow, stricken in the belief that it had been said automatically. Something had happened during the weeks they had been apart. Had he met another woman? She could think of no other reason why he had set up this barrier between them. Yet he had risked his life for her, cared for her tirelessly through Mrs. Webb's treatment, which was so exhausting for patient and nurse alike, and carried out every kind of intimate duty that a sick-room demanded, all of which could have been left to an underling. She had planned to greet him at their London home with an outpouring of her heart that he had never heard from her before, but that opportunity had been lost. Yet if it had come about and she had met him as he was now, her words of love would not have been spoken, stemmed by that withdrawn air of his that was something new and strange and frightening. Her eyelids closed of their own volition, but her night was restless.

Day by day she became stronger and still he showed no sign that he would succumb to the infection. Their hours passed peacefully. At first, leaning on his arm, she reached the door and sat outside in the shade of a tree with him. Soon afterwards they took short walks together and Mary brought the children to wave to them from a safe distance. Every one of the women from the cottages came in pairs or groups, all calling out that they would be glad to get back to work again. They had enjoyed being in the country, but they missed London and were not used to being idle. Since they were now out of quarantine, she asked Mary to find them some work at Briar House. The next day it was reported to her that all the women had cheered up and were glad to be earning money again.

In the evenings Julia and Adam played chess or cards, or read. There were times when his gaze would leave his book and settle on her, she unknowing as she sat reading herself. He knew the distancing between them was of his making, but it was not through loving her less; quite the contrary. She had cried out only for Christopher when she had been at death's door, but it had not been proof of unfaithfulness, simply an unconscious utterance of caring until her last breath. It was during those horrifying moments when the plague had almost snatched her from him that he had experienced a new dimension of love sweeping through him to eliminate all that had ever seemed important before. In that instant he had accepted the compromise that she had created for herself as if somehow it might give her the extra strength to sustain her in her tenacious fight for life.

He looked back at his book without taking in what was printed there. Let her have unchallenged what she wanted most. Never again would he question the allegiance of her most tender feelings to her life-long love, for that sentimental yearning had no realism and in their living together they had far more than most couples ever glimpsed.

Yet that meeting of her halfway, about which she knew nothing, had subtly changed their relationship. He had felt the difference in himself when he had come into the cottage when she had thought it was her maid who was there. Although he had tried to tell himself at first that the change was too slight to be of any importance, it had become clear that the rapport between them had gone. He had to face the fact that it might never come back.

# NINETEEN

*W*HEN AUTUMN CAME the plague was still raging in London and there were more outbreaks in the provinces where the pestilence had been carried by those who had slipped the net. The realm was being ruled from Oxford, there being no question of the King risking his life by returning to Whitehall, particularly as the Queen had not yet given him an heir and concern was growing that she was to prove barren. Parliament continued to be prorogued and both Lords and Commons made the most of being at their country seats, hunting and shooting and caring for their estates as they did in any case during the months when Parliament was in recess. Unlike their French counterparts, Court life was not the be-all and end-all for the English nobility and gentry, entertainments being as pleasurable in the green countryside as in London. Although normally there would have been parties and balls throughout these times when people were at their country seats, because of the plague large gatherings were discouraged. On the whole, only local friends and acquaintances gathered together in small numbers for any occasion.

Adam's days followed the same pattern. Outwardly everything was well between him and Julia, but they did not laugh together as often as before and their quarrels, previously lively and often leading to love-making, took on a sharp, unhappy twist. Julia wanted to talk everything out with him as they had done when problems had arisen in the past, but each time she tried to broach the subject she became choked emotionally, fearful as to how he would answer her.

She had hoped desperately at first that the change in him had been temporary, the result of tiredness from his solicitous nursing of her, but that was not it. Since then she knew with her whole being, tuned in every nerve to Adam, that the special and adoring spark in him which had been dedicated wholly to her had gone. Extinguished like a candle-flame, it had left his attitude towards her as previously hers had been towards him. Everything due to a wife was being given, but he had withdrawn his soul from hers, which previously he would have laid at her feet.

She accepted that it was just punishment, all the harder to bear, she realised, because he was unaware that she had sensed what had happened, further proof of how everything between them had deteriorated. It had not been a deliberate revenge that he had taken, but after five years of marriage his love had failed to find the reciprocation that should have been his from their wedding night if she had come to her senses then and not at Versailles upon hearing that he was in danger. That was when she knew she could not live without him, that he was everything to her and had been all unconsciously from a certain moment that she could now pin-point. It was when she had been dressed for her marriage in the Elizabethan gown and had looked at her image in the mirror. She had asked aloud, right out of her heart, if Adam would find her beautiful. It was what she had wanted above all else and had not understood that it sprang from love.

When she had kissed Christopher in the Cour Royale it had been a long overdue farewell to a first love that should have faded with her emergence from adolescence. Katherine had given her sound warning and it was the only time she had paid that sensible woman no real heed. In that final embrace Christopher had exchanged a special, loving look with her. He had understood what was happening, just as he had so often comprehended her hopes and fears in the past, and he had been glad for her.

One night when Adam had been particularly tender in his love-making she had gazed into his beloved face on the pillow beside her and, with effort and with trepidation, she had whispered the words she should have said long ago.

"I love you, Adam."

He had looked back at her for a long moment and then he had smiled wryly. "Of course you do."

She had seen that he did not believe her, that he thought she was making some effort in response to his special cherishing of her body. It was clear that he was more hurt than pleased that she should say then what she had never before said to him.

"I do," she persisted, aware of blundering on, but wanting to convince him. "I didn't realise until I thought you were in London in danger of the plague."

He drew a finger along her jawline and then placed it against her lips. "You'd have felt the same about anyone you knew well in that situation and proved it in bringing Katy and those women out of London. Sleep now, my love. I've kept you awake too long." He snuffed the candle and turned away from her, something which he never did, and she thought her heart must break. She lay awake until he slept and then curled up against his naked back, sliding her arm around his waist and resting her head against him. The woman who had estranged him from her was herself. She had worn out his love, not appreciating what he had given her from the start. When he had been so set on winning through to make her his wife, she had responded with a compromise she now saw to be utterly wrong. For any other man with feelings less deep than Adam's it would have worked, but he was too passionate and strong-willed to be content with liking and fondness from the woman he loved. At some time he had finally come to the moment of truth and met her on her own terms.

She pressed her lips to his spine in a kiss and breathed softly, "I love you, my darling. It's become my turn to try to win you. I shall have a harder battle, because when love fades it can't easily be revived."

He slept on and in the morning had no knowledge of what she had poured out to him in the darkness of the night.

JULIA HAD FAR MORE TROUBLE than she had anticipated from her London workers. They were used to working together, but not living under the same roof in somewhat cramped quarters. They quarrelled and sulked and several times some of the younger ones fought like wild cats. With the exception of Alice and a few who had found sweethearts in the village, three already wed, they were tired of the countryside and longed for the more vibrant atmosphere of London. Neither did they like working with the local hands, mocking their Sussex dialects, and those in turn were shocked by some of the rough language used in their hearing. Since there was no longer any likelihood of Michael's coming home from France to stay, Mary had no need of Briar House and Julia turned it into separate workshops for her London and village hands. The extra rooms also supplied more spacious accommodation and things became better generally for all but two of the women. They were so homesick that their work had become slack and Julia found them alternative employment and housing with a prosperous Chichester dressmaker. Although they received much lower wages their compensation was in living again amidst the bustle of streets and markets, albeit there was no comparison between the great capital and the small city of Chichester.

With no outlet for her ribbons in London, and not prepared to accept lower prices in the provinces, Julia wrote to Michael about selling them in Paris. He told her to send whatever she had and keep up a steady supply, because he could sell her ribbons through his own silk channels and would find as great a demand for them as she had known previously. Mary produced designs incorporating $L$ for Louis XIV and fleur-de-lis in gold and silver thread, but Anne's flower ribbons and designs proved equally popular with rich French customers. A well-to-do shopkeeper who rented one of the exclusive little shops at the château of Versailles and other of the royal palaces increased his orders steadily for Pallister ribbons, the nobility being much taken with the extravagant novelty of them.

Sophie bitterly resented this new line in ribbons going out under the Brissard reputation. She broke her usual silence with Michael when they were on their own to storm at him.

"We've always dealt only in the best Lyonnaise silks, not in fripperies such as any pedlar might sell! You must be out of your mind to degrade my father's wares in such a manner."

He cut her tirade short. "I had to remind you once before that I'm the head of Brissard's now. The ribbons are of faultless silk and sell as fast as they are delivered and the orders stockpile. I've started sending Julia's wares out with silks that tone with the various designs and this is proving successful. When you have sound advice to offer instead of wanting to cut off a new selling source simply to cling to old ways, I'll listen and not before."

It seemed to Sophie that he crossed her at every chance. She tried to think how she might thwart this new sideline. If she let it be rumoured that the ribbons came from plague-stricken London, instead of Sotherleigh, she would not be deviating greatly from the truth, for she knew that Julia had simply evacuated her workers for the time being. France was as used to outbreaks of plague as everywhere else on the Continent and a summer never passed without its flaring up somewhere, but never to her knowledge had there been such a scourge anywhere as was presently diminishing the population of London, and fear of its crossing the Channel continued to be high. One reason why Julia had been kept in the dark over it was because there was a superstition that even to speak of it was to invite its presence.

Sophie gave considerable thought to how best to put her plan into action. She decided to let her outburst at Michael subside well before she took action or else he would suspect her and she never wanted to experience again the ordeal she had been forced to endure as a result of driving him to the end of his tether. The trouble with easy-tempered people was that when they were finally driven into a rage they were worse than anybody else and made themselves ill over it. She had seen Michael looking haggard for days afterwards. It had been her only consolation.

After waiting a month, Sophie rode in her coach to the cemetery as she always did and spent her usual time at the graveside, for nothing should disturb the time she spent there. Then she returned to the gates to send the coachman on an errand to collect a garment she had specially ordered from her dressmaker for this day.

"It will take me a couple of hours, Madame."

"No matter. I shall wait here."

She watched until the coach was out of sight and then hailed the bearers of a sedan chair that took her to a shop that sold Pallister ribbons supplied by Brissard's, which she had never patronised before. It was located in a part of Paris that had become unfamiliar to her through new buildings and street planning since she was last there. It made her realise how long it was since she had ventured anywhere, either with Michael or later when the cemetery had become her only destination. The shop proved to be full of customers and she took a quick look round, but there was no one whom she knew and in her mourning veils nobody would recognise her again.

As always her elegant air commanded immediate attention and she asked to see embroidered ribbons. She was shown some that she knew instantly.

"These are very beautiful," she remarked, trailing one of snowflakes on a midnight-blue ground over her gloved hand.

"They are Brissard ribbons," the assistant informed her, finding it easier to impress customers with the name of Brissard rather than the unfamiliar and foreign-sounding name of the maker.

Immediately Sophie gave a scream, aware of every head turning, and she dropped the ribbon as if it had become red-hot. "They are imported from plague-stricken London! I heard that only yesterday!"

Pandemonium broke out. The assistant himself shot back from the ribbons; women shrieked and exclaimed in dismay. Sophie wrenched off her gloves, having had them in contact with the wares, adding to the panic. Then she was pushed and jostled as customers vied with her in getting out of the shop first.

"Plague goods!" she heard someone shout in the street and several more took it up.

Smiling to herself, she entered a glover's, had an agreeable time selecting a new pair of gloves and then took a chair back to the cemetery. She had ten minutes to spare and then the coach came to take her home again. Once there she awaited events.

At supper Michael looked abstracted and worried. She guessed someone had been sent to the office wanting confirmation or denial of what had been said about the ribbons, but since she and Michael did not normally converse at supper, Jean-Robert already in bed, he did not tell her and she could not ask.

At first Michael was able to appease those who came with the rumour, but within twenty-four hours it was out of his hands. By law, plague goods had to be burnt and officials, keeping a distance from him, came to question him at his office and study custom papers and ledgers concerning the ribbons. While this was going on Jean-Robert arrived with a footman, it being the child's pleasure to call in and see his father at work sometimes. He liked the warehouses where there were no little children struggling with difficult tasks, and if the men working there were not too busy he would get a ride on one of the hand-carts. For the first time his father did not give him a welcome, but an anxious frown instead.

"You can't stay today, Jean-Robert. Go now! Quickly!"

"Wait!" One of the officials held up a hand. "Is this your son, Monsieur Pallister?"

"Yes."

"Then he stays here. We do not doubt your honesty or that of your sister, but there is plague in the provinces now in England and in view of the many complaints laid at our door since yesterday we must take action to protect the city of Paris from the slightest risk. We shall not order your wares to be burnt yet, but we must seal up your premises here and your home for a period of two months."

"No!"

The official ignored the interruption. "If at the end of that time nobody has fallen sick of the pestilence, then we shall re-open your property and you may sell such wares as are now in store."

Michael, holding his son close, with the footman, two clerks and twenty packers and loaders, watched as outer doors were locked and padlocked. A watchman was placed by each.

At home Sophie was getting ready to go to the cemetery when a maidservant came rushing to her, eyes wide with fright.

"Madame! There are men sealing up the house! They say we may have the plague here! We are to be isolated for two months!"

Sophie almost fainted. She clutched at a bedpost for support. "That's not possible. They can't do that."

"But they are, Madame!"

She pulled herself together. "I'll speak to them." Downstairs she found the entrance door already padlocked. As she opened a window to speak to the men carrying out the work they thrust it back into place and began setting a bar into place across it. "Stop!" she cried through the panes. "There's no truth in the Brissard ribbons being infected with plague! I know the person who started the rumour. It was done as a joke! For vengeance! Out of rivalry! Who knows? But it was a lie!"

She dared not confess to being the culprit and in any case they were not listening. Wild with fury she hammered her fists on the panes and wept. This was not at all what she had expected. She had thought the sales of Pallister ribbons would fall off so drastically that Michael would be forced to stop importing them. This was disaster beyond anything she had imagined. Then to her horror she saw that the men, wary that she might break through the glass, had begun to board up the windows.

She drew back sharply and fled out into the hall where she dithered like someone in a maze, remembering she would not find her father in his study or upstairs. The only place she could be with him was no longer accessible. She uttered such a scream of frustration that the servants, who had gathered gloomily in the kitchen to discuss the distressing events, rushed into the hall in a body, thinking she was being attacked. When they reached there she had already dashed up to her bedchamber and slammed the door. They stood at the foot of the flight, able to hear her crashing about and the drumming of her heels in helpless fury.

She came down to supper white-faced and red-eyed. Those waiting at table saw her halt with a startled look on the threshold at not finding her husband waiting for her. It was apparent to them that she had been so wrapped up in her own misery that she had not given a thought before now to either him or her son. Neither had she deigned to utter a word to her domestic staff trapped in the house with her, as any normal employer would have done. There was not one servant from the housekeeper to the kitchen boy who did not resent it. Without her being aware of it, she had become still more isolated in the midst of isolation.

At the Brissard business premises Jean-Robert was thoroughly enjoying himself. It was like being a soldier at camp with make-shift beds for his father and himself in the office, the footman and the clerks in the outer office and the workers in the stockrooms. The bedclothes and feather beds had been brought to the door to the watchmen, together with the food and wine that went on his father's account at the suppliers. They had all eaten together at one of the packing tables in the warehouse and an initial shyness among the workers had been dispersed with the wine.

"This is fun, Papa!" he declared before he slept. "I'm glad I'm here. But do you think Mama will be worried?"

"No. One of the senior officials has promised me he will take a message to her to say that you are here with me. She will know that we're safe, just as we know she will be. None of us is going to fall sick, of that at least we can be certain."

By the end of the first week time had begun to drag for everyone. Michael's banker came in answer to a message to shout through a window. Michael arranged that the workers' wives should be paid weekly. Some of the women came with their children to wave to their men at the windows, but the watchmen would not let them draw near. Michael had to keep everybody occupied and when the last scrap of work had been done he had the premises cleaned and repainted, a project long overdue. For relaxation there were games of boules in a warehouse, chess, draughts and cards, but he forbade gambling for money, not wanting the men to fall out, and they played for counters instead, marking up debts against one another to be settled later when wages would be theirs again and not in the hands of their wives. Books were brought in for Jean-Robert and Michael gave him daily lessons, including English, which in spite of Sophie's opposition had always been part of his curriculum. Occasionally there were violent quarrels among the men that resulted in bared chests and fisticuffs, which Michael supervised as if it were a public fight on an English village green. There was such cheering and shouting on these occasions that the din could be heard in the next street. As one week followed another tempers were more easily frayed and the fights became more frequent, a safety outlet which, when organised, Michael did not discourage.

Sophie had no such responsibilities, for her staff organised their own pastimes, the housekeeper making sure that there were no idle hands. Drink had become Sophie's escape. She had always liked cognac, having been given her first sip by her father, but in adult life she had never indulged, restricting herself to the occasional small glass and knowing that it would be all too easy to make it into a daily habit. Now she had to have some outlet from this impossible situation or else she would go mad.

She passed her time pacing about the house like a caged beast or sitting for hours by her bedchamber window, gazing out with a glass in her hand. Normally she liked to read and there was some half-finished embroidery on a trestle frame that she could have finished, but she was too possessed by hatred for Michael to take an interest in anything. It was entirely his fault that this terrible predicament had occurred. If he had listened to her and dropped the ribbon-selling she would not have had to resort to her trick and be shut up now like a prisoner in the Bastille.

She put a hand to her aching brow. It was such a long time since she had had one of those devastating headaches that she had begun to hope they were gone for ever, but since the first day of incarceration one had been threatening like thunder in the far distance and giving warning of a storm to come. But it was coming on her now. The signs were all too familiar. She had tried to stave it off by lying quietly most of the day on the couch in the salon that had once been her father's, the nearest she could get to him since Michael had swept away her shrine and she was prevented from going to the graveside. She would have to get upstairs to bed.

With a groan she sat up slowly. Swords pierced through her brain. On a sidetable by the couch was a half-full decanter and glass, which she picked up to take with her. At a slow and careful pace she made her way from the room in the direction of the stairs. In the kitchen some of the servants were playing cards. It was an exciting game and the rest were watching, only the housekeeper absent, having a nap in her room. Nobody saw Sophie making her way with painful slowness up the long, curving flight.

She was swaying on her feet by the time she reached her bedchamber door and felt horribly nauseous. Almost blindly she found the key to her cupboard and with every nerve in her head and neck shrieking with pain she opened its door and took down the bottle of tincture that always gave her relief. At this stage she should have relocked the cupboard and sum-moned her lady's maid to administer to her, but she was desperate for the dose and let the drops fall into the glass of cognac that she had poured. She had no idea if the spirit would diminish the tincture's effect and added extra for good measure since it was harmless. She drank the mixture down in three gulps and then sank thankfully back on her pillows. It was a little while before she felt the first twinge of stomach pain.

WHEN SOPHIE WAS FOUND DEAD by her lady's maid it was thought at first she had died of the plague and the servants were panic-stricken. The housekeeper alone kept her head. With the two months nearly up she knew they were all well out of danger as Madame would have been. She had no fear in examining the body and saw for herself there were no plague-blains or signs of swelling. Seeing the decanter she wondered if it was an excess of cognac, but that was for the doctor to decide.

He sniffed the bottle of tincture and put a taste on his fingertip. Both the lady's maid and the housekeeper were able to confirm that Madame had had the only key to the cupboard where she kept her tinctures and lotions and nobody knew where she had kept the key. The doctor soon made up his mind as to the cause of death and informed the staff, who were gathered in the hall, that their mistress had poisoned herself.

"But," he added when their murmurs of shock had died down, "I think there's every likelihood that she may have taken the dose from the wrong flask in error."

At this point one of the young maidservants fainted. The doctor soon brought her round, saying kindly that it was natural that distress for Madame should so affect her.

When he reported the death to the public coroner, he showed the bottle of poison, pointing out how the label simply said *Lotion,* and since all the bottles were similar he did not think it was suicide but accidental death.

"Why should she keep poison in the cupboard in the first place?" he was asked.

"It's a whitener for the skin and could have caused her demise through constant use had she but known it," the doctor explained. "She was a beautiful woman and had a range of herbal aids to beauty in her cupboard among medical decoctions for the usual women's ailments. It's my belief she had been drinking too much cognac and, feeling unwell, sought some relief and thereby made her fatal mistake."

His evidence saved Sophie from a grave in unconsecrated ground. She was buried with her father and her name was added to the ornate headstone that she had chosen for him herself. Jean-Robert was heart-broken. Michael encouraged the boy's memories of the loving side of Sophie that she had often shown their son and tried to cheer him with the promise of seeing Sotherleigh when it could be arranged. Julia had written that there was an outbreak of the plague in Chichester, and Michael considered it was too near home to expose his son to the risk.

WINTER HIT HARD at the plague. Frost and flurries of snow brought the numbers of dead down to double figures and hope rose that the end might be in sight. Julia had wondered anxiously about the Webbs as well as Abigail and her husband, who if they had survived would be longing to see their four-month-old son.

Boy was thriving and living at Sotherleigh where Anne and Mary had him and Katy and Patience under their joint wing. Another boy who was getting along very well was the embroiderer's brother who had objected to taking his clothes off by the river. He had found work on a local farm and lived with the farmer and his wife, who had lost their two sons at the Battle of Naseby and were fostering him as if he were their own.

Only with Adam and Julia was the situation becoming gradually more strained. He went no fewer than three times to Oxford during the winter. She would have liked to have gone with him and visited Faith, as well as Susan and her husband at Bletchingdon, while he was at Court seeing ministers about whatever government business had taken him there. But he did not suggest it and she did not dare to ask, not wanting him to suppose her purpose was solely to see Christopher and thus exacerbate the painful relationship between them.

Christopher had much to keep him busy. The majority of the members of the Royal Society had gravitated to Oxford to escape the plague if they were not already living in the vicinity of the University and the meetings continued. He went often to Cambridge where his chapel was still being built, as was the Sheldonian Theatre, which he visited daily, and if all went well the King would open it in a few months' time. He also had several interesting commissions, some to be started in the near future, three nearing completion and a number still at the planning stage. A board of councillors wanting a new Town Hall, and seeking prestige for themselves by commissioning the eminent Dr. Wren, had rejected his first plans, declaring that the wide stone canopy over the entrance would never bear its own weight and was likely to fall and crush those unfortunate enough to be beneath.

"But I assure you, gentlemen," Christopher had replied, "that nothing could dislodge that canopy in a thousand years."

When he proceeded to explain why, crisply and clearly in his tutorial manner, he might as well have been speaking a foreign language for all they understood. The chairman cut him off quickly to save general embarrassment.

"We really wanted a grand portico, Dr. Wren."

Christopher could have been offended. There was grace and elegance to the canopy as it was, its structure totally in harmony with the rest of the building, and to add anything else would be unnecessary. But even as he reached out to gather up his plans and depart, his sense of humour got the better of him. It was not often that an architect had the chance to play a little joke, but he had done it in the painting of the ceiling of the Sheldonian Theatre and he would play another on this pompous assembly.

"Very well, gentlemen."

"You'll add the columns?"

"Six should suffice."

They all looked pleased and nodded approval. The chairman was most genial. "You have satisfied us completely as to the safety of the canopy, Dr. Wren."

Christopher could not stop chuckling to himself as he returned to his rooms at Wadham College. He planned to order the columns to be an inch shorter than the height they should be. The gap might never be spotted in the councillors' lifetime, or his own, but the canopy would continue to hang free of any visible support, and in years to come there would be many a laugh when it was seen what he had done.

He would share the joke with Faith when next he saw her. He liked to see her laugh. Amusement would start in her eyes, bring out her dimples and then her laughter, which was like a sweet-toned bell. That reminded him. This evening he must pen his weekly love letter to her.

Nell Gwyn, passing in a gallant's coach, saw him and waved, but he failed to notice her, lost in his own thoughts. She gazed after him. He was an attractive man, but although he was gracious and smiling towards her, it only came from his natural courtesy. She had met him first in London's Mermaid Tavern, where members of the Royal Society sometimes gathered for beefsteak and ale after a meeting. It had been the haunt of actors and playwrights since Will Shakespeare and Ben Jonson had roistered there, and it was natural that she and fellow players should have made it their own. Christopher had been holding forth on some discourse and she had listened in fascination, wondering how any man could know so much. Then she had mimicked him very accurately and he had laughed and applauded as much as anyone else. She had liked and respected him for that. Since arriving in Oxford she had seen him several times at a distance.

"What are you thinking about, Nell?" her escort asked her. He was good-looking, rich, periwigged and fun to be with. She had met him after her arrival with the rest of the players from the King's Playhouse and the Duke of York's players when they had fled from the plague, she bringing her mother with her. Mrs. Gwyn's drinking still kept Nell short of money, but she accepted the situation as good-humouredly as she had always done, loving the old woman and taking care of her. Yet she was longing to get back on the stage and start earning again.

"How glad I shall be when we can all go back to London," she answered on a cheerful sigh. "I was just getting my first good roles when the plague came. At least the King has lifted the ban on dancing rooms and playhouses here in Oxford for Christmas, but there are too many of us players looking for work for me to get a role anywhere. I'm bored with performing in playlets at parties." Her eyes danced wickedly at him. "As you know, I do vary that by singing for my supper sometimes."

He answered her in the same vein with a long and smiling look. "You always sing the sweetest of songs, Nell."

She laughed and pouted a kiss at him that was full of promise. At sixteen she was as experienced in the ways of the world as any actress twice her age, but he was certain she would keep her girlish, mischievous charm to the end of her days.

IN FEBRUARY the King moved back to Whitehall. The plague still simmered in the slums of Wapping and Stepney, which made many of the Court wary of accompanying him, but he was impatient for life to return to normal. Adam followed the King's example, as did hundreds of others, and left Julia at Sotherleigh while he went ahead to get their London house aired and fumigated and put to rights before she came.

Like everyone else who returned at that time he was saddened by the state of London. Every street had many shops and houses boarded up where the occupants had perished. There had been so little traffic that grass had grown amidst the cobbles, giving even main thoroughfares the look of country lanes. It was now estimated that a hundred thousand had died and in places a stench still came from the mass graves that had not been properly covered in the haste with which the dead were buried.

But London was stirring again. The King's return revitalised it and people cheered him wherever he went. Coaches and wagons and carts and drays began bringing citizens back again. Many new faces came with them. London had had always been a magnet for the young and enterprising, and now there was a flood of eager workmen and craftsmen, freshly out of their apprenticeships, who realised there would be many gaps that they could be filling in among the city's reviving trades. On all sides windows were thrown wide in houses and tenements as homes were reclaimed and shutters were removed from shops. Bonfires burned in every street and alley as bed linen, clothes and anything else that might still be harbouring infection were burned. Strange aromas filled the air as perfumes, herbs, pitch and brimstone were used to purify premises. Once again at the passengers' steps up from the river the ferrymen's cry of "Next oars!" was heard. In the Port of London ships stranded by the plague set out for foreign harbours ready to accept them once more.

Adam made enquiries on Julia's behalf and was able to let her know that although Abigail and her husband had both contracted the plague they had been pulled through by Mrs. Webb. Boy was then restored to his parents by one of the nine evacuated embroiderers who wanted to return to their London homes without delay. Later Julia heard what a joyous reunion there had been and although Boy was baptised Arthur after his grandfather, who had not survived the pestilence, she was always to think of him by his nickname whenever her thoughts dwelt on those days.

As for Katy, Michael had legally adopted her by proxy for his mother's sake, for Anne had no authority to sign such papers. The child's predicament had been explained to him by letter, there being no relatives that could be traced, and no less important was the fact that Anne had become as devoted to her as to Patience, thinking that Katy was another daughter. Michael understood what it would mean to his mother if for any reason she should be separated from the child. It puzzled Anne at times as to why she could not recall giving birth to Katy. Then Mary would prompt her memory gently to the true facts, which she would remember for five minutes and then forget again.

The news of Sophie's death was withheld from Anne. She could get deeply distressed if she believed anything was affecting one of her children, and she would have grieved for Michael's loss in a way that would be detrimental to her state of mind. Only to his sister had Michael written of the true facts and Julia realised how narrowly he must have come to receiving a fatal dose the first time it had been administered to him. Much as she wanted to see him, she had had to advise him about the flare-up of the plague in Chichester, for it had been fierce and a mass grave had been dug outside the city walls.

Mary did not care to think what her future might be now that Michael no longer had a wife. Men did not always want to marry women they had made their mistresses when at last the chance opened up for them. It was some comfort that he had sent her a very affectionate message in his letter to his sister. At least Julia's warning of the plague should keep him away long enough to be able to consider everything carefully before he came to Sotherleigh again. There was no reason to imagine he would visit more often than before in any case, for he was the owner of a most prosperous business in France and it would be his son's after him.

It was June when Julia returned to London. She had hoped for a new beginning with Adam, but as soon as she arrived at their house she became unsure again. All the rooms that had been despoiled by the looters had been refurbished and anything that might have remotely reminded her of her terrible experience had been removed, but the light-hearted atmosphere that had prevailed before had gone. She supposed the cause lay within Adam and herself, a cloud under which she woke each morning and slept again at night. She thought so often of Katherine, who had seen the folly that lurked in her nature. Many times she wished that her grandmother was still at Sotherleigh with some wise advice to steer her out of her present troubled path.

Her workshop in Carter Lane was exactly as it had been left. For safety's sake she felt obliged to have the ribbons there and any of the raw materials that might have been handled by the plague victims put to a bonfire.

Fortunately a large stock had been building up in Briar House and on a date that was set, these were delivered to Carter Lane. That same day all nine of her workers, who had left Sussex earlier than the rest, arrived to start work again. Alice's old aunt had died not long before and she herself was shortly to be married in Sussex. As a country-bred girl she had no wish to return to the City. By the end of a week Julia had three-quarters of her old work force at their tasks again. She went personally to her previous contacts, who had always bought from her. The shops were open, but in some cases sons or nephews had stepped into the shoes of owners taken by the plague. All knew of her ribbons and were willing to buy, although until commerce recovered the orders had to be moderate. The ban on centres of entertainment was still in force, no fairs allowed, and the Court had not fully regathered. The war with the Dutch had flared up again, but a splendid victory at sea had settled that for the time being.

By chance Julia had good news of the Webbs. Both had survived the dangerous risks they had taken and he had been given a living at a church in Manchester where they could continue to care for the poor and the sick. In the meantime they were at Wapping, a few cases of the plague still festering there, and they would not leave London until they were no longer needed. Another piece of good news was that the Needhams had also escaped infection despite some at the Heathcock having died. Their sons were now back from the country, the family reunited and the inn open again.

Julia had suffered considerable financial loss throughout the plague. What she had banked for Michael had dwindled fast while she had kept work and wages going with no outlet except the Parisian one. That had helped considerably before coming to an abrupt standstill, and now it was uncertain if it would ever revive. Michael hoped to start selling her ribbons again after a period, but at present they were still associated with the plague in French people's minds, a fear it would take time to over-come. He also warned that Louis XIV was discouraging the import of foreign goods, wanting France to create for itself in all luxurious crafts. She began to wonder how secure her business was even in England, for fashions were changing and the excessive use of decorative ribbons was on the wane, people much sobered in outlook by the plague. Yet it was not time to sell the business either and she must keep going as best she could.

There were moments when she could have believed that Adam had some project of his own that was keeping him amused and interested. He seemed much happier than in recent months, the brooding, sombre look gone from his eyes. It made him easier to live with, for they quarrelled less, and she responded warmly to this change in him, even though the invisible gulf between them did not diminish in any way.

He took her to the King's Playhouse when it reopened in August, the ban on some divertissements lifted at last. Nell was not in the production, being in rehearsal for a play in September, but she came to their box during an interval to chatter about her prospects after first recounting how she had spent the time of the plague in Oxford and wanting to know how Adam and Julia had fared.

"I'm getting my first leading role in *The English Monsieur!*" she exclaimed joyfully, leaning back in the chair Adam had vacated for her and kicking her feet with delight as if splashing them in a pool. The chair tilted and would have toppled if Adam had not acted promptly in grabbing it and saving her. She barely noticed in her exuberance. "I'm to have my own dressing-room too! They say the King will be coming to the first night. He's never paid me any attention before that I know of, but he should this time! Have you seen my cloak?" She stood up and whirled around in a swirl of crimson velvet and wool. "It's my royal livery! All of us players here at the King's Playhouse have been granted the right to wear it as favoured servants of His Majesty!"

"It's very grand!" Julia said.

Nell twinkled at Adam, always provocative towards attractive men. "Does it suit me, do you think?"

"Handsomely," he grinned.

"Say you'll both be here for my opening night!" Merrily she struck a dramatic pose, her hands pressed to her heart.

"You know we will!" Julia laughed, extremely glad that Nell should be getting her big chance.

"We'll be in this very box!" Adam promised.

A trumpet sounded, announcing the continuance of the performance and Nell left them to rejoin friends in the pit. Adam sat down again and reached for Julia's hand and held it. She glanced at him. He was looking at the stage, his face illumined by the lights into planes and shadows, a smile still on his lips. Everything had eased for them during that ten minutes of Nell's light-heartedness. If only it could be the start of their drawing close again! This time she would have so much more of herself to give, for it would include her whole heart.

It was the Saturday morning of the same week of hearing Nell's good news that Julia spotted Christopher standing on the steps of St. Paul's. She was in a sedan chair and on her way to Carter Lane for a morning visit, but told her bearers to halt. Paying them off, she went up the flight to him. He had his back to her, his feet set apart, his elbows jutting and his hands on his hips as, with his head tilted back, he gazed upwards at the Cathedral's classical portico. It had been added to the medieval edifice over a quarter of a century earlier by Katherine's old enemy, the cutter-up of Queen Elizabeth's gowns—Inigo Jones. Dedicated to the patron saint of London, the edifice had stood here since 1087 when it replaced a wooden one built in 604 that had burned down.

She hesitated for a few moments before speaking. It was to be the first time they had seen each other since parting in the Cour Royale, although they had exchanged letters at Christmas. She found her voice. "Good day, sir."

He turned swiftly, knowing her voice anywhere, and his face broke into a broad smile. "Julia! Of all the most welcome surprises!"

As he took up her hand to kiss it she realised it was the first time she had not felt almost faint with excitement at being with him again. Instead there was the warmth of affection that one directed towards a good friend, known over a long period of time.

"Are you about to start the restoration work that you told me about?" she asked, glancing at the Cathedral. "I suppose the plague delayed you."

"It did, but I intend to spend all my time here now from this first day of September to at least the middle of the month trying to solve a few more of the problems that I've discovered since my preliminary inspections."

"I shouldn't hinder you."

"Nonsense! We haven't talked for a long time and I want to hear about everyone at Sotherleigh. Come into the Cathedral with me. I have a couple of fellow surveyors measuring up there."

They entered the Cathedral to a buzz of noise. These great edifices were always the hub of community life, for when religious services were not demanding the whole expanse of the buildings the aisles were used for commerce. Stalls were set up and marketing and bargaining took place. Libertymen and Freemen of the various guilds sometimes held meetings there for convenience and in winter chestnuts and potatoes were baked over braziers of charcoal, providing heat and refreshment at the same time. By one of the memorials those seeking employment would stand hopefully, a tool of trade in hand to announce their calling.

Christopher and Julia were met by one of the virgers, who escorted them up the main aisle to the stalls in the choir where they sat side by side and talked for quite a while about Anne and Mary, of Sophie's dreadful fate and whether Michael would come home more often in his changed circumstances. Julia had had a recent letter from Faith and knew that life in Bletchingdon was continuing its peaceful course.

"And what of Adam and you, Julia?"

She meant to answer him lightly, but the unhappiness of the past months had built up in her to such an extent that at his quietly voiced question her composure cracked. Tears started to her eyes and she pressed the back of her hand against her suddenly trembling lips.

"I took too long to discover how much I loved him. You know why, Christopher." There was no point in not speaking frankly. "As a result I've driven him from me."

"That's not possible. He risked his life to save yours."

"And he would again, I know. But what could have been between us is lost."

He shook his head. "That is something I can't believe. You're mistaken. All marriages have setbacks. This will prove a passing phase. You're not in total disagreement?"

"No. There are moments when I imagine that things have improved slightly, and then I'm uncertain again. Maybe I'm looking too hard, searching for a will-o'-the-wisp that isn't really there." She broke off, her throat aching with the tears she was holding back, anguish in her face.

He leaned towards her. "Listen to me. We've talked of your childhood dream before. Do you still have it?"

"Never. It's gone and perhaps all I ever really wanted has gone with it."

"Try to think that I've been keeping your share with mine. It will come back to you." He took her hands in both of his. It was as if he were trying to instill hope in her from some inner knowledge that belonged to him alone. "All will be well in time. I'm sure of it."

She managed a wan smile, wiping the glitter of unshed tears with the back of a finger from one eye and then the other. "At least I feel better through talking to you."

"If you want to talk again I'll be here at St. Paul's, as I told you, for the next two weeks."

EVEN IF Julia had wished to take advantage of Christopher's offer to talk it was not to prove possible. She was awoken in the early hours of the following morning by the rattling of an inner shutter that had not been fully folded back on its hinges by the open window. Careful not to disturb Adam, who lay deep in sleep, she lowered her feet to the floor and padded across to the window, pushing her hair back with both hands. A coolish easterly wind billowed her nightgown through the open window and, as she pressed the shutter back into place, she noticed a sinister reddish glow in a little patch against the sky somewhere in a distant part of the City.

Resting her hands on the window ledge, she stood for a few minutes trying to judge whereabouts it was, but it could have been in any one of a hundred streets or alleyways. Fires were not unusual and sometimes a whole row of houses would burn down when they were joined without party walls as so many were, Alice's old home and that from which she had rescued Katy being typical of thousands. She could imagine the scene with hand-squirts taking water from the conduits, bucket chains in progress and men with hooks pulling down parts of the burning buildings to keep the fire from spreading. As she went back to bed she hoped for the sake of everyone in the area that the fire would soon be extinguished. It would not be a peaceful Sunday for either the fire-fighters or those who had already lost their homes.

When she stirred again it was morning. Adam had left the bed and was tying the cords of his robe as he stood by the window, his attention caught by what he could see from there.

"There's quite a bad fire somewhere in the City," he said with a frown.

She took up her own robe from where Molly always placed it nightly across a chair near her bed. "I saw it when I woke in the night."

"What was it like then?"

"Just a small fire." She reached his side and she gasped at the sight that met her. Great clouds of thick, black smoke were billowing upwards over the City. More streets than one had fallen to the fire. "Where do you think it is?"

"It's certainly near the Bridge. Unless this easterly wind changes there should be no danger of the fire reaching the gunpowder that is stored at the Tower, but I hope the fire-fighters are making sure the flames don't reach any of the warehouses. They hold every kind of inflammable goods from barrels of lamp oil and tallow to sea coal, timber, tar, pitch and resin."

She thought also of the stores of hay and straw at the stables of every tavern, and the byres where milking cows were kept, the wine shops with casks of spirits and printers with reams of paper. And everywhere the weather-boarding and wood that the dry summer had turned to tinder. "Do you suppose my workshop is in any danger? I have a very valuable stock of ribbons waiting for shipment to Michael and equally large supplies ready for the most important orders I've had since the plague."

"We can hail a ferry-boat and take a look later to see exactly where the fire is located, but you need have no fear that it is anywhere near Carter Lane. See!" He pointed to the tower of St. Paul's, which could be clearly seen on the brow of the building-covered hump on which the City was centred. "The fire is nowhere near there."

While he went to bathe and make ready for the day, Molly came to attend to her and was full of what she had heard about the fire. "They say it started in the small hours at a bakery in Pudding Lane, my lady. Soon it had spread the length and breadth of Fish Hill Street. Rows of houses there are built back to back with those facing Bread Street and they all went at the same time. The fire melted the lead pipes of the conduit there, cutting off water where it was most needed, and it burnt up the water-wheels."

"They were near the Bridge. What of that?"

"Saved by a gap in the buildings on it, which also prevented the fire from crossing the river."

"How do you know all this?"

Molly hesitated. She could not give away the footman who had wit-nessed the start of the fire through staying late at a tavern before creeping back into the house through a kitchen window. He had even seen the Lord Mayor arrive on horseback and fall into a temper at having been awoken from sleep for what at first sight appeared to be a smallish out-break. Declaring to the fire-fighters that it could be pissed out, the Lord Mayor had ridden off to his bed again. She did not doubt that he had more than changed his mind now.

"The milkmaid could talk of nothing else when she was here with her buckets about half an hour ago," she replied truthfully.

"Where is the fire now?"

"Taking loaded barges at the quayside and the warehouses in Thames Street while the church of St. Magnus is burning like a torch."

Julia shook her head at such dreadful tidings. "Let's hope there's no great loss of life."

Later that morning Adam hired a ferry-boat and they were among many going by river to see what was happening. The smell of smoke became strong and wafted down over the wind-rippled water as they drew nearer the Bridge, bringing with it the yeasty aroma of ale boiling in vats at the burning breweries. The roaring flames were chasing people out of buildings everywhere. None of them paused to make any attempt to save the properties, but bundled their possessions down into waiting ferry-boats and other small vessels that had come to take advantage of the situation. One man whose coat-tails were on fire jumped into the river and was rescued by a waterman, who hauled him up into a boat.

With a splash of oars a waterman brought Mr. Pepys alongside the Warrenders' boat. "This is a sad and sorrowful business," he said, his face grave. "I've just come down from a high viewpoint in the Tower and it was a terrible sight. One of our finest Livery Halls in the City, the ancient Fishmongers' Hall, is burning and I'll have no more dinners at the Swan Inn." He heaved a sigh. "I'm going now to report the state of the fire to Whitehall. At that end of London nobody can have any idea what is happening here."

"I agree." Adam gave a nod. "From our house we could see that this fire was more than usual, but we had expected to find it under control. In this case the old law is at fault. I mean the one that decrees if a man pulls down another's house he must rebuild it, that must be proving a deterrent to creating the necessary fire-breaks."

"I intend to mention that. Now I must away to the King and afterwards to bury my wine and some good cheese in the garden in case my wife and I have to move hastily with whatever possessions we can take with us."

"God speed you, sir."

Upon returning home, he and Julia found a friend waiting, whose house was one caught by the fire. He had a waggonload of goods behind his coach that he wanted to store temporarily in their cellar. They agreed and offered him hospitality as well, but he declined the invitation. His coachman was driving him back to his daughter's house in Cannon Street in case it should prove necessary to evacuate her and her children should the fire spread, whereupon he would take them to his country seat. Apart from this visit, Sunday passed much the same in the Strand as it did everywhere else in London not affected by the fire. Church bells rang for services. Adam and Julia were among one of more than a hundred congregations gathering quietly while in a few less fortunate churches the flames were bringing bells crashing down and melting altar plate that could not be saved in time.

That evening Adam and Julia went again to view the fire. It had spread widely since the morning and the heat was so great that there was no question of getting close, for even in the middle of the river it scorched their faces and there was constant danger from firebrands hurtling through the air to plunge hissing into the water. The river was a throng of boats of every kind carrying people, their belongings piled high, to safety at

Westminster or across to the other side. Julia found it touching to see what had been grabbed in flight. Many had taken lutes and violins, clocks and rolled-up rugs. One woman, gazing blankly with shock, clutched a bird-cage. Dogs and cats had been taken too. The whole scene was as bright as day from the fire's awful glare, the moon being almost eclipsed by the pall of smoke.

By morning every Londoner realised the extent of the danger, for the fire had spread so rapidly in the night that the streets had become a flow of people fleeing from its relentless path. Julia realised what Adam was going to do when she saw he had donned a leather jerkin and gauntlets before thrusting an axe into his belt. He saw her anxious expression and grinned, flicking the end of her chin with his finger.

"Don't worry. I have to give what help I can. Too many people have been made homeless and I can't stand by and see more of London's treasures lost."

"All I ask is that you take care!"

"I will. Every one of the men-servants has volunteered to come with me. I shall report to one of the fireposts being manned throughout the City and we'll be directed from there to points where we are most needed."

She flung her arms around his neck and kissed him as if he were going off to war. His mouth responded passionately to hers and as they drew apart he gave her a deep and searching look.

"There are times, Julia, when—" Then he broke off brusquely. "I must go. Every minute counts. I'll be back when the fire is under control."

She went outside to watch him leave by the main gates into the Strand with the men-servants, who were not in their velvet livery today, but protectively attired. Then she turned about to run down the sloping path between lawns and flowerbeds to peer over the parapet at the riverside and watch him board one of two ferry-boats drawn up by steps where she had landed when coming home from France in the plague. Although she waved he did not see her, not expecting her to be there in any case. She stayed by a parapet until the two boats disappeared into the smoke wafting up the river.

That night Adam did not come home. She stood at the window for a long time, wondering where he might be and aghast at the horribly increased width of the expanse of flame that created an arc of fearful light across the City. During the day there had been optimistic talk with those who had called on her from Whitehall that the flames could be checked by fire-breaks, the King having given orders for any means of halting the fire to be used, and it seemed certain it would never reach Carter Lane. None of her workers would have been at the workshop in any case, for the entire life of the City had stopped as if the hands of a clock had been checked. At least she could be sure that they were all safe, for none lived where the fire had started and they would have had sufficient warning to leave their homes, unlike the time of the plague when danger could come without notice. She gave a sympathetic thought to Nell, whose chance to play a major role before the King would have to be postponed, and who could say when the time for play-going would come again?

Unable to sleep, she wandered to look out of a landing window at the Strand. It was as busy in the moonlight as it had been all day with people removing what possessions they could from fire-threatened properties. Sick people were carried on stretchers if there was no transport available, for again, as in the plague, anything on hooves or wheels was in enormous demand, any price paid. Lanterns and flares bobbed along as if some festive procession were going by. Surely no city had ever suffered two such vastly different tragedies as London had during the space of fifteen months?

By morning, after sleeping for a little while, Julia resolved to try to save her precious stock of ribbons. Months of work had gone into them and she would have almost nothing left if the fire took them. According to Molly, who was helping her dress, merchants had been transporting goods all the previous day from the great commercial street of Cheapside, which was a good indication of the new sweep of the fire, and Cannon Street had now become a target. Julia fumed to herself that she had not gone the previous day instead of trusting in fire-breaks that had only scattered timber seized on by the flames like stepping stones.

"You're not going to Carter Lane!" Molly exclaimed in disbelief when Julia told her to fetch one of the coachmen's spare leather capes, normally worn in bad weather.

"Do as I say!"

While the cape was being fetched Julia found one of her winter hats with a stout brim that would shield her face from sparks just as the cape should protect her from any chance burning splinters flying through the air. Some blackened ones and scraps of burnt paper had landed on the lawn, giving an idea how far the wind was bearing them. She could not bury her ribbons as some people had done with their wine, for there was only a cobbled yard at the back of the workshop. But there was a dry well with a cover jammed over it to prevent accidents that had been there for years, but still had a rope to it. If she lowered the boxes into the well and shovelled what earth there was over them, they should be safe until the fire had passed by.

Even if there had been someone to drive her, a horse could not be taken anywhere near the fire, and she managed to summon a waterman after only a short delay. He refused to take her to the steps she wanted, saying the fire might have drawn too near, and landed her at a flight slightly to the west. It meant covering an extra length of another street, but she intended to run all the way.

As she emerged from the side alley leading from the steps, she came into full view of St. Paul's and cried out in distress at seeing it was ablaze. It was as if the heart of the city had been taken! But she had no time to linger and set off at a run to Carter Lane. So many people were fleeing from that direction that she was bumped and jostled against, nobody having time to make way.

When she reached Carter Lane she saw why so many were in flight, for the fire was approaching at the far end, the swirling smoke giving her glimpses of houses beyond that were sheathed in flames. The heat was tremendous as if the fire were sending out a warning to be clear of its path. She could not possibly take the risk. It would be madness. A fire-brand had fallen on the workshop roof, which was smouldering and adding to the danger. Disappointment surged through her. To be so close to saving her ribbons, even able to see the window behind which they were stored on the shelves of large cupboards, was frustrating in the extreme, but sparks were showering down like fireworks and she dared not go nearer.

Then, just as she was about to withdraw from the street and join those retreating from the flames, she hesitated, certain she had glimpsed some-body in that storeroom window. Gazing upwards, she became sure there had been a flick of a cape as someone had taken a swift glimpse to check the nearness of the fire before vanishing again. Immediately she thought of two or three of her workers whose loyalty was such that they cherished the finished ribbons as much as she did. They would know what it meant to lose vital stock. Whoever was in there probably had no idea that the roof was already alight. She must go in herself and get that person out of the place while there was still time!

Lowering her head to gain the maximum protection of her hat-brim against the sparks and keeping her cape tightly about her, she bolted for the workshop, dodging flaring firebrands lying on the cobbles where they had fallen. When she reached the workshop door she saw that although it was pushed shut an entrance had been forced, enabling her to swing it open at a touch. She plunged into the smoke-filled interior, shouting the names most likely to gain a response.

"Martha! Beatrice! Peg! Come quickly! This place is on fire!"

No reply was forthcoming. No footsteps resounded. She began to cough and drew a handful of the cape over her nose and mouth. The firebrand must have taken a greater hold on the attic than had appeared from outside. Suppose one of those women had already collapsed from the smoke?

She darted for the staircase and pounded up the flight to dash through the weaving room to the storeroom, but as far as she could tell nobody was there in that thick and billowing smoke. Coughing violently, she wrenched open the cupboard doors and saw that they were empty. Once again she called to the same women, wanting to be sure that nobody was trapped or had fallen somewhere gasping for breath. She searched carefully and then again in the weaving room, but both were deserted. Maybe it had been a trick of reflected light against the window panes that had made her believe someone was upstairs here. There was no time to wonder whether her ribbons had been taken a day or two previous by trusted hands or by looters, because her own life was at stake now.

A sudden dreadful cracking sound made her look up sharply at the ceiling where the plaster was beginning to give way before the heat above. She screamed and darted in the direction of the stairs. On the way she saw, as if caught in a nightmare that had suddenly slowed down, the whole ceiling of the weaving room disintegrating into huge slabs of jagged plaster about her. A triangular piece struck the back of her head and she fell amidst thick smoke and choking dust into blackness on the floor. Above her the revealed flames no longer crept but burst into a lively roar in the draught that had been created.

In the yard behind the workshop Adam was at work with a coal shovel, which was all he could find to dig up earth from around the tree that grew in a corner there. He was shovelling it into the dry well where he had lowered all the boxes of ribbons in a length from one of the rolls of linen used for packing, not wanting to risk them bursting open by landing too heavily.

He had been fighting the fire near at hand when he heard it was advancing on Carter Lane. The King was at his side, although he had not recognised him at first, for Charles was as blackened by smuts and ashes and as charred in his clothes as any other man beating out flames with pieces of carpet or throwing water, or hooking fallen timbers out of the fire's path. The Duke of York was equally unrecognisable, except for his stentorian voice with which he competently gave commands, having taken charge. It was he who had shouted that Cannon Street was lost and the Old Change beyond saving, thereby causing Adam to remember Julia's ribbons and their importance to her. Since he had not taken a rest for several hours he broke away to use that time in going with great haste to the workshop, thinking how the ribbons might be saved. His heel had smashed a way into the premises and a quick inspection had shown him that the well, half filled with ancient rubble, was dry.

Now, just as he had finished his task, he was almost certain he had heard a woman call out from the upper rooms of the workshop. Knowing the roof was alight there now, he flung down his shovel and ran inside to the foot of the stairs as the ceiling gave way in the weaving room. He threw himself up the flight and saw Julia lying as if dead in a great cloud of choking white dust amidst a rubble of chunks of plaster, flames curling down from the rafters and one of the looms already burning.

With an agonised shout he dashed to her. She had fallen close to a loom and a great slab of plaster had fallen at an angle against it or else she would have been crushed. He shoved it aside and it shook the floor as it fell. Coughing from the smoke, he scooped her up in his arms, rushed with her down the stairs and out into the street. There he ran like a man demented to bear her away from the fire, for the flames, as if encouraged by the workshop's flaring like a torch, had leapt raging to meet it, firing both sides of the narrow street as it came. Turning into a side alley that was only half burning, he bore her in the direction of the river, seeing that other ways were now cut off. He dived through a passage-way, the walls of which were oven-hot. As it caved in behind him, he came out on the waterfront and saw that the fire was devouring one by one the row of the warehouses to his left, and to his right it had taken possession of Blackfriars, trapping him in both directions.

There were ferry-boats on the river, but they were all a great distance away, mostly close to the opposite side of the water. He stood there with Julia in his arms and shouted with all the power of his lungs.

"Oars! For mercy's sake!"

He was not heard, but he was seen by a gentleman with a spyglass, who had come up from the countryside beyond Southwark like many other sight-seers to view the Great Fire. He ordered the waterman in whose ferry-boat he was sitting to pull for that section of the waterfront immediately. When his order was not obeyed he showed a gold coin, intent on having this unexpected adventure with which to regale friends and acquaintances for years to come. The waterman pocketed the coin and began pulling on his oars across the river.

Seeing the boat coming, Adam went down the steps that had been placed there for the passage-way and sat down on the lower step where he soaked a handkerchief in the river and bathed Julia's face. When the boat came alongside, the gentleman exclaimed with dismay. "My dear sir! She's not—?"

"No," Adam answered huskily, "she's alive and will stay so, thanks to you and your waterman."

Julia was lifted into the boat and then Adam held her again as they were rowed all the way to the Somerset steps. From there he carried her home.

# TWENTY

*A*T SOTHERLEIGH that night Mary stood on the lawn in the moonlight looking in the direction of London. Although it was sixty miles away there was a pinkish glow rimming a patch of the horizon that told of the furnace the fire had become. Servants had gathered silently on the lawn behind her. They were all concerned for the fate of those at the house in the Strand. Mary tried to tell herself that Adam would have made sure that Julia, and all in their charge, were safely away from danger, but not knowing definitely made it impossible not to worry desperately about them.

News of the fire had reached Sussex quickly as elsewhere. There were tales of people camping in the fields around the City, of noblemen and wealthy merchants who had hindered the fire-fighters by refusing to have their fine mansions pulled down to create the necessary fire-breaks, and of roads out of London filled with refugees. Mary had started to keep watch for Julia's return with Adam, hoping every time there were hooves in the drive that she would see them safely home again. Perhaps tomorrow they would come.

It was mid-morning the next day when from an upper window in the house, Mary happened to see a coach emerge from the elms as it took the last curve of the drive. She had just returned from taking Anne and the two children to Warrender Hall for the day, but had come back herself in the certainty that Julia and Adam would soon be arriving. Gathering up her skirts, she ran in excitement and relief that they should be safely home and dashed downstairs and out through the door already opened by a footman to greet their arrival.

Then she stopped abruptly on the top step, her heart leaping. It was Michael who had alighted from the coach and with him was a handsome little boy to whom he was pointing out aspects of the house. Then he saw her and held her eyes.

"I've brought Jean-Robert home with me, Mary. We're here to stay."

A sob of gladness rose in her throat. As he and the boy came up the steps hand in hand she knew that all she had ever wanted was about to come true. When he came level with her he drew her into an embrace and kissed her lovingly. Then he presented his son, who bowed deeply to her. The boy's English was faultless.

"I'm honoured to meet you, madam. Papa has told me that you are to be my stepmother and the new mistress of Sotherleigh."

She put a hand on his shoulder, looking down at him. "Welcome to the home that has been waiting for you, Jean-Robert. You will be happy here, I know, and my happiness will be all the greater through your becoming a son to me." Then she looked at Michael with eyes full of love and joy. "This is the second most important day in my life."

He smiled, putting his arm around her waist as they went indoors. "What was the first?"

"The day you rescued me from the scaffold and I loved you from the first moment you spoke to me."

He paused in the middle of the hall to kiss her again. Jean-Robert sprang up the stairs to the first landing and studied the portrait of Queen Elizabeth that his father had told him about. He knew all about the gold she had given his great-grandfather to build Sotherleigh, and how her seamen had defeated the Armada and that the last of her gowns was in his Aunt Julia's keeping. He turned on the landing to face the hall, his feet apart and his thumbs hooked in his belt as he imagined Great-Grandfather Ned had done when sailing triumphantly into harbour after a long voyage.

Dinner was served in the Great Hall, Michael seated at the head of the table. Towards the end of the meal, Jean-Robert, too excited to eat much, had been allowed to leave the table and go and explore the gardens. Then Michael told Mary of how he had sold Brissard's for a very high price, many bidders being after the business.

"It was a decision I did not take lightly, but Jean-Robert has been set against the silk industry ever since I took him to Lyon. Although he might have felt differently towards it later on, it was apparent to me that his heart would never be in it as his late grandfather and his mother would have wished. There was another factor that weighed with me too. By being able to tell Julia that my financial future is secure I can release her from her aim to recoup as best she could the lost Sotherleigh fortune." He reached for Mary's hand. "Above all else I wanted to share Sotherleigh with you and to see my son and our children grow up here."

She had not known it was possible to be so happy.

After dinner she and Michael walked with Jean-Robert by way of the short cut to Warrender Hall. Patience and Katy were playing with Meg's three youngest children on the lawn, Anne trying to organise them. She did not hear Michael's approach across the grass, Jean-Robert at his side. Then, when she happened to turn her head and catch sight of him, she did not show the least surprise.

"Thank goodness you're here, Michael. You can settle the game of football the children want to play." Although he bent his head and kissed her cheek, she took no notice, her attention focused smilingly on his son. "Who is this?"

The boy answered for himself. "Your grandson, Jean-Robert."

"Then why are you Frenchifying your good name? Robert was good enough for your grandfather and it shall be for you." At that she put a hand to her head, panic in her eyes as sometimes happened when an incident jerked her out of her tranquil state, and she turned at once to Mary on whom she had come to rely. "He looks a good boy. I know I love him, but why can't I remember his mother?"

"She lived abroad and she died some time ago. The boy was born in France."

"Was he?" She looked astounded.

"He's to be my stepson. Michael and I are to marry."

Anne was overjoyed. She kissed Mary and embraced Michael and then stooped down to give her grandson a hug. "What a good thing you are here now, young Robert. Do you know how to play football?"

"Papa taught me. Shall I take over the game?"

"Please!"

He went running to join the other children and Anne straightened up to tilt her head sideways as she studied Michael. "I'm sure you've grown three inches since you were last at Sotherleigh?"

He laughed softly. "You've said that to me at many homecomings."

"Are you going away again?"

"No, Mother. Never again."

Anne heaved a blissful sigh. "That's splendid news. Let's go and tell Meg. She's waiting to pour me tea."

"Why not invite her to the wedding at the same time," he suggested.

"Oh, yes!" Chattering happily, Anne led the way into Warrender Hall.

IT TOOK JULIA thirty-six hours to regain her senses. By then the fire had been defeated, due mainly to Mr. Pepys, who had the idea of bringing in seamen from ships of the navy. They had created fire-breaks with gunpowder, sometimes blowing up a whole row of houses at a time. It had saved the fire spreading out beyond the City walls into the Liberties and devouring everything as it went. Virtually the entire City had been destroyed from the Tower in the east to the Temple in the west, the destruction stretching out roughly in the shape of a fan from the river to Cripplegate and only a hair's-breadth from Moorgate in the north.

Adam walked into what was left of Fleet Street the morning after the Great Fire's end and in whichever direction he looked there was nothing but smoking, charred and blackened ruins. He could see people wandering about as if in a desert, some trying to find where their homes had been, and he was drawn to walk through a great part of what had once been the greatest and most thriving capital in the world. During the fire-fighting there had been no time to assess the losses being sustained, but with shock and sadness he estimated that over a hundred churches had gone and that St. Paul's, where once Queen Elizabeth had given thanks after the victory over the Armada, stood as a broken shell. Over fifty Halls of Companies, all of which had been magnificent palaces, marvellously adorned and constructed, had gone with the flames, together with many other historic buildings, including the Elizabethan Custom House, the Royal Exchange and Gresham College where, with one of the odd tricks the fire had played, the statue of the founder, Sir Thomas Gresham, stood untouched. There was a second oddity he spotted, which he took note of to tell Julia. On another scale there was the loss of priceless medieval libraries and other heritage treasures that could not be saved. A tragedy in itself was the loss of thousands of homes belonging to every class of person from the nobleman to the beggar.

Adam constantly lost his bearings where whole streets had become a flat area of ashes and debris. In places the cobbles were too hot to step on, cellars were still burning and water hissed as it boiled in the conduits. After great difficulty he located the well where the ribbons lay, for as with other narrow streets, the heat of Carter Lane made it impassable and he had to approach it from the rear. He saw that a piece of still smouldering timber had fallen across the well, half demolishing it, but he thought he had thrown in a thick enough layer of earth to have kept the boxes well protected.

When he returned home he had to change all his clothes and bathe and wash his hair to remove the stench of the fire before he went to Julia's bedside. She was still deathly white and felt unwell. The doctor had recommended a rest at Sotherleigh as soon as she was able to make the journey. Adam drew up a chair and held her hand.

"I've two things to tell that will please you," he said.

She looked at him listlessly. "What are they?"

"The first is that amidst all the destruction of the City, Queen Elizabeth's statue still stands untouched on Ludgate."

"Grandmother would have been pleased about that too." Her voice was weak and only just audible, but a smile touched her lips.

"I'm also certain that your ribbons have been saved."

"I should never have gone there." Her drawn face was full of unhappy self-reproach.

"I've good reason to be glad that you did on my own behalf," he said with a smile. "I was at Whitehall earlier today and the King told me that had I returned to the fire-fighting at his side I should not be here. A wall gave way unexpectedly and he only just escaped being crushed. I should not have stood a chance."

She closed her eyes tightly on the tears that sprang there in relief at the escape he had had. "I wouldn't have wanted to go on living without you."

"Nor I without you," he replied softly.

She had soon recovered enough to make the journey back to Sotherleigh. Michael had come to London out of anxiety about her and Adam, which enabled him to take her back when he returned to Sussex, Adam having to stay on at the House of Commons to deal with the chaos that the conflagration had left. It was exactly six days after the end of the Great Fire when Julia left with her brother. On that same day Christopher Wren presented his plans for a new and beautiful London to the King at Whitehall.

IN THE GOOD AUTUMNAL AIR of Sussex Julia soon recovered completely. There was a wonderful atmosphere at Sotherleigh that nothing had ever destroyed, and Anne's tranquil happiness seemed to lighten it everywhere just as the gracious windows filled it with air and sunshine. Due to Michael's insistence that he was as wealthy as if the Sotherleigh treasure had never been lost, Julia accepted that her days of business were over. A Chichester merchant took over her village stocks and employed her workers in their own homes and, being a fair man, he kept on Mr. Mather as his inspector and agreed to pay the same adequate wages. As for London, Julia knew her workers there would have no difficulty finding employment, for soon the demand for skilled workers in sewing and weaving would be enormous to replace all the goods that were lost. The marriage of Michael and Mary was to take place in the village church and had been arranged for early November when Adam felt he could get away for the ceremony.

Mary made her own wedding garments. Julia had offered her the Elizabethan gown, but Mary felt it was too splendid and regal for the quiet wedding that she and Michael wanted, although she did accept the loan of a trimming for her gown of some of the beautiful drop-pearls, on the day itself. On the eve of the marriage Julia awaited Adam's return as if she were a bride herself, full of trepidation and love.

He usually called in at Warrender Hall to check that all was well before coming on to Sotherleigh and this time Julia had made a special arrangement with Meg. Servants were to be posted along the short cut between the two estates to signal to her when he had arrived there. He was late and everyone else at Sotherleigh had gone to bed as she continued to watch from a window for the first flicker of lantern light. She hoped that for once Adam would not decide to come straight to Sotherleigh instead, because that would ruin all that she had planned.

Out of the darkness a light suddenly glowed. The chain of lanterns had reached the gate there. Already in her cloak, she raced down the stairs and outside where Charlie stood ready saddled for her. The groom helped her up and she was away, galloping across the park and through the gate that stood open for her onto Warrender land, the first time she had ventured on it since her chance meeting with Adam on the slope above the house when his friends had made such sport of her.

She overtook the returning lantern-bearers and when she reached the Hall a groom was waiting to take Charlie from her. The door was swung open at her approach and she rushed into the candle-lit hall. At the head of a great carved Tudor staircase Adam stood talking to Meg. He looked down at Julia in astonishment and disbelief. His sister melted away into the shadows.

Julia went slowly to the foot of the staircase, her face upturned to him. "I've come home to you, Adam."

He moved down the flight to her. Cupping the side of her face, he gazed at her tenderly. She seized his hand to press the palm passionately to her lips while she leaned against him and rested her head against his chest. Without a word he swung her into his arms and carried her up the flight to the master bedchamber where, long ago, he had planned to possess her.

It was a bed even wider than that of the master bedchamber at Sotherleigh. They used every inch of it in the abandonment of their love-making in the glow of a single candle that by dawn had drowned in its own wax. They slept late. His caresses awakened her. The sensual bliss of being made love to when still drowsy was always one of special delight to her and it was particularly pleasurable after the night they had shared. This was the time when he expected no active response from her, content to touch and stroke her erotically while she feigned sleepiness a little longer until her own body gave her away as it did now. Her arms reached for him. This morning, as she blended with him in their mutual passion, it seemed to her when the supreme moments hurled them into total ecstasy that she had conceived at last.

As they lay together with their heartbeats subsiding, she turned her head slightly to look into his face. His eyes were closed and she traced with a fingertip the scar on his cheek made by the mirror-frame she had thrown at him on the day he had come riding to Sotherleigh.

"This is my seal on you, Adam Warrender," she whispered softly, her voice imbued with love. "It bound me to you then and for ever. I loved you always, but it took me far longer than it should have done to discover it. I believe I gave my heart to you that day in Chichester when you rode into my life on a pearl-white pony. Why else should I remember every detail of our meeting from that moment onwards? That you should have remembered it too is surely proof that we were destined for each other. I love you. I know I said that many times to you during the night, but I say it again now and will do the same with my last breath."

His arm had tightened around her and he opened his eyes to look at her with such depths of love and joy in his eyes that she caught her breath in wonder. "My beloved," he said huskily. "You have been and always will be my life."

Simultaneously each sought the other's mouth in a kiss of such loving intensity that their embrace did not bring them close enough and once again he entered her in a passion enriched now by the new happiness they had found together.

ONLY THE FAMILY and a few close friends were to attend the marriage of Michael and Mary. It meant that all would be able to sit at the one long oaken table in the Great Hall and there would be none of the riotous junketing such as Julia and Adam had had to endure. Christopher was Michael's groomsman and it was the first time the two friends had seen each other since they were in Paris.

"I trust you will be groomsman to me, Michael," Christopher said before the ceremony.

"Gladly! When is it to be?"

"In exactly three years. By then I should be settled in London with no more travelling to and fro between Oxford and the City like a jack-in-the-box."

"How goes it with the London plans you told me about?"

"I had strong competition and my plan as a whole has not been accepted, but I am to have licence in some areas and have received a great commission to rebuild many of the lost churches to my own designs."

"That's splendid news!"

Christopher nodded very seriously. Then he spoke almost shyly. "There is still more, Michael."

"What could that be?"

"I'm to rebuild St. Paul's. I beg you to pray for me that I may be worthy of this commission and raise a cathedral that will be a hymn of praise to the glory of God."

"My prayers will be for you, my friend." Michael shook his hand firmly and they clapped each other on the arm.

The village church was full when the bride entered at Adam's side to be taken up the aisle to where Michael awaited her. She was in forget-me-not blue satin, her wide-brimmed hat trimmed with a bunch of Anne's ribbons embroidered with the tiny blooms and she carried a small posy of late flowers gathered from the Knot Garden. Anne sighed romantically and turned her head, expecting to catch her husband's smiling eyes. In confused bewilderment she saw he was not there, but young Robert was and he took her hand.

"I'm here, Grandmother," he whispered. He had learned fast how to calm this sweet lady, whose sudden dithering was a sign she needed reassurance.

"So you are," she whispered back, full of smiles.

Faith, present with Susan and William, let her eyes rest on Christopher as he waited to hand the ring to the Rector for its blessing. She was content that they had a wedding date now and three years should soon pass.

It was a week before Julia and Adam left for London again. During that time she came to know Warrender Hall. It was an old and beautiful house in its starkly early-Tudor way, but in spite of losing her aversion to it she knew it would never mean anything to her as a home. Although she was mistress of it, she felt she was usurping Meg, who belonged to it far more than she. Not once did she execute her authority in any way and it gave her an understanding of how it must have been for her mother at Sotherleigh when Katherine had held sway.

The November weather was cold with sharp frosts, which enabled the journey to London to go at good speed over stone-hard roads. To Julia's surprise, when they came to the cross-roads that would have led them towards Westminster and the Strand, the coachman followed the sign to Chiswick village.

"Why are we going there?" she exclaimed.

Adam grinned at her. "I've a surprise for you."

It was a charming village with many trees and thatched cottages clustered by the river. The coachman drove through open gates into a park only recently landscaped to a newly built mansion. Adam sprang out first to help Julia alight, and she paused on the coach step to look in delight from the house to him and back again.

"It's ours, isn't it?"

"I've sold the Strand house. It is equally convenient here to go by boat to Westminster. I shall have my own oarsman."

She stood and gazed at the classical frontage. Built of mellow-toned brick it was three storeys high with handsome windows, those uppermost framed in stone drapery, each topped by a lion's head. As for the wide and welcoming entrance, it was flanked by two columns supporting a friezed doorway elaborately ornamented. It was a house both simple and grand, its splendour restrained and yet glorious. Without being told she knew its architect. She turned to Adam, her face shining with joy.

"How did you know I once made Christopher promise to design a house for me?"

His eyes twinkled. "You told me yourself, without knowing it, when you were delirious with the plague. I made up my mind then that one day you should have your wish."

"I'm going to love it more than Sotherleigh! I can't pay it a greater compliment than that!"

"I'm glad, because this is our home now. Several times when I left you on what you supposed was political business, it was to meet Christopher in order to discuss plans and then later on the site of the house when he supervised the building himself."

"What of Warrender Hall?" She did not want it to be abandoned.

"I've signed it over to my eldest nephew. It was never the place for us. If ever you want a country seat we'll build another house."

"I don't want any other than this one and here we are in the country already. Let's call it Chichester House to remind us always of our first meeting."

He nodded smilingly. "Whatever pleases you."

She caught his hand eagerly. "Let's go in! I can't wait any longer to see inside."

Hand in hand they went swiftly up the steps into the house.

# EPILOGUE

*I*N THE LATE SPRING of 1723, a few weeks after Christopher's impressive funeral, Adam took Julia to St. Paul's to see his tomb. They were both in their eighties; she was still spry and he rode daily, only having recently retired from many distinguished years in politics. In Chichester House, which she still loved as much as the day she had first seen it, she had borne him five sons, who in all had given them more than a quiverful of grandchildren, resulting in a mounting number of great-grandchildren, with frequent visits from them all. She thought sometimes that the house, which their eldest son, an eminent lawyer, would inherit, had rarely been without some happy sounds of singing or laughter or music. There had been sad times too, as happened in any family, but through it all adults and children alike had sustained one another and remained united.

As she alighted at the huge flight of steps leading up to St. Paul's Julia hesitated, not because she was daunted by the effort of ascending the flight, but because memories were flooding back to her. This beautiful Cathedral, with the double portico of Corinthian columns and the twin towers displaying a classical formality, had taken thirty-five years to build, its magnificence surpassing anything else of its time in Europe. Surmounting the portico with its bas-relief showing the conversion of St. Paul, was a statue of the apostle himself. With the massive pearl-shaped dome rising three hundred and sixty-five feet high, the cathedral dominated the skyline through the sheer power of its glorious architecture.

Just fifteen years earlier she had been standing almost at this spot. Then she had been gazing up at the dome against a ribbon-blue sky to see a tiny speck, which was Christopher's grown son, who bore his name, placing the last stone on the lantern topped by a ball and Cross to complete the building. At the moment it was done the mighty bells began to chime out for all of London to hear. Christopher, who was standing on the steps, had sought her eyes, and she had answered the smile he gave her with one of perfect understanding. His half of the dream had come true in his masterpiece just as hers had come to fulfilment in her love for Adam.

Adam's voice brought her back to the present. "Shall we go into the Cathedral now?"

She gave him a fond look and took his arm that he was offering her. He was still a handsome man and the grey periwig draped down to his broad shoulders suited him well. He still found her beautiful, but then they had ever looked at each other with the eyes of love.

As she took the steps, holding her tawny velvet hem free of her rosette-trimmed shoes, her thoughts turned to Faith, whom she missed sadly, nothing able to fill the gap left by a dear friend. As arranged, Christopher and Faith had married in the year he had been given the honoured position of Surveyor of the King's Works, but after only six devoted years together she had died of smallpox just a few weeks after giving birth to their son. Soon afterwards Christopher had married again. His second wife, Jane, had much the same gentle nature as Faith, and she had borne him a daughter and son, but over the years he had lost all three of them and did not marry again.

He had become President of the Royal Society, which he had helped to found, but in another sphere in his latter years he had had a great deal of stress. After years of loyal service to the Crown and building many beautiful churches, palaces, colleges, mansions and hospitals, he had fallen from favour with King George and had been dismissed as the Royal Surveyor. He had retired to his apartment at Hampton Court and from there he had come often to sit in St. Paul's, a small frail old man not noticed by those who came to view and worship in its dazzling magnificence.

There were tears in Julia's eyes as she reached the great door, but she dashed them away. Christopher would not have wanted her to cry. She held up her head, her stateliness set off by her cream-coloured hat. Wide brims had never gone out of fashion and it suited her well. The musical thunder of the organ seemed to hang in the air as she and Adam entered the vast glory of the Cathedral, two tiny figures amidst a wonder of colour, gold and stone. It was full of light that streamed down from the dome, which was supported by eight great pillars, and from many lovely windows. She remembered Christopher telling her of the day he had been marking out this huge new edifice and had called for a lump of the old masonry with which to set a central guide for the whole project. A stone had been picked at random and when the workman had dropped it into place Christopher saw that engraved on it was the word RESURGAM, meaning *I shall rise again*. St. Paul's had risen again with greater beauty than ever before and she hoped with all her heart it would remain undamaged by fire or anything else throughout the centuries to come.

Adam gave her his arm as they went down the steps into the crypt, which was arched in Gothic style and lay beneath the floor area of the whole Cathedral. At first Christopher's tomb was hard to find. They searched individually in various directions until at last she found it.

"He's lying here," she said quietly. "He always was a shy and retiring man."

The plain, unadorned tomb was in a secluded corner that could be easily missed. Buried nearby was his daughter, Jane, who had been so dear to him. The inscription on his tomb read in Latin: *Under this stone lieth the Builder of this Cathedral, Christopher Wren, who lived for more than ninety years, not for himself but for public good.* Then, most poignantly, there followed: *Reader, if you seek his monument, look around you.*

"How apt," Adam said, putting his arm around Julia's shoulders. "No man has ever done more to enhance a city or his own land than he."

They stayed a little while and then left again. On their way home to Chiswick they passed many of the lovely churches with their soaring spires that Christopher had set like jewels about London. He had never allowed any of his workmen to swear when building a holy place, each church an expression of his own committed Christian faith. If his plan for the City had been accepted, it would have been a capital of graceful avenues, each converging on a piazza on which would have stood one of the beautiful buildings that he had had to build elsewhere, such as the Royal Exchange and the Custom House, but there had been opposition on grounds of expense and through legal difficulties over land and property rights, which had defeated his purpose. Nevertheless London had risen again in brick and stone with wide streets, leafy parks and much architectural splendour to become the cleanest city in the world, with sewers instead of open drains and much good water supplied. It was also again the wealthiest with nothing to show of the great calamity that had flattened it.

Among the Wren buildings that Adam and Julia passed on their homeward journey was the Royal Hospital at Chelsea, which was a home for maimed and retired old soldiers that had been commissioned by Charles II at Nell's instigation, for with her soft heart she had always been touched by the plight of those who had fought well and been left to beg on the streets. The inmates toasted that merry monarch on every Founder's Day and never forgot to salute the memory of pretty, witty Nell, who had achieved fame on the stage and finally won the King's heart, outliving him by only two years.

Julia thought to herself how swiftly the years had gone by. She was about the age now that Katherine had been when displaying the treasured Elizabethan gown to her at Sotherleigh. It was high time she did something to ensure its preservation, but much as she loved her granddaughters there was not one she could single out for the task and her great-granddaughters were as yet too young. There was only one course open to her and, always practical, she decided to carry it out that day.

Upon arrival home she hurried up to what she thought of as her casket room, for it was where she kept in carved boxes ribbons of every design that Anne had ever embroidered. It was a craft that had faded away now, woven ribbons having become very fanciful and elaborate and quite lovely. Also in the casket room was the old black chest in which the Elizabethan gown had always been kept. She had not wanted to remove the gown from it and Michael had had it transported from Sotherleigh to Chiswick for her shortly before Mary gave birth to the first of their three daughters.

Now she lifted the lid and picked up the box with the ruff and farthingale and the golden shoes, all of which she carried through to the bedchamber that had become known as the Elizabeth Room. Because of its charm her granddaughters had always competed to sleep there, establishing a tradition that seemed bound to continue. Proof of this was when her three-year-old great-granddaughter on a recent visit made a special request.

"Please, Grandmother! May I sleep in 'beth's room?"

"Me too!" echoed another young one.

That pleased her. She had her reasons for making the room a link with Sotherleigh. She placed the items she was carrying on a chair and then returned to gather up the gown in its soft lawn coverings to bear it through to the Elizabeth Room. There she uncovered it and laid it across the bed exactly as it had been when first shown to her. Patience and Katy had both worn it on their wedding days, but it would have fitted none of her daughters-in-law and in any case they had not been interested, all being young and frivolous young women at the time. Neither had young Robert's bride worn it. She was a Frenchwoman whom he had met in Paris when visiting his childhood haunts, and she had been married from Sotherleigh in a gown of such Parisian elegance that all these years later it was still spoken of when the family reminisced.

Julia went to some beautifully carved mouldings that framed the panels of the walls, informal garlands of flowers that gave the room such charm and caused it to be so enchanting to young girls, who liked to think themselves in a bower as they preened and primped before the mirror there.

She touched one carved leaf and then another, which sent a cunningly concealed drawer to emerge from the panelling at waist level. It was typical of Christopher's ingenuity that he should have designed such an unusual hiding place.

"It's for the Elizabethan gown's safe-keeping," he had said when first revealing it to her. "I know how much it means to you."

As she laid the ruff and the farthingale into the secret drawer, together with the golden shoes, she happened to knock the brim of her hat against the wall and realised that in her eagerness she had forgotten to remove it. She went across to take it off in front of the mirror with the stump-work that she had embroidered long ago. The girls loved the little door with Queen Elizabeth on it, which was why it was hanging here in this room. It reflected now a face that was an older version of that of the fifteen-year-old who had first looked in it. She could see a likeness to her mother, as happened with women as the years advanced. Sweet Anne, who had lived to a considerable age, getting a little more vague all the time, had simply closed her eyes one day like the flower she had been embroidering closing its petals for the night.

Julia took her hat through to her bedchamber. In the anteroom she sat down at her bureau and wrote a brief history of the gown and how it came to be the only one belonging to the royal lady that was saved. When she had sealed what she had written, she returned with it to the Elizabeth Room where she stood to look again at the gown that had played such a part in her life. She touched the embroidery for the last time and smoothed a hand over the shimmering satin. It showed its age now, but the flower slips still looked as fresh as if the blooms had been plucked and embroidered only a few days before.

As for the drop-pearls, their lustre was undimmed. She slid her fingers under them and was as full of wonder at their beauty as when a child she had viewed them for the first time. Now she knew that they were mellow with the dreams of the women who had worn the gown they adorned.

Slowly she swathed the gleaming gown in its lawn wrappings. Lifting it up carefully over both arms, she carried it across to lay it full length in the secret drawer. Lastly she placed the sealed history beside it. Then, with one slight twist of another carved leaf, the drawer went sliding away out of sight.

She did not linger, except to pause in the doorway and send a little kiss of farewell from her fingertips in the direction of the treasure she had concealed. Then she went downstairs to go outside where Adam was waiting to stroll with her in the rose garden.

It was her fervent hope that in many decades to come one of their descendants, maybe a girl much as she herself had been, with chestnut curls and a sense of history, would discover that secret place with its treasure within. Then the pearls, which had linked up the past, would draw the future into a gleaming circle. In her mind's eye she could almost see the young face full of wonder. Surely such a girl would find a way to share the beauty of the great Tudor Queen's gown with another century and a new age.